EMPIRE OF SILENCE

THE SUN EATER: BOOK ONE

CHRISTOPHER RUOCCHIO

DAW BOOKS, INC.

DONALD A. WOLLHEIM, FOUNDER

1745 Broadway, New York, NY 10019

ELIZABETH R. WOLLHEIM
SHEILA E. GILBERT
PUBLISHERS
www.dawbooks.com

First Paperback Printing, June 2019
1 2 3 4 5 6 7 8 9

To my grandparents:
Albert and Eleanor. Deslan and James.
This took too long to finish.
I'm sorry it's late.

ACKNOWLEDGMENTS

The word *author* conjures up impressions of solitude, of the rugged individualists of the mind. One imagines the old and near-blind Milton hunched over his writing desk by candlelight. But while solitude is certainly a mainstay of this profession, it is a mistake to imagine that anyone is truly alone. It is fitting, therefore, that I take this small space to thank all those persons who have helped me to see this through.

Any such list that did not begin with my parents—Paul and Penny—would be a mistake. Though I did not always appreciate it, they always supported me, no matter my bad behavior or ingratitude. I am truly blessed to be their son, and humbled, too. My brothers deserve special mention as well. Matthew, Andrew, and I were not always friends, but we are now, and that has been unspeakably important to me in recent years. If I were to list every family member to whom I owe some depth of gratitude, I would have to publish a genealogy, so here's a short list: to Uncle John, for his help understanding contracts; to Brian, for reading the book before anyone else in the family; to Uncle Pete, for indulging my requests for artwork when I was little and for showing me it was possible to be an artist and a success in life; and to my mother's mother, Deslan, who bought me my copy of *The Lord of the Rings,* which along with *Star Wars* made me want to tell these stories. And to everyone else, for being truly the best family—and a better family than I truly deserve.

I would be remiss in mentioning family without mentioning my friends, the additional family that I have chosen, or who have chosen me (for reasons I don't quite understand). As with my true family, I have been more fortunate than I feel I deserve. To Erin G., my oldest friend and chiefest critic; to Marek, D'Artagnan himself; to Anthony; Michael; Jordan; and Joe—brothers all; to Victoria, captain of the beta-readers; to Jenna, for all her help and hard work on my website (and for much more besides); to Erin H. and Jackson; and to Madison and

Kyle, for their long friendship and support. And to Christopher-Marcus—from whom Tor Gibson took his name—perhaps most of all, for a lifetime of discussion and illumination. Arete, my friend.

To certain of my teachers I owe special thanks: to Anne Sweeney, Diane Buckley, Chris Sutton, and Nikki Wright, for encouraging my proclivity for literature. To Priscilla Chappell, for enduring four years of me in high school—when I was at my most insufferable; to Dr. Joe Hoffman, for putting history in a context and clarity I had not imagined possible; and to Craig Goheen, for showing me there was far more in science fiction and fantasy than the likes of Tolkien and Herbert. To Drs. Marvin Hunt, Cat Warren, and Etta Barksdale, for making college worth the time and money. Extra special thanks should be paid to Sam Wheeler, for helping me figure out exactly how one might eat a sun, as well for helping with other physics problems well beyond this English student's abilities; and to Dr. John Kessel, for his mentoring, his help with my query letter, and for telling me to cut out that stupid frame narrative.

Lastly, I should thank all those involved in the production of this book. First, to Betsy Wollheim and Sheila Gilbert of DAW and to everyone on the team there, most especially to my editor, Katie, for her insight and her patience in dealing with me. To Sarah, my first editor, and to Gillian Redfearn and everyone at Gollancz. To my agents, Shawna McCarthy, Danny Baror, and Heather Baror-Shapiro for their incredible support. I could not ask for better agents, truly. And finally to Toni Weisskopf and all my co-workers at Baen, and not just for employing me.

Thank you.

[text in constructed/fictional script]

BEING THE ACCOUNT OF THE SUN EATER,

HADRIAN MARLOWE

OF THE WAR BETWEEN MANKIND

AND THE CIELCIN.

TRANSLATED INTO CLASSICAL ENGLISH

BY TOR PAULOS OF NOV BELGAER

ON COLCHIS.

CHAPTER 1

HADRIAN

LIGHT.

The light of that murdered sun still burns me. I see it through my eyelids, blazing out of history from that bloody day, hinting at fires indescribable. It is like something holy, as if it were the light of God's own heaven that burned the world and billions of lives with it. I carry that light always, seared into the back of my mind. I make no excuses, no denials, no apologies for what I have done. I know what I am.

The scholiasts might start at the beginning, with our remote ancestors clawing their way out of Old Earth's system in their leaking vessels, those peregrines making their voyages to new and living worlds. But no. To do so would take more volumes and ink than my hosts have left at my disposal, and even I, who has more time than any other, have not the time for that.

Should I chronicle the war, then? Start with the alien Cielcin howling out of space in ships like castles of ice? You can find the war stories, read the death counts. The statistics. No context can make you understand the cost. Cities razed, planets burned. Countless billions of our people ripped from their worlds to serve as meat and slaves for those Pale monsters. Families old as empires ended in light and fire. The tales are numberless, and they are not enough. The Empire has its official version, one that ends in my execution, with Hadrian Marlowe hanged for all the worlds to see.

I do not doubt that this tome will do aught but collect

dust in the archive where I have left it, one manuscript amongst billions at Colchis. Forgotten. Perhaps that is best. The worlds have had enough of tyrants, enough of murderers and genocides.

But perhaps you will read on, tempted by the thought of reading the work of so great a monster as the one made in my image. You will not let me be forgotten because you want to know what it was like to stand aboard that impossible ship and rip the heart out of a star. You want to feel the heat of two civilizations burning and to meet the dragon, the devil that wears the name my father gave me.

So let us bypass history, sidestep the politics and the marching tramp of empires. Forget the beginnings of mankind in the fire and ash of Old Earth, and so too ignore the Cielcin rising in cold and from darkness. Those tales are recorded elsewhere in all the tongues of mankind and her subjects. Let us move to the only beginning I've a right to: my own.

I was born the eldest son and heir to Alistair Marlowe, Archon of Meidua Prefecture, Butcher of Linon, and Lord of Devil's Rest. No place for a child, that palace of dark stone, but it was my home all the same, amid the logothetes and the armored peltasts who served my father. But Father never wanted a child. He wanted an heir, someone to inherit his slice of Empire and to carry on our family legacy. He named me Hadrian, an ancient name, meaningless save for the memories of those men who carried it before me. An Emperor's name, fit to rule and be followed.

Dangerous things, names. A kind of curse, defining us that we might live up to them, or giving us something to run away from. I have lived a long life, longer than the genetic therapies the great houses of the peerage can contrive, and I have had many names. During the war, I was Hadrian Halfmortal and Hadrian the Deathless. After the war, I was the Sun Eater. To the poor people of Borosevo, I was a myrmidon called Had. To the Jaddians, I was Al Neroblis. To the Cielcin, I was Oimn Belu and worse things besides. I have been many things: soldier and ser-

vant, captain and captive, sorcerer and scholar and little more than a slave.

But before I was any of these, I was a son.

My mother was late to my birth, and both my parents watched from a platform above the surgical theater while I was decanted from the vat. They say I screamed as the scholiasts birthed me and that I had all my teeth in my head. Thus nobility is always born: without encumbering the mother and under the watchful eye of the Imperial High College, ensuring that our genetic deviations had not turned to defects and curdled in our blood. Besides, childbearing of the traditional sort would have required my parents to share a bed, which neither was inclined to do. Like so many nobiles, my parents wed out of political necessity.

My mother, I later learned, preferred the company of women to that of my father and rarely spent time on the family estate, attending my father only during formal functions. My father, by contrast, preferred his work. Lord Alistair Marlowe was not the sort of man who gave attention to his vices. Indeed, my father was not the sort of man who *had* vices. He was possessed by his office and by the good name of our house.

By the time I was born, the Crusade had been raging for three hundred years since the first battle with the Cielcin at Cressgard, but it was far away across some twenty thousand light-years of Empire and open space, out where the Veil opened on the Norma Arm. While my father did his best to impress upon me the gravity of the situation, things at home were quiet, save for the levies the Imperial Legions pulled from the plebeians every decade. We were decades from the front even on the fastest ships, and despite the fact that the Cielcin were the greatest threat our species had faced since the death of Old Earth, things were not so dire as that.

As you might expect from parents such as mine, I was

given into the hands of my father's servants almost at once. Father doubtless returned to his work within an hour of my birth, having wasted all the time he could afford that day on so troubling a distraction as his son. Mother returned to her mother's house to spend time with her siblings and lovers; as I said, mother was not involved in the family's bleak business.

That business was uranium. My father's lands sat atop some of the richest deposits in the sector, and our family had presided over its extraction for generations. The money my father pulled in through the Wong-Hopper Consortium and Free Traders Union made him the richest man on Delos, richer even than the vicereine, my grandmother.

I was four when Crispin was born, and at once my little brother began to prove himself the ideal heir, which is to say that he obeyed my father, if no one else. At two he was almost as large as I was at six, and by five Crispin had gained a head on me. I never made up that difference.

I had all the education you might expect the son of a prefectural archon to have. My father's castellan, Sir Felix Martyn, taught me to fight with sword, shield-belt, and handgun. He taught me to fire a lance and trained my body away from indolence. From Helene, the castle's chamberlain, I learned decorum: the intricacies of the bow and the handshake and of formal address. I learned to dance, to ride a horse and a skiff, and to fly a shuttle. From Abiatha, the old chanter who tended the belfry and the altar in the Chantry sanctum, I learned not only prayer but skepticism and that even priests have doubts. From his masters, the priors of the Holy Terran Chantry, I learned to guard those doubts for the heresy they were. And of course there was my mother, who told me stories: tales of Simeon the Red, Cid Arthur, and Kasia Soulier. Tales of Kharn Sagara. You laugh, but there is a magic in stories that cannot be ignored.

And yet it was Tor Gibson who made me the man I am, he who taught me my first lesson. "Knowledge is the mother of fools," he said. "Remember, the greatest part of wisdom is in recognizing your own ignorance." He always said such things. He taught me rhetoric, arithmetic, and history. He

schooled me in biology, mechanics, astrophysics, and philosophy. It was he who taught me languages and a love for words; by ten I spoke Mandar well as any child of the interspace corporations and could read the fire poetry of Jadd like a true acolyte of their faith. Most important of all, it was he who taught me about the Cielcin, the murderous, marauding alien scourge chewing at the edges of civilization. It was he who taught me a fascination with the xenobites and their cultures.

I can only hope the history books will not damn him for it.

"You look comfortable," said Tor Gibson, voice like a dry wind in the still air of the training hall.

Moving slowly, I pulled out of the complex stretch I'd folded myself into and flowed through the next position, twisting my spine. "Sir Felix and Crispin will be here soon. I want to be ready." Through the small, arched windows set high in the stone walls, I could just make out the calls of seabirds, their noise muffled by the house shields.

The old scholiast, face impassive as a stone, moved round into my line of sight, slippered feet scuffing on the mosaic tile work. Stooped though he was by time, the old tutor still stood taller than me, his square face smiling now beneath his mane of white hair, side whiskers making him look like nothing so much as the lions the vice-reine kept in her menagerie. "Looking to put the little master flat on his ass, are you?"

"Which ass?" I grinned, stooping to touch my toes, voice creaking a little with the strain. "The one between his ears?"

Gibson's thin smile vanished. "You'd do well not to speak of your brother thus."

I shrugged, adjusting one of the thin straps that kept my dueling jerkin flat over my shirt. Leaving Gibson where he stood, I crossed barefoot to the rack where the training weapons waited on display by the fencing round, a slightly elevated wooden disc about twenty feet across,

marked for dueling practice. "Did we have a lesson this morning, Gibson? I thought it wasn't until this afternoon."

"What?" He tipped his head, shuffling a little closer, and I had to remind myself that though he moved well, Gibson was not a young man. He had not been a young man when his order commissioned him to tutor my father, who was himself nearing three hundred standard years. Gibson cupped a gnarled hand to one ear. "What was that?"

Turning, I spoke more plainly, straightening my back as I'd been taught in order to better project. I was to be archon of that old castle in time, and speechcraft was a palatine's dearest weapon. "I thought our lesson was later."

He could not have forgotten. Gibson forgot nothing, which would have been an extraordinary quality were it not the basest requirement for being what he was: a scholiast. His mind was trained to be a substitute for those daimon machines forbidden by the Chantry's holiest law, and so could not afford to forget. "It is, Hadrian. Later, yes." He coughed into one viridian sleeve, eyed the camera drone that lurked near the vaulted ceiling. "I was hoping I might have a word privately."

The blunted backsword in my hand slipped a little. "Now?"

"Before your brother and the castellan arrive, yes."

I turned and placed the sword back in its place between the rapiers and the sabers, spared the drone a glance myself, knowing full well that its optics were trained on me. I was the archon's eldest, after all, and so subject to as much protection—and scrutiny—as father was himself. There were places in Devil's Rest where two might have a truly private conversation, but none were near the training hall. "Here?"

"In the cloister." Distracted a moment, Gibson looked down at my bare feet. "No shoes?"

Mine were not the feet of a pampered nobile. They looked more like the feet of some bondsman, with sheets of callous so thick I had taped the joints of my largest toes to keep the skin from tearing. "Sir Felix says bare feet are best for training."

"Does he now?"

"He says you're less likely to roll an ankle." I broke off, all too aware of the time. "Our word . . . can't it wait? They should be here soon."

"If it must." Gibson bobbed his head, short-fingered hands smoothing the front of his robe and its bronze sash. In my sparring clothes I felt shabby by comparison, though in truth his garments were plain: simple cotton, but well dyed to that hue that is greener than life itself.

The old scholiast was on the verge of saying more when the double doors to the training hall banged open and my brother appeared, grinning his lupine grin. Crispin was everything I was not: tall where I was short, strongly built where I was thin as a reed, square-faced where mine was pointed. For all that, our kinship was undeniable. We had the same ink-dark Marlowe hair, the same marble complexion, the same aquiline nose and steep eyebrows above the same violet eyes. We were clearly products of the same genetic constellation, our genomes altered in the same fashion to fit the same mold. The palatine houses—greater and lesser—went to extravagant lengths to craft such an image so that the learned could tell a house by the genetic markers of face and body as easily as by the devices worn on uniforms and painted on banners.

The craggy castellan, Sir Felix Martyn, followed in Crispin's wake, dressed in dueling leathers with his sleeves rolled past his elbows. He spoke first, raising a gloved hand. "Oy! Here already?"

I moved past Gibson to meet the two. "Just stretching, sir."

The castellan inclined his head, scratching at his skein of tangled gray-black hair. "Very good, then." He noticed Gibson for the first time. "Tor Gibson! Strange to see you out of the cloister at this hour!"

"I was looking for Hadrian."

"Do you need him?" The knight hooked his thumbs through his belt. "We've a lesson now."

Gibson shook his head swiftly, ducking into a slight bow before the castellan. "It can wait." Then he was gone, moving quietly from the hall. The doors slammed, sending a temple-hushed *boom* through the vaulted hall. For half

a moment, Crispin did a comic impression of Gibson's stooped, lurching step. I glared at him, and my brother had the good grace to look abashed, rubbing his palms over the coal-dark stubble on his scalp.

"Shields at full charge?" Felix asked, clapping his hands together with a dull, leathered snap. "Very good."

In legend, the hero is almost always taught to fight by some sunstruck hermit, some mystic who sets his pupils to chasing cats, cleaning vehicles, and writing poetry. In Jadd, it is said that the swordmasters—the Maeskoloi—do all these things and might go for years before so much as touching a sword. Not I. Under Felix, my education was a rigor of unending drills. Many hours a day I spent in his care, learning to hold my own. No mysticism, only practice, long and tedious until the motions of lunge and parry were easy as breathing. For among the palatine nobility of the Sollan Empire—both men and women—skill with arms is accounted a chief virtue, not only because any of us might aspire to knighthood or to service in the Legions, but because dueling served as a safety valve for the pressures and prejudices that might otherwise boil into vendettas. Thus any scion of any house might at some point be expected to take up arms in defense of her own honor or that of his house.

"I still owe you for last time, you know," Crispin said when we had finished our drills and faced one another across the fencing round. His thick lips twisted into a jagged smile, making him look like nothing so much as the blunt instrument he was.

I smiled to match his, though on my face I hoped the effect was less swaggering. "You have to hit me first." I flicked the tip of my sword up into a forward guard, waiting for Sir Felix's say-so. Somewhere outside, I heard the distant whine of a flier passing low above the castle. It rattled the clear aluminum in the windowpanes and set my hairs on end. I placed a hand on the catch of my thick belt that would activate the shield's energy curtain. Crispin mirrored me, resting the flat of his own blade against his shoulder.

"Crispin, what are you doing?" The castellan's voice cut across our moment like a whip.

"What?"

Like any good teacher, Sir Felix waited for Crispin to realize his error. When the realization didn't come, he struck the boy on his arm with his own training sword. Crispin yelped and glared at our teacher. "If you rested highmatter on your shoulder like that, you'd take your arm off. Blade *away* from the body, boy. How often must I tell you?" Self-conscious, I adjusted my own guard.

"I wouldn't forget with highmatter," Crispin said lamely. That was true. Crispin was no fool; he only lacked that seriousness of person that predicts greatness.

"Now listen, both of you," Felix snapped, cutting off further argument from Crispin. "Your father will hand me to the cathars if I don't make first-class fighters out of the both of you. You're damn decent, but decent won't do you any good in a real fight. Crispin, you need to tighten your form. You leave yourself wide open to counter after every move, and you!" He pointed his training sword at me. "Your form's good, Hadrian, but you need to commit. You give your opponents too much time to recover."

I accepted the criticism without comment.

"En garde!" Felix said, holding his blade flat between us. "Shields!" Both of us thumbed the catches to activate our shields. The energy curtains changed nothing where the human speeds of swordplay and grappling were concerned, but it was good practice to get used to them, to the faint distortion of light across their permeable membranes. The Royse field barrier would deflect high-velocity impacts with little difficulty; it could stop bullets, halt plasma bursts, dissipate the electrical discharge of nerve disruptors. It could do nothing against a sword. Felix dropped the blade like the headsman he sometimes was, dull point clipping the floor. "Go!"

Crispin boiled off the line, blade tucked back to put the power of his elbow and shoulder behind it. I saw the blow coming from light-years away and ducked under it as it whistled over my head. Spinning, I came back to

guard at Crispin's right with a perfect angle to strike at his exposed back and shoulder. I shoved him instead.

"Stop!" Felix barked. "You had a perfect opportunity, Hadrian!"

We continued in this vein for what felt like hours with Sir Felix laying into us at intervals. Crispin fought like a whirlwind, striking wildly from above and the sides, aware of his greater range of motion, his power and strength. I was always faster. I caught the turn of his blade against my own each time, stumbling back toward the edge of the round. I have always been grateful that my first sparring partner was Crispin. He fought like a freight tram, like one of the massive drone combines whose arms sweep entire fields. His superior height and strength prepared me to do battle with the Cielcin, the shortest of whom stood nearly two meters high.

Crispin tried to trap my blade, to force it down and so allow himself time to strike my ribs. I'd fallen for that gambit once already and could feel the bruise blossoming beneath my jerkin. My feet scraped against the wood, and I let Crispin have his way. All the force behind his blade made him slip, and I clouted him on the ear with an open hand. He staggered, and I struck him a blow with my sword. Felix clapped, calling a halt. "Very good. A bit less focused than your usual, Hadrian, but you actually hit him."

"Twice," Crispin said, rubbing his ear as he returned to his feet. "Damn, that hurt." I offered him my hand, but he swatted it away, groaning as he rose.

Felix gave us a moment, then squared us up again. "Go!" His blade clipped the wood floor, and we were off. I circled right as Crispin charged, sweeping to my right and into the first parry to bar his attack as he slipped by me. I clenched my jaw, whirling—too late—to strike his back. I heard Felix expel his breath through his teeth.

Crispin spun wildly, slashing a wide arc to clear space between us. I knew it was coming and leaped away. Sword low, I lunged. Crispin slapped my blade down, aimed a cut at my right shoulder. Recovering, I turned my wrist and parried, catching Crispin's sword with mine. He kept hold of his sword but twisted, exposing his back.

"Crispin!" The castellan purpled in frustration. "What the hell are you doing?"

The force of Sir Felix's voice gave Crispin pause, and I thumped him soundly across the stomach. My brother grunted, glaring at me from under heavy brows. The knight-castellan stepped up onto the round, dark eyes fixed on my brother. "What part of 'tighten your form' do you not understand?"

"You distracted me!" Crispin's voice went shrill. "I was getting free."

"You had a sword!" Sir Felix shook his open hands before himself, palms up. "You had another hand! Go again."

He sprang off the starting tape, sword high in both hands. I pivoted to the right, slapping hard to the left to block my brother's wild slash. I cut in, striking at Crispin's back, but my brother turned and caught my riposte on counter-parry. His eyes were blazing, his teeth bared. He knocked my sword aside and rammed into me with his shoulder, crouching to throw me up and back off the round. I hit the floor, the wind knocked out of me. Crispin loomed over me, six feet of angry muscle dressed all in black.

"You got lucky, Brother." His thick lips quirked into that jagged smile. He threw a kick at my ribs, and I winced, gasping for air. I ignored him as he continued, saying how if I'd fought fair, I never would have hit him. If Sir Felix said anything at all, I took no note of him. Crispin was close, towering over me. He finished talking and turned to go. I hooked one foot around Crispin's ankle and pulled. He came tumbling down, landing face-first on the edge of the fencing round. I was on my feet in a second, snatching up my sword. I planted one bare foot on Crispin's back and tapped him on the side of his head with the edge of my sword.

"Enough," Sir Felix snapped. "Go again."

CHAPTER 2

LIKE DISTANT THUNDER

THE NARROW WINDOWS OF Gibson's cloister cell stood open, looking twelve stories down upon an inner courtyard where servants tended the topiary in the rock garden. White sunlight streamed in from an eggshell sky, casting highlights on the clutter in Gibson's study. The walls were given over to bookshelves stuffed so to bursting that they leaked paper onto the floor like snow, the sheaves fallen amid piles of yet more books. Some shelves held racks of crystal storage and spools of microfilm, yet all of these were outnumbered one hundred to one by Gibson's books.

The scholiasts read.

Technological injunctions filed against their order for long-ago heresies forbid the scholiasts unfettered access even to the limited technologies permitted Imperial houses by the Earth's Holy Chantry. They were allowed only the pursuits of the mind, and so books—which are to thoughts as amber to the captured fly—were their greatest treasures. And so Gibson lived, a crooked old man in his flattened armchair, taking in the sunlight. To me he was a magus out of the old stories, like Merlin's shadow cast forward across time. It was all that knowledge which stooped his shoulders, not the passing of years. He was no mere tutor but the representative of an ancient order of philosopher-priests dating back to the founding of the Empire and further, to the Mericanii machine-lords, dead these sixteen thousand years. The scholiasts counseled

Emperors; they sailed into dark places beyond the light of the Suns and on to strange planets. They served on teams that brought new inventions and knowledge into the world and possessed powers of memory and cognition beyond the merely human.

I wanted to be one, to be like Simeon the Red. I wanted answers to all my questions and the command of things secret and arcane. For that reason I had begged Gibson to teach me the language of the Cielcin. The stars are numberless, but in those days I believed Gibson knew them all by name. I felt that if I followed him into the life of a scholiast, I might learn the secrets hidden beneath those stars and travel beyond them, beyond even the reach of my father's hand.

Hard of hearing as he was, Gibson did not hear me enter, and so he started when I spoke from behind his shoulder.

"Hadrian! Earth's bones, lad! How long have you been standing there?"

Mindful of my place, that of the student before his teacher, I performed the half bow my dancing master had once taught me. "Only for a moment, messer. You wanted to see me?"

"What? Oh! Yes, yes . . ." The old man noted the closed door behind me and tucked his chin against his chest. I knew the gesture for what it was: the deeply ingrained paranoia of the palace veteran, the impulse to check for camera drones and bugs. There should be none in a scholiast's cloister, but one could never be sure. Privacy and secrecy: the true treasures of the nobility. How rare they were, and how precious. Gibson fixed one sea-gray eye on the brass fixture of the doorknob and shifted languages from the Galactic Standard to the gutturals of Lothrian, which he knew none of the palace servants understood. "This should not be said. There are orders, understand? It is forbidden to speak of it."

That held my attention, and I seated myself on a low stool, pausing only to displace a stack of books. Matching my tutor's Lothrian, I said, "It's a mess in here."

"There's no correlation between the orderliness of one's work space and that of its mind." The scholiast flattened his flyaway gray hair with one hand. It didn't help.

"Is not cleanliness next to godliness?" I struggled with the strange language. The Lothrians had no personal pronouns, recognized no identity. I had heard their people did not even have names.

The old man snorted. "Lip today, is it?" He coughed softly, scratching one bushy sideburn. "Well, enough. This news won't wait. It was received last night, else it would have been shared sooner." He sucked in a deep breath, then said in measured tones, "There's a retinue from the Wong-Hopper Consortium due here within the week."

"Within the week?" I was so stunned I forgot my Lothrian for a moment and said, "How is it I've not heard?"

The scholiast eyed me seriously along the crook of his nose and replied in Lothrian, "The QET wave only arrived a few months ago; the Consortium diverted from its usual trade routes to make the trip." What Gibson said next, he said without preamble, without softening. "Cai Shen was hit. Destroyed by the Cielcin."

"What?" The word escaped me in Galstani, and I backpedaled, repeating myself in Lothrian. *"Iuge?"*

Gibson just kept looking at me, his eyes intent on my face as if I were an amoeba in some magi's petri dish. "The Consortium fleet received the telegraph from the Cai Shen system just before the planet fell."

Strange, isn't it, how the greatest disasters in history often feel hollow and abstract, like distant thunder? A single death, wrote one ancient king, is a tragedy, but a genocide can only be understood through statistics. I had never seen Cai Shen, had never left my own homeworld of Delos. The place was only a name. Gibson's words carried the weight of millions, but my shoulders carried none of it. Perhaps you think me monstrous, but no prayer or action of mine could bring those people back or quench the fires on their world. Nor could I heal every man and woman mutilated by the Chantry. Whatever power I had as my father's son stretched only so far, and only so far as he allowed. Thus I took the news without eulogy, my ini-

tial shock ebbing into numb acceptance. Then something deeper, something cold and pragmatic, took hold of me, and I said, "They've come for a new source of uranium." I sounded like my father.

The scholiast's ghost-trace of a smile told me I was right even before he admitted it. "Very good!"

"Well, what else could it be?"

Gibson shifted noisily in his seat, groaning from some complaint of time. "With Cai Shen destroyed, House Marlowe becomes the largest licensed supplier of uranium in the sector."

I swallowed, leaned forward to rest my chin on my folded hands. "They want to make a deal, then? For the mines?" But before Gibson could form an answer, a darker question settled on me, one I couldn't ask in Lothrian, and instead I whispered, "Why wasn't I informed of this?" When Gibson did not respond, I remembered his earlier remark and breathed, "Orders."

"*Da.*" He nodded, trying to pull me back into Lothrian.

"Specifically?" I sat back sharply. "He said not to tell *me*, specifically?"

"We were instructed not to share the news with anyone not cleared by the propaganda corps or without the archon's countenance."

I stood, and forgetting myself, still spoke in Galstani. "But I'm his *heir*, Gibson. He shouldn't—" I caught the scholiast glaring at me and returned to Lothrian. "This sort of thing should not be concealed."

"I don't know what to tell you, my boy. Truly I don't." He switched smoothly to Jaddian, glancing out the window as a maintenance worker ascended on a scaffold past stained glass in the shadow of a buttressed wall. If I craned my neck I could almost see the vast gray expanse of the Apollan Ocean beyond the curtain wall, stretching east to the bending of the world. "Just keep acting like you know nothing, but prepare yourself. You know what these meetings are like."

Frowning, I sucked on the inside of one cheek, and following his language change, said, "The Cielcin, though? They're sure it was a raid?"

"I saw the attack footage myself; the Consortium broadcast the last news packets from Cai Shen along with their visit announcement via the wave. Your father had Alcuin and myself up all night reviewing with the logothetes. It was the Cielcin, no mistake."

We sat there a long while, neither one moving. "Cai Shen's not in the Veil," I said at last, referring to the frontier beyond the Centaurus Arm of the galaxy comprising the bulk of the war front against the Cielcin. I looked down at my hands. "They're getting bolder."

"Latest intelligence says the war's not getting better, you know." Gibson turned his misty eyes away from me again and looked out the window and across the deliberately antique merlons and purely symbolic ramparts that hemmed in my family's house. The servant was still out there, polishing the glass by hand.

Again silence reigned, and again I broke it. "Do you think they'll come here?"

"To Delos? To the Spur?" Gibson eyed me pointedly, bushy brows contracting. "It's nearly twenty thousand light-years from the front. I'd say we're safe for now."

Still in Jaddian, I asked, "Why does Father insist on keeping secrets from me? How does he expect me to rule this prefecture after him if he won't keep me involved?" Gibson did not answer, and as it is the peculiar nature of youth to be deaf to silences, I did not take his meaning or see the answer presented there. I forged ahead, caught in the gravity of a question I could no longer shake: "Does Crispin know? About the Consortium?"

Gibson gave me a long, pitying look. And then he nodded.

CHAPTER 3

CONSORTIUM

BY THE DAY OF the Consortium's arrival, the castle could no longer hide the signs of preparation. Wong-Hopper, Yamato Interstellar, the Rothsbank, and the Free Traders Union: these institutions transcended the boundaries of our Empire and bound the human universe together. Even in far-flung Jadd the satraps and princes bent to the demands of industry, and for all his greatness, my father was only a petty lord. Every stone and tile of the black castle I called home was made ready, and every uniform of every servant and peltast of the house guard showed immaculate. All preparations that could be done had been done: the gardens were trimmed, the hangings beaten, the floors waxed, the soldiers drilled, the guest suites brought online. Most telling of all: I had been banished from the premises.

"We simply do not have the equipment, lordship," said the Mining Guild representative. Lena Balem flattened her hands against the desktop, wine-colored nails gleaming in the ruddy overhead light. "The refinery at Redtine Point is badly in need of repair, and without increased attention to containment, worker death is likely to exceed five percent by the end of the standard term." From her file, I knew her to be about twice my age, just on the far side of forty years standard. She looked so old. Her plebeian blood—undoctored by the High College—betrayed her in the graying of her golden hair, in the creases at the corners of her mouth and eyes, and in the softening of the flesh of her jaw. Time was already taking its toll on her,

whereas she was little more than a child measured against the centuries I anticipated. I must have stared, or else been too quiet for too long, for she broke off abruptly and said, "I'm sorry, but I thought I was meant to be addressing your lord father on this matter."

I shook my head, sparing a glance in the mirror above and behind her desk at the black-armored peltasts who awaited me by the gray metal doors, all leaning on the hafts of energy lances taller than they were. Their silent presence gave me pause, and it was all I could do to keep the crooked smile from my face. "My father is irretrievably detained, M. Balem, but I am happy to field any of your concerns. Though if you would prefer to wait, I can take whatever problems you have to him directly."

The Guild representative's brown eyes narrowed. "That isn't good enough."

"I'm sorry?"

"There has to be money to replace some of these machines!" She thumped the table with one hand, scattering a tangle of storage chits. One fell from the desktop at my feet. Without being asked, I stooped to collect the chit for her. It was a mistake, not a thing one of my rank ought to do, and I imagined the shade of white my father's face might have turned to see his son so help a plebeian. Not commenting on my gesture, Lena Balem leaned across her desk to face me. "Some of the radiation suits for our miners are twenty, twenty-five years old. They're not adequate to protect our workers, M. Marlowe."

Without being prompted, one of the guards took a half step into the room behind me. "You will address the archon's son as 'sire' or 'my lord.'" Her voice was flattened by the visor of her horned helmet, vague and impersonal in its threat.

Balem's prematurely sagging face whitened as she realized her mistake. I felt a strong urge to wave the soldier into silence, but I knew deep down that the woman was right. Father would have ordered the mining representative beaten for the offense, but I was not my father. "I understand your concerns, M. Balem," I said carefully, focusing my attention on a spot just over the woman's

slumped shoulders, "but your organization has its mandates. We require results." Father had been precise in describing what I was allowed to say in this meeting, what was acceptable to command this woman's obedience. I had already said it all.

"Your house, sire, has kept quotas at the same level for the past two hundred years, all while doing nothing to recoup the losses to our equipment. We're fighting a losing battle, and the more uranium we extract from the high country, the deeper we inevitably must go. We lost an entire drill rig to cave-ins along the river."

"How many workers?"

"Excuse me?"

I placed the recovered data chit back on the edge of her faux-wood desk with the utmost precision, labeled side up. "How many workers did you lose in that cave-in?"

"Seventeen."

"You have my deepest condolences." Surprise flickered in the eyes of the peasant woman, as if the last thing she expected from me was anything resembling the faintest human kindness, hollow and meaningless as it was. Words are often that way. Still I felt it was on me to try. This was a tragedy, not a statistic, and the woman before me had lost people. The surprise held her mouth open a moment.

Then it was gone. "What good are your condolences to the families of these people? You need to do something about it!" Behind me I heard the peltast who had spoken earlier edge forward, and I headed her off with a gesture that went unseen by Balem, who continued, "It's not just accidents, my lord. These machines are ancient—some of them as old as my grandfather, Earth take him. It's not just the drill crawlers either but the refineries, as I've said, and the barges we use to sail the yellow cake downriver. Every part of the operation is on the edge of breaking down and falling apart."

"Father does love his profit margins." The pathos, the bitterness in my voice surprised me. "But you must understand, I am not empowered to offer reparations at this time."

"Then there has to be money to replace at least a portion of these machines, m'lord." She reached across her desk and dragged a small block across stacks of paper. "As it is, we've got men and women working down those tunnels with pickaxes and hand spades. Thirteen-hour shifts." Her voice grew louder. "Do you have any idea how many people it takes to match the output of those machines?"

I felt my smile falter as it dawned on Balem that she had just raised her voice to one of the peerage. I imagined Crispin ordering his guards to strike her and set my jaw instead. I was not Crispin or my father. "M. Balem, those machines are produced offworld." I wasn't certain where. "With the Cielcin harrowing the colonies in the Veil, interstellar commerce comes at a premium. It's very difficult to—"

"There must be *something*." She cut me off, turning the cube over in her hands. Only a paperweight, I realized, staring at it. For a moment I had thought it was a storage crystal of the sort used to hold sim games and virtual environments. But no, the lower class was not allowed such things. They were forbidden even the technical know-how to replace their battered mining equipment. The means of production were left entirely in the hands of the noble houses and the handful of artisan-manufacturers who worked for them. High technology, even entertainment devices like sim games, were the province of the elite. This was a paperweight and nothing more.

"There very likely is." Keeping my voice soft, I shifted my eyes away from the steel in hers.

Before I could continue my thought, Lena Balem cut in, "And the current mines will only last for so long, m'lord. Without those drills we've no way of cutting new shafts, unless your father wishes for us to use our hands."

He may wish that, I thought, swallowing. "I understand, M. Balem." I drew another breath.

"Then why is nothing being done to fix the problem?" Her voice grew in volume again. I was losing control of the conversation, if I hadn't lost it already. One of Lena

Balem's hands closed around the steel cube, red nails like bloody claws closing around a heart.

"The Guild representative should remember that she is speaking to the son of Lord Alistair Marlowe." The other peltast this time; both of them were watchdogs for my father.

The color fled Lena Balem's cheeks, and she caved back into her seat. My father's name had that effect in his lands and on the rest of Delos. Though ours was but one of 126 lesser houses in-system sworn to the planet's vicereine-duchess, ours was by far the richest, the noblest, and the closest in council to Lady Elmira. Father had spent increasing periods of time in Artemia at the vicereine's castle in recent years and had even served as her executor years and years ago, when she was offworld. It was not impossible that before long we would be asked to leave Meidua and Devil's Rest to take up a fief and title on some new world all our own.

"I beg your pardon, m'lord." Lena Balem set the paperweight down as if it had burned her. "Forgive me."

I waved her apology aside, resuming my politest smile. "There is nothing to forgive, M. Balem." I bit my lip, thinking of the soldiers behind me who *had* thought there was something to forgive. "I shall of course take your complaints to my father. If you have projections regarding the cost and benefits of these replacement machines, I think both Lord Alistair and his councilors will want to see them." I checked the time on my wrist terminal, eager to be off. I still had a chance to catch the arrival of the Mandari visitors. "M. Balem, I also suggest you prioritize your needs before speaking with my father and his advisory council. But I must beg your pardon." I made a show of checking my terminal again. "I've an appointment to keep." My chair scraped the tiled floor as I stood.

"That's not good enough, m'lord." Lena Balem rose as well, looking down her overlarge nose at me. "People are dying in those mines *regularly*. They need at least adequate environment suits. My people are dying from radon gas, radiation . . . I have photos." She rummaged through

the collected sheaves of printouts on her desk, glossy images of lesioned torsos and scabrous flesh.

"I know." I turned away as my guards moved forward to place themselves at my sides. I felt the point of my parrying dagger bump my leg. I felt in that moment that this woman might attack me. She would never behave like this with father. I had been too soft. Father would have this woman whipped, put in the stocks along Meidua's Main Street naked. Crispin would have beaten her himself.

I merely left.

"Success, my lord?" asked the young lieutenant after our flier took off from the Guild complex in the lower ward of the city below the limestone cliffs. We rose slowly above the tiled rooftops and past the sky-spires of Lowtown, ascending to join the sparse air traffic. Below us the city of Meidua unrolled like an anatomical sketch along the seaside beneath the mighty acropolis on which my ancestors had raised the ancient fastness of our home.

I risked a glance at the lieutenant, shook my head. "I'm afraid not, Kyra." The shuttle passed through a plume of white steam rising from a seaside nuclear plant as we banked wide over the water to approach Devil's Rest from the east. Atop its acropolis of white stone, the black granite of the curtain wall and Gothic spires within drank the gray sunlight, looking out of place against the limestone bluff on which it stood, as if some inhuman power had pulled the stones still smoking from the heart of the planet, as indeed it had.

"Sorry to hear that, sire." Kyra tucked a bronze curl up under the lip of her flight cap. I glanced sidelong at the two peltasts seated in the back of the shuttle, feeling their eyes on me.

Leaning forward against my straps, I said, "You've been with us for some time now, haven't you, Lieutenant?"

"Yes, sire," she called back over one shoulder, briefly looking my way. "Four years now!"

The afternoon sun streaming in through the front canopy edged her face in snowy fire, and I felt a pang for her. There was something in her that struck me as somehow more real than the palatine ladies to whom I'd been introduced, more alive. More . . . human.

"Four years . . ." I repeated, smiling at the edge of her face visible from my place on the back benches. "And did you always want to be a soldier?"

She stiffened, something in my voice putting her on edge. The accent, perhaps. I have been told several times since that I speak like the villain in some Eudoran opera. "I wanted to fly, sire."

"I'm glad for you, then." My attention could no longer stay on her face, and flushing, I looked out the window at the city—my city—taking in the tangle of it, the way the streets spiderwebbed across the bluffs beneath Devil's Rest and above the sea. I could see the verdigris dome of the Chantry with its nine minarets like lances thrust at the sky, and at the opposing end of the main street the great ellipse of the circus, today open to the elements. "It is beautiful up here." I knew I was babbling, but I found it distracted me from the thought of what I was flying toward: my father and the Mandari guests he'd meant to keep from me. I thought of Crispin and his jagged smile. "Nothing to worry about."

"Only the other fliers, lordship." I saw the corner of her mouth rise and, briefly, the milky flash of teeth. She was smiling.

I smiled too. "Yes, of course."

"Do you fly, sire?" she asked before adding demurely, "If his lordship does not mind my question."

Turning in my seat, I looked pointedly at the two peltasts sitting by the exit ramp at the back of the flier, their gauntleted hands clasping support loops that drooped from the gray-paneled ceiling. "I don't mind. And yes, I fly. Not so well as you. Ask Sir Ardian about it sometime."

She laughed. "I will."

Unable to shake the cloud settling on me, I changed the subject, now looking pointedly at the short-carpeted

floor of the cabin. "Has the delegation arrived at the castle yet?"

"Aye, lordship," the lieutenant answered, pushing our flier into a steep descent that brought us below the crown of the bluffs where the living rock ended and the imported black granite began. Somehow, looking at the old place from beneath like this, I always imagined the crash of thunder. "Some hours ago."

It was as I'd feared and expected: I was going to miss the ceremony. "What does your father do, Kyra?" I had not meant the words to escape me, yet they had—small things, and dangerous.

"Sire?"

"Your father," I repeated. "What does he do?"

"He works the city's light grid, sire."

My lips twisted, formed a poor joke. "Do you want to trade?"

The castle at Devil's Rest, product of an age grander than our own, was itself large as a city, though less than a tenth the number of souls dwelt within it than clambered about and below its walls. When its first walls were raised, the Sollan Empire sat heavy on the stars, unopposed in might and majesty, the sole human power in the cosmos. While those halcyon days of blood and thunder were long since gone, still she endured, a confusion of buttressed spires and knuckled masonry rising like so many weathered bones from the hill above Meidua. Grand as she was, the old fortress was small by the standards of the day. The Great Keep, a massive, square-sided bastion of steel fronted in dark stone, rose only fifty levels above the plaza in which it sat. Still it dwarfed the other structures in the castle, even the minarets of our own private Chantry. The small, twelve-storied tower of the scholiasts' cloister looked pitiful in its extreme corner by the gardens and the outer wall. I strode toward the Keep, passing through the shadows of a colonnade, boot heels clacking on the mosaic.

I'd lost my two guards in the landing hangar and left Kyra to finish powering down the flier. But I was not alone; light-armored peltasts and hoplites with body shields and full ceramic plate were posted at intervals along the colonnade and the grand stair that led to the viaduct that fed into the plaza at the base of the Keep. There I rubbed shoulders with a throng of uniformed logothetes of the house staff who administered our little slice of empire. Even had I been the only one on the path, I would not have been alone. None of us was ever alone. The cameras were ever watchful.

I passed the statue of Julian Marlowe—long dead and mounted on his horse, sword held defiant against the heavens—and ascended the sweeping white marble stairs. I continued through the main gate, pausing to acknowledge Dame Uma Sylvia, the knight-lictor on watch at the door.

"My father?" I asked, the question ringing clear in the afternoon air.

"Still in the throne room, young master!" Sylvia replied, not breaking her perfect attention.

I crossed the white-and-black tiles of the floor, darting straight across the copper sunburst of the Imperial seal and toward the inner stair. Black banners hung heavy on the high walls, and the noise of foot and trumpet echoed up the hollow shaft in the center of the space for thirty of the Keep's fifty levels. That noble banner, sigil of my fathers unto the very deeps of time, sullied now by my hand. Perhaps you've seen it? Blacker than the black of space, its red devil capering, trident in its hands above our words: *The sword, our orator.* Two such devils faced one another beside the wrought-iron doors to my father's hall, dwarfing the pointed arch there and the men guarding it.

Strange things, those doors—weighty things of poured iron, raw and treated with some dull resin to guard against rust. Each door was three times the height of a man and several inches thick so that the confusion of human forms done in relief upon each surface stood out sharply. Each door must have weighed several tons, but they moved

gently, balanced by slow counterweights so that even a child might open them.

"Master Hadrian!" said Sir Roban Milosh, a furtive, dark-skinned man with tightly curling hair. "Where have you been?"

My eyes narrowed, and I was a moment collecting myself, breathing a scholiast aphorism under my breath: "Rage is blindness." *Rage is blindness.* To Roban I said, "I was detained with the Mining Guild, father's orders. Are they inside?"

"For about the last thirty minutes."

Uncomfortably aware of my disheveled appearance, of the wild tangle of my too-long hair and the wrinkled imperfection of my formal jacket, I clapped the knight on the arm. "That just means we're through the boring part. Let me by." I moved to pass him, pressing one palm flat against the door. Roban's counterpart stepped forward and seized my arm. Outraged, I whirled and glared at the hoplite. His helmet, like the helmets of most combat suits, had no visor, only a ridged carapace of solid ceramic that hid his face. Cameras piped images to a screen inside his mask, giving the impression that he was a statue and not a man at all.

"Lord Alistair says no one's to enter while he's receiving the director." He released me pointedly and firmly. "Sorry, young master."

Working to contain my sudden surge of outrage, I repeated the scholiasts' aphorism in my head, trying not to let myself focus too much on the persistent dread rising in me. I should have turned and walked away. It would have been easier.

Instead I cleared my throat. "Soldier, stand aside."

"Hadrian." Roban put a hand on my shoulder. "We have orders."

I turned, and I confess that my frustration undid me. "Get your hands off me, Roban." And I shoved the door open before either the knight-lictor or his lieutenant could stop me. The door made no noise as it swung inward. The damage done, I turned and glared at the hoplite, who was

halfway to seizing me. I had the same eyes as my father and knew how to use them. The man quailed.

No fanfare accompanied my entrance, unless one counted the nods of the peltasts just within. There is a limit to the vastness of space which the human eye and mind can fully appreciate, beyond which the impact of grandeur overwhelms. The throne room exceeded that limit, being at once too tall, too wide, and too long. Rank and file of dark columns retreated left and right, supporting frescoed vaults depicting the death of Old Earth and the eventual colonization of Delos. Though human senses could not detect it, the distance between floor and ceiling subtly shrank between the doors and the dais at the far end so that the supplicant was deceived into perceiving the archon as larger than any human ought to be. It is said the Solar Throne on Forum makes use of such a trick, that the Emperor might dwarf even the lordliest duke of his constellation.

The throne itself sat wreathed in shadow, and the two curving horns at its back—in reality the ribs of a great brass whale—towered halfway to the distant ceiling, blocking the light from the rose window behind the throne so that the figure seated upon it was veiled.

The Consortium retinue stood assembled before the throne, standing tall at the base of the dais, their silhouettes absurdly stretched by the microgravity of the ships they lived aboard. There were seven of them, all in matching robes, attended by two dozen soldiers in matte gray, each carrying a short rifle instead of the energy-lances favored by my father's troopers.

"Forgive my lateness, father." I used my speaking voice, bringing the full force of the rhetorical training Gibson had given me to bear. "The Mining Guild representative went on a little longer than intended."

"Why are *you* here?" The sound of that voice in this place curdled within me, and I felt a cold wind blow through my soul. Not only had Crispin known about the visitors from the Wong-Hopper Consortium, he had been invited.

I ignored Crispin's petulant question and approached within ten paces of the line of Consortium guests as they stood beneath my father's throne. I was not yet in the shadow of that great chair, and my father was only a darker shape amid the blackness of that ebony and wrought-iron seat. Going to one knee before the throne, I bowed my head before the Mandari visitors. "Honored guests,"—the practiced depth of my voice pleased me after Crispin's whinging—"forgive my lateness. I was detained by local matters."

One of the tall visitors took a couple of steps toward me. "Rise, please." I did, and the Consortium representative turned to look up at my father. "What is the meaning of this, Lord Alistair?"

In his throne, my father stirred. "My eldest son, Director Feng." His voice, which ought to have been as familiar as my own, was as a stranger's to me.

The woman who had addressed me nodded, letting spidery hands fall to her sides in a rustling of gray sleeves. "I see." The other Consortium members shuffled on slippered feet.

"Take a seat." My father slowly resolved into focus as my eyes adjusted to the deep shadow of his throne. He was more like me in appearance than Crispin; the genetic looms had built father thin and lean and hard with an aquiline face, all sharp edges and hard angles. Like myself, my father eschewed the local fashion. His hair was long and combed straight back so that it curled slightly below his ears. His face was clean-shaven, thick-lipped, and cold, and his violet eyes watched all that was below him, unfeeling.

I swallowed and brushed past Director Feng and her associates, my attention on a line of three chairs below and to the right of the high seat. Crispin sat there alone on the seat nearest Father. I stopped, staring down at my brother as surely as Father was staring at me. "Move over, Crispin." I kept my voice low.

My brother only raised his eyebrows, gambling—quite correctly—that I would not push the issue in front of our

guests. I didn't. I was too much the gentleman for that. But I was enough the child to pick up the small bloodwood chair next to him and carry it two steps up onto the dais. I sat, ignoring the muted outrage I could sense pouring from my father on his dark throne.

CHAPTER 4

THE DEVIL AND
THE LADY

"NOT YOUR SMOOTHEST PERFORMANCE,
Hadrian." My mother's voice carried well through the
darkly paneled door that separated my closet from my
bedchamber. Contralto; rich with the accents of the
Delian nobility; polished by decades of speeches, formal
dinners, and performances. She was a librettist by profession, and a filmmaker.

"Crispin wouldn't move." It was all the response I
could muster as I fussed with the silver buttons of my best
shirt.

"Crispin is fifteen and ill-tempered to a fault."

"I know, Mother." I flipped my braces up over my shoulders, tightened them. "I don't understand why Father
didn't . . . didn't include me."

From the dullness in her voice, I could tell Mother had
moved away from the closet door and toward the high
window that overlooked the sea. She often did this. The
Lady Liliana Kephalos-Marlowe had a tendency to drift
toward windows. We shared this—that desire to be somewhere else, anywhere else. "Do you really have to ask?"

I didn't. Instead of answering, I slung on my silk-and-
velvet waistcoat, smoothed the collar down. Sufficiently
dressed, I opened the door and stepped out into my bedchamber, seeing that Mother had indeed moved to the
window. My rooms were high in the Great Keep, built into
the northeast corner of the square tower. From there I had
a commanding view of the seawall and the ocean beyond,
could see for miles to where the Wind Isles lay dim against

the horizon, though they were invisible at sea level. Mother turned to face me. She never wore black, never adopted the colors and the heraldry of Father's house. She had been born of House Kephalos; her mother, the vicereine, was also the landed duchess of the whole planet, and she wore it proudly. For this occasion—the banquet welcoming Director Adaeze Feng and her party—my mother wore an elaborate gown of white silk so tight it must have been synthetic. It fastened over one shoulder with a gold brooch fashioned in the shape of the Kephalos eagle. Her honey-bronze hair was pulled up in the back, left to fall in tight ringlets before her ears. She was beautiful in the way all palatine women are beautiful. An image of forgotten Sappho cast in living marble, and just as cold.

"Your hair is atrocious."

"Thank you, Mother," I said evenly, pushing my curling fringe behind my ear.

Lady Liliana's red-painted mouth opened, searching for words. "It was not a compliment."

"No," I agreed and shrugged into my frock coat with the devil of my house embroidered above the left breast.

"You really ought to cut it." She moved away from the window, reaching out to straighten my lapels with white fingers.

"Father confuses me with Crispin enough as it is." I let her adjust my collar without comment save my most cutting glare. Her own eyes were amber, warmer by far than Father's. Even so, I could not feel that warmth. I knew if she had her way she would be back in Artemia with her family and her girls, not with us Marlowes in this dim and ashen place. Us Marlowes with our cold eyes and colder manners, her husband's coldest of all.

"He does no such thing." From the muted haste in her tone, I guessed that she had missed my point.

"Then does he mean for Crispin to take my place?" Still I glowered at her as she smoothed the shoulders of my jacket.

"Isn't that what you want?"

I blinked at her. I had no way to answer that, not without breaking the delicate balance of my world. What

could I say? No? But I didn't want my father's job any more than I wanted to be First Strategos of the Orionid Legions. Yes? But then Crispin would rule, and Crispin . . . Crispin would be a catastrophe. I did not want to gain my father's throne—I wanted Crispin to lose it.

Mother peeled away and returned to my window, heels clacking on the tile floor. "I can't claim to know your father's plans . . ."

"How could you?" I drew myself up to my full and unimpressive height. "You're never here."

Mother didn't flare up, didn't even turn to look at me. "Do you think anyone would stay if they had a choice?"

"Sir Felix stays," I retorted, shrugging my jacket more tightly about my narrow shoulders, "and Roban, and the others."

"They see the possibility of advancement. Lands, titles of their own. A small keep."

"Not out of loyalty to my father?"

"None of them *knows* your father, save perhaps Felix. I married him, and I can't say I know him."

I knew that, but hearing it—hearing that my parents were strangers—shattered me every time. I allowed the smallest of nods, then realized my mother could not see it with her back turned. "He doesn't inspire familiarity," I said at long last, frowning in spite of myself.

"And neither should you, if you rule in his place." Lady Liliana half turned to regard me through bronze curls, her amber eyes hard and tired. I think it was then that I first marked her age—not the early adulthood she wore outwardly, but the nearly two centuries she held in truth. The effect vanished in a snap as she continued, "You will have to lead your people, not stand beside them."

"If I rule?" I repeated.

"It's not a foregone conclusion," she said. "He may yet choose Crispin or order a third child from the vats." Anticipating my response, she added, "Just because House Marlowe has always honored the eldest child does not mean it must. The law permits your father a choice of heir. Assume nothing."

A bit stung, I said, "Fine. It doesn't matter, that's—"

She cut me off. "Quite right, it does not matter. Come now, we're nearly late."

Stars, I thought, were born and died before dessert. I maintained my silence through the toasts, through the salad course, through cycles and cycles of servants setting and clearing the table. And I listened, all too aware of the anger that, like gravity, bent time and space around my father. Privately I was grateful the director and her contingent had displaced me far from my customary place at Father's right. A day had passed since my late arrival to the throne room, and my father had yet to speak to me. That in itself was nothing strange, but that I had done what I'd done and not been reprimanded filled me with unease.

So I ate and listened, studying the strange, almost alien faces of the Consortium dignitaries. The plutocrats spent their lives in space, and the centripetal imitation of gravity aboard their massive spinships did not stop them from changing. Were it not for gene therapies almost as rigorous as my own, they would not be able to stand on Delos—with its one and one-tenth standard gravity—but would be crushed and gasping as boned fish upon the strand.

"The Cielcin have gone too far, pressing beyond the Veil," said Xun Gong Sun, one of the Consortium junior ministers. "The Emperor should not stand for it."

"The Emperor is not standing for it, Xun," said Director Feng mildly. "That is why there is a war on." I studied the director. Like all the members of the Consortium party, she was utterly hairless, her cheekbones and the shape of her brows enhanced to accentuate the slant of her eyes. Her skin was darker than that of the others, almost the color of coffee. She turned to speak to my mother and father where they sat at the head of the table. "The Prince of Jadd has committed twelve thousand ships to the war

effort under the command of this grandson of his, this Darkmoon. Even the Tavrosi clansmen have set sail."

My father set his glass of Kandarene wine down on the table, pausing a practiced second before responding. "We know all this, Madame Director."

"Yes, indeed." She smiled, lifting her own wine cup. Her fingers were like stick insects waving. "I only mean that all these ships will need fuel, my lord."

The Lord of Devil's Rest stared hard at the director, teeth sliding against his lower lip, and folded his hands on the table. "You don't need to convince us. There'll be time for it all soon enough." This elicited mild laughter from the ministers at the foot of the table, and across from me Crispin smiled. I glanced at Gibson, raised my eyebrows. "Fortune passes everywhere, and the current situation accords us a moment of advantage, despite the recent tragedy on Cai Shen."

Often I had observed my father in this mode, didactic and imperious. His eyes—my eyes—never settled in any one place or on one face but drifted over all that surrounded him. His basso voice carried far, resonating in the chest rather than in the ear. He had an air about him, a cold magnetism that bent all who listened to his will. In another age, in a smaller universe, he might have been Caesar. But our Empire had an abundance of Caesars. We bred them, and so he was doomed to suffer Caesars greater still.

"Is it true the Pale eat people?"

Crispin. Blunt, tactless Crispin. I felt the muscles tighten in every person at that long table. I shut my eyes and took a sip of my own wine, a Carcassoni blue, waiting for the storm to break.

"Crispin!" Mother's voice carried in a stage whisper, and I opened my eyes to see her glaring at my brother where he sat regarding the Consortium director. "Not at table!"

But Adaeze Feng only smiled sidelong at my mother. "It's quite all right, Lady Liliana. We were all children once." But Crispin was no child. He was fifteen, an ephebe on his way to manhood.

Completely unaware of his faux pas, my brother said,

"I heard from a sailor once that it was true. That they use people for food. Is it true?" He leaned in intently, and for all the gold on Forum I could not have said that Crispin had ever looked so interested in something.

Another of the Consortium executives spoke up in a voice deeper than the trenches of the sea. "Like as not, it is true, young master." I turned to watch the speaker where he sat beside Gibson and Tor Alcuin midway along the length of the dining table, near a bowl of steaming fish soup and a collection of wines in red-figure ewers. He was the darkest man I had ever seen—darker than the director, darker even than my hair—which made his teeth appear white as stars when he smiled. "But not always. More often they carry off a colony's native population and use them as slaves."

"Oh." Crispin sounded disappointed. "So they aren't all cannibals?" His face fell, as if he had been hoping the aliens were all monstrous, man-eating, murderous.

"None of them are cannibals." Everyone looked at me, and I realized it was I who had spoken. I drew a slow breath, composed myself. This was my area of expertise, after all. "They eat us, not one another." How many hours had I dedicated to studying the Cielcin with Gibson? How many days had I spent dissecting their language, extrapolating from those few texts and communications intercepted during the three hundred years of war? They had fascinated me ever since I could read—perhaps even sooner—and my tutor had never balked at the extra lessons I asked of him.

The dark-skinned scholiast nodded. "The young master is quite correct." I wasn't, I later learned—the Cielcin ate one another as readily as anything. It was only that no one knew it in those days.

"Terence—" Junior Minister Gong Sun placed a hand on the dark-skinned fellow's sleeve.

The other man, Terence, shook his head. "It is an ugly matter to discuss at table, I know. Forgive me, Sir Alistair, Lady Liliana, but the young masters should understand what is at stake. We've been at war for three centuries now. Too long, some would say."

I cleared my throat. "The Cielcin are nomads and carnivorous almost to a fault. Raising livestock in space isn't easy, even if you simulate gravity. It's easier to take what they can from planets. And the average Cielcin migratory cluster averages about ten million strong, so surely they can't have taken all the people on Cai Shen."

"It was a very large cluster, the reports say." Terence's nonexistent eyebrows rose in surprise. "You know the Cielcin well."

Gibson's reedy voice carried from farther down the table. "Young master Hadrian has had an interest in the Cielcin for many years, messer. I've been teaching him the aliens' language as well. He's quite good."

I looked down at my plate to hide the smile that had flickered onto my face, afraid Lord Alistair had seen it.

Director Feng twisted in his seat to look at me. I sensed renewed interest in the foreigner, as if she were seeing me for the first time. "You've an interest in the Pale, have you?"

I nodded, not trusting myself to speak until I remembered my courtesies. This was a director of the Wong-Hopper Consortium speaking to me. "Yes, Madame Director."

The director smiled, and for the first time I noted that her teeth were metallic, reflecting the table's candlelight. "Most commendable. It is a rare interest for a palatine, particularly for one of the Emperor's own peerage. You ought to consider a career with the Chantry, you know."

Unseen beneath the table, the knuckles of my left hand whitened against my knee, and it was all I could do to force a smile. Nothing could have been further from my desires. I wanted to be a scholiast. One of the Expeditionary Corps. I wanted to travel on starships, to go where none had gone before, to plant the Imperial flag across the galaxy, and to see things wondrous and strange. The last thing I wanted was to be chained to an office, least of all to the Chantry. I tossed a glance at Gibson, who offered a weak smile in return. "Thank you, madame." A brief look at my father was enough to know I should say nothing else.

"Or with us, perhaps, if your father could spare you.

Someone will need to do business with the beasts once the war's over."

Father had been notably quiet during all this, and I could not help but feel his wrath was imminent. I looked to him where he sat beside my mother, head slightly bowed as he listened to a footman who'd come to relay a message. Father muttered an instruction and was thus distracted when Crispin said, "You could sell them food!" My brother's face split with a macabre grin, and the director smiled sharp as a scalpel blade.

"I expect we will, young master. We sell everything to everybody. Take this wine, for instance." She gestured at the bottle from which I'd been drinking, a Carcassoni St-Deniau Azuré. "An excellent vintage, Archon, have I said?"

"Thank you, Madame Director," Father said. Without looking, I knew his eyes were on me. "Though I do find it curious that you have such an open mind where the Cielcin are concerned, particularly given the recent tragedy."

The director waved the suggestion away, setting her knife and fork on her plate. "Oh, the Emperor will be victorious, Earth bless his name. And Mercy's cup is overflowing, or so the priors say."

One of her junior ministers—a woman with golden streaks tattooed on her pale scalp—leaned round the director and said, "Surely after the war is ended the Pale must become subjects of the Solar Throne."

"Must they?" asked my mother, elegant brows arched. "I'd feel better with them gone."

"That would never happen," I said sharply, knowing I had made a mistake. "They have an advantage over us." Both my parents' faces had gone hard as stone, and from the tightness in Father's jaw I knew he was about to speak.

But the Consortium junior minister spoke first, smiling sweetly. "Whatever do you mean, sirrah?"

"We live on planets. The Cielcin are like the Extrasolarians," I said, referring to the backspace barbarians who plied the Dark between the stars, always moving, preying on trading vessels. "They have no home, only their migratory clusters—"

"Their *scianda*," said Gibson, using the Cielcin term.

"Exactly!" I skewered a morsel of pink fish with my fork and ate it, pausing for effect. "We can't ever be certain that we've wiped out the Cielcin. Even if we break a whole cluster—an entire *scianda*—all it takes is a single one of their ships escaping to ensure their survival. They're atomic, Protean. You don't crush that with military force, Mother. Messers, ladies. You can't. Ultimate extermination is impossible." I took another bite. "Now the same is true of us, but most of our population is planetbound. We suffer attacks harder, is it not so?" I looked to the director, counting on the lifelong sailor's vision of the Empire to vindicate me.

She seemed about to do just that when my father said, "Hadrian, enough."

Adaeze Feng smiled. "Not to worry, Archon."

"Do let me worry about my son, Madame Director," Lord Alistair said softly, setting down his crystal goblet. A servant hurried forward to refill the glass from a clay ewer decorated with wood nymphs. Father waved the woman away. "Particularly when he flirts so with treason."

Treason. It was all I could do to keep the surprise from my face, and I clamped my jaw more tightly. Across from me, Crispin pulled a face and mouthed something that looked rather like "Traitor." I felt the flush creeping up my neck and the embarrassment running down like so much wet clay.

"I didn't think—"

"No," Father said, "you didn't. Apologize to the director."

I looked down at my plate, glaring at the remains of my baked salmon and roasted mushroom—I had avoided some of the more exotic fare prepared specially for our offworld guests. Glowering, I held my silence. It struck me then how my own father never called me by name, how he spoke to me with commands or not at all. I was an extension of himself, his legacy made flesh. Not a person.

"There is nothing to forgive, sir," the director said, glancing briefly at her juniors. "But enough of that. This

has been a lovely meal. Sir Alistair, Lady Marlowe . . ."
She bowed her head low over the table. "Let us forget this
conversation. The boys meant no harm—either of them—
but perhaps we could return to business?"

CHAPTER 5

TIGERS AND LAMBS

THERE WAS A CLEAR pattern of events emerging, but I was little more than a child, and could not see it. Perhaps you do; perhaps you understand exactly what was being done to me. Why I did not see it when I had been trained for such things almost since I could speak, I will never know. Perhaps it was arrogance, the sense that I was better than Crispin, better suited to rule. Perhaps it was greed. Or perhaps it was because we are blind until the knife first takes us, because we believe ourselves immortal until we die. The world into which I'd been born was a wilderness of tigers playing at lambs. A wise man once told me that flesh was the cheapest resource in the human universe and that life spends more easily than gold. I laughed when I heard that and denied him.

I was a fool to do so.

How little I knew.

The arch that led into the rotunda beneath the Dome of Bright Carvings stands forever in my mind, imperishable, as the symbol of my failure. Awoken late by a maidservant, I hurried through the outer gate and into the circular gallery that enclosed the council chamber, moving with deliberate haste toward that awful portal. Poisoned sunlight fell in strange colors through the stained glass mosaic in the roof above, casting sickly shadows on the ancient statues—their bright paints cracked and fading—that decorated that curious place. It had been the custom in my family for generations to commission wood carvings from all the peoples of our prefecture every

decade. The greatest of these decorated the room, standing in niches and upon shelves, bolted to the wall, or suspended in the air on wires so that their shadows cut the colored sunlight to ribbons. The rest were given to the flames at Summerfair.

It was as if someone had taken all the color from our dark castle and pressed it into this one place like some dreadful secret. Birds and beasts, men and ships and demons all cavorted about the space, lit only by the filtered light of Delos's sun. The door was worst of all. Like most doors in our castle, its arch was pointed, and on the keystone—carved from brass whale ivory—was the likeness of a human face, aquiline and severe. It might have been my own, but it was the perfect twin of the face on the statue before the Great Keep, the face of Julian Marlowe, who raised the castle and our name to glory. Other faces clustered about his, pressed to the wall and down the frame so that thirty-one watched from about the doorway, all bone-white but for their violet eyes. Funeral masks taken from the catacombs where my family's ashes lay interred.

I knew them all, had memorized them as one of my earliest lessons.

My forebears, their features locked in time, put up for all to see.

The guards at the doors did not resist me as they had outside the throne room but opened the heavy wooden doors at a sign from me, their hinges quiet so that the only sound was that of my shoes scuffing the flagstones. The sound was lost at once beneath the murmur of conversation that rose like the tide to meet me, and I stopped short as half the faces at the round table looked up at me. Only Tor Gibson smiled, though it was brief and strained, smoothed away almost at once by his emotional discipline. The Consortium ministers regarded me with cool indifference, and Crispin—for there he was, seated to father's left—grinned that jagged, toothy grin of his.

My father did not even break stride. ". . . license permits us sole ownership of all uranium mined in the Delos system, not just from along the Redtine. The outlanders in

the belt can be brought up to quota with the right persuasion." He glanced over his shoulder at Sir Felix, who stood on guard behind his lordship. The castellan wore his best armor, the Marlowe sable and crimson cut with the bronze of his own lesser house. "Send Sir Ardian if the workers continue to hold out on us. He'll know what to do."

"The belt workers are in rebellion?" asked Adaeze Feng, her rich voice carefully modulating surprise and contempt. "I'd been given to understand you were a bit firmer in your grip than that, Lord Marlowe."

My father's face evinced less reaction than a scholiast's might have. He smoothed his hair back with an idle gesture. "The belt workers are always in rebellion, Madame Director. They make their puerile complaints, we grant them a few concessions, then take them away when that generation fades out of the workforce."

"Life expectancy amongst asteroid belt miners is only about sixty years standard," added Tor Alcuin, the pitch-skinned scholiast who was my father's chief advisor. "We can afford to cycle concessions in and out for new workers over the next century or so to keep their rebellions to a minimum. Take and give." While he spoke, I seated myself between two logothetes of the family treasury a full quarter turn around the massive round table from Father's oversized chair. I sensed the tension in the logothetes, saw the blond-haired woman at my left briefly turn in my direction. I ignored her, hoping to keep my lateness off the table as a matter for discussion.

The minister with the gold tattoos on her scalp frowned, looking directly at Tor Alcuin. "The vicereine approves of this?"

"The vicereine," Crispin interrupted, putting his tablet facedown on the table, "is content to let us do her dirty work. If we're putting down rebellions at home, that allows Her Grace to manage the sector." It was a struggle to smooth the surprised frown from my face. Crispin had these moments, these startling instants of clarity.

"Our true focus must be on the Cielcin," said Eusebia, the Chantry prior in Meidua. "All this must serve the Earth's chosen Emperor." The old woman was frighteningly pale,

like moonlight, her face seamed as crumpled paper, her voice like the blowing of spiderwebs in a slow wind. I caught Gibson watching me, and he shook his head, scratching one cheek. I knew what the Chantry was. Power dressed as piety.

The director waved one ringed hand, precious stones glittering as she smiled with those silver-metallic teeth. "Of course, Prior, but thought must be given to the situation *after* this war is over. When the war is won"—here she splayed that hand flat against the petrified wood of the tabletop—"we wish arrangements with Delos and House Marlowe to be as . . . amicable as possible."

"When the war is won?" Eusebia's soft voice rose in pitch and volume, and her cloudy eyes widened. "And should we not attend to the small matter of securing such a victory, Madame Director?"

Adaeze Feng's smile did not falter. "That is a question for the Legions, surely. And your Emperor. I am a businesswoman, Prior. I am here to make a deal with the archon for a share of his exports, not to strike at the heart of our mutual enemy."

"The Cielcin grow closer every day," said a minor functionary in the black robes of the Chantry seated not far from aged Eusebia. "Lord Marlowe, I must urge you to consider the alternative. You must arm the vicereine's legions with atomics."

Lord Alistair Marlowe did not look the Chantry toad in the face, but his deep voice undercut the sudden burst of chatter that followed. He did not raise his voice, did not shout, but spoke beneath the others and so undermined them, saying, "The Lady Elmira pulls fifteen percent in raw materials off our yield every standard quarter. She does not need more atomics, Severn, nor do we. The system is armed." He glanced at Gibson. "Scholiast, how many ships is Elmira capable of fielding in-system?"

The old man coughed, surprised to have been called on. "At last inquest by the Imperial Office? One hundred and seventeen ships total, discounting lighter craft." He rattled off a list of demographics, citing the subdivisions of that list by type of ship.

My father gestured for Gibson's silence with an open

hand, his attentions now squarely on Eusebia. "You see, Prior?" He returned his attentions to Adaeze Feng. "Is there something about the state of local affairs that disquiets you, Madame Director?"

Feng looked hard at my father for a moment, sucked on her words before answering. "The offworld workers . . ."

"Will accede to our demands the moment they start to starve on those airless rocks they call home," my father finished, resting his chin on his folded hands. "The planeted workers are a larger concern. The Mining Guild claims a series of systemic breakdowns in their mining and refinery equipment. The enrichment centers are of gravest concern—we lack the means to replace them and so must buy them from your manufactories."

"And we've a Guild factionarius here who wishes a word, Director Feng," Alcuin added. "She has the details of the situation among the planeted miners."

Junior Minister Sun leaned forward. "What proportion of uranium . . . er . . ." He broke off, murmuring to his neighbor in Mandar, the Consortium trade language. Apparently finding the word he wanted, Sun said, "Harvest. What proportion of the uranium harvest comes from planeted mines?"

"Thirty-two percent," said Gibson and Alcuin in tandem, the trained mechanics of their minds responding with nearly identical degrees of precision, but it was Gibson who went further, saying, "We're not operating near that capacity at present, sad to say. The attrition rate amongst the miners in the absence of proper drilling equipment has increased threefold in the past century."

Lord Alistair rapped the tabletop with his knuckles. "Enough, thank you."

The director pursed her lips. "Delos is not so rich a vein as Cai Shen was; repair to those enrichment crawlers is absolutely necessary. You wouldn't want to fail *our* quotas, after all. Would you?"

A piano-wire smile bled across my father's face, and the silence went tight as a garrote. Threatening the Lord of Devil's Rest had a long history of failure. Once when Father

was little older than I, the vicereine—my grandmother—had been called to attend the Emperor at Forum. Thirty-seven years she was away, and she left the recently orphaned Lord of Devil's Rest in her stead as executor. It had taken House Orin of Linon less than three years to begin refusing Father his tribute, and by the next year Lord Orin had raised an army among the exsul houses to depose my father and the absentee vicereine-duchess. They'd swarmed in from the outer planets in-system, falling from the sky like rain.

There had been no second year of Lord Orin's rebellion, and the castle at Linon was home now only to ghosts, a shattered ruin in a twilit crater on a distant moon at the edge of Delos's system. My father ordered the deaths of every member of House Orin, smashed their genestock, and raided their family atomics. He would have sown the earth with salt if it would have done any good on airless Linon. As it was, he only opened the windows of the sealed fortress and let the air out of the castle.

I think the director realized her mistake, for she ran a hand over her scalp and had the grace to look away. Father knew, I don't doubt, that he was not dealing with some exsul house—that this was a director of the largest interstellar corporation for ten thousand star systems—but he did not so much as change his expression. "I remind you, Director, that I am not the one who diverted my starship several parsecs to have this meeting. You are. If you believe you can obtain uranium on a scale comparable to that which is mined in-system here—and that you can do so legally—then I will not stop you. If, on the other hand, the unfortunate tragedy on Cai Shen means you must do business with me and my infrastructure, then I ask that you stop playing these games and tell me what it is you need."

I sat in silence, regretting that I had attended at all. The meeting broke up, and Alcuin led the Mandari party away to meet with the Mining Guild factionarius, leaving the logothetes and Chantry personnel to scatter more slowly.

"You." Father's voice did that alarming thing again,

sliding softly beneath the other sounds until it latched, adder-like, onto my attentions. "Stay."

I slumped back into my seat, looked away to watch the retreating backs of Eusebia and young Severn, the old prior leaning on the arm of her subordinate. They moved like a pair of witch-shadows, robes darker than the black armor of the house peltasts who moved to shut the doors behind them. In the moment before the doors closed, I saw Gibson's stooped figure leaning on his cane, frowning a frown he did not smooth away. That bothered me more than anything else: that he did not master his emotion as he should have done.

Then I was alone with my family.

"Mother didn't stay for the meeting?"

Father sniffed, adjusted the cuffs of his white sleeves beneath his dark jacket. "Your mother has gone to Haspida."

"Again?" Crispin set his tablet down and threw his hands in the air. "She only just arrived."

Lord Alistair waited a moment, drumming long fingers on the tabletop. His eyes were fixed on a spiked, heart-shaped wooden mask that formed the centerpiece of the decoration on one wall. The instant I glanced away to look at the ugly thing, he said, "You promised them assistance."

Unsettled, I looked round, eyebrows raised. "I'm sorry?"

"The Guild factionarius meeting with Feng. You promised her new mining equipment."

"Balem?" I sat straighter. "I did no such thing."

His deep voice deadly calm, Lord Alistair cut off any further protest. "You gave the damned woman assurances that we would do more to aid her workers."

"We should, Father!"

"Have you *any* idea how much one of those enrichment crawlers costs, boy?" When I did not answer him at once, he said, "Just under fifteen million marks, and that's before the import costs and the tithe to pay the Chantry." He leaned in over the table, eyes narrowing, "Do you know how many of the crawlers have been reported damaged in the past three standard decades?"

Crispin made a noise, and I turned to look at him

before answering. He was watching me with the same violet eyes as my father. I thought of the masks outside the door, the faces of my forebears. They filled me with disquiet, the sense that all of us were born to order, cut from the same violet-eyed cloth. But I did know the answer to Father's question, as it happened, so I shut my eyes and said, "Nine."

Crispin whistled. "Nine?"

"It's the Chantry," I said. "If we had the technical capabilities to effect large-scale repairs . . ." But that was impossible. In those days the Chantry controlled the use and trade of any and all complex machinery. They were seeking daimons, the intelligent machines with which the Mericanii had oppressed the rest of humankind long ago and which had oppressed them in turn. No such monster had emerged in Imperial space in more than two thousand years, but still the Chantry was watchful. When a lord stepped out of line—built a private datasphere, harbored foreign technicians, traded forbidden technologies with the Extrasolarians, or purchased one too many uranium enrichment crawlers without the permission of that system's grand prior—there were consequences. Daimons were everywhere, they said. Ghosts in the machine. The abominations were only waiting for a foolish magus to summon them from silicon and ytterbium crystal. Those lords who dabbled with that blackest art were subject to the Inquisition, to torture at the hands of the Cathars. In the worst cases, whole planets were sterilized, subjected to nuclear fire or to plague, to whatever horrors the black priests kept in their arsenal.

Aware of this deadly threat, Father's lips went white. "Do you want an Inquisition, boy?"

"I was only saying that—"

"I know what you were saying." Lord Alistair stood, looking down his hawk nose at me. "And I know you know how dangerous that is. Do you think Eusebia or that Severn fellow would hesitate for a moment to put any of us under the knife? We walk a fine line here. All of us do."

Crispin twisted in his seat to look at Father. "We've not done anything wrong."

Leaning back in my chair, I folded my arms. "I'm aware of our obligations to the Chantry's Writ, sire. I only think that if authorizing the purchase of new equipment is what it takes to restore planeted mining operations to parity, then we have to do it, regardless of the costs. Perhaps I could sit down with the director before she leaves; let me take Gibson. She needs our mining operations as much as we do, and maybe we can make a deal."

"A deal? You?" Lord Alistair turned away, his full-length coat belling as he did, a swirl of damasked black and red, his attentions on an ancient oil painting of a gondola approaching an island walled in by whited sepulchers.

To my surprise, Crispin cleared his throat. "Why not, Father? He's good at it." I opened my mouth to reply, shut it again, and found myself staring at Crispin in numb confusion. Had he just spoken in my defense? I just sat there, looking at my square-jawed little brother, the gaming tablet again in his big, blunt-fingered hands.

"Because your brother made this embarrassing situation that much worse with his meddling." Father half turned, feet still planted so that his body twisted as he regarded me from beneath hooded brows. The colors of him dimmed, lit only by the faint sunlight through the oculus in the dome above with its darkly frescoed images of conquest. "I gave you a simple task: placate the Guild factionarius. You agitated her instead and cut negotiations short to get back in time for that farce in the throne room."

I gripped the runners of my seat so tightly I felt my tendons groan. "You shouldn't have cut me out."

Father actually turned now. "Do not presume to lecture me on politics, boy." And for the first time that day, Lord Alistair raised his voice, those heavy brows contracting to form a slim crease just above his nose. Not quite a shout, but it was enough. Even Crispin cowed. "I know your uses, few as they are."

My wounded pride outdid my fear, and now I was standing. "Few? I thought I was being coached on diplomacy, Father. Gibson says—"

"Gibson is an old fool who forgets his place." My father

was all lord in that moment, dismissing the scholiast's three centuries of service with a wave of one glittering hand. "It's high time the old man retired. We should find some cloister for him in the city, or perhaps in the mountains—he'd like that."

"You can't!"

Father blinked once like a glacier cracking, his voice suddenly, dangerously soft. "I believe I told you not to lecture me." He turned away again, back to his contemplation of the painting with its deathly isle and the small white ship. "We will do nothing precipitately. Like yourself, the old man has his uses. I understand your study of languages is going well."

Sensing a trap but not yet seeing the shape of it, I said, "Yes. Gibson says my Mandar is excellent and that even my Cielcin is conversant."

"And your Lothrian?"

The trap was well and truly closed. How had he known? There were no cameras in the scholiasts' cloister. There couldn't be. Anything more complex than a microfilm reader wasn't allowed within arm's reach of an unsupervised scholiast. Had someone bruised his ear at the keyhole? Or . . . I remembered suddenly and smiled. There had been a servant cleaning the windows above the courtyard, hadn't there? I stood a little straighter, imitating a soldier's parade rest and hoping to hide my surprise. "Quite good, but not so good as to send me to the Lothriad—the Commonwealth." I exaggerated my small smile, hoping to mask my understanding with a joke. "I know enough to ask for the bathroom, but I might get lost elsewise."

Crispin laughed, and Father glared sidelong at him before addressing me. "Do you think this is a game?"

"No, sire."

"The scholiast revealed the visit to you, did he not?"

No use in denying it. "He did, Father."

"He's getting old. He forgets his place."

"He is wise and experienced," I snapped.

"Do you defend him, then?"

"Yes!"

Shrugging, Crispin offered, "He's not a bad teacher, you know."

"He's a great teacher," I said, thrusting my jaw out. "He did what he did only because there's no sense in keeping these things from your son, sire. If I'm to rule after you, I need to be involved."

"If you're to rule after me?" Lord Alistair blinked and shook his head, genuinely confused. "Who ever said you were to rule after me?" On reflex more than anything, I looked at my brother. No. No, it wasn't possible. It didn't make any sense. But Father wasn't done. "I haven't named a successor and won't for many years, by Earth. But if you continue like this, boy, I can tell you one thing." He paused, his back still to me, framed by the painting of that dread little isle. "It will not be you."

CHAPTER 6

TRUTH WITHOUT BEAUTY

ON THE FLOOR OF the coliseum, a team of four douleters worked with stun rods to bring the azhdarch to heel
while three others worked to clear the remains of the
slaves who had been sent out to fight the offworld beast.
I watched one work with a spade to throw sawdust on the
bloodstains, since like many people I found the alien
predator hard to look at. It was something in my cells, a
deep memory of what life ought to look like that stemmed
from the days when the curve of Earth bounded our collective universe. And the azhdarch was just wrong. In
many ways it resembled a pterosaur, those bat-lizards of
antiquity, with its leathery wings. In other ways it resembled a dragon out of fantasy with its long, spine-covered
tail and hooked claws. But the neck—nearly twice as long
as a man—was open from its vestigial head to the start of
its thorax and lined with hooked, snarling teeth that
hinged open and closed like the mandible-leaves of a fly
trap.

I saw one brave douleter—a red-haired young woman—
lash out with her stun rod and catch the thing in one leathery flank. It let out a gurgling howl and lunged sideways,
dragging the other three douleters by the great chains
they held. The crowd gasped and cheered, and the beast
blew sputum from its open throat. Even from the safety
of the lord's box above the shield curtain, I could see the
blood in it.

"Devils are up next," Crispin said, punching me in the
arm. "You ready?"

"As I'll ever be." I turned back to the book in my lap, rubbed the blade of my right hand. The charcoal there had started to smudge the image, clouding the profile I had drawn of Lieutenant Kyra's face. We'd been sent, Crispin and I, to attend the opening day of the Colosso season in Father's stead. He was away with our grandmother in Artemia, discussing matters of state.

As a boy I'd hated the arena. The bluster of it, the blood and circumstance. The violence offended me. The shouting and screaming all battered my ears as the trumpets blared from on high, amplified by the coliseum's massive sound system, and the announcer's voice cut above it all. The smell of unwashed bodies mingled with that of grilled artificial meats and the iron stink of blood assaulted the nose even as the screaming did the ears.

Yet it was the offense against life that wounded me most, the callous spending of humanity. The fighters were slaves, I knew, and perhaps that excused the violence for many, but I had just seen three men torn to ribbons by a flying xenobite monster and seen children squealing with delight and terror in the stands. Bare-chested men, their bodies painted red and gold or red and black, beat on each other and sloshed cheap beer onto themselves, shouting and laughing at the spectacle. The sight of blood sickened me as the news of Cai Shen and the massacre had not. For here was something immediate, concrete. And the people reveled in it.

I often wonder what the ancients would think of us, of our violence. I have heard it said that those generations that killed Old Earth had derided such violence in their everyday lives. It was ironic that the same people who had enacted nuclear war on the Homeworld, who presided over the refugee camps and rotted the ecosphere, had balked in the face of blood sport. Would they call us barbarians, those men of ancient days?

I darkened the line at the edge of Kyra's face with my pencil. Enough philosophizing. Crispin was cheering now. "I get to go on after the first bout!"

"What's that?" I did not look up from the image on my lap, accentuated one curl of hair. My mind was on other

things. On Cai Shen, on my father. On Crispin himself. In my mind I kept hearing my father's words to me beneath the Dome of Bright Carvings. *Who ever said you were to rule after me?* It was meant for Crispin after all. Every bit of it. I was to be discarded, packed away. Married off to some Baron or Baroness like an ornament or forced into the Legions.

"I get to go on!" Crispin smiled, looking genuinely excited at the prospect. "Father said I get to fight today."

"Oh." I looked at him only briefly. "I knew that. You keep saying." I pressed the pencil so hard against the page that the charcoal snapped, marring Kyra's slim nose. I cursed inwardly, realizing that I resented my brother. I already hated him, but hatred is something pure, like a fire in the belly. Resentment, though, sat in me like a cancer. I did not want what was his. Rather, I resented that he had taken something that I had implicitly understood was mine. I did not wish to win my father's throne, as I said. I only wanted Crispin to lose it.

"Father says I can only fight the slave myrmidons, but I could take Marcoh, I know it. Couldn't I take Marcoh, Roban?" Crispin stood up in his seat. My brother had dressed in armor for the occasion, in a suit of titanium and ceramic accented a deep red. Black leather had been stretched over the muscled breastplate, the Marlowe devil embossed there, drinking the light like blood. He wore a half cape over his left shoulder, all rich velvet, crimson where it caught the light, black where it did not.

The round-faced knight ran a gloved hand over his tightly curling hair. "I'm sure you could, young master."

"He favors those big swords—what do you call them?" Crispin took a drink from a glass of some blue energy drink, snapping his fingers at Roban.

"A montante," I said. I scratched Kyra's name in small, neat letters in the bottom right of the picture above the date with a second pencil removed from the leather kit between my feet.

"That's the one!" Crispin burbled a low laugh, grabbing another pair of olives from the china bowl on the small table between us. "They're so slow."

Roban did not stir from his place by the door. "The young master is quite right."

"Short sword and main gauche are better," Crispin declared, planting one foot on the table and upsetting the bowl of olives. It shattered on the floor, olives bouncing and rolling across the tile. Crispin ignored it, ignored the servants as they rushed forward to collect the fallen olives and smashed china. "Do you know who they have for me to fight?"

Sir Roban shrugged. "Just some of the slaves, I imagine."

"More than one?" Crispin's teeth flashed in the dim overhead lighting. His back was to the coliseum floor, his face in shadow.

"Perhaps, sire." Roban jounced his helmet under his right arm. "I was not informed. They left that up to the Colosso's vilicus. I was told he would come looking for us when they were ready for you."

Crispin swung back down into his seat and snatched up his drink with a gauntleted hand as he leaned forward over the rail. On the field below, the Meidua Devils emerged from a lift along the right side amid tumult and the sounds of trumpets. They were dressed in the ivory and scarlet of Imperial legionnaires, their faces blank armored swaths the color of bone, their names stenciled in red across their backs above identifying numbers. Tom Marcoh stood in the middle, the number nine huge on his back. He was a broad man with stripes on the white ceramic of his upper arms to mark him as a centurion, not that he was any such thing. He was a performer, a toy soldier, and as nothing next to the true soldiers I had known.

"It was the summer of '987!"

The announcer's voice filled the coliseum, rebounding off the cheering masses with their banners and hand-painted signs, screams and shouts of "Devils! Devils! Devils!" nearly drowning out the artificially amplified tones. It was enough to wrench at even my attention. I knew the date, knew what it was we were about to see.

"The last men of the 617th were stranded on Bellos, their ship crashed, their brothers and sisters slain! No one was coming to save them!"

On cue, the lift at the far end of the platform was raised, spilling thirty men and women out onto the field. Slaves, all. They were felons to a man, it being the practice on Delos—as in much of the Empire—for felons to be forced into such a life. Their nostrils were slit to mark their crimes and their foreheads tattooed with their offenses. Some lacked a hand, others an eye or both ears. All had been shaved bald, their bodies painted white to make them look more like Cielcin. Though it was impossible to tell in their black jumpsuits, I knew the male slaves had all been castrated and that the breasts of the female slaves had been removed to make them more like the Cielcin—neither woman nor man—and to demoralize them. They were meant to die there on that day. Meant to fit the narrative in which the survivors of the 617th Centaurine Legion repelled a Cielcin horde that had ravaged Bellos colony.

The seven men of the Meidua Devils wore body shields and armor; the slaves had none. The Devils carried plasma rifles and lances, set low so as to cause only superficial burns. The slaves had crude steel blades and cudgels—the Cielcin abjured firearms. It was not a fair contest. But then, it was not meant to be.

This was the Colosso, the great sporting event of the Empire, and it was a bloody thing. First the baiting with the azhdarch; then this melee, a chance for the conquering heroes to get their blood up; then the smaller bouts, champion against champion. And first among those battles would be Crispin, the young and dashing son of their lord, resplendent in his finest armor, gallant with his bright sword and stylish hair. The whole thing struck me as perverse in that moment. Perhaps the ancients were right. Perhaps Valka was. Perhaps we are barbarians. I wanted away, wanted my rooms back in Devil's Rest.

"See our noble heroes surrounded by the Pale beasts!" the announcer continued. With their stun rods, red-uniformed douleters prodded the slaves into a ring about the seven Meidua Devils. "See our noble heroes, the only thing standing between the poor people of Bellos and their fate as food for the monstrous Cielcin! See them make their heroic stand!"

A gong sounded, filling the arena: sonorous, doleful, oddly serene. The ringing of that gong echoes within me still, shadowing my own future. The crowd shrieked with ecstasy. I turned away, flipping to a new page in my book and sharpening my broken pencil on the little scalpel I carried in my kit.

The first shouts as the plasma fire cut into the attacking slaves burned me. They could not do anything but fight. The douleters around the perimeter had glowing lances that would drop them in an instant, force them to fight another day or kill them where they fell.

I shivered.

Beside me Crispin was entirely out of his seat, brandishing his unsheathed sword, the ceramic blade gleaming razor-sharp above the heads of the groundlings below our box. He shouted incoherently with the crowd, spurred on by the violence. I thought of Sir Felix then, of the boxing round the ears he would've given Crispin for drawing his sword so needlessly. I'd worn no weapon myself save a long knife, telling Roban I needed no defense other than his presence. That had gladdened the knight, but I felt foolish and terribly small, underdressed beside my brother, armed and armored as he was.

One of the Meidua Devils brought his foot down on the face of a slave, breaking the man's nose. Red blood ran down his cheeks and chin, carrying flakes of white paint where it went. He brought his foot down again, and the crowd gasped, then cheered. The boot rose, stamped again on the slave's face. The slave didn't move. He was dead— had been dead. This was showmanship: gratuitous, meaningless. It was not for me. It was for creatures like my brother, like the hollering serfs and plebeians in the stands with their kebabs and spun sugar delicacies, their sweetened drinks and cheap beer.

"Young master Crispin." A harsh, masculine voice sounded from the back of the box. I looked around the side of my chair and was surprised to see that it was a woman who had spoken: squat and with sharp brown eyes, her hair a tangled, sandy whorl cut just above her ears. Her ugly, windburned face twisted into a grotesque

smile. I reached up and grabbed Crispin by his absurd half cape.

He sloshed blue drink onto the floor as he turned, leering at the sight of the ugly woman. "Is it time?"

"Yes, young master."

Crispin practically wet himself with excitement, abandoning the drink on the table and almost running to where the fat douleter stood just inside the open door to the hall. The sounds of the crowd wafted in through that open portal, clearer, sharper without the muddying effect of the box's shields to help block the noise.

"Are you coming, Master Hadrian?" Sir Roban took a step forward.

"No, Roban." I turned away, rubbing at the smear of charcoal on the blade of my hand and succeeding only in dirtying my left thumb in the process. I fixed my attentions on the page before me and not on the bloody work on the killing floor. The truth was that I would gladly have gone with Roban if the lictor were bound for any place other than the gladiators' annex at the entrance to the field.

"Shall I stay here, then?"

"No, no. Crispin will need you more than I. The box locks."

"Yes, sir."

Alone in the lord's box, I sat in the chair meant for my father while below seven men kitted out as Imperial legionnaires butchered thirty prisoner-slaves with plasma burners and energy lances. The smell of burned flesh and singed fabric began to rise from the killing floor, mingling with the smells of kebabs and popcorn rising from the stands. It was an unsettling, disgusting aroma. I flipped through the pages of my sketchbook: images of people and places around the castle.

I had loved drawing ever since I was a child. As I grew up, however, I realized there was something singular about the process. A photograph might capture the facts of an object's appearance, colors and details rendered perfectly at a higher resolution than any human eye could appreciate. By the same token, a recording or RNA memory

injection might convey a subject with perfect clarity. But in the same way that close reading allows the reader to absorb, to synthesize the truth of what he reads, drawing allows the artist to capture the soul of a thing.

The artist sees things not in terms of what is or might be, but in terms of what *must* be. Of what our world must *become*. This is why a portrait will—to the human observer—always defeat the photograph. It is why we turn to religion even when science objects and why the least scholiast might outperform a machine. The photograph captures Creation as it is; it captures fact. Facts bore me in my old age. It is the *truth* that interests me, and the truth is in charcoal—or in the vermilion by whose properties I record this account. Not in data or laser light. Truth lies not in rote but in the small and subtle imperfections, the mistakes that define art and humanity both.

Beauty, the poet wrote, is truth. Truth, beauty.

He was wrong. They are *not* the same.

There was no beauty in that arena, but there was a truth. There, while men shouted and died on the killing floor, executed for the diversion of seventy thousand spectators, I saw it. Or heard it, rather—heard it behind the screams and cheers and laughter of the adoring public as Crispin stepped onto the field amidst smoke, as the douleters and servitors dragged the bodies of the dead slaves toward the lift. A silence. A profound, echoing quiet. Not a quiet in the ears but in the mind. The crowd—for it was a singular being—was shouting to drown out the loud silence in their souls.

I heard it, but I did not understand what it was. What it meant.

Buttoning my jacket, I turned, crossed to the door, and left the box. I needed air. All at once I found I could stand to watch the tableau no longer. It was not my world, not a thing I wished to inherit along with the rest. The peasants cheered as I left the box, cheered for Crispin.

He was welcome to it.

CHAPTER 7

MEIDUA

THE AIR WAS COOLER outside, and the sounds of tumult from the Colosso were muted and far away. Afternoon was settling toward evening, and the hulking, pale sun reddened on her haunches above the low towers of Meidua. In the distance our acropolis and the black castle of my home loomed like a thunderhead. And I was alone. The men and women ambling along the street outside the arena and the circus grounds might have been members of another species, so distant did they seem.

Perhaps my father was right to doubt me. If I could not endure the violence of the Colosso, how could I be expected to rule a prefecture as he did? How could I be expected to make the hard and bloody choices that are the soul of ruling? As I hurried from the coliseum, past the hippodrome and the grand bazaar, my mind turned to House Orin, to the shattered halls on Linon half a system away. I told myself I could not have done such a thing, that I was not so strong or so cruel. I thought of the dead slaves, of the gladiator's boot smashing the whitened flesh until the head crunched beneath it. I walked faster, wishing I could walk fast enough to leave the world entirely.

Immediately beyond the circus grounds, the city rose to loftier heights, its street lamps already lighted as the towers carved their shadows on narrow streets. A shuttle winged its way overhead, and in the far distance I could just make out the fusion contrail of a lifter rocket streaking heavenward. I wished I were aboard it, bound for somewhere—anywhere—else. I knew I should be heading

back—to my own shuttle at least, if not to the box and the
games—but the thought of returning to the coliseum, of
seeing Crispin at his bloody game, filled me with disquiet.
I stopped a moment in the shadow of a triumphal arch,
watching groundcars move past as they wove slowly
through the heavy foot traffic this near to the coliseum. A
stiff wind blew up from around the bend in the road, carrying with it the scents of salt and sea and the cawing of
distant birds. The fading day was fair with a faint chill
hinting at the end of summer, and I shrugged my jacket a
little closer about me. I would walk home, I decided, and
damn Father and what he'd have to say about it. It was not
too far to the castle: a few miles west and north up the
winding streets, hooking around a bend in the limestone
bluffs toward the stairs and the Horned Gate.

So I set off along the esplanade, moving parallel to the
Redtine and up toward the falls with their great locks.
Beside me the river thrummed with little fishing junks
and heavy barges carrying trade goods from upriver. The
sound of men's voices carried far over the water, raucous
and rough. I lingered there a moment, watching an old-
fashioned galleus crewed by serfs go by, pressing against
the slow current of the great river on its way back toward
the distant mountains. Faintly over the waters I heard the
cry of their oarmaster and the banging of the drum. "Row
on for home, my lads," he cried, words in time with the
drumbeat. "Row on for home."

I stopped for a moment, watching the old-style ship
until a freight tanker painted with the Marlowe devil
blocked it from sight. The serfs didn't stand a chance.
They were forbidden the technologies allowed to our
guild workers, and so they made do with the sweat of their
brows and the strength of their arms.

I had half a mind then to turn back, to make for the
wharfs and the fish market I'd often toured in my youth.
There was a Nipponese man there who rolled fish with
rice in a corner store, and in Lowtown there were per-
formers who pitted animals against one other. But I was
mindful of my danger, a palatine nobleman walking
openly down the street dressed in the finery befitting his

station. I twisted the signet ring on my thumb self-consciously and fiddled with the slim bracelet of my terminal. Instinct told me to call for backup, to at least alert Kyra that I was not going to meet her at the shuttle.

But I was protective of my privacy, as are all young men faced with difficult periods in their lives. Turning away from the riverside, I waited until the groundcars stopped rolling and crossed the front street, following a winding avenue upslope past blinking storefronts and stands selling produce and Chantry icona of printed plastic and false marble. I politely declined one woman's offer to braid my hair, then ignored her angry shouts that someone with my long hair must be a catamite. It was fashionable in those days for men to wear their hair short, as Crispin or Roban did, but I—and perhaps this was an emblem of my failures as an heir—preferred to ignore the populace. I wanted to point out to the woman that her archon wore his hair long, too, but I restrained myself and left her screaming on the corner.

As I said, I felt almost a part of another species. Because of my family's long history of genetic modification, I was—despite my short stature—taller than most of the plebeians I passed, my hair darker, my skin paler. Though I was still but a child, barely twenty years standard, I felt ancient beside those prematurely aged merchants and laborers, not because I was ancient but because I knew those wrinkled faces and leathered hands were scarcely older than my own. Their bodies had already betrayed them. Perhaps it was the barbarity of the Colosso, or perhaps my feelings have been clouded by what followed that walk, but thinking back to that moment I remember the faces of the Meiduans as little more than caricatures. Each seemed but a child's sketch or primitive carving done by one who had only the barest inkling of what a human was meant to be. Their heavy brows and large pores, oily skin mottled and sun-leathered as mine would never be. I did not then stop to ask myself which of us was truly human. Was it me, with my College-tailored genes and regal bearing? Or were they more human than I could ever be, their state the state of nature? I believed at the time that it was me, but as in

the parable of the sea captain who repairs his ship plank by plank until it is new again, I cannot now help but wonder how many lines one can rewrite in the blood before a man is no longer a man, or human at all.

The next street I found wound up and to the right, its limestone-and-glass facades curving around and artfully grown over with grape vines, though it was the wrong time of year for them to bear fruit. I passed the offices of several goods importers and a place where the commoners could pay to have someone replace their rotten teeth. Theirs did not grow back indefinitely and did so imperfectly, I'd been told. I had always found that strange, but then I thought of Madame Director Feng and her stainless steel implants. Why had she opted for such when white ones were available? This thought utterly absorbed me, and so I did not take the gunning of the bike engine for what it was or suspect the coming blow until it took me in the back.

My breath was knocked from my body, and I struck the paving stones with a grunt, my long knife under me. My back ached, and it was all I could do to get my arms under me and rise to my knees. Too-black hair fell into my face, and suddenly I understood the utility of Crispin's shorter style. That almost made me laugh, but too much of my mind was absorbed in what was happening. Where had everybody gone? And where was the vine-fronted street I had so admired moments ago? I must have wandered, entering a broad alleyway that angled steeply upward toward the face of the bluffs and our acropolis. High above, the towers of Devil's Rest still looked like the uplifted palace of some turbulent god.

Distantly I heard the bells in the city Chantry begin to chime the sunset, and the chanters' voices, amplified by massive speakers both in the temples and on tent poles across Meidua, began to pipe the call to prayer.

"Get him, Jem!" a voice called. Something heavy and metallic smacked stone, and I turned just in time to see a big man on a powered cycle gun his throttle, the primitive petroleum engine belching poison into the air. Where he

had gotten the thing—from some guild motor pool or back-alley deal—I never knew. He clutched a length of pipe in one hand, and from his posture I knew he had just struck the ground with it. The pipe also must have been what had struck me down. But it was the man's face that caught my attention. The left nostril had been clipped, sliced up to the bone so that the thing gaped awfully in the light of the burning streetlamps. And on his forehead, text proclaimed the man's crime in angry black letters: *ASSAULT.*

"Get him!" the other boy cried out.

I snapped my attention sideways to where two other men on bikes waited at the end of the lane ahead, egging on the man with the pipe. I held a hand up, staggered to my feet. "I yield!" I said, remembering my lessons about situations such as these, then discreetly thumbed the panic button on my wrist terminal. "I yield." Dimly I recalled instructions from my childhood, a reminder to surrender when unarmed or outmatched and to hope for ransom. Any palatine house would honor such a request as part of the rules of poine.

But these were no palatines.

"Fuck that!" said one of the two men behind me. "Fuck yielding."

The other said, "You're a pat, ain't you? Fine clothes like that?" He ran his tongue over his crooked teeth. "All kinds of money on you, I'd bet."

No answer I could have given would have satisfied that greed. I had only a second to take in my surroundings. The man with the pipe opened up the throttle of his bike, rear wheel spinning in place, kicking up dust and stone chips loose on the road. Then he rocketed toward me, pulling his arm back for another swing. Almost all my years of combat training fled me then, and I lurched sideways up onto the sidewalk, hoping the small bit of curb there would slow my attacker. During the scramble I thumbed the activation box on my shield-belt, felt the dry hum of the energy curtain coalesce around me. The sounds around me all went muddy, but it occurred to me that even on his bike my attacker would be too slow for the shield to do any

good. The threshold of a Royse field's usefulness was faster than any human could move. It would protect me if one of the bastards had a gun, but from that length of pipe? No.

The man's blow went wide, and he turned his bike into a skid, laughing as he wheeled about to face me again. I should have run, but I stood my ground instead and drew my main gauche. The knife was only about as long as my forearm, its ceramic blade milk-white in the red of twilight. "Who sent you?" I demanded, adopting a defensive crouch. Absurdly my mind went to the azhdarch-baiting I had witnessed earlier that afternoon, but I realized quickly how little that situation had in common with my own. The flying xenobite had outmatched the slave gladiators with ease. This was more like the bullfights of old, which were still practiced when the Colosso lacked for more colorful monsters.

And I was a poor matador without even a proper sword.

"Who sent you?" I repeated, now more challenge than question. The other two men flew at me on their own vehicles, one brandishing a prefect's blackjack, the other an aluminum bat such as children played ball with. I threw myself forward, counting on the fencer's strategy of closing distance to save myself from the assault. It only worked in small part, and before long I found myself flat on my backside. Clotheslined—that was the word. Surrounded, I rolled onto my knees and recovered my ground, tapped the panic button on my terminal again. Roban must have gotten the alarm, along with Kyra and the other guards. I tried to imagine peltasts piling into Kyra's shuttle, imagined energy-lances opening like jewel boxes into attack mode.

"Take his rings, Zeb!" said the man with the pipe. "You see them things?"

No, I realized with a start. *Not a man. A boy.* My assailants were all children. Ephebes no older than Crispin, their faces patched with sad little twisted hairs and pockmarked by acne. Common street rats. A gang. But where had they gotten the bikes? Such things could not come cheap, surely, even though they weren't regulated by the Chantry.

The Chantry . . . the sanctum's infernal bells were ring-ing all over the city now, and above in Devil's Rest Eusebia would be preparing for that evening's Elegy. People were praying, or else worshipping the bloodshed at the Colosso. I imagined Crispin standing in the dusty ring of the coli-seum as rose petals showered down upon him and his van-quished foes. Somewhere Sir Roban would be homing in on my location, but around my little knot of chaos, the world went on unchanged.

I held my knife out. "Fight me fairly!" I called, foolish and naïve. This was no duel, no refereed, back-and-forth, man-to-man fight with matched weapons, the tide of com-bat dependent solely upon skill.

"Thought you yielded!" said one of the other boys— Zeb, maybe. I never learned which was which. The two behind me circled closer, bikes idling. "Fucker probably lives in one of them spire palaces up in Hightown, and he talks about 'fairly.'" The boy spat. "Knock him down again, Jem. This ain't his turf."

"This is my—" I was about to say *city* when the big lad with the pipe drove straight at me. I lunged sideways, aim-ing to bring my knife around—too slow. The pipe caught me in the arm just above the wrist, and I dropped my knife. Howling, I went to one knee, knowing my wrist was shattered. The two other boys whooped and jumped off their bikes. Clutching my broken arm to my chest, I scrab-bled across the concrete, chasing my dropped knife.

"No you don't, pat!" Someone seized me by the back of the coat. I twisted, cracked the serf in the chin with my good hand. I heard him cry out and bared my teeth in satisfaction, nostrils stretched, chest heaving. The other boy snarled and pounced. Thinking of Crispin—how he would fight almost the same way—I snapped out with a kick, taking the peasant between his legs. He winced and stumbled back, according me enough time to get back to the knife. I recovered it just as the boy with the pipe joined the fray.

I knew I couldn't win. Maybe with both hands I could have bested three hoodlums in the streets of Meidua. Maybe. If I were armed properly with a sword? Certainly.

But as I was? Broken and ambushed and with only my knife? All I could do was play for time. I was lucky, and the boys got in one another's way more than, say, three legionnaires of the Imperial forces would have done. So I stood, abandoning all my breeding and education like the troglodytes who abandon civilization and live as beasts.

The one with the pipe—Jem, I think—came at me first, and I slipped backward even as one of his friends circled round behind me. I slashed at him, but I was too clumsy and slow with my off hand. I was many things, but left-handed was not one of them. Something clubbed me in the back—the blackjack or the stickball bat—and knocked the wind out of me. I staggered and fell, and a boot slammed hard into my ribs. What little air was left to me fled, and I gasped, tried to rise. Another foot slammed down on my good wrist—not hard enough to break it, but enough that I dropped the knife. I lost consciousness for a moment. They must have kicked my head. Something hit my back again, but only with the immediacy of distant cannon fire. I think my spirit tried to rise even as my body ran itself to ground and darkness. Dimly I washed back to faint awareness, heard one voice hiss, "Ought to teach you to come down here like you own us!"

"Take his rings, Zeb!"

"He's got a terminal, too! Snag it!"

Hands tugged my signet ring from my left thumb and started on my terminal's magnetic clasp. Then I heard it: "Guys, we're fucked. Look." I smiled, though my face was in the pavement. I knew he was showing them the ring. "He's a fucking Marlowe. We're fucked." I wanted to smile, but my lips would not respond. A palatine's ring is everything. It holds his identity; his genetic history, both of his family and his constellation; his titles; and the deeds to his personal holdings. If they took it and tried to use it anywhere on Delos, Father's men or Grandmother's would find them.

Fools.

I don't remember anything else except darkness and the absolute certainty that I was dead. Crispin would rule. No question about it now. Let him have his throne, his

place in the Imperium. Let Father grow to lament his choice. I didn't care.

Certain scholiasts teach that each experience is only the sum of its parts. That our lives may be reduced to a set of equations, that they may be factored, weighed, balanced, and understood. They believe the universe is one of objects and that we are only objects among objects. That even our emotions are no more than electrochemical processes carried out in our brains, accessories to the pressures of Bloody-Handed Evolution. This is why they struggle for apatheia, the freedom from emotion. This is their great failing. Human beings do not inhabit a world of objects, nor did our consciousness evolve to live in such a place.

We live in stories, and in stories, we are subject to phenomena beyond the mechanisms of space and time. Fear and love, death and wrath and wisdom—these are as much parts of our universe as light and gravity. The ancients called them gods, for we are their creatures, shaped by their winds. Sift the sands of every world and sort the dust of space between them, and you will find not one atom of fear, nor gram of love nor dram of hatred. Yet they are there, unseen and uncertain as the smallest quanta and just as real. And like the smallest quanta, they are governed by principles beyond our control.

And what is our response to this chaos?

We build an Empire greater than any in the known universe. We order that universe, shaping outward nature in accordance with inward law. We name our Emperor a god that he might keep us safe and command the chaos of nature. Civilization is a kind of prayer: that by right action we might bring to pass the peace and quiet that is the ardent desire of every decent heart. But nature resists, for even in the heart of so great a city as Meidua, on so civilized a world as Delos, a young man might simply take a wrong turn and be set upon by brigands. No prayer is perfect, nor any city.

It was suddenly very, very cold.

CHAPTER 8

GIBSON

IF I HAD DIED in that alley more than a thousand years ago, things would be a good deal different. There would still be a sun in the skies above Gododdin; there would still be a Gododdin. The Cielcin would not be forced to live as our thralls, in our alienages. But then, there would still have been a Crusade. I know what it is they say of me. What they call me in your history books. The Sun Eater. The Halfmortal. Demon-tongued, regicidal, genocidal. I have heard it all. And as I have said, we are none of us one thing. As in the riddle the sphinx asked of poor, doomed Oedipus: we change.

If you seek my baptism, look to that moment when I lay dying on a lonely street in Meidua, my hand and ribs shattered, my skull cracked, my spine fractured. Seek the time when I was cut down while Crispin ascended to glory and the adulation of the crowd. I would watch the holos later, recovering in my rooms in Devil's Rest, and see how flowers and banners were hurled at Crispin on the coliseum floor, how the people laughed and cheered for the gallant son of their archon and his stupid cape.

I awoke to painted constellations. Ebony rails embedded in cream plaster, the stars' names shining in brass inlay. Sadal Suud, Helvetios—the constellation Arma, the shield. And just beyond it, *Astranavis*, the starship. My room, the curved vaults of the ceiling done up in homage

to the Delian skies. My room. That was wrong. I was dead. How could I be in my room? I tried to move, but I couldn't. Shifting produced only a dull ache in my bones. I could move my head, though, and I looked round. A slouched figure in green sat by my bedside, head bowed as if in prayer. Or sleep. Beyond him were only the familiar bookshelves, the gaming station, holograph plate, and the painting of the broken starships in white paints on black canvas. An original Rudas, that one.

"Gibson," I tried to say, but could only groan with my dry throat. My eyes widened, seeing the device clamped to my hand. It was like a gauntlet or a skeleton's hand, a loose assortment of metal plates like the petals of an orchid—or of some medieval device of torture.

"Gibson . . ." This time I produced an infant's approximation of a word. There were needles, hair-fine and flexile, pressing down from the gauntlet rigged to my ruined hand. A similar device, more closely fitting, prisoned my ribs, and both sites almost glowed with warmth. Someone had strapped my good arm and legs to the bed frame to protect my injured parts. I imagined those flexile needles curving through my bones, branching as roots branch so that the accelerated healing process could take place.

The old man stirred, moving with the exaggerated slowness of the exhausted returning to consciousness and a groan like the creaking of trees. His cane slipped, the brass head striking the tiles. He ignored it, leaning forward in what a non-scholiast would call excitement. "You're up."

I tried to shrug, but this tugged against the hellish contraption about my chest and forearm, and I bit back a ragged gasp. "Yeah."

"What in Earth's name were you doing in the city alone?" He didn't sound angry. He never sounded angry. A scholiast's first training was in the suppression of emotion, the elevation of stoic reason above the winds of mere humanity. And yet . . . and yet there was concern in those gray and misty eyes and in the way his papery lips turned down at their wrinkled corners. How long had he been sitting there, slumped in his chair?

I took in a rattling breath and instead of answering, I mumbled, "How long?"

Inarticulate, that. Vague. The leonine old man at last stooped, grunting, to recover his fallen cane. "Almost five days now. You were nearly dead when they brought you in. You spent the first day in suspension while Tor Alma worked to rebuild your damaged brain tissue."

I felt my brows contract involuntarily. "Damaged?"

Gibson almost, *almost*, cracked a smile. "No one could tell the difference anyway."

"Was that a joke?"

The old man only stared at me. "You're to make a full recovery, Alma says. She knows her business."

I waved my good hand, tugging on the strap. My head felt as if some perverse surgeon had packed it with cotton and cleaning alcohol, so light was it, and my eyes throbbed. "Think I'd rather be dead." I let my head fall back against the pillows, grunting.

The scholiast's eyes tracked over my face, one beetling brow cocked. "You shouldn't talk like that." He glanced past me and out the narrow windows to the sea.

"You know I don't mean it."

He sniffed, wrapped his long, gnarled fingers over the head of his cane. "I know." I tried to move again, and Gibson reached out to set a hand on my shoulder. "Don't move, young master." I didn't listen, tried to sit up. Pain flared white behind my eyes, and I fell back again, unconscious.

When I woke, Gibson was still sitting beside me, eyes closed, humming softly to himself. There must have been some change in my breathing, for the old man cracked one eye open like the owl he so resembled. "I told you not to move, didn't I?"

"Was I out long?"

"Only a couple of hours. Your mother will be glad to know you're back with the living."

Feeling more cogent than I had on my last waking and somehow more brave, I said, "Will she, now?" I glanced round the room, moving only my eyes this time for fear I'd repeat my earlier mistake. "Is there water?" With surgical

care, the scholiast stood, leaving his cane propped against
the chair he'd vacated, and tottered across the room to a
sideboard where a silver beverage service dispensed a cup
of cool water. Gibson found a straw and moved to my bedside, proffering the drinking cup. "Tell me, Gibson: If
mother cares so much, where is she?" I drank, the water
tasting finer than Father's best wine. I knew the answer
already, but I plowed on. "I don't see her."

Gibson's face fashioned itself into a thin mask over pain.
"Lady Liliana is still at the summer palace in Haspida."

I made a small "Oh" sound, more an outrush of air
than a proper word, akin to the Cielcin word for *yes*. Haspida, with its orchards and clear pools. I thought of Mother's suites there with her servants and her girls.

"I wish she were here, too." Gibson rubbed at his eyes.
There was a deep tiredness in him, as if he had been sitting up for days. *Five days,* I told myself. *Too long.* "For
your sake, she should be here."

My brows contracted. It was not his place to say what
my mother *should* be doing. But this was Gibson, so I let
it stand. "How bad is it?"

"You completely shattered your right hand, broke five
ribs, and did considerable damage to your liver, pancreas,
and one kidney." Gibson's face flickered with disgust, and
he smoothed the front of his robes. "And that's to say
nothing of the head trauma. I'd take it slowly, or you'll
tear things again."

Nodding weakly, I allowed myself to sink back against
the pillows, eyes drifting closed. "What happened?"

"You don't remember?" The scholiast frowned. "You
were attacked. Some lowlifes by the warehouse district.
We pulled the surveillance footage and found them." He
inclined his head toward the side table. "Ardian led the
prefects. They found your ring." I followed his gaze, and
there it was—my signet ring with the Marlowe devil laser-
etched on the bezel sat there amongst odd medical instruments, my terminal beside it.

"I see," I murmured, tipping my head to drink from
the water again. Strange that when you've no need of
water, it tastes like air. You never notice the taste, the

glorious taste, until you're parched for it. "They're dead, then? The three of them?"

Gibson only nodded. "Sir Roban found you just in time. He brought you back. He and that lieutenant of yours."

"Kyra?" Against caution I tried to sit up straight again, regretted it as the pain turned eloquent within me.

Gibson grew quiet, and I thought for a moment that he had passed out standing up like a narcoleptic, overcome by the soul-deep tiredness that pervaded him. But as I settled back into place and the pain faded, I saw that his eyes were open, watching me.

"What is it?" I asked, wincing as I turned, tugging at the place on my stomach where Tor Alma had fixed the corrective.

The old scholiast drew in a deep breath, fussing with the cuff of one voluminous sleeve. "You father wants to see you whenever you're well enough."

"Tell him to come see me," I spat reflexively. It hurt. Neither of my parents was here, nor was Crispin. Only Gibson, my tutor. My teacher. My friend.

A small, nearly warm smile stuttered into place on Gibson's seamed face, and he patted me on the shoulder with one spotted hand. "Your father is a very busy man, Hadrian. You know that."

"Someone tried to kill me!" I gestured against my bonds at the patch below my ribs. "You'd think he could take the time to check in on me. Did he come at all? Even once? Did Mother?"

"Lady Liliana has not bestirred herself, no." Gibson sucked in another breath. "She left instructions that she was to be notified in the event that your condition worsened. As for your father . . . well . . ."

That was all I needed to hear. "He is a very busy man." There was a hollow, brittle quality to my words, like a pane of safety glass cracked by a bullet, its pieces held together only because the shards had fallen *against* one another, ready to topple at the slightest disturbance.

"Your father . . . asks that you consider how your injuries might reflect on the dignity of your house." I will always remember how Gibson would not look at me as he

said those words, almost as much as I remember the sting of them.

I shattered, shut my eyes to hold back the tears I sensed were coming. It was one thing to know intellectually that one did not have the affection of one's own parents, but it was quite another to feel it. "He told you to say that."

There was no response, and that confirmed it. Looking again, it struck me just how tired Gibson was. There were dark circles beneath the old man's gray eyes and a fine stippling of beard between the fierce side-whiskers. I reminded myself that this man had been sitting in that chair for almost five days, for the entire duration of my recovery. I had a father of a sort, but his face would never hang beneath the Dome of Bright Carvings.

"You should sleep, Gibson."

"Now that I know you're all right." And with that the scholiast took my water away, setting it back on the side table with my effects and the medical instruments. "As soon as you can, speak to your father."

"Gibson . . ." I reached out with my good hand and seized his loose sleeve by the cuff, belts straining, fingers thick and weak and numb. "He's giving it to Crispin."

The aged scholiast looked down on me, his eyes gone flat as mossy stones. "Giving what to Crispin?"

Not caring about the cameras, the microphones, whatever else lurked in my room, I shrugged and flapped my good arm, wincing. "Everything."

He tapped his cane against the tiles, pensive. "He hasn't declared an heir."

"But he did make some sort of announcement, didn't he? After the Colosso?" I felt certain that I was right and would have closed my hands into fists had one of them not been imprisoned in the gauntlet.

"Nothing as such." Gibson tapped his cane on the ground again. "Between your assault and your brother's turn in the Colosso—which was a frightful piece of work, as I understand—he's not had time to say much else. The plebeians are in a furor over your brother. I hear Crispin was quite the . . . the gallant."

"Gallant?" I almost laughed, feeling the sudden urge

to spit on the floor. "Black Earth, Crispin's a maniac, Gibson! Unstrap my left hand so I can drink myself, damn it!" He did, passing me the cup. The feeling was ebbing back into my hands, and I squeezed my left around the clear, heavy plastic. The capering Marlowe devil hanging on my wall almost looked to be laughing at me, and I clenched the cup so tight the plastic creaked. "He has to know! He heard what Father said."

Gibson tipped his head at an angle. "What did your father say?"

I told him everything: my failure with the Guild factionarius, the council session, everything. After a moment I shut my eyes, letting my head fall back against the feather pillow for what seemed the hundredth time. Then I asked the question I feared above all others, deciding it was better than letting it fester in me. "What is to be done with me, then?"

For so weighty a question, Gibson answered it with surprising swiftness and control, and I had to remind myself that the man was a scholiast, trained to hold logic above all other things. "That has not been announced. Your father never declared you his heir, so if what you say is true, there's no legal difficulty, not truly. And the commons are rather taken with Crispin, as I say. For the moment at any rate."

"We'll see how long that lasts."

Gibson laid one spotted hand on my shoulder, light as paper. "Your father has always thought you too kind, Hadrian. Too soft to rule."

"It's the Mining Guild factionarius . . ." I reached up to set the cup on the windowsill by the bedside, turning on my side as best I could while Gibson regained his seat.

"It isn't just about the Guild factionarius." Gibson leaned against the back of his chair, his eyes slipping again from my face to the view of the sea through the high window. "Your father is a carnivore, Hadrian—a true predator. He believes all lords must be thus."

I did sit up then and winced at the pain in my side, pressing a hand to the medical seal. "There are people dying in those mines, Gibson. The radiation . . ."

My tutor acted like he had not heard me and continued to speak, his voice never rising above a muted whisper like the rasp of wind through weathered stones. "He believes dominion must be hard, your father." His voice changed suddenly, crackling with a pedagogue's intensity. "Hadrian, name for me the Eight Forms of Obedience."

I did. "Obedience out of fear of pain. Obedience out of fear of the other. Obedience out of love for the person of the hierarch. Obedience out of loyalty to the office of the hierarch. Obedience out of respect for the laws of men and of heaven. Obedience out of piety. Obedience out of compassion. Obedience out of devotion."

"Which is basest?"

I blinked, having expected some question more daunting than this. "Obedience out of fear of pain." He only wanted to make me say it, to make me feel the weight of those words.

Gibson smiled. "The law of the fishes. Quite right. Your father commands thusly, and Crispin will be more of the same. That is why he believes in your brother and not in you. Do you see? It is a compliment he pays you, though he does not mean to."

Lacking an answer, I let the empty cup drop from my hand and turned away in disgust. The whole business was sour. Wrong. "That is no way to command a people."

"All your father wants is to squeeze. To earn enough from his mines to buy a barony off the Imperial Office and elevate your bloodline among the houses of the peerage."

"But why?" I murmured, feeling the pain in my side more sharply then, though it was yet a dull and warming ache. "More dirt and serfs to dig in it. More of the same . . ."

Gibson's voice shifted, sounding suddenly far away. "Once the lords of men all thought as your father does, counting all resources as fuel for progress. It destroyed them and cost the Earth her life. In your father, this callousness is excusable only because there are other worlds he might move to when this one is spent."

As he spoke, my vision started to darken about the edges, and it was all I could do to reply, "That's not an excuse."

The scholiast patted my shoulder. "And there's the difference between you."

If I had a response to that, it never came. The darkness at the edges of my vision crowded in, falling like sand.

In my dreams I was alone, passing under the narrow arch that led from the necropolis to the mausoleum where my family's ashes lay interred. How many times have I walked that way in dreams, who in life stood there only once? That had been for the funeral of my father's mother, Lady Fuchsia, when I was yet a boy. I had not known her well, but hers was the first body I had ever seen. My first encounter with Death. The stink of it and the memory have never left me. It haunted me, and often when I witnessed Death again I recalled the cloying smell of myrrh, the smoke of the incense tapers, and the drone of the chanters and of old Eusebia as she led the funeral march down the echoing steps to our necropolis. To my young mind it was less that my grandmother had died and more that Death had visited us, so that each death that followed hers recalled that procession, those steps, that walk into the underworld.

In the dream, Father went first behind the prior, carrying Grandmother's ashes, while we, her family, followed with the canopic jars. I had her eyes, suspended in cerulean fluid; mother had her heart; my uncle Lucian—dead now seven years himself, killed in a flier crash—carried the brain. A shroud of some hue darker than black concealed the statue of my grandmother erected on the rough floor amongst the stalactites. I could hear the water dripping from the stone ceiling, dropping into pools flat as mirrors. In my dream, when I tore that pall away, it was my father's statue beneath and not Grandmother's at all. And it lived, watching me with eyes like dying stars. And I dropped the jar of eyes I carried, which smashed upon the cavern floor.

His stone hands seized me, lifting me bodily from the limestone. The cavern melted around us, turning to smoke

and darkness until only the red eyes of my father's ghost remained. I fell away from them, back out and through some unseen portal ringed by the funeral masks of thirty-one Lords Marlowe, white and fading in that endless shadow. I felt as one swimming in crushing depths, frigid and smothered, bereft of direction. A gripping terror held me in her talons, and I seemed to wake, finding myself whole and healed. Gibson was still there, standing straight and tall as he had never stood in memory, his crooked spine straightened, his hair neatly ordered, his eyes sharp as scalpel blades.

All this I easily discounted, distracted by the slit nostril marking my mentor as a criminal. Sometimes I think my memory has failed me, lost somewhere across the long centuries since my youth. From time to time I wonder if I my later memories rushed backward and clouded that childhood nightmare. Yet if I were again threatened with beheading, still I think I would swear that it was so: that I saw Gibson's injury *before* it was inflicted upon him.

I was old and young again before I understood.

CHAPTER 9

BREAD AND CIRCUSES

A WEEK PASSED BEFORE the corrective brace came off my ribs, and though my hand was still trapped in its own device, I had an order to obey, so I dragged my fragile self from my bed. Shoes proved too difficult with only the one working hand, and not wishing to order a maidservant to put them on for me, I went without and took the lift-tram from my suites down to ground level of the Great Keep. I had been fussed over enough, and besides, I wanted Father to see the state of me. I descended into a series of underground tramways and up again into the offices of the prefecture capitol, a deltoid building near the castle barbican crowned by a central dome and three square towers styled like the bell towers of ancient cathedrals. Barefoot and attracting stares and whispers from the gray-uniformed logothetes of the various ministries, I crossed the great Marlowe seal on the floor beneath the rotunda and moved toward the highest of the three corner towers.

Father's office was at the pinnacle, accessed by a circular metal door guarded by Sir Roban Milosh and a decade of lance-toting hoplites, faceless men and women in liquid-black ceramic armor and red capes. The knight-lictor grinned. "Young master! It's good to see you on your feet." He stepped forward. "Here to see your father?"

I bobbed my head, numb, exhausted, and conscious of the awkward weight of the medical corrective clamped to and laced through my flesh. I hid the grizzly thing behind my back, suppressing a wince as the exoskeleton bumped

against my backside. "I understand I've you to thank for my life, sir."

Roban waved that off with his usual ill grace. "Doing my job, sire."

Not one to be rebuffed, I set my good hand on Roban's armored shoulder—as much to steady myself as to thank him—and rasped, "All the same, sir. You saved my life." I bowed my head. "Thank you."

"Your father has been expecting you, my lord," was all Roban said in answer, perhaps not knowing how to take such gratitude from one of his palatine masters. Or else the sight of the corrective on my hand offended him. The man was patrician himself and of decent birth, if not an exalted one. His genetic enhancements were coarser, after-market things, applied upon his ascension to knighthood. A mutant, as were many of his caste. "He's inside."

I took my hand away, sighed. "Well then." I straightened my back. "*Morituri te salutamus*, eh?" I looked round at the decade of armed hoplites with their energy lances glittering. *We who are about to die salute you.*

"Sire?"

"Latin, Roban," I said, limping forward, my heavy callouses scratching against the mosaic work on the antechamber floor. I did not give him the translation. "Can you get the door? I . . . well . . ." I lifted my injured hand, noting again the little dots of dried blood crusted where the hair-fine needles pierced my warmed flesh.

"Aye, young master." He reached forward, the articulated armor plates of his suit opening to bare his palm, which he pressed against a translucent hemisphere in the center of the door. The device scanned the veins within the knight's hand, and heavy bolts slammed. That done, the door rolled sideways into a slot in the wall, and Roban called within, "Hadrian is here to see you, my lord."

My father's basso voice came from within. "Send him in." Curious that he did not address me, though I was well within hearing. But then, he did not look up either or at all bestir himself from the constellation of holographic diagnostics that englobed him at his monolith of a desk. I crossed from the mosaic onto Tavrosi carpets an inch

thick. Father's high-backed seat was framed by a massive round window that looked out over Meidua and the arcing seaport. The sky across the southern country was streaked by the contrails of rockets carrying payloads into orbit and beyond. The two side walls were packed with bookshelves. But where the shelves in Gibson's study were stuffed, described by the chaos of long use and loving attention, my father's were ordered and—I suspected—only free of dust because of the fleet of house servants who tidied the place.

I stopped almost in the precise center of the square room, just on the edge of the high-angled sunlight, kneading my toes into the carpet. Like a penitent before the altar of a jealous god, I waited, head bowed.

At long last he noticed me, setting his tungsten stylus on the black glass desktop and dismissing the holographs with a wave of his hand. With the light behind him, he sat in shadow. He did not speak at first but contemplated me in silence. After what felt like eons, he only said, "Take a seat."

I stood for a moment, a beat, no longer than a couple of seconds. Father just watched me, unmoving, unspeaking. So I relented, falling into a low, round-backed chair opposite my father in his grand old confection of red leather and brass. Silence filled a single, acid moment between us, stretching time in its unfeeling fingers. I waited him out. Patience is a common trait amongst the peerage—and indeed amongst any of the nobile castes— but whereas I had the whole day open to my recovery, Father had doubtless allotted only a small amount of time for our appointment. I had the luxury of patience where he did not.

Presently he spoke. "Why were you in the city?"

"What?" I felt my shoulders tighten as if expecting a blow. "No, 'How are you feeling, Hadrian? Are you all right?'"

"Of course you're all right, boy." The gray hairs at Sir Alistair's temples and forelocks glinted silver in the high sunlight. "That's why I've put off this conversation. No point in having it until you were all right."

"You could have visited."

My father sniffed. "You have not answered my question."

"I was walking home." Mid-answer, Lord Alistair's eyes drifted from my face to the fine enameled globe of the planet at the extreme corner of his desk. It was of the sort made for wealthy collectors, lighting itself in real time with the rotation of the world and Delos's twenty-six-hour day, weather systems and cloud banks rendered in exquisite holography.

"Walking. Home." Somehow each word was a manifesto, a condemnation. In my drug-addled state I struggled not to shrink from him. He did not raise his voice. He almost never raised his voice. That was one thing that made him so terrifying. "Do you know what you've cost us with this little misadventure of yours?"

"Misadventure?" My voice cracked as I slid forward in my seat, robe belling open at the chest as I repeated, "Misadventure? I was attacked, sir."

The Lord of Devil's Rest drummed his fingers on his desktop, upsetting a few loose sheets of formal vellum. Contracts, I supposed, if not writs of fealty. The truly important documents were all still done by hand. "The offenders have been apprehended and given to the Chantry for punishment."

I held up my left hand for his examination, the signet ring screwed back onto the thumb. "So I'd guessed. Did you cut it off the poor bastard's finger, I wonder?"

Father smiled. "The minute a peasant can harm one of our own is the minute our house ceases to be feared. This isn't like the ancient days, son. We rule, *ourselves.* Not as a body politic, not in the name of or with the consent of the governed. Our power is *ours*—do you understand? And that power is *ours* only so long as we can hold it."

"Obedience out of fear of pain," I spat, remembering Gibson.

"That is the only way a man can govern a dog, boy." He leaned back against his seat, the red leather crinkling. Taking a leaf from his book, I glanced past him to watch the distant ground traffic in the city below our acropolis and the tilt of white sails in the harbor.

A sick feeling formed in the pit of my stomach as I asked, "What have you done?" I strained, half expecting to see a burning city block or a blackened glass crater where the offending suburb had been.

"Placed a curfew on the district and shot anyone in violation of it."

"You can't do that!" I objected, shaking my head. "It will only make things worse."

"You still haven't answered my question." Lord Alistair briefly fixed his attention on my face again. Before I could articulate a clarifying question, he said, "Why did you leave the Colosso?"

Half talking over him, I rolled my eyes and spat, "The bloodshed disagreed with me, Father."

"Disagreed with you?" His lordship visibly sneered, lips pulling down and away from his lower teeth. "Disagreed with you? And you wonder why there is a question as to whether you or Crispin will succeed me?" He stopped his globe spinning with a slap of his hand.

"Because I don't want to sit through Colosso?"

"Because people *saw* that you didn't sit through Colosso. That box isn't opaque, you idiot child." I was about to speak, but Father held up a hand for silence. "While you were busy trying to leave, your brother was standing his ground with the best of my gladiators, standing for his people." He banged a hand on the desktop. "And do you have any idea what your departure says to them? Do you know what message that sends? And then to be wounded by *churls*!" He shook his head, lips curled as if the last word had put a foul taste in his mouth. "They won't fear you after this!"

"And they fear Crispin?"

"And they fear Crispin," Lord Alistair repeated, drumming his fingers on the tabletop again. "It should have been you in that coliseum, boy. Felix tells me you're the better fighter." I tried to contain my surprise at this statement. It was true, but I'd never expected to hear Sir Alistair say it. In the voice of a grim magistrate, he asked, "Do you understand what you've done?"

"Gotten myself beaten."

"Forget the beating." Father waved a hand, leaned back in his seat like a Chantry inquisitor about to issue judgment.

Forget the beating. I looked down at my hand prisoned in the corrective brace. *Would that it were so easy.* Eyebrows raised, I said, "I'm having difficulty with that at the moment."

"Be quiet." Father leaned forward so quickly it made me jump, prompting a spasm of pain across my torso. "The people love those games. The Colosso. You've now publicly spurned them. It was on the Meidua Broadcast, did you know? Ran for five hours before Tor Alcuin and I could suppress it." His cold eyes narrowed to mere slits, and he swung out of his seat, moving toward the window.

He was treating me like a child, and perhaps I deserved it. What he said made sense, and I should have seen it— would have but for the pain in my arm. Still it seemed unwise to speak, so I held my silence, watching Father as he surveyed his domain. "Bread and circuses, boy."

"I beg your pardon?" I recognized the quotation as a very old one. From Juvenal, a man so dead I thought only the scholiasts remembered him or his kind. But then, I was the fool who'd spoken Latin to Father's men mere minutes before, and Father had secret depths to him.

"Imperial law forbids the planetbound serf class from operating anything more complicated than a groundcar, discounting anything required by the disparate guilds. They're made to grub around with livestock and combustion engines, and do you know why?"

"Because they might rebel?"

"Because they might start to think they have a right to."

"Excuse me?" I took offense to that, a blow to common decency I hadn't known I could feel.

My father did not turn, did not bother to acknowledge the shock or the outrage in my tone. "Look at the Eudorans, the Norman Freeholds, the Extrasolarians. Do you know what they have in common?" Before I could answer, my father slapped his hand against the frame of that round window. "They have no leaders. No order. The Empire is

order. Us." And here he turned, pressed a ringed hand to his thin chest. "It's the same with the Jaddian princes, the Lothrians. Order. Without that, civilization on a galactic scale is impossible. It breaks down."

"The Eudorans get on just fine!" I objected, thinking of the nomad caravaners with their net of asteroid stations spread throughout human space. "And the Freeholders."

"Please." Lord Alistair sneered. "Those inbreds can't hold a single planet together, much less a thousand." And with an impatient hand wave he dismissed billions of human lives from our conversation as one shoos away a fly. "Do you know that some of those Freeholder worlds have *countries?* Nation-states like those from before the Exodus? Some of those little colonies can't even build starships! They fight themselves as much as they fight anyone else."

I shrugged. "And we don't?"

"The rules of poine have their admirers in the Imperium, I'll grant. But the Chantry regulates our actions, minimizes collateral damage."

"They threaten dissident lords with biological weapons, you mean. What has any of this to do with circuses?"

The Archon of Meidua thrust his chin out. "We aren't like those other nations, son. There's no congress, no body politic here. When I make a decree, *I* make it. Personally. No proxies, no fallbacks. The old systems of democracy and parliament only allowed the cowards to hide. Our power depends not on the consent of the people but on their belief in us."

"I know all this," I said, shifting forward to the edge of my seat. My nostrils flared. I had not forgiven the man for abandoning me to my injuries. He was my father, in Earth's name. My father. And I was being lectured because I had been brutalized. Still, he was right. I was not *just* a boy. I was his son, and there was a responsibility on me to carry the weight of my house. There was power in that responsibility and an accountability, too. It is for this reason that a lord was better than parliament. A lord had no excuse. If he abused his power, as I feared Crispin might, he

would not rule for long. If he was cold in the application
of his power, as I knew my father was, he would not rule
easily.

"No, you don't," the lord snapped, smoothing a curling
lock of hair back behind one ear. "We have to engage with
the churls. We have to show that we are people, boy, not
some abstract political *concept*. That is what they understand. That is why I sent you and Crispin to the Colosso
while I treated with Elmira. I am patriarch to the people
of Meidua, and you both were sent to represent me and
our house. Personally. Crispin played his role admirably;
the people love him now because they see him as part of
their world. He fought in *their* Colosso, while you . . . you
turned your back."

While he spoke, Father drew a small crystal chit from
inside his sleeve. It was perhaps four inches long, one and
a half wide. He turned it over in his fingers like a blind
man trying to figure out what it was, as if he were weigh-
ing a gold hurasam in his hand to determine if it was
counterfeit. "It would have been bad enough if you had
just left, but you managed to get yourself hurt as well. Our
power is intensified when our people understand that we
are above them. And you damaged that understanding."

"By bleeding?" I couldn't keep the incredulity from
my tone.

"Yes." Father snapped the chit down on the table and
retook his seat. I could see his seal plainly visible on top,
the red devil glinting against its dark background embossed
on the bluish crystal.

"I thought we had to show that we are men, not ghosts."

"We have to show that we are not abstractions," he
corrected, "that we are tangible powers. Not that we are
human."

In vanished Egypt, the pharaohs were expected to
behave like gods: placid and impartial, above the fever
and the fret of mortal life. When a pharaoh failed to
match these expectations, he revealed his mortality to his
subjects, and in so doing invited reprisal from those who
had served and worshipped his divinity. We were little
different—no lord was. With our genetic tailoring and

enhanced lifespans, we were like gods in ways those long-gone pharaohs could never have dreamed. Though he was a mere archon, a provincial governor, Father's domain was greater than the size of storied Europe, and our family's distant relation to the Imperial family only elevated us further. My mother's mother ruled not only a planetary palatinate—a duchy—but an interstellar province. She was vicereine of all the stars in Auriga Province, some four hundred in all, and reported directly to the Solar Throne and the Emperor, who was her distant cousin. Through my mother, I too was cousin to His Radiance and in line for the throne, though several thousand steps removed from it. My father too shared royal blood, but more distantly, as it had been several generations since House Marlowe last wedded into the constellation of the Imperial House. Despite our old blood and considerable wealth—the envy of many newer and more powerful houses—only a scant billion people owed their allegiance to my father or were owned by him: planetbound serfs and artisans and slaves.

"I am sending you to Lorica College on Vesperad to enter the seminary."

"No!" I actually rocketed to my feet then, knocking the small, delicate chair to the floor with a dull thud. "No, you can't!"

Lord Alistair Marlowe watched me with only mild surprise, genuinely perplexed. "I thought this would please you. Your faculty for languages would be quite useful there; the Chantry always needs new ambassadors."

"New missionaries, you mean." I could barely contain my sneer. I knew what the Chantry was, and I despised it. No true religion, as among the adorators who yet keep the old gods. Only the fist in the Imperial glove, anointed with holy oil. Only the cynical posture of faith, its prayers memorable but hollow, dripping with unearned tradition. It was an instrument of terror and holy awe, the largest circus under Sol. *Obedience out of piety.* A certain amount of suffering will ever be a part of the human universe, but I call such terrors by their names and love them not.

"Words, words," muttered the archon distractedly.

The larger implications of his decision washed over me. "You're disinheriting me?"

The lord's face darkened, brows drawing down, casting his familiar violet eyes in craggy shadow. "I never declared you my heir."

"But I'm the eldest!" I objected. I was unable to stoop and right my fallen chair; the mere act of standing had sent a horrid spasm through my chest, and I imagined spiderweb fractures redressing my mended bones, still brittle from their stem cell treatment. I knew that mine was a weak objection, that birth order meant little in the Imperium, less than the decree of the respective lord. "Crispin . . ." I couldn't get the words out. "Crispin . . ."

Father found them for me. "Your brother will remain here at my side and take my place in his time, provided he continues to prove himself."

I nearly choked on the thing in my throat that would not declare itself a laugh or a sob. "Prove himself? By beating another serving girl? Or killing another eunuch in the coliseum? There aren't two connected neurons in that boy's head!" I was right up against the edge of the desk now, staring down at my father where he sat. He rose like a bolt of thunder and slapped me mightily across the face. Lightheaded, already unsteady, I went reeling to one knee, then tried to push myself back to my feet. In my haste and confusion I used my injured hand, and though the hellish contraption kept me from flexing my fingers, the mere pressure pushed on all the needles in my flesh and sent pain flashing up my arm. I howled and half expected Sir Roban to come see what the commotion was. But no one came.

"Crispin is your brother. I will not have you speaking of him like that."

Rather than respond, I recovered my footing, summoning up every last scrap of my dignity. "I don't want to be a priest, father."

"You will address me as 'sire' or 'my lord!'" my own father said, coming round his desk like a stalking panther.

Lacking other options, I swept into my lowest bow, one meant for a planetary lord. A petty vengeance, as he was not one.

As I straightened, swaying, I said, "I want to be a scholiast."

The second blow took me on the other cheek, but I was ready for it and turned with the slap, keeping my feet this time. "Is that really what you want? To be an adding machine for some borderworld baron?"

"I want to join the Expeditionary Corps, to travel the stars like Simeon the Red," I replied, using my good arm to support myself on his desk.

"Simeon the . . ." Father repeated, trailing off. He snorted, and why not? Even to me it now seems a childish dream. He changed tactics, falling back on logic. "The Chantry exercises real power, Hadrian. You could be an inquisitor, perhaps even one of the Synod." His jaw tightened, lips barely moving. "We need someone in the Chantry, boy. Someone on our side."

Something hollow and sucking formed in the pit of my stomach. *By the Dark,* I thought. "You've been planning this?" I shook my head. "I won't do it."

My lord father stood more than a head taller than I, and he stood a mere inch away, looking down that hawk's beak of a nose at me, eyes narrowed to microns. "You will." He pressed the crystal chit into my hand. "You leave for Vesperad at the end of Boedromion." He referred to the local month that marked the beginning of autumn.

"That's just three months from now!" I objected, fearing another blow.

"This incident has accelerated our plans. I need you out of the public eye before you cause me more embarrassment."

"Embarrassment!" I could have screamed. "Father, I—"

"Enough!" And for the first time in the whole conversation, he raised his voice, nostrils flaring, eyes wide. "It is decided!" His lips curled in contempt as he took in the corrective brace on my hand. "Get out before you injure yourself further."

It was all I could do not to scream, to howl in his face, to take up the small chair I'd knocked over and smash it across his Grecian sculpture of a face. I sucked in a deep breath—as deep as my aching ribs would allow—and, drawing myself up to my unimpressive height, turned on my heel.

CHAPTER 10

THE LAW OF BIRDS
AND FISHES

I SAT IN SULLEN silence, glowering at the sea. A fortnight had passed since my meeting with Father, and in that time I had done my utmost to avoid him. So I sat beneath the shadow of a sheltering spur of rock on the stony strand that passed for beach at the base of our acropolis. There, away from the cameras and the eyes of the watchful guards, a boy could sulk as nature intended. My hand fully healed, I reclined against the cliff face, scratching at a page in my journal, rendering a profile of the deep-sea trawler making her placid way to port, dwarfing the little fishing junks—red-sailed and white— that dotted the sea from shore to sunrise.

A gull dove through the salt air and pierced the ocean's surface, emerged dripping with a fish in its beak. I watched it go, then watched the ship I was drawing slip farther into the distance, rounding the cape and the lighthouse toward the city and the mouth of the river.

The corner of Father's crystal chit cut into me through my pocket, and I was reminded acutely of the encoded holo it held: a recording of my father, verified by terabytes of authenticating code, declaiming my qualifications for the proctors of the Chantry school on Vesperad. I had watched the recording half a hundred times in the past two weeks. Each time my private stash of the house wine was diminished; each time my journal grew another page.

Frustrated, I shut the book on my pencil and leaned my head back against the stone. My hand still ached

where it had been shattered, though I knew that would fade in time. I massaged it with my left hand, noting the collection of tiny pinhead scars that stippled the pale skin from fingertips to mid-forearm. They shone in Delos's silver sunlight, and I flexed the creaking fingers, baring my teeth a little at the discomfort. Tor Alma, my family's physician, swore the bones were back in working order, but I swore in turn that they'd grown oddly, were as uneasy as new teeth.

"Is this where you get to when you want no one to find you?"

I didn't need to look round to know who it was. "Apparently not."

Tor Gibson, leaning heavily on his ash-wood cane, bobbed into my view from the right, having just descended—incredibly—a flight of several hundred steps cunningly masked by the craggy randomness of the cliffs. The hem of his fine viridian robes trailed in the sand, though if he noticed he did not seem to mind. "You were late for your lessons."

"Impossible. It's ten in the morning." I shut my eyes and rested my head back against the stone. Still I sensed him looming above me, and I cracked an eye to see the almost, *almost* bemused expression on his wrinkled, leathery face.

"It was three hours ago," my tutor replied with a desultory nod. "It's nearly noon."

I stood so fast an onlooker might have thought I'd burned myself, or else been stung by one of the anemones common along the seacoast. "I'm so sorry, Gibson. I didn't realize. Must have lost track of time. I . . ." I fumbled for an excuse, had none.

The old man raised a hand. "Don't worry about it. You didn't really need another rhetoric primer."

I made a face. "Perhaps not."

With exquisite slowness, Gibson lowered himself onto the last of the steps that ascended the cliff face toward the castle. I hurried to help him, but he waved me away. "That's the second time in as many weeks that you've

missed a lesson, Hadrian. It's not like you." I only grunted in response, and Gibson let out a great rush of air. "I see. Maybe you could use that rhetoric primer after all."

Scowling, I turned away and walked out to where the stone ended and the sand ran down to silver-glass waters. With no moon to pull at it, the sea was always placid, eddying only a little over the beach. "I still can't believe it. The blasted *Chantry*, Gibson." We'd already had this discussion. Twice.

"You could be great, you know."

"I don't want to be great, damn it." I kicked a stone with the inside of my foot, sending it skittering out over the water. Out there, another gull dived. "I told Father I wanted to be a scholiast. I told you that, didn't I?" There was utter defeat in my voice, tempered by mocking self-criticism, as if only the Emperor's own fool would do such a thing.

The other man was silent a long while—for so long, in fact, that I almost repeated my question. At last he quavered, "You told me." Looking back over my shoulder, I found the scholiast—his green robes blown by the sea wind—sitting with his chin propped on the brass handle of his cane, misty eyes glassed over in thought. "You have the aptitude for it. You're sharp enough. I've spoken to your father about it myself on a couple of occasions. He rejected the idea out of hand."

Glossing over this additional news, I pressed, "But I could do it? Be a scholiast?"

Gibson shrugged both shoulders. "Given time, they could teach you to think properly, aye. But Hadrian, you should not challenge your father in this thing."

Affecting my best face of patrician contempt, I said, "It's my burden to bear. Is that what you're saying?"

Abruptly switching to Classical English, the scholiast said, "If survival calls for the bearing of arms, bear them you must."

I raised an eyebrow at the man and in my native tongue asked, "Shakespeare?"

"Serling." He looked up at the sky, at the threaded clouds like windblown gossamer in the white sunlight.

"Though I suppose the quote would be more fitting if it were the Legions your father were sending you to join."

"There's the Inquisition," I said, scowling. "They're worse."

Gibson rocked his head in the affirmative, keeping his chin planted squarely on his cane. "True enough." He scratched one leonine sideburn, speculation in his shriveled face. "I don't see that there's a way out of this for you, my boy. If your father's gone to the trouble of drafting the letter on that chit, you can bet he's waved it on to Vesperad. The deal's done. Sealed."

My head shook without my telling it to do so. "I can't accept that."

Gibson caught the nervous tension in my face and pointed a knobby finger at my chest. "That way lies madness, Hadrian."

I looked up sharply. "I'm sorry?"

"Fear is death to reason." The words were a reflex, his mind's automatic response to the named emotion both in himself and in others.

I blinked, stopped my search for a stone to throw, and said, "I'm not afraid."

"Of joining the Chantry? Of course you are." He looked me plain in the face, his own no different than that of a statue, the only creases there those of time, not of expression. He might have been cast from bronze. "You want to be a scholiast? Master that fear of yours or you're no better than the rest of them." Here he waved a hand in the vague direction of the castle as if to encompass all of lay humanity. "Imitate the action of the stone. Never let the future disturb you. You will meet it if you have to with the same weapons of reason which today arm you against the present." I failed to recognize the quote at the time: Marcus Aurelius. Another Roman.

Smiling, I quoted back, an aphorism from *The Book of the Mind*: "The frightened man eats himself."

Any other sort of man might have smiled, but Gibson's mouth only quirked as he nodded his approval. "You know these things, but you haven't learned them." Another silence fell between us, and I turned back to

watch the birds at their hunting. They were proper gulls, descended from seed stock brought to Delos with her oceans countless centuries ago. True terranic gulls, white and gray, such as plied the shores of Old Earth all the way back in Sargon's day and beyond. "The Chantry's not a bad option. You'd stand above the lords of the Empire. *See* the Empire, the Commonwealth, maybe even the Tavros Demarchy. You'd have an opportunity to put your training to good use."

"I was supposed to be training in diplomacy, not . . . not . . ." I couldn't find the word.

"Theology?"

"Propaganda!" I sneered. "That's all it is. They keep everyone in line with fear, Gibson, even Father. You know he said that's why he's sending me to them? He said he needed someone there 'on his side.' Like he was planning something illegal." I ground my teeth again. "Is that all I am? A tool? Is he trying to cheat his way into a proper title?"

As I waited for a reply, I watched the scholiast, who sat like the icon of Ever-Fleeting Time in our Chantry sanctum, wasting away, hunched over his cane. But it was the scholiast who replied, and not the man beneath. "In the technical sense, all the palatine houses have children for precisely that reason. It's about strategy."

"Chess pieces." I spat on the strand. "I don't want to be a pawn, Gibson. I don't want to play." I have always hated that metaphor.

"You have to play, Hadrian. You've no choice. None of us has."

"I'm not *his*." I said the words as a snake might, glaring at my teacher, venom dripping from my tongue.

The scholiast's dim eyes narrowed. "I never said you were. We're all pawns, my boy. You, me, Crispin. Even your father and the vicereine-duchess. That's the way the universe works. But remember!" His voice cracked upward, and he jounced his cane against the weathered white stone. "No matter who tries to move you, be it your father or any man of power, you have a choice, because your soul is in your hands. Always."

It was strange to hear Gibson—to hear any scholiast—talk of souls. Not knowing what to say, I looked away again, back to the birds and their predation. I moved across the strand back to the stone where I had been sitting and scooped up my journal, wincing with pain as my sore fingers closed on the black leather volume. "What choice is that?" I didn't look back at him, returned my attention to the birds and their hunt.

Gibson didn't answer. I knew why. Even here, away from the castle and its pricking ears and prying eyes, he could not speak treason. The instinct for obedience ran too deeply in the man. *But what form of obedience?* I wondered, and I wonder still. Instead he asked, "What are you looking at?"

"The fish."

"You can't see the fish."

"Not until the birds get them," I answered, pointing, though I supposed the old man could not see even then. I realize now that I do not know how old dear Gibson was. His skin was like old parchment, drawn and stretched. And his eyes—do you know how old a man of high birth must be to begin to lose his vision? I have known men more than five hundred years old whose sight was sharp as flensing knives. Sometimes I think my beloved tutor was the oldest man I ever knew, discounting only myself.

Ever the Socratic, the scholiast asked, "And what, pray tell, about the fish has your attention at a time like this?"

In a muted voice, I breathed, "It's fate."

"What?" Gibson asked, the knee-jerk query of the deafening man.

I was glad he hadn't heard me; I could imagine the abrading I'd have gotten for daring to reference something so tawdry and mystical as fate. I spun to face him, shrugged, and reframed my thought. "They have no say in being eaten. Pawns again. Biology is destiny."

Gibson cocked one bushy eyebrow as he snorted. "Must everything you say sound like it's straight out of a Eudoran melodrama?"

"What's wrong with melodrama?" I brightened, relieved at the faint breath of humor.

"Nothing, if you're an actor."

"All the world's a stage." I spread my hands, attempted a smile, entirely certain that this, at least, was Shakespeare. Weakly I tried to laugh, but I stopped almost as quickly as I'd begun. Gibson shut his eyes for a two-count of breaths, a gesture I had learned from long experience was the man exerting his psychic faculty to suppress his own bout of laughter. *The mind must be like the sand in a garden, raked clean,* wrote the scholiast Imore in the third millennium. "I just feel like one of those damned fish right now."

The old man pressed his lips together. "I don't know what to tell you."

"I don't want to go to Vesperad, Gibson."

"Why?" Not an argument but a probing question. *Damn Socrates to the Outer Dark for all of time . . .*

I opened my mouth, closed it again. Looked up at the castle. Opened it again and said, "Because . . . because it's all a load of horseshit. The Cult of Earth, the icona. None of it's real. The Earth's not going to come back to us green and pure again if we repent for the sins of our ancestors." I shook my head and spat the next words out like bile. "Bread and circuses." I felt dirty just saying it, owning that piece of Father's tradition. I was hard on religion as a boy where I should have been hard only on the Chantry.

Gibson's mouth did twitch then, forming a fractional impression of a smile. Was it triumph I saw there? Then it was gone, and he said, "You should really keep that to yourself, you know."

"You think I don't know that?" I pointed up at the tenebrous mass of Devil's Rest far above. "I didn't tell *him* that! Earth and Emperor, man! Do you think I'm an idiot?"

"I think," Gibson replied with extraordinary care, "that you are an archon's son and lack a commoner's caution."

I barked a short laugh at that, cold and humorless. "Caution? Gods in hell, Gibson, have I not shown enough caution? I've tiptoed around Father and Crispin for years. And Eusebia and Severn and the other chanters. I need

to do something . . ." A mad grin stole over my face then as I realized what that something was.

"I don't like the look of that at all." The scholiast almost scowled at my display of emotion.

The scheme assembled behind my eyes, thudding into place one lumbering component after another. "I'm not going." I said the words like a prayer, small and certain and powerful. "I'm not going to Vesperad."

"You have to."

"No!" I pointed at Gibson, brandishing my journal at him. "You said I have a choice." I looked down at the crumpled man on the steps, a feral grin lighting my eyes. "You could draft a letter of introduction to the athenaeum primate on . . . Teukros, say." Wearily Gibson looked up at me, a curious expression in those cloudy gray eyes, dangerously close to a coherent and lingering feeling. He pressed his lips together and stood, grunting with the effort. My proposal unanswered, momentarily forgotten, I moved forward to help him stand. Even with his back bent by untold centuries, the scholiast was taller than me, clear evidence that his was some antique bloodline old as empires. Into the reborn quietude I said, "You could, couldn't you? For me?"

We both knew what it was I asked. It was an act of treason, a betrayal of his lord and of centuries of service here in Meidua. Gibson had known my father all his life. Perhaps they had stood on this same strand, the scholiast advising a young and frigid Alistair on how to cope with the difficulties of ruling. Father had been barely fifty, after all, when a homunculus—a gift from one of his Mandari competitors—had killed my grandfather and thrust the title of archon upon him. Old Lord Timon had died abed, strangled by that artificial person while in the throes of lovemaking. It had taken Father the better part of a century—and the Battle of Linon—to make the lords of the Delos System forget that embarrassment. Part of me wondered if Gibson had counseled that attack, if the air had been blown from House Orin's castle at his suggestion and the bloodline destroyed by his word.

Voice ragged, the words broken pieces of themselves, Gibson replied, "I can."

I threw my arms around the man who was dearer to me than my own father, trying to suppress the warm joy in my chest. "Thank you! Thank you, Gibson."

Living as I did in a world of servants and masters and politics, I was a stranger to real friendships. My relationship to my parents could not at all be described as a loving one. So too my relationship with Crispin was characterized by my distaste for him. My bonds with the others of my father's court—with Sir Felix and Sir Roban, with Tor Alma and Tor Alcuin and Eusebia the Prior and all the rest—were only the attachments of student and teacher or of master and servant. Even my nascent feelings for Kyra—though I did not know or appreciate all of what that meant—were passed through the sanitizing membrane imposed on my life by my station. Only Gibson had broken through. He was, as I have said, the closest thing to a father I ever had.

And that damned us both.

CHAPTER 11

AT WHAT COST

I THINK NOW THAT the old rascal wanted me to do it, that even during our little conversation by the strand he was pushing me, needling me so that I'd come round to my convictions on my own. I set myself quite privately to the business of escape, having only the vaguest notions of how to accomplish such a thing. I, who had never once been out-system, dreamed up ways to charter or steal starcraft and pilot them somewhere besides Lorica College on Vesperad. I entertained notions of bribing the sailors aboard whichever ship Father chartered for the voyage or of slipping away at some intermediate stop on our long cruise and lighting out for the territories. I knew it had been done, but the logistics were quite beyond my limited experience.

As I understood it, I had two essential problems: figuring out how to get offworld and how to pay for it. Perversely, the second problem proved far easier to solve than the first. I was, after all, the son of a palatine lord, and I had access to certain avenues of wealth that the peasantry couldn't even imagine. You will imagine, perhaps, chests of precious gems and gold diadems. While gold retains enough value for its scarcity as well as for its myriad practical functions, it is a relatively common thing, and the coined specie of the Imperium—gold hurasams, silver kaspums, and the rest—circulate primarily amongst the lowest strata of our civilization. Gemstones, which are little more than carbon in most cases, have not held value in elite circles since before the rise of the Empire. Cut

diamonds, sapphires, rubies, and the rest could be had cheaply by anyone with access to an alchemist.

Instead, the fortunes of the palatine caste are backed by the collected chemical wealth of the Imperium. Gold is one such trade-worthy material. Uranium is another, and a far worthier one, particularly because one required a license issued directly from the Imperial Office to mine it legally. Thus, whilst a single hurasam is available to anyone, the Imperial mark—nominally the standard currency of the Empire—is something available only to those whose occupations lift them from the dirt and engine grease at the base of our society.

Marks are worth much more, one-to-one, and they are much easier to move than a shipload of gold, being only data in an account. The trick was moving them unnoticed. Father's logothetes and the secretaries of his various ministries—to say nothing of the house treasury—had enough to keep track of as it was, but there was always the chance that one overzealous clerk might glance too closely at my allowance and the various emergency accounts banked in my name. And there was also the possibility—slim, I thought—that Father might be keeping a special watch on me.

Three months.

How little time that truly is, even though Delian months ran longer than standard ones, and our days were longer, too. Even for a palatine—perhaps especially for a palatine—the days pass quickly. I had to act just as quickly and turn to the one avenue of action to which I knew my lord father—for all his vaunted coldness—could never object.

Charity.

"You want to what?" The Guild factionarius looked like I'd just slapped her, her deep-set, muddy eyes wide in her prematurely aging face.

Calmly I repeated my offer from across her cluttered desk, trying not to think of Kyra and the other two guards waiting just outside the office door, as if thinking of them

might draw their attention to me and what I did. "I want to make a donation to the Guild. From my personal accounts."

Lena Balem's common face narrowed in suspicion. "Why?"

Not able to meet her eyes, I looked past her to the holograph on one wall displaying a bird's-eye view of the Redtine Valley region in three dimensions. Its mining sites were marked with the yellow glyph of radioactivity, regions shaded by their corresponding levels of risk. I'd been out that way many times before. Despite the best efforts of biologists, only the hardiest plants took root in the hill country above the river. The consensus was that some massive collision deep in the geologic past had brought to ground the region's uranium deposits, which were then exposed again during the subtle cataclysms of our long-ago terraforming.

At last I asked, "You've heard I'm leaving Delos?"

Taken aback, the Guild factionarius leaned forward, elbows on the edge of her cheap desk. "It's true, then? They were reporting it on daytime broadcast, but I thought . . ."

I shook my head. "It's true. I'm leaving aboard the *Far-worker* on the thirty-third of Boedromion. But in light of all that's happened in the past few weeks, I, uh . . ." Here I managed to look her in the face again, conscious that it was the opposite of what my father would have done. "I felt bad about how I left things here. I understand the Consortium was able to meet some of your needs while they were here?"

She snorted. "One refinery crawler and a couple of drills. It'll offset some of our losses, but we've still got people down those shafts with hand equipment." Distracted, or else trying to find her focus, Lena Balem reached forward and rustled an assortment of papers on her desk. "I have to ask, Lord Marlowe. Why the sudden interest in our operations?"

I spread my hands, all innocence. "I just want to correct a mistake I've made." I waited a couple of seconds before adding, as if it were an afterthought, "And where I'm going I won't need the money. Father's sold me to the

Chantry." Before she could have time to think about the implications of these words, I plowed on ahead. "So I want to make a donation. One hundred and twenty thousand marks."

Her eyes went wide as dinner plates. "You're serious?" Had her jaw dropped off like that of poor Yorick's skull and hit the desk, I wouldn't have been surprised. Perfect—exactly the reaction I wanted from her.

"You could outfit a dozen work crews in hazard suits with money like that, couldn't you? New ones? Electron shielding and all?" I shook back the sleeve of my frock coat, checking the time on my terminal.

Lena Balem reached under her desk and drew out a packet of T-free cigarettes. She paused a moment, as if asking permission, before lighting one up. When I raised no objections, she put the thing to her lips, the end glowing cherry-red as she lit it and blew smoke between us. "We could, but that still doesn't answer my question."

"Which question, Factionarius?"

"Why are you doing this?"

"I told you," I said with feigned exasperation, ramping up to the truth. "I don't want those men's deaths on my conscience. If my father won't pay for the equipment, I will." I inclined my head at the desk, as if to indicate some nicety of paperwork. "Draw up a contract if you won't take my word. You can have it in writing. In fact, I insist." More smoke clouded the air, and I tried to clear it—coughing—with a wave of my hand. I knew the game she was playing, trying to discomfit me. I smiled, exhaled sharply. The gene-tailored tobacco wouldn't leave deposits in the lungs, but it smelled foul. I should have told her not to light it. Maybe I was too soft.

She rummaged around on her desk, located a file bound in false leather, and, opening it, produced a crystal tablet and rubber-tipped stylus. Her cigarette held in her yellow teeth, she said, "Here." Silence hung on us a moment, save for the sound of ground traffic in the street beneath the Guild hall windows.

Now for the delicate part.

I took the tablet and filled out the simple form with

ease, tapping the screen with the stylus as it converted my handwriting to Galstani's neatly ordered script. Then I repeated the process in a new tab. My work nearly finished, I paused, knowing my moment had come, and set the tablet down on the table. "You know, M. Balem, it occurs to me that we could help one another out." I gave her my best, least-Marlowe smile.

Her weak-chinned plebeian face darkened. "How is that?"

I maintained my politest smile. "You agree that one hundred and twenty thousand is an . . . adequate sum, yes?" With the air of one waiting for a Eudoran sorcerer to complete his bit of hand magic, she nodded. Once. Slowly. Saying nothing. "What would you say to one thirty?"

Absurdly, my mutinous heart beat faster against my still-sore ribs. I had spoken softly, felt sure that my guards had not heard me from the hall. Not through the plain rolled steel of the door. Why should I fear? I held all the power here; I had the money, the name. The Guild factionarius had . . . what? The means to expose me? But that would only implicate her, if she accepted. And she would accept. I knew she would accept, and knowing this, I spoke my offer. "I will sign *this* contract in the amount of one hundred and *fifty* thousand marks if"—and here I swiped my hand across the tablet twice, shooting the pair of documents across to the wall holograph—"you sign this parallel contract for one hundred and thirty, which I will keep on my person. Unfiled." I saw confusion in her eyes and pressed on. "I want you to give me the difference on a universal card, or—even better—in hurasams, if you have them."

"Do you know how many hurasams that is?" Balem sounded incredulous. "Do you have a lift palette?"

Chastened, I waved this away. "The card, then."

"You're asking me to launder money."

"No, I'm not," I insisted, hoping I could keep up with the ploy in my own head. "I'm asking you to . . . to feel guilty about the large sum of money I'm gifting you and to return a paltry amount of it to me quietly. To salve your conscience." I smiled, only this time it was the crooked

Marlowe smirk. Carefully I unscrewed my signet ring from my left thumb, held it ready to seal the two contracts and so pass on the terabytes of formal encryption keys. I thought of all the ring signified: my name, my blood, my genetic history, my personal ownership of twenty-six thousand hectares of land in the Redtine Mountains.

Balem glanced from my face to the contracts on the wall holograph, then at the door. I could see the cupidity alight in her muddy eyes. Her cigarette was burning down in her fingers, momentarily forgotten. "And if I refuse?"

Did I have to spell it out? "That's what the other contract is for. I file it with the treasury and say someone on your end must have hacked the contract file and amended the sum. Who do you think will be believed? Father's already rather cross with you after that mess with the Consortium." I saw her rough complexion go a shade paler. "Of course, you're welcome to turn down my offer."

She bared her teeth, eyes aglow with contempt. "This was never about charity."

I smiled sadly, a proper smile again. "I do want to help, M. Balem. Whether or not you believe that doesn't matter, but you must help me as well. These are my terms." I held the ring up, ready to apply it to the two documents. "Shall we?"

With twenty-thousand marks writ to a numbered universal card tucked into the inner pocket of my coat and the data for both the public contract and the one I thought of as my insurance policy stored in the matrix within my ring, I sat in the rear of a flier as we took off again for Devil's Rest. The old fortress looked like a thunderhead above the city today, itself beneath skies overcast with the threat of summer storms.

"It's decent of you to donate to the miners like that," Kyra said over her shoulder.

From her of all people, this statement filled me with shame. After all, I hadn't done it for the miners, had I? My

tongue felt suddenly thick, and I turned my face away. "Thank you." Should I say something to her before I went? Tell her she was beautiful? Strong? My hands clenched into fists in my lap, the right one aching horribly, bones sore. But I forced the pain on myself, feeling somehow deserving of it. I had read once that the priests of one religion or another would scourge themselves with knotted cords that their pain might redeem their sins. I have not found it to be so, only that pain so often feels like justice.

"Lieutenant," I said at last, voice hushed.

"Sire?"

"Could you change course, please? Take us to the city penthouse."

One of my two guards objected. "Sire, do you really think you should go into the city after the last time?"

Midsentence, I turned and glowered at the man, glad perhaps for the first time in my life that I had the same eyes as my father. I spoke over him. "Corpsman, I remind you that I am your archon's son." There was a sudden venom in me, brought on by my newly grown sense of shame. "I appreciate your concern, but let's consider the damage from that affair done, shall we?" I snapped my attention back forward. "The penthouse, Kyra, if you would." I did not want to go back to the castle, not that day.

Now I had the other problem to consider, and it was by far the more complicated one. In a sense I had less right of travel than the meanest plebeian. Any common dock worker or urban farm technician not planetbound by blood might earn passage offworld, or else enlist in the Legions—there was a war on, after all. But I . . . I was scrutinized, guarded, protected. At least when I wasn't getting myself pummeled nearly to death by a bike gang in the streets of Meidua. And yet that particular episode did inspire in me a measure of confidence. I had slipped away from my watchful sentinels once, hadn't I?

I could do it again.

The sun was sinking, yellowing to gold above the western mountains, and below and about me the lights were coming alive in the city of Meidua, the snaking trains of groundcar traffic slowly flicking their running lights into night mode. A holograph panel taller than a house began to glow brightly from the tower across from me, first advertising the Meidua Devils—the gladiators—and then displaying a recruitment ad featuring a strong-jawed woman in the bone-colored armor of the Imperial Legions. I leaned heavily against a carved stone balustrade, sagging against the rail. Already my guilt over blackmailing the factionarius was fading, and a part of me was giddy with my success. I had twenty thousand marks in my possession, totally unknown to my father, and when or if the logothetes and the house bankers checked my accounts, they would see only my generous donation to the Meidua chapter of the Delian Miners' Guild.

Who could object to such civic piety? I was going to be a priest, after all.

Weakly, I laughed into the crook of my arm, hoping that Kyra and my guards could not see me. My actions that day had left me with a powerful need to remain unbothered, unobserved. Alone with my thoughts. As much as I longed to leave my ancestral home, I feared that parting just as much. The stars blossoming in the growing dark pressed themselves upon my mind, looming as Devil's Rest never had.

The ancients had a saying, a kind of curse, that reads: *May you live in interesting times.* I suppose I did. With the sun setting and the black of space becoming visible above, I felt somehow that the Cielcin grew closer. I felt almost as if I could see their vessels descending like castles in the night air, though I had never seen one in truth. In my mind their towers stretched like the fingers of frigid hands, delicate structures rimed with ice that shone like a palace of grim faeries. Was it a vision or a waking dream? Or else the future pressing on my present? Perhaps it was only a dull fist clenched around my soul—the aching terror that I was about to leave home.

It only began to hit me then. Father's declaration that

I was to join the clergy had never felt *real* because I had rejected it so handily. But with the plastic of the universal card tucked into my breast pocket and the taste of blackmail still sour on my teeth, the thought that I was leaving that miserable city—the only home I'd ever known—came upon me sharp and sudden as those plebeian thugs on their motorbikes.

"My lord?"

"Lieutenant?" I started, stepping away from the rail. Kyra stood primly just outside the door to the penthouse proper, hands clasped before her, eyes downcast. "Is something the matter?" I smiled at her and found that hers was a face I could keep looking at without glancing away as I must with Father. Her hair was the color of beaten bronze, curling like some Petrarchan vision about her heart-shaped face, the curves of her body gone to slimness.

"I only came to tell you the suite's locked down. No one's coming in or out without triggering house security."

"What?" It took the words a moment to penetrate the clouds in my brain thrown up by her beauty and my shame. "Oh, yes . . . Very good, Kyra." I smiled again, more weakly this time. "Tell the two hoplites they may retire, then. Or take up shifts, if they wish."

"Sir?"

"The shifts thing," I said, wagging a finger. "Have them do that."

The lieutenant pressed a fist to her breast in salute. "Of course, sire." She turned to go.

"Kyra." She stopped, shoulders tense, though the meaning was lost on me.

"My lord?" Her voice was soft. Then a moment of bravery: "Why do you do that?"

"Do what?" I blinked, genuinely lost.

Her back still to me, she said, "Call me by my first name. It isn't proper."

My father's voice echoed within me, cold. *It isn't proper, my lord.* I silenced it, unsure how to answer that. But caution outweighed desire, and I said, lamely, "I wanted . . . to feel close to someone, is all." She turned back, and

there was understanding in her green eyes—understanding and . . . fear? Surely not. "I'm sorry if I've given offense."

"I am your servant, sire. You've no need to apologize." She shook her head fiercely, then shut her eyes and asked, "But . . . why me?"

"I'm sorry?" A flier swung low overhead, coruscating the penthouse shields so that the air shimmered with disturbed lines of force. Briefly I turned to watch it go, running lights blinking red and green in the twilight.

The lieutenant stood a little straighter, thrusting out the fine point of her chin. "You've ordered me to take you about on your errands for weeks now, even before the accident."

Accident, I thought bitterly, ordering my face into stillness as I recalled my mugging.

But Kyra was not finished and repeated, "Why me?" Her face was still downcast, eyes closed. I crossed the infinite space between us, reached down and clasped her small, calloused hand. She grew tense as a coiled spring and stopped—I think—to breathe. Braver then than I had ever been and lacking any words to explain, I kissed her.

She froze.

I squeezed her hand in what I hoped was a comforting way. I was barely more than a child and didn't really know what to do. They say time freezes in these instants, but it is only your breathing that does.

And Kyra. Kyra was still as stone.

I drew away, embarrassed and afraid. "I'm sorry, I shouldn't have. I . . ." One of her hands pressed against her breast; the other still clasped in mine. I let it go, stepped back. Her tanned skin had drained of its color. Still babbling, I looked away, formal again, and said, "Lieutenant, I . . ."

In a dead, dry voice, a voice that confirmed her deepest fears about me, she said, "If my lord wishes, I . . . I could . . . I could join him in his . . ."

I never heard her say "bed," for I shouted, "No!" Not like this, damn it. Not like this. I froze too, realizing that it could have been no other way. I was palatine, the son of

an archon, slated to be a prior of the Earth's own Chantry. How could she, a lieutenant in household guard, ever refuse? I felt sick, cheap. A coward. I brushed past her into the suites without another word, not trusting myself to speak.

CHAPTER 12

THE UGLINESS
OF THE WORLD

I HAD NO NOTION of how I was going to get myself offworld. I toyed with the idea of shipping out on a merchant vessel, working my way to Teukros or Syracuse or any world with a scholiasts' athenaeum. But I was no sailor, nor had I any particular skill that would make hiring me attractive to a ship's captain. Besides, such a posting would doubtless have called for a blood scan, which would have instantly revealed my high birth and flagged my father's office. Any passenger liner would require a scan as well, lest our planetbound serfs escape in violation of their bond.

Thus logic called for a less scrupulous class of businessman, even as prudence argued against the same.

And yet what other choice did I have?

In my youth and ignorance, I had hoped Kyra might share whatever childish hopes I had of some dalliance or tryst. In my long life I have known too many palatines, men and women both, who so abused their underlings. There are words for creatures who so abuse their power, but none shall ever be applied to me. In the innocence of my affections, I thought I was different. I had not thought that I could be no different. No amount of honesty or honest intent on my part could close the gap between Kyra and myself, and if she submitted, it would not be from desire but out of duty—or worse, out of fear. I had made a grievous error and been—if only for a moment and against my intentions—the very worst sort of man, which is almost no man at all.

So I hid from her and from much of the castle, save my teachers. Tor Alma administered a battery of medical tests before my departure, subjecting my already substantial immune system to a series of slight enhancements that would protect my cells against offworld pathogens and the subtle radiation common even in the quietest parts of space. Sir Felix and I concluded our martial appointments a month before my departure when it was announced that I was to leave by way of Haspida, spending my final week planetside with my mother at the summer palace. And of course there was Gibson and our frequent walks about the castle grounds.

"Pirates are a terrible idea!" Gibson said, grunting as I helped him up the stairs to the rock garden below his cloister. "Leastways hiring one off the street is. They're not . . . well, they're not the most reputable sort, are they?"

I conceded this point with a shrug, letting the scholiast lean on my arm as we crossed the courtyard, careful that we might not again be overheard. We were speaking Jaddian, the lilting syllables tripping like confused poetry so quickly that even the attentive might mistake seven words in ten. "I can't think of anything else," I said, turning to look the old man in the face and speak more directly into his deafening ears.

"Well, you may not have to," Gibson replied, then pressed a crooked finger to his lips for silence at the approach of three passing servants in the deep red uniforms of the housecleaning service. One man bowed as I passed, but I waved them all on with a thin smile. We held our silence while we moved into the shadow of a colonnade, the inner pillars overgrown with ivy so dark it was almost blue. Anxious, I glanced up at the watchful little cameras studding the shallow vaults above, hidden but not completely concealed by the neat scrollwork in the molding. Thence we passed out into the topiary garden. The bushes—fantastically clipped into the shapes of men and dragons—appearing almost black in the silver sunlight.

Keeping up with our Jaddian, I said, "What do you mean, I might not have to?"

Gibson shook his head, hiking up the hem of his heavy viridian robes so as not to trip over them on the stones as we mounted an inner stair up to a wall-walk that fed into one of the castle's many raised viaducts. "Not just yet. Wait." Then, "Are you nearly ready to go?"

"I've finished packing, more or less. I'm not sure what to take. No matter what happens, I don't expect to have very much to my name." I did not mention the twenty thousand marks charged to my new universal card. "I can't keep anything, can I?"

Gibson stopped a moment, and I hung back as he caught his breath, waving me away with a flapping hand. "The Chantry permits you one chest of personal effects, as I recall. Wasn't that in the instructions your father passed along?"

I blinked. I hadn't even read them. I'd been thinking that as a scholiast I would be expected to forswear everything I owned, so I hadn't made any serious preparations. At last I admitted, "I'm sorry, I haven't read them."

Gibson looked at me long and hard, switching from Jaddian to Classical English. "You had best see to that." He raised his eyebrows in such a way that said, *Or else people will start asking questions.* Once Gibson started walking again, we passed a pair of peltasts with high lances gleaming in the sun. They saluted as we left them and rounded an exterior spiral staircase that curved around a tower leading up to the seawall.

On seeing the sea, people believe it is the water that first captures their imaginations, that first transports them and makes them dream of sailing and of lands unknown and undescribed. They are wrong. The sea's first actor is not its waters but the wind. And that struck me first and fully as we mounted the huge, nearly semicircular arc of black stone that formed the easternmost expanse of Devil's Rest. Though the age of siege warfare had died long before the vanished Earth, my ancestors had raised this massive wall as if to defend against armadas. The ramparts snarled with triangular merlons like the teeth of a

saw blade, and between them even a small man could look out on the steel-gray waters where they broke on the cliffs below.

I took in a deep lungful of the wind and sighed, speaking in Standard for the first time that day. "I wish it would be all over with, Gibson. Everything decided."

Safer out here than in many parts of the castle, Gibson matched my Standard, if only for a moment. "I understand that particular pain. Periods of change can be most upsetting, but they present the most opportunity for growth, I find. You'll face what comes—"

"Or I won't," I cut in.

The scholiast sniffed, permitted me to lead him down the wall toward the knobby finger of Sabine's Tower, almost a full mile around the arc of wall from the scholiasts' cloister and the lower gardens. After a second of this progress, Gibson—in Classical English again—breathed the words, "Fear is a poison, my boy."

"Another aphorism?" I smiled my best Marlowe half smile.

"Well . . . yes," Gibson almost grumbled, "but it applies."

"Don't they always?" I mused, detaching myself from the old scholiast's grip and switching to Lothrian as a patrol moved past—though this part of our conversation, at least, was entirely innocent. We made a habit of switching like this, cycling between Standard, Lothrian, Jaddian, and Classical English, sometimes supplementing with the mongrel Demarchy languages. Occasionally we even practiced the Cielcin language, which I spoke almost fluently even in those early days. That we usually reserved for more private lessons, as anything to do with the Pale xenobites drew suspicion from the Chantry devout.

"Teukros is far warmer than this place," Gibson said, matching my Lothrian. "There wasn't enough cometary mass in-system to start a lasting water cycle when it was terraformed. The settlers use sand plankton there to regulate the air because the surface temperatures run high enough in summer to bake more delicate flora." Switching back to Classical English, he added, "You'll want to lose those ridiculous coats of yours."

I shrugged my long coat more tightly around me, its high collar close to my face. "I think I'll keep this one." The truth was that I knew I would soon be parted with the garment and given either the white and sable of the Chantry or the scholiasts' viridian. "If we meet again, I'll be in green like you."

"We won't meet again." He did not say it cruelly. From a scholiast, it could be no more than a plain admission of fact. But it stunned me as much as my father's blows had done, and I said nothing, taking the time to let this sobering realization sink in. I had known that I would never see any one of these people again. The Empire was vast and the human universe vaster still, and I was traveling across that quietude, frozen in fugue for years. I'd leave them all behind.

Into that silence Gibson injected the magic words, "I've written your letter."

I brightened at once. "Have you?" I had to compress my joy, to stamp it into apathy as Gibson did to keep it from bleeding forth.

"And some ideas about getting offworld, aye. Ones that don't involve gambling on the charity of pirates." The old man tucked his chin against his chest and advanced to stand in the shadow of one massive merlon, looking for all the world like some green-feathered owl, his robes flapping in the wind. His hands were tucked into his voluminous sleeves, and they fidgeted with something concealed there. "Do you know, my boy, that we live on a truly beautiful world?"

That was not the sort of question one expected of a scholiast, even of one as human as Gibson of Syracuse, and so I was taken aback and turned to look at him. There were dark circles under his eyes and a profound weight upon his stooped shoulders. He seemed an aged Atlas, nearing the end of his heroic struggle to carry the weight of the world. Overcoming my surprise and the previous moment's grief, I said, "Yes, I suppose we do."

Gibson smiled, a gesture fine as gossamer in the burnished light. "You sound unconvinced." Against my wishes, I turned back and looked at the edifice of black granite

and mirror-glass that comprised the Great Keep and bastion of my home. That same sunlight that frothed the sea to silver glass had no luster for the castle of my forefathers, which—though it was perfectly sunny—seemed cast in cloud-shade. I heard the scholiast laugh. "I suppose you don't believe me, but you haven't seen this." And without looking, I knew he meant the ocean.

"I've seen it."

"*Kwatz,*" the scholiast spat, rebuking me. "You are only looking. You have not seen."

I looked.

The ocean was as I have told you: a sheet of rippled glass edged with leaden fire. The Wind Isles were invisible at this hour and from this altitude, and what few clouds there were cut deep shadows on the sea, turning the silvered water to a black that gleamed like the deep of space. Gibson was right—it was beautiful.

"In spite of all that's happening out there around the farther suns," Gibson intoned, hands still fidgeting within the sleeves of his robe, "and in spite of events here . . . In spite of all that ugliness, Hadrian, the world is beautiful." He drew his hands out, and I saw that in one he clutched a small, brown leather book. "Hold that tight." Gibson took in a deep breath. "A final lesson, then, before you go."

"Sir?" I accepted the book and read its title aloud. "*The King with Ten Thousand Eyes?* Kharn Sagara?" I flipped the front cover open, turning the book to its first page. Tucked in tight against the binding was a small, off-white envelope. The letter I had asked Gibson to write to the scholiasts. I shut the book quickly, fearing that a camera drone might fly overhead at any moment, though the air was clear save for the distant circle and cry of the gulls. "The pirate king? Gibson, this is a novel!"

Gibson raised a hand to quiet me. "Just a gift from an old man, eh?" He waved that raised hand in dismissal and self-deprecation. "Now hear this. Here's a lesson no tor or primate of the college will ever teach you, nor any Chantry anagnost—if it even can be taught." He turned again and looked out to sea. "The world's soft the way the ocean is. Ask any sailor what I mean. But even when it is

at its most violent, Hadrian . . . focus on the beauty of it. The ugliness of the world will come at you from all sides. There's no avoiding it. All the schooling in the universe won't stop that." So overawed was I to hear a logician like Gibson speaking like this that I did not stop to wonder what he then meant by *the ugliness of the world*. Now I wonder if he knew what that very day held for us both or how quickly the boot would descend, as it had on the face of that poor slave in Colosso. "But in most places in the galaxy, nothing is happening. The nature of things is peaceful, and that is a mighty thing."

I did not know what to say, but I was spared at once when Gibson closed the subject, saying, "You'll do well, whatever happens."

I slipped the book up into the crook of my arm and acting on impulse, again hugged the old man who was better to me than a father. "Thank you, Gibson."

"I don't think you'll let any of us down." I made an objecting sound low in my throat, but before I could get the words out, Gibson added, "Your parents, either. They will learn it after you've gone."

"I'm not so sure." I released the old man. I had two weeks to make my preparations, to say my farewells. But aside from Gibson, there was no one much worth saying farewell to.

Gibson smiled, showing a rank of small white teeth. "None of us ever is."

Was it my imagination? Or some trick of the silver light? I thought I saw a shadow fall across Gibson's face, as though the sun had gone behind a cloud. When I bring Gibson's face to mind, it is as I saw him in that moment, stooped and wind-tossed on the battlements of the sea-wall, shrunken and sad. An old man leaning on his staff. To recall him in any light other than that of that beautiful day is somehow sacrilege, as though all our other days were ugly.

CHAPTER 13

THE SCOURGING
AT THE PILLAR

MY WORLD CHANGED WITH the ringing of the bells. Deep as the cracking of stones beneath the earth they rang.

High in my chambers, I dropped the white shirt I was folding for my trunk and listened. The sound shook the very stones of the mighty keep, clear and low and loud. I checked my terminal. It was nearly an hour before noon but not on the hour. That was my first clue that something was wrong before even I recognized the bells calling for special assembly. Hurriedly I stuffed the book Gibson had given me, *The King with Ten Thousand Eyes,* into the footlocker that was to accompany me into exile. I threw my coat over the top of the contents and shut the lid. I had an uncanny feeling that those bells tolled for me. Was this to be my father's formal declaration that Crispin would be his heir? It would be like him to perform such a ceremony while I was still present.

But I went, descending in the lift and emerging into the atrium and the shadows of the twin banners, the Marlowe devils capering with their tridents. Boot heels clacked on the copper mosaic depicting the Imperial sunburst. I was halfway to the massive doors when a realization struck me. The plaza would be filling with castle staff: red-uniformed servants and black-armored guards, the gray and brown suits of the various logothetes, with here and there the white-and-black-striped cassocks of Chantry anagnosts hurrying to their prayers and the brighter costumes of the guilders up from the city for

business. All eyes would be on me if I came through those doors onto the balcony above the plaza. I looked round, half expecting to see my father and his lictors emerging, already shielded, from the green room kept ready just beside those main doors.

No one appeared. I would have heard Father orating had he already been outside, but the only sound through those massive doors was that of the murmurous crowd roiling. I lingered for a moment in the hall, ignoring the five hoplites by the throne room, then went out through a postern door instead, down a narrow stair, and out into the yard. Mindful, I activated my personal shield with the control pack on my belt, felt the energy curtain come online around me. Then I pushed out into the crowd, dressed plainly enough that I did not attract an enormous amount of attention. A few stares came my way, but enough members of the crowd were used to seeing me that they held their places and their silence. Though I did not know it then, a trio of peltasts—unshielded and in light armor— peeled off the perimeter and shadowed my steps.

Short as I am, the plebeians in the crowd were shorter, and I could see over their grayed and balding heads to the main doors and the railed balcony I had spurned. New instinct kept my hand clasped about the leather hilt of my knife. The whole population of the castle was in evidence, clustered around Lord Julian's statue, packed shoulder-to-shoulder like legionnaires slumbering in the fugue creches of a troop carrier. I pushed forward, trying to get a better view of the platform just outside the doors to the Keep. Someone had brought the huge ebony podium out of the green room and set it at the balustrade, and hovering camera drones tagged with the decals of the Meidua Broadcast drifted above the crowd. Ten hoplites in full battle armor stood at attention along the double staircase approaching that platform, their energy lances at the ready, shield curtains glimmering.

The bells ceased, and a herald—a red-skinned and leathery little man—emerged carrying the Marlowe banner on a silver staff. "Presenting the Lord Alistair Diomedes Friedrich Marlowe, Archon of Meidua Prefecture by

the order of Her Grace, the Lady Elmira Kephalos, Vice-reine of Auriga Province, Duchess of Delos, Archon of Artemia Prefecture; and by the will of His Imperial Radiance, the Emperor William the Twenty-Third of the House Avent, our Lord of Devil's Rest!" Its clear, high voice marked it for a homunculus, one of the little androgyns—not quite human—bred and tailored for such roles as this. The sound system on the platform amplified its voice a dozen times over, and it filled the plaza unto the walls of the encircling colonnade.

Recorded martial trumpets played from the court speakers, and their fanfare clashed against our dark towers, rebounded off buttressed walls and pointed windows to drown out the unquiet crowd. My father appeared, bracketed by Sir Roban and Sir Ardian in their best armor, Dame Uma and the other lictors behind him, their lances held ready in defense of their lord. Crispin was there too beside Tor Alcuin and the ever-present Eusebia and Severn, dressed like Father in the black frock coat and red toga expected for such formal appearances, his block of a face oddly expressionless. No one had sent for me. Had I been forgotten already? And where was Sir Felix? Surely the castellan ought to be among the assembled party.

The trumpeting ceased at a raised hand from Father, and I could just see the shield glimmer faintly around his party. Father's eyes took in the crowd but skipped right over me unseeing as he lifted up his voice and said, "My people, I come before you with disturbing news." He paused, ever the master, just long enough to allow the possibilities to begin forming in the minds of the gathered hundreds, building up until they leaked out in whispers. He allowed just enough time to let them believe it was the Cielcin and that their world was ending. I believed it, too. Believed that an invasion had come, if only for a second. But it was only my world that was ending. "As many of you know, my eldest son, Hadrian, is set to be leaving us in but a few days' time." I almost missed his next pronouncement, for I stood transfixed. He had used my name. Lord Alistair never used my name. A pit opened in my stomach, yawning and cavernous. "He will be

taking the journey to Vesperad to take his rightful place as a pious member of the Holy Terran Chantry."

I clenched my hand around the hilt of my long knife, the fingers aching with remembered pain. Pious indeed. But Father was still speaking, his words growing softer, perfectly amplified and modulated by the plaza sound system. His sudden hush dragged the crowd in closer as he said, "This noble plan was jeopardized by a *traitor*." Here he curled his hands into fists before his face before lowering them to the podium. "A traitor who would have seen *my son* kidnapped and sold to the Extrasolarians."

"What?" I cried, pushing forward, drawing surprised expressions from the logothetes and servants around me. But my words were lost in the sudden tremor of the crowd, the mounting rumble as they conferred with one another, questioning with one voice. What was Father on about? I looked around sharply, as if to find an answer writ on the faces of those gathered hundreds. There was none. And then I saw it. A simple wooden post, half again as high as the tallest palatine, stood slightly crooked between those sweeping steps, slotted into a hole in the ground, its bent shadow pointing nearly straight at me.

A whipping post.

My heart froze in my chest, and I turned to glare up at my father at his podium in time to hear him say, "Had this plan not been uncovered, my son would have been delivered into the hands of those barbarians, maybe even to the Pale themselves." He shook his head. "Bring him out."

I turned, eyes wide and wild, to see four hoplites dragging a piteous, white-haired figure between them. A white-haired figure in green robes. "Gibson!" It wasn't true; it couldn't be. I tore sideways through the crowd, shoving the plebeians aside. The trio of guards I had not seen hurried forward and seized me by the arms. The scholiast looked up at me, and I swear he smiled. Not the sardonic little ghost of a smile that crept its way onto his face from time to time, but a true smile, small and sad and sure. I strained against my guards, but the old man shook his head. I turned, wanted to scream that it wasn't true, but then I remembered the letter secreted in the

pages of an old adventure novel. Gibson's meaning was plain enough. I choked back my objections and looked wide-eyed at my father, and so I did not see Gibson's thin arms being lifted, manacles rattling as they were looped onto the hook atop the whipping post.

The guards at my side cleared a wedge through the sea of gray and red uniforms, frog-marching me up the white marble stairs to the platform. Father watched my progress with hooded eyes. "Tor Gibson," he said, "you have been caught colluding with barbarians in the kidnapping of my son!" As Father spoke, the guards pushed Gibson to the ground, so that he sprawled beneath the balcony like a puppet with its strings cut.

Some clinical, detached part of my soul reflected that this was precisely what Tor Gibson had referred to that morning—was it just that morning?—when he spoke of the ugliness of the world.

Father was still speaking. "Three hundred and seventeen years you have served us, Gibson, and our father before us. Three hundred and seventeen years you've been with us." My father advanced toward the railing, spread his hands on the balustrade. "Is it true that you intended for my son to be delivered into the hands of these backspace barbarians?"

Gibson clambered to his knees and looked up at us on the balcony. He caught me staring and shook his head sharply, pointedly. "It is true, sire." He shook his head again, more brusquely this time, and I realized the gesture was for me. The contrast between word and action was lost on those gathered round, even on Alcuin or Alma, who should have noticed. It was meant for me so that I would know the truth and not interfere.

I've had years to think about this. This moment. Years to work out Gibson's reasoning. To work out why he did what he did, why he took the blame for my attempt to flee. Perhaps you see it? He must have known about the money or deduced that I had done something like what I'd done. If Father and his intelligence corps believed that the plan was Gibson's, they might not look so closely at me. His confession saved me from further scrutiny and made

everything that followed possible. Oh, Father would blame the *idea* of fleeing on me, but in his mind, so grand a plan would require a conspiracy. The sort of thing a scholiast might concoct.

There was no conspiracy.

There was only me.

I've said it before, but Gibson was the closest thing to a father I have ever known. And this moment cemented that fact more than any other. Gibson died for me. Not there, not then, but on the distant planet of his exile. He gave his life for me, gave up his comfortable place in my father's court so that I might have a chance at the life I wanted. I am glad he did not see my future, for it was not a future either of us would have chosen for me, fraught as it was with hardship and suffering.

"You do not deny it?" My father's voice betrayed no emotion. He might have been talking to an enemy taken in the field, not the man who had tutored his children their entire lives and been his tutor before.

Gibson found his feet. "I have already confessed it, sire."

"Indeed you have," said one of the guards on the platform above, and I recognized Sir Roban's voice. Sir Roban, who had saved me from the highwaymen outside the coliseum, my father's faithful lictor. "I had it from him myself, my lord." He keyed a playback function on his wrist terminal, his armor interfacing with the plaza's sound system.

Gibson's reedy voice played from every corner of the yard, artificially amplified like the voice of some aged and quavery giant. "Hadrian never would have reached Vesperad. I'd made arrangements . . ." The clip severed abruptly, cutting, no doubt, just in time to preserve Father's choice fiction involving the demoniac Extrasolarians.

A ripple ran through the crowd. Scholiasts were regarded with suspicion by the uneducated, as is the fate of every man of learning in every age. There was something of the machine in the scholiasts, a relic of the order's ancient history and its founding by those few Mericanii who survived the Foundation War. And in every age there is a stigma attached to extreme intelligence, for there are

heights to which the human mind may be pushed that astonish those at sea level.

Ever they have been the first targets of pogrom and Inquisition.

"Tor Gibson, for attempting to kidnap my son, I, Alistair of the House Marlowe, Archon of Meidua Prefecture and Lord of Devil's Rest, do deny you and banish you from my lands and from all this world."

The scholiast slumped, rattling the chains on the whipping post he clung to.

"It's not true." Everyone on the landing and everyone below who had heard turned to look at me.

"It is true!" Voice ragged, Gibson took a half step forward, straining his arms in their manacles. "A priest, Alistair? You would throw your son to those charlatans? Your son—"

"Heresy!" shrieked Eusebia, pointing a gnarled finger down at Gibson. "Kill him, lordship!"

Lord Alistair ignored the prior. The familiarity in Gibson's voice tipped him beyond composure—none of his servants called him merely *Alistair*. Not ever. "He is my son, scholiast! Not yours."

One of the soldiers kicked the old man in the back of the knee, and Gibson fell like a tower toppling. The chains stopped him, and he groaned as he hung there. An involuntary cry tore from my throat, and I moved to the railing. "Let him go." I rounded on my father, tears in my eyes. "Please."

"I am letting him go." Father did not turn to look at me this time; he lifted one hand to snap his fingers. "We are merciful as Mother Earth is merciful," Father declared to the crowd. "Gibson has served our house long, and in memory of that service, we withhold the White Sword." He overrode an objection from Eusebia, who caved so quickly I knew their arrangement was preordained. "Sir Felix."

The castellan emerged from the shadows, and I paled. Sir Felix, who after Gibson had been my greatest teacher, was dressed not in combat armor but in religious white and black. Beside him was a blindfolded cathar of the

Chantry, his head shaved, his skin like porcelain, a black muslin band obscuring his eyes. Unspeaking, Felix led the torturer down the stairs toward where Gibson stood lashed to the post.

"Stop!" I screamed as I stumbled for the stairs. My guards grabbed me above the elbows, held me back with armored fists. The cathar advanced on Gibson, producing a fine blade that glowed star-hot in the daylight. He did not hesitate but slipped the needle-fine blade up into Tor Gibson's nose and pulled, plasma-coated edge slicing a wedge in the old man's nostril all the way to the bone. Gibson let out a yelp and a gasp of pain as he slumped. The wound would mark him a criminal all his life. The plasma knife had cauterized the wound even as it cut, leaving his face bloodless.

Sir Alistair waved his hand, and the two peltasts holding Gibson tore his robes. It fluttered like two broken wings from his thin shoulders, pale flesh visible between them. Sir Felix accepted a three-thonged lash from the cathar, acting as Father's proxy for the punishment that was to come.

"Mercy, Father." I strained against the men holding me. He ignored me.

The two soldiers forced Gibson against the post, one pressing his face against the rough grain of the wood. The castellan swung, tearing the scholiast's flesh like cheese-cloth. The sound Gibson made shook me to the marrow: a mewling, wrenching yowl. I couldn't see his back from where I stood, my arms pinioned, but I could imagine the bloody stripes the lash traced against his skin. It fell again, and Gibson's sobs turned to cries. For a moment I saw his face, transfigured. Gone was the kindly old man I had known all my life with his endless stream of quotations and quiet admonitions. The pain had reduced him to something less than the shadow of a man.

The lash fell again and again. Fifteen times it fell, each time punctuating the old scholiast's sobs with another cry. I have never forgotten his face. By the end he had ceased even to cry but set his jaw and bore the pain of it. When I think of strength, it is not of the armies I have seen that

come to mind, nor the fighting man. It is of Gibson, stooped and bleeding but unashamed.

Father looked down on him, unspeaking. When Sir Felix was once more at his side, the lash in hand, the Archon of Meidua said, "Take him away." Then to all the gathered logothetes and secretaries of the court he said, "Back to work! All of you!"

"Why did you do that?" I broke free of the guards who held me, cracking one in the face with an elbow. Below the landing the crowd was draining back into the castle, crushed into silence by the display. As much fun as the sight of blood was in the Colosso, the comedy and the glory of it vanished when one of their own was so abused.

"Because, *Hadrian*," my father said, voice low, no longer amplified by the plaza's sound system, "it couldn't be you."

I drew up at this, stunned. Stunned less by the cruelty of this revelation than by the fact that my father had used my name again. Father waved Felix back, lacing his hands before him as if in prayer. He had worn his full set of rings that day. Three rings on each hand, all with huge bezels set with rubies or garnets or carnelians, each a symbol of his office or power in some way, red on silver. I did not see his wedding band. I never did.

"Me?" I finally managed, my voice sounding small and high, like Crispin's.

"I know you asked the old man to find a way to get you to an athenaeum," Sir Alistair said in muted tones. The last of the crowd retreated through the Horned Gate to the path down from our acropolis. "I don't know how he planned to do it—something involving a shipboard scholiast, I don't doubt."

You believe that, I thought, trying to keep the venom from my face. I thought of Gibson's letter and knew that a part of it was now useless. Whatever the scholiast had planned, it was uncovered now.

The Lord of Devil's Rest took a couple of steps nearer, looming over me. Crispin stood off to one side, watching with bright eyes, a small smile quirking his fat lips. "You will not be a scholiast. Do you understand?"

I had no words. Nothing. I was leaving in five days,
leaving and never coming back. And I had nothing. "Go
to hell."

Father struck me full in the face again, with a closed fist
this time. One of his rings caught my cheek, tore the meat
there in a thin, ragged line. "Take him to his chambers. He
won't learn his lesson." As the two hoplites seized me by
the arms again, my father turned and led Crispin up the
stairs to the keep. Presently Father stopped, turned with
his hand on Crispin's shoulder. "Do this again, and I will
kill the scholiast. You understand?"

I spat on the tiles at the base of the stair and looked
away.

Alone again in my chambers, I had no room for tears. I
fell back against my door, sank to the floor, chest heaving.
I shut my eyes for a long time, my mind retreating past
sleep and madness to a place of utter stillness where rage
smoothed itself to a quiet burning. I sat there a long time,
legs splayed out on the tile before me. I could feel the
blood in me moving and the tears starting to come. Dimly
my dream came back to me: Gibson standing tall, his
nose cut. I wondered at that and at myself and so opened
my eyes.

My wonderment vanished at once, buried by cold fear.
My coat—the one I had thrown across the top of my
footlocker—lay on the furs at the end of my bed. That was
wrong. Half crawling, I hurried to it and threw open the
lid of my footlocker. I threw clothing and the gathered
detritus of my life every which way. I had to punch my leg
to stifle a sound that was at once a wail of grief and a howl
of fury and a sudden conviction that I too was whipped.

The Kharn Sagara book was gone.

CHAPTER 14

FEAR IS A POISON

I DID NOT LEAVE my chamber for three days, commanding the household staff to bring and clear away my meals. I do not think I spoke a word in all that time, and I could not have felt myself more a prisoner had I been a guest in any of the Chantry's bastilles. A frigid, slimy fear had me in its coils, poisoning me with the certainty that I would fall next. Surely Father's agents had taken my book with its incriminating letter, acting on suspicions or from evidence in security footage from times that Gibson had not been *quite* careful enough. I hadn't even read the letter. I hadn't had a chance.

Ideas that don't involve gambling on the charity of pirates. That was what he had said. Gibson would not have contacted the Extrasolarians. How could he? Father's theory—that he'd worked out some deal with a shipboard scholiast to spirit me away—seemed more plausible. What I would have given to read that letter, to learn the truth of Gibson's plan. His *compromised* plan, I had to remind myself. Whatever contacts Gibson might have engaged or suggestions he might have enclosed were now well and properly in the hands of Father's agents. Those doors were closed. The scholiasts would never admit me without a letter from one of their own.

So I would join the Chantry. I would learn their hollow prayers and empty rituals. I would be taught the procedures for inquisition and the protocols of interrogation. I would become a torturer, a propagandist. I might see the

universe as I had dreamed, but it would only be to crush it under my heel. The thought alone was poison. I have lived a tragically long life, long enough to know the evil that they do and why. I have seen heretics burned and crucified by the score, seen lords brought low by the Inquisition and the vast empires bow to the whim of the Synod. They, who police mankind, who keep her from the sins and the dangers of high technology, command technologies as foul as those they hunt down.

It was hypocrisy, and I was disgusted as only youth can be by the sins of age and establishment. In my youthful cynicism, I had glimpsed one of those great truths: that for all the Chantry's talk of faith, they believed in nothing. They committed that ultimate and atheistic error: thinking that there is only power and that civilization arises only from the abuse of the innocent by the powerful. There is no more evil thought, and it was the soul of their false religion. And so I could not be a chanter or prior.

But I knew I would be.

The day of my departure dawned foul as any I had seen: overcast with the threat of storms. I was to take a suborbital shuttle south to the summer palace on my grandmother's land at Haspida to see my mother for what I knew would be the last time. My father was not there to wish me farewell, nor was Felix or any of the senior counselors. A soft rain already licked at the airfield out beyond the city walls in the lowlands where the suburbs died. Crispin was coming with me, eager as I was for a chance to leave Devil's Rest for a time.

Devil's Rest waited on the horizon, a black smear above Meidua's foggy lights. A strong gust blew across the flatlands to the eastern dunes and the bald limestone formations that crested from them like the hulks of shattered seaships. It gathered my long coat in its fingers and set the awning snapping above us. The concrete darkened with rain.

"Ready to say goodbye to Mother?" Crispin asked.

"What?"

"Are you ready to go and see Mother again?" he repeated, watching me from under those square brows of

his, a thin crease forming just above his nose. I wondered what he was watching for in my face, and the paranoia that had grown over the days of my self-imposed exile commanded my muscles to stillness. For a moment I thought I heard Gibson speaking, reminding me that fear was a poison.

So I stilled my fears and answered, "Ready? Yes, I suppose. I'm surprised you're coming along."

Crispin clapped me on the shoulder. "Are you kidding? I love the summer palace. Besides"—he leaned in, conspiratorial—"home's a bit of a mess right now. You know?" I just stared at Crispin, not sure what to say. He seemed to shrink before me, the armored gladiator he had been in Colosso became only my younger brother. I stared too long, for he raised those thick brows and said, "What?"

I pushed a fall of ink-black hair from my face, turning away as I settled my hands into the deep pockets of my coat. My fingers brushed the universal card tucked into the lining of one pocket. Useless now. The scholiasts would accept no one as a novitiate without a letter from one of the order, and tradition demanded that letter be handwritten in a cipher known only to the order itself. I swallowed and shook my head, undoing the work I'd just done on my hair. "I don't want to go."

"What? You'd rather stay here?" Crispin wrinkled his nose, taking in the decade of house troopers standing at attention not far off. "You won't miss much." My words failed me, and it took an effort to clamp my jaw shut. I wanted to hit him, to break his jovial composure. I could see it in the casual shrug of his shoulders. He didn't want to rule. "I hope Father gets his way. He's angling for a barony in the Veil, you know? Says our house might move offworld when I'm . . . well." He trailed off, aware enough to realize that his succession might be an upsetting topic for me.

Through the rain the shuttle appeared. It fell like a raven upon a carcass, the whine of its engines bleeding over the quiet rain. A hollowness sounded in the pit of my stomach, an emptiness that echoed like an abandoned

temple. I have felt that desolation several times, but only as strongly one other time: in the dungeons of our beloved Emperor, awaiting my execution.

Crispin brightened. "But you're going out there! That's . . . that's good, isn't it? Maybe you'll see the Pale."

I sniffed. "All I'll see is the inside of an anagnost's training cell."

"Anagnost," my brother mused, scratching at the fine stubble on his jaw. "Odd word."

I grunted. "It'll be miserable."

"Sure!" Crispin replied, adjusting the wine-red jerkin he wore over his black shirt. "Until you become an Inquisitor and you start dropping atomics on the Pale." He grinned. "They might even have you advising the Legions at the front."

Turning away, I made a face. "I wish we'd make peace with the aliens." Crispin was uncharacteristically silent then, and sensing his flat eyes on me, I turned and found him watching me intently. "What?"

"You really think the Pale are worth saving?"

"The Cielcin?" I narrowed my eyes, then turned away from my brother in favor of watching the approach of the shuttle. Our guards moved slightly, adjusting their posture in preparation, their armor flexing, plates scraping softly. "They're the only other spacefaring civilization we've ever encountered. Don't you think they deserve a bit of"—I gestured at the sky—"all that?"

Crispin spat on the concrete. "Heresy."

I raised my eyebrows at him, sighed heavily. "I don't want to be a priest."

"Father told me." I could hear the frown turning Crispin's voice downward.

"You've spoken to Father? Since Gibson's . . ." I couldn't get the words out, had to shut my eyes to stem the sudden upwelling of tears. I tried again. "Recently?"

My brother shrugged his ox's shoulders. "Only for a moment. You should be honored. I hear the Chantry doesn't take just anyone."

"*Ekayu aticielu wo,*" I said. *I am not just anyone!* He

did recognize the language, though, and his pale flesh went paler. "I wish I were going to the scholiasts instead."

Clearly thrown off by my little show of Cielcin language, he said, "Heard that too." The shuttle alighted just beyond our pavilion. Four of our guards hurried forward to secure the craft. "Can't really fathom why anyone would want that. Shutting down your feelings like that. Don't you think it's weird?"

I kept my silence a moment, fixing my eyes on the distant city through the worsening rain. Devil's Rest appeared almost a part of the storm, a blacker shape amid all that grayness. The way I felt—the creeping terror that Father was not yet done with me—made me wish I *were* capable of the scholiasts' mastery of emotion. I wished I could sink into the stillness of their apatheia and forget myself. "It's a tool, Crispin."

"I know it's a tool, damn it." He took a few steps toward the edge of the awning and the approaching shuttle. "I only asked if you thought it was weird."

"No." I pushed my long hair back again, squinted through the rain. I wanted to remember this moment, the way the shadowy castle faded into the rain. I had my sketchbook and pencils in the red leather satchel propped by my footlocker. "There are stranger things out there." I jerked my thumb at the sky beyond the awning.

That brought another silence, and my attentions were captured by the descent of two of the guards from the shuttle's ramp. They gestured an all-clear sign to their fellows in the coded hand-talk unique to our house guard. At once the others turned to take up our luggage. One passed me my satchel with a soft-spoken, "My lord."

I looped its wide strap over my head and shifted the pack into place. Dogged as ever, Crispin said, "I mean, they're all a bit off, aren't they? A bit mechanical. I heard Severn say once they ought to round up the scholiasts for heretics, so maybe it's good you'll be on the other side." He smiled at me, uncertain. I see now that Crispin was trying to be conciliatory, but at the time . . .

"Heretics? You're honestly going to stand there and tell

me that the Earth died to inspire the Exodus? That it sacrificed itself so that we might spread ourselves out among the stars?" I rounded on my brother, glad that most of the guards were out of hearing range.

Crispin—not truly pious, I think, but acting with that strange defensiveness the faithful always find when challenged—thrust out his chin. "Why shouldn't it have?"

"Because it's a planet, Crispin." I waved one hand in a circle. "A rock somewhere out in space. It's not coming back, it doesn't answer prayers." I tightened the strap on my satchel. "It isn't coming to save us." Behind me I heard two of the peltasts suck in their breath, and I turned in time to see one make a warding gesture with his first and smallest fingers. I was past caring just then.

Crispin called after me, "You can't say that, Brother!"

I ignored him and mounted the ramp, coming up out of the rain and into the cramped shuttle compartment. I did not have to duck under the bulkhead, and ignoring the salutes of the flight crew in their drab uniforms, I seated myself in an armchair by one window. I was seated by the time Crispin joined me. I could feel him glaring at me across the aisle. After I stowed my satchel beneath the seat, I leaned back to watch our escort file aboard.

After the last of them had passed, Crispin hissed, "You really can't say things like that, you know."

Lightning flashed, and the heralded thunder came on swift and sudden, rattling the shuttle before the light had faded. "Or what?" I murmured, no longer caring for this conversation or for time with my brother.

"They'll throw you to the cathars, just like they did our old bitch of a tutor."

My fingers tightened into claws on the arms of my chair, my fear momentarily abandoned. "Let them, then. I won't serve them." My words were hot as my anger. The way I saw it, I had nothing to lose. In a week I would be dropped into cryonic fugue to slumber until my decanting in Vesperad orbit. Years would have passed by then, and light-years, and all the stars would have changed.

Even at this distance I could hear the bells of the city chiming and the massive carillon in Devil's Rest. The

shuttle began rolling, and a female voice informed us that we were preparing for departure. Thunder rolled again, and the jangling chorus of the bells stilled, making space in the sound of rain and whining engines for the chiming of the hour. One. Two.

We were leaving right on time. If Crispin meant to argue with me still, our rapid acceleration drove it from his mind. The bells in the castle banged again: Three. Four. Five. For a moment I felt the thrill I'd wanted, a brief and shrilling glee as the shuttle burned hard and lifted into the air. Six. Seven. We were pushed gently into our seats for only an instant, and then the shuttle's suppression field came online and countered our change in inertial mass. More distant than the thunder, I could still hear that massive bell ringing. Eight times it rang. Nine. Ten. Though my inertial mass felt normal again, I imagined that my heart sped on forward, launched from my chest and out into the storm, soaring up and away . . . and was gone, leaving me entirely. While I would come down again, it vanished as a ship at warp, slipping faster than light toward worlds I would never see. Below the mighty bell rang on.

The clock was striking thirteen.

CHAPTER 15

THE SUMMER PALACE

MOTHER DID NOT MEET us at the landing field nor at the gate of the great palace with its glass domes. This came as no surprise, and Crispin and I were shown to our quarters in adjoining rooms overlooking the water gardens. With summer nearing its end even in the south, the water lilies were dying, and the red-and-white spots on the green waters faded even as sunlight flashed iridescent off the koi in the waters. My sketchbook lay open on the table, depicting Devil's Rest as I had last seen it.

"Memory betrays most people." Gibson's words echoed back to me so clearly that I could see the man standing by the arched window, back stooped and face withered. "It fades, leaving them with dull, soft impressions of a life more like a dream than history." He always said I was so sharp I'd cut myself, but looking back at the portraits I have drawn from memory—of Gibson or of any other—I have observed one thing: No two are the same. A nose hooked in one image is straight in another, sloped between brows both beetling and narrow in turn. It is said that the scholiasts never forget a thing, that all they are and experience is held hard and unchanging behind their eyes. I never mastered that trick, and so cannot say how long I lingered by that window, watching the birds wheel above as Mother's serving girls bathed in one of the clear pools.

My memory is to the world as a drawing is to the photograph. Imperfect. More perfect. We remember what we must, what we choose to, because it is more beautiful and

real than the truth. I can hear Gibson scoff at that, saying, "Melodrama is the lowest form of art." I never had a rebuttal for that.

A knock sounded at the door, dismissing my botched rememberings.

Crispin came in. I could tell it was him without even turning or regarding his reflection in the window. No one tramped as heavily or heedlessly as Crispin. He walked like a whole platoon, clangoring and clamoring. "Mother's not here."

That got my attention. "What?" I turned from the window, attempting to right the maladjusted shirt I was wearing. "Where is she?"

My brother shrugged, threw himself unasked into a green armchair, one leg draped over the arm. He held an unsheathed ceramic knife in one hand, waved the milky blade about the room. "Your room's bigger than mine."

"Where is she, Crispin?"

"Euclid, apparently." He shrugged again, sinking lower into the chair with a squeak of leather on leather. "No idea why. The girls told me." By *the girls,* I knew Crispin meant the women of the vicereine's harem. There were, last I'd heard, thirty-seven concubines kept in the summer palace, men and women and one who was both, if the rumors were true. Most lords maintain such persons as a symbol of their wealth. "You know she's got a homunculus now? Blue-skinned. You wouldn't believe the hips on her." He made an obscene motion. I looked away, thinking of Kyra, of my shame, almost forgotten in light of the hole that Gibson's whipping had left in me.

"You really have no idea why she's in Euclid?" That was miles to the south. It was just like Mother not to be around at a time like this.

Crispin blinked. "The blue girl? She's not, she's just back—"

"Mother, you ass," I snapped, eyeing Crispin's knife. I wished Sir Felix were there; he'd have given Crispin a lashing for brandishing the weapon like that. Then I remembered Felix whipping Gibson and promptly changed my mind. "You didn't get anything out of the girls?"

A bit confused, Crispin frowned, looking at his knife hand as he replied, "That's rather the wrong way round . . ." I glared, watched him splutter into silence. A splash sounded in the gardens below, followed by clear laughter.

I smiled. "Things are different here. Less . . ."

"Boring?"

"Cold." I walked over to where I'd left my journal open. I picked up the pencil, sucking on my teeth. I'd worn the charcoal down to a stub during the three-hour flight from Meidua. "Can I borrow your knife?" I held out a hand. Crispin looked thoughtful for a moment, nervous, so I snapped my fingers. "I'm not going to stab you with it. In Earth's name!" After another moment's hesitation he handed the ceramic blade to me. I seated myself by the table and began sharpening my pencil with the knife, dropping the shavings onto the tabletop. "Sometimes I think maybe it's just home that's drunk on politics. When I'm here . . ." I gestured. "It's hard to imagine there's a war on."

"There is, though," Crispin said, adjusting himself with one hand as he slid further down in his seat. Then, "Don't they make a tool or something to sharpen those things?" He indicated my pencil with a lordly wave of one blunt-fingered hand.

"Not as good. I want a better point," I said dismissively, not looking at him. "I've got a set of scalpels in my crate, but . . ." I trailed off, blowing the dust off the end of the pencil and wiping the blade on my pants. I placed the knife back on the table. "Was there any information about when Mother would return?"

Crispin frowned, eyes flicking to the knife he'd lost. "Tomorrow, I think. They didn't really say."

I grunted my understanding, set the pencil back in the fold of my open journal. "Is that why you came back up here? To let me know about Mother?"

"Well, yes," he said, smiling. "But I thought . . . since you're leaving . . ." He cleared his throat. "Why don't you come down to the harem with me? You have to see this blue girl, really."

"No."

Unabashed, Crispin said, "They've got boys too, if that's for you. Is it?"

Fifteen years, and he never asked. How disjointed the palatine family is. A cabal of strangers bound by something thinner than lowborn families. Not blood, not really—only our genetic constellation. My mother and father weren't parents so much as donors, my brother and I classmates, acquaintances who happened to share the same base genetic code. I have observed many palatine families in my life, and almost always it is so. Yet another way, I think, in which our plebeians are more human than we. My brother did not know me.

"No, thank you." Now I realize that Crispin was trying to befriend me, to give us one shared experience before I left forever. I could have proposed an alternative. A hunt in the hills above the lakes, racing fliers. We could have played a blasted sim game, even. Instead I glared and returned his knife hilt-first.

Mother did not return the next day, or the next. With each passing hour my heart sank deeper into the earth. One simple fact alarmed me more than all the rest: she hadn't called. She could have called even if she'd gone offworld. She might have used a quantum telegraph or even just called via the datasphere comms net. And she wasn't even offworld, if Crispin's intelligence was correct. I suppose I might have called her, but I was the one leaving, and wanted to matter enough to her that she would call. Perhaps that was petty, but I'd hoped to have one parent care enough to try.

I was having difficulty enduring anything by this point, so I found myself sleeping as much as I could. As I have grown older, I find I need sleep less, but in those early days I found it a blessing, a way to escape the worldly indecency of time. Asleep I could forget my nervousness and the blind terror of my situation. I could forget what I was. Not a man, not the palatine son of a prefectural archon, but a

pawn. Whatever my feelings about that literary conceit, it was applicable. On Delos, and in Meidua especially, I was only an extension of my father. His piece to move. Plebeians rarely understand this. They see wealth and think it power, but they are beneath the notice of the powerful and so are often free to make their own decisions, however limited they may be. As my father's son, I was not. Without Gibson's letter I was trapped and would be sent to Vesperad no matter my objections.

No one as observed as I was is free. Like light particles, the unobserved man is free to become whatever is in him and the world allows. But beneath the eye and auspice of the state, he can be only what his betters demand of him. Pawns, knights, bishops. Even the king may move but one step at a time.

I had half a week before I was due to leave the hill country retreat of Haspida for the spaceport in Euclid. Half a week before I shed the gravity of my home for the alien pull of another world and the dark sacrament of the Chantry's faith. I imagined the prison cells in the bastille at Lorica College on Vesperad packed with the screaming and the tormented, the flayed and broken prisoners who had once been great lords of the Empire or barbarian kings. I imagined some shaved-pate proctor of the seminary putting a knife in my hand, commanding me to slit a man's nostrils, to tear skin from flesh and flesh from bone in accordance with the dictates of some prior or magister of the faith.

All this and more pushed its way through my brain like a medical probe or the thread-like needles of the corrective braces whose scars still glistened about my hand and ribs. All this hounded me as I took my habitual morning run up and around the ornamental fortifications that made up the perimeter of the palace proper. Haspida itself was small by the measure of the palaces of the palatine nobility, covering a mere seven hectares including its inner gardens and the central domes of the greenhouse conservatories. That was less than a third of the area of Devil's Rest and not even a tenth of the ducal palace at

Artemia. Rustic, if a twenty-four-hundred-room palace could be such a thing.

My lungs were aching as I bounded down a stairway and onto a flattened sweep of earth paved with crushed white stone. I was sweating badly, the synthetics of my running gear clinging to my back, my hair plastered here and there to the skeletal planes of my face.

And so I felt filthy and totally underdressed when a servant in the white-and-blue livery of the vicereine's staff hurried from a gap in the hedges and stopped me in the shadow of a bent tree. "Master Hadrian, we've been looking all over for you."

Rocks sprayed under my heels as I slid to a halt. "What is it, messer?"

The man bowed hurriedly. "Your lady mother, sire. She's returned, lordship, and requests your presence in her studio."

I glanced up at the sky, then down at the chronometer on my wrist-terminal. "Is there time for me to wash, messer?"

"She said it was most urgent, lord." The man bobbed his jowly head, rubbed both hands flat against a slight paunch in his rumpled uniform. "She said I was to bring you directly."

Mother's suites were in a detached villa apart from the main house, built long after the initial construction of the summer palace. They were only a century or so old and patterned to her needs as a librettist and composer of holo-operas. I followed the portly house attendant through a deep tunnel in one hillock, past one portion of the arboretum with its blue-black leaves and pale grasses lush in the fullness of the day.

The villa itself evoked a more ancient mode, being of that style which enthusiasts call Pre-Peregrine: all clean, straight lines and right angles. It looked totally different from the Rococo scrollwork and idle embellishments of the summer palace itself, wholly removed in color and substance from the Gothic weight of Devil's Rest. A water feature poured free and easy over one wall into another of the palace's omnipresent koi ponds. A quartet

of legionnaires in the Imperial ivory bearing the emblem of House Kephalos on their left arms and the Imperial sun on their right saluted as I came into view, and before long we were inside.

CHAPTER 16

MOTHER

LILIANA KEPHALOS-MARLOWE STOOD AT her holography booth, her back to me, moving through the ghostly image of a fencing duel, a light-pen in her hand, an entoptics monocle screwed over her left eye. The booth was a disc about twenty feet in diameter, mirrored by another on the ceiling that sketched a three-dimensional world within its boundaries. Mother's workspace—glass-walled on the far end and with a commanding view of the domes and slim towers of the summer palace—appeared to contain a portion of grassy sward with a crowd of onlookers in period dress witnessing the doom of an antique musketeer. She couldn't have been back long, and she was already back at her work. I didn't know whether to admire her dedication or to hate her for it. Like Father, she had so little time for her children.

The servant bowed, tapping his feet together. "Hadrian Marlowe, ladyship."

My mother turned, arching one bronze eyebrow until the monocle popped out of her eye. "There you are!" She stopped the monocle swaying, pressed it into a small pocket on her azure blouse. She waved the light-pen, banishing the hazy cloud of holographs with a quiet click. The sward and musketeers vanished, leaving us standing in gray emptiness.

I stood straight, tugging my running shirt down to smooth it. "Here I am? Mother, I've been here for days. You know I'm leaving at the end of the week?"

A faint smile flickered over Mother's porcelain face.

"Yes, yes I know." She turned to the servant. "Mikal, you may leave us." The man bowed and departed, sealing the front doors behind him with a bang. She smiled then and, unknowingly evoking Hamlet, said, "Now we're alone." She crossed her arms, surveying me with an expression I could not quite place: lips pursed, brows contracted, amber eyes narrowed. Were it not for that slight motion, I might have thought her another frozen holograph, an image cast in light as a statue is from bronze. "Would you care to tell me what in Earth's name you think you're doing?"

I blinked, genuinely surprised and not expecting this tack. I looked around. "What are you—"

"Don't play the fool with me, Hadrian." She whirled, green-and-bronze skirts fanning as she did, and crossed the holography platform to a sideboard littered with the instruments of her trade. I spied a pair of heavy entoptic goggles as well as an old-style computer console and a pair of crystal hand tablets nested in a charging station beside the controls for the lights and the polarizing controls for the bank of windows. Liliana Kephalos-Marlowe seized a nylon strap and hauled up a small attaché case such as high-security couriers of the Imperium used. Without ceremony, her jaw clenched, she threw it at me. I caught it on reflex. "Open it."

I did and nearly dropped the pack. Just barely catching it, I looked up at the woman who had given me her genes and said, "It was you? How?"

"I keep eyes on you," she said coolly, thumbing the wall console that turned the bank of windows from transparent to an opaque, metallic gray, shutting out the world. "Especially after the incident at the Colosso."

Gingerly I removed the item at the bottom of the attaché case, drawing it out as if it were a viper or a severed hand. "How did you get this, Mother?" It was the book, of course—the little brown leather volume Gibson had given me that day upon the seawall. *The King with Ten Thousand Eyes,* purporting to be the autobiography of the ancient pirate Kharn Sagara, King of Vorgossos. I opened it, withdrew the yellow envelope Gibson had placed

beneath the front cover. My name was written on the packet in Gibson's spidery hand. Someone had opened it, and I peered within, tucking the book under my arm.

"He'd made plans with one of Lord Albans's scholiasts," Mother said, moving a little closer to me. "Apparently the woman knew a merchanter vessel that'd take you to Nov Senber on Teukros." She scowled. "Not the best plan in the world. You can read about it in there."

A hundred little questions formed and burst, foaming within me. The most important rose to the top. "How did Father find out?"

"About the letter?" She smiled. "Oh, Al has no idea. Lord Albans's people alerted his office when the man's scholiast flagged unauthorized transmissions with the merchanter in high orbit. The plan unraveled on the other end." I placed the letter back inside the novel while she spoke, intestines turning Gordian within me. "Your father knows you had a hand in it, but he figures he's won after . . ." She trailed off, a strange expression clouding the aristocratic severity of her face. "I'm sorry about Gibson, by the way. I know the two of you were close."

"Do you know what happened to him?"

She shook her head. "Packed aboard some cargo freighter headed Emperor-knows-where. Your father had him listed on nine ships' manifests, four of which are heading out-system. I can't wave them until they come out of warp, and even then I'd have to clear a telegraph wave with either my mother or your father." I grimaced. Telegraph waves were expensive and carefully monitored by the Earth's Chantry, being dangerous technological artifacts.

"He's gone, then."

"Alive," Mother replied, "if that helps." It didn't. I looked down at my feet, at the self-lacing gray running shoes. My words fled me, retreating through the opaqued windows and over the towers and glass domes of the palace to vanish in the next valley's glades. Then something happened that I have never forgotten, something that changed my world as surely as if a passing comet had altered my orbit. My mother wrapped her perfumed arms around me, not speaking. I stood there paralyzed. Not

once in nearly twenty standard years—not once—had either of my parents shown me an ounce, an instant of physical affection. That one embrace made up for nearly all of that. I didn't move for the longest time, and it was only with a sort of shellshocked slowness that I moved to embrace her in return. But I did not cry; I did not make a sound.

Mother said, "I want to help you."

I pushed away, looking up at her from closer than I think I had ever looked at her before. "What do you mean?" Nervous, I looked around the room, sighting the cameras high in the smooth metallic walls.

Seeing this, Mother smiled, smoothing her cerulean blouse. "Cameras are all off in here." Her smile widened. "Privilege of running the household." Nearly two decades of experience cast doubt thick and heavy over me, but she smiled and repeated, "The cameras are off." Still numb, I nodded and swallowed, but before I could speak, Lady Liliana said, "You still haven't answered my question."

"Which one?" My knees felt weak, and I crossed to sag onto the divan beside the attaché case that had held *The King with Ten Thousand Eyes*.

"The one where you explain what on Earth you think you're doing."

Reassured by her promise about the cameras, I told her everything. My fear of the Chantry, my hatred of them, my desire to be a scholiast and join the Expeditionary Corps. She winced when I told her Father had struck me, and her eyes glazed over when I recounted Gibson's treatment in Julian's plaza, but she listened attentively and never once interrupted or raised objections. As I spoke she found a low stool in a distant corner and wheeled it just across from the divan where I sat. When I was done she pressed her lips together, reached out, and took my hand, repeating the words that had barely registered the first time I'd heard her say them. "I want to help you."

Youthful petulance cracked its whip within me, and I snapped, "How, Mother? How? It's over. Father's gotten his wish. In four days I'll be on a ship for Vesperad." Crispin's little laugh came back to me then, rattled me.

Anagnost. Odd word. I wondered where Crispin was in that moment. I hoped he was far away in the arms of his blue-skinned girl and not wondering why I wasn't in the main palace. "He's won. It'd take days to come up with some kind of plan . . ."

She squeezed my hand. "Where do you think I've been, hmm?"

I straightened as if Mother had shocked me, felt my eyes go wide. "You're serious."

Lady Liliana only looked at me. "I was in Euclid tracking down a Free Trader, someone to take you offworld."

"A Free Trader? That's no better than a pirate. You can't trust people like that."

She raised a placating hand, letting mine go. "Director Feng vouched for him herself."

That caught me off guard. "The director is still on Delos?"

Mother smiled, rubbing her thumb along her lower lip. "Why do you think I was in Euclid, of all the godforsaken places in Mother's domain?" I wondered at that and at the distant look in Mother's eyes. "No, this fellow's good. A Jaddian. Ada says he used to run Lothrian orbital checks for some of their . . . more sensitive cargo."

I raised my eyebrows. "Ada?"

"Director Feng," Mother amended, looking away. She stood smoothly, pacing toward the foggy windows.

"I got that," I said. "But 'Ada?'"

Lady Liliana smiled a private smile—an expression I understood all too well. "You want to do this or not?"

Seven words. A single question. I was as a man balancing on a wire, ready to fall either left or right. Never to climb back up. "What about you?" I asked, looking up at my mother from my place on the divan. "Aren't you worried about what Father will do once he learns that you helped me to escape the Chantry?"

She turned back from where she stood by the opaqued windows. It suddenly struck me how much taller than me she was. It was from her bloodline that Crispin got his monstrous size. She towered like some alabaster Venus, or like an icon of Justice blown from white glass upon a Chantry altar. "My mother"—she tipped her head back, summoning

all the aristocratic hauteur she could muster—"is the duch-ess of all Delos *and* one of His Radiance's own vicereines. She has your father's balls in her hand."

"Why are you doing this?"

She thrust out her chin. "Al never once asked me about this Vesperad business. So damn him to the Outer Dark. You're my son, Hadrian." She ran her tongue over her teeth like a bored lioness, her attentions captured by something only she could see. "Is this what you want? Life as a scholiast? With the Corps?"

I cleared my throat, desperate to stifle the swelling of emotion the words *You are my son* had placed in me. "Yes."

CHAPTER 17

VALEDICTORY

THE DAY BEFORE MY departure came at last, dawning a sunny silver and painting the green-black countryside with its glow. The sky above was the color of turbulent, storm-tossed seas, but it was sunny and fair as any I'd ever seen. That seemed wrong to me—the rain and storms I'd encountered leaving Meidua struck me as by far the more appropriate weather for such an end. Officially I was to be on a shuttle the following morning, carried up to the trading cog *Farworker* for a steady circuit of the inner Imperium that in time would bring me to Lorica College and exile on Vesperad. Officially. I had it on good authority that I would vanish sometime in the night and instead be transported to the island city of Karch in the middle of the Apollan Ocean, back east of Devil's Rest, to meet Mother's mysterious contact.

Attempting to appear casual, I waited near the landing field for the approach of Father's shuttle, the orbital lifter meant to take me to my rendezvous with the *Farworker* and my fate. Emissaries from Devil's Rest were coming to see me into exile, and propriety begged that I greet them. Crispin stood beside me—whether out of boredom or genuine interest I couldn't have said. He had been astonishingly quiet for the past several minutes, allowing me time to order my mangled thoughts. I was thinking of the scholiasts' meditations, of the apatheia. I was trying to carve out as clear an image of this moment as I could, to take in every detail. *Focus blurs,* Gibson used to say. *Focus blinds. You must take in all of a thing by seeing the*

totality of it, not by focusing on minutiae. This is as important for a ruler as it is for a painter.

A lump settled in my throat as I stood with my brother watching the approaching shuttle. It appeared at first as a tiny shape, birdlike, a blur at the edge of my vision, falling from the sky like a lance. The bird shape grew, became a dragon, and brought with it a scream of metal fury grinding at the sky—first a low rumble like thunder, then the sound of several hundred swords being sharpened on the firmament. It slalomed back and forth across the sky, shedding massive amounts of speed with every turn, just as we had on our arrival.

"I wish they'd let me go up with you," Crispin said. "I've never been to orbit."

I didn't answer him but shielded my eyes in time to see the shuttle's retrojets burst for a moment, killing more speed as it hurried in for its final approach. Around us and on the landing field below, technicians in Kephalos livery hurried about, preparing. Thirty Imperial legionnaires, their white armor immaculately polished, their faceless, eyeless visors down and helmets sealed, took up position at parade rest, rifles in hand, standing shoulder to shoulder with the ten Marlowe hoplites we'd brought with us from Meidua.

The shuttle slewed into its approach vector, canted upward as its attitude jets helped it shed more and more velocity, aided by the shuttle's onboard suppression field. The craft looked more like a knife blade than an aircraft, not at all like the carrion-bird that had brought Crispin and me to this place. Twenty meters of black adamant, the hull bonded to a titanium chassis, capable of withstanding micrometeor impacts even without the shield projectors mounted fore and aft, little concave dishes shining like quicksilver.

The underside of the hull still smoldered from the friction of reentry as it settled onto the landing field, the ship wreathed in tongues of smoke like some evil dragon. Technicians ran forward to cool the glowing adamant with chemical sprays, and the whole thing hissed like a

nest of adders as the gangway descended. For one terrible instant, I felt sure that Father's broad-shouldered silhouette would come stumping down that ramp, that Mother's carefully laid plan and Gibson's sacrifice—and the money I'd secreted—would come to naught and all would be lost.

But it was only Tor Alcuin with his shaved head and dark skin, his voluminous robes flapping from his shoulders like an embassy of flags. Sir Roban, just as dark, followed in his wake, not armored but dressed in simple semiformal blacks, his highmatter sword swinging free from his shield-belt. My farewell party. A trio of lesser functionaries followed them down the ramp, followed by a senior flight officer . . . and Kyra. The lieutenant looked out of place in their company, younger than the others by a decade or more. I marveled at the unhappy odds that had ensured that of all my father's pilot officers, she had been chosen to fly the shuttle. It was almost enough to make me believe that there was a God and that he hated me.

The young scholiast and the functionaries bowed deeply. Roban saluted, his fist pressed to his breast, and the other officers followed suit. "It is an honor," Alcuin said in unctuous tones, "to accompany you on your journey from Delos, Lord Hadrian."

I inclined my head, eyes darting momentarily to Kyra in the back of the party. I looked away quickly, praying I had not reddened. Emboldened by Father's absence and Mother's plan, I said, "I would be more honored, Counselor, if Gibson could have joined us." If I had expected a reaction from the scholiast, I was disappointed. Alcuin's dark face remained impassive, his eyes flat and smooth as agate. The others all betrayed disquiet in the uneasy way they shuffled about on their feet. Deep beneath my surface, an ember of hot ash blew into flame, a fury with this man— this adding machine—who felt nothing, nothing at all for the brutality visited upon his comrade and brother-in-arms by the man they served. Alcuin must know the story, must know that Gibson's treatment was a gross injustice.

And he didn't care—couldn't care. Caring was an alien notion to him, as alien as the Cielcin xenobites in their

labyrinthine worldships. As alien as any of the coloni races, enslaved on their own worlds. As alien, indeed, as the dark gods that whisper quietly in the night. He only said, "Gibson's treason was unfortunate."

"Hadrian," Roban said, stepping forward and offering a hand, "it's good to see you again before you go."

I clasped Roban's hand, but my attentions barely flickered from Alcuin's face. "It's good to see you, too, Roban." I trailed off, finally peeling my gaze away from the scholiast to look the knight-lictor in his blunt-featured face, at the wide nose and deep-set eyes beneath the heavy shelf of brow. Feeling at once awkward and still, I said, "I should have thanked you more . . . more appropriately for saving me. And for everything." Remembering suddenly, I craned my neck to speak to Kyra past the three uniformed functionaries. "And you, Lieutenant. Thank you."

She bowed slightly, and Roban clapped me on the shoulder. "One last trip, then, you and I. Are you all packed?"

Giving the lictor a smile that I fear failed to reach my eyes, I said, "Of course!"

"I know that this is not the future you envisioned for yourself, young master," said Alcuin, voice like dry leaves, "but your role with the Chantry will serve the greater glory of your house. A Marlowe in the Chantry will allow—"

To my surprise, Crispin cut him off. "He doesn't need the speech. He knows."

Alcuin went stiffly silent, bowed his head. Eager to inject some calmness back into the proceedings, I said, "I understand the necessity, Alcuin." And I smoothed all expression from my face, watching the scholiast—my father's chief advisor—with an expression as apparently empty as his own. Only my serenity was skin-deep, a layer of ice atop turbulent waters. Alcuin was frozen solid. I could hear Gibson's cries of pain as the lash bit into him resounding in my ears and felt myself slipping further away from this meet-and-greet on the landing field. I felt an instant need to be alone.

"Of course you do, young master." Tor Alcuin bowed

past his knees, tucking his hands into his flowing sleeves before him. "Forgive me."

Coldly I said, "There is nothing to forgive, Counselor." I had another mystery to unravel, and so I turned, blood creeping into my face, to speak to Kyra. "Lieutenant, I am surprised to see you here." *What are the odds?* I wanted to ask, to joke, to try and salvage a bad situation, to smooth over my earlier mistake.

Kyra averted her gaze quickly, bowing her head so that the short bill of her flight officer's cap hid her eyes. "I was told I was personally requested."

I felt the blood drain from my face. "By whom?"

She looked up sharply, and there was nothing of the fear I expected in her face, only something lean-edged and hard. "By yourself."

She's lying, I thought, smiling at her. We both knew it. I could see it in her face, in the way she held my gaze as she had not done before. Often I have found that liars do this: they watch their dupes closely, searching for the moment when belief sets in. Conscious of the onlookers, I said, "Oh, yes! Of course, I'd forgotten! I'd like a private word, when we have a moment." Inwardly I frowned. Something was going on, but what it was I didn't guess. I had known the delegation was coming, but even so I did not relish the task of escaping the Haspida palace—however Mother intended to see it done—under the noses of Roban and Tor Alcuin.

"Where is Lady Kephalos-Marlowe?" Alcuin asked, taking a mincing step forward.

Crispin moved to join the counselor, pivoting to indicate the domes of the palace on the hills above us. "Just this way, everyone. Please."

CHAPTER 18

RAGE IS BLINDNESS

THE FIRST KNOCK CAME late that evening, when the silver sun had fattened to gold and was setting over the western hills. For what seemed the thousandth time, I sat on the floor of my suite in the Haspida palace, sorting through and repacking the items I was meant to take to Vesperad—or to Teukros, if Mother and I had our way. I straightened a stack of books, called over my shoulder, "Enter!"

Crispin sauntered in, barely waiting for my permission to do so. He had a half-eaten apple in one hand, his gray shirt only buttoned partway.

I stood quickly, upsetting a stack of carefully folded shirts. I swore under my breath, hurried to straighten them. "What do you want?" The presence of Father's watchdog committee made me nervous, Alcuin especially. The man was sharp as nanocarbon wire and just as dangerous to someone moving fast and carelessly.

"You're leaving in the morning," Crispin said, spreading his arms. "*Early* in the morning. I . . . well, I guess this is goodbye. For a while, at least."

I crouched, replacing the clothing in the bottom of the heavy plastic trunk. "You know, it's about eleven years to Vesperad. By the time they pull me out of fugue, you'll be the older brother." I stood up, smoothing the front of my shirt and fixing my fringe of dark hair.

Crispin's jagged smile pulled at one corner of his mouth, and he chuckled quietly. "Yeah, I'd not thought of that." He looked down at the things collected on the

floor—the books and data crystals, the shoes and the pair of long knives. "This is all you're taking?"

I shrugged. "The Chantry doesn't really want us taking more than we need. We're supposed to be leaving our lives behind as much as we can." *And the scholiasts will expect me to surrender everything.* Remembering the cold emptiness of Alcuin's eyes, I shivered, feeling again the shadow of doubt.

"That part sounds miserable. I thought Eusebia had those great apartments in the Belling Tower. Isn't all that hers?"

"Sure," I said, using a stack of language books to compress my packed clothing. I sat on a low footstool, cracked my knuckles one careful joint at a time. "But she's not a student, is she? The rules are different."

"I guess that makes sense." Crispin spoke around a mouthful of apple, then dropped again into my armchair. I was glad that this time at least he was not brandishing a naked blade. "Still, I didn't realize it was going to be that rough on you."

My attention wandered across the view out the window, over the low lily ponds to the distant black-leaved cypress under the golden twilight. "They're just things, Crispin. They aren't important."

Crispin laughed, a coarse and braying sound without music in it. "If you say so, Brother." He set the half-eaten apple down on the spindle-legged table beside his armchair and tugged one leg up to adjust the cuff of his boot. "But you're still the one going out there, you know? You're getting to see the Empire."

"I doubt it'll be very glamorous," I said dryly, still not looking at my brother. "Like I said, I'll be looking at the inside of a training cell for years. That's it." It came to me then that I was imitating Mother's habit of staring out of windows, of drifting as far from the locus of conversation as politeness and architecture allowed. I wanted desperately to be gone. I wondered if at that moment, in some secret corner of the grounds, there wasn't a shuttle being fueled and checked for a night voyage to Karch, ready to meet the Consortium's Free Trader contact. The plan

made me nervous, but if Mother was willing to stake my safety on the honor of this ship's captain, then I supposed there was nothing for it. Unless I wished to become a holy torturer and inquisitor. Gibson's face swam up before me as if reflected in the armored glass of my window.

I did not wish that.

Crispin had been silent for a long moment, a fact I didn't notice until he broke his silence, calling attention to the absence of words between us. "So you and that lieutenant, huh?"

"What?" My head snapped round, brows contracting.

"The skinny one with the curls and the small tits." Crispin mimed breasts with his hands. "The pilot officer."

I felt my face go ashen. "Kyra."

"Kyra," Crispin repeated, grinning that awful grin. "Is that her name, then?" He picked at his teeth with a fingernail, wiped the finger on his pants. "She something special, then? I guess that's why you didn't want to go to the harem with—"

"That's enough, Crispin." Emulating Father, I did not even turn to look at my brother as we spoke, did not raise my deep voice above a whisper. "Leave her alone."

My brother raised his hands defensively, then ran them through his short hair, agitated. "Calm down, Hadrian. I get it. Mind you, she's pretty enough, I guess. A bit boyish, but if that's your thing, well . . ."

"I said that's enough." I stood, pushing the footstool out from behind me. The hairs on the back of my neck stood on end, and I ground my teeth, glowering at my brother.

Crispin paused, recovered his apple. He looked down at his lap, speaking to his hands. "Look, I'm sorry. I just . . . I wish I were the one going. Father did always like you best."

Had I been drinking, surely I would have spat the liquid out. "What?" I spluttered. "Emperor's blood—what?" I nearly stumbled on a pair of old boots left beside the open trunk.

"He's sending you to Vesperad, and I get Devil's Rest. What do I want with Devil's fucking Rest?" He took another bite, following my gaze out the window. "You get

to be out there fighting, hunting down treasonous lords and Cielcin . . ." He trailed off. For a moment I felt I had misunderstood Crispin. For a moment I realized that being the younger brother, he had expected to come into nothing. Just as I had thought Devil's Rest had always been Crispin's, he had believed it mine. He had toiled in my shadow, and I in his, neither of us knowing the shadow was really just that of our Father, drowning us both.

"Don't get your brain eaten."

"Wasn't on my list of things to do." I couldn't tell if he meant it as a joke or if it was a serious concern in the younger boy's mind. Or perhaps he mentioned it deliberately to remind me of the dinner where my final slip from Father's grace had begun. Crispin's blunt features betrayed nothing of the mind sparkling behind his flat eyes, and my own blood ran cold.

My brother kept chewing, lips smacking open and closed, cow-like. At last I ventured, "Why are you here, Crispin?"

He blinked. "I told you! I wanted to say goodbye!" He stood, moving close enough to clap me on the shoulder with one hand. "It'll be a while before I see you again." We stood there a moment, shoulder to shoulder, looking out the window. Crispin took another noisy bite of his apple. "Last few months have been . . . really something. Father says I can fight in the Colosso again." When I only nodded, turning to scrape my journal and the priceless copy of *The King with Ten Thousand Eyes* off a side table, Crispin added, "Shame what happened to Gibson, though. I can't believe the old bastard turned traitor like that."

I stood immobile, the ice in my veins turned to granite. Through a jaw so tight it might have been wired shut, I hissed, "I don't want to talk about that."

Oblivious, dumb, blind, Crispin took another bite of the apple. "Did you see his face, though? Disgusting. He looked like a prole." I slammed a hand against the polished mahogany window frame, rattling the alumglass like a drumhead. Turning, I saw Crispin's eyes widen under square brows, one cheek puffed out absurdly around the food there. "Why are you so mad?"

He didn't understand. He really didn't understand. "Gibson's gone."

"He was just some servant." Crispin swallowed, shifted the apple a little to get a better bite. I slapped the apple out of his hands. It hit the tile with a thud and bounced away toward the door. Crispin looked at me, surprise stretching those thick lips. "What did you do that for?"

Rage is blindness, I told myself, Gibson's voice rolling over in my head, muttering the old scholiasts' mantra. But another voice—my own voice—answered Crispin. "He was my friend."

Crispin looked at me, incredulous. "He tried to ship you off to be some limp-dick scholiast. He was going to give you to the Extras!"

"That isn't what happened, you imbecile." My nostrils flared, and I could feel the muscles in my face tighten dangerously, hardening into a grimness two steps from fury. I knew as I spoke that I should not have said it, that some officer of the house intelligence corps could hear and alert security, but I was past caring.

Crispin colored red, face flushing all at once, a startling transition from his accustomed paleness. "Don't you dare."

"Call you an imbecile?" I stepped inside the reach of Crispin's arms. The bones of my right hand ached, drawing attention to themselves and the danger I was putting myself in by coming within striking distance of a larger Marlowe. But I was leaving the next day—that night, if I had my way. It needed to be said. "You're an imbecile."

The poets speak of rage as a fiery thing, consuming, destroying, twisting a soul to mistaken action. They sing songs of revenge, of lovers killed in the night, of passions inflamed, of houses torn asunder. But there is little heat in rage. The scholiasts have it right. Rage is blindness. A red color blurring out the world. It is light, not fire. And light, when finely tuned, can cut as surely as steel. I saw Crispin's lips curl, preparing some cutting remark that never reached my ears. It never left him. I smashed him in the side of the face with the heavy books in my right

hand, sending him staggering to the ground, his arms beneath him.

"He was helping me, you bastard." I dropped the books into my chest and moved to stand over my brother. "I asked him to do it." Crispin was on his hands and knees, shaking his head as if to clear the ringing from his ears. "I told you when we left home, Crispin: I don't want to be a prior. I don't believe any of it." Or that's what I would have said, what I meant to say. Crispin launched himself from his knees, slammed into me like a battering ram, his arms about my midsection, a rabid cry rising in his throat. We slammed against the huge window, the back of my head cracking against the alumglass, the wind knocked from me. Crispin's momentum undid his footing, and he stumbled, lacking the advantage I had in the wall of glass at my back.

I shoved, and he caromed away, spinning round to right himself, coming up with fists raised. "You're going to pay for that!" he said. "You hear me?"

Rage is blindness, I told myself. But it didn't matter. It all came boiling up then, shining from the back of my skull and washing out my reason. Gibson's scourging; my embarrassment in the streets of Meidua; my mistakes with the Mandari delegation. They all spun up out of that inner darkness, alloyed themselves with my fury at my disinheritance; my dispossession; my anger at Father; my contempt for the Chantry; my jealousy of Crispin.

Crispin swung wide, and I blocked the blow with my arm. It would have been easy, pure child's play, if the boy were not so monstrously strong. We were both palatines, taller and stronger than common men, but Crispin had more than a head on me and at least twenty pounds more muscle. I struggled to hold him at bay, to fend off his left jab, to take a glancing blow to my shoulder, to accord myself an opening to kick Crispin in one poorly positioned knee. He staggered, snarling, and I said, "Get out of here, Crispin."

"No!" He lunged again, and I danced sideways as he lurched into the heavy alumglass window. Crispin steadied

himself against the glass, leaving a big, sticky handprint there. I was glad, even impressed that furious as I was, I was not like Crispin. Even with my blood up and my jaw clenched so tight it sang, I held myself tight. Cold. Perhaps rage *was* heat for Crispin; perhaps there is no such single thing as rage. He barreled at me again, blows falling like hail, like rain, like legionnaires diving from space in armored drop-carriages. I took a vicious blow to the side of the head, rolled with it. Dropping low, I curled into a crouch and spun round to strike Crispin in the chin with the heel of one foot. The blow stunned him, and he stumbled backward, keeping his feet only through an effort of concentration.

Again he shook his head, gave a bull's anxious snort. "You think you're better than me!" he shouted and jabbed a finger at the floor. "You always have!"

Grateful for the moment to recover, I wiped at my nose with my thumb. It came away bloody. "I think you're an ass, Crispin." I shook out my hands, settling into a boxer's guard. My brother swung at me wide, but I ducked, hit him once, twice, three times in the belly. He grunted, brought an elbow down on my shoulder. I slipped to one knee and had to roll sideways—tangling on a stack of laundry I'd left ready to be repacked—and came back up on my feet in time to grab Crispin by the wrist. He smashed his free arm down on mine, and I released him. "Just stop," I said, chest heaving. "Get out."

"You hit me." He lashed out with one foot, the kick taking me in the hip and sending me scrambling backward, trampling the detritus of my life, the clothes and papers, the stupid things I'd brought along. He repeated himself more darkly: "You hit me first."

"Don't be a child." I sneered, unable to stop myself. "That was a cheap shot. Try it again."

I saw the whites of Crispin's eyes as he reared back for another straight kick. He'd meant it to spite me, to surprise me, but I knew my brother, knew he would rise to the bait. My fingers closed round his ankle, unbalancing him. Crispin toppled, dragging me down on top of him. I fell with one elbow aimed at Crispin's gut, winding him.

Without hesitation I struck him hard, a glancing blow across the face. With Crispin momentarily stunned, I managed to regain my feet.

"Stay down," I said, backing off, hoping the distance between us would calm him where he lay.

Through gasping breaths, he wheezed, "Fuck. You." He had fallen near my crate and might have cracked his skull on the corner had he been only slightly less lucky. Crispin grasped it, using the lip of the box to haul himself into a sitting position, head lolling, his back against the heavy box.

I stood ready, hackles up, prepared to kick him across the face if he tried anything stupid. Chest still heaving, my voice suddenly shrunken and drawn, I said, "Just stay down." It was not the voice of a nineteen-year-old, but the voice of a ghost, of an old man tired and frail. "Stay down, Crispin."

Crispin sat, rubbing his jaw with one hand. His words thick and furry, he said, "When you're gone, that little girl of yours? The lieutenant? She'll get what Gibson got. And when that's done—"

I never heard the rest. Anger's light washed me out. Whether childish or righteous or just plain stupid I cannot say, but I launched myself at Crispin.

He leaped at me, hurling his massive body from the cluttered and broken objects on the floor as from a trebuchet. I ducked low, taking him about the legs, using all that mass and momentum to lift my brother up and over my shoulder and to send him crashing back to the tile, spread-eagle. I heard the air go out of him in a spasming rush. I did not hesitate, did not stop to think about what I was doing. I struck Crispin in the head with my boot. He went limp. Unconscious.

It was over so quickly. But violence is always over so quickly. No decrescendo, as in music. It only ceases. Stops. As a light snuffed out.

Breathing hard, I tried to quiet my thoughts, tried to still the waters cascading within me, spiraling ever downward into blind grottoes of panic. I do not know how long I stood there, heart hammering. An hour? A month?

Minutes? It could not have been long. Every atom, every quark in me thrummed, rattling like a violin string twanged and tightening to stillness. I tried to practice one of the breathing exercises Sir Felix had taught me as a boy, tried to focus on the palatial structure of memory and fact Gibson had tried to teach me to build, to seek solace in myself, anything to still the tattoo rattling through my blood. I crouched, one hand to Crispin's lips. He was still breathing, at least. That was something.

I had not killed him. He was alive.

The cameras had seen everything, surely. I looked at one, at the little aperture glittering like a dark eye in one corner, watchful as a murder of crows at the gallows. I bared my teeth in a snarl, unknowingly echoing an expression which to the Cielcin conveys the deepest joy, and gathered my scattered belongings, stuffing them madly into the case that I was meant to take into one exile or another.

"Hadrian!"

The voice was transformed by shock and horror and so was alien, but it had used my name.

Lady Liliana stood stunned in the doorway, one hand forgotten on the latch. By chance or by the grace of some unknown god, she was totally alone. No guards, no retinue. Alone. "What did you do?"

"He attacked me," I lied, no longer caring. A moment later I hedged my bets and said, "He said things. Words about Gibson. About the lieutenant." I glanced over my shoulder at Crispin's supine form. "Why are you here? Is it time?"

She looked at Crispin soberly. "It is now."

"Mother, I'm sorry. I wasn't expecting him. I was just waiting for your people like you said and—"

She placed gentle hands on each of my shoulders and made a shushing sound. "No, this is fine. This is good."

"Good?" I practically screamed the word. "Good? How in Emperor's name is this good?"

Ever the storyteller, Lady Liliana looked at me as if I were one of her holograph actors, and in a voice small and serious and sad, she said, "You've given me an out. I'll say

you stole my shuttle and fled in the night. You can fly one, can't you?"

I nodded. "Sir Ardian's been teaching me since I was seven."

"Good. But take my people anyway," she said. "You may need the help."

"Won't that get you in trouble?"

"Your father wouldn't dare touch me. It's my house that rules here, not his. You need to hurry. Take what you can."

She gave me a little push, back toward the heavy foot-locker I'd brought with me from home. Stooping, I tugged a pair of trousers out from under Crispin and bunched them into the case, began tossing things pell-mell atop the pile. A thought, unbidden but pressing, came to me. "They'll review the footage. They'll see us talking."

"They didn't see you talking to Gibson the day of his torment, did they?"

I froze, two pairs of wine-red socks in my fingers. "That was you?" By Earth, she couldn't have raided the security storage at Devil's Rest, could she?

"You can thank me when you're safely out-system. Now hurry up." She pressed a key on her terminal.

Dropping the socks into place, I obeyed, pausing only a moment. "Mother?"

"Son?" There was a wryness in her tone that I have never forgotten—a tiny audible smile.

Slamming the lid of my trunk, I turned. "Why are you doing this?" Mother froze, became marble. I thought her caught as light is caught across the horizon of a collapsed star, for a piece of me felt she might never move again.

On the ground, Crispin groaned. "Mother?"

A terrible, fractured smile broke over that stone she called a face. Ye gods, in another life she'd have made a better scholiast than Gibson. After an eternal several seconds, she said, voice breaking, "You always were my favorite."

I was saved the necessity of a response by the arrival of two Kephalos legionnaires . . . and Kyra. The lieu-tenant accorded Crispin's form only a moment's note. "Master Hadrian, come with us at once."

"Kyra?" I looked at Mother, everything crashing into place.

She shook her head, all business. "No time."

"*You* are Mother's eyes?" I glanced at Mother, who smiled.

"We have to go!" Kyra snapped.

I allowed the legionnaires to take up my trunk. Their faces obscured behind those blank white visors, they seemed somehow unreal. Like part of a dream. A play. I locked eyes with my mother. "Thank you," I said. Those were the last words I ever spoke to her, and as it always is with last words, they were not enough.

CHAPTER 19

THE EDGE OF THE WORLD

THE FREE TRADER WAS not at all like I'd expected—but then, I hadn't been sure what I expected. Demetri Arello was Jaddian and thin as a rapier with skin the color of oiled bronze. He smiled, flashing teeth so white I knew they had to be ceramic implants. "Strange for a nobleman to be so desperate as to stoop to my level." He chuckled self-deprecatingly and leaned back in his seat, ruffling his star-bright hair. It was brighter than his teeth: a luminous, vivid white.

"Your level?" I asked, pouring my own wine from the glass carafe. Outside the arched doorway, the day was hot and steaming, and I could hear the heavy sounds of construction from the half-finished apartment building rising near the docks. "What do you mean?"

Arello smiled. "My ship is fast, but she is no luxury cruiser." He took me in with an appraising eye, bit his lip intently. "You may not be so comfortable." The trader stroked his smooth chin with one ringed hand, his smile not faltering.

"I'm not looking for comfort," I said. "Just passage to Teukros."

He interrupted me, eyes taking in Kyra where she sat between us. "Clearly comfort is not your goal, else you would be bringing this one along with you, eh?" He smiled again. He was always smiling. Kyra offered no response. I could sense the urgency coming off her in waves. She wanted this done with, and quickly.

"If I were looking for comfort, messer, I'd be staying at home."

"Quite. Though as I understand it, you are not having a home to stay in, yes?" He tipped back his tumbler of wine and grimaced. "How do you Imperials drink this horse piss? I ask you . . ." He shook his head. "In my homeland we'd stone the man who dared sell this."

Apparently past her limit, Kyra said, "Your ship's fast?"

"Fast enough for the lady who chartered me." Despite his protestations, the man seized the carafe and refilled his tumbler with the thick, red-black liquid. He took another more speculative sip. "It's strong, at least." He set the glass down and leaned back and sideways, stretching the loose folds of the green-and-orange robe he wore over his otherwise bare and hairless chest. "Listen, if you want to get to Teukros, then the *Eurynasir* will get you to Teukros. We go by Obatala and Siena. A thirteen-year journey."

"By Obatala . . ." I trailed off, my frown deepening. "It's not a direct journey?" I looked at Kyra, who was here only to see that I arrived on the trader's ship. She'd changed out of her pilot's uniform and into simple street clothes, tight leggings and a loose-fitting tunic printed with the Albans salamander and the name of some Colosso gladiator. It suited her.

Arello's snowy brows contracted. "Direct? To Teukros? That's a fucking long journey, my friend. I'm not looking to put myself out on a long trip up-spiral the one courier job. I've got crew to feed and pay, and if we're going so far, you bet your pasty palatine ass we're stopping for trade. War's driven up all sorts of demands—a man could make himself a king."

Kyra leaned toward me and whispered, "I really don't like to be wasting time like this, my lord. I'll be missed soon." Against my objections, she had insisted on accompanying me into the wine-sink to meet with the Jaddian captain despite the five-hour flight back to Haspida. The morning was well on now, and by the clock on one wall there was only about an hour before my scheduled departure from the summer palace for the *Farworker* and Ves-

perad. I had abandoned my terminal in the summer palace, not wanting to be tracked by its signal.

"They've probably already missed you," I said soberly, still unwilling to look her in the eyes. Junior or no, she was a pilot officer and would have been expected to show up for systems checks. I only hoped that Mother would have the wits to play for time. Perhaps she'd say I had stunned Kyra too in my escape, that I'd left her in some out-of-the-way place where she'd not be found. She'd come up with something.

"Is this a private conversation?" Demetri asked, his lilting accent almost feline in its lazy drawl. "Or can anybody step in, hmm? I dislike this idleness as much as any of you, but I need to know we have an understanding." Here he placed a hand against his heart like a vassal swearing an oath to his liege.

Very serious, I narrowed my eyes. "What sort of understanding? You've been paid, am I right?"

"Yes, yes." Demetri Arello nodded vigorously. "Five thousand hurasams in advance with the promise of nine thousand marks from your bank on Teukros when you arrive." He waved a hand as if to dismiss these thoughts like so many bloat-flies. "This is all well and good, but how am I saying this? You are a nobile. Nobiles are uh . . . how you say?" He looked pointedly from my face to Kyra's. "Complicated?" I stared back, each of us waiting for the other man to blink. Silence, I've often found, is the most effective tool in any conversation. So I waited the merchant out. The clamor of morning construction subsided a moment, and I heard a man calling out in some street argot. "You are not some sort of criminal, are you?"

Taken aback, I raised my eyebrows at the man. "What? No." What had Mother told him?

"It is only that I do not wish my people endangered," Demetri explained, keeping his eyes locked on me as he refilled his glass, unable to mask the disappointed sneer at the sound of the liquid spilling into his cup. "We have sufficient troubles of our own without dabbling in Delian politics."

I glanced sideways at a faded opera poster featuring a naked, black-skinned woman holding a highmatter sword, one bare foot planted on the face of an Imperial legionnaire. *Tiada,* it read, *The Princess of Thrax.* "You're taking me away from Delian politics." When Demetri looked to be on the verge of arguing, I switched to Jaddian and said, "Listen, you're from the Principalities, yes?"

The foreigner blinked, surprise coloring his sharp face. "Yes, yes. *Si.*" He watched me with hooded eyes.

"How do you feel about the Terran Chantry?" Demetri's jovial expression faltered, and he made a face like he'd had more of the dive's sour wine. Satisfied, I said, still in Jaddian, "That's what I thought. Well, as it happens, I feel the same way, *mi sadji.* I was being sent to seminary. You're helping me escape." I smiled again, the grin unintentionally crooked, as all my family's grins were. I was conscious then of my accent, the polish of the old Imperial elite, scion of the elder houses of the inner worlds. It was a voice associated with villains in the sort of operas portrayed on the rather tasteless posters that plastered the wine-sink's walls.

Demetri set his pointed jaw. He leaned in over his wine and hissed, this time in Imperial Galstani, "Sticking it to the Chantry, is it?" He glanced over my shoulder, across the common room to the pair of jubala addicts at their hookah. The smokers were the only other people in the dismal bar, either the first customers of the day or the last of the night. He kept his eyes on them. "I have heard this already from our friends in the Consortium. I only want to make sure it is not more than this thing. Nothing . . . messy."

Crispin's unconscious form lying on the floor blossomed flower-like in my mind. From the look on Kyra's narrow features, I saw she was thinking the same. "No, no. Nothing like that."

If Demetri could tell I was lying, he didn't seem to care. He slammed back his wine in one gulp, gasping at its foulness. Then his eyes narrowed, and in a lower voice he asked, "Who are you?"

"I told you," I said. "My name's Hadrian."

He wagged a long finger at me, and I noted a faintly

reflective tattoo glittering on the back of his hand. "No no no no no. I may not be from your Empire, but I am no mongrel to be kicked and lied to. You are Hadrian *some-one*." He turned the finger on Kyra. "This little female of yours is no friend. She's a servant, no? A bodyguard, maybe?" When I hesitated, his huckster's grin widened, and he sat back, laughing softly to himself as he fingered the triangular gold medallion about his neck. "Which house? Feng wouldn't say." Not seeing the point in denying it, I tugged the ring off my thumb and showed it to him. Foreign as he was, he frowned. "I should have turned the bitch down."

"If you go quickly, there won't be a problem," Kyra snapped, jaw tight. I think the word *bitch* in reference to my mother—her secret master—lit something in her.

"Marlowe . . ." Arello was ignoring her, turning his wineglass on the tabletop so that it rattled. "Marlowe . . . Weren't you attacked? Some time ago now? Mugged coming out of a brothel, was it?"

With Kyra there, this rankled especially. I slapped the table with one hand, the rage I'd felt the night before flaring up. "It wasn't a brothel!"

Demetri laughed again, a polished-wood sound that drew the eyes of the two jubala smokers by the arch that led to the outer balcony. "So it was you, then!"

I scowled. Oldest trick in the book, that. "It was the Colosso."

"Whatever." Demetri waved a hand, refilled my glass for me. "Your lovely bodyguard is right, *domi*. We should be going. And now." He raised his empty glass in imitation of a toast. "But my grandmother said never to waste wine, even goat's piss like this. Your health, *mi sadji. Buon atanta.*"

"*I tuo,*" I replied and stomached the swill.

Karch lay at the edge of the globe, as far from civilization as was possible on a planet like Delos. If our cartographers had shared the romance of the ancients, they might have

drawn dragons and sea serpents in the waters encircling her. Where Meidua was tall, her proud towers stretching like supplicating fingers toward the gray heavens, Karch was squat, a rambling tangle of two- and three-story buildings along the stony rise above the bay. On those blue-gray waters, floating like so much garbage, lay a tangle of pontoon bridges and floats anchored to concrete piers like bones in a fish. A great many ships gathered there: sail and steam and star.

And the people. Earth and Emperor, the people. The terrible crush of them, the weight and stink and sound of them. For once I was a tall man, standing nearly head and shoulders above the tallest plebeian in the throng. So I took to slouching, my satchel slung over one shoulder, my shirt unbuttoned to the sternum in the uncommon heat. Mother's two legionnaires, dressed in simple clothes but with pistols hanging from their shield-belts, carried my trunk between them, following at a respectful distance. Kyra hurried along ahead of me, moving with a deliberation that parted the crowd all on its own. The pontoons rocked beneath our feet, bobbing on the gentle swells.

Demetri had gone ahead of us, and so when we approached the low, dark lozenge of his ship where she squatted on the waves, he stumped out to greet us. He'd undone his orange-and-green robe, and the silk billowed about him. He raised a hand, waved. I acknowledged the gesture and hurried forward, ducking around two broad-chested sailors unloading their small freighter. I barely saw them, my attention entirely given over to the matte-black hull of the ship pressed against the surface of the bay.

The Jaddian ship reminded me of a catamaran, with two swollen runners making up each of her flanks, running a little to the fore and aft of her nearly forty-meter length. Between them, the body of the craft arched out of the water. An alumglass dome—like a hooded eye— peered from between those runners, and at her rear a slim conning spire rose between heavy air fins that doubled for rudders when the ship was down in water, as then. Every inch of her was dark as space, the hull a composite of

adamant and high-impact ceramics with pieces of alum-glass and exposed titanium here and there. Saying all this, perhaps it sounds glamorous, and if I were some backwater farm technician with barely two hurasams to rub together, perhaps it would've been. But to me—to the son of a landed archon—it was . . . worrying.

Hairline fractures veined the ceramic in places and were in places caulked or welded. A mural of two cupped hands peeled near the front of the craft, the fingers cupping the flowing Jaddian letters of a single word: *Eurynasir.*

Salt from Delos's ocean caked the lower regions of the hull, and the smoke trailing from the warming fusion lifters in the back made me think of some ancient wood-burning locomotive. If she had suppression field generators, I could not see them.

"Fine ship, Captain!" I called, lowering my hand. "I hope I've not kept you waiting." It had been perhaps half an hour since we'd parted in the dingy wine-sink with its jubala-scented air. The air on the pontoon pier stank of ozone from the fusion drives and diesel fuel from outboard motors.

Demetri Arello smiled, white teeth flashing in the light as he tied a green sash about his slim waist. "You are just in time. Hurry." He caught sight of the two plain-clothes soldiers carrying my trunk, and his smile faltered as he said, "If ever I had doubts about what you were, this would end them." He watched the two soldiers put the case down. "We can carry it inside." He bit his lip again, looking me over as if I were a specimen under glass. His fingers drummed against his legs.

"One moment." I turned to Kyra. "You've done all you can, Lieutenant. Take the others and go. With luck, you've not been missed."

She shook her head, hooked a thumb through the belt of her tunic. "It's too late for that."

At once the toe of my boot absorbed all of my attentions, and I spoke to it instead of the woman before me. "I'm sorry." I wanted her to say something. Anything. To

tell me it was all right. I thought of Crispin's threat against her and said, "Mother will protect you. I swear it. Ask her for a posting with my grandmother. Anywhere away from the castle." *From my brother.*

"I'll be fine," she said defensively, and she turned to go. I could not blame her for hurrying.

But I caught her wrist. "Kyra, wait." She looked back, still half turned away, her hard eyes glaring at the spot where my hand held her. I wonder now if she thought I was going to kiss her again. I did no such thing. I knew this moment was important, that hers was the last familiar face I would ever see, the last human piece of my life before childhood's end. I wanted to say something she would remember. But I let her go, pressed my fist to my chest in salute, and could only repeat what I had already said: "I'm sorry."

I wished she would speak. But she didn't. Instead she nodded, turned, and was gone, passing between the two legionnaires, who mirrored my salute and melted into the crowd. In memory, I stand watching as the three soldiers dressed as common men faded into the throng on that bobbing pier. But that is a dream. Not a second passed before Demetri grabbed my shoulder, fingers insistent. "Hurry, boy. We waste time."

"Yes," I said faintly, craning my neck, patting myself down to check the contents of my pockets: my knife, my static identification, a few hurasams, the letter Gibson had written for me, and the universal card I had won from Lena Balem and the Mining Guild. Twenty thousand marks was a precious thing. Once I was offworld, away from my father and his prying eyes, it was enough to start almost any kind of life. Despite Gibson's letter, I could go *anywhere.* Twenty thousand was enough to buy passage on a ship. On several ships. Between that and my blood, I could buy a ship on credit, turn merchanter or mercenary. I imagined sailing to Judecca like Simeon the Red, breaking bread with the avian Irchtani, seeing the universe. I could not help smiling.

Teukros first.

Stooping, I helped Demetri with my trunk, walking down the boarding ramp and into the cool, sterile dimness of the airlock and out—for the last time—from under the silver sun and sky of my home.

CHAPTER 20

OFF THE MAP

"WE READY TO SHIP out?" a husky, feminine voice asked when Demetri and I finished wrestling my trunk into a space amidst wooden crates and steel drums in the low-ceilinged hold. The air aboard the *Eurynasir* was frigid, as the air aboard so many starships is, and the lights were dialed low and golden, casting dim highlights on the black walls and scuffed metal floors. The place smelled like spent gunpowder, like engine grease and burnt metal. Rust. Not a clean smell, and not one that inspired confidence. The ship had been around a long time—decades at least, and perhaps longer.

Turning, I saw a woman in a dull gray jumpsuit approaching. She had the same bronze skin as Demetri, the same star-bright hair, though hers was nearly twice as long and waved almost to her elbows. So similar were they that they might have been cousins, siblings, were it not for the way Demetri's face opened up as he bounded to her and gathered her into his arms, making a low sound in his throat as he pressed his lips to hers. "Juno! Come and meet our new friend!" He stretched an arm toward me. "Has Bassem got the engines ready? I want to dust off at once." The woman, Juno, followed Demetri and extended a hand. I looked at it a moment, confused. Into my confusion, Demetri said, "This is Hadrian Marlowe, my lady."

"My lady?" I bowed, my confusion temporarily forgotten, adhering to an almost genetic need for propriety. The lady's hand waited another moment—I knew not why—but after a few more seconds she let it fall.

They both laughed, but the woman said, "I am no lady; Demetri here is only trying to be charming. He is like this." She put a hand to her breast. "No noble blood here." She could have told me she was a princess of Jadd, and I might have believed her. In Jadd the eugenic obsession with beauty was raised to a moral imperative, and even their middling classes bred themselves to beautify and so glorify their people. Neither her nor Demetri's hair could have been natural. It must have been an aftermarket modification, the first sign that I was leaving the tightly tended garden of Imperial life.

"Except for him," Demetri said, one hand close to his mouth, thumb tracing the line of his lower lip. "The lad is royalty. Son of some archon or other."

The woman brightened, eyes shining amber in the yellow light from overhead. "Really? I've never met an Imperial palatine before."

Abashed, I looked away. "I'm not a palatine any longer, madame."

"Juno, please," she said, moving forward to have a look at me, squinting up in the dimness. I had thought Demetri tall when we'd met in the quayside bar, but neither of the Jaddians was tall as I was. I did not know how to categorize them by Imperial standards. The hair bespoke some changing in the blood, so I could not call them plebeian. Patrician, then? Augmented like Sir Roban and Father's other knights?

A series of rising notes chimed through the ship's speakers, slowly ascending like the peal of a clock striking the hour. Then a voice rang through: deep, masculine, thickly accented as Demetri's. "Is the passenger aboard, Captain?"

"Aye, Bassem!" Demetri called out. He started off toward the rounded bulkhead and out of the frigid hold. "Don't waste time asking for permission to take off—just go. Out to sea and up. You know the way. We'll be right there." He turned back in the doorway, both hands pawing the metal frame like an actor preening onstage. "You'll want to see this."

Up.

The word resonated within me, humming in spite of all the things that could still go wrong. I grinned and followed after the trader, through the bulkhead and up a rattling metal stair, past the sealed glass door to the ship's infirmary. A pair of pale women, their faces streaked with grime, peered out from the shadow of one cabin, and someone called a question to the captain in what I thought was one of the languages of the Tavros Demarchy, but Demetri let it stand unanswered.

"How many crew have you got, messer?" I asked.

"Call me Demetri," he corrected, leading me into a low common room, "or Captain, if you like." An ellipsoid metal table dominated the low space, its benches crudely welded to the deck. The place was completely bare, the random items of human habitation squirreled away and packed up. "Only six, not counting yourself." He indicated Juno, following hard on my tail. "You've met my lovely wife. And there's Bassem, the twins, Doctor Sarric, and old Saltus:" He stopped short, frowning. "I guess I make seven, sorry."

A starship. She was a true starship, not one of the suborbital shuttles I was used to; those were barely fit to scratch the top of the sky. My heart pressed against my throat. A true starship. And I was on it. I had dreamed of this moment since I was a boy, since I'd learned that Delos was not the world but a planet island in it. The *Eurynasir* lurched beneath us, and I could make out the muddy sound of water churning below. I stumbled at the movement, thrown against the concave wall of the corridor, and nearly tripped down an open hatch descending to the floor below.

"Hey!" A small face, shriveled and with skin the color of ash, peered up from a hatch in the floor to one side. At first I thought it was a child, though no child had so wizened a countenance. Even Gibson, whose life had retreated so far into age that it was lost within it, looked young next to the little goblin. Surely he was a homunculus: a genetailored replicant like the little herald Father kept or my mother's blue-skinned houri. The gaunt creature spoke

again, his voice improbably high. "Are we underway, Demetri?"

"Aye, Saltus." The Jaddian turned. "Best strap yourself in. We're for the up-and-up."

The little man pulled himself up and out of the hatch, wrinkling his already wrinkled face. At his full height, the man could not have been more than four feet tall, and he was built in a way that recalled the orangutans I'd seen in my grandmother's menagerie. His arms nearly dragged on the ground, and there was thick gray hair on them and on the backs of his hands. His legs were short and bowed. Saltus smiled, running one of those huge, wrong hands over his hairless scalp until he grabbed the gray-black queue that sprouted from the base of his skull. He twisted the rope of hair in his hands as he spoke. "This the passenger?"

"Of course he is, *haqiph*," Juno put in, voice scathing. She sounded as revolted by the creature as I was myself, though there was a worn quality to her disgust.

The homunculus, Saltus, squinted up at me, twisting his hair in an awful parody of a little girl. "You didn't say he was like me."

I started, nearly jumped out of my skin, hackles rising. "What do you mean?" I had to will my fists to unclench. We couldn't have been less alike if the little monster had been Cielcin. Homunculi weren't human, not truly. They represented a loophole in the Chantry's technological regulations—their religious decrees—and like all loopholes, greed and human cruelty poured into that space like wine. Homunculi were bred for tasks that normal men, even the planetbound serfs, found distasteful. To have one compare itself to me . . .

"We are both homunculi!" he said brightly, and he offered me his hand as Juno had. I didn't take it, not then understanding the gesture. "Both children of the tanks."

Aristocratic reflex made me lunge forward. "I'm not a homunculus!" I couldn't keep the disgust from my voice.

Demetri cut in, "Quiet, Salt. We'll be having no lip. The man pays better than you."

"Smells better, too," Juno put in with a rounded grin. Beside and behind us, the *Eurynasir* began to whine, her engines shifting from a low and crunching growl to something high and steady, as if deep water were coursing through the veins of the world. "You would best be getting comfortable, Salt," the sailorwoman said archly, crossing her arms.

The homunculus grumbled something, and the woman urged me on after her brightly dressed husband to the end of the corridor, down a short flight of stairs, and out into the forward-facing glass dome I'd seen from outside. The bridge—for bridge it surely was—was arranged on an outthrust finger of steel in the center of that dome so that the glass blister stretched out and around us on all sides, according us an equal view of the silver sky and sea. Saltus had vanished back down its hatch in the floor, and a huge, broad-shouldered man with skin and hair black as my family's banner sat behind the controls in a seat far too small for him. As I entered, the ship crossed one of the sea's rare swells and bounced, throwing me against the padded ovular entryway and thence into a bank of quietly blinking instruments.

"You're late," the man said, deep voice rumbling beneath the sound of the music thrashing from his command console. "We're almost to speed."

Demetri took the chair beside him, strapping himself in even as the huge man keyed a series of red switches above his head, moving left to right. "Any trouble from traffic control?"

"In a pissy little backwater town like this?" The helmsman snorted. "Not that I heard." He turned and grinned at Demetri. "But then again, I closed the comms. Got sick of all the chatter." He broke off a moment, calling up a glittering line of blue-white holographs in the air before him. With the ease of long practice, he looped his finger through a glowing reticule and spoke into the air before him, voice carrying over the ship's sound system for the benefit of the homunculus and the others we had passed. "If you bastards aren't belted down, now'd be a real good time."

The ship bucked again, bouncing out of the waves for

a good two seconds. When it hit, I fell sideways onto one of the low crash-couches waiting there. Juno tried to catch me—somehow she'd kept her feet. Things were relatively smooth for a stretch thereafter, long enough for me to turn around and strap myself into my seat.

"Closing the dome!" Demetri said, reaching across his massive copilot to throw a small lever. Fingers danced across his arc of console as if it were a piano, the music still blaring and rattling as outside huge flower petal–shaped pieces of hull closed over the dome, leaving us in darkness. So enthralled was I by this mechanical precision—and at such speed—that I failed to note that I had seen the surface of my world for the last time, vanishing as light does through the aperture of a camera: split into wedges, then slivers, then darkness. And Delos was gone, the inside of the dome filled instead with the holograph model of flight trajectories, ship's telemetry, and the pulsing sound of Bassem's grindingly metallic song.

And there it was: the faint sensation of my stomach dropping away through blind depths, the rage of the twinned fusion drives far to aft. We were flying. Rising along the curve of an invisible chain through air and darkness toward a darkness greater still. What I would have given for a window in that moment. "You'll be really feeling it in a second, boy!" Demetri called over the music and the howl of fusion fire.

He wasn't wrong. Acceleration fell upon me, a terrible boot grinding me into my couch. I was seated facing the middle of the ship at a right angle to the axis of thrust, and so I was pressed sideways into the headrest of my seat. I felt my flesh hanging on my bones, felt the weight of it as hooks in the meat of me; Delos would not let me go. My vision blurred and spat, eyesight guttering like candles. I groaned, but the sound was lost in the thrashing of artificial guitar and the growling of foul tongues from the ship's console.

And then it was over, vanishing into nothing. Even the music stopped.

"Hey!" the helmsman snapped, punching his captain in the arm. "I was listening to that!"

"And we need to make sure no one is sore about that unauthorized dust-off, and I can't focus with that *skubus* you call music in my ears, Bassem," Demetri snapped, using the Jaddian word for shit. He danced through a series of commands at his controls, hunched to study the readouts. "Not seeing anything that flags. You?"

Bassem shook his head. "Nothing yet. We've got a few hours before we can get to warp, though." He glanced back at me, speculation in his eyes. "I hear you say something to Salt about the boy being royalty?" He swallowed, throwing the lever Demetri had moved back into place before unlocking his own chair and half turning to better look at me. "You don't think the ODF will be on us?"

"The Defense Force? Not if the codes that lady passed us check out," Demetri shot back. "Keep them on reserve in case someone flags us. Don't want to draw attention early."

I almost heard none of this. I was distracted—not by what was happening but by what was gone. Gravity. I floated in my restraints and relaxed my arms to watch them drift, stick-like, in the air before me.

A thin laugh escaped me, and I hid my face in my hands. Juno had strapped herself into the couch beside mine and peered around the headrest to look at me. "Why do you laugh?" Her brow furrowed, and she glanced over to Demetri for support. The captain did not see her, as he was entering the commands to open up the dome's shielding again. For the first time I noticed that the whine and roar of the engines was gone, the silence punctuated by deep-boned metallic clanking as the fusion reactor quieted and the radiation sinks opened. I had not heard them earlier, but with all sound fled into that endless night, they rang clear as Chantry bells in my ears. And where minutes before that iris had closed out the light of my home world, here it opened onto a blackness total and absolute.

I dragged my hands down across my face, hoping to still the emotions there. Gibson's voice rasped in my ear, so close I almost felt him at my shoulder. *Joy is a wind, Hadrian. It will pick you up only to smash you against the*

rocks again. I latched onto the beginning of that statement, murmured, "Joy is a wind."

"Excuse me?"

The feeling of weightlessness vanished all at once as the suppression field slammed on. I had never before felt one without the influence of Delos's gravity—I had only ever experienced the Royse field effect as a means for counteracting inertia in high-acceleration flights—and so I was unprepared for the queasy feeling of it. My arms fell to my sides, and my weight collapsed back into the seat. It felt as if a stiff, wet blanket had been draped over me. The few loose items in the air—a light pen, an empty drinking can, a box of playing cards—all fell, but I still felt weightless. The suppression field was not proper gravity or even true artificial gravity. It only pinned us to the deck as butterflies are pinned under glass.

I felt suddenly green, mumbled, "Think I'm going to be sick." Instantly Juno produced a paper bag, which I held before my face, breathing carefully.

"The hell was that about winds?" the big helmsman asked, turning about and unbuckling his restraints.

I looked past him, out at the untellable beauty of the cosmos: eternal, untouchable, and clean. "Something my tutor used to say," I replied. When the three merchanters kept watching me, I added, "He was a scholiast."

Bassem looked startled, but Demetri and Juno both nodded. The captain spoke, saying, "That would explain our destination."

"What's that?" the helmsman asked.

Demetri pointed a finger at my chest. "Boy's going under the ice until we make planetfall on Teukros."

"I know that shit," Bassem snapped, standing and stretching out his back with a groan. No matter his blood, the man was certainly taller than me—was nearly as tall as my father—and he knew it. You could see it in the way he looked down at his captain beside him and at me. "What's that got to do with the *hudr*?" That made me blink. I'd never heard the scholiasts called that before. *Greens*.

"We're supposed to drop him at Nov Senber," said

Demetri, switching to Jaddian, then back to Imperial Galstani as he swept a hand to encompass me. "Our friend here is to join the *hudr*."

Bassem frowned at me, deep creases framing his gray lips. "Why?" The disgust in his voice was so thick it was almost solid, hitting me like a slap.

I did not speak at once. Somehow I couldn't really see the big man but rather saw past him to the disc of the planet visible through the clear dome. Delos. Her gray seas stretched away wide and wild below us, the mono-chrome more pronounced by the pitiful contrast accorded by the white smattering of cloud. Only the land relieved it: here brown, here green-black or ochre. Here dun, there an angry red or burning umber. I imagined Father's globe, the one floating on his desk in the prefectural cap-itol building. From our high orbit it was easy to imagine that it was only that globe I saw, not the world. It felt as if at any moment, Father would strike me across the face again, and it would not be my crash-couch I fell into but his desk, the bloodwood chair splintering beneath me.

At last I shrugged. "Better them than the Chantry."

"You want your brains scooped out?" Bassem asked, disgust curdling his momentarily friendly face. "You want that head of yours stuffed full of kit?"

"That isn't how it works!" I stood then, looking up sharply at the huge sailor. "They aren't demoniacs. They just study for centuries. Train their minds to work better, more efficiently."

"By turning themselves into fucking soulless pricks, that's how." He glared down at his captain. "I don't like it, boss."

Demetri shrugged, wrung his hands like Pilate over the water basin. "You don't have to like it, Bassem. We've got nine thousand riding on it, and all we need to do is drop him off."

CHAPTER 21

THE OUTER DARK

THE FUGUE CRÈCHES LINED one wall of the ship's medica, and something about them—perhaps their arrangement like pillars in a hall or the vaporous chill of the room—put me in mind of the mausoleum of my forebears beneath Devil's Rest. There were twelve of them, each fronted in dark glass half cylinders, the chassis all polished metal darkly gleaming, indicator lights slowly pulsing red and green and deepest violet to no rhythm I could see. Two at the far end were occupied, their lids frosted over, vital monitors glittering in white-blue holographs. The others all were empty, quiescent. I remembered carrying my grandmother's canopic jars, her eyes staring sightlessly from suspension in their blue fluid, and I heard once more the *drip-drip-drip* of water from the limestone stalactites clinging to the ceiling above the perfect black of the funerary statues.

I shuddered, folded my arms across my chest. "How does this work, then?"

"Well, we'll be making the jump to warp just as soon as we're clear of Delos's shipping lanes, then making the five-year trip to Obatala. Then two more to Siena, and then from there the final jump to Teukros." He slapped a hand on the cover of the crèche. "You won't be noticing a damn thing, though. These beauties were Imperial-issue Legion tech. Salvaged them off a crashed destroyer on one of the moons of Bellos. You could be sleeping a thousand years in one of these crèches and never gray a hair."

Taking careful steps, I edged a little farther into the

room, boot soles crunching on the delicate sheen of frost no one had bothered to scrape away. "All I need to do is get in, then? Now?"

"Your mother didn't cover room and board," Demetri said, his customary smile prominent on his face as he leaned against the nearest crèche. How he hadn't frozen to death in his loose-fitting silks I had no idea. "But then, neither did any of us. We don't have hold space for thirteen years of rations, and I never was any good at gardening. So we'll all be in right after you." He checked his own terminal. "It'll be . . . 16149 by your Imperial calendar next time you breathe free air again."

That stilled me. The simple fact of it. I was no stranger to the technicalities of space travel; such was common knowledge at the court of any lord in the Imperium. And yet to have it recounted so, spoken plain and simply, without feeling, shocked my naïve mind to alertness. It was called slipping in those days, the way a sailor lost time—perhaps it still is. Thirteen years would just melt away, and I would not even notice.

I signaled my understanding, eyes locked on the cold machines. At length I thrust my chin in the direction of the two occupied machines. "Who are the others?"

"Hmm?" Demetri looked back over his shoulder, hair almost sparkling with the movement. "Oh, them?" He made a dismissive gesture. "Norman migrants—an urban farm technician and his husband. Been on board twenty-one years. They're for Siena, when we get there."

From where I stood I could just make out two faces—one pale and one faintly copper-toned—beneath the frosted dark glass. Suspended as they were in darkness, I thought of biological samples, flayed and plastinated or else packed in formaldehyde, pickled like onions and left on the shelves of some mad scientist's laboratory. They looked dead, and in a sense they were: the processes of their lives suspended, forwarded to another day. I had known this moment would come, and yet nothing could have prepared me for the unnatural horror of it. *Fear is death to reason,* I told myself, and again it was Gibson's

voice, quieting me with the familiar words. *Reason, death to fear.* This was only cryonic fugue, routine and commonplace. I wasn't going to die. Not there. Not today.

I took in a deep breath, and when I exhaled it, I nodded. "I'm ready."

"Good!" Juno's voice sounded from behind me, and turning, I saw her enter, leading a wax-faced, mustachioed man with lank blond hair pulled back into a tail. To my disgust, the little homunculus followed thereafter, knuckles literally dragging on the floor. "Sarric, prep the casket."

The blond man with the mustache bowed his head silently and rubbed the geometric tangle tattooed onto his too-high forehead, diamonds and triangles interlocking. "Just a moment." The man—the doctor whom Demetri Arello had mentioned in passing before—brushed past me, moving almost silently, exhaling little breaths of steam into the chilly air. He busied himself with the fugue crèche nearest the two occupied ones.

"Putting you back in the bottle, eh?" asked the homunculus, lifting his dragging queue and draping the disgusting rope of hair over his shoulders like a shawl. He tittered. "Back where you came from."

Juno kicked the creature in the back of one knee, sharply but not hard.

I ignored the little hobgoblin and the woman both. "You," the doctor said, clapping his hands together to crush out a series of holographs. "You must disrobe." He didn't look up as he spoke, crouching to examine a screen embedded in the wall beside the crèche. "There a locker here for him, Captain?" His voice was strange, crackling and throaty. Tavrosi, I decided, thinking back to the language I thought I'd heard from the grubby girls I had seen in the ship's hallway before dust-off. The man was one of the clansmen of the Tavros Demarchy, which explained the tattoos. Valka had such tattoos. They told the man's genetic and personal histories in a symbolic language I'd never learned to read.

"Over there!" Demetri pointed to a bank of dinted metal storage lockers. "Put everything in there."

I froze, taking in the grinning captain, his beautiful wife, the wax-faced doctor, and their little pet monster. "Could I get some privacy, then?"

Except for the doctor, they all laughed, and Saltus said, "We'll all be able to see your little cock once you're in the freeze, cousin. No point getting shy now." The creature bared its too many teeth. Juno kicked him again, and he yelped, falling sideways into the wall.

"Leave the boy alone, Salt," she said, reaching down to grab the homunculus by the scruff of his neck. "Go on now." And she half pushed, half threw the little man back toward the door.

Obedience to necessity already had me removing my coat, the long jacket that Gibson had told me I wouldn't be needing. Demetri prized open one of the lockers, held it open while I hung the coat neatly inside. As I swung it into place, the universal card I'd extracted from the Mining Guild factionarius tumbled out and clattered to the floor. I lunged for it, hoping to grab it before Demetri could see what it was. I shoved it back into the lining of the coat, caught the captain watching me with pale eyebrows raised. "Get me to Teukros, and it's yours." I wouldn't need it anyway. "I swear it."

The doctor was watching us. "What was it?"

"A bank card," Demetri replied. "How much?"

"Plenty."

At last I was naked, shivering in the air, gooseflesh pimpling my pale skin. I held my hands over my sex, trying not to meet the eyes of the woman and the two men around me. The doctor moved forward, placing a dry hand on my shoulder. "Come on, now." He guided me toward the open crèche and helped me step inside. I pulled myself up with one hand, using the other to cover myself. Seeing my ring, the doctor caught my free hand. "You will want this off. 'Twill burn you."

I shook my head vigorously. "Then it burns me." I looked at the locker, thinking of the universal card. Mother had hired these people, and apparently Adaeze Feng had recommended them, but that didn't mean I had to trust them. And the ring was all I would have left of the boy I had been:

a single loop of silver, the carnelian bezel with its laser-cut devil sigil masking terabytes of crystal storage. It held both copies of the contract I'd made with the Mining Guild as well as all manner of other documents, my identification not the least of them. I would not part with it.

Doctor Sarric snorted. "Imperial barbarian foolishness."

"Leave it, Sarric," Demetri said, stepping closer, fists planted squarely on his hips. "We're not trying to rob you, boy. We aren't pirates. Pirates would have dumped you out the airlock the moment we left Delos."

The white plastic padding at the back of the crèche clung to my bare skin, and I shuddered, standing there naked. "It's not that, Captain. It's . . . it's a palatine thing."

That made him laugh. "You really don't want to be wearing that ring when you go in."

"I'm keeping it." I tightened my jaw, lay my head back in the cradle meant for it. "Let's get on with it."

The doctor glanced to his captain, scratching his head just above one small ear. "Demetri?"

The Jaddian merchant waved a hand in dismissal. "The lad can do as he likes, Sarric."

The physician pushed air through his yellow teeth. "As you wish, then." And without preamble he slapped a sensor tape to my chest, then another. A third. He barely looked at me as he did so, then pulled a self-sterilizing needle from a slot inside the crèche beside me. It hissed as it pierced my arm, and he fastened the securing strap about my biceps. "'Tis going to get cold rather fast."

It already had. The freeze crept from the needle site in my arm, the blood transmuting, cells hardening without tearing. My brain began to go fuzzy, and as if from far away I heard Doctor Sarric say, "He's ready. Seal the crèche." I heard rather than saw the dark glass slam down over me, trapping me as in a sarcophagus. Something coolly gelatinous began to rise about my ankles. Darkness blossomed behind my eyes, and through that darkness I again perceived the funeral masks of my ancestors as they hung above the doors to the council chamber beneath the Dome of Bright Carvings, their violet gaze accusatory and unkind.

The preservative gel rose about me even as I froze from within. I wanted to scream, to slam my fists against the walls of the tank, but the strength was already gone from me. I was drowning—I knew I was drowning, knew there was nothing I could do. I was going to die in that tank. And then the worst part of all happened.

My breathing stopped. The fluid was not even to my chin, and my breathing stopped. Then it was in me, black water thick as oil flooding down my throat, up my nose. That outer dark took me, and I plunged into blackness and cold.

And when I awoke, my world had ended.

CHAPTER 22

MARLOWE ALONE

THE FIRST THING I noticed was the stink. Wherever I was, the stench of rotting fish and raw sewage was overpowering. Then it was the heat, damp and oppressive, clinging to me like wet canvas. And light. There was light. A universe of it, almost as bright as the light of Gododdin's sun; perhaps it was that light, cast backward across time to blind me in my childhood, to turn me back. I could not see.

"He's alive." The sound was wrong, remote, as if I were hearing that voice down a long rubber tube or washed along with the surf of some moon-tossed sea. "Someone get water!" I could just make out the sound of bare feet slapping on stone, and then someone was propping me up, forcing me to drink water from a clay bowl. The white universe faded a little, graying and reddening to indistinct blurs. I coughed, felt the water spill onto my chest. Then I doubled over, shoulders heaving as I forced something glutinous and sour from my lungs and throat. The same someone held my shoulders, kept me from falling. "In Earth's name, girl, get a fucking mop!" the voice called out. "He's coughing up more of that shit again."

It was all I could do to breathe, to still the sudden pounding in the capillaries of my skull. Groaning, I allowed myself to be pushed back against the linens. I was in a bed. Gods, but I was heavy. My limbs felt like they were made of stone. "Where?" I rasped, voice barely more than a croak. "Where?"

A rough hand settled over my eyes, testing my forehead. "You're safe. You're safe now. Got you in off the street."

"Street?" It didn't make any sense. But a more pressing thought came to me, and I said, "I can't see."

The voice—that of an old woman—said, "Fugue blindness. It will pass." I heard another person shuffle into the room, followed by a slopping sound. Someone had found that mop the speaker had shouted for. "The boys found you lying in an alley near the starport. Terrible business. Still, one sees it all the time in cases like yours." I wanted to ask what she meant by cases like mine, but my tongue felt thick and swollen in my mouth, and I didn't even try. "Terrible business," the raspy voice repeated. "But at least they didn't sell you for meat, eh? Abandoned is better." She jostled me by the shoulder. "We can fix abandoned."

It was a good minute before I found my words again, during which time I came to distinguish a rusted blur above and to my right. It might have been the shape of the old woman. "Teukros?" I wheezed, coughing into the air above me; I felt flecks of spittle fall on my naked chest. "Was going . . . going to Teukros."

"Teukros?" The ragged voice went paper-thin, and the rusted blur leaned in closer, so close I could smell the alkaline bite of verrox stimulant on the speaker's breath. "Bless us, no. This is Emesh, in the Veil."

"No." I felt myself shake my head, but it seemed to be happening to someone else. "No no no . . ." I squeezed my eyes shut, willing them to work better, as if the strain would force the delicate muscles there to tighten, to sharpen again.

The stranger's hand settled again on my shoulder. "It'll be fine, lad. You'll be all right. You'll see." The water again, tepid and oily. I drank it greedily, spilling more of it onto my chest. It didn't matter. Hands on my arm, my face. I think I dozed. It is true what they say about fugue: you do not dream. I felt . . . what? Displacement? Disconcert? Yes and yes, but it was something more than that. I felt an incredible sense of discontinuity, the way I imagined an infant might feel if it possessed the faculty and

the language for complex thought. There was no sense of what had come before, as a sleeper feels upon waking. I had no sense of yesterday and so felt hollow and blank. Distant, as if I were only then beginning to dream.

As if to confirm that supposition, I saw Tor Gibson's face peering at me when I opened my eyes, the scholiast's wrinkled visage comporting itself into a frown, the only clear point in all the blurry world. His lips moved, but I could not hear him, and when at last I blinked, he was gone, leaving me awash in a place of indistinct color.

At least my words had found me. "Where am I?"

"You deaf?" the old woman asked, clicking her fingers beside my ear to prove her point. "I said you was on Emesh, didn't I?"

Grunting, I said, "Specifically."

There was a creaking of wooden joints. "In my clinic. The boys found you left for dead in an alley. I'd say it was a horror if we didn't pull castoffs like you out of the gutter every other Tuesday. Ships dump their passengers all the time, pop them right out of their crèches and drop them where they think no one will look." She sighed, throat rattling. "And with the war on, people are bringing in all sorts—the streets get more crowded every day. Empty ships found smashed on the trade lanes . . . You're lucky you're here." Above me the whirling of a ceiling fan came into dull focus, and around it the shape of a dingy red-brick room. My savior stood over me, a hunched, hook-nosed beast with warts stippling her red face. I think she saw my eyes gain focus, for she smiled then, not unkindly. "You have a name, lad?"

"Hadrian," I said, more on reflex than anything else.

She whistled. "That's a proper fancy name for some-one found naked in a gutter." She squinted at me, her right eye gone blind and crusted over with some red growth near the nose. "You some sort of lord?" Her white hair fell lank past her hunched shoulders almost to her navel, though she had tried in vain to tie it back. She looked like the witch character in Eudoran mask theater, and I half expected to see a black cat in her arms.

"No," I said too quickly. "No, I'm not." Then I noticed

the small girl behind the witch-woman. She couldn't have been more than fifteen, willowy and fair but thin. So thin. And those freckles—they were plebeians, no doubt about it. Perhaps even serfs. Wherever I was, wherever this *Emesh* was exactly, I had washed out at the bottom of it. "What happened to Demetri? To the *Eurynasir*?"

"That your ship?" The crone pulled a spindle-legged chair from one corner of the baking, dingy little ward and seated herself beside me. Down the hall someone moaned, and turning I beheld several more beds like mine, a dozen or more. Most were empty, but three toward the far end had men lying on them. The old woman snapped her fingers. "Maris, go and see if the poor bastards' beds need cleaning." When the girl didn't move but seemed glued to the spot, the old woman snapped her fingers again. "Damn it, girl! I'll be fine with his lordship here, thank you!" She waved a dismissive hand, and the young woman scurried off. When she'd been gone a moment, the old woman grunted, folding twisted, thin-skinned hands in her lap. I didn't like the way she'd said *lordship*, the word edged in mockery. "This won't be easy for you to hear, lad—ships dump people. All the time. Captain gets a better price for his berth, changes his flight plan, decides your scrawny arse ain't worth the fuel or the time-debt."

Even as she was speaking, I was shaking my head again. "No, not this one." It didn't fit, wouldn't fit. Demetri had nine thousand marks to collect on Teukros, to say nothing of my universal card. And there was my mother to contend with. Oh, the Empire was vast and the galaxy vaster still, but one did not simply cross the scion of an Imperial vicereine. There must be some reason, some explanation. Somehow it all had to make sense. I clamored for the calm of the apatheia, yearning to see as a scholiast sees, but my pretenses there were only that: pretenses. I bunched my sheets in my fists and shut my eyes. "He hadn't been paid yet. Something must have happened."

"Well, if you say so, lad. If you say so." She peered past me out the unglassed window at a world I could not see. She didn't believe me. "When you're well you can go to the starport, have yourself a good look round. You'll find

your captain long gone. I bet dumping you was the last thing they did before dust-off."

That silenced me a long while, and I shifted uncomfortably on the linens. Something scraped my hand, raw and painful, and looking down I saw a white bandage wound around my thumb where my ring had been. "How long?"

"Until you're well? Tomorrow."

I shook my head. It hurt. "How long was I . . . frozen? What year is it?"

"It's Year 447 of the Dominion of House Mataro."

"No." I tried to raise a hand but failed. "No good, what's the standard year?"

The old woman's expression soured. "I look like a spacer to you? What good's the Imperial star date to me?"

A new thought smashed its way into my universe. "My things?"

"You didn't even have pants on when they found you. You've bigger things to worry about than what happened to your effects. We'll find something for you in the back; poor dead bastards leave enough lying around to clutter the whole fucking Empire."

"But my money!" I said, sitting up straight so quickly it made my head swim. "I have to pay you!"

The old woman smiled, baring her crooked teeth, the enamel stained the mint-green of the serial verrox abuser. "You're a lord, ain't you? It's writ all over that pretty white skin of yours." She traced a finger down my exposed arm as she spoke, and I yanked it away. "You got to have an account. With Roths or the Mandari or some shit. I don't know."

Then she left, still muttering, heaving herself onto her feet and passing down the hall to join her servant.

An account. I cannot easily describe the fear that thought put in me. An account; my family. The old woman had said this planet—Emesh—was in the Veil. That would have to be the Veil of Marinus, where the Norma Arm just began to stretch its way around the galactic core and away from the Empire's heart in the old Spur of Orion. The crest of the wave of colonial expansion that had

brought our mighty civilization into contact with the Cielcin. The gods only knew how far I was from home, how lost, and how much time had fled from me. I shut my eyes, squeezing out tears as another more horrible realization struck me. Worse than my situation; worse than the fact that I was lost and alone on a world I had never heard of; worse than the loss of my hard-won universal card.

I had lost Gibson's letter.

The letter of introduction he had drafted to the scholiasts at Nov Senber. The letter of introduction without which I would never gain admittance at the athenaeum. I'd be turned away at the gate. I tried to tell myself that a scholiast would not cry. But I was not a scholiast, would never be a scholiast. I slammed my fist into the mattress. Once. Twice. I hit my thigh, wordless sounds leaking out from between my teeth, anguished and accursed. Maybe it was only a dream. It had to be. It all had to be a dream, some awful nightmare. Maybe you did dream in fugue. Maybe I was dreaming then. Maybe I would wake up in a minute to Demetri's irrepressible grin. On Teukros.

I never did.

The thought of my family consumed me. Of orders shunted by QET wave between the stars. I could imagine my father demanding the local prefects hold me until I could be retrieved. I wondered where he would deliver me. To Vesperad? Back to Delos? Or simply out an airlock? I had shirked my duties, abandoned my role as a son. By the Great Charters, by all the laws of the Empire, I was his to command. *Hadrian, name for me the Eight Forms of Obedience.* I wouldn't. Somewhere in the nameless city, the bell towers of a Chantry sanctum began to chime. I wondered if I had dozed again, drifted off toward the deathlike state I had occupied for uncounted years until that day. For a mad instant I thought they were the bells of the Chantry sanctum in Meidua and that I was home again, that my father might come striding up that ward, through air stinking of rotting fish and old mold.

And I knew. Knew I could not let anyone scan my blood. The moment my genomic fingerprint hit the system on this world, I would be flagged, and there was nothing

in the universe I could do to stop that information from reaching all the way back to Meidua. The instant my genes turned up on some census, the moment I tried to pull funds from my out-system accounts, they would know in Devil's Rest. Interplanetary extradition was such between Imperial worlds that whoever it was who ruled this sweat-soaked rock the old surgeon had called Emesh would have no choice but to jail me and pack me off on a return journey to Delos.

So I had to disappear.

Night fell with astonishing speed, and soon the bleary red-gold light through the open windows was replaced with the inconstant yellow sputtering of the ward's lamps. The men at the end of the hall moaned incessantly, their trauma the only sound apart from the rumble of groundcars outside. I slept fitfully, my whole body feeling like someone had struck me with a meat tenderizer. When I woke, it was to that awful smell and the sight of the ugly crone and her willowy assistant walking up or down the aisle of that desolate place. During one of those waking cycles it struck me at last that I had seen no sign of proper medical equipment: no drip-bags, no monitor equipment, no scanners. Thankfully I saw no corrective braces. I felt as if I had wandered out of the world I'd known and into some meaner universe such as the fantasies in Mother's holograph operas, places where the printing press was magic and healing meant draining the blood from a man. I half expected those guttering light fixtures to be gas lamps.

"Is he really a lord, ma'am?" The girl looked back over her shoulder from under flaxen hair, her voice hushed and breathy. I closed my eyes to the merest slits, pretending as only the truly tired can to be asleep.

I heard a tinny rattling, then the sound of those bony jaws crunching something. The old woman's verrox leaves, I didn't doubt. "I think he is, Maris. Yes."

"He's very tall," the girl said, voice even lower than before. "Do you think he's a prince?"

The old woman shook her head, limp hair flipping about her face. "Princes all have fiery hair. Everybody says so. We'll find out who he is when the money comes in, girl. Leave the poor boy alone."

Something oily twisted its fingers in my guts, and I turned my head away, unwilling to continue looking at the two women who had helped save my life. I might have thrown up again if I'd had anything left in me worth losing. The fishy soup they'd fed me was little more than broth, and it had stayed down. But I couldn't stay.

I couldn't pay them.

In the near silence, I thought I heard the dripping of the water in the mausoleum of my forebears, the march of soldiers in Marlowe livery. I could not go back. I had beaten my own brother nearly to death and fled in the night. For that alone, my father . . . I do not like to think what my father might have done to me. But it was more than that. If I feared Lord Alistair's fury so much, I would never have left home. No, it was for my mother that I feared. What might happen to her if Father knew what part she had played? I hoped my grandmother would protect her.

Night came, as night must. True night, so that even the street without grew hushed, and I—who had slept most of that day and for untold years before—pulled myself naked from beneath my sheets. My muscles felt slack, weak, heavy as lead weights, and I slumped against the aluminum bedstead as I stood. I was grateful that I was alone in my nakedness, remembering how the mutant Saltus had mocked me. Where had they gone? What had happened while I'd slept frozen? What had changed? The crone who ran this clinic—I never learned her name—swore that this was typical of Free Trade vessels, that passengers were tossed aside like so much chaff. I couldn't quite make myself believe that it was so.

Fearing the poor girl would choose that moment to enter the hall, I dragged my sticky sheet off the bed and

made a toga of it, holding it shut with my hands, grateful for the thick callouses on my feet from years of training. My bandaged thumb ached, my head swam, and I swayed against one peeling plaster wall. I had to find clothes. I couldn't go out into the city in naught but my skin. Leaning against the corner of the landing at the midpoint of a narrow flight of stairs, I thought back. The woman had said she would find clothes for me in the back. The back. A storeroom? A closet? Surely there was something lying about.

There was, as it happened, behind a dinted green metal door on the first floor, past a supply closet and a pair of drinking fountains. The room smelled of fungus and rot, as if it had been underwater more than once and never properly aired. Never cleaned. I didn't want to waste time, fearing that Maris or the crone would find my bed empty and come looking. I found a shirt, a gray pullover with a black star inked on the chest. After several attempts, I found a pair of trousers that fit well enough at the waist. They were baggy, their dun legs covered in mismatched pockets, variously stained. Of shoes, socks, or undergarments there was no sign. But nearly fifteen years of fencing barefoot and of running the walls at Devil's Rest and Haspida unshod had turned my soles to horn. Those hardened soles slapped the grimy floor as I left the medica, moving toward the double doors. A ceiling lamp flickered, highlights glittering over the white-and-black-checked tiles. A rat scampered across the space, causing me to start. I watched it go; so like myself it was, stealing into the night.

I squeezed my fist around my bandaged thumb, pain lancing up my arm to my teeth. With a grunt, I set my jaw. Whatever had happened, the bastards had taken my ring along with all the data it held. All the proof I was who I said I was, of my titles and holdings. There were people for whom the mere sight of a palatine seal opened doors, greased palms. That ring might have helped without putting me on high society's damned genetic map, might have kept me off Chantry and state registries.

The doors moaned as I threw them open, pressing

against the wet night air. It hit me like a wall, like a wave. I had thought it hot and humid inside the musty clinic, but I was mistaken. Breathing the heavy air was like sucking in a lungful of water, and I felt my stolen clothes start to stick to me.

Something smashed against the floor behind me, glass and metal and the clatter of wood. I turned and caught Maris staring at me from down the hall, the remains of someone's meal—mine?—shattered and spilled on the checked tiles. She looked ready to scream, to cry. She bit her lip, hands twitching before her, and I knew then that she knew I was running, stealing the help they had given me, leaving them with nothing. I thought of the rat again and ran. She did scream then, but the word was lost in a sudden gust of night air.

I ran then, ran for blocks, splashing through filmy puddles in the warped and sagging tarmac, past the neon windows of storefronts and under the overhangs of the upper stories of short buildings that looked rust-colored in the light of orange street lamps. Rain fell soft and warm on my downturned face, and though I knew it was wrong, I ran anyway, chest heaving, head pounding as my blood, long still, became reacquainted with the necessities of living. At long last I stopped, slumped against a rubbish bin outside a bakery, a lone figure in stolen clothes, crouched against the night. Nowhere to go. Nowhere to hide.

And I realized that it was not rain on my face, but tears.

CHAPTER 23

RESURRECTION IN DEATH

I SPENT THE REST of that night hiding in a loading dock behind a warehouse, huddled among a set of unmarked steel drums. Sleep never came, but how could it? The very air felt as if it would choke me, so thick it stuck in my lungs. Some artifact of antique terraforming, perhaps? Or of natural ecology? I knew nothing of my new world, this Emesh. The gravity was undoubtedly stronger, which explained the leaden weight in my limbs. I'd heard a story once about a man, a magus who advised the Emperor, who could gauge a planet's gravity by the rate at which a pocket bandalore fell and returned to his hand. I had never learned the trick of it, but at a guess I was pulling more than thirty percent what I had on Delos.

When day came at last, the sun was wrong. Delos's sun was a tiny point, half the size of a silver kaspum, no bigger round than the cross-section of my smallest finger. Emesh's sun, by contrast, was an angry, weeping red eye the size of my fist. It baked the streets, turning the low brick structures of my new home into the walls of an open-air oven, rippling the air with whorls of heat visible to the eye. My stolen clothes stuck fast to my frame, and I felt the water being burned out of me beneath a sky dappled orange and ocher and pink, streaked with high and inconstant clouds.

The city itself was a curiosity, a low sprawl of unknown scope. Its buildings—most no more than three or four stories high—stretched like netting over an equally low landscape. What little earth I saw between the concrete was sandy and pale. Once or twice I caught sight of the

sea between the buildings, peering at me from down
crooked streets and over the heads of the growing crowd.
Only it too was wrong. The waters shone a sickly green,
patched here and there with blue and no silver at all.

Emesh, I later learned, was tectonically dead, and its
air and water had more in common with Earth's sister
Mars than with the Homeworld herself. But for one continent, her rare landmasses—little more than islands by
the standards of any planet worth the name—were low
sedimentary accretions built upon the backs of shoals and
coral reefs or else dredged and mounded up from the bed
of Emesh's shallow world ocean. The city itself, Borosevo,
was built on steel pilings rammed deep into the earth, and
over the long years this obtuse architectural fact revealed
its folly in spiderwebs of cracks in walls and pilings. You
could see the count's palace, though, standing above the
low mass of the coliseum and the nine minarets of the
Chantry sanctum with its copper dome and grim bastille.
The palace sat upon a concrete ziggurat gray as the ocean
of my home, a fat, topless pyramid a thousand feet high
that dominated the low, tin-roofed sprawl of Borosevo. Its
spires were glass and sandstone, its roof red-tiled and
bright beneath the bloody gaze of the sun.

Using that massive building as a landmark, I worked
my way around the city's edge, reasoning that the starport
must be close. The kindness of strangers is one of humanity's proudest miracles, but it has limits, limits that told
me whoever had found me would not have brought me far
from whatever alley I'd washed out in and that the alley
likely would not have been far from the ships. My jaw
tightened with rage at the thought even as my stomach
tied itself tight into knots of hunger. Yet it was the thirst
that really started to get to me, and when at last I found the
starport near noon, I was dry as an unused sponge and
flagging badly.

A pair of ornithons took flight as I approached, the six
winged snakes rolling their way up and through the air to
join the steaming contrails of distant shuttlecraft. I
watched the creatures go. My dry mouth hung open, for I

had never before seen such things. Here was something more tangible, more real than the gravity and the soupy air. Strange creatures, strange climes.

The cold air of the starport terminal—kept in by a static field—hit me like a breaking wave, and I became a fish gasping at the thinner, drier air, doubled over, hand on my knees just inside the entry. What a sight I must have been: bare and muddy-footed; the legs of my baggy trousers already torn and stained from my midnight run; my long, coal-dark hair plastered down my face almost to the chin. A pair of women in purple business suits skirted me as widely as they could, collapsing matching umbrellas that held the sun at bay. I was unsure how to proceed. My whole life, shuttles had been arranged for me and people had cleared out of my way. I'd never had to come at this sort of situation from outside. From below.

"Messer?" came a polite voice, intruding on my confusion and indecision. "Messer, you can't be in here." Looking round, I found a young man in a sort of uniform kaftan, his hands clasped in front of him, peering up at me from a respectful distance from beneath the brim of a flat cap. "You're upsetting the clientele."

I stared at him, mind gone entirely blank. "Upsetting?" I repeated, looking round at the moon-blank faces of the people around me, at the way they tried not to stare. Understanding broke over me, and I said, "Sirrah, I . . . forgive me. I was on a ship, the *Eurynasir*. Perhaps there was some mistake. I awoke in the city, in a clinic . . ."

The honorific surprised the man in the kaftan, and he glanced uncertainly at the two khaki-wearing security officers who bookended him as lictors might a great lord of the Empire. He repeated the word softly to himself: "Sirrah?" Then he said it again more strongly, a tight smile stealing over his effete, fine-featured face. "On a ship, you say?" Something in his manner, in the cold exactitude of that smile, told me that even if he understood, even if he believed me, it didn't matter.

I drew myself up to my full height. Such as it was, I had a few inches on the little plebeian in his flat cap and

flowing robe. "Yes," I said, planting hands on hips. "The *Eurynasir.* Sailing out of . . . out of . . ." I racked my memory, trying to dredge up the names of the planets Demetri had mentioned, but at last I surrendered. "Out of Delos. Check your flight logs. The captain was a Jaddian. Demetri Arello."

Something in my voice, in my face—perhaps even in my use of the subordinating honorific—gave the man pause. He shook back his sleeve, glanced sidelong at the square-jawed woman in khaki to his left, and called up a holograph display from his wrist-terminal. He frowned, cycling through panel after panel. Still bent over it, he said, "I'm not seeing a ship by that name." His small smile sharpened until it could've cut glass. "You're sure you have it right?"

"Eurynasir," I repeated, spelling it out for him, a shade breathless. I paused, composed myself. "It has to be here." I lowered my voice, took a half step closer to the man. When his two guards tensed, raising telescoping batons, I froze, held my hands innocently visible. "Look, I was dumped in an alley, sirrah." I glanced around, trying to make absolutely certain no one could hear me, and for a moment the coolness of the air distracted me, breaking my train of thought, and the words that escaped me came out breathless. "I'm trying to figure out what happened." The man made a gesture, and his two guards bulled forward, each seizing me above the elbow. "You have to listen to me!" I snarled, trying to free myself, but the woman with the lantern jaw struck me in the gut.

"Get him out of here," the man in the kaftan said, waving a dismissive hand and turning to go.

Weak as I was, I snapped my arm free and lunged forward. "It has to be here."

The man in the kaftan froze and made a slashing gesture with one hand. "Maybe they scrapped the junker." Then the lantern-jawed woman struck me again, full in the belly. I doubled over and stayed there. The man smiled that glass-cutting smile. "Don't come back here, you understand?" The smile was a thing of beauty, its

condescension so flanged, so precise. I said nothing, permitting myself to be dragged away down a white-tiled hall, past high windows rattled by the distant takeoffs of lifter rockets from blast pits that dimpled the concrete mass beyond the terminal, orange beneath the blighted sunlight. The tinny music piped over the terminal speakers jangled meaningless in my ears. They hurled me out a back door onto a loading dock much like the one where I'd spent the previous night. Only after the door had locked behind them did I rise and limp back into the city.

I'm not seeing a ship by that name. The words resounded in me, and I bit my lip, thinking, nursing the bruise I was sure was forming on my belly. My stomach turned, gnawing on itself. I hadn't eaten since the thin broth they'd given me in the clinic, and before then I had had neither food nor drink since the wine I'd had with Demetri in Karch. *Not seeing a ship by that name.* What did that mean? Did that mean the *Eurynasir* had not put down in the starport? I lowered myself onto a low concrete wall in the shade of a leafy palm tree, listening to the steady thunder of a distant fusion rocket as it burned its torch for heaven. Did this city have a second starport? It didn't seem likely, given the distance needed to isolate the city folk from the crushing sound of those rocket engines cracking at the sky.

My mind plugged through the steps of understanding with mechanical slowness, my thoughts bent by the heat and by hunger. But I had not yet abandoned hope. For all I knew, Demetri and his crew were waiting, lurking in some blast pit or other on the extreme edge of the starport landing field. *Or,* a little voice said within me, sounding too much like Crispin, *or . . . they're all dead.* That thought stilled me, chilled me in spite of the heat of that infernal planet. Like Cid Arthur, I sat a long time in the shade of that tree, watching boats wend their way up the canal opposite me. *Row on for home, my lads. Row on for home.*

I'm not seeing a ship by that name.

Not the starport, then. Not the starport.

Maybe they scrapped the junker.

It took the rest of the day and an exacting conversation with a city prefect to find an answer. The woman had been on the edge of arresting me for vagrancy, but my manner kept her from pulling the trigger on the stunner at her hip. Growing up, there were always stories, you see. Tales of crews gone missing in the depths of space, their empty ships scudding into ports and into systems on dying warp wakes. Men said it was pirates, the Extrasolarians preying on merchant vessels, kidnapping the crews to serve aboard their massive, black-masted ships, forcing machines into their flesh to enslave them.

I have seen those black ships, have stalked their halls. I have seen their deathless armies, machine-men hollow and unfeeling. There is truth in those tales. Still other men say it was Cielcin that preyed on the wandering ships, harvesting the crews the way you or I might net a school of fish from the sea. I suspect both are true, and more besides. I suspect that ships disappeared in the throes of poine, in interhouse warfare, the familial vendettas that typify our Empire. I suspect misfortune, mismanagement, mistakes, or perhaps an accident that caused the captain to abandon his vessel.

It does not matter what happened, and I am now too old to care. There are always empty ships and dead sailors. As the ancient sea was cruel, so too is that blacker sea, vaster by far, that fills the void between the suns like water. But I cared then, and so I found myself—ravenous and in pain—at the gate of a massive series of hangars that sat upon the very margin of the sea and the city. The orange disc of the sun rippled in the afternoon sky, distorted and shimmering in the thick air. I almost felt I could hear the steam rising off the frothing, turbid waters and from the scummy canals, green as forests, that veined the great city. And from myself.

The hangars had not been easy to find, and so rather than repeat the episode at the starport, I ignored the two guards lazing in the guardhouse by the main road and approached the high fence that cordoned off the reclama-

tion depot, following it to where the chain terminated against the wall of an outbuilding. The fencing was cheap stuff, poor and antiquated, the sort of defense one would never have found on an old Imperial world. Unsophisticated, utterly without artifice. It wasn't even electrified. I climbed it easily, grateful for the first time since waking on Emesh that I had no shoes as my toes helped me climb the linked bands of metal.

I proceeded along the convex arc of the shoreline, moving from the shadow of one hangar to another, peering into grimy windows and around open doors. I tried my best to walk with purpose, to appear that I belonged, which was difficult when one took my ragged appearance and palatine height into consideration. But no one stopped me, and aside from three old men standing around in the shade of a steel awning, drinking from brown bottles and laughing, wiping their hands on faded brown coveralls, I saw no one.

Each hangar held a ship, the larger ones two or even three, all lighters like the *Eurynasir*, space-to-surface craft. Black-hulled and white, their ceramic and adamant shells all showed signs of damage: friction burns, meteoroidal impact scars, the carbon scoring of weapon-fire. Empty ships. There are always empty ships. They whispered to me, droning of battles, of pirates, of xenobites howling out of the Dark. Of old, such sunken vessels were lost at sea, swallowed by harsh waters and destroyed by the weight of them. Space sought no such equilibrium, allowed its wrecks to remain pristine, untrammeled. There were whole corporations dedicated to the salvage of such damaged ships.

None of the ships I found in the first hangar was the *Eurynasir*, nor in the fifth. With evening coming on, huge flies began to emerge from their diurnal haunts and filled the air with a droning. I swatted them aside, calloused feet scraping on the burning tarmac.

Starting to panic, my stomach cramping from hunger and the need for an answer, I rounded a parked forklift just outside one of the massive buildings and nearly slammed into one of the old men I had seen earlier. He

was short and nearly so broad as he was tall, all muscle and hair. His scalp was bare and the color of old bronze, his face lost in such a profusion of beard as I had never seen. Hair sprouted on his cheeks almost to his eyelids, and his arms reminded me of those of the homunculus, Saltus, reaching almost to his knees. He glared at me, alarm and outrage bubbling to the surface of that expressive, hairy face. "Who in Earth's name are you?"

Instead of answering, I pushed my sweat-soaked hair back from my face and said, "I was on a ship. The *Eurynasir*. Is it here?"

The big man blinked, looked sidelong past me into the open sky above one shoulder. "What's it to you?" He spat on the white concrete at his feet.

Trying not to lose my patience in light of the heat, my exhaustion, and my hunger, I repeated myself, more slowly and precisely this time. "I was *on* the ship, messer."

At first I had thought the man old, judging by the way his face creased, the skin beneath the matted, graying beard pinched and scaled, but age among the plebeians is a tricky thing. He might have been younger than forty, and these Emeshi were all squat and muscled like bulls from the weight of that added gravity. He squinted up at me, ham fists planted on his hips.

"Skag!" another voice called. "Where'd you go?"

"Here, Bor!" the dock worker called back over his shoulder. "That fish we threw back's come round again!" Another man rounded the corner, this one paler than the first, his skin red and peeling like the skin of the old crone in the clinic's had been. There seemed something wrong in it, but it wasn't sunburn. Scars? The mark of some sickness long passed?

I raised my hands, trying to appear peaceable. "Gentlemen, I don't want trouble. I just want—" I broke off, catching sight of the silver band the second man had wrapped around his smallest finger. A silver band with a carnelian bezel. My voice tightened in my throat, coming out high and petulant. "That's mine!"

The dock workers looked at each other, neither knowing how to respond. I gathered their victims did not often

return. Maybe I was the first. In the end, they did answer, but not with words. I felt suddenly as if I were on the streets in Meidua again, facing down those thugs with their bikes. The first blow, when it came, caught me by surprise, cracking my jaw and sending me reeling. By the second blow I was ready, rolling away as the foot descended so that the man's heel came down on concrete instead of bone. I found my feet. I was not going to die, was not going to let myself be victimized the way I had in Meidua years and weeks before. I bared my teeth, spat. The sputum came up red.

"There's a letter," I said, keeping open hands up between me and the two men. "Handwritten. That's all I want." And after a moment, I added, "And my shoes." My eyes betrayed me, for even as I said the words, my eyes went to the signet ring—my signet ring—on the hand of the other dock worker.

On a good day, I could have taken the two men. If I had been hale, whole, uninjured, well rested, well fed. If we had been on Delos, where the very effort of standing did not beggar the muscles on my bones. If perhaps the two men hadn't each been behemoths corded in sheets of muscle from a lifetime of hard labor in this gravity.

Perhaps.

I blocked the next blow, giving ground, stumbling a little as my callouses scuffed on the uneven earth. I was lucky; the two got in one another's way, their blows wild and uncoordinated but frighteningly strong. In my weakened state, I less blocked their attacks than deflected them, knowing full well I could not stop a blow directly. Memories of a thousand sparring lessons with Felix came to mind, with Crispin. They retreated just as fast, fading as distractions must in the heat of such moments, retreating until the only memories were those of muscle and blood. A wild hook took me in the ribs, sending me staggering. *Too slow,* I thought, more angry than in pain. *Too weak.*

The man with my stolen ring on his finger hurried into the opening I'd created with my backward stumble, and even as I thought to run, the sight of it caught like embers in dry wool. I turned my stagger into a whirl, grabbing the man's wrist, twisting so that all the weight of me fell on

that pronated arm. The elbow went out with a revolting crunch, and the man's yell turned to screaming. The sound stalled the other man, the hairy one who had first accosted me, long enough that I was able to tug the ring free. My chest worked like a bellows. There wasn't enough air. Or there was too much air. My vision was going out at the edges, bruised with shadow.

I must have looked like an animal, standing above the man with the broken arm. I was an animal. Footsteps sounded around the corner of the far building, and through clenched teeth I said, "I just want my things back."

"The hell's going on?" asked a rough, feminine voice.

Not taking his eyes off me, the bearded man called out, "Bastard broke Bor's arm!"

The others appeared then, seven of them as like the first two as one could imagine, like clay sculptures pressed from the same mold: all squat and square-shouldered, muscled identically from identical lives. The woman who'd spoken was bald but for the faintest dusting of stubble shadowing her scalp, her unpleasant face marred by an ugly wine-stain birthmark. She took in my face, and something there gave her pause, but after a moment she smiled. "Go the fuck home, boy." She glanced at the injured man still groaning on the ground, his crooked elbow starting to purple. "Or you'll get worse."

The man on the ground spoke through gritted teeth. "He broke my damn arm, Gila. Call the prefects, for Earth's sake."

I jammed my ring onto my uninjured thumb. "You were the ones who pulled me out of my ship." It wasn't a question. "You don't want the prefects here, do you?" I held the ring up for inspection, using it to make my point. I didn't want to say anything, to call attention to what that ring meant. Doing so would have opened me to reprisal. If they called my bluff, I would have to reveal myself to the authorities, to my father. I walked a thin line, razor-sharp and with the threat of violence looming like the sword of Damocles. "I just want my things."

The woman—Gila—spat just as the bearded man had

done. "Ship's gone. Moved up-well for refitting this morning."

The moment's respite had granted me some time to recover, and my breathing slowed. My hair was still plastered to my face, half covering my eyes. I tried to flip it out of the way, but it wasn't coming free. "You're lying." The injured man recovered his knees, helped up by the bearded man and one of the others. "Give me my effects."

"Your effects?" one of the dockworkers sneered. "The hell are you? The Prince of Jadd?"

I didn't rise to the bait. "What did you do with the salvage? The crew?"

"Ship was empty when it came in-system," Gila said. "Crew bugged out, took the shuttles and ran, left your sorry ass in the freeze."

I licked my dry lips. "You admit it then?"

"Fuck you, boy." She waved a hand. "Get the fuck off my worksite."

I took a step closer, and to this day I can't say if it was a calculated move or just blind aristocratic stupidity. "There was a letter, a handwritten letter."

"Love note from your girlfriend, is it?" the bearded man said. "Or are you the girlfriend?" Laughter bubbled from the rest of the crowd, and somehow the sound was more threatening than a snarl. I checked my advance. Part of me, the sensible, rational core, whispered that I should run. Not to the fence, but to the open gate I had seen with the guards languishing in their air-conditioned hut. None of the dock workers had called for guards. It was possible, but it wouldn't be easy. I was still weak. I needed water. I needed to eat. I had only bested the idiot cradling his broken arm because of my training. I'd been lucky.

Gila spoke then. "Threw everything out. Go look on a rubbish barge." One of the men beside her moved forward, but she grabbed him by the front of his filthy jumpsuit. Her small, dark eyes darted to my ring, knowing what it signified, the danger she was in. She was smarter than the thugs from Meidua, or maybe just less brave. "Now get out."

I knew they'd be on me the moment I turned around, for the ring if nothing else, so I backed away. I wanted to say something clever, something cutting, something to rattle them in their boots the way my father might have done. Something to freeze their blood. I had nothing. I said nothing.

At least I was fast.

I have always been fast.

CHAPTER 24

THOSE MINDLESS DAYS

THREE DAYS AND NIGHTS have passed since last I put pen to vellum. Long have I pondered how to proceed, how best to relate those days and years lost to the streets of Borosevo. They say that when he was a boy, the prince Cid Arthur was kept in a pleasure palace by his father's faithful archon, isolated from death, disease, and poverty, for a vate had prophesied that if he should see the ugliness of the world, Cid Arthur would renounce his father's throne and become a preacher himself. I had always wondered at this, for I had grown up in a palace myself, and I knew of poverty and sickness and had had my own brushes with death—first with my grandmother, then later when Uncle Lucian had died in his shuttle crash. I could not understand how Arthur had been so blind.

I understood it now.

Just as there is a difference between the news of a distant planet's destruction and the bloody death of a coliseum slave, it is one thing to know there is poverty and illness and another to walk among the poor and suffering. Often I saw beggars covered in black sores and peeling skin beseeching the Chantry for deliverance not from evil, but from sickness. The Rot was rampant in the city, the gift of some alien animalcule very like a bacterium. It blackened skin and wasted flesh and hardened lymphs and lungs. The city prefects piled bodies in squares and burned them, and the smoke carried votive lanterns to a heaven that seemed deaf to all prayer. My own palatine

blood defended me, but there was no defense from the horror of it.

My father's face haunted me at night, his and the funeral masks of our forebears and the screaming of nameless prisoners in the bastille he wished to send me to. For their sake I suffered, and for my mother. I dreamed I saw her dragged to the whipping post, lashed by a blindfolded cathar in unfeeling black. When I awoke, sweating and sobbing in a cardboard pile between a clothier and a bakery, it was to thoughts of Gibson. The old man had suffered for nothing, was exiled for nothing. For there I was, rotting on the edge of the Empire and the Veil in a system looking out on the Sullen Gulf between the Arms of Centaurus and Norma.

But I forced myself to go on.

Like Cid Arthur on his quest for the Merlin Tree, I did what I had to do to survive. I ate fish raw from the canals, raided compost bins. I depended upon the kindness of street vendors—a class of men not much noted for their charity—and I learned to beg. I will not say I was good at it, but desperation eventually broke down the dregs of my palatine dignity.

I suppose I might have surrendered at any moment, submitted my blood and ring to the count's authority and waited for my father to collect me. I was tempted—sorely tempted—those first weeks most of all. The years slipped by in squalor, and the days were long. Mad as it sounds, despite the misery and the struggle, despite the prefects and the gangs . . . I was happy. For the first time in my life I was truly free. Of my father. Of my station. Of everything.

It was not enough. Free I might be, but to be free and less than a serf is small consolation. Each night the stars called to me through Borosevo's haze. They had never felt so far away. All I needed was a way offworld. I longed to find some unscrupulous merchanter who would hire a man without the necessary papers, but I couldn't get within half a mile of the landing field. Trespassers were shot on sight.

In time, whatever lofty dreams I had faded into dreams of food. I missed wine with a passion I find difficult to

describe, and fruit, and hot meals . . . and water most of all. Do you know what it is to miss *water*? I was made to siphon off rain barrels. All the while I brooded on my fate, on the utter destruction of my hopes and dreams. In my mind I saw Gibson's letter afire, black smoke curling from its corners as it twisted like a dragon devouring its own tail.

I was never going to Teukros.

I was never going anywhere.

CHAPTER 25

POVERTY AND PUNISHMENT

I CROUCHED ON THE old drinking cooler I used as both treasure chest and chair in the storm drain I had called home for the past ten nights, eating half a smoked eel I had stolen from a street vendor outside the coliseum. The meat was tender, brushed with garlic and soy sauce, vaguely smoky. I had been a thief now for the better part of a week and had decided I was good at it, though my whole body ached from gravity fatigue.

It was a good spot. Dry, unless one counted the channel in the bottom of the storm drain. Enclosed, unless one counted the open mouth of the tunnel that spilled out onto a canal some twenty feet below. It was one of dozens built into the side of the White District, so called for the color of the lime-washed bulwark that separated it from Belows. The White District clustered about the base of the castle ziggurat, fifty feet or so above sea level, relic of the days when the Empire seized Emesh from the Norman United Fellowship, which had colonized it. There lived the planet's wealthy, its patricians and offworld plutocrats, the guild factionarii and important businessmen, local celebrities and gladiators. The Chantry sanctum was there, a copper-domed structure beside the brutalist concrete mass of its attendant bastille. We beggars were not tolerated in the White District save on the day of the High Litany, which cycled through the week as Emesh's day-and-night cycle failed to tally with the standard calendar.

I sat on the very edge of the drain, looking down and

out upon Belows, the warren of canals and low buildings
with rooftop gardens. The sun was going down, bruised
and bloody into the blackened sea, and I dangled my bare
and aching feet over the edge, airing them. I ate the last
of my eel with something resembling contentment, wishing I had something more than rainwater to wash it down.

A flight of terranic pigeons rose from the street corner,
and I watched a paper votive lantern rise above the rooftops. They were always rising from the city, carrying
prayers toward Mother Earth, entreaties for the souls of
the Rot's victims. I leaned against the side of the drain-
pipe, resting my head on the whitewashed concrete.

"You!"

How is it you can always tell when a word is directed
at you? Every muscle in me tightened like a bowstring
ready to fire, and I looked round, terrified for a moment
that someone had come through the barred grate behind
me. But no. I saw the culprits at once: a man and a woman
in the dun khakis of the urban prefects. They were standing on the edge of the sidewalk by the canal, hurrying
toward the accessway that arched over the water to the
ladder bracketed into the wall.

"Come down!"

I scrabbled to my feet, tripping back and falling over
the cooler in my panic. It was a damnably stupid thing to
do. One of my spasming feet caught the cooler I'd been
sitting on and kicked it right over the ledge. I felt a yell
choke off behind my teeth, dismay and frustration coloring my surprise. Everything I had in the world—excepting
my clothes and my family's ring—was in that little blue
crate. My extra food, the two magazines I'd lifted from a
newsstand three days earlier, the empty bottles I used for
collecting rainwater. And my money. I had managed to
scrape together a few dozen steel bits until I had nearly so
much as a single silver kaspum. That kind of money could
have bought me a night in one of Belows's many flop-
houses. I was saving it for shoes.

A ragged yell escaped me, and before I could much
think on it, I hurled myself down after it, diving feet first
toward the green water of the canal. The prefects yelled,

but the sound fell away in the liquid rush of air past my ears.

I hit the surface of the canal like a boulder, my legs tucked up around me. When I surfaced, I cast about for the heavy plastic of the cooler. I hadn't seen where it had fallen. Had it sunk? Had it managed to fall on the street instead of in the water? Damn it, I'd acted too fast. Stupid, stupid, stupid. There it was, bobbing low in the water by the concrete wall I'd leaped from. I swam to it, mindful now of the shouting behind me. "What were you doing up there?"

Maybe I could talk my way out of this. Treading water, clutching the cooler's handle in one hand, I pushed off the wall of the White District and made for the sidewalk just above the canals. The prefects both hurried from the arched access bridge to intercept me, but I was faster, vaulting onto the sidewalk, trailing green and stinking seawater. A line of schoolchildren hurried by under the watchful eye of their teacher, pointing and laughing at the dripping man with his wild hair. "Just enjoying the view, ma'am. You can see the whole city from up there." I tried to smile, tried to pass off my wild state as the fault of my spectacular dive, not of more than a month spent without a wash.

The prefect glowered at me, black eyes measuring as she tapped her stunner in its thigh holster. "Them drains is off-limits to the public. Everyone knows that."

"Yes, ma'am." I bobbed my head, taking a step back, clutching my cooler to my dripping chest. "Sorry, I—"

"Papers," the other prefect snapped, holding out a hand. "Let's see your identification."

I took a step back. "I . . ." What could I say? "I don't have it with me."

The second prefect sighed. "You'll have to come with us, then." He held out a hand.

Crispin's unconscious shape moved just beneath my vision, haunting me. What was I supposed to do? My signet ring seemed to hang more heavily about my neck, and I glanced from side to side. There was a small alley wedged between two shops not far off. If I could make it to that alley . . .

"Come on, you." One of the prefects made a grab for me. I took a violent step back. The prefect seized my wrist. I panicked, swung the still-dripping cooler in a wide arc that took the officer in the side of his head. He reeled back, released me with a cry of surprise and pain. And the lid sprang open. Coins and magazines and half an old sandwich fanned across the two officers, damp banknotes and napkins sticking to the inside of the box. I choked back a sob and turned and ran.

I didn't make it far.

The stunner bolt grazed my leg, and the muscle there went slack as old rubber. I stumbled, lost my grip on the now-empty cooler. It clattered away across the pavement. I struggled to stand. Before I could so much as reach my knees, a boot slammed down on my shoulder, pressing me to the earth. My vision went dark as my head struck the pavement, and it was all I could do to crawl forward. The stunner had only grazed me. I could still run, if only I could ignore the needling sensation humming up my leg, if only I could find my feet. Someone kicked me below the ribs, and I winced. Visions of that night in Meidua spasmed in me, and my breath came hard and caught. The ragged sound of my blood pounding in my ears drowned out the prefects' muddy swearing. Something battered me across the head, and my vision blurred again. I lay quiescent, flat on my face, and gritted my teeth to keep from sobbing or crying out.

I felt hands patting me down, turning out my pockets. They found a pair of steel bits and a coupon from a chain of fish carts promising a discount. They did not find my ring, did not so much as bother to turn me over. "Bastard's poor as dirt," the woman said.

"He's gutter trash, Ren," the other prefect said. "Ain't worth booking." He spurned me with his toe, and I bit down on my tongue, tasted iron blood. "Should have run faster, *neg.*"

She swore, and I felt a pressure on the back of my neck. Something hard slugged me square on the back of my head, but I didn't black out, just groaned. The stunner fog turned my whole side warm where it had skimmed me, and now I

doubted I could have so much as walked in a straight line, much less made a break for the alley. I thought of how I'd trashed that dockworker a month before and felt shame rise in me. The prefect was wrong. I shouldn't have run faster. I shouldn't have run at all. I bared bloody teeth and spat on the cement beside my head.

Just then the woman seized me by the hair and peeled me off the concrete. She crouched close, breathed in my ear. "Don't let me catch you where you don't belong again, *neg*, or you'll regret it."

A retort—something about laying off the illegal horse hormones—formed and fell from my lips. I let it go, struggled toward a calm like the apatheia. I went limp, felt my face bruise as she dropped me to the pavement. I do not know how long I lay there or why none of the passing men and women stopped to help me.

CHAPTER 26

CAT

THE RAIN SHEETED OFF the canted roofs, over choking gutters, and into canals so bloated they swallowed the roads. I splashed over an elevated walkway, glad of the fresh water despite the storm. Whole sections of Borosevo—the poorest—drowned whenever the storms came in. Lightning spasmed across the underbelly of the sky, caroming from one cloud to the next. I leaned against the plastic rail, shoved my hair from my eyes to protest the gusting winds.

I needed shelter. I needed food. I needed to stop hurting.

The streetlights went out, and the swinging chain of lights strung over the bridge with the power lines died too. Darkness stole over the raised street, and I scrabbled on, bare feet scuffing the worn cement. I tarried a moment in the leeward face of a shuttered grocer and contemplated smashing the windows. The prefects were not likely to risk action in a hurricane, not even for burglary . . . but no, no.

Out beyond the dark shapes of low buildings and the tiered sprawl of the city, a bolt of lightning struck the sea, turning all that darkness to gleaming glass. The thunder shook me to the marrow, rattled over Borosevo like the descent of starcraft. A striped awning snapped above my head, rain bouncing off it like the beat of a thousand tiny drums. Driven by instinct, I curled myself up on the stoop and hoped to wait out the storm. From my vantage point, I could just make out the looming mass of the palace ziggurat rising over the city, its black shape crouched over Borosevo like a dragon on its hoard. The lights in its high

towers flickered. Even the count's power systems shivered in the wake of Emesh's fury.

We had storms on Delos, blown in by the sirocco across the sea to our eastern shores, but they were nothing—*nothing*—next to the storms on Emesh. Cloudscapes vast as empires towered over the city, filling the sky and burying all the stars. Despite the heat and steaming air, I shivered. A light flicked on behind me, and a beet-faced man slammed on the glass with his fist, shouting dull words. I got the message, lurched awkwardly to my feet. How long had it been since I'd last eaten?

Rain lashed the concrete, pelted off glass storefronts and off tarps shielding boats broken and bobbing in the swell. I hurried on, darting into an alley in the hope of finding some loading dock left open by mistake. But the people of Borosevo were diligent, well used to their storms, and I was left to wander. Old garbage stuck to the soles of my bare feet as I scuffed along, leaning against the tin wall of a shed a block back from the front street. I clutched my ring on its chain through the front of my soaking shirt, held it as a sorcerer might a talisman.

As a child I had wished for an adventure. I had wanted to see the galaxy, to plumb the hidden depths of the human universe and prize secrets from the darkness between the stars. I had wanted to travel like Tor Simeon and Kharn Sagara in the old stories, wanted to see the Ninety-Nine Wonders of the Universe and to break bread with xenobites and kings. Well, I had gotten my adventure, and it was killing me. At least the buildings in the alley overhung the street. It wasn't much, but the hanging eaves allowed for a stretch of space about a meter deep that stood dry. Drier. Trying again, I pressed myself down between two garbage bins, shielded from wind and water as much as was possible.

Why had it all gone wrong? What had happened to Demetri? It wasn't fair. I had done everything I was supposed to do, followed Mother's plan as carefully as I could. I should have been on Teukros in a scholiasts' cloister by now, listening to lectures on warp-space math and the

diplomatic ties between the Empire and client states among the Normans and the Durantine Republic.

"What you doing?" I thought I had imagined the voice at first, so small was it, hissing sharp beneath the pounding of the storm. "You!" I looked up—all the way up—to the roof of the building across from me. A small, dark face peered down at me, plastered with sodden hair. I wanted to slink away, to vanish. I had not spoken to anyone in weeks, not since the time a sailor on shore leave had given me half a sandwich when I asked for a kaspum. You may think it odd, but if you have ever been well and truly alone for any length of time, you will know how hard it is to come back to the world of people. So I just stared at her.

"Are you stupid or something?" When still I didn't move, she added, "They didn't sandbag the alley, *rus*. Fall asleep there, and they'll have to fish you out of the lagoon come sunrise. Climb up!" She jerked her head at a broken gutter that ran up one corner of her building.

I almost bolted. Maybe I would have if I had been healthier, if my ribs didn't still ache from my third beating in as many weeks. But when I stood pain lanced up my side, and I keeled sidelong into the nearest garbage bin. The huge plastic tub slicked on the drenched concrete, fell sideways with a dull bang. I swore, apologized to no one and nothing. The girl's face had vanished from the lip of the building. Had I imagined her? I clambered to the gutter. Its bulky brackets were nearly as good as a ladder, but they were far apart, and the sheet metal was slick. I only slipped twice, biting my lip as I splashed in the nearly two inches of water that pooled at the base of the building.

The third time a small, strong hand seized me by the wrist. "The fuck's wrong with you?" She wasn't strong enough to haul me up, but she bought me time to plant my feet again, time enough to finally seize the lip of the building and pull myself over. A light flier passed overhead, running lights blinding in the close air. "You some sort of idiot?"

"I'm not!" I snapped, baring my teeth. She recoiled,

wiping the rain from a face suddenly poisoned by fear. All at once the wind went out of me, and I said, "Sorry . . . I . . ." I bowed my head, darted a glance back at her. "Thanks for the leg up." She was younger than I, perhaps sixteen standard, copper-skinned and round-featured, her eyes smiling out of her rough, plebeian face despite the wary set of her jaw. Her clothes were patched and torn worse even than my own, suggesting a body lean and undernourished. She was like me: homeless, helpless in the storm.

She cocked her head to one side. "You're not from here, are you?"

I shook my head, looked away, taking in the rain-swept rooftop. A bank of dinted solar panels marched along the far edge, and a washing line hung barren and swinging in the wind. Another peal of thunder shook the world, echo of some unseen lightning. From our meager vantage point the low sprawl of Borosevo unrolled like trash caught in a gyre.

"You offworld?" she asked.

"Yes." I eyed the bank of solar panels at the far edge of the roof, shuffled toward them. With the girl's help, I lowered myself beneath one of them. The roof was still wet, but at least the rain no longer fell directly on our heads.

She slunk in after me, making me budge aside to make room. "You hurt?"

"I ran afoul of some . . ." I was about to say *local color*. ". . . people."

The words sounded lame even to me, and the girl made a face. "Ran afoul?" she repeated. "That mean yes?"

I grunted in answer and leaned back, ducking my head where the panel canted backward at an angle to face the south. The concrete roof felt unspeakably good just then, and I lay flat on my back, not moving. "Nice spot you've got here." For a storm, I was hard-pressed to think of a better one. The solar panels proved a good cover from the rain, and the rooftop was clean and above any level likely to flood.

To my surprise, she brightened, revealing crooked teeth when she smiled. "Got lucky—owners ain't in." She

went quiet then for a moment. "Why you trying to drown yourself in the street like that?"

"I was just trying to sleep." My eyes were closed, my breathing deliberately shallow, protesting the pain in my sides. The waif didn't say anything for five seconds. Ten seconds. After half a minute I cracked one eye, found her crouched, watching me. "What?"

"Ain't you got money?" she asked, confusion obvious in her tone. "Offworlders always got money. You could get a room." Was that hope in her voice?

"I don't have anything," I said, forcing my hand not to grasp my ring through my shirt. The last thing I needed was to give the little street rat an excuse to rob me. After another unsteady silence, I asked, "What's your name?"

This earned me a sharp look. "What's yours?"

I opened both my eyes but did not sit up. "Hadrian."

She made a face that to this day I can't describe. "I'm Cat."

"Is that short for Catherine?"

Her nose wrinkled. "No! What sort of name's 'Catherine'?" She ripped a strip of tape off the roof beside her, exposing an old wire that ran down from the solar panel overhead. "It's just Cat." After another pregnant silence, she echoed, "What sort of name's 'Hadrian,' anyway?"

I shrugged. "An old one. Mine." My unfortunate gruffness stalled the conversation out again, and I pressed a hand to my ribs, wincing at the hot pain there. The girl moved, unsure how to help, hands hovering above me. Thunder rolled. The roof was drenched beneath me, but it didn't matter. For once I was grateful for the uncomfortable warmth and the weight of the air.

"How bad you beat?"

"Two fractured ribs, I think." Remembering what had happened that night after the Colosso in Meidua, I added, "I've had worse." Only this time I wasn't going to be given medical correctives. I groaned. I had thought I could get away with stealing from a group of teenagers. They'd been stronger and meaner than I could have believed, and there had been twelve of them.

She bit her lip. "Can't do nothing for that."

"No," I agreed. I listened to the lashing rain a moment, fighting the blurred vision of encroaching sleep. "Why'd you help me?" It didn't seem like a smart thing for a girl alone to do.

Cat sat a little straighter. "I wouldn't leave no one in the low streets in a storm, *rus*." She gave me a speculative look. "Can you even swim?"

"Maybe if my ribs weren't broken."

"My ma said some offworlders ain't even got water. I weren't sure . . ." She trailed off, playing with the little strip of tape.

I offered a thin smile, hoping it would go some way toward repairing the damage I'd done by glaring at her. "I grew up by the sea. I can swim, I just . . ." I cast about the rooftop with my eyes. "Everything's different here. Air's all wrong, gravity's too strong. People are strange . . ." I winced. I was rambling.

She wadded up the tape and threw it out into the rain and looked at me with a sudden intensity I found almost frightening, and I shied away despite the pain in my chest and arms. "You talk funny, Hadr-Hadrian." She stumbled on my unfamiliar name. "Where you from?"

"Delos," I said, as if the name could mean anything to her.

You talk funny. That thought stopped me short of saying anything further. It was so obvious now that I'd had it pointed out to me. Whatever I looked like, I still spoke like a Delian nobile, like a palatine of the Imperium. I should have noticed that—no wonder the others among the city's poor mistrusted me. I stood out like a broken finger.

"Where's that?"

Only a few of the unfixed stars peered through the storm, watchful and timeless. Around one of those lights was home. I could not say which, for though I knew the names of the stars, their positions were strange here. It could be any of them or none, my home lost under cloud or in the Dark. But the truth is poor poetry, and my mother had taught me better. I bit my lip—in part to subdue another wave of pain from my burning side—and pointed.

"See that star, there?" I coughed. She nodded. "You can't see it, but there's another star behind it. Much, much farther away. That's where I come from."

"What's it like?"

"My turn for a question!" I interjected, trying to sit up. No good. As is so often true in cases of exhaustion or hurt, rest was the best and worst thing for me. I couldn't make myself move. "You don't have any painkillers, do you? Nothing heavy. No narcotics."

She shied away, face darkening. "I don't . . ." I wasn't sure if she was answering me or not. Her voice broke. Was it fear? Why? I couldn't understand. "I don't know these words."

"Drugs," I said. "Medicine?"

"What exactly happened, anyway?"

That brought a grimace to my face. "Tried to steal off the back of a lift-palette from some bastards with white armbands." I gestured to my left biceps.

"Rells?" Her dark face went pale. "Shit, *rus*, you are crazy."

"Seemed like a good idea at the time." I laughed weakly, trying to undercut my own foolishness. I waggled my toes. "I wanted . . ." My voice trailed off, broken by exhaustion, by pain, by the interminably long night.

. . . *shoes.*

I must have passed out. When I awoke, the Emeshi night stood deep upon the world. The clouds had rolled on, and the fierce squall had diminished to gentle rain. I was alone, unmoved from my spot beneath the solar panel. Cat was nowhere to be seen, and I lay aching and soaking and cold on the hard rooftop. Whatever comfort I'd felt in the place before going to sleep was gone, replaced by a bone-deep stiffness and a dull throbbing at the base of my skull. I lay a long time before Cat came back, watching the underside of the solar panel and the swirl of clouds along the horizon. The storm passed away

north, lightning now only distantly visible, thunder reduced to the dullest drumbeat.

"You're not dead," she said, small mouth going up at the corners.

"I wasn't that badly off."

She placed a plastic shopping bag on the roof beside me and opened it, one of the heavy sort sailors and housewives insisted on never throwing away. "Any of this help?"

I had to grab one of the solar panel's support spars to haul myself into a sitting position. The bag was full of half-emptied medicine bottles, the labels torn or blurred or written in foreign scripts. I began sifting through them. "Where'd you get all this?"

"Trash," Cat said simply. "Might still work okay."

I was in no position to be choosy. I set five bottles of vitamins aside as well as three with labels written in a form of Mandari strange to me—no sense playing dice. At last I found a bottle written in the distinct blocky Lothrian alphabet. Naproxen. I shook it before unscrewing it. There weren't many left. "You sure I can have some?"

She made a throwing away gesture and went out into the still drizzling rain. I took three of the pills, ignoring the bottle's recommended dosage, and left the bag beneath the solar panel. It took a great effort to make myself stand again and more to peel off my soaked shirt, which I left hanging from a bar beneath the panel. I paused a moment, taking my ring off the cord round my neck. I stuffed it into a pocket of my soaking pants instead. A moment later I sagged onto the ledge overlooking the city. The water had risen nearly a foot and a half in the alley below, and I averted my eyes. Tired as I had been, I might not have awakened until it was too late.

Cat and I sat there a long while, unseen by the world, seeing all of it. At last I asked, "Why did you help me?"

"Told you," she said, making the throwing away gesture again. "Ain't gonna let anyone drown in their sleep like that." I held her gaze for a good long while, and something in my face must have spoken to her, for she added, "And you was crying. I know what that's like. Being alone."

"You said something about your mother," I put in, curiosity overcoming tact.

Cat's face crumpled, the pretty, common lines drooping. I felt something in me break for having caused that sadness as she said, "She's dead. Sick. The Rot, you know . . ." She tossed something over the side of the building—a chip of the concrete ledge, perhaps. "You got a family?"

I shook my head, resisted touching my ring where it lurked in my pocket. "No."

CHAPTER 27

FORSAKEN

"SHE HAS FORSAKEN US!" the vate shrieked, reaching gnarled fingers up to the sky in the raised square before the massive dome of the Borosevo Chantry in the White District. The holy madman stood on a scaffold ten feet above the paving stones, crying out to all who would listen. Most days the people hurried past such as he, scurried out from the canals or up from the sealed parking lot for those few citizens wealthy and vapid enough to purchase groundcars in a place like Borosevo, where the roads were few. But it was Friday, and the weekly Litany was being celebrated by the system's grand prior, an aged priestess called Ligeia Vas who put me in mind of withered old Eusebia. Because of this, the plaza was flooded with worshipers who could not fit into the Chantry sanctum and who would instead watch the prior from screens hung between pillars depicting the Four Cardinals.

Beggars crowded the entrances to the plaza and clustered about the pillars that stood before the double doors, young and old alike. Many were bandaged, sores weeping from Gray Rot. Yet more bore the marks of the Chantry's justice: missing fingers, thumbs, eyes, tongues. You could see their crimes tattooed in black lettering on their foreheads: *ASSAULT, THEFT, ASSAULT, HERESY, HERESY, THEFT, RAPE, THEFT, ASSAULT.* The more naked among them showed the signs of whip scars on their backs or ugly wheals and burn scars bright as new metal. A disproportionate number of them were men, though the Rot showed no such prejudice. Some among

the standing congregation wore masks over their faces or else wore gloves despite the heat of the day.

The crowds also meant conditions were right for begging. With an icon of Charity carved above the doors of the sanctum, even the most hardhearted of the faithful thought twice before spurning us with a toe. Whether they gave us any spare steel bits or quarter-kaspums was something else entirely, but I bobbed my head in placid gratitude all the same, kneeling like a penitent alongside Cat near a street corner leading into the plaza. The vate still screamed from his pulpit, naked and stinking. "Our Mother, the Earth Who Was and Will Be Again, has turned Her face from us. These Pale devils are Her punishment for the vanity of our ways! Mark me, brothers and sisters, children of Earth and Sun! Mark me, for the punishment is coming! A cleansing fire that will wash away all our sins! Repent! Repent! And be clean again!"

A man dropped a coin into Cat's begging bowl; she looked small and terribly forlorn beneath one of the city surveillance cameras. "God and Emperor bless you, messer," she said, bowing her face over the bowl. I couldn't help but notice that she had nearly three times the coin I had. I grimaced. At least my ribs had healed.

"You're sharing some of that with me, aren't you?" I asked, smiling. I kept my voice down but was wholly incapable of keeping the playfulness from it.

"Gods no," Cat spat back. "Get your own!" She swatted at me, smiling so that the light caught her crooked teeth. I chuckled softly. It felt good to laugh again, to be given a reason to laugh. Her hand lingered a moment on my knee, fingers warm and damp with sweat through my trousers. The day was hot, the air thick and steaming. We stayed there all morning, as we did each morning on the day of the High Litany. A woman in a violet suit walking beneath a bright paper parasol placed a whole silver kaspum into Cat's bowl with a smile. The girl nearly cried and stood to bow in thanks.

I looked down at my own bowl, at the paltry collection of steel bits and the crumpled twelfth-kaspum note there. The smile on that woman's face has never left me, though

she never said a word. When I think of kindness, it is to the shape of that mouth with its cheap red lipstick that I turn.

"We have rejected nature!" the vate cried. "We bend the knee and the neck to lords made less than human!" And here the naked madman clutched his own member with a gnarled hand, beard blowing in the wind atop his scaffold. "The Mother knows! Knows the nobiles have forgotten Her, have worked Her from their blood!" The part of me that had been an archon's son twitched, half expecting to see the prefects—or even soldiers in the green-and-white of the count's service—march in to take the sun-crazed old preacher away. None came, for it is said the mad are close to Earth.

CHAPTER 28

WRONG

ALREADY NUMB FROM A stunner graze and clutching my useless left arm, I slalomed round a street corner and up onto a set of crates, using them to springboard over the parked float-palette that blocked the road. The gray concrete glowed with heat, but my scarred and grimy soles could not feel it. I cannot say which day it was or how many months or years of my life had washed into those canals like so much garbage.

I heard shouts behind me and shrugged the straps of the stolen purse into the crook of my still-working arm. Gasping, I darted up a set of stairs and into an alley so narrow my broad shoulders almost scraped the sides. The buildings hung close above my head, piping and ductwork exposed and bracketed to metal walls. My shirt snagged on a bolt and tore, doubtless gashing my unfeeling arm in the process. The electric crackle of stunner fire and shouts of, "Stop! Thief!" followed me like the hounds in one of my late uncle's foxhunts. My chapped lips pulled into a mean grimace, hair blowing in my face. I turned, shouldered past a pair of women carrying shopping baskets on their heads and onto a high street running along the saline bend of a canal.

Though my instinct was to run, though years of bruises and broken bones badly set by backstreet hacks screamed at me to keep going, I knew that would only make me stand out. Many's the time I watched a crowd turn against a fellow thief, the brightly dressed throng transmuted into a wall of solid flesh as the prefects brought him down.

Instead I slipped around an iron railing and settled at an empty glass table at the edge of a cafe's sitting area. Holographs for ordering flickered on the glass surface, and I made a show of riffling through *my* purse—no mean feat with one of my arms stunned and useless. I did not doubt that there was a camera somewhere on me, but I didn't think that information would make it to the prefects before they slipped by me. I ignored the universal card in the purse and the identification forms, both belonging to the powdered man in the low-slung sarong I'd stolen it from. I found a pair of slightly ovoid glasses—silver-rimmed with lenses of ruby glass—that I shoved onto my nose. I took a moment to gather back my long hair and bind it with an elastic band, also courtesy of the bag. What's more, I found a full half-kaspum note and nearly another kaspum in steel change. These I stuffed into my pocket with a small smile before setting the purse down beside my chair.

Behind me, I heard the drumming of boot heels on the pavement, but I did not turn. I bowed my head and pretended to look over the menu embedded in the table.

"Don't worry," a rough voice said. "I won't say a thing."

I looked up to find an older man smiling at me from the next table over. He raised his eyebrows and smiled over the rim of his drink. We were the only clients for three tables. An old book sat closed beside one fist, and he wore an indigo jacket cut in Nipponese fashion, square sleeves patterned with gold and black diamonds about the cuffs. His graying hair was pulled back into a greasy topknot, frayed and bristling like a calligrapher's long-abused brush.

I decided to play dumb. "I'm sorry?" My voice came out ragged, masking somewhat the effect of my clipped Delian accent.

"Your arm's gone stun-lame and you're breathing like the Duchess Antonelli's prize racehorse. Don't take a scholiast to figure you've done a runner." He wasn't Nipponese either, judging by the craggy lines of his face or the tenor of his words. Indeed, I couldn't place his accent. Durantine, maybe? Or one of the Norman freeholders,

though he didn't have their coloring. I stood sharply, turned to go. "Don't be that way. Old Crow ain't going to say a word. Why don't you sit awhile?" He kicked a chair out with a sandaled heel. When I didn't answer or move, he sighed, slipping a loose lock of graying hair behind his ear. "How long's it been?"

"How long has what been?"

"Since you was stranded, boy! You got the stink of space all over you, and anyone with eyes can see you're no Emeshi."

I let my numb arm fall and swallowed the impulse to object to being called *boy,* but I didn't take his offer of a seat. "I don't know," I said. "Couple of years."

Old Crow frowned. "Couple of years . . ." He shook his head, topknot wavering. "That's hard."

I risked a glance over my shoulder to where the prefects—four of them—were working their way through the crowd. Suddenly nervous, I slunk into the chair opposite the other man.

From his complexion and the strangeness of his dress and accent, it was clear he was as Emeshi as I was, so I asked, "Where are you from, messer?" I could have kicked myself. The *messer* made me sound more than half-educated, not the common thief I seemed.

Crow smiled as if he understood, waving a hand around noncommittally. "Oh, lots of different places." He peered over my shoulder, watched the prefects press on down the high street toward one of the many bridges that arched over the canal. "But I'm *bound* for Ascia, in the Commonwealth. You?"

I chewed my lip, looked down at the table. I didn't want to answer. I regretted sitting down. At last I said, "I'm from . . ."

He slapped the table. "Not that. Where are you *going*?"

Slowly I raised my eyes to his, confused. "Nowhere. What do you care? I shouldn't even be talking to you. Whatever you're selling—"

"Not selling a damn thing," Crow said, scratching behind one ear. "Just seeing a man in need's all, only I ain't got nothing to give, neither." He groaned, leaning in

over the table. "Bones don't thaw like they used to. Damn fugue creches." Despite his complaints, he looked to be on the near side of middle-aged. I couldn't guess his caste, or even if he had one. He splayed a hand on the tabletop, and only then did I realize the man was at least a little drunk. "A man's got to be going somewhere. That's why Old Crow here . . ." He gestured at the sky, trailed off. "Anyway . . ."

I rose to leave, checking my pockets for the coins I'd taken from the stolen purse. They were still there, and I crumpled the half-kaspum note in my fingers. The prefects had vanished around a bend, and I peered out through the lenses of my pilfered red glasses, seeking them. The sailor made no objection to my leaving but said, "This planet's a shithole, you know? How's a man supposed to breathe? Even the whiskey's wrong." He made a face at his mug.

Wrong.

It was precisely the word I'd thought of a hundred times since my rude awakening on this world. It was all wrong. The sunlight, the two moons, even the air. I could not have imagined my current state from the comforts of Devil's Rest nor wished them on even the lowliest peasant. At once the stolen coins seemed a terrible weight in my pocket, a yoke upon my shoulders.

The drunken sailor was still talking, though less to me and more to the world in general, it seemed. "Listen to Old Crow here. A man's got to have a fire under him."

"How'd you become a sailor?" I asked without thinking. There was a better life, one I might aspire to in my meanness. Thoughts of Simeon the Red—of traveling the unending night—filled me. Even if I would never be a scholiast or part of the Expeditionary Corps, the adventure and mysteries I sought and the prestige of exploration need not be barred from me.

Crow cocked his head at me, scratching at his ear again, a look on his face like I'd asked him a hard question. "I was born one. So many are." He pointed a finger at me, jerked his thumb like the hammer in an antique firearm. He winked, then squinted at me. "You ain't thinking of signing on, are you?"

My heart leaped into my throat. The thought of again being on a cold ship, clean and fed, positively swelled within me. I darted a glance over the cafe rail to the street, keeping an eye out for the khaki uniforms of the urban prefects. Interpreting my quietude for an affirmative, Crow said, "That's a hard life, brother. You'd be better off getting a job in the hothouse farms than sailing. Black Earth! Be a fisherman. Fishermen make an honest living without all the damn freezing." He rubbed at the back of his neck, grimacing. "Say, you thought about the pit fights? Strapping lad like you . . . They got no shortage of need over in the Colosso. Someone's got to fill in for the dead boys."

"Are you a recruiter?" I asked.

"Am I a recruiter?" he repeated. "Shit no, just like a good fight." He leaned forward, pointed at my chest. "You'd be great, though. Got the build for it." Old Crow looked sourly at his drink and said, "Remember, though— be a myrmidon, not a gladiator. Girls don't like the professional killers."

That struck me as odd. Girls loved the gladiators in no small part because they were killers. Heroes. Real men. No one liked a corpse. Looking back, I suppose it was prophecy, or perhaps it was just because the old bastard was foreign.

"I'll consider it." I took a mincing step away, making for the gate to the street, aware now that my standing was drawing the attention of a few other diners. The impulse to run warred with my desire to stay, and I must have looked a fool, dancing as I was from foot to foot. If I did, the sailor paid no mind. He was again in his cups, one finger tapping on the ordering service built into the table. I thought I saw a flash of khaki in the crowd and jerked back. My movement drew the other man's attention, and for a moment all the drunkenness seemed banished from his craggy face.

"You can't go on like this, brother." He waggled a finger at me. "That's no way for anyone to live. You're lucky it were me this time, but next time you duck into a cafe with some lady's purse"—he kept his voice low—"someone might just call the guards."

I looked down at my bare feet, at the mud caked there. I wanted to ask him to take me with him, but I thought of Cat—about her smile and her crooked teeth—and I bit my tongue.

"You don't know me," I said sharply.

"Sure don't," Crow said. "But folk ain't that different, one-to-one, no matter what's on the outside. Doesn't even matter where you been. Hurt the same, need the same. Need someone to remind them they're human." He scratched at his ear thoughtfully. "You got means, boy, even when you got nothing. You got you. And I don't mean blood." From the way he cocked his eyebrows, I swear he knew me then for what I was: nobile, palatine, scion of the peerage now fallen. But then he grinned, a gold tooth flashing, and the impression that here was a man wise as sages was shattered and obscured by all that roughness the way an ancient bit of shattered pottery only hints at the vanished empire that crafted her. "Who you are don't mean shit. Don't mean enough, anyhow. It's what you *do* as matters, you hear?"

He spoke the truth, but I was not really listening, and it was a long time before the drunken sailor's words penetrated that armored bunker I called a skull. But I was nodding, craning my neck all the while to get a look round the street corner through the windows of the cafe.

From behind me I heard a shout from the high street, and looking back saw one of the prefects pointing straight at me. I felt the blood tighten in my veins even as Crow raised his cup in salute. "Run," he said. "But run *somewhere*, eh?"

I ran.

CHAPTER 29

LESS WINGS TO FLY

WITH OUR POCKETS UNUSUALLY heavy from a trade with a less-than-scrupulous pawnbroker, Cat and I stopped and bought sandwiches with slabs of vat-beef thick with juices from a shop whose owner did not turn us away on sight. We came to the back door, as she had said to do the time before, and ate on the street corner in view of the canal, watching little boats go by, poled or motored across the stagnant channel.

"Tell me again about your castle, Had," she said when she had finished half her food.

I had told her, of course. Who I was. What I was. She hadn't believed me at first, thought I was just another lying sailor abandoned on a strange world. But I had shown her my ring, and she had believed with the innocence of someone whose personal world was bounded by the margins of a city, of someone to whom the vastness of the Empire and the galaxy was only a fairy story.

I finished my bite, wiped the juice from my mouth with the back of my hand. "Not much to say, really. You know the story." I had explained a bit about why it was I'd fled. Just a piece.

"Not the story!" She poked me on the cheek, turning my head away. "What was it like?"

Smiling, I set my sandwich back in its little paper tray and looked at her intently, my head cocked at an angle. I tried to speak, then looked away abruptly and clapped my hand on her knee. I have never been much of a poet, and so the words came haltingly. "It was cold, and everything

was clean. It wasn't the sort of place that felt like people lived in it, you know? Everything had a place, and everyone, too." I shook my head. "It's hard to explain."

"What did it look like, though? Were there towers?"

I barked a laugh, pulsed my grip on her knee. She slid a bit closer, laid her hand on mine. "Yes, there were towers, all granite and black glass catching the sun . . ." I watched her as I shared with her the story of how Julian Marlowe had raised the old pile after he helped Duke Ormund secure power on Delos. As I spun stories about the ancientmost days of the Empire, I caught the light in her honeyed eyes and felt the caul of ice in me crack. Just a little. I was remembering a night some few weeks before, kissing her beneath a bridge leading up into the White District. She had kissed me. "And when the clouds were right," I said, "you could feel them like a roof just over your head and see the sunlight playing on the gray sea."

"You want to go back?"

"What?" I froze. I pulled my hand away and looked down at the sandwich in my lap, then at the fraying front of my shirt where my ring hung. "No. God, no."

"But you make it sound so beautiful."

I couldn't remember when I'd clenched my fists, but it took an effort of will to unclench them. "It was, but . . ."

"You can't . . . can't like *this*." She flapped a hand around at the street. "This is shit, Had. You don't belong hereabouts." I looked up at the sound of something fragile in her tone. The way she ran a self-conscious hand over the knee of her threadbare dress, right where I had touched her, broke my heart. "You should be up and up, you know?" Cat jerked a thumb skyward. "Way you talk, you belong in a castle."

"I don't!" I said, recalling the dream I'd had of my father's statue in the crypt with its red eyes like dying suns. I had not dreamed that dream in years, not since I'd awoken to this strange and stinking world.

"Well, you don't belong here," she said flatly, then leaned her head on my shoulder. Her hair tickled the side of my face, and I put an arm around her, as if by that gesture I could prove her wrong. I couldn't think of anything

to say. She was right. "If you could go anywhere—anywhere in the whole great Dark—where would you go?"

Teukros, I almost said. *Nov Senber*. That answer died sharp and sudden on my tongue, and I picked at the few roast potato chips in the bottom of my lunch tray. "Have you ever heard of Simeon the Red?" She shook her head. I forced myself not to blurt a panicked "What!" at her and said instead, "He was my greatest hero. Simeon was a scholiast. No court vizier, but a ship's science officer and part of the Expeditionary Corps. This was . . . oh, thousands of years ago, back when the Empire was young. His was one of the first ships into Centaurus, surveying worlds for future colonies. Mostly they found freeholders, barbarian men who preferred the frontier to civilization, like the Normans today. These they let be or traded with or conquered in the name of the Emperor, striking ever outward into the Dark. There they found a strange new world, a freezing, craggy place ruled by giant birds and by a race of flying xenobites."

"What were they like?" Cat asked. "The xenos?"

"Like birds themselves. A little smaller than us but with great wings for arms and short beaks."

"And talons?" She leaned her weight against me.

"Oh yes," I said, gesturing. "And claws at the end of their wings that they used to wield cutlasses tall as I am!" I raised a hand to indicate how tall those weapons were. "So Tor Simeon led missions to the surface, trading with the natives. The Irchtani, they called themselves. He learned to speak with them and to understand the sign language they used, and all was well between our people and theirs.

"But they had sailed too far for the crew. The men were sick at their guns and for want of home and human women. And while Simeon was on the ground with his guard and his science team, the crew mutinied, killed Simeon's captain and the other officers, and were going to take their ship out to the freeholds and live like pirates. But they made a mistake."

"They forgot Simeon?"

"Oh no, they didn't forget him. They wanted him. Simeon could speak to the Irchtani, see? He could persuade

their chieftains to sell their enemies to the mutineers as slaves. No one in the galaxy but them had seen an Irchtani before. Imagine the price one of them would fetch! For research at an athenaeum, or in Colosso, or sold to some old-blooded lord. They meant to be rich, you see, and they thought Simeon would help them. No, the mistake they made was thinking Simeon could be bought. He couldn't. Simeon was a scholiast and renounced wealth when he donned the green robes of his order. Worse, Simeon had befriended the Irchtani princes and banded with them to fight the mutineers when they came in their shuttles to find him. Simeon had never been a soldier, but he led the xenobites against the human traitors all the same and helped organize their retreat to the temple at Athten Var, the holiest of holies to the Irchtani people."

"What was it like?"

I waved a hand. "They said their gods built it all of black stone on the highest mountain on the world and that it could be defended. That was where they made their stand. Simeon and the Irchtani were victorious, the mutineers were thrown off the mountaintop, and Simeon retook his ship. And as a gift the Irchtani gave to Simeon a great cloak such as their princes wore. 'It is like your robe!' the Prince of the Birds said, but it wasn't. The Irchtani do not see color like men do, and the cloak they had made was red, not green. And thereafter Simeon was called 'The Red' for the cloak of the Irchtani, and he called the planet Judecca for the treason that was suffered there. The Empire named him captain and furnished him with a new crew, and they traveled farther into the Arm of Centaurus and brought to many other worlds the light of the Imperial Sun."

"And what happened to the xenos?" Cat asked. "When the Empire arrived? Are they gone now?"

"They're still there," I said. "I forget which house rules Judecca now. Calbren, maybe? Or Brannigan? There are actually Irchtani auxilia in the Imperial Legions, fighting the Cielcin. I once heard talk that the Emperor was considering citizenship for those who served the standard twenty-year period."

"Really?"

"Really!" I said, squeezing her with one arm. She had finished eating as I spoke, and she stole some of my potatoes despite my weak protests. Realizing I'd not answered her original question, I deflected, saying, "What about you? Where would you go?"

She shrugged. "Ain't going nowhere. Nowhere but here, that is."

"Neither am I." I plucked at my threadbare shirt.

"You *could*, though," Cat said, sitting up to look at me with her bright eyes. "You could show that ring to any old trader, and they'd have to do whatever you said. You could take me!" She smiled sweetly, displaying her crooked teeth. There must have been a look on my thin face, for her own fell, and she breathed, "I know you can't."

We were quiet then, and after a moment I finished the last bits of my sandwich, passing the remaining potatoes to Cat. We sat awhile then, watching a group of well-dressed people our own age hurry by, laughing and joking, uncaring and unconcerned. After a long while, Cat said, "I'd go to Luin. Ma always said there were fairies in the woods there and silver trees taller than that." She pointed to Castle Borosevo, its sandstone towers and walls an artful riot atop its terraced concrete ziggurat. "She used to say the fairies guided people through forests to magic pools that no one else had ever seen before." She smiled up at me, and I smiled back, knowing deep down that the phasma vigrandi of Luin were actually luring insects closer to the flesh-eating trees that made their world so beautiful. Not fairies at all.

"I want to see xenobites," I said breathily, leaning back on my elbows to look up at the lurid green-orange sky. Suddenly I recalled the sailor, Crow. Inspired, I said, "I wish I had my own ship, that I could travel. That way Father and the Chantry would never find me. I'd sail to Jadd, to Durannos, to the Lothriad, and the Freeholds, too. I want to see *everything*." It was a good while before I noticed I was still talking. I must have babbled for five minutes. For ten. It felt good to dream again out loud, to lay bare the naked wantings of my heart.

I hadn't realized that what I'd said was true until I'd spoken it. I wanted a ship, wanted the freedom of the stars. If I could not be a scholiast and learn secrets written down and stored, I would seek out truths where they lived. If only I could find the coin. Between Cat and I both we had less than a single silver kaspum, and that would not buy me shoes to walk in, much less wings to fly. Cat never stopped my gabbling, never interrupted. That was more than passing strange. She was watching me carefully, as if unsure of what to say or how to say it. A small crease formed between her eyebrows, and she bit her lip.

"What is it?" I asked, prodding her in the shoulder. "It's not like you to go all stiff."

In a papery voice she said, "You really want to leave, don't you?"

I blinked, looked round at the sweating canal and trash plastered to the roadside. "Well . . . yes." I waved a hand. "I've just got to find a way offworld is all. Someone who'll take us away in secret, you and me. I've just got to find the money."

Cat shook her head. "I can't leave. I'm planetbound." She'd grown very quiet, and I wondered at that.

"I'm not going to leave you here!" I murmured, nudging her with a shoulder. "Do you really think I'd just abandon you? We'll figure something out. Then we'll see Luin and meet the Irchtani. I'll even buy you a dress that's not all torn."

"You don't got to leave Emesh to see xenos." She looked down. "You can stay right here."

"What are you talking about?" I asked, sitting up.

She made a face. "You don't know dust about us, do you?" Cat stood then, leaving the ruins of her lunch on the curb. "We got xenos on Emesh."

CHAPTER 30

THE UMANDH

BOROSEVO HAD ITS URBAN farms, grand towers of glass that filtered the bloated sunlight into something kinder for the cultivation of terranic life, but they were not enough to feed the metropolis's five million people, and man does not live by vegetable matter alone. The rest of the local food came from the ocean, brought in from the fisheries to docks along the southern face of the merchants' quarter. Most of the city's homeless stayed away: its cripples, its orphans, its broken men. But not us.

"You really don't believe me?" Cat asked, scratching at her hair, rough where she'd hacked it shorter. Before the Rot reduced her, before the plague that swept the city in my second year laid her low, she was bright and fiery. She was *happy*, truly happy, content to ply the streets and scrounge and steal, as happy in her ignominy as I was in my freedom. It was what bound us together. "I swear, they're real."

Following her, I rubbed my permanently smooth chin—the follicles there had been burned out on my thirteenth birthday in accordance with Delian custom. I shook my head. "I just haven't seen them." Had Emesh even been on the list of planets Gibson had quizzed me on? I struggled to remember.

"I haven't seen this planet you say you're from," Cat pointed out, smiling in a way that hid her teeth, "but I'm sure it's there."

"That's different," I said chidingly, following her down into an open culvert that would take us under an indoor bazaar for offworld tourists and to the warehouse yard

and packing houses where the fishing trawlers brought their catch. The fishing trawlers with their allegedly inhuman crews.

"The coloni are real, Had." She squeezed my hand. "They're why the others don't come this way." She meant the others of the city's poor. The fishery warehouses were poorly guarded, it was said, but everyone was terrified of the planet's natives. The Umandh. From what I had heard, the creatures were squat, monstrous, and wholly unlike a man in shape: three-legged with flesh like stone or coral, their mouths thick with filaments like strong arms.

Rather than answer her, I gestured to the rough mortar above our heads. "Is this going to fill completely when the tide changes?"

She grinned, this time revealing her teeth. "It will a little, yeah."

"A little?" I repeated her words, tone twisting upward to turn them into a question even as the old Marlowe grin twisted my lips.

"Move your ass and you won't find out." She laughed, shoved me down the flooded culvert.

We walked on for the better part of five minutes, knee-deep in seawater. The water rose in gentle waves that brushed our thighs, and a fish swam past us, frightened by our passage. "Why don't the others come this way? If it's as easy to steal fish from this place as you say it is . . ."

"The coloni scare them!"

"Why?" I asked, genuinely perplexed. I had seen several holograph films on the coloni before: the subject-races of the Imperium, the primitive aliens who had been captured and downtrodden. We had found intelligent creatures on forty-eight worlds: some bright, some dim, others strange. Forty-eight times we had enslaved them, for none was more advanced than the discovery of bronze. The Cavaraad on Sadal Suud, the Irchtani of Judecca, the Arch-Builders of Ozymandias. There were more, many more. Some protected, others extinct, ground into the dust by the necessity of human expansion. Only the Cielcin were different. Only they were strong enough to resist.

The ancients used to complain that the stars of heaven

were too numerous to suppose that we were the only life, the only inheritors of the universe. They used to think it strange that no other races cried out into the darkness, their radio waves and noise blasting across the unending Dark. The truth we discovered when our long ships plied the oceans of night and planted flags on far shores was simple. We were the first. The Chantry took that fact to heart, declaring loudly and often that the stars were *ours*. That they belonged to the Children of Earth. They built their religion on that essential fact as much as they did on a fear of the corrupting power of technology and the pollution of the human form. We had a right to conquest, they claimed, as the ancient Spaniards had claimed when their sad ships crashed ashore.

Cat hadn't answered my question but had walked on ahead of me in silence, a sudden tightness in her person belying a nervousness that betrayed her in the shaking of her small-boned hands, in the taut line of her shoulders beneath the ripped dress she wore over her scant frame. I repeated myself. "Why do the coloni scare them?"

She looked back over her shoulder at me, brow furrowed as if I were the stupidest man she'd ever met. "They're demons, Had. Why don't they scare you?"

I had no answer to that. Only a glimmer of the curiosity and excitement that had moved me through books and holographs as a boy. "You think we can do this?"

"Steal from the coloni?" She shrugged, pausing at a fork in the culvert to get her bearings. Dimly I could hear the tread of several thousand feet in the bazaar above our heads, dull and constant thunder covering up the susurrus of human voices, bleeding down through stone as from another world. "It's not hard. They don't guard the fish." She moved down the path to the left.

I followed after her, kicking my knees up to move more precisely in the water behind her. My added height was a boon and made my progress easier even as my head threatened to scrape the ceiling. "What's the problem, then?" I kept my eyes on the swaying of her narrow hips in the gloom, on the way the damp fabric of her dress clung to her frame.

She looked back at me, eyes flashing in the gloom. "You ain't listening. They're . . ." She shook her head. "They're wrong."

The first thing I noticed was the droning. At first I thought it was the flies; such a plague of the ever-present things was common in the blighted city. Only this sound was deeper than any insect's patter, deeper than the deepest human voice. All the air resonated as if we stood packed beneath the skin of some mighty drumhead, making all the little hairs on my arms tighten and stand alert. Cat shrank back at the sound, cowering toward the spot where we'd clambered up onto the pier outside the tin-walled warehouse. For a moment I thought the sound was coming from the rockets streaking overhead. This sound had no apparent direction, though it was obviously close. Two great fishing trawlers waited at the end of the pier, bobbing on the surf, their white-painted hulls long chipped and speckled with salt and rust. I darted across the pier, dragging Cat behind me into the shadow of a stack of refrigerated crates, steel-sided and slick with condensation. I pressed my forehead to the metal, grateful for the cold and the brief feeling of cleanliness the brush of that fresh water brought to my salt-caked skin. Looking up, I found what I was looking for: a fire escape, the brown metal structure bolted to the tin siding of the warehouse. I chewed my lower lip, gauging the height, the distance.

The droning had only grown louder. Cat's jagged fingernails cut into the flesh of my arm, and I looked down at her. How clearly I remember that face. The smooth lines of cheekbone and brow beneath brown skin mottled by sun and salt; the eyes wide and alive and afraid; the small nose; the crooked teeth of her smile, which was absent then, washed over with fear. I squeezed her hand. "We'll be fine. In and out." She didn't say anything. "You can wait here."

"Alone?" Her amber eyes widened. "What if one comes out?"

"This was *your* idea!" I hissed, craning my neck to peer over the refrigerated crates and back at the ships. A pair of human douleters descended the gangway, khaki uniforms sticking to their fat frames, bald heads shining. I ducked lower, watching. One man carried a long lash coiled in his fist, the other a stun baton such as the prefects sometimes carried.

Cat averted her eyes, looked down at her bare feet, at the gray sand crusted there. "I know, I . . ." I saw her jaw tighten, resolve stealing over her, through her. She released my arm, and I kissed her forehead before vaulting up onto the crate behind me, fingertips catching on the rubber seal that kept the cold air in. I turned, reevaluating the distance to the collapsed ladder hanging above. "Hadrian, wait! Help me up!"

"I'll pull the ladder down!" I said back, struggling to keep my voice low. Turning, I leaped into the empty air, hands closing around a strut at the base of the ladder. My few months in Borosevo had boiled all the softness and extra weight from me, and merely moving in the increased gravity had strengthened me. Still, I was lucky not to be seen and luckier still that the horrible deep droning helped to mask the clangor and squeal of the ladder as it came down. I gestured for Cat to hurry up, and before long we were on the roof, the sea wind tearing over us. For a second it was like being home again, above and surrounded by the sea. The smell of salt was the same, though the pink-umber sky and the angry orange sun were wrong. The rippling, turbulent shadows of the air spun arabesques against the white gravel that covered the rooftop. We hurried to the door, opened it slow and steady onto an unlit stair, followed it down onto a catwalk of the same rickety construction as the fire escape.

The songs and operas, the holographs and poems and epics all say that the moment of revelation is a shock, a climax, an instant of crushing realization that alters the world. They are not wrong. Ask anyone who stood with me at Gododdin, who saw that murdered sun go down in fire, and they will confirm the truth of those tales. And yet we are quick to overlook the quiet revelations, the

moments that dawn not from the chaos of the world but from a hollow seed in the pit of one's stomach.

Cat and I looked down from that catwalk onto open crates packed with small, silver fishes in salt and larger ones on ice. We looked down on uniformed douleters with lashes and batons in hand and on their charges. I am not sure what I expected from the coloni, from the indigenes who had owned Emesh before it was a province of man, but it was not this.

The Umandh stood like pillars swaying in an unfelt wind, like walking turrets as tall or taller than a man, each balanced on three bowed legs that emerged radially from what I suppose one might call their waists. Where true towers had crenellations, crowns of time-eaten stone, these coralline creatures with flesh like white-pink rock had fleshy cilia wide as a man's arm and nearly three times as long. Without being told I knew that they were the source of the omnipresent droning. Despite the baking heat within the warehouse, I felt a chill wash over me, whispered, "They're singing."

Cat looked at me sidelong, but I did not linger to watch her. I only had eyes for the inhuman things below us. I had spent years, countless hours, in study of the Cielcin: their language, their customs, their histories. Suddenly they—the implacable enemy of man—seemed very human to me indeed. The Cielcin had two eyes, two arms, two legs, two sexes, however bound up one was in the other. They had a spoken language, wore clothes and armor, ate at tables, talked of honor and family. They had blood that moved through veins in shapes so like our own.

The Umandh were different, as if Red-Handed Evolution, in her caprice, had wrought the Emeshi natives as a critique of our similarity with the Pale Cielcin. Two of the creatures lifted one of the crates with their cilia, twining them round the massive carrying bars. Their trunks vibrated, changing the pitch of the droning song. For the first time, I noticed the thick collars tight about their midsections, the metal chafing their gnarled, pearlescent flesh an angry red. They put me in mind of trees about

which a wire had been tied so that as time passes and the wood grows, it cuts deeper and deeper still.

One of the humans cracked his whip in the air. "Faster, you dogs!" he shouted, rough voice recalling for me Gila and the dock workers who had robbed my unconscious body and looted Demetri's ship. The huge creatures lurched, their steady droning flexing like a plucked harp string with the effort.

"They'll be taking it to a barge to go into the city," Cat whispered, her breath hot on my neck as she leaned in close. "One of those boats. We need to hurry."

It was my turn to grab her by the arm. "Wait until they're outside again." She sucked on the inside of her cheek, torn between hunger and fear. "And give me the sack."

She glared at me. "I can do it, Had."

"I know you can, but let me." I kept watching, a frown deepening on my face. "Why are they using them as slaves? You'd think there would be easier ways."

"They can live in the water," Cat said. "They walk the seabed."

"Shepherds?" I frowned again. "For fish?" The droning shook my whole body as I snatched the plastic sack from Cat's fingers and shook the water of the culvert off it. We wouldn't need much. A sackful would last the two of us a week, longer if we could find something to brine the fish in. As I watched, one of the douleters lashed out with his baton, striking the narrow trunk of one Umandh. The creature let out a cry like an elephant's trumpeting, like a whale song, like a choked human sob. I cannot describe it. No human word was meant to capture that alien agony. It lurched, going to one of its three knees, trunk sagging, wilting like a flower in the first rush of summer heat. The huge wicker basket it carried upended, spilling fish out onto the floor of the warehouse.

The douleter swore. "The fuck's wrong with you, Seventeen?" While he spoke, a man with a heavy console twiddled a pair of dials, altering the pitch and frequency of the great droning hum that filled the air. He was translating, I realized, and an ancient, half-forgotten part of

me grinned within, forgetting the horror of the moment. I wanted nothing more than to take the box apart, to sit and talk with the man and with the creatures he was trained to speak to. Was it a language, then? Or something else entirely? I wanted to know. Had to know. Until my stomach turned over within me, groaning with the hunger that had become a part of me, of my life.

The timbre of the drone changed again as the stumbled Umandh worked to pick up its fallen fish, tentacles grasping, shuffling across the smooth concrete floor. It was strange, for most of the alien song remained unchanged, the difference something fine, something minute—counterpoint in a symphony whose notes were so indistinct I could not make out one from the next.

The man with the console spoke. "It's apologizing, Quintus."

"It had fucking *better*," the first man said, and he struck his charge again. The Umandh let out another groan, though the droning never ceased. "Look at this, fish all over the Earth-burning floor," he hissed past his teeth. "You fucking . . . beast!" He kicked the spindly creature to the ground between the second word and the last, stomped on its midsection. Though it had no face I could see, I was reminded of that day—it felt like ten thousand years ago—when I had watched our gladiator stomp on the face of a mutilated slave in the Colosso. Here it was again: the face of our species, raw and red and exposed. The douleter, Quintus, spurred the fallen Umandh in the ribs. "Stand up!" It didn't stand.

I tell myself now that I could have stopped it, that I could have stepped in, dropped off that catwalk and onto the hot-blooded overseer. It is hard remembering those brief years of powerlessness after all the power I held in the war. The gears of the Empire grind their human chaff to powder, and it is only the rarest creatures who endure. Who grow. Who rise. We sing songs, spin tales of Sir Antony Damrosch—born a serf himself—or of Lucas Skye, stories I had shared with Cat by night a hundred times. We like to imagine it is easy to rise, to stand. The be a

hero. It is not. This was not my moment. I was not a hero. Am not, or was not then.

I was only a thief.

"Stand up!" the douleter commanded, his assistant twiddling the dials to add this tone to the song. "Stand up, damn you!" The stony flesh was not stone, and it cracked under the man's boot, leaking something yellow and glutinous that filled the air instantly with a stench like the deepest pit of hell. When the Umandh didn't stand, the man swung his baton down like a lictor's sword. Once. Twice. Three times. The creature's groaning ceased, collapsed into blubbering as it bled onto the floor.

"Quintus, stop!" The other overseer let his console fall, dangling by the strap about his neck as he hurried to stop his companion. "Leave the beast alone!" Something in my guts unclenched, untangled, for there it was: the other face of humankind, Mercy. He caught Quintus by the shoulder, pulling him back before he could strike another blow. "Boss will have your bonus if you kill the *colonus*."

The thing in my guts twisted back into place. Not the other face of humanity at all. Only old greed. Cat whispered beside me, "We need to hurry."

"Not yet!" I said, resting a hand on her leg where she crouched at the railing beside me. "Soon." I gritted my teeth, watching as the second douleter—with the help of another of the coloni—helped the wounded creature back to its three splayed feet.

The droning shifted, rose in pitch, ululating, pulsing like a heartbeat. The second douleter checked the screen on his console, said, "They wish to take Seventeen to the surgeon, Quint."

"Fucking . . . ." The slavemaster shook his head. "Fine! Do it! Engin will have my ass if we lose another one." He massaged the arm that held his baton as if it pained him, as if it and not he were responsible.

Then they were gone, passing out the door and into the afternoon light. "I'll be right back." I patted Cat's leg, dropped down the nearest ladder, hit the floor next to one

of the open crates. Acting fast, I dropped two large fish—tuna, I thought—into the plastic sac, along with two snake-like creatures whose names I did not know. I proceeded in this fashion, stuffing fishes into the sack. I had enough for three days, then four. Enough to feed the little orphan boys Cat cared for when they couldn't beg bread from the chanters.

Grinning, I mounted the ladder and climbed.

CHAPTER 31

MERE HUMANITY

CID ARTHUR FOUND MORE than poverty when he escaped his father's palace. He found sickness, too. As did I. The Gray Rot had been on Emesh for some years, brought by some unscrupulous trader from offworld. The natives had no immunity, and the animalcule chewed through them like paper and festered in the street. I was palatine. I was immune, Mother Earth have mercy on me.

Have you ever stopped to think about what it would be like to sit in the belly of an epidemic, untouched by it? I felt like a ghost. My body's almost-alien biochemistry—the legacy of tens of generations and of millions of Imperials marks' worth of genetic recombination—preserved me from every weeping sore, every bout of necrosis, every bleeding cough. It sounds like a blessing. It is no blessing to watch other men die, even less to watch the ones you love waste away. When I started this account, I thought to skip this part, so painful was my loss of Cat. But I was wrong. She matters. She must matter.

She held on longer than most, longer than could have been believed for someone so small.

It stank in the storm drain where I had left her on a high ledge above the main track of tunnel. We were beneath the stock exchanges on High Street and so elevated above the level of the canals. Night had fallen, and the light of Emesh's two moons—one white, one green from the nascent terraforming projects scrambling across its surface—bled up the track of the storm drain to where the girl lay on a damp cardboard palette. Beneath the

smells of moss and rotting garbage I could make out the sweet and rotting pall of sickness, the rot from weeping sores. You could smell it on every street, in every canal, on every rooftop in that city. I had to pause at the base of the stainless steel ladder a moment before climbing up to where I'd left her, long enough to marshal my forces, to quiet my stomach and settle my nerves.

We'd been together—partners in crime—for just under two standard years. That was all ending now, I knew. Had known for weeks.

Cat shivered beneath a thin sheet that had once been the curtain of an abandoned tenement. We had spent a week in that house as it crumbled into the sea, playing as tramps might at the lives of common folk. Cat might have gotten a job if she'd wanted. I was doomed. Any employment, even the base-level jobs guaranteed by the count's Ministry of Welfare, would have required blood-typing from me. They would have wanted to screen for health risks, for congenital defects, for drug addiction and mental deficiency—anything to deny me honest work. They would have discovered who I was, and I would've been packed off to a tower cell to await the word and envoy of my father. Cat and I had been happy that week—happy and naked and clean. The patterns of purple hyacinth printed on the curtains, which in the broken window had appeared bright and beautiful, now lay upon her like funeral garlands. But she was not dead, not yet.

Nor did she notice me. Instead she mumbled in her sleep, shuddering like a candle flame. I had never known sickness in Meidua, in Devil's Rest. When I was small my grandmother's mind had been faded, but Lady Fuchsia Bellgrove-Marlowe had been nearly seven hundred years old; my father was the child of her age and the same birthing vats whence I had been decanted. Cat was eighteen, younger than I had been when I left Delos, when my life truly began. And her life was over. Proper medicine was in short supply, so I had spent what cash we had on compresses and new bandages. I had seen the broadcasts; images of beautiful newscasters on screens wrapped round street corners declared the disease proof against

antibiotic treatment. Whole chunks of the city had been cordoned off, canals dredged for corpses, bodies burned in city squares when the morgues reached capacity.

"I brought you soup," I said, placing the paper cup on the stone beside her sleeping form. The liquid was cool by then. "No carrot, I promise." I drew the curtains back, wrinkled my nose at the brown-green stains on Cat's bandages. She stirred but did not wake. "Broadcast says they think the plague's running its course, burning itself out. I heard one man say he thought the plague was a Cielcin weapon . . ." My voice trailed away down some corridor in my soul, and I sat in silence for a long time. "I wish I knew how to help you better," I said at last, picking at an innocent scab on my forearm.

Still Cat didn't answer. I laid a hand on her forehead, feeling the sickness there, a fire under her skin as if one might expect there to be magma in her, not blood. I knew she didn't have long. A day or two. A week. No more. It wasn't fair. I started undoing the bandages on one arm, revealing the chewed, diminished triceps, the way the brown skin had turned gray and blistered green and liquid yellow. I threw the ruined bandage aside, tore open a packet to apply a new medicine-soaked one. Lacking the words I needed, I hummed as I went about my work, binding up the wounds on her arm and thigh and breast.

She did not wake, and her soup remained uneaten; whatever heat it might have had bled into the tepid, unmoving air. Water in the channel below us ran at a trickle. Here and there condensation on overhead pipes dripped back to ground, its droplets marking out the nonsense seconds of nature's timeless clock. I thought—as I often still do—of Lady Fuchsia's burial and Uncle Lucian's. There would be no funeral procession for Cat, no canopic jars. No one to remove her vital organs or to burn her flesh to carbon. No true burial. No ashes for the Homeworld. No votive lantern released to the skies.

"Had?" The word was small as angstroms, the voice soft as the turning of a page.

I squeezed her hand as I had a thousand-thousand times. "Right here."

After an infinite second, she rasped, "Why . . . here?"

My brows furrowed of their own accord, and my words came unbidden: "What do you mean, why am I here?" She nodded weakly, as if in answer. "Where else would I be?" I smiled, tried to laugh. "I don't like anyone else on this whole planet."

Her laughter turned to coughing, and I cradled her head as pink sputum spattered the bandages over her ruined breast. I bit my own tongue to force back the tears, hoping—almost praying—that she would stop. She did after a moment. "Sorry . . ."

"Don't apologize," I said, shaking her gently, reaching up to move the stringy hair away from her sweat-streaked forehead. "Don't apologize. You'll be fine soon. You'll see. I'll help you."

Slowly—so slowly—she reached up, cupping a hand against my face. Cat made a shushing noise. "Don't have to stay," she murmured, lips exposing gaps where her teeth had fallen out. "Not got long . . ."

"Don't say that." I tried to smile, but I could tell the expression was only pained. "You'll get better." We both knew I was lying. She was half a corpse already, her once-fiery eyes soft with fog. One, I thought, was blinded or else had gone beyond sight. How fast she had changed. Weeks before—mere weeks before—she had been whole and hale and healthy. Who was this ghost?

"No." The echo shook its head. "Promise me . . . Promise me one thing."

"You are going to be fine!" I insisted, helping to lower her head back against the wadded scraps of cloth that passed for pillows.

Her hand closed on my leg. "Promise me you won't let them burn me." She meant in the huge pyres, I knew. The bodies piled in squares.

We believe our lives are coherent things. That they have meaning. Direction. Weft. That there is a purpose to us as there is a purpose to a player in a drama. That, I think, is the soul of religion, why so many people I have met—even my own brother—believe the world must be controlled, the universe planned and guarded. How comforting it is to

imagine that there is a reason for all things. Millions of theologians and magi, the cult-priests of a thousand dead gods, have taught this lesson. Cat taught me something else, dying in that storm drain for no reason at all. I am wiser now, but know that no matter what I said, I could not help her. I could not even die with her.

I could only watch her die.

"Tell me . . ." She lost her words for a moment, and perhaps her wakefulness, and for a moment the only sound beside the dripping and the quiet runnels of water was the ragged, wet breathing in her throat. Before I could move, could grab for water or for the rag I used to clean her face, she continued, "Tell me a story, would you? One last time."

My fingers found her weak ones, closed between them. "You shouldn't talk like that." She did not reply, turned her thin face away. She was done arguing with me. We sat in silence a long while, hand in hand. I watched the mingled moonlight that leaked into the storm drain, the color of pale jade. My other hand went to a corner of the curtains patterned with hyacinths. Her blankets. Her shroud. I remembered how we'd torn them from the wall in the heat of the moment and how Cat had stolen them when the prefects staved the doors in, answering reports that we'd been squatting there. That week, that perfect week . . . Had it only been two months ago?

Not even two.

"All right." I sucked in a rattling breath, held it so it wouldn't come out a sob. "I'll tell you a story." A year passed, it seemed, or a century before I chose a story for her as I had countless times. It was one she'd heard before and one I knew almost as well as Simeon's. "Once upon a time, on an island far from Earth, upon the margins of untrammeled space, there stood a city of poets. The Empire was young in those days, and the last of the Mericanii were broken.

"The city of poets had been built as a haven, as a place for men to hide from the Foundation War and compose their arts in peace. The city had only one law: that none may use force against another. So the city flourished and

was made beautiful by all the artists who dwelt behind its walls and prospered by their fellowship."

"Except for Kharn."

"Kharn had not chosen the city for his home but had been born to it, the child of a great poet. And as the children of great warriors are often not warriors themselves, so he was no poet. He dreamed of being a soldier, a hero like those in the epics his people composed. His people would hear none of it. 'We have no need for soldiers here, nor the burden of arms,' the poets said, 'for we are far from Earth, and the walls of the city are strong.'

"'Those who will not live by the sword will die by one,' Kharn insisted, for so the poems said. But the poets did not believe their own words, believing stories to be dead trifles under their command. Yet truth is neither opinion nor its slave, and the day came when the sky was darkened by sails. The Extrasolarians had arrived. Men like monsters in the Dark, the children of the Mericanii in their black-masted ships. And they burned the city and the poets in it."

"Except for Kharn."

Here I paused to brush the hair from Cat's face and to mop her brow. That accomplished, I continued, "Kharn fought them, and the Exalted—who are kings among the Extrasolarians—recognize only strength. So they spared him even as they cut the hearts from his people and set their bodies to crew their vile ships. They spared him. And Kharn lived among them for many years and with them pillaged other cities, other worlds."

I do not know how long I spoke or how long I held her hand. I told the whole story. How all the while Kharn Sagara harbored vengeance in his heart. How he turned the Exalted against one another, slaying their captain and taking command of their ship for himself. How he set a course for their home: the frigid Vorgossos and its dead star. I told her how he took their planet for himself, how he made himself king of that dark and frozen world. It was the story from the book Gibson had given me, *The King with Ten Thousand Eyes*. It was not a happy story, nor was it a short one.

Somewhere in the middle of it Cat's fingers went slack, then steadily colder. I did not weep or stumble in the telling. I had had enough of weeping, and she would not have liked it if I had stopped. Instead I squeezed her fragile hand, kissed it, said, "The end." Only it wasn't. Funny thing about endings—until the suns burn down and all is cold, nothing is ended. The players only change.

Though Cat's story had ended, the sun was rising, promising another day of Emesh's eternal summer. I wrapped her body in the flower-dappled curtain. Death had reduced her to skin and bones, and she was light in my arms. I didn't burn her. I carried her through back alleys and along access tunnels and the semiflooded walkways that ran along some of the side canals right at the water's level. It wasn't right that she should be gone so soon, so young. It wasn't fair. I laid her to rest in the waters, as in the tale of the Phoenician sailor, and weighed her frail body down with stones. I never found the place again, never returned to light a votive lantern and send a prayer for her soul drifting skyward to the vanished Earth.

Then, truly alone, I turned away and made my way back to the world of the sick and living.

My own story was not yet done.

CHAPTER 32

STAND CLEAR

THE PREFECTS' STUNNERS TOOK two of Rells's minions in the back, dropping them into a deep puddle at the end of the winding street while I watched, crouched in the shadow of a cluster of dishes and antennae on the roof of the corner store we had robbed together. I still clutched the purse: two hurasams, perhaps fifty kaspums, and a fistful of steel bits. A small fortune to the creature I'd become. Not enough to buy my way offworld—not nearly—but it was all mine. I had tripped the store's alarm while the bastards beat the shop girl. Hypocritical, perhaps, as I had stabbed the manager in the shoulder. I still held the knife, the blood wiped imperfectly from its scarred surface. The older woman would live, or so I hoped. I'd missed the heart and hit bone. It must have hurt.

Seven prefects, sweating in their khaki uniforms and blue windbreakers, fanned out to corner the two boys and one girl still standing. "Stand down!" called their leader, a tall man with hair almost as dark as my own, his eyes hidden behind bright lenses. He held his stunner square on Tur, the biggest of the three still on his feet. I could see the stunner's aperture glowing its icy blue, a narrow vertical stripe of light at the end of the dark weapon. "On your knees, all of you!"

"Kaller's drowning, you bastards!" cried the girl, cowering behind Tur's massive shoulders. She pointed to where one of the two stunned thieves had gone down, his face buried in the puddle. The bespectacled prefect-inspector didn't move, but his partner—a small woman with her dark

hair in a bob—moved off to pull Kaller from the mud. I didn't move. I might have been carved from stone, a gargoyle such as decorated the walls and buttresses of Devil's Rest.

The female prefect checked Kaller's pulse, his breathing. "He's alive, Gin."

The man in the glasses didn't so much as nod his head. He didn't seem to care. Behind him, the only other woman in the group of seven prefects moved off to help her counterpart, hauling the other stunned thief from the mud. The crowd waited behind holographed cordons projected from subintelligent projection drones allowed by Chantry religious law, the kind that had human operators back in the prefects' office in the palace complex above and at the heart of Borosevo. The drones looked like little more than dustbins studded with sensor and projection equipment balanced on single rubberized spheres. They were not rolling now but standing sentry about the active crime scene.

For a moment I lost track of the conversation below me, could only hear the repeating recorded feminine voice broadcast from each and every one of those cordon drones: "This is the Criminal Response Division of the Borosevo Prefects' Office. Please stand clear. A crime is underway. Please stand clear. Repeat. This is the Criminal Response Division of . . ." The words retreated beneath hearing, becoming—like the sounds of water and of aircraft—a part of the ambiance of the scene.

"We should stun them, Gin," said another of the prefects, a gangly man with thick sideburns, beanpole thin and tall as a palatine. "Bag them and take them in for conditioning."

"Bleed that!" Tur growled, spreading his arms to cover his girl companion. "Don't want you fuckers fucking with my head." He brandished the hooked length of pipe he always carried. "Stay the hell away, you Earth-bleeding sons of *whores*!"

The man with the sideburns shot Tur square in the chest, stunning him. He toppled backward, nearly crushing the poor girl beneath him. She shrieked and cowered

against the painted-glass storefront, and the other thief—
I forget his name—rushed to her side. "Stay down!" the
man with the glasses said, training his stunner on the others. "I don't want to have to shoot either of you." Then, to
his associate: "Ko, hold your fire."

"The guy was rabid, Gin," the other man said.

"I said hold your fire," the prefect-inspector snapped,
glancing back at his associate. "Where's what you took?"
he asked the thieves, looking at their empty hands; my own
tightened about the stolen purse.

The girl thrust out her chin. "Gone, lawman." She
grinned. "You bitches are too slow."

"This is the Criminal Response Division of . . ."

The prefect-inspector thumbed some switch on his
stunner, and the blue line of the emitter glowing brighter.
"On your knees. Surrender."

"So you can take us to the bonecutters and get our
heads straightened out?" the man responded. "I'm with
Tur on this. No thanks."

The prefect-inspector took a step forward. "Surrender,
and you don't have to. You can go to the Colosso; they
need more walking corpses." The thief's bronze skin went
white, and he said nothing. Beside him the girl was even
paler. Still I didn't move, hidden as I was among the antennae, hoping my one-time accomplices would not see me. I
needn't have feared. No one ever looks up.

". . . Division of the Borosevo Prefects' Office . . ."

The girl was shaking her head. "No. No, I'll take the
bonecutters." I thought of the slaves in our own Colosso in
Meidua, the mutilated men and women dressed as Cielcin
dying at the hands of professional gladiators. I could not
blame her for fearing. Even the peasants who entered the
ring voluntarily didn't usually last long against those pro-
fessionals. The Colosso was a death sentence, and a humil-
iating one, to go to one's end mutilated by the cathars:
noses slit, foreheads branded.

I did not blame Tur and the others for changing their
minds.

The prefects didn't take chances. At a signal from the
prefect-inspector, the man called Ko opened fire, dropping

the other two thieves. I thought of the bruised shop girl and the manager I had stabbed, nodded my approval. Rells's gang was a bunch of vicious thugs, worse than I ever was. What happened to them felt like justice. And when at last the criminals and prefects had left the street, after the holograph cordon and the projector drones had packed up and rolled away, it was not the public address that had repeated so many hundreds of times during the incident that stuck in my head. Instead it was what Prefect-Inspector Gin had said to Tur. *You can go to the Colosso.*

They got no shortage of need over in the Colosso. The words came back to me with a strange, lucid insistence. That old sailor, Crow—he had suggested I might fight in the games. It would be a way to earn a living, maybe to earn enough for passage offworld. It would be dangerous, but what other choice was there? At once that chance encounter took on prophetic proportions, and I leaned back against the rooftop antenna cluster.

Why hadn't I done it sooner?

CHAPTER 33

TO MAKE A MYRMIDON

THE VOMITORIUM WAS COLD compared to the outdoor swelter, and through the static field that held that temperate, thinner air in, I could see the heat ripples from the baking street outside the arena. During all my years in Borosevo I had avoided this part of town, never having looked the part. But the coin I had stolen—the theft that had put five of Rells's thugs into reeducation at the hands of the Ministry of Welfare and the cathars—had been more than sufficient to kit me out in new clothes, plain but functional. I had paid in cash. I'd even sprung for a room in a flophouse near the starport that had once thrown me out on my ear. The room was little more than a shelf, just tall enough to lie down in, but I was sleeping in a proper bed for the first time since before Cat's death.

On a whim I'd regretted almost instantly, I'd purchased a cheap razor from a dispensary in the hotel lobby, glad of the cool air and the safety and the fact that no man or woman looked at me with suspicion. My hair was a nightmare, a monstrous tangle controlled by a rubber cord that kept it pulled back behind my head. I shaved it off, every scrap, until I was bald as an egg, then cast the leavings in an incinerator just outside one of the hotel's pay toilets, glad I no longer looked like a complete fool.

Indeed, the figure I cut striding up the vomitorium beneath hanging banners painted with the jade sphinx of House Mataro was one gaunt and terrible to behold. I caught glimpses of my reflection, distended in the massive brass gongs that lined the crowded space. Thinking back,

I half looked like a Cielcin, all height and lean muscle, my skin still pale despite the past years of abuse. I lacked only the horns and massive eyes.

A line of women with casks balanced on their heads moved out of my way, and even one huge homunculus in the red uniform of the Colosso service backed away, bowing its head in something like deference. My ring hung heavy on its cord about my neck, reminding me of its presence, almost calling out to be worn again. But that would have been disastrous. I knew this plan of mine would get me off the streets of Borosevo, but I would need to be extremely careful. I could not enter as a proper gladiator. I had no references and did not want to be subjected to rigorous examination. What I did have was nearly two standard decades of combat training, to say nothing of my years on the street dealing with Rells and his gang.

So I stopped the first Colosso staff attendant I could find, a woman as bald as I. I put my hand on her arm and said as politely as I could, "Are you all taking in people for the fodder pool?" I forgot to smile for a good five seconds, then failed disastrously—if the look on the poor woman's face was any indication.

The woman's eyes went wide as she took in my appearance: the way my white shirt clung to whipcord muscle and the hard lines of my bones. After a moment she nodded.

I sat on the edge of the examination table atop a sheet of sanitary plastic, naked and unafraid. One light flickered in the corner of the low ceiling, sending shadows over the banks of quiescent medical equipment. If you are not from my Empire, then perhaps you are unfamiliar with our greatest game, its mechanics and rules, its traditions. There are gladiators: the heroes of a million operas, champions of the sporting season. Children know their names, wear their colors and their numbers, follow their efforts. Even in wartime the people treat them as heroes almost equal to our knights and soldiers. They fight one another gloriously, one-on-one or in small groups. If they

are wounded, they are escorted from the field, given over to scholiasts for treatment before they resume combat another day.

Then there is the fodder pool, the myrmidons. They come as criminals, as slaves. They come starving for the promise of a meal and the hope that they might survive a round or two. They come desperate or intoxicated or drugged. On some worlds the less scrupulous lords of the Empire kidnap their own serfs from the streets to feed to lions and chimeras and azhdarchs. The myrmidons are broken men, mad men and desperate. They are angry men and suicidal ones. I was none of these things. I was a rarer sort of fool. I was determined.

In truth, I'd expected them to take me for Colosso fodder without so much as a single page contract waving the rights of any kin for retributive legal action against the games' proprietors, namely the House Mataro of Emesh and its count, Lord Balian. But I did sign such a contract and was made to submit to a physical exam.

The Colosso medic wore the bronze collar of a slave and had the slit nostril of a criminal and a punitive tattoo on her forehead that marked her offense clearly: *DESERTER*. There were other tattoos on her arm: an armorial hawk on the inside of one wrist, a coiled snake on the other to hide what appeared to be burn scars.

"Another for the fighting pits, is it?" She eyed me from under too-long brows. One eye was clearly glass and pointed the wrong way. The other shone dark in her hard and wizened face. The word inked on her forehead wrinkled as she looked at me with that one good eye, hands on her hips. "What's your reason? Fame or fortune?" She sniffed, pushing back her grubby sleeves and pulling on sterile examination gloves kept in a bin on the counter.

I cleared my throat. "Just trying to get by."

"Trying to get by, is it?" The woman sniffed again, sidled closer. "What? Does the Ministry of Welfare not need thugs to beat the Umandh into submission anymore?"

A flash of the old aristocratic hauteur flared beneath the surface, and I bridled. "I'm not a thug."

"Oh, excuse me," the woman said, biting off each word

like dried meat. "I thought you were trying to get into the Earth-damned fighting pits. Don't tell me you're not a thug." She slapped my arm. "Budge along. No need to hide your cock, lad. No one here cares." I moved my hands away slowly, not looking the old woman in her face. "Well, you're a strong lad, and no mistake." She prodded at a scar along my ribs. "History of violence, is it?" When I didn't answer at once, she poked me again.

"Few fights," I allowed.

"No need to be so fucking terse." She glared at me, glass eye looking off at something I could not see. "You have a name?"

"Had."

"The fuck sort of name is Had?" She broke away, crossing to the counter at the opposite wall, returning with a stethoscope and a scanning probe in her crooked fingers. "Short for something?"

I held my silence a moment, watching as the woman counted my heartbeats. At last I said, "It's Hadrian."

That single black eye watched me, colored with suspicion like a sheen of oil on the sclera. "Hadrian, is it?" She frowned. "Fancy fucking name for a thug." My instinct was to deny that I was a thug for a second time, but I sensed danger here. I could not see a camera anywhere in the examination chamber, but that didn't mean we were really alone. No one is ever truly alone, not in the Sollan Empire. Not anywhere. So I only shrugged, and the doctor said, "Well, have it your own way then." She pulled the stethoscope out of her ears, left it swinging from her neck. "Name's Chand, not that you were wondering."

"Chand," I repeated, trying to place the name's provenance and the heavy gutturals in her accent. "Don't you have somatic scans?" I indicated the stethoscope. "You really need to use that?"

"Nosy for a thug, too. Scanners get confused." She held up the scanner in question, a metal cylinder long as my hand. "Better to listen, but we're still going to run the full battery. Stand up."

I complied, followed her gesture to the scale at one corner, allowed myself to be weighed and measured. She

took other measurements, too, besides my height. "Want to get armor as fits you," she said by way of explanation. Then, "You're proper fit, aren't you? I've seen actual gladiators in worse condition than you."

"What did you mean, 'full battery'?" I asked, slapping her hand away.

"I mean you're getting a proper physical, boy. I may not look it, but I've been chief medic here since before you were a dram in your daddy's balls, so how about we cut the questions, eh?"

Undeterred, I asked, "Including blood work?" Without replying, the doctor reached up and flicked my ear. I yelped.

"Thought I said to cut the questions." She glared up at me, the tattooed word on her forehead crumpling as the leather-brown skin creased. When I didn't break eye contact with her, she laughed. "You're a tough one, aren't you? That's critical, that is. A proper myrmidon. Crowd likes the ones that don't piss themselves first time they see the Sphinxes squaring off with them in full kit. You'll give a good show of it." I had no response for that. I hoped she was right. When she caught me still glaring at her, she said, "Yes, it includes blood work." She eyed me seriously. "Any reason it shouldn't? You a user?"

"User?"

"Drugs, boy." She directed me back to the examination table and began to measure my reflexes, to check the dilation of my eyes with a penlight.

This brought a renewed frown to my face. "Why's the Colosso care if its sending addicts to the fodder pool?"

"They don't," she said, tutting over another thin scar on my leg, "but if you *are* a user, they want to make sure they get that pretty nose of yours clipped. Make you more fearsome." She pulled a face, baring snarled and yellowing teeth. Glancing at my shaved head she said, "Well, at least I can say you don't have lice. Shame."

I looked down at her, unsure how to respond to this latest confounding piece of conversation. At last I opted simply to repeat her word. "Shame?"

Chand pulled a smile so wide it buried her face in

wrinkles, reducing her glass eye and her black one to mere slits. "Never known a palatine with lice before, have I?" The last two words fell flat, choked off as she backed against the wall, retreating as I rocketed to my feet. I realized mid-action that this was precisely the wrong thing to do, that it would serve only to confirm whatever suspicions the doctor had about me. I hunched my shoulders, turning half away from the slave woman, who laughed. "I take it I'm right, then? I can tell one of your lot a mile away. Have to be an idiot not to."

I didn't deny it, but I didn't answer her, either. Suddenly my brilliant plan to enter the Colosso as a fodder myrmidon struck me as incredibly foolish. Snatching up the pair of pants I'd folded on the counter, I made to dress myself.

"Where in Earth's holy name do you think you're going?" Chand asked, an unseen frown evident in the lining of that guttural voice. She hurried past me to stand against the door, one true eye trained on me as I slipped on my pants.

I could have moved her aside, struck her, thrown her down in an instant, but I waited, worked on the fastenings of my new boots. "You can't help me. This was a mistake."

"Mistake, was it?" The slave's face arranged itself into a thoughtful expression, tattooed crime distorting as she cocked an eyebrow. "Never met a palatine as didn't want his name trumpeted from the temple minarets."

"I'm not a palatine," I insisted, eyes trying to pick out the surveillance gear I felt certain was in the dingy little exam room.

"And I'm not a slave. I'm the meretrix of the Imperial harem and get my ass oiled by muscled bronze eunuchs every second Thursday." She did not move from the door. "Answer my bleeding question, boy. Ain't no one here but us."

I stopped midway through the act of buttoning my shirt. "What question? You haven't asked one."

"Why aren't you shouting your fancy-ass name from the temple minarets?" she asked, rephrasing an earlier statement. "We could be fitting you for a proper suit of armor

upstairs right now, your lordship." There was an odd note of mocking in the slave doctor's voice when she said those last two words, something that jerked me upright, forced me to my full height.

"I'm not a lord," I said again.

She snorted, put a hand against the door to stop me from leaving. As if she could. She stood tall as she was able, her wispy white hair swaying in the air from the vents. "Answer the question, *momak*."

It finally clicked. The strange accent I couldn't place. Durantine. She was of Durannos, or had been. The tattoos on her arms were Imperial Legion, plain as day. An auxiliary? I wanted to laugh, to cry. A plan had come from nowhere, sprouting full formed like Pallas Athena from my head.

"Ti si od Resganat?" I asked, speaking the heavy tongue of that distant Republic. *You are from the Republic?*

The woman's eyes went wide, and in the same language, she said, "You speak Durantine?"

"Haan," I replied, inclining my head. I had to play it carefully, though I had an advantage already in that the woman was hearing me out. Perhaps she was bent; perhaps she let myrmidons into the fodder pool unqualified all the time. I reached into the back pocket of my new trousers, fingers skating over my ring on its tangled cord. I fished out one of the hurasams I'd stolen with Rells's gang. I held it out for her to see, the Emperor's aquiline profile gleaming in the light. "Take it."

The doctor looked like she wanted to spit. "The fuck do I want with your gold, boy?" She hooked a finger under her collar and pulled, indicating her slavery and how little coin was worth.

Offering money like that was exactly what she would have expected of me, and I didn't want to disappoint. That offer made and rejected, I plowed ahead, counting on the republicans' stiff-necked assertion that class and caste meant nothing. "Fine, then. Look." I paused, sucked in a deep breath. "I don't want to be a lord."

She eyed me with her one good eye. "Why's that, then?"

I was perfectly happy to lie to her. "No one should be."

She snorted, clearly disbelieving. "The worst that happens is I get killed in the pool and the universe will be short another palatine. You were a soldier, right? An auxilium?" I indicated her tattoos. "Here's your chance to order a nobile to his death and not the other way round."

She gave me a very strange look, said, "Why would you want this?"

"I don't have anything else," I said. She looked about to argue, and I said, "I've been sleeping on the streets in this city for three years now. I don't have *anything* else." Maybe she took pity on me, or maybe it was delight at seeing a nobile in a position like my own, but I sensed she was on the edge of a decision and added, "Put me in the pool. Please."

CHAPTER 34

MEN OF GROSSER BLOOD

"YOU OVEREXTENDED ON THE thrust again, Switch!" I called, ducking a blow from Siran, one of the other myrmidons on the team with which I'd been barracked. The red-haired kid didn't listen, throwing himself at Kiri, who parried with the haft of her dummy lance and struck the young man in the back of his knee. Switch toppled into the dirt with a grunt, his short sword beneath him. Farther off, the other myrmidons laughed.

Ghen called over, "Leave him alone, Had. Let the boy figure it out. It's not our problem."

Holding up a hand for Siran to stop, I pulled off my helmet and scratched at the shadow of stubble growing back over my scalp, trying not to think about how much I surely resembled Crispin. "It will be if he goes down at the end of the week, Ghen."

"They're giving us shields!" Switch said. "I heard the techs saying. We're getting shields." The boy had opted against wearing a helmet, and his huge ears stuck out from beneath his angry red hair.

"They ain't giving us shields!" called one of the others from across the yard. "Shields is for the proper gladiators. Got to protect their investments!"

"They won't matter none if you fall on your fool face, anyhow," Siran said. She wasn't the oldest of our little platoon, but she'd been in the pits the longest, more out of a talent for keeping her head down than out of any particular skill in combat. An offworlder like me, she was paler than most of the natives, though still much darker

than myself: her skin a warm brown, hair cropped short under her brass-plated helmet. Her face was marred by the gash in her right nostril, same as Ghen's, each for some crime minor enough not to merit a tattoo on their foreheads—or else they'd paid the fine to avoid that fate.

Switch was an offworlder too: a milk-skinned, freckled catamite off one of the deep-space commercial haulers, his muscles all for show. He'd been trained to dance, to serve tea, to entertain the men and the rare woman to whom his master sent him. He wasn't a fighter, not by a long shot. By contrast, Kiri and Ghen were both native Emeshi, their skin darker than Cat's had been but from the same plebeian stock. Ghen had the thick arms and thicker neck of a day laborer and a strong, square jaw that made me think he'd spent his life chewing stones and not food. Kiri was an oddity, a plebeian woman in early middle age. Not a criminal like Ghen or Siran nor a vagrant like myself or Switch, but in the pits because she wanted to be there. "Trying to put me son through the service exams," she'd said brightly my first night in the barracks when I'd been introduced to the team by Doctor Chand. "He's so clever, Dar is."

"We're fighting as a team," Siran said, speaking to the problem at hand, running her tongue nervously over her teeth. "The boy's a liability."

"Not with a shield-belt on, I won't be!" Switch tapped his sword anxiously against one armored calf. Without warning I threw my steel helmet at the boy. I meant to strike him in the breastplate, but the unbalanced thing slipped in my hands and took him in the belly instead. Switch doubled over, wincing, spluttering for words. He dropped his sword. The others all froze, none of them sure how to respond. Kiri sucked in a breath, surprised. "The hell was that?"

"His Radiance has finally gone mad," Ghen said, laughing his deep laugh. I wanted to snarl at him, but the big convict was not our weak link—the boy was. So I ignored the nickname, crossing the open ground of the quadrangle, kicking up clouds of dust as I went. I may have been a poor thief and a poorer beggar, but I'd been

schooled for the sort of formal combats common in the Colosso. I may never have liked it, but it takes more than a couple of years to take the shine off muscle memory.

"A shield-belt wouldn't have stopped that helmet!" I shouted. "It won't stop swords or thrown spears, either." Stopping about five paces from Switch, I spoke softly, emulating Gibson more than Felix in that moment. "We aren't getting shields, Switch. Whatever you think you heard."

"I don't *think* I heard anything!" Switch said, color rising in his freckled cheeks. "I heard that—"

"Even if we were getting shields, they wouldn't help us." I kept a piece of my attention on the others in the yard, listening to the clangor of their arms as they sparred, swords and spear-shafts tangled in the geometries of combat. "Shields are for high-velocity weapons: firearms, plasma burners, lances. They won't help once you're in range of the long knives."

"You should listen to the Emperor here, whore-boy. Help him shove that stick farther up his ass." Ghen barked a laugh, made an obscene gesture with his thumb. He never took his eyes from Switch's face. "You won't last a nanosecond when the shit hits." The big man tapped the flat of his sword against his shoulder, the metal slapping the interleaved plates there.

Ever the mother, Kiri hurried forward and placed a hand on Switch's shoulder, offering mute support. She murmured something to the boy, something soft. Siran punched Ghen in the arm. "Would you shut up?"

"What?" The big man rubbed at his ruined nose, trying to hide his embarrassment. While they bickered, I took a breath to compose myself, in small part regretting throwing my helmet at Switch. Since I'd come to the coliseum two weeks earlier, I'd come to realize how hard-edged my time in the streets had made me. Those weeks, those months since Cat's death had done their damage. I recalled the robbery I'd carried out with Rells's gang—the way I'd betrayed them and the knife I'd buried in the shopkeeper's shoulder. The temperate edges that had separated me from the others in my family had been chipped away, a

mosaic defaced by the iconoclast. These past days amongst
the myrmidons had made that clear, had become an exercise in reconstruction. I held that breath a long time, glad
of the cooler night air, thick with the haunt of flies and the
hiss of ornithons. I wiped the sweat from my brow.

At last I spoke, my baritone restored to a portion of its
former polish—one of the benefits of proper food and
clean water. "Look, you must shore up your footwork."

"Oh," Ghen cackled, "you *must*. You hear that, whore-
boy? You *must*."

"Shut up, you," Kiri put in. "Leave him alone." The
woman took a couple of steps closer to the big man, a
fierceness in her that I wouldn't have challenged had I
been called to do so. A mother's fierceness. A thing I'd
not truly seen before, except the once.

"Or you'll what?" Ghen said, pressing toward Kiri so
they stood chest-to-chest, the laborer-turned-convict
staring down his wide nose at the woman below him.
"Old bitch like you?" Kiri didn't move, didn't strike the
bigger man. She didn't retreat either. She just fixed her
jaw and glared at him, her amber eyes flinty.

Siran moved forward. "The hell's gotten into you, Ghen?"

The big man broke away from Kiri, looked to his fellow criminal. "This is the worst group we've had since we
got here, Siran. Look at them!" He gestured, taking in
Switch, Kiri, myself, the others scattered in training knots
about the field. There were a few scarred veterans like
himself, like Siran, mixed into that group. Most were
criminals. Borosevo had produced a terrific multitude of
criminals since the plague, and many had found themselves in the coliseum's hypogeum, in the sweat-soaked
concrete dormitories we called home. Better that than
hang or face the full extent of the cathars' corporal punishments.

A part of me started to question the wisdom of my
scheme. When at last I'd convinced Doctor Chand to sign
off on my application, listing me only as Had of Teukros,
I imagined that I'd be put on a team replete with leathery
convicts. Men of grosser blood. I hadn't expected the desperate, the hungry of Borosevo. I hadn't expected the

concerned mother, the male prostitute, or the one-armed gondolier who, lacking for family, had come into the coliseum to go out in glory. I wondered what Father might have said about the company I kept now. I suppose he'd have been glad to find me in the Colosso at all. I suppose there is an irony there. My disgust with the fighting pits had—in a dramatic sense—started off my whole misadventure, and now there I was, dressed in the nearly medieval armor of a fodder myrmidon. *Not even a proper gladiator*, I reflected, imagining Father's contempt.

Ghen was still talking. "This is a shit show, Siran. You know it; I know it. Banks knows it; Pallino knows it." He jerked a finger at a pair of older myrmidons training opposite fresher meat. "And you can bet your ass the promoters know it too. They'll be advertising our slaughter on public broadcast." I had seen such advertisements, plastered on the huge screens that dominated street corners all over the city. He cast his eyes around at Switch and Kiri, at a few of the other myrmidons who'd peeled away from the crowd to hear what all the ruckus was.

I kept my mouth shut through all of it, watchful not of Ghen but of the gathered dozen myrmidons in their scratched and dinted plate. No two suits of armor were quite the same, though the faces the men made were identical. Each had the same drawn-lipped, wide-eyed look of a deer in sight of the hunter. One didn't have to be a Legion psychologist to see that Ghen was scaring them. None of the other veterans were in the little knot of onlookers, I noted. All were green as I.

"Maybe it won't be so bad," Switch said, no real conviction in his high voice. I was struck by how young he was. Younger than me—young enough that his beard grew in patchily on his narrow jaw. I was young myself, though how young was a mystery. Twenty-one? Twenty-two? I had only ever seen local calendars, wasn't sure of the Imperial Star Date. How many years I'd been in fugue aboard Demetri's ship I could not say.

Ghen's hairless eyebrows rose, incredulous. "Maybe it won't be so bad?" He sneered the words, repeated them more loudly. "You'll go ass-up for the enemy the minute

you get a chance." The great ox pushed forward past Siran with an outthrust arm. He seized Switch by the throat. "I don't want to get plowed, boy. Do you?"

There. That was my cue. I laughed. Not boisterously, not so much as to deliberately call attention to myself. I confess I learned the trick from my father, if not the laughter. The quiet noise caught in a brief space of silence, snagged and yanked Ghen around. The nearest trainees cleared a space around me, and I shook my head to dispel the canned laughter. The yard had gone deathly silent, and the only sounds came from the other groups training at the far side of the yard, steel clashing in the shadow of the columns.

"Did I say something funny, Your Radiance?"

I laughed again, more shortly this time, and spread my hands. "You're the only one here talking about being plowed, Ghen. If I didn't know better, I'd say you were lonely," I said. Siran barked a short laugh, and a couple of the trainees tittered nervously.

The big man shoved Switch back, letting the younger man tumble into the dust and the dry grass. Ghen rounded on me and drew his sword with a rasp. "You want to do this, boy?"

"What?" The man was so predictable he might have been reading off a playbill. "Right here? In front of everyone? Without even dinner first?" The laughter was a little stronger this time, strong enough to make Ghen angry. To make him stupid. "You're hardly for me . . ."

I saw the blow coming from parsecs away, a wild slash that would have cleaved my bare head in half had it come anywhere close to landing. I ducked the blow easily and sprang back up, catching the man by the wrist and by his hyperextended shoulder. My own sword bumped my thigh in its sheath as I torqued the bruiser's weapon down and away, overbalancing him. He staggered, and I seized the opening to draw my own blade. "Too slow, friend."

When Ghen whirled, he found me waiting, sword held in a high guard, angled before my face in the warm air between us. The whites of his eyes stood out in his dark face, as did his bared teeth. He didn't speak, just charged

me again. It was, I noticed, much like fighting an angry Crispin: all size, no sense. He fought like a man used to winning and winning quickly. My years on Emesh had hardened me, but Ghen was born there, his flesh shaped by its invisible hand. He was built like an ancient tank, square and squat and solid.

That solid mass fell on me, and for a moment I nearly folded under it. Then I slipped sideways, bringing my sword in hard to slam the man in the stomach. Ghen gasped, but his steel breastplate took the brunt of the attack. The blade was blunted anyhow: a training implement. I danced behind Ghen, planted a booted heel on his ass, and kicked him into the dust. All too easy.

Instinct would have had me speak only to Ghen at my feet, but I was moved by greater necessities, so I held my blade threateningly beside Ghen's face as he lay quiescent. Instead of addressing the beaten man—he was only a symptom—I raised my voice, calling on hundreds of hours of oratory training at Gibson's hand. "Would you divide our strength when we need it most?" Like my father, I let my eyes strafe over the crowd, fully aware of what I was doing and who I was emulating, my heart going leaden in my chest. But I was not my father. I did not want them to fear me. The faces of the recruits watching me—men and women as new to this as I was—were jaundiced with that same skin-tightened expression of fear I'd observed moments before. "People are expecting to watch us all die. You!" I pointed at a young woman with pale hair, her skin red and peeling in the sun, nearly obscuring the word *THIEF* tattooed across her forehead. "And you! And you! And me." I struck my chest with my fist in imitation of a salute. "I aim to disappoint them."

"Brave words from a first-timer!" shouted Banks, a lantern-jawed, leather-faced man near the back of the crowd. This was met with cries of agreement from the more seasoned gladiators, all but Siran, who watched me with an unreadable expression. "You don't have the gravitas for command, son!"

"Gravitas?" I smiled. "Fancy word." But I'd expected the response, had even guessed it would be Banks who'd

say it. It would have been Ghen, but embarrassment and rage had the other man seething at my feet. "I don't have any fancy words for you all," I said, "only desperate ones. I don't want to die, do you?" I paused only for the barest instant, hoping someone would respond but not counting on it. No one did. "None of us would be here if we had another choice."

"That pretty nose of yours says different!" said the pale woman with the peeling skin, voice older than I'd expected.

This surprised me, and for a moment I stood, blade still pressed against the side of Ghen's head, chewing on my tongue. "That doesn't mean I'm here by choice. We've all got our reasons. I think Kiri is the only one of us here who doesn't have to be." I waved my free hand to take in the peasant woman, her dark face lined with care. How old was she in truth? Forty standard? Fifty? So young. My own mother was nearly three hundred and appeared almost less than half this woman's age. "But even she is here for a reason. We all are."

"Shut your mouth, lad, or I'll shut it for you!" called Pallino, an old veteran with the solid build of a career soldier and a leather patch over one eye.

Planting one foot on Ghen's back, I raised both arms, sword still in hand. "You are welcome to try me, sirrah." I took my foot off of Ghen and stepped forward, a little closer to the crowd.

This pronouncement sent a surge of whispers through the gathered crowd. One small, rat-faced man leaned toward his companion and murmured, "Bastard." I ignored the whispers, narrowed my eyes at the one-eyed veteran.

The distant scream of a flier passing toward the massive shadow of the palace ziggurat filled the air. Pallino didn't step in to challenge me. When the droning of the flier had ceased, I stooped, offered Ghen my hand. In a stage whisper aimed at the man I had bested, I said, "Here, man."

Ghen rolled onto his side, caught sight of the lowered hand. He seemed to chew his thoughts, to literally work them in his teeth like he was worrying at gristle. Then he

took my hand and allowed me to help him up. "You're fucking fast, Had."

I allowed myself a shadow of the old Marlowe grin. "That's 'Your Radiance,' to you, old-timer."

I should have been a librettist, a playwright like my mother. The man's emotions played in him precisely— *precisely*—as I'd imagined, as I'd hoped. I should have been an actor. I should have been . . . something else, anything other than whatever I was or became. A soldier? A sorcerer? An explorer like Simeon the Red?

Ghen looked for a minute as if he wanted nothing more than to strike me. Then the emotion was gone, crashing back beneath the surface or behind a cloud as a wild grin stole over his coarse features. He laughed, not as I had moments ago, but loud and long and clear. Pallino's threat was forgotten, erased by that clarion instant. "Back to work, everyone!" Ghen bellowed, clapping me on the shoulder. "The kid here's right. It's those cowards in the nice armor we mean to kill, not each other!" A half-hearted cheer went up from the gathered trainees, overwhelming the quiet veterans. Ghen sauntered off, Siran peeling off with him for a spate of quiet conversation.

Groaning, I stepped forward and stooped to collect my helmet by the broad flange that guarded the neck. It was an ancient-looking thing, more than medieval, made of beaten steel and shaped in the same fashion as the helms of the Imperial legionnaires. Only where theirs had faceplates of seamless white, mine was open, the cheek guards swinging off hinges at the temples. This one wasn't forged, of course, but had been printed in the coliseum armory, the steel threaded with carbon wire—finer than the finest hair—to strengthen it. I screwed the thing onto my head, tapped Switch lightly on the leg with my sword. "Come on, we've got to sort out that footwork."

"I need practice," Switch moaned, not looking up from his boots.

"Aye," I agreed, glancing over at where Ghen and Siran were talking to three of the raw recruits. Siran had found a long spear—a dummy lance without the plasma burner housing attached—and was leaning her weight on it. Seen

from the left without the scarred ruin of her right nostril, there was something in the lines of her face, in the shape of the high cheekbones and the narrowed eyes, that made me think of royalty. She was nothing like Cat had been. Thinking of Cat darkened my mood, and I chewed my tongue, distracted. "We all need practice, Switch. That's why we're here. We've got a week."

He shook his head, red hair fanning about his face; he'd forgotten his own helmet in the barracks when we'd all kitted out to practice in the quad. "It isn't enough time, Had. It isn't."

Pressing my lips together in mute conciliation, I clapped the younger man on the shoulder and stalked away. I whirled into a low guard: knees bent, back straight. Earth and Emperor, to hold a sword in my hand again! I had not thought I'd miss it. The blood was still pounding in me, drumming as surely as the beat of some martial parade drum. Brief as it had been, my fight with Ghen had been a proper fight, not some back-alley squabble. I suppressed a grin and lied, "Of course it's enough time. We've got a week, Switch. You can do loads in a week. Here, front foot forward, and keep your back straight—that's why you're overextending. Makes you lean. See?" I showed him, performing a wild, vaudeville impression of his mistake, unbalancing myself so that I dropped to one knee, entirely too vulnerable. That accomplished, I repeated the move correctly, careful to keep my back straight. "Your go. Show me."

CHAPTER 35

PROPER MEN

I DID NOT SLEEP. Could not. I sweated instead. No rarity on that sweltering world, save that the sweat ran cold as the blood in me. I left the other contract myrmidons to their fitful dreams and wandered out into the corridor where sconces flickered in the dull cement walls, solid and close. I did not mark it as I padded into the hall, but mine was not the only bed left empty in our vaulted and pillared hall. I was not alone in my dreamlessness.

The world was different at night, and the coliseum hypogeum even more so. By day it churned with activity, with the shouting of men and the braying of beasts and monsters. Ghosts, I thought, were only the echoes at night of that which we expected to find by day, haunting our consciences.

The coliseum was built somewhat above sea level. In most coliseums, the dormitories, kennels, and dungeons of the hypogeum were literally that: underground. But Borosevo had its peculiar quirks, built as it was on a marshy atoll. Still the stone walls dripped, and here and there runnels of condensation could be seen collecting on the metal piping of overworked climate control systems and on weeping windowpanes. The arched ceiling hung so low above me that I could trail my calloused fingertips along the smooth stone, and I did. I walked a long time, heart in my throat as it had never been before. I felt as the prisoner feels on the eve of his execution, praying that the prior or his lord will pardon him—a feeling I know all too well now.

Cat's plague-shrunken form seemed always to lie at my feet or just behind my back, and I found my gaze dragged constantly downward. It didn't seem real, death. None of it did. Not the coliseum hypogeum, not the city without, not the rotten years since I'd awakened there in chaos and in fear. If you have ever awakened in the dead of night and questioned the cosmos down to the space between its atoms, you will know how I felt. In my dread and in the sickness of my heart, even the flesh of my own two hands seemed alien. I found myself thinking of the morrow's combat—my first—but I could not dwell on it, and always I would retreat to some other memory. To Mother's operas, to tales of Simeon the Red and Kharn Sagara. To Gibson's lessons, to sparring matches with Crispin. To Cat's smile and our time in that abandoned tenement. I remembered the pain of broken ribs and the night when Rells's thugs had dragged me from my cardboard hutch in the streets of Borosevo.

I stopped outside the entrance to the showers, listening. There was a faint sound of water running, droning over something scuffling, snuffling—an animal sound almost too quiet to hear. I froze then, cocked my head. The door was open, and it swung silently inward, spilling harsh white light in a wedge upon the opposite wall. Barefoot as I was, I made almost no sound as I stalked into the gray bath chamber. The shower stalls ran along the far wall, each fronted by an oily white curtain. The last one in the row was running, belching steam into the quiet air, not quite masking the animal sound I'd heard from the hall. There were no clothes upon the single metal bench, nor any other sign the place was occupied by anyone but my ghosts.

But once I was inside, the scuffling noise was clearer.

It was weeping.

"Hello?" I decided I'd best announce myself, feeling suddenly that I'd intruded too far upon something private. I cannot say what made me do it or why I did not simply leave. Perhaps it was my native curiosity, perhaps I was simply nosy, perhaps . . . perhaps I was lonely and very, very scared.

The occupant of the shower started, and I heard a dull thunk followed by a curse, a sniff. "What?" After another moment of snuffling, "Is that you, Had?"

It was Switch, of course. I moved to shut the door to the hall. Ghen was secure in the prison block on the lower levels with Siran and the other criminals, but I dreaded the thought of someone like him interrupting. Not that night, not before a combat. In a voice pressed as dried flowers, I said, "Switch? Yeah, it's me."

The young boy cleared his throat. "I . . . I couldn't sleep, you know?"

Seating myself on the low steel bench between the bank of showers and the bank of lockers, I nodded, not thinking that the younger man could not see. After a moment had passed in silence, I said, "I know. I've never done this before either. Fought in the Colosso, I mean. I had a chance once, a long time ago, but . . ." The words caught in me, and I looked down at my hands. I heard Switch suck in a breath, and I knew I'd made a mistake. The younger man was just starting to believe in me, and here I was undermining that.

"I'm going to die, Had." He said the words with a lack of emotion that shocked me. "Why did I do this? Why am I here?" Switch made a choking sound, and I was about to say something—to commiserate—when he said, "Maybe I should have renewed my contract with Master Set after all. It's better than dying. Ghen's right—I'm not a fighter. I'm just some whore."

My head between my hands, I looked up, glaring at the featureless white plastic of the shower curtain. "Ghen's an idiot, and that's exactly what he wants you to think."

"It's the only thing I'm good for!" He sounded almost defiant in his self-loathing.

"Well, you're rubbish at sword work." I tried to smile, sensing that even a bad joke was better than pity. When the younger myrmidon did not reply at once, I reached out and slapped the edge of his stall. "No one's going to die, man. And you've gotten a lot better since we started."

Switch kept his peace a long moment. "I should have stayed on. Master Set wasn't tired of me yet. I could have

done another tour, held out for better pay. I thought this was going to be better, but . . ." His conviction lagged. "But at least I wasn't going to die there."

"Hmm." I grimaced, glad Switch could not see. Switch couldn't have been more than eighteen standard. How long had he been in this Set's employ? A year? Two? Five? It was honest work, legal, which was more than could be said of my past few years of living, but the thought of what he'd been offended me. Sold into indenture by his parents and only a child . . . No child should have to live like that. Again, I did not offer him pity. I did not think he would accept it. "So . . . how'd you end up in this fix, eh?"

"In the pits?" Switch asked. I could hear him moving in the shower cell, just out of sight. "Thought I'd make a change, only none of the other ships'd hire me. I can't fly or do hydroponics or nothing. Just . . ." I imagined Ghen making an obscene gesture to fill the silence. "I figured it was this or go back to Master Set. And I'm done with him." He spat loudly, and there was a hint of fire in his words as he said, "Filthy old man. This seemed like a better idea at the time. Thought I'd learn to fight like . . ." He broke off, embarrassed.

"Like what?"

"I can't say." A dull thudding came from Switch's shower cell, and I guessed he was hitting his head on the wall. "You'll laugh."

I quirked a small, unseen smile. "Try me."

The words seemed almost squeezed out of Switch's chest. "I wanted to fight like Kasia Soulier, you know? You ever see those films? Or Prince Cyrus, maybe. I wanted to be a man, you know? A proper man. Someone who could stand up for himself."

I did laugh then and pinched the bridge of my nose. I could hear the embarrassed silence boiling off the younger man, and I said, "I know exactly what you mean. I wanted to be Simeon the Red."

"Simeon's not a fighter."

"No," I agreed, thinking of the time I'd told Cat his story that day on the canal. "But he had to be, when the time came. That's what I'm saying. It doesn't matter what

you *are*, Switch. You have to stand when the time comes, and the time is coming." I told him a bit about my mother, about her storytelling, her art. For a moment it was as if all the torment and pain the past few years had gone behind a cloud and I was lit by the rosy light of childhood. "I don't know if there's such a thing as a proper man, Switch. My father wanted me to be a priest, but like I said . . . I always wanted to be like Simeon." I grinned. "I wanted to see the universe."

It was his turn to laugh at me, by rights, but he was quiet a long time. "Guess we're both in the wrong place," Switch said, a weak humor in him.

I snorted. "I guess so. But a man's got to make a living. Money's not too bad here if you can collect."

"If we survive," the younger man corrected. "We're not really paid until the end."

"None of that," I said, perhaps too sharply. "We'll be laughing about it this time tomorrow." I broke off, glancing at the clock above the door back into the hall. There were just about two watches left of the night—five little hours. So many and too few.

"No, we won't." A tiny choking sound broke from the shower stall, part laugh and part sob. "It's hopeless."

"It's not," I snapped back, glaring intently at the shower curtain as if I might burn a hole there with my gaze. "Don't worry about hope. Hope is a cloud." It was one of the many balancing aphorisms Gibson used to maintain his scholiast's apatheia. It felt strange to say such things again. Strange, but right. Looking around that low concrete room, I felt a sudden pang for the loss of the old man. What I wouldn't give to see him again, to speak to him. But that too was not of the apatheia, and I tried to grind it away, though it would not go. "You'll do what you have to do. We all will. Hope doesn't enter into it."

"But what if we don't make it?"

"What if we do?" I countered, struck by a thought. I pulled my legs up under me and sat like a sage beneath a tree in meditation. "What if you make it through the year and earn your keep? Did you give any thought to that, or did you come in with a death wish and the hope of a few

decent meals?" He wouldn't be the first who had. His silence betrayed him. The boy had no plan, no ambition. Just a dumb, vague hope and a childish fancy—not unlike some other young man I knew. Well, he wasn't the first for that, either. A heavy sigh escaped me. "Tell you what," I said, slashing against the fear in his broken voice. "Why don't we stick together, eh? I don't have any friends here either. I could use one."

"I'd like that," the other man said. "You're the only one who hasn't mocked what I was."

I was thinking of what I'd told Cat so long ago: *I wish I had my own ship, wish I could travel.* "I don't want to stay here. I'm trying to save up for a ship, or we could at least sign onto one as hands."

"I don't know anything about that!"

"After a year you'll know how to fight!" I snapped back. "Ships need security! Guards! You just haven't thought it through! A year's a long time." I couldn't bear his hopelessness, having so recently overcome my own.

Switch twitched the curtain aside and glared up at me. He was sitting all curled up at the bottom of the stall, fully clothed, his back against one wall, red hair plastered to the sides of his face. The boy narrowed his eyes at me. "That sounds a lot like hope to me. I thought you said not to hope."

"I said hope was a cloud," I countered. "That doesn't mean there's no hope."

CHAPTER 36

TEACH THEM HOW TO WAR

THE LIFT CLATTERED AS it carried the twenty of us up into the first event of the day's Colosso, each fighter sweating and stinking in the confined space. Switch stood beside me, muttering a prayer to himself, a mantra invoking the Chantry icon of Fortitude. "Bless me with the sword of your courage, O Fortitude," he breathed, voice barely a whisper. "Grant me strength in this time of need. Bless me with the sword . . ." I shut my eyes. Courage is the first virtue of fools, the patron of those too afraid to run.

The myrmidon on Switch's other side nudged him with an elbow. "Can it, will you?"

Switch looked at the man, muttered an apology. I grimaced, adjusting the antique-style round shield I'd been given, same as everyone else's, a three-foot carbon-fiber hoplon. For all my encouragement, Switch was right about himself—it would take far more than a week to make a fighting man of him. And Ghen wasn't wrong, whatever Siran and Kiri said. The boy wouldn't last a nanosecond. I clenched my teeth, biting back a reprimand as the aged and hissing speaker system in the lift carriage let out a high screech and Pallino's rough voice rushed in over our heads. "Hold together like we rehearsed. Groups of five. Don't let the enemy surround you."

"Do we know what they're packing, boss?" asked Keddwen, a local boy who'd made it through a few fights already, distinguishable by his bleached, ropy hair. He had to shout to be heard, his voice hoarse.

Pallino called back, "Same shit we've got: swords, spears, round shields. But it's Jaffa's team, so expect the fuckers to be throwing javelins."

"We'll throw them back, then!" Siran shouted, summoning up enough raw energy that the men at her end of the carriage cheered, lifting their weapons in the grimy orange light.

Sensing Switch's nervousness, I leaned over and knocked on his round shield. "At least we have shields, right?"

The younger man grimaced, tamped down his helmet over his wild red mane. "Not funny, Had." I understood him perfectly. I'd have given my left arm for a proper Royse shield.

There came a moment before every one of my fights in the Colosso, right before we all marched out onto the sand-dusted brick of the killing floor, when all I wanted was to be somewhere else. Anywhere else. I felt it for the first time then. My bowels twisted into knots; the blood hammered against the anvil of my skull. I stared up at the steel girders that supported the arched ceiling at the top of the lift tube, counted the massive bolts that held them in place. Why was I doing this? There had to be other ways to earn passage offworld. *It's for your ship*, I told myself, imagining. I *could* leave the Empire then, leave it and never return, lose the Chantry and Father and the rest. I could travel to Judecca, meet Simeon's Irchtani, and see Athten Var. I could become a trader in the Outer Perseus. I could turn pirate. Mercenary.

But the few hurasams I'd stolen from that corner store wouldn't have bought a broom closet aboard a star cruiser, and anyway I was contracted to the coliseum for a standard year. Sixty-five combat engagements, and any one of them could be lethal. And any attempt to breach that contract, to run, would end with my feet lopped off, my nose slit, my body dragged into the Colosso and thrown at the mercy of the great beasts, fodder in the purest sense of the word. The sponsors—Count Balian Mataro not least of all—would get their value out of me one way or another.

Standing there, trying to compose myself while my

neighbor's bladder emptied down her thigh, my thoughts turned to our enemy. They would be armored and shielded—truly shielded, not merely given the old-fashioned antiques we carried. We were dressed like it was Homer's Troy we meant to attack, not five gladiators in advanced sensor armor. The whole exchange was a farce. Our blunted weapons could only dent their armor. The suits they wore would interpret the blows mathematically and inhibit their wearers in simulation of damage without ever truly causing harm. True gladiators rarely died; professional athletes such as they were too great an investment. We could only immobilize them.

"Shock and awe, Hadrian," I murmured to myself, kneading my eyes with my knuckles, running my fingers through the sharp stubble of my hair. "Blood and thunder." A groan escaped past my teeth. I missed Gibson. I missed Roban. I even missed Felix. The castellan would have known what to do, could have thought of at least a dozen ways out of whatever it was we faced. A hundred. I felt suddenly that I should have paid more attention in tactics. I hadn't learned all I needed to know. Now I never would. Felix was hundreds of light-years away, and Gibson—well, only my father and Mother Earth knew where Gibson was. I took a moment to secure my helmet, tightening the jaw strap.

The lift juddered to a halt, and almost at once the huge, heavy doors ground their way open, metal grating on stone. I swear the sound hit us before the sunlight did, the great, crashing squall of it deep and crushing as the sea. The animal sound of eighty thousand human voices screaming, shouting with drunken delight and the joyous rage of spectacle. That sound affected each man in a different way, flattening him or lifting him up.

Fear is a poison, I told myself, repeating the old words as Switch had done his prayer. *Fear is a poison*. I felt that poison like ice in my veins. Rising, I followed Ghen and the veterans out into the sickly orange sunlight, hefting the carbon fiber shield as I drew my short sword for combat. The floor of the arena stretched nearly a hundred yards long and was perhaps half as wide. We had entered into a forest

of stone pillars distributed at random throughout the arena, according the combatants cover. No two were the same, their heights and diameters variable, but all thrust from the brick floor, crowding what otherwise would have been level and open ground.

Ringing the massive expanse of the arena rose a sandstone wall twenty feet high, pierced at intervals with steel lift doors like the one from which we had emerged. A high-class energy shield shimmered above us, washing out a portion of the cheering, the bellows, and the jeers. It was there to protect the crowd from weapon fire, as it had been on the day I'd seen thirty slaves butchered on stage by the Meidua Devils. Couldn't have a stray plasma burner slicing up the wall and into some watching logothete or guild functionary.

None of that registered. The spartan battlefield was so much dead space, mere foreground for the overgrown jungle of color and movement that was the crowd distorted by the Royse field blur. And there they were, arrayed by a gate at the far end of the field: five gladiators dressed in the armor of Imperial legionnaires, the white plate ceramic painted green and gold. Each held a spear taller than he was and watched us through faceplates of solid green, unjointed and without details or eye slits. Patient as mossy stones.

"The shield's up," I said, grabbing Switch by the triceps as we all hurried onto the field.

Distantly, as if I were hearing her from the bottom of a deep well, I could make out the muddy words of the Colosso master of ceremonies, though what she said was lost in the cheering and the murky effect of the field. We had no need to hear it. We knew why we were there.

Switch leaned closer. "What did you say?"

My attention was split: half on the gladiators opposite us, five of the Borosevo Sphinxes in full kit, and the other half on the lord's box at the midpoint of one wall and on the man seated in it behind still more layers of energy shielding. Balian Mataro, Count of Emesh. I had seen him on city broadcast screens, but there he was in the flesh, seated between his lictors and his Umandh slaves. Even as

we entered, a pair of the alien creatures was helping their human douleters drag the corpse of some cephalopoidal land predator through a side gate and onto another lift, trailing green blood on the bricks. We weren't the first event after all. I made Switch hang back, waited for Kiri and Pallino to join us with a recruit I did not know.

I jerked a thumb upward, repeated, "They have the prudence shield up."

Pallino squinted up at it one-eyed. "Oh, fuck me," the veteran swore just as the first shot struck the bricks above our heads, violet plasma scorching the wall black. Off to one side, Banks was forming up his cluster of five—three spearmen and two swordsmen—all crouched low to make as much use as possible of their carbon fiber shields.

"Get down!" I screamed, throwing my arms around Pallino and Switch, dragging them down with me as a salvo seared through the air above our heads. "Will these stop lance plasma?" I asked, propping my shield up in front of me to afford my body some cover where I lay in the dust.

Pallino grunted. "Aye, but don't depend on it long."

"Then let's not take long, sirrah," I said. Kiri and the raw recruit ran forward, somehow having avoided the shots that had nearly claimed us. They kept their shields up even as they helped us all to stand. "This way!" I pointed toward one of the many pillars that rose from the arena floor, hoping to put an obstacle between us and the gladiators with their energy lances.

"It's a cull!" Pallino spat on the dirt as we took cover behind the pillar. When I just looked at him, uncomprehending, he jerked his chin to indicate our fellow myrmidons. "Thinning the herd." Switch had gone deathly silent. Pallino seized me with his free hand. "I should have killed you when I had the chance."

My mind went blank. "Me?" I spluttered. "What in Earth's name has this got to do with me?"

"They saw your little speech in the yard. Must've done." The other man released me, drew his sword again. "They're taking us down a peg."

That was an understatement. We were about to be

slaughtered. I tried to slow things down. To think things through. To breathe. "Fear is a poison," I murmured, trying to calm my fast-beating, mutinous heart. We outnumbered the gladiators four to one, but their armament outmatched ours by millennia. Already I knew the original plan would fail. If we clustered into little fighting units the way legionnaires did in ground assaults, fighting shielded, back-to-back, we would all surely perish. "We need to split them up. Try and isolate them." I peered out from behind the pillar, saw Siran and Ghen pinned down behind another massive column. There was a chance. The pillars were certainly not a default part of this coliseum's construction. They would have gotten in the way of the horse and dog races common in such places and certain forms of the combat. "Switch, stay with me. The rest of you break left; keep the pillar between you and them."

"Since when are you in charge?" asked the raw recruit, the man I didn't know.

Fate chose that moment to interfere, and a bolt of plasma fire took the man in his chest. It singed my clothes as it passed, followed by the chemical stench of molten metal and cooked human flesh. The man didn't even have a chance to scream. I wanted to scream, to cry. Something. Anything. But all I could think was, *What is the point of all this armor, then?* I gave Switch a shove with my shield, pressing him forward and away from whoever it was who'd saved me the trouble of answering the recruit's question. Above the floor of the Colosso, the master of ceremonies' high voice narrated events in rapid-fire, her words still lost through the prudence shield.

Five. They'd sent five men to kill us. Five professional toy soldiers in their fancy armor, each doubtless kill-ready, blood soaked in testosterone supplements. Five Crispins. That thought nearly brought a smile to my lips even as I half pushed, half dragged Switch around another of the columns. We needed to put space between us and the man who'd killed the recruit. Pallino and Kiri hadn't followed, had peeled off another way. Whether they'd taken my advice or just been swept away by the chaos I never knew. In memory that first day hangs as if in a

cloud, some moments outlined in brilliance, silver-edged and radiant. Others are shadowed, burned, as if those gray pillars were smoke and the clamor of the ground a distant, primal thunder.

"Split up!" I called, seeing a knot of our myrmidons crowded behind pillars. "Groups of two or three! Fan out!" I didn't stay to see if they heeded me. Someone screamed, and I thought, *Now we are eighteen.* I hoped I was right, hoped I'd not missed another death in my haste. Switch had gone nearly catatonic beside me, frozen, eyes wide with fear. I shook him. "Snap out of it!" I pushed him against the pillar with my shield. "I need you here!" The boy's eyes focused slowly, and I punched the wall beside his head with my sword hand. "I need you if we're going to get out of this!"

"Get out of this?" Switch echoed, looking round. "How?"

"I have a plan." It was only half a lie. I had an idea. A feeling.

Banks's voice cut through the din. "You two! With us!" The leather-faced veteran stood with a group of six behind the fattest pillar on the field.

I shook my head. "You need to break up, Banks! We have to outflank them!"

"What?" he shouted, brows furrowed beneath the lip of his helm. "Are you insane?"

"Are *they* fighting together?" I called back, leaning on the word for emphasis. "Do you want to line up for them, or do you want to fight back?" Just then I spotted one of the gladiators—a tall woman in the characteristic green and gold—passing between two pillars. She hadn't spotted us in the chaos, had her lance leveled in pursuit of another target. Without waiting, I dragged Switch along to the next pillar, dogging her steps.

Banks saw this and snarled, following with two of his myrmidons. They fell in behind a pillar opposite ours, leaned around to take stock. The gladiatrix stopped a moment, the bayonet end of her lance lowered as she fussed with some setting on the shaft and ejected a heat sink with a tinny ring. "I hope you know what you're doing," Banks spat.

"I'll draw her fire. You hit her from behind."

"Behind, eh?" Banks bared his teeth in a feral grin.

I felt my face flatten of expression. "Do grow up." I turned to Switch. "Stay right behind me, got it?" The boy nodded, then looked down at the sword in his hand as if it were some deadly tumor. He didn't answer, just kept looking at his sword. I cursed myself. Ghen had been right about him. For the second time I shoved Switch against the pillar. "You don't have to fight. Just stay with me." I didn't wait for him but tore off across the bricks, the sound of my armor slapping against itself drowned out by the noise of the crowd. I could only hope she wouldn't hear me.

The gladiatrix had her lance raised and pointed at some target to my left, the haft tucked into the crook of her arm, the weapon at eye level as she sighted along it. Blood pounded in my ears louder than the crowd. I slammed the flat of my blade down on the length of the lance even as she fired. Violet plasma coughed against the bricks at our feet, turning the loose silicates in the sand to molten glass and filling the air with a chemical smoke. The woman let out a surprised sound and whirled, trying to take me across the face with the butt of her lance. I smashed down with my round shield, the whole thing ringing unpleasantly as the handle jounced my hand. I grimaced but pressed forward, backing her toward Banks and his people. Switch had vanished somewhere in the madness. I ground my teeth hard, lashing out with my sword.

The weapon actually caught the gladiatrix in the leg, and I heard an artificial whine. She staggered on her next step backward, and she tried to bring her weapon to bear on me. It was too long, a bad option in close quarters. And now her suit had betrayed her, registering my strike on her leg as battle damage, protecting her own precious, well-paid flesh. She let out an angry growl through the speakers in the neck of her underlying skin-suit and dropped the lance, hands going for the long knife at her hip. Brave move, sensible. It might have worked against Switch or even Kiri. It might even have worked on me, strung out on nerves as I was.

But Banks crashed into her with one of his myrmidons, one blade crashing through her energy shield—unaffected for its human slowness—and ringing against her helm. She swore vilely as the jade suit of armor seized up, knocking her out of commission. I thought of the cephalopoidal monstrosity the slave Umandh had dragged from the field, imagined the stony, three-legged xenobites dragging this woman to a side lift to have her armor unlocked. She'd lose a bonus for this upset. The crowd let out a roar, above which the muddy, shield-flattened words of the compere narrated the whole thing.

Banks was grinning like a fool as he said, "All right, we'll use your plan."

"There's still four left!" said his nearest companion, the woman with the peeling skin. "Can we use that?" She pointed at the lance the gladiatrix still held in her seized-up fingers.

The veteran shook his head. "They're made to interface with the suit gloves. Won't fire if we try."

"We have the numbers!" I craned my neck. "Where's Switch?"

"The slut?" The woman shrugged. "No fucking clue."

I pushed past her, hurrying back the way I'd come, calling out for Switch. I silenced myself quickly, realizing our hunters were as like to hear us as anyone. I passed two of our bodies smoking on the bricks—was that the one I'd seen die earlier? Or were they both new? Were we sixteen then? Or seventeen?

"Oy, Your Radiance!" Ghen's deep voice carried above the sounds of the crowd. "Over here!" He crouched as he cut between the pillars, hiding as much of his bulk behind his carbon shield as was possible.

Back braced against one of the pillars, I waited for him to approach, Siran in tow. The two convicts fell into place beside me just as—distantly—someone screamed. The part of me that thought in Gibson's voice ticked another one off, dispassionate. *Fifteen?* Keeping my eyes out for another attack, I said, "We got one. Banks and me. I lost Switch."

"Saw him with Keddwen and Erdro just a second ago," Siran said. "He looks like he's about to piss himself."

"Heard someone already did." Ghen grinned.

I shook my head. "It wasn't Switch. He's just scared. What's the score?"

Siran shrugged. "They've got four of ours, I think?" She rubbed her ruined nose with the back of her sword hand, ducked her head to look past Ghen.

"I counted at least five," I said darkly. "We can't spend five people to one of theirs. Banks and I caught one alone. Hammer and anvil."

Ghen nodded. "I'd be fucking surprised if Pallino's not done one in already. Bastard's been working over the Sphinxes for five years now."

"Come on," I said. "Let's go."

The big myrmidon turned out to be right. We passed the locked-out body of the second gladiator sitting against one of the columns not far off, and my heart went up a little lighter, then sank when we found the bodies. One was decidedly Keddwen, the local boy with the ropey hair who called Pallino "boss." The other was not Switch but a local girl who looked too much like Cat for my comfort. *Only three left.*

We found three more of our dead before we found the other gladiators—all men—standing back-to-back-to-back in a tight legionnaire's triad. I had heard of such a thing, would see it countless times on many battlefields. The proud soldiers of the Emperor's service: white ceramic gleaming, crimson surcoats snapping about their knees, their faceless white visors impassive in the face of incredible challenge. The Cielcin, whiter still, pressing in on them from all sides. It was we who pressed here, ducking behind pillars to avoid plasma fire. One of the three men had lost his lance and held one of our swords in each hand.

The crowd above, I realized, had gone oddly quiet, holding their collective breath. I'd fouled my count somewhere in the struggle. Thirteen of us remained at a glance. There was Switch, huddled, crouched in the shadow of a pillar with Kiri. I breathed a sigh of relief. "The fuck's

everyone standing around for?" Ghen barked. "They'll drop the pillars if we don't move."

I didn't have time to ask what this meant, for Pallino shouted, "They'll have to come to us."

"That's not going to happen!" Siran snapped. I agreed with her.

A series of ratcheting clicks sounded deep in the floor below us, and with a grinding roar the concrete pillars began to sink. They would descend until they were flush with the level of the floor, leaving us exposed. I glared at Pallino, at Ghen, looking round. "We have to go now, or they'll be able to pick us off at their leisure."

"At their leisure?" Pallino repeated, scorn evident in his tone. "That's what this is, boy. That's what this all is."

"Fine," I snarled, turning to Ghen. "I'll do it. You with me?"

The big man looked down at me, brows furrowed beneath the lip of his helmet. He nodded. "We're running out of time anyway."

"Me too," Siran said. "What's the plan?"

I hefted my shield. "Leave the one with the swords for last."

"That's not much of a plan," said a nameless myrmidon who'd moved to join us.

"No," I agreed and sheathed my sword. Ordinarily one attacked the enemy himself. But for now I needed to strike his weapon. That gave me a notion, a mad one.

We didn't shout. Shouting as one charged only drew the enemy's attention. I wanted as little of that as possible. Ten paces of open space separated the knot of gladiators from our shrinking cover, plenty of time for the trained killers to fix their two lances on us. I saw the muzzles glow blue-hot, heard the whines as the weapons sucked in air to heat their plasma. One of the slow-action models, air-fed, without ammo reserves. Good. He'd have only one shot.

The weapon spat fire.

When you fight—no matter the cause—you make a choice. You choose to set aside everything else for that moment. Choose to funnel everything you are, everything

you've been, and push it through the eye of a needle. You risk everything. The plasma charge broke on my shield, heating a patch of the carbon fiber until it glowed. The second gladiator panicked, his own shot going far wide. The gladiator with the two swords turned, stunned, just in time for Kiri and Erdro to come tearing around from the right flank, emerging even as the pillars shrank to naught. Someone behind us shrieked as a plasma shot from the second gladiator caught her. I didn't turn to look.

I closed distance between the nearest gladiator and me, passing my shield from my left hand to my right, clutching the glowing disc by the rim. Then—disregarding the common sense of a thousand generations—I ground to a halt, counting the seconds until I thought the man could fire again. The lance whined as it sucked in air, and Ghen and Siran drove past. I saw the gladiator's thoughts scanning behind that faceless visor, sensed him trying to pick a target. The Royse field barrier of his shield shimmered in the distorting heat of the day, crackled with static from the dirt and grit. I threw the shield, the light carbon slicing the air like a discus in the Summerfair pentathlon. The man ignored it, some well-trained part of his mind perhaps expecting his energy shield to deflect the blow without incident. It didn't. Fast as it was, my round shield was too slow for the man's energy curtain. It struck him in the chest, jerking his arm up even as he fired again, spraying the round up against the prudence shield. He staggered.

Then Ghen was on him. And Siran. I drew my sword and cut in and past them, positioning myself so that Ghen's bulk shielded me from the second still-armed gladiator. I heard the whining of servos in the man's chest as his armor seized under Ghen's assault. Siran kicked his lance away. I lashed out with my blade, striking the second lance-wielding gladiator so hard in the arm that his suit forced him to drop the lance. His arm swayed at his side, joints frozen, the polymers of the skin-suit hardened to something like stone. Not yet giving up, he drew his belt knife, whirled to stab me. It was nothing a real opponent would have done. My blow might have severed the arm of

a man dressed as we were, but the gladiator was himself not truly injured. His attack caught me off guard, and the weapon skirted off my breastplate, leaving a deep furrow.

"Not left-handed, then?" I asked, and I stabbed the man in the thigh. His suit whined and hobbled him, but he didn't fall as a man ought, and I had to snap a neat seconde with my sword arm, elbow cracking the blade down to disarm the man before I finished him with a ringing blow to the head.

Then it was over—the final gladiator had fallen to Siran and one of the others. As with Crispin, I expected there to be some glorious instant, some swell to mark the end of battle. Nothing came. It never does. The fight ends, the needle is threaded, and all you were before comes crashing back. For a moment all I could hear was my blood still drumming in my ears; all I could feel was the weight of my armor cutting into me by its leather thongs. All I knew was the rise and fall of my chest in time with breaths labored in the thick and dripping air.

Then the prudence shield snapped out of existence, and the ecstatic triumph of the crowd swept us along, giving me my moment of crescendo. An upset. A titanic upset. I wondered how many people had expected us all to die. Only eight of us had died. Twelve stood. Amid the clamor I looked up at the count's box. Beneath the striped gold-and-jade awning, Balian Mataro stood, a great bull of a man with another slender man at his side. I could just pick out the black witch-shadow of a Chantry prior not far from him. He raised a hand, his image projected on screens beside his box—screens I had not even noticed until that moment. The crowd's tumult subsided until at last the nobile's amplified voice carried over it, rich and superlative.

"Well fought, my myrmidons, well fought!" He was clapping, and even thirty feet below him I could see the gold glittering on his fingers, on his forehead, at his throat. The metal stood out sharply against his coal-black skin. He was as ostentatious as my father was spare, a true aesthete, and his voice was like strong wine. "I can truly say none of us gathered here thought to witness so great

a surprise as this." He leaned against the blond wood rail of his box.

I looked up, for the first time noting the swarm of camera drones orbiting the field. I stooped to collect my burned shield, stumped over to where Switch was standing. We exchanged words, enough for me to know the younger man was all right. Looking round I caught sight of a look on Ghen's face. The big man was grinning, but there was something in his wide eyes other than joy. He caught me looking, nodded, and kept on smiling. Was it respect? I wasn't quite sure, but I didn't think I had anything more to fear from the big man. Kiri pushed forward to embrace me, murmured some soft congratulations. "That thing with the shield," she said as she hugged me, "was damn clever."

"I'm just glad we made it," I returned, extricating myself from her embrace. One-eyed Pallino grinned at me, and I saw he'd chipped a tooth in the fight. The one-time legionnaire pressed his fist to his chest in salute, bobbed his head. I returned the gesture with a slight bow.

The count was still speaking, addressing the crowd more than we the victors. "Such a fight we have not seen in many seasons! Many seasons. We are well pleased, and hereby award each of you a sum of fifty hurasams for your gallantry!" The cheer that went up was engineered, a palliative to wash the taste of plague from every heart and mouth.

I touched the spot on my breastplate beneath which my house's ring still hung on its cord.

Bread and circuses.

CHAPTER 37

MIGHT NEVER DIE

WE CELEBRATED IN THE city, taking our bonus
purses to one bar after another until money and darkness
ran out and the sun came up in fire. Many of my companions would remember nothing of that victorious evening,
but to me it is forever bright. I bought nothing, saving every
bit and every crumpled five-kaspum note of my share of the
bonus. I had a ship to think of. Still I did not want for drink.
None of us did. It was only that the others spent as if they
had not thought to see tomorrow. I thought of little else.

You might think it was a sad occasion, glasses raised
to Keddwen and the others we lost. But while there was
some of that, and while there would be offerings burned
before the icons of Death and Fortitude in the Chantry
the next day, we rejoiced, for we were young and strong,
alive, and assured in that moment of our immortality. We
raised a glass to our dead and several to ourselves, and
though many of us said we wished we were dead the next
day, not a one of us meant it. Headaches be damned, for
they are fleeting, and we felt we might never die.

It was the first of many such victories, and in time our
little band of myrmidons became known, celebrated by
the fans who greeted us. And so I walked upright down
streets where once I had run or cowered in fear of the
prefects and my fellow criminals. I will say no more of that
celebration—or of any other—but for a moment we had on
the road back to the White District and the hulking mass
of the coliseum. For by the wan, red light of morning we
passed a small cafe with an iron rail. The sky was dark,

bruised only slightly with day's fire, and the night wind was still cool and damp as the breath of a cave. The sight of that cafe lit something in me, rekindled a conversation I'd had earlier with Pallino and Elara, another veteran of the pits. She had not fought with us that day, being on another team, but it was well known that she and Pallino were lovers, and he had brought her with us.

"But look," I said, words slurring only slightly as we weaved, "we can't be doing this forever." I made a vague gesture with one thin hand. "Switch and I've been talking. When this contract's up, we're going to take our pay and get a loan on a starship." As I said this, I staggered against the cafe's rail, not three yards from the table where Crow had helped hide me a lifetime before.

"After only a year?" Pallino scratched his stubbly jaw, steadied by Elara hanging on his arm. "You couldn't afford a damn leaky tub on six thousand. You'd need a hell of a lot more."

I smiled thinly, staggering a bit. "That's why I'm talking to you both." I lay a hand on Pallino's shoulder. "You were a legionnaire—a thirty-year man, was it?" I undershot the number on purpose. "You must be tired of this life!"

"Twice twenty years, and you know it, lad!" Pallino groused, pulling Elara closer. She yelped, and the old myrmidon proclaimed, loud and drunkenly, "My sword was first wetted on Sulis!"

Elara swatted him. "Everyone knows, dear."

"Killed forty of the Pale for His Radiance!" Pallino said to all who'd listen. He put an arm on my shoulder. "For the Emperor, yeah? Not you, Your Hadrian-ness. Ness . . ."

I knew it wasn't the time for a conversation like this, but we were all drunk and riding high on the taste of blood and victory. "Switch and I were thinking you two might want to join us. Look. We buy the ship jointly, divvy up shares—"

"We can talk about it," Elara said, looking over her shoulder to where a mostly sober Switch helped a sick Erdro along. "If the whore boy don't bite the dust come Summerfair."

"I won't!" Switch bristled, face red as his hair, flush with wine and the courage of his survival. "I'll make you eat those words!"

"Hope so, lad!" she shot back not unkindly, ignoring Kiri's shouts to leave Switch alone. "But a year's a long time. Miracle old Pal here and I are still kicking after five and three!"

Pallino's one eye widened. "Miracle? It's no such thing, woman. It's skill!" And from there the old veteran swung into another of his too-familiar tirades about how the gladiators were no proper soldiers and no match for those who were. He beat his chest in an approximation of the Legions salute. "Cost me my good eye to stay alive, it did. That's more than those green-armored boy-fuckers can claim." He coughed a bit, stopped to sway uneasy on his feet despite the woman supporting him.

I shook my head, exasperated. I liked Pallino. The old soldier had a gruff charm and bravado in him that spoke to a certain atavistic part of me, as if he were—to use Switch's term—a proper man, back when that meant only one thing. For all that there was an honorableness in him that ran deep, and he'd kept his head in the thick of the fighting, as befit a veteran of forty years. I wondered at his age and reasoned that he must have a drop or two of patrician blood in him. He had to be older than sixty standard, perhaps halfway to seventy, and yet he moved like a man of fifty, a construct of horn and hardened leather.

"Look, Had," he said, seeming suddenly more sober. "It ain't a bad notion, but you don't know how much money it takes to get even a pissy old lighter spaceborne and staying there. Even with what the woman and I have stored away, you're not going to get anything new." He shook his head, and by the tone of his voice I knew I'd pressed far enough, so I ducked my head and followed him. I hadn't planned on buying anything new. It just needed to fly. "You ain't going to buy nothing with six kilos in specie. A decent ship's worth the price of a township, son." We went on in the droning, slurring noise that passes for quiet among the truly drunk and happy. After a few blocks Pallino seized my arm again. "Don't buy

nothing with VX-3 ion engines. Norman crap'll shake you right out of the sky." And I knew I had him, at least for now. It was a start, the first step down a road that would take me off of Emesh and into the heavens, away from this long, dark purgatory of the soul. I said no more, but Pallino's words had lit something in me. *The price of a township.* Well, I still had something worth that much, didn't I? How could I have forgotten?

So I did not press the matter but sang softly with the others from "Between the Worlds So Shining Bright." And for once—perhaps for the first time—I knew what it was to be among friends and was content.

CHAPTER 38

BLOOD LIKE WAX

I NEVER LOST A round of single combat in the Colosso, never had to kneel beside one of the professional gladiators or my fellow myrmidons to await the judgment of the crowd. Not in five engagements. Not in ten. After seven months and a particularly clever turn using sand from the coliseum floor to short out a gladiator's shield-emitters, I'd garnered quite the reputation. I'd not been made to kill anyone either. The proper gladiators were not permitted to die, and on the rare occasion that I battled one of my fellow myrmidons, I disarmed them. The commons loved the gallantry of it. Most of my fellow myrmidons lacked the proper training I had, and one-on-one duels were where I was most at home.

The risk of death only came in the group actions such as that first combat I have described. To consecrate each day of combat to Earth and Emperor, those of us not fighting in the small pools or single-combat tournaments would shed our blood in the opening melee. Call it tradition. I participated several times, scraping by sometimes by the skin of my teeth and sometimes in spectacular triumph. Once we came through without losing a single man. Another time only Switch and I remained. Kiri left the Colosso shortly after I arrived, and Banks died shortly after that, killed in single combat with the gladiator captain Jaffa when the man's spear struck a joint in his armor.

The Umandh were made to fight too. Once I watched a droning quartet of xenobites battle a pair of panthers

brought from offworld. One of the beasts fell quickly, the great cats goaded by hunger and hormone shots that drove them mad. The others—learning that the alien things were predators—panicked and tried to defend themselves, their tentacles lashing at the massive cats. They succeeded, but not before another of their number was critically wounded, leaking its noxious green blood onto the bricks. I'd never fought one of the creatures myself. They were not permitted to battle against the human myrmidons. Even without proper combat armor the creatures stood a chance of victory, and it wouldn't have done for a child of Earth to fall at the hand—or what passed for hands—of a xenobite barbarian.

The myrmidons' dining hall in the coliseum dormitories stank of sweat and vat-grown meat and smelled of home. After nearly a year in the Colosso, after fifty-seven of my contracted group engagements and nearly as many nonlethal single combats, the musty place with its shallow-arched ceiling and sputtering lamps was more a home than Devil's Rest had ever been. I was always greeted with friendly waves from Elara and the others who knew me and with whispers from the rawer recruits. The Legion troop carrier *Obdurate* had limped into port recently, discharging a few foederati contract soldiers who wanted out of the war. For them the lives of myrmidons at Colosso on a strange new world was a vacation, paradise after the rigors of real combat.

"Nearly wiped the Pale out at Wodan," one was saying as I walked past. "First Strategos Hauptmann led the sortie himself."

"Really?"

The foederatus nodded over his bottle of energy drink. "Sure. How do you think we took so many of the demons hostage?"

I stopped, listening. Cielcin hostages. The thought stirred a long-dead piece of me. Scattered words of their

language played in my ears. Grubbing as I had in the streets, I had forgotten the war. Always it had seemed so remote, so distant. The monsters had seemed painted at the fringes of the map. They snaked their way closer now, worming their way out of the Dark.

"Hostages?" It was Switch, seated at the table with the foederati. He caught sight of me and waved. "Had! You've got to hear this." He urged me over, and though I'd already eaten, I moved to sit on the bench beside him. "This is Kogan; he's a mercenary."

"Was a mercenary," Kogan said, speaking in a thick accent I didn't recognize, doubtless that of some hinterlands minority on some planet I'd never heard of. He offered me a hand. I had finally learned the commoners' gesture and shook it. "Kogan."

"Had." I glanced sidelong at Switch. "You were in the war?"

"Battle of Wodan, forty years back. Just ditched my contract with the Legions, left my company." He scratched his beard. Kogan was—like me—a good deal paler than the Emeshi, though he wore a plasma burn high on one cheek that turned the plane into a sheet of bubbled scar tissue. His thick neck crawled with tattoos partially concealed by body hair nearly so dense as his beard. "Seized one of their worldships. What's left of it, anyway. The demons scuttled it in orbit before their leader fled to warp." He raised his plastic drinking bottle. "Score one for Earth." He looked at me, speculative. "You're the one, then? This Had I keep hearing about?"

This had ceased to surprise me, though it never ceased to discomfit me. I answered it as I might have done in my father's court. "I don't know what you've heard, but I'm the only Had here that I know of."

"I hear you're quite the duelist. Seen it, too. Your fight against that gladiatrix with the red hair. What's her name?"

"Amarei," Switch said, unconsciously patting down his own red mane.

"That's the one." Kogan drained his bottle. "I hear you've got palace training. That you're some sort of nobleman."

I studied Kogan, eyes narrowing in spite of myself.

"I've been hearing that a lot." Eager to get the focus off of me, I asked, "You captured Cielcin at Wodan?"

"Only a couple hundred. Hauptmann gave them over to the LIO," Kogan said with a conspiratorial tilt of his head, referring to the Legion Intelligence Office. He leaned further in. "I was just telling your boy here that before I left my company, Commandant Alexei—that's my old boss—retained a pair of the prisoners for sport."

"Sport?" I frowned. "Never heard of anyone trying to keep Cielcin slaves."

"Guess that shit about you being a lordling's shit then." Kogan grinned. "Way I hear it, the palatines have been trading Cielcin since the war began."

One hand flitted up to press my ring to my chest through the fabric of my tunic, and I paused for the space of a breath to stop myself saying something stupid. I'd never heard of any such thing, but that didn't necessarily make M. Kogan a liar. Rather than disagree with him or say something that might have laid open any sort of truth about myself, I asked, "Which company were you with? The Cousland Drakes?" I'd heard mention of such a company attached to the *Obdurate*, their vessels stored in the massive carrier's holds. Switch had been drinking in news of the orbiting battleship as if he'd been parched all week.

Kogan actually spat on the floor, raising more than a few eyebrows from the next table of myrmidons. "The Cousland fucking Drakes? I was with the Whitehorse under Sir Alexei Karelin. Do I look like one of Arno Cousland's pillow-biters? No." He slapped the table. "I've done seventeen years of active service with Whitehorse Company. Nearly one hundred twenty years standard." He was referring to his time in and out of cryonic fugue. "Served no fewer than five Legion contracts in seven major engagements. Cousland's bitches just shoved paper around and marched in Hauptmann's fancy parades."

I stood slowly so as not to be perceived as a threat and bowed fractionally. "I didn't mean to cause offense, messer."

"Offense?" Kogan shook his head, suddenly amiable. "No, you planetbound saps can't offend me none. Just correcting your mistake."

Some days later I left sparring practice and hurried out into the hall, grateful for the climate control system that worked its best to keep the place a little cool and even more grateful for the sudden solitude. Kogan had been regaling our team at length about his exploits in the Battle of Wodan, how his foederated company had assisted the 437th and 438th Centaurine Legions—under the direction of Duke Titus Hauptmann—in destroying one of the Cielcin worldship fortresses. It might have been a good tale if the teller hadn't been a belligerent and erratic one.

I thought plaintively of a bath in the common area for the freed myrmidons. At the dinner hour it was likely to be nearly empty, and I had no combats scheduled for the next week. My mind wandered as I walked, recalling my previous bout, the one Kogan had mentioned against the gladiatrix Amarei. It had been my twenty-seventh single combat—my twenty-seventh victory—since registering with Doctor Chand and the Borosevo Colosso. It had nearly been a defeat, in truth. She was as good as any fighter I had ever seen. I'd only won because I'd started gaming the suit, not fighting like it was a proper duel. Amarei had been armored in a combat skin-suit, same as all the proper gladiators. The suit had no way to simulate damage other than to seize up, and so repeated scrapes to her arms slowed her suit's programmed response time. Underhanded, perhaps, but she wasn't the one with the weeping red lines on the inside of one arm and on her chest. She wasn't the one bleeding her life's blood into the ring.

I descended a flight of metal stairs and exited into a curving hallway, passing lines of dormitory chambers, names glowing on wall panels above palm-locks. Following the hall, I reached the place where it intersected with a tunnel that ramped up onto the street and the complex landing field, then crossed that path into the baths complex near the holding cells where the convicted myrmidons had their block. I rounded the corner at a brisk walk and nearly knocked over a tall man in black robes.

Not black. Darker.

He spluttered, falling back on a guard in a strange brown uniform with cream epaulets. "Watch where you're going, slave!" He straightened, taking in my appearance and my simple attire, pressing a perfumed cloth to his face in the rank tunnel.

Cautious, I bowed deeply, straightening my right leg out before me. "Forgive me, Your Reverence, but I am no slave."

The chanter lowered his kerchief, revealing a hooked nose wrinkled in disgust. "No, no, I suppose you're not, sirrah." There was a lisping, aristocratic drawl to the man's voice, a liquid hauteur that tightened my fists. He stood tall almost as myself. At a glance I'd thought him palatine, short for that exalted caste. But continued study revealed that he was patrician; the slight surgical treasons that were the hallmark of that lesser, artificially enhanced caste betrayed him.

No, not patrician either. My jaw tightened, and my skin began to crawl.

There was something *wrong* about the priest. Something off. In the scant light, I could see that one eye gleamed a piercing blue while the other was black as pitch. He had a head of thick blond hair, oiled and combed straight back from a square face and heavy jaw; his nose was bent, his broad shoulders hunched. The high blood that ran like fire in my veins stuck in his like wax. Half a hundred tiny imperfections evidenced themselves in his face, in his posture and carriage, more so even than in the bulk of the serfs and plebeians I had known. "Out of the way," he said.

Dutifully I stepped aside, back against the wall, and focused my attention on the quartet of guards. The uniforms were completely unfamiliar. Dark brown jackets belted at the waist, high black boots. Each bore a patch on his right forearm, an armorial white horse rampant against that brownness. Kogan's words came back to me. The Whitehorse Company. Free mercenaries. Foederati. They marched a standing fugue cylinder on a carriage between them, the heavy device buoyed several inches from the floor. It stood empty, quiescent, the running

lights dim. They'd come up from the prison section. Standing against the wall, I glanced back down the way they'd come, bit my lip.

I made a decision and cleared my throat. "Forgive me, messers. You're not with the Whitehorse Company, by chance, are you?"

The chanter's escort turned, slowed up a little. The robed man went on a little farther, then stopped as the oldest of his four guards said, "We are."

"Under Alexei Karelin?"

"Walk away, pissant," the chanter said, narrowing his eyes in that broad, unhandsome face as he glared right at me. "Right now."

"*Sir* Alexei Karelin," a younger soldier corrected, pride overriding his master's command.

"Forgive me." I bowed, not quite so formally as I had moments before, buying a moment to examine the floating fugue crèche floating in its suppression field. It was far too large for any man, a floating lozenge large enough for a cow. If Kogan had been telling the truth, I knew what had been in that crèche. Not a cow, but no human either. "Forgive me, I'd not realized the man was a knight." I paused, licked my lips. The top one was still split from where Amarei had broken it with a punch the week before. "Are you hiring?" It was an idle question, not one I truly expected to get me anywhere.

The chanter produced his kerchief from his sleeve again and pressed it to his face, those mismatched eyes suddenly hard as he moved toward me. Ah, the look of aristocratic contempt. I'd seen it so often in my own father. No—this was more like the light in Crispin's eyes, rampant and feverish. "Are you deaf, boy?" He seized me by the shirt front, slammed me against the wall. I'd had worse, so much worse, and tried not to smile at the effort. Let the man think he was in control. "I said walk away."

Pointedly I ignored the priest holding me and spoke instead to the four guards. "I speak eight languages, five of those well, and I've almost a year's Colosso fighting experience." The thought had literally occurred to me as

I spoke it, yet there it was: a way for me to leave Emesh, and soon. Switch could come with me, and Pallino and the others, if they wanted. The foederati shifted uneasily, eyeing the angry priest. Still I hoped business was business. It was the soldiers I needed to listen, not the Chantry's man.

It might have worked, but the priest slammed me back against the wall again. My head struck stone. I winced, losing focus for a second as he stepped back, wiping his hands on the front of his synthetic black robes. Still I didn't fight back. The man was a priest of the Holy Terran Chantry, anointed with the ash of the Homeworld herself. No matter my blood, it would have been death to strike him. He made a gesture to his guards. "Stun him."

"Reverence?" one of the guards asked, glancing from the priest to his superior.

"Stun him!" the priest shouted. "And leave him here!"

I don't even remember the weapon coming free of its holster, nor do I remember hitting the wall.

Something struck my face, forcing my eyes open and admitting the damned light. All I could see was brightness. For a mad instant I thought I was waking up in the accursed flophouse by the starport landing field, that I would see the red-faced old woman and her twiggy assistant, that my time on Emesh had begun again. "The hell'd you go passing out for, *momak*?" An old woman's voice, thickly accented. She slapped my face again, shone the light in my eyes. But it was only a penlight, checking my pupils for head trauma. It was only Doctor Chand. Switch stood behind her, worry evident on his face, his arms crossed, chin tucked.

"Is he all right, Doctor?"

"The priest," I said, the whole world swaying as I tried to sit up. Chand clamped her hands hard against my arms to steady me, nails biting flesh. "Ow! Let go, damn it!"

"Only if you stop trying to move." She let go of my

arms, brow furrowing, blurring her tattoo. The slave-doctor checked the scanner on the floor beside her, then pressed it to my skin. It tingled, sent a short pulse through me. "Conductivity's up. If I weren't wise on so much common sense, boy, I'd say you were stunned."

"I was stunned!" I insisted, allowing myself to rest against the rough stone at my back. "By the priest. Where is he?"

"What priest?" Switch and Chand asked at the same time.

I described him, massaging my face with my hands. My side ached, a portion above the ribs still thick-feeling and sluggish. My clothes all clung to me. I ran a hand up through my shaggy hair, which had grown back in the months since my indenture in the Colosso began. When I broke into a fit of coughing, Chand passed me a bottle of the blue-green drink they always served at the coliseum. I drank it down, grimacing at the cheaply sweetened chemical taste of it. By the time I'd finished recounting the episode, Switch had gone the color of milk—or would have, were it not for the omnipresent freckles. His fine-featured face looked drained. He sucked the inside of one cheek, arms still crossed over a chest broadened by months of fighting and strength training. I knew he was having the same thought as I, and I said, "If what that Kogan fellow says is true, I think there's a Cielcin in the prison block."

"But why?" Chand closed her medical kit, snapped her fingers up at Switch.

He didn't move, just stood there nodding, pale eyes wide as he worried at a thumbnail. "I hope you're wrong."

Before I could answer, Chand glared up at the younger myrmidon. "What's the point of all those muscles, lad, if you won't help an old woman off the floor?" Mollified, Switch helped her stand. I swear I heard her bones creaking. She sucked on her teeth, leaning on Switch's arm. "I'd say let it go, lads. Chantry ain't worth fucking with."

Still sitting with my back to the stone wall, I looked back up the hallway, following the direction the nameless chanter and his Whitehorse guards would have taken out

of the complex, back to the street and the Red Canal.
"Any idea who he was?"

"You said he was a hunchback?" Switch asked.

"Eh?" Chand looked up at Switch; next to her the boy
looked half a giant, she was so small. She patted the boy's
arm absently. "Patrician blighter, was he? Face that makes
you want to step on it?"

Unbidden I thought of Severn, old Prior Eusebia's
aide. The knife-faced chanter had possessed much the
same air of cruel dignity, and I had no difficulty imagining that Eusebia herself must have sneered thusly in her
youth. Perhaps they learned that at Vesperad, in seminary. "Golden hair, two-colored eyes." I pointed at my
own eyes, waggling my fingers.

Chand hissed air through her teeth. "That's the grand
prior's bastard. He's in all the time with the count's party."

"The grand prior's . . . bastard?" I frowned. That
didn't make any sense. Palatines didn't have bastards—
not often, at any rate—and the grand prior was certainly
palatine. It simply wasn't done. The High College vetted
every palatine couple's request for a child, ensured that
the parents' extravagantly altered genetics did not result
in a stillbirth or in just such a monster as this. That was
how the Emperor kept the control of his nobiles: by con-
trolling their genetic destiny through their children, by
ensuring that any palatine seeking an heir would have to
kneel and scrape before the throne. I thought of the myriad failings of the priest's flesh: the hunched shoulders,
the crooked nose, the swollen brow and mismatched eyes.
Mutations caused by the untended flowering of his palatine genetic inheritance, the excess chromosomes soured
in his blood. We have a word for what he was. "He's an
intus?"

"Don't let him hear you say that," Chand said sharply.
"Gilliam Vas sits on the Count's council. He'd have you
pilloried before you could bow an apology."

"No, he couldn't," I snapped. "You don't get pilloried
for slander. The Indexed punishment is no more than
twenty lashes." No more than fifteen, in truth—I had to

consult a copy of the Index. There was a time when I knew the formal punishment for every sin, crime, and disobedience in the Chantry canon. Father had insisted. That was long ago. I have forgotten much that once I knew. "And it's not slander if it's true." The soreness from the stunner charge was ebbing, turning into a pain more akin to hate, thick and ulcerous. Groaning, I tried to stand but gave up with a shake of my head. I had to push Switch and the doctor away. "Just stay here a minute," I murmured, shutting my eyes. A moment later, I asked, "Is it true?"

"About Chanter Vas?" Chand spat, grunted something in Durantine that I didn't quite catch. "Reckon so. I mean, you saw the man. Something's clearly crossed in his nucleotides."

We humans have always ascribed moral virtue to beauty, we palatines most of all. I wonder now if such mockery and abuse shaped Gilliam in spirit to match his mutation or if his petulant cruelty was native-born. I can almost, *almost* pity him now, but the stunner ache and aching pride made such emotion impossible for me at the time.

I wasn't listening to her; my attention had gone back to the hall, the one leading down to the prison section. Sweating as I was from the stunner bolt, I wanted that bath, but now the place was likely to be crowded with the other myrmidons, and I was still enough the palatine to seek solitude for such things. My old curiosity had me in its talons, and something of it must have bled onto my face, for Switch said, "Had, don't."

"Don't what?" I looked up at him and Chand, trying to sound innocent.

"Leave it be," Switch said, prising himself free of Chand to stand over me. "Kogan's full of shit."

I didn't answer him but sat in silence, legs thrown out across the hall. Dimly I thought I heard the sound of sandals scuffing on the rough floor, but when I looked up there was no one. Unbidden I thought of Gibson, whom I had not thought of for months. Kogan's story. The chanter. The foederated companies. The Legion carrier in orbit

around Emesh. Rumor, truth, or total fiction: each datum was a piece of colored glass, a mosaic's tessera. Gibson would have had me step back and try to discern the complete picture. I was not a scholiast, but still I glimpsed what was going on.

"There's a Cielcin in the coliseum dungeon."

CHAPTER 39

A KINGDOM FOR
A HORSE

"THESE OLD ANDUNIAN MODELS will outlast
the sun," Gila said, wringing her hands in a servile fashion that clashed with my memory of her from my first days
in Borosevo, when her workers had tossed me out after
salvaging the *Eurynasir.* She had no memory of me, Earth
be praised, though in her defense, I was no longer barefoot, no longer a recent-thaw, scuffed and cryoburned. I
wore my best, which while not especially fine still set me
far enough apart from the urchin I had been. She was as
ugly as I remembered, her balding head scabbed and covered in uneven patches of black-and-gray hair, her
squashed face purpled by a wine stain across her nose and
one cheek. She was as plebeian as they came, her jumpsuit
soiled, the green patches of the Mataro County service
peeling from its shoulders.

I, on the other hand, pretended I held some vague
higher status. Despite what I'd said, I was not there to buy
that day but to get a sense for what sort of ships one could
find in salvage. The *Eurynasir* was long gone, and I stood
beside the squat crew boss on the cargo ramp of a Blowfish-
class Andunian light freighter. She was an ugly bird, fat-
bellied and cast of pitted adamant. Flat-nosed and
inelegant, she had all the qualities of a brick.

"You know, I'd heard that about these old beasts," I
said, running a hand along one of the huge pistons that
raised and lowered the ramp.

Switch was nodding, arms crossed. "How much will
she carry?"

"Payload?" Gila asked, rubbing her chins as she checked something on her terminal. "Just under three hundred tons. She's a good old-fashioned workhorse."

I bit my lip, stumped up the ramp to stand on the cusp of the echoing hold. It was all square lines, ugly as the outside and just as plain. Rings of rust glowered like eyes from a floor scraped clean as could be, and the whole thing stank of use and age. "How old is she?"

Gila swore. "Mother's bones, man, that's a question." She broke off, narrowing her eyes at a pair of her subordinates as they hurried by on the tarmac outside. "Andun shipyards ain't made shit in four centuries, easy. Ilium put them out of business, and Monmara."

"Fucking Normans," Switch said, sounding disgusted.

It must have been some manner of joke—a sailor's meme, perhaps—for Gila spat, "Fucking Normans. Build cheap, build fast, but only Empire's built to last." She said this like it was some kind of slogan, but I didn't know it. Switch was nodding, and the two of them went on in this vein for a moment. I was glad I'd brought the other myrmidon, though it had taken some convincing.

What's the point? he'd said. *We've still got months left!* I was even considering renewing my commission with the Colosso—another six thousand hurasams wouldn't hurt, after all. But I had a powerful need for more information. I had to do *something*. Now that I had a plan, I couldn't just waste time loitering about the coliseum. I needed action, needed to do whatever I could to move a step closer to escape. Though the threat of them had faded in time, I still feared the Inquisition, still woke up sweating in terror of whatever punishment might befall my mother if her role in my escape were ever discovered.

I fingered my family's ring through the front of my shirt as if it were a talisman that might keep them away, not a lodestone to call them down upon me. I turned a thought in my fingers, one that had been growing for months. The same thought that had brought me back to these criminals and this chop shop on the edge of Borosevo. My secret weapon, if I played it right.

"These things are ancient!" Switch exclaimed, shaking

me from my reverie. "I'd come out grayer than my grandfather if I rode in one of these!" He knocked on the acrylic
lid of a fugue crèche. I couldn't guess what the boy was
seeing, but Switch had spent his entire life aboard starships,
and between his nights of entertaining he'd acquired a fair
bit of practical knowledge—so much that he had the mak-
ings of a fair spacer, whatever he thought of himself. He
and Gila argued about the crèches for a long while, and I
made a show of wandering around the hold, examining the
place up and down before returning to the entry ramp.

I looked out over the tarmac where I'd once broken a
man's arm to the low line of hangars opposite. There was
the one where the *Eurynasir* had been all those years ago.
As I watched, one of the hangar doors rolled upward,
rattling in accompaniment to the shouts of the work crew.
And there it was.

It was a ship, but it was as unlike the Andunian lighter
in which I stood as my grandmother the vicereine was
unlike the plebeian woman at my back. For a moment my
hands ached for want of my pencils to capture the image
of her in the orange sunlight, her crimson hull—dinted
and scorched—turned the color of wine. She was no yacht,
not gaudy and rare, but beautiful in the way that a sword,
well made and unadorned, is beautiful. She was vaguely
deltoid in shape, like an arrowhead or one of the mantas I
have seen in the aerial rivers of the Mandari stations with
viewports of mirrored alumglass. She had no wings, for
her whole body was one large one, lifted not by fusion
burners but by Royse repulsors silent as space itself.

"Hadrian!"

"I'm sorry?" I turned around and was almost surprised
to find that I was not alone. "Did you say something?"

Gila opened her slash of a mouth, but Switch spoke
first. "Do you want to see the rest of the ship?"

"What?" I glanced at the other vessel across the way.
"I . . . What about that one?"

The crew boss frowned. "The Uhran? That ain't hardly
a cargo hauler."

I waved her away and hurried across the yard toward
it, only half listening as the crew boss rattled off a list of

specifications: payload, acceleration, maximum warp.
"How much?" She said a figure. I almost swore; it was
nearly twice the price of the Andunian, which was still
several times more than the paltry six thousand hurasams
Switch and I each had been promised as chattel myrmidons. In a pained voice I asked, "And what's the price in
Imperial marks?"

"That *was* the mark price," Gila said, shrugging. "The
county won't take specie unless you're willing to pay in
full up front." My heart sank: 3.2 million Imperial marks.
Even with Pallino and Elara, we couldn't hope to put so
much as a down payment on the ship—either ship—much
less pay for the whole thing. I might have despaired—
would have but for one little thing.

I crossed my arms, tucking my chin as I looked up at
the red sweep of the Uhran lighter. I had badly misjudged
the price of a starship. Father had always talked of such
purchases with a cool detachment bordering on disinterest. But I still had my secret weapon. Nervous, I eyed
Switch. I hadn't mentioned it to him, and I wasn't sure
how he would react.

"I don't suppose you'd take a loan from the Rothsbank?" I said without much hope. "Or set up a payment
plan with a Mandari account?" I had neither and no way
of getting either, but it was all part of the dance. Switch
was watching me, arms crossed. Was I losing him? Surely
I was. There was no way we were going to come up with
3.2 million marks—not by year's end, not by the end of
the decade. Not in a hundred standard years.

"That is the normal way of doing business," Gila said,
moving to stand beside me as I admired the Uhran lighter.
"Only had one man—a Lothrian—pay in hard coin in all
my years working for the county. Damnedest thing." She
was shaking her head. Behind her Switch was slashing at his
throat, silently asking me to cut it short. It made sense. This
was always meant to be just an exploratory visit to confirm
my suspicions.

As a young man I'd witnessed my father and the house
staff bargaining with the Consortium, with other Mandari
trading houses, with others of the Imperial houses'

palatine. I knew how business was done. What's more, I had been a beggar, and I knew the intonations and the mannerisms of the desperate as intimately as I knew the languages of the Commonwealth and of Jadd. I'd misstepped in my obvious appreciation of the Uhran starcraft. I ought to have continued my mask of disinterest. "That's still rather more than my associate and I are willing to pay." Unwilling, but not incapable. Switch's face went studiously blank. I imagined the conversation we were bound to have later.

We don't have any money, Had! Not any! Did you forget?

"What about trade?" I asked, fingering the fine chain about my throat.

Gila took half a step back, looking up at me. "Excuse me?"

I hesitated a moment, glancing up at the rafters of the hangar and searching for cameras. I did not see any, but this impound shop belonged to House Mataro and the Empire. Just because I couldn't see them did not mean they weren't there. But then, perhaps there were no cameras. These were, after all, the very criminals who had left me for dead in some back alley. *You should be up and up, you know?* Cat's words turned over inside my chest, and my fingers tightened around my family's ring. *Way you talk, you belong in a castle.* Well, I had belonged once. I looked at Switch for a moment, and I felt a smile touch my lips, thin and ghostly as hope. But hope didn't enter into it. "I have the title for twenty-six thousand hectares of land on Delos, held in my own name under the seal of the prefecture government and the sector vicereine. It's worth more than either of these." It was worth both, worth more than that.

For a moment Gila's eyes widened in surprise. Surprise, I hoped, and greed. Her commission would be handsome, I guessed. Then that dream died, smothered by the narrowing of her eyes. "You're not serious."

This was the critical moment. You see, there was a chance that Gila had seen my ring years ago. I drew it out, held it before her slitted eyes. They widened, dark and muddy as a dried-up puddle. There was fear there, but no

rage. No recognition. Switch said nothing, but over Gila's shoulder I saw his eyebrows shoot up. His eyes darkened to something terrible even as Gila's widened in surprise. For the first time in a long time, the crooked smile stole across my face. I put Switch's reaction aside a moment and focused on the woman before me.

"This real?" Gila asked, reaching out to touch it.

I jerked my hand back, summoning a piece of Crispin's ire. "Don't touch it!" I nearly slapped her hand away, as would have been only proper. My uncle Lucian, dead before his time, used to carry an antique riding crop for just such occasions. I'd hated the man, but a piece of him moved me. After a beat had passed, I said, "Can a trade be made? Would you be willing to hold the ship until such time as my business in Borosevo is complete?" She made to speak, but I raised one finger. "Before we proceed, be honest: is this even a transaction you're authorized to make? Or shall I fetch the logothete pluripotentis?" At home, use of a pluripotentis incurred a fee that was levied not from the buyer but from the merchanter's commission. It was meant to prevent or at least curtail predatory practices on the part of the salesman and was a privilege reserved only for palatine and patrician customers.

Gila bowed with surprising grace. "I'd not realized sire was palatine." She stayed bowed. "My apologies." The crew boss paused for a sour moment, then glumly said, "The county might trade offworld holdings, but as your lordship says, that's not for me to handle."

I nodded. "That's all I need for now. You can hold it for me?"

"It's still being repaired," she said, wringing her stubby hands. "It isn't for resale. Not yet."

"Capital!" I said, speaking as if the issue were decided. "It's good land—been in my family for generations." My gaze flicked to Switch. His expression was inscrutable. "Father left it to me when my brother inherited, you understand." I did not so much as look at Gila as I spoke, knowing my father would not have.

Even if Father had frozen my assets on the occasion of my disappearance, the ring would still register my

ownership of them. He hadn't had an opportunity to change that. The ring carried the authority and weight of my house and name. If I used it to promise something, House Marlowe was legally bound to deliver on that promise. Because of this, the merchanter would not delay *me* and *my* departure, for it is the privilege of palatines to be trusted in such transactions even as it is our duty to uphold the pledges we make under the sign of such a ring—pledges enforced by the very Inquisition I hoped to avoid.

But Father would doubtless contest the trade. I didn't doubt he'd already reclaimed my land holdings following my disappearance. I hoped he had—that would rob Emesh of any gain in this situation. What's more, I could be on my ship and on my way out of the Empire before Gila or the Emeshi pluripotentis realized what I'd done to them, before the news of the sale even reached Delos and home. The Chantry would come and discover that the dock workers had not only abetted my escape but had decanted the missing lord Marlowe in the first place. In a single stroke I would buy myself a ship with land I had no right to sell and revenge myself upon the very people who had thrown me into the street and robbed me of Gibson's letter.

As revenges go, it would have been perfect, had it ever played out.

CHAPTER 40

A MONOPOLY ON SUFFERING

"YOU COULD HAVE SAID something!" Switch hissed when we left the lot. The sun hung near its zenith, and the daylight beat on me like a rain of fists. I drew out my stolen dark glasses and pushed them up my nose, tucking my shoulders as I hurried along the canal, eager to be home. I had a lot to think about, but Switch granted me no time to think. The younger man seized me by the shoulder and turned me around. "Why didn't you tell me?"

"Tell you what, Switch?" I demanded. I wasn't playing stupid. I knew what he meant. I just didn't know how to say it. "Tell you what?"

His cheeks flushed nearly red as his hair, pointed jaw working as if he were trying to crush a pebble between his molars. "I get wanting to play the merchanter, but you could have told me!" He twisted the fabric of my shirt in his fist, then repeated more softly, "You could have told me you were one of *them*."

He said that last in barely more than a whisper. Almost on reflex I pulled myself up to my full height, angling my chin so that I looked down at him. I'd not registered it until that moment, but I was much taller than he. Had I grown so used to being surrounded by plebeians that I was now blind to their smallness? I am not tall—not by the standards of the court—but I felt myself a colossus then, and clung to my palatine height like the emblem that it was.

But Switch was not cowed, not the scared boy he'd been a year ago. He jabbed me in the ribs, eyes wide.

"You're supposed to be my friend, Had." I can still hear the reproach there, see the way he bared his less-than-white teeth. "You're supposed to tell me these things."

Something twisted in me, a fraction of the old nobile's rage brought on by bargaining with the dockyard foreman. "Tell you what? About this?" I drew the ring out and held it up for Switch's inspection, the silver transmuted to bronze by the bloody sun. "What did you want me to say?"

The younger man worked his jaw again, struggling for words that would not come. He looked away, up at the looming wall of the White District fifty feet above our heads. A series of cable cars bobbed overhead, carrying people from the richer part of the city down into Belows. I felt I should say something. Anything. Everything. About my father, Crispin, Kyra. About Gibson and what had been done to him. About my mother and what I feared might be done to her. About the Chantry and what I was sure they'd do to me.

In the end I told him none of these things.

Instead I said, "It . . . didn't seem important." The words sounded dismissive to my ears, shadows cast by these higher concerns. They were small things, and I was made smaller by saying them. "It doesn't matter."

"Didn't seem important?" Switch still hadn't let me go. He shook me. "Didn't seem important?" His voice shot up, drawing stares from a passing courier and a young couple in matching sarongs. "Why are you even in the Colosso? You don't need the fucking money!"

My jaw clamped shut, and I placed a conciliatory hand on Switch's arm. "It's not that simple, Switch—"

"Of course it is!" he hissed, pulling so that I bowed at the waist. "You're one of *them*. Don't tell me it doesn't *matter*." I saw something move just beneath his face, a shadow coloring it. The memory of what he'd been came to the front of my awareness, and recalling the houris in the vicereine's harem and the way Crispin and my mother used them, I shuddered. What had Switch's experiences of the palatines been like? Thinking of Kyra, of how she had frozen in my arms, I froze in turn. "Is this a

game to you?" he demanded. "Slumming it with the rest of us?"

"No!" I snapped. "Damn it! No. Don't be absurd!" *Absurd.* It was not a plebeian word. Switch's face twisted at it, or perhaps at my clipped Delian accent—recognizing it now as a token of what I was.

"Ghen was right about you, Your Radiance," he sneered, and he shoved me back.

"It's not like that!" It was all I could do not to scream at him. A couple of people were staring openly now, so I hissed, "I wouldn't use this unless I had no other choice. The minute I do it'll be nothing but trouble until I leave the Empire! Do you understand?"

Switch was practically snarling. "What'd you do? Beat one of your father's concubines when you couldn't get it up?" That touched a nerve, lighting on my grandfather's murder at the hands of one of his concubines.

"I never touched one. I never would. I don't know what you went through, Switch, but it wasn't at my hand. Do you think we're all monsters, is that it? I am the same man I was two days ago. The same man who saved your ass in the coliseum a hundred times over. The same man."

"You're not," Switch said. "You're one of them, and you lied about it."

"I couldn't tell the truth!" I spat. "I can't. It's too dangerous."

"It didn't look dangerous when you were waving that ring around!"

I did not have the patience to discuss the finer points of financial transactions between planetary houses. "They would have *had* to give me the ship because of who I am. They would have *trusted* the ship to me."

"Because of who you are," Switch sneered.

"I was trying to steal from them, to put one over on my father and these Mataro people," I growled, gesturing to the grimy street and the tin-roofed houses and storefronts around us. "You think I want to be here? You think I wanted this? Do you really think I'd be here if I had another choice?" It was the worst thing I could have said.

"What's so wrong with us?" Switch countered, barely

keeping his voice at a growl. "This is what life's like, Your Radiance. Real life. You don't know!"

"I don't know? Really? Me?" I countered, but choked on my explanations. I could feel the blood pounding in my head. My lips were pulled back in a rictus more snarl than smile. "You're not the only person who ever suffered! Three years I ran around this city sleeping in gutters. I've been beaten, stabbed, nearly raped. I survived the damned Rot. I buried my . . ." My what? My lover? My friend? "I lost people in this city. Just because some perfumed merchanter buggered you up and down the spaceways doesn't give you a monopoly on suffering!" From the way Switch's face went white, I knew that *this* was truly the worst thing I could have said. I felt all my explanations, justifications, and pride rush out of me. I could handle my pain; I shouldn't need it to make a point, even a fair one. I folded like a jewel box closing, shoulders caving in. How I wish I could say that it was my father's voice speaking from my mouth. How I wish I could say it was Crispin's, my mother's, Uncle Lucian's . . . but it was only my own.

I didn't see the blow coming until it landed square against the side of my chin. It snapped my head back, and I almost lost my footing, staggering back against the wall of a bakery. Someone gasped, and as my vision adjusted I saw two young men in the silver livery of some ship or other fiddling to get their terminals out to record. I spat. Was there red in it? Or was that only the indecent sunlight? For a moment I was made especially conscious of the way my clothes stuck to me in the damp and smoking air. I did not respond at first, just straightened my brown shirt. Switch was glaring at me, the color slowly rising into his face. He held his fists at his sides, but they remained clenched. The scholiasts tell us that the flow of time is absolute, but standing there with half the street looking on, I felt the seconds dripping by like eons.

"I'm sorry," I said at last. Weakly. However I had suffered—and I had suffered—it didn't give me a monopoly on suffering. I thought of that night Rells's gang had dragged me from my hovel, of the many times I'd been

stunned and beaten by the city prefects. We were not so different, Switch and I, whatever our breeding. And here I was, accusing him of exactly my failure. "I'm sorry. I just can't talk about it."

"Why not?" Switch glowered at me.

I rubbed my mouth with the back of my hand. "That was a good hit." I looked at my arm. There *was* red in the sputum. "I deserved that."

"Why won't you talk to me?" Switch moved a step closer, blocking the sailors recording on their terminals from view as they circled like the masked crows in a Eudoran dumb show. He practically whispered, "Did you kill someone?"

I shook my head, glaring past him at the onlookers, the vacuous fools with naught in their lives but to peck at the lives of others. I sucked air past my teeth and shook my head again. The first was a denial, the second a refusal to say more. Switch spat—not quite at my feet, but near enough as made no difference. My jaw ached, and I wondered with some detachment if I'd lose a tooth. One felt loose. It would grow back. I am palatine. They always grow back.

I cleared my throat. "Switch, I . . . I can't. I'm sorry, I . . ."

He raised a hand. "Save it."

Then he turned and went away. I watched him go, lowering myself slowly until I sat with my back against the wall of the shop, just like the beggar I had been.

CHAPTER 41

FRIENDS

SWITCH WASN'T SPEAKING TO me. It had been two days, and he hadn't said a word, not even at practice. I couldn't blame him. To his credit, he had not betrayed my secret to Pallino or any of the others that I knew of, for even in the depths of his displeasure he was loyal, the sort of friend everyone wishes for but no man deserves. A cloud hung over me. I had lost my only true ally and with him my momentum. It was like losing Gibson's letter all over again, but worse because I had done it to myself and my friend.

Three myrmidons—newcomers all—stood opposite me with blunted short swords. They wore printed steel armor and looked like medieval impersonations of Imperial legionnaires in their knee-length red tunics, their scratched plate painted pale ivory, flaking in places. The first rushed me, eyes wide. I sidestepped him easily, kicked him to the ground as he passed. The second came in then, blade held high. I caught the blow against my vambrace and rang the girl's helmet like a bell. She tumbled away. The third fared a little better. I parried a blow with a neat twist of my wrist and lunged. He managed to outdistance my riposte, but I caught his wrist when he followed through and yanked him forward, laying the edge of my blunted sword against his throat.

"Yield!" he said, voice surprisingly high.

I shoved him away, face turned up in disgust. "Is this it?" I demanded, looking round. "Is this all?" I held my arms akimbo, laying myself wide open. A black humor

was on me, an anger difficult to dismiss. I glowered at the three of them, two sprawling in the dust of the training yard. "You three won't last five minutes in your first bout." I flapped my arms. "You have a distinct advantage, you know?"

The girl had her feet under her, and she advanced, more cautious this time. I kept my arms wide, willing her to make her move. She slashed at my head. I didn't parry. I leaned. The blade whistled by my ear, and I twisted away from a second blow. She was so slow. It wasn't her fault. She was only human. She fell again in due course, cursing in the dust. I rotated, taking in the other two myrmidons-to-be. I flew at one, batting his sword from his hand, turning just as the other tried to catch me from behind. I seized him by the cuirass just under the arm and hurled him away from me.

"None of you seems to get it," I sneered, taking a few lurching steps toward the one who had yielded. He staggered back, jerking his sword up to guard. Laughing, I turned aside. "There are three of you! In Earth's name! You're meant to work as a team!" I turned on my heel, letting them surround me in the light of the lamps. Above us, the sky hung dark and pondering, the two moons like mismatched eyes half-closed in shadow. "We *always* outnumber the proper gladiators. It's our only advantage!"

"That and our winning personalities." Pallino's voice cut the night like a whip. "Back off, Had." The old legionnaire glowered at me with his one dark eye, white hair standing on end in the thick breeze. He helped the girl to her feet. "You three go clean up. You've got time before your first bout. We'll get you straight before the time comes for knife work." He watched them go, and I spied Elara and Siran hanging back in the shadow of the pillars that ringed the training yard like actors waiting in the wings. When the trainees were gone, Pallino rounded on me. "What in nuclear hell's gotten into you, boy?" I stood, momentarily dumb, my sword in slackened fingers. "Those firsters don't need you beating the piss out of them. Damn it, you're supposed to be training them!" I expected him to hit me. I wanted him to hit me. I wanted him to try.

"They won't last a round," I said finally, my words as measured and controlled as I could make them.

"I seem to recall a certain red-haired boy Ghen used to say the same about."

That stopped me. I cast my eyes around at the nearly empty yard, then down at my hands. They'd toughened in the years since Delos, thickened. They almost looked like Crispin's hands. I swallowed and let the rage ebb until I could see again.

"Don't talk to me about Switch," I growled, guarding my shattered pride as I sheathed the practice sword at my hip.

The two women were advancing as I spoke, and Elara's eyebrows arched. "Lover's quarrel?" I glared at her but said nothing. "The boy's been downright sulky the past few days. Should have realized you'd be at the bottom of it." Though silent, Siran was smirking at me in a way I did not like. "What'd you do?"

"What do you mean, what did I do?" I twitched my chin up, an unconscious gesture of defiance. "He's the one who has a problem."

"You're the one's gone all backed up with rage, though," Elara said, clapping a hand on Pallino's shoulder. "Says guilty to me."

I held a finger up to respond, opened my mouth. The words wouldn't come, though, so I shut my mouth again. The finger remained, a broken metronome. "Did he put you up to this?"

"Up to what?" Pallino crossed his arms.

"This . . ." What was the word? "This!" I waved my hands in a broad sweep, then tugged my helmet loose, hair streaked across my high forehead. There was something in their eyes. Pity? Suspicion? No. "We went to look into buying a starship. Visited one of the repo docks down in Belows."

Pallino sighed through his nose, derision made plain. Siran cocked her head. "What were you looking at ships for?"

Pushing her short fall of hair back from her squarish face, Elara cut in, "Had here and his pretty friend been planning to jump offworld fast they can once their term's up."

The prisoner-myrmidon looked affronted. "Why didn't you say anything?"

I blinked. I hadn't wanted to tell Siran—or Ghen, or any of the prisoners, for that matter—for the simple reason that they wouldn't be allowed to come. They were not here by choice, and only a writ of pardon from the count's office could have unchained them. "I . . ." I looked again from one face to the next, trying to decipher that strange tightness of expression wound up in the three of them. I sighed. "I'm sorry. I didn't want you feeling left out."

"So you left me out?" Siran smiled wryly, and I could feel that I'd lost the exchange already. And yet she didn't seem hurt. That was one relief, at least.

At once the scuffed toe of my boot was very interesting, and I studied it with a concentration Tor Gibson would have praised. "I'm sorry. Switch and I . . . We'd been keeping it private. Didn't want everyone just jumping in, you know?"

"Only person I can think you'd not want is Ghen, and he can't go anyhow. Same as me." Siran was smiling openly now, and in the lamplight her slit nostril almost vanished.

I conceded that point with as much grace as was left to me.

"The hell were you looking at ships for?" Pallino interjected. "Thought I told you you don't have the money and not to fuck with it."

"Technically you told me we'd talk about it when the year was up."

The older man swore, glancing from Elara to Siran like he couldn't believe I'd said that. "Twice twenty years on the Emperor's coin and this is what I get? Lip?"

"Had's been off since that priest stunned his ass," Elara put in, drawing an icy glare from me.

Pallino's blue eye widened. "What's this, now?" He looked round at his paramour, reaching up to adjust his rough leather eye patch.

The last thing I wanted was to relate that particular tale right now. But I sighed, recounting in brief the incident with Gilliam the intus and his foederati compatriots.

Much as I hated to admit it, I was glad of the reprieve, the momentary distraction from Switch and the damage I'd done. Despite what you may think reading this account, I do not enjoy reliving my mistakes, and that one still stung.

"The hunchbacked one?" Pallino frowned. "That's the prior's by-blow, ain't it?"

"It is," I agreed somewhat darkly.

"You think they've really got one of the Pale squirreled away down there?" He looked at Siran, who was after all a prisoner herself, free only here in the training yard. Siran only shrugged. I shifted my helmet from one hand to the other, unsure what to say. I had about half a dozen notions of how I could break into the coliseum's gaol to see if there was any truth to what the mercenary Kogan had told Switch and me what seemed like months ago. Looking back, I suppose it was that brush with the outer Dark that pushed me back to Gila's repo shop, that had driven me to unlock a piece of my palatine identity, if only for a moment.

"Maybe," I replied.

"It's not important now anyway, Pal," Elara said, putting a hand on the older man's shoulder. Eyes on me, she asked, "You going to be all right there, Had?"

"I wasn't entirely honest with him," I said. "With Switch, I mean." I was certainly not about to be entirely honest with these three either. Let them think I'd tried to swindle him on our deal. I did not mind being thought a cheat. I had been called far worse. What I planned to do to Gila's crew and the Mataro County should have been proof enough of that.

"Is that all?" Pallino shrugged his shoulders, leaning against the nearest of the squat pillars. "Black Earth, boy, I thought it was something more serious, the way these two were going on . . ." He waved a hand at Siran and Elara, who bridled. "Look, we've got knife work to do here, like you was saying to those poor sods. Get your shit together, Had. I don't want you pulling any of this berserker nonsense in a real fight. You're not a fucking Maeskolos. You can't fight three at once, and thems won't be trainees you're tussling." I wasn't entirely sure how to

respond to that, but I didn't have to. Pallino wasn't done. "We may be your friends, boy, but if you throw yourself into a mess next time we're on the floor, I'm not jumping in after you." He drew a line across his throat to emphasize his point.

Ashamed, I bowed my head in understanding.

"We're just worried about you, lad," Elara said, putting a conciliatory hand on my shoulder.

I shrugged her off and made for the door. They were right, but I didn't have to say it.

"This isn't a game, boy! Not for us!" Pallino called after me. "Oy, we're talking at you!"

It was too much. There comes a time past each of our mistakes when we must decide to stop adding to the weight of our errors. It comes before we are willing to carry that weight but after we take it on ourselves. I set my jaw as I turned to glare back at them. My mistake with Switch did not wash out the necessities of my condition. I needed that ship. I would have done anything to get it.

Siran cut in, a voice of reason. "Can't you just talk to Switch? He's been downright unreasonable . . ."

"Then maybe *you* should talk to him," I countered, glad of the simple riposte.

It was only after they left me alone as I deserved that I realized what the strange expression was that I had caught flickering candle-like on their weathered faces. It *wasn't* dislike or suspicion or even pity. It was concern. They feared for me. Not in the life-and-limb way Cat had done, nor out of white-knuckled fear of my father. They cared because they chose to, and they did so with a gruff but quiet indelicacy that propped me up in my despair and whispered that this was what it was to have a family. A ragged and blustering one, beyond a doubt, but I'd not have traded them for my natural one, not for all the ships in the sky.

And yet . . . and yet I was leaving them. Was trying to leave them, at least. I had been trying since before I'd met

them, since I met the sailor, Crow, that day in the cafe. Kogan's tale still spun in my ears, his words catching in me as Crow's had, like sparks in tinder. I was remembering the boy I'd been not so long ago. Hadrian Marlowe. I wanted knowledge, knowledge like Simeon the Red had. That was where I had first erred, wasn't it? In the forgotten Latin, to err was to wander or stray, not to make a mistake. I had staggered from my father's vision of my life and—like the sinner in the old prayer—fallen from the narrow way into some unfortunate hell. I had wandered, but I was not lost. I had my way out. More than that, I had friends who cared enough to irritate me and hurt because of me. And I was close—I suspected—to one of the Cielcin. There was knowledge of the most special kind. Something even ancient Simeon had not seen or spoken to.

That was something else entirely.

CHAPTER 42

SPEAK LIKE A CHILD

THE CROWD APPLAUDED WHEN we survived. My chest was heaving. The creature's blood clung to my face, ran into my eyes, cobalt and stinking of copper. I still had one spear in my hands, forgotten, and the other three were lodged deep in the dying creature's back. I never knew its name—some pelagic beast dredged up from the seas of distant Pacifica. In truth it reminded me of the Umandh, all tentacles and teeth. In death it deflated like a balloon, the thousand tiny hearts that kept its blood pressurized and its body rigid pumping that same blood into the morning air.

Ghen was cheering, pounding Switch on the back. Even Siran looked pleased, smiling as she stared up into the sky. I spat, sending a gobbet of phlegm mixed with the alien's blood onto the sand. It tasted like burnt metal, like acid and smoke. I stank of the same, drenched as I was in it. Mine had been the blow that had finally cleaved a rent in the chitinous plates of the beast's hide and opened a major blood vessel.

In the box above us, the count was standing, clapping as he had on each of the rare occasions he'd been in attendance. His husband, Lord Luthor Shin-Mataro, a plutocrat from an old Mandari family, stood beside him, a slim figure in silver-green. "Well fought, well fought!" The count leaned against the parapet, speaking directly to us myrmidons. In the shadows behind him, a pair of Umandh waved a series of paper fans to cool the count and his man, as well as the two children and the collected

advisors and counselors who had that day been invited to the royal box. A useless gesture, as the box was doubtless climate-controlled within its nested shield curtains. The count launched into another rote demonstration of our skill and gallantry, this time without the reservations he usually made for loss of life and glorious sacrifice.

None of us had died.

None of us had died.

"You are all exemplars of your craft." He cast an object down from his box, a leather pouch that struck the bricks with the clang and jangle of gold. "A gift." I was closest, so I approached to take the bag.

In the moment before I spoke, my eyes found the count's, and he bowed his head, inclining it in the slightest deference, which from so great a lord as he was a measure of high respect. By all accounts, Count Balian Mataro was a man of classic passions. He enjoyed hunting—though there were no forests on Emesh—and fighting—though no subject would give him a fair contest. Yet whenever his rigid schedule allowed, he witnessed a fight in his coliseum or a race in his circus. Whenever impressed, he doled out bonuses. The others—or those free to leave the coliseum complex—would take the money into Borosevo and spend it on whores and drugs and entertainments of all description. It was my third time receiving such a dispensation. The gold from the previous two remained in my private locker, secured with my few personal possessions, namely my house ring and the new journal I had purchased. It was a luxurious thing: fine white paper and black leather with silver clasps. I missed my drawing, you see.

This time, Pallino was not here to say the words, and so I went to one knee in the dust, a pain reporting in my sliced thigh, and said, "We thank you, Your Excellency, for your generosity. Truly we are not worthy of such honors." It was a pittance, really, less than a fraction of what I had once swindled from Lena Balem—and lost in epic fashion. I chafed to grovel like that and chafe more at remembering it. A knee so unaccustomed to bend as mine does not bend easily. Yet they were just meaningless

words, expected of my station and the context in which we found ourselves.

But, when in Rome . . .

Though it was in part a prison, the coliseum complex in Borosevo was not like the dungeons of the bastille on Vesperad or the Emperor's prison planet on Mars. It held its secrets in slack fingers, and time and imprudence jostled them. Rumor was that the priest, Chanter Gilliam Vas—sometimes in the company of a blindfolded cathar, sometimes not—had been seen in the coliseum warrens many times since the *Obdurate*'s arrival and the influx of foederati and legionnaire dropouts to our ranks. The word was that they were keeping something in the solitary confinement ward of the underground prisons amongst the madmen and the murderers who died in Colosso in the most spectacular of ways. Some said it was an Exalted, one of the demoniacs who ply the Dark between the stars, as in the tale of Kharn Sagara. I heard various descriptions: it had two heads, or else six arms, all jôinted steel and exposed bone. Still others said it was a traitorous lord, some maniac who'd turned against mankind and the light of Mother Earth in favor of the Cielcin. They said he broke bread and meat with them and supped on the bones of human children.

They have said the same of me.

Many times I'd pointed out the obvious theory, the one we'd heard from Kogan: that the count had purchased a captured Cielcin from the foederati who'd sailed to Emesh aboard the *Obdurate*. That theory had caught in the minds of the myrmidons and the gladiators both.

Sweating from a round of exercises in the yard, we all marched back into the musty cool of the coliseum hypogeum. Switch was ahead, laughing with one of the younger recruits. His once-slim form had filled out in the months of our indenture. He looked a proper fighter. Siran made some passing remark to me before she and Ghen—along

with five more of our number—were marched back to their cells in the prison block. I waved farewell, returning Siran's jest with a wry remark of my own.

"Now what?" Switch's recruit friend asked. "Food?"

Surprising him and most of us, Switch wrapped an arm around the recruit's waist. "We need to get you clean first!" The recruit elbowed him in the ribs, and Switch bent over, groaning. Pallino and the others all laughed at his expense, and I smiled.

"You two can go wash yourselves, then," Pallino said, passing his helmet off to one of the others with a knowing look. He always seemed to have a mock attendant at hand, a squire of sorts. The grizzled veteran adjusted the strap of his leather eyepiece and said, "Food for us, then. And none of that shit they serve upstairs. I'm cooking." That evinced a small cheer, for Pallino was as fine a cook as any I'd ever met, in his plebeian way. It always surprised people, learning that of the leathery old man. I watched him go, smiling at the others, but I didn't move, for a notion had struck me.

One of the others jostled me, and I came to, looking round. "What's that?"

Erdro, who had been with us since the beginning, repeated his question. "You coming?"

"I . . ." I looked away, down the hall at Switch and his recruit's retreating backs. "No, no. You go on without me."

Erdro frowned. "You'll lose mass if you don't eat, man."

"Yeah, yeah." I waved him off. He wasn't wrong, but the loss of a single meal would hardly devastate me.

One of the girls grinned. "He's going to go bathe with Switch."

"You wish!" I shot back, grinning crookedly. This hit too near the mark, for she blushed. "No, I'll catch up to you. Might take some of our bonus for that last win into town, get something that's not vat-grown." Unbidden, I felt a pang of longing for the sea markets and the bazaars of Meidua, for the old Nipponese man and his fish rolls. I missed the taste of game brought in from our forest and from the valley of the Redtine. Real food, honest and true, was a thing enjoyed only by the wealthy, who could

afford it, and the destitute, who were so close to it that no one could take it away.

"All right then, Had." Pallino sketched a salute—his polite farewell—and drew the others off and away. Over his shoulder he called, "Practice tomorrow at eighth watch." I returned the salute with Imperial precision, as if the man were a tribune or legate of the corps. He didn't see it, but he didn't have to. They were gone.

I couldn't have asked for a more perfect time. The convict-myrmidons would be frog-marched through their short shower cycle and returned to their block in time for the evening meal. I knew they weren't locked into cells after the fashion of a palatine's dungeon or a Chantry bastille but simply confined to a dormitory under lock and key.

That key was held by one of two guards in a duty station at the end of the hall where weeks before Gilliam Vas had ordered me stunned by his foederati. Constantly bored, the two gaolers lounged behind their desk, wearing tired expressions and khaki uniforms with the Mataro sphinx embroidered on their sleeves. I passed them, walking with purpose up a narrow side ramp and into one of the stainless steel–paneled service corridors that led to the kitchens. If I was right, the food trolleys would be along with their variously flavored protein pastes and watery vegetables at any moment, pushed in a train by several of the coliseum staff, plainclothes men who had drawn the short straw that day and so were made to make the long and tedious circuit of the prison block.

I mussed up my hair, changing the lie of it, and on a whim adopted an impression of the chanter's hunched shoulders, thrusting my head a little forward on my neck to disguise the face of Had of Teukros just a little. You would be surprised how much a little change deflects even those men who account themselves astute. Once I fooled an Imperial auctor with little more than an accent and a pair of colored lenses to hide my violet eyes.

"You there!" A thickset plebeian man in a white-striped chef's costume poked his head out of a side door, framed with steam from a huge pot simmering on a heating

element and glowering in a way that showed off his pronounced underbite. "Boy, come here!"

"Messer?" I frowned, effecting a Durantine accent, Chand's face and tones coming so readily to mind.

All in all, this disguise would not have fooled an Imperial auctor—it might not have fooled an astute child. But the man wasn't quite as bright as are most children, and so he swore, "Bloody offworld shit-lickers. You! Yes, you! Are you deaf, boy? Come here." He pointed, gesturing violently with a spoon. Committed momentarily to my scheme, I stumped in after him, helped him to hoist the steaming pot into a cradle atop one of the rolling trolleys I'd come to find. Behind him, farther into the kitchens, a team of cooks worked under the big, ugly man to finish the meal. I was early, so I spent the next few minutes taking the man's orders in silence, all the while maintaining the hunchback as best I could.

After perhaps ten minutes, a round-faced local woman poked her head in from the back hall. "Protein's thawed out, Stromos."

The monstrous chef with the underbite practically snarled at the woman. "Not ready here."

"They're prisoners, man. You're not cooking for the count."

"More's the pity," the man grumbled. But in short order the food—finished or otherwise—was packed into heated pans and marched into the hall. To himself, Stromos said, "No one appreciates food anymore." My heart went out to him.

I grabbed the sleeve of an attendant as he was leaving the kitchen with a cart of some noodle dish in brown sauce. "I'll take it."

The man eyed me, confused. "Really?"

I smiled. "Yeah, you look dead tired, and I got a girl in there. You know?"

"One with the slits?" He picked at his nose, indicating the mutilation. "Why?" He made the question sound one of genuine confusion, as if he couldn't imagine anyone wanting one of the felons for any reason whatever.

"Look at me!" I shrugged my sloped shoulders, sinking into the character of the hunchbacked plebeian, and grinned. "And I don't really have to look at her face, you hear?" I grinned, more a snarl than anything, and the other man laughed and clapped me on the shoulder.

A part of me danced inside when I made it over the threshold, following the line of food workers down a narrow hallway lit by roundels high on the left. Mirrored panels on the ceiling concealed cameras and recording equipment. Whether or not anyone was watching was another question. The dancing part within me turned over, slowing as I contemplated my next step. I'd been guessing that this would work for months. I wanted only to see it, to know it was really here. If Kogan's story was true—and I put the odds strongly in the one-time mercenary's favor—I only wanted a glimpse.

Gibson had taken me to one of the teaching rooms in the old library at Devil's Rest, called up a holograph from the archive's memory. The Cielcin had appeared from nowhere, materializing in the center of that blank, dark space, glittering in robes of silken fabric, sable and sapphire and white, every inch covered in circular glyphs that overlapped, interwove, linked. If you have never seen them, the Cielcin have crests that rise like crowns above and back from their foreheads at a steep angle, the same white as their milk-pale flesh. They terminate just past the spots where their ear holes are, and the back halves of their skulls grow a thick, white hair.

"They have six fingers!" I remember saying, reaching up to transfix the holograph with a finger. "Why do they look like us?"

Gibson had frowned at me then, given me a long and careful look. "What makes you say that?"

Evolution or some power stranger still had fashioned them like us. If one looked past the cosmetic differences, past the epoccipital crown of thorns, past the fangs and the massive, unfeeling eyes, one might almost see it. A kinship between us in the lines of arm and finger, in the face and the general body plan and in the hair that grew

upon both our heads. They were far more human than the strange and sub-thinking Umandh to my young mind. That closeness, that similarity somehow made them more alien to me, more exotic and appealing because already there was a road to understanding them. The Umandh I did not understand, so like were they to corals and trees. The Cielcin I longed to understand.

I have since paid for that mistake.

We set up the trays in a low-ceilinged common space, folded metal side tables from the stainless carts, and locked the wheels in place—couldn't these border-world primitives spring for suppression floats? Then we stepped back, our preparations complete, and withdrew into a side room at the behest of our guards, who said it was for our own protection. That was lucky—the last thing I needed was Ghen running his mouth just then. After a moment I faked a need for the bathroom, then faked an inability to understand the douleters when they objected. I gesticulated and shouted in Durantine, reciting stock phrases in the guttural language of that client republic. "Where is the library? Hello, my name is . . . Yes, yes. Where is the library?" And so on. The bastards didn't understand a word. Needless to say, they let me go. For a moment I feared my guard would follow me, but when I none-too-gently jostled him into the door frame, he tottered back, clutching his bruised forehead and gasping. *"Izvinit,"* I said, still speaking Durantine. "You are . . . all right? *Straf?"*

The man swore, pushed me away. "All right? Shit . . ." I moved to help. "No! You go," he hissed between his teeth. "Around the corner on your right."

When I rounded that corner I straightened, rolling my shoulders and setting my jaw back in its proper place, shedding my disguise of posture and accent. Smoothly now, I hurried down the hall, guessing at the place's layout, the pattern of it. I hurried past the single-occupant bathrooms clearly intended for the guards and down a switchbacked stair. The cameras were bound to see me, and I was sure that there had to be guards on the Cielcin, or whatever Gilliam Vas and the Whitehorse foederati

had down there. But I figured I could always claim to have gotten lost. What could they do? Lock me in the coliseum? *Already here, boys.* And if it came to it, if things became truly desperate, I would put on my ring and face whatever came.

As I have said, the convict-myrmidons were not confined in oubliettes or pilloried, nor were they kept in cold cells, but rather permitted to share the common space and the dormitories behind. At first blush, not depriving their felonious charges of the warmth of human contact could be construed as an act of kindness on the part of the gaolers. The reality, as in all of our Empire, was double-edged. That very openness exposed the convict-myrmidons to assaults, rapes, and molestations, all the cruelties and privations the human mind might contrive. Yet the prisons of the Borosevo coliseum also held a deeper, more icily calculated cruelty.

Recall that Borosevo was a city built upon a coral atoll, on sandbars, and in the lagoon in which these petty masses gathered. Easy to forget, having lived for so long in and around the sunken concrete fastness of the coliseum. Yet the sea was never far. On a hunch I descended another flight of stairs, knowing now that I must be well below the high-water mark, and followed an arched corridor past empty chambers separated from the hall not by sealed doors but by classic iron bars. The stench of sewage hung ripe upon the air as in midsummer, baked by ambient heat. And something else . . . salt? Seawater, that was it. Seawater. Something wet and soft struck stone inside a cell to my right, splashing. I stopped, listening. Far above and distantly, I thought I could hear the groan and drag of human feet: the evening crowd awaiting that night's skiff jousting. I had nothing to do with the sport, Emperor be praised. It was for gladiators only. The smell of raw sewage intensified, and I looked in growing horror on the muddy trenches carved into the sides of each cell.

It clicked.

There were holes in the ceilings of the cells, shafts doubtless leading up to the public privies just inside the coliseum vomitoria. The prisoners here were literally shat

upon by the plebeian and serf clients of the Colosso games. I scowled, distracted by a deep-throated lowing from around one far corner, followed by the hoarse whisper of a man. I set my teeth and moved on, trying not to smell the salt and rotting feces.

Holding my nose, I reached a place where the path split at right angles from where I had entered. The smell of seawater blessedly strengthened, cutting the gutter stink to a manageable level. The cells all stood empty— had there been any great culling action on the killing floor lately? I could not remember. I felt there should be more guards, but with no prisoners but the rumored one, what need was there for such?

The dull sounds of human voices echoed up from my left, washed out by the misplaced groan of the sea. That was wrong, I decided. It should not have been audible, not this far underground.

"It's looking at me again," a gruff voice hissed. Then more loudly, "What did I say about looking at me?" The ringing of metal on metal sounded up the hall, punctuated by soft splashes and the strange alien lowing I'd heard earlier.

Then a deeper voice replied with words like broken glass: *"Yukajji! Safigga o-koun ti-halamna. Jutsodo de tuka susu janakayu!"*

I froze mid-step. The words sounded completely different from a native speaker than they did from old Gibson or myself. Rougher, smoother, harder, edged with a razor's brilliance. The guards both stepped back from the bars, appearing round the bend in the hall. "Earth and Emperor!" one swore, then lunged at the bars again with his shock-stick. "Priest ain't paying enough for this shit."

A long, startlingly white arm pressed out from between the bars and seized the guard by his wrist. It might have been a human hand sculpted by some intelligence only vaguely informed on the subject of the original. It was far larger, for a start, the six thin fingers too long and with too many joints. The guard shrieked as his partner surged forward to help. *"Yusu janakayu icheico."*

"Let him go, demon!" The other guard's voice broke

as he slammed his shock-stick into the exposed arm. The
Cielcin howled, released the gaoler, and withdrew that
too-long arm back into the cell. It spat a series of alien
curses into the air.

"Iukatta!" I screamed. *Stop!* It was the command
voice I'd learned, Lord Alistair Marlowe's voice, ringing,
resolute, clear, and hard as iron. The Cielcin was only
going to get itself hurt.

The guards both turned, sticks raised. "Who the hell
are you?"

I ignored them both. I wanted to see. They didn't resist
as I moved forward, something Imperial in my bearing
moving them to momentary silence. And there it was,
cowering in the muck at the back of its narrow cell, clutching its flash-numb arm, baring its snarl of translucent,
glassy teeth. I wanted to laugh, to weep. To run. I had just
gotten what I'd wanted—a glimpse of the Cielcin—and I
needed then more than anything to be away, to be anywhere else.

It was strangely smaller than I expected: a stick sculpture of a man, arms and legs of bundled twigs or of bone.
Yet that smallness was an illusion of its posture, and even
as I watched, it uncoiled limbs too long for its small and
pigeoned torso. Someone had sawed the horns from its
brow and sweeping crest and sanded the nubs to the quick.
It looked at me with eyes the size of tangerines, black as my
grandmother's funeral shroud. I discerned something in
those eyes, but it was no human feeling. I felt only cold.

Whatever spell of command I'd held over the two
guards promptly evaporated, and the nearer man laid a
hand on my shoulder. "Who the hell are you? No one
comes down here without the count's express permission."

"Tell that to Gilliam Vas," I said, drawing the name
from memory. It had its intended effect, lie that it was.
The two men shied away, cowed by the mere mention of
the hunchbacked priest. Shrugging his hands from my
arm, I pushed forward, well within reach of the creature's
grasping talons. In its own language, I asked, "You are a
soldier? You were taken in battle?"

"Taken?" the creature repeated, then flared the four

slitted nostrils in its weathered face where a nose might have been. *"Nietolo ti-coie luda." You speak like a child.* I smiled, the expression meaningless to the creature. It was right, but I was grateful my words were coming at all, however haltingly. Glad that the Cielcin could speak in a tongue I understood, unlike the Umandh.

Settling onto my haunches, I suppressed a thrill. I was speaking to a Cielcin—a true Cielcin, not Gibson or the sub-intelligent computers back in the Devil's Rest library. "I have never spoken to one of the People before." When the creature in the cell did not respond, only shifted, dragging one pale leg through the grime spattered on the stone floor, I pressed, *"Tuka namshun ba-okun ne?" What is your name?*

It sat there watching me for what felt like half the life of the sun. Its face was so like a human face—like a skull, with those huge eyes. It resembled nothing so much as a statue left for generations in the rain, its nose and ears worn away—or it would, were it not for the bony crest that evoked some cell memory of saurian creatures bellowing in some jungle out of geologic time. It was cruelty that had sanded that crest to naught, not time. "Makisomn."

"Makisomn," I repeated, tripping over the nasal digraph, knowing I was wholly incapable of trilling the sound the way they did—I lacked the muscular control of my nasal passages their species depended on to make that difficult sound. I pressed my hand to my chest and introduced myself. *"Raka namshun ba-koun Hadrian." My name is Hadrian.*

Where I had failed to pronounce its name, it failed to say mine. The anthropologist I never was might have grinned, and indeed the faintest smile pulled at my lips. "You speak its language?" one of the guards asked, ruining the moment.

I twisted, looking up into the guard's flat, dim face. There was a light in those dark eyes, dull and cold and uncomprehending. *Fear,* I realized. *This man is afraid of me.* Through my teeth I said, "Obviously." I knew I couldn't keep this up long, that soon the guards watching the other food servers would come looking for me. They

would haul me either onto the street or into a cell. And it had been so easy—too easy. Well, I was too deep in now, and my curiosity had gotten the better of me. I never could resist.

"Why is it here?" I gestured at the creature.

"Thought you were from Gilliam." The second guard narrowed somewhat sharper eyes at me. "Don't you know?"

Where before had I played the role of a Durantine serving man, now I played my father, standing to my full height, aware of my sweaty clothes and that I did not truly look the part. "And do you know what will happen to you when Gilliam Vas and his mother discover how easy it was for me to walk straight into this prison and up to this cell without ever once being detained? Answer my questions, or you will answer them for one of the cathars." *That's done it,* I thought. *A proper threat. Put the fear of God in them, Marlowe.*

The second guard—call him Slow—stammered out a response. "He's a gift, messer. For the count's son's Ephebeia. The beast's to be sacrificed in triumph in the Colosso."

A dram of contempt passed my lips, and I turned away. At least it explained why the beast was here, not in the palace dungeons. Here at least it was close to the action, to the place where it would die. I crouched, eyeing the creature through the crooked iron bars. Behind it and high up, a slitted culvert open to the elements sloshed seawater down the back wall of the cell, coating the bricks with salt. "It," I said.

"What?" asked the other guard—call him Slower.

"You called the Cielcin 'he,' " I said to Slow, not looking at him. "The Cielcin are hermaphrodites. It." If the guards cared at all about this correction, they didn't say anything, and I crouched to speak to the xenobite in its own language. *"Ole detu ti-okarin ti-saem gi ne?"* Do you know why you are here?

The creature bared its glassy fangs in a snarl, exposing blue-black gums. *"Iagamam ji biqari o-koarin."*

I shook my head. "Kill you? Not me, no. But someone will."

"Begu ne?" It asked. *How?* Was that fear in its voice?

In all the stories they have told of me—all the ones I've heard, even some of the ones I've started—no one has ever gotten this scene quite right. My first encounter with the enemy. I have heard it said that I slew the beast in Colosso for all Emesh to see. I have heard it said that it was not in Borosevo at all, that my first meeting with the Cielcin was at Calagah in the south, with the Ichakta Uvanari, amid the ruins. The operas and holographs sing my praises in battle or curse me as a sorcerer, a magus tipping poison into the Emperor's ear. None imagine—none believe—that our first meeting was amid sewage in the basement lockup of a sweaty coliseum gaol. The meanest, most provincial of circumstances, entirely without pomp.

"How?" It asked again.

"Sim ca," I said, choosing honesty over comforting illusion.

Not well.

I never heard Makisomn's reply, because someone—Slow or Slower, I never learned which—thrust his shock-stick between my shoulder blades, and the world went black.

CHAPTER 43

THE COUNT AND HIS LORD

WAKING, I EXPECTED RESTRAINTS, but found none. I was seated, slumped in a fat armchair in a chamber dimly lit and climate controlled. I could not recall ever being quite so comfortable and sore at the same time. The shock-stick—it was all coming back to me—had not been nearly so gentle as the Whitehorses' stunners. I felt almost as bruised as I had in Meidua after that gang had nearly killed me. I was only glad to be without corrective braces this time. A quick series of motions revealed no broken bones, and I set myself to studying my surroundings. After several years amid the mass-produced, neon-and-plastic world of the plebeians, the room was a sybaritic revelation, sumptuous beyond all my dreams. The walls were paneled not in imitation print but in genuine teak—so much of it that it had to have been flown in from offworld. The minutely tiled floor was draped in Tavrosi carpets in shades of green and gold and brown, showing hunting scenes in timeless fashion. Silk hangings billowed around an open set of double doors, stirred by winds slowed by the faint shimmer of a static field. All of it looked hand-made, for in our world of machined perfection where even gemstones can be generated to order, craftsmanship is the greatest treasure.

"You're awake." That deep voice—operatic basso profundo, darkly polished as the wood paneling on the walls. I knew it, but from where? "You must forgive my men, Lord Marlowe. They were under orders to protect Chanter Vas's little prize." Count Balian Mataro walked slowly

into view, a snifter clutched in one massive hand. His scalp shone where it had been recently waxed, black as a chess piece, and he glowed in a pale-green-and-off-white suit whose jacket trailed almost to the floor, held shut by a fat silk sash detailed in gold and cream. "Though I understand you nearly had them fooled. A fine performance, by the way. I've been watching the recordings." He drummed one fist in applause against a sideboard as his lictor—a wiry woman with skin nearly so dark as his own—moved into position by the billowing curtains. "Though I must confess I am a bit confused as to why the son of a Delian archon is playing myrmidon in my Colosso. What is it you call yourself? Had of Teukros, isn't it?"

Of course he knew. The moment I was unconscious and in his power, he would have had his scholiasts blood-type me and checked the entry against the High College's Standard Registry. He knew I was palatine, knew which house I was from, what year I'd been decanted. Knew my family history, my relations. Knew I was part of the Imperial peerage, my blood distantly conjoined with the Emperor's own. A thousand stories, all lies, spun like prayer wheels in my mind. What could I say? The man had read my blood. There were no lies I could tell at this point, no matter how clever I thought I was. Sometimes, if you're very, very unlucky, there is only one answer.

"No, lordship. It is as you say—I am palatine. My name is . . . is Hadrian Marlowe. Of Delos." I swallowed, the words strange, almost painful on my tongue. Still sore from the shock-stick, I realized that I had not answered his question, though it was only after the big man raised sardonic eyebrows, gold chains tinkling about his bull's neck, that I added, "It is a long story, lordship." Those eyebrows did not lower. I had to remind myself that this was a palatine, that patience was his native language.

Lacking in options, aware of the lictor to my right, her muscles like whip-cord, and imagining hidden guards behind the hunting tapestry on the inner wall, plasma burners trained on my chest, I told him. About Demetri, about the flophouse clinic and the old woman, about Cat

and the plague, about Teukros and the letter Gibson had
written for me. It took less time than I imagined, nearly
three years of my life covered in some twenty minutes. I
left out the adventure with the Umandh and any reference to truly criminal activity. I was not about to confess
to the near murder of a plebeian shopkeeper or serial
theft in the count's hearing. But in short order I was done,
and after a brief pause, I asked, "You haven't waved
Delos, have you, lordship?"

Balian Mataro at last ceased his pacing—he hadn't
stopped the entire time I'd spoken—and settled himself
against a sideboard that glittered with crystal liquor bottles. "Should I have?" His skin was *too* dark, I decided.
Too dark in precisely the same artificial manner in which
I was too pale, both of us without blemish, fashioned, as
it were, from two opposing kinds of stone.

In all my narration I had not given him a reason for
leaving Delos, and he had not asked. "No, lordship."

"They—my guards, I mean—said you *spoke* to the
Cielcin."

With some effort, I sat a little straighter in the chair. I
still wore my clothes from the practice yard, and my sweat
grated in them, dry and granular. "Yes, lordship." I ran
tired hands through my hair. "My first study was languages. I'm no master by any means, but I can speak to
the creature if need be." I laughed, a small, weak sound.

"What's so amusing?" The count placed his emptied
snifter on the sideboard.

I slid forward in my seat, shaking my head as I tried to
stand. The lictor tensed in her place by the curtains but
stayed where she stood. "It—the Cielcin said my pronunciation was terrible."

Balian Mataro smiled, stroked the thick, woolly swatch
of beard on his square jaw. "That bad, is it?" Despite my
unease, I found myself still smiling. The count turned,
poured himself another drink from a crystal decanter.
"What else did it say?"

"It asked if it was going to die, lord." I did stand then,
though I was careful to keep my distance from the royal

person. Orienting myself so that I still faced his lordship and keeping my huge chair between myself and the thin lictor, I pressed ahead. "I told it that it was."

Lord Balian tipped his snifter back and took a long drink before replying. "Well, you did not lie." He licked his lips, a curiously thoughtful expression pulling at the muscles of his face.

Thinking of the parade they would hold, the one the guards said would culminate in the Cielcin's death, I blurted out, "A triumph, Your Excellency?"

"For my son's Ephebeia." The big nobile tucked his thumb into his paisley sash, pointed past an arched wooden door into what must have been the rest of the palace. "He will be twenty-one standard in September."

Five months. I thought of the Cielcin—of Makisomn—trapped in that sewer-cell for five months. I was not sure I'd last five hours, which was of course my greater concern in that moment. "My congratulations. You must be proud."

"Of course!" the lord count said, emphatic. "He is my son." He spoke the words with endearing force. It was, I decided, how a father ought to speak of his children. "But you haven't truly answered my question, Lord Marlowe."

Behind the chair, my back to the corner of the sitting room and to a glassed-in case containing antique projectile weapons, I sketched a careful bow. "Forgive me, lordship. Which question was that?"

"Why are you here?" Before I could reply, he raised one massive slab of a hand and spoke evenly in that operatic basso of his. "I understand *how* you come to be here; it is why that most interests me. That and what exactly you were doing in my gaol." There it was at last—the dreaded question, fallen on my neck like a sword. The count's shadow might as well have been that of the executioner—and that was just the problem. "I am not in the least acquainted with your house. If this is an act of *poine*, some covert vendetta, I know of no reason why—"

"It isn't *poine*, lordship," I said simply, spreading my hands. "My father sold me, and I ran."

The count took this in stride, relief spreading beneath

that beard of his. "Sold you? To some baroness?" When I didn't answer or nod, he cocked an eyebrow. "Baron, then? Well, that has its charms as well." He grinned toothily, and the count's lord husband sprang to memory, the willowy Mandari man with the long black hair.

I folded, might literally have crumpled on the back of the armchair before me were it not for the aristocratic iron that held up my spine. "It's not like that at all, lordship." Count Mataro waited me out, his noble patience asserting itself in light of my laconic turns. When the silence stretched and broke in me at last, I said, "I was to go to the Chantry."

His momentary relief forgotten, the count froze. Gray-faced, he managed to find his words after only some small grasping about. "No one knows where you are?"

That's done it, I thought, smelling an opportunity if not an advantage. "Not unless you waved my lord father." Even as an abstract concept, the Chantry was doing what the Chantry did best: putting the fear of Gods and Earth into men. Everything I'd seen for three years—every cloud and sunset, every street corner and serving woman, every square scrap of land on this overweight world— belonged to the colossus standing opposite me. When he died, they would carve a statue of him for some temple, some mausoleum like the one in our necropolis at Devil's Rest. He would be portrayed with his booted foot planted on Emesh, a show of the power he'd held in life. Real power. The man could have ordered me dead in seconds, and here he was moved to silence by the thought of a ghost half a galaxy away.

He hesitated a moment before replying, toying with one of the massive rings on his fingers. "I've ordered no communications by QET," said the lord count, referring to the entangled telegraph network that bound the Empire and the human universe together. "I'll ask again: Does no one know you're here?"

"The ship on which I arrived was abandoned, lordship, as I told you. I was bound for Teukros, not Emesh. I could not have predicted coming here." The lictor was watching

me with hard eyes, the hilt of her deactivated highmatter sword in her fist, ready and waiting. Gambling, I said, "The wise thing to do would be to kill me, of course. Hide all evidence that I was ever here." That said, I looked slyly up at the palatine, making it clear that that could not be less true, as if merely saying the words aloud could dismiss the notion.

It worked. His black eyes narrowed, and his jaw tightened beneath that thatch of beard. "Do you think me so great a fool, Marlowe?" He'd omitted the "*Lord.*"

Got you. Half a dozen quips on this point danced in my mouth. I bit down on them, indeed bit my lip to keep from smiling, from sighing a breath of relief. *No executions today, not for me.* I struggled to reply for a moment, but before I could speak, the door opened, admitting a rapier-thin Mandari man: the count's husband, Lord Luthor Shin-Mataro. "You started without me, my lord?" He raised a fine eyebrow, a tight frown carving channels that framed his small mouth. Lord Luthor had the bronze complexion and high cheekbones familiar to anyone who has seen an interstellar plutocrat; the same blue-black hair; the same astonishing, forest-green, almond-shaped eyes; the same frigid composure. Those eyes . . . were they an after-market mutation? The Consortium had their bone-cutters too, their surgeons and magi, and they were less interested in the boundaries the Chantry imposed on human modification. The color mattered little, but there was something about Luthor's eyes that suggested he saw more than other men. Into the ultraviolet, perhaps, or the infrared. I couldn't say, nor was I certain the Chantry would take exception to Luthor's eyes and pluck them out. I know only they disturbed me.

"The boy woke earlier than Tor Vladimir expected, Luthor," the count answered, taking me in with a sweeping gesture that displayed one flared and finely textured sleeve. "We have only just decided that our best course is to see his head off and be done with it." The curtains blew in a little, pressed by the slow exchange of temperatures across the static field in the open doorway.

The thin foreigner paled. "Balian, you can't!"

The lord count's broad face broke into a grin, and he dissolved into bass laughter. "No, of course not," he said, still chuckling, "but by Earth, the look on your face." He pointed, smile unabated, before turning to look at me. "Hadrian Marlowe, may I introduce my lord husband, Luthor Astin-Shin-Mataro, formerly of the Marinus office of the Wong-Hopper Consortium, and my Minister of Finance."

Remembering my courtesies, I turned and said in perfect trade Mandar, "*Rènshu ni hěn róngxong shun*, Zhu Luthor." A formal greeting, polite. I bowed deeply, nearly at a right angle to the ground, a bow befitting the man's exalted station. At once I regretted the gesture as blood pounded in my ears and the bruises on my back and neck reported horribly. I had to clutch the armchair to right myself.

Politely ignoring my difficulties and clearly surprised, the foreigner raised his perfectly sculpted eyebrows and responded in Galstani, doubtless for the benefit of his husband. "You speak Mandar very well. Where did you learn?"

"I had a scholiast tutor as a boy. As I have told your lord husband, sire, my first training was in languages. I speak Jaddian as well, and Lothrian, Durantine, and Classical English, and I've a smattering of some of the Tavrosi languages. Nordei and Panthai, mostly."

The Mandari man whistled his approval. "All this in addition to the Cielcin tongue? Most impressive."

"Indeed." The count frowned. "Our interloper is full of surprises." *Interloper.* I imagined someone taller, more mysterious, probably with a black cloak and a cloth mask. Sensing that this was not the moment to interrupt, I maintained a diplomatic silence and tried to picture my parents—a more traditional couple by some outmoded standards—having a discussion such as this. The vision wouldn't come. I kept imagining them trying to outdo one another in impersonating a glacier. "You were in the fighting pits to . . . what? Earn money?"

Glad for a concrete question to answer, I brightened. "To buy passage offworld." Almost too late, I added, "Your Excellency, sire."

"To go where?"

"Tavros, I think," I said, deciding on that answer only in that moment. Beyond those polities that knelt at the Chantry's altars, amongst the technocrats and demoniacs at the galaxy's edge, I might outlive Father and any Imperial interest in my future. "Anywhere the Chantry won't look for me."

The Mandari consort exchanged glances with his husband. "The Chantry?"

"The boy is a seminarian, Luthor," the count intoned. He put his glass on the sideboard again, then turned to his lictor. "Camilla, please open those damned curtains. It's dark enough as it is." The hard-eyed woman saluted, somehow managing the action without peeling her eyes from her nobile charge. Impressive. Beyond, night was falling over Borosevo and the surrounding ocean, the sky bruised, tattooed with cloud. Turning back to his husband, the count said, "We've got a truant on our hands."

"A truant?" echoed Lord Astin-Shin-Mataro, green eyes widening with fear more than interest. "From Komadd?"

I shook my head. I had never even heard of Komadd. Some provincial Chantry-controlled world, no doubt. "Not Komadd. Vesperad."

"Vesperad?" the count and his husband said in shocked unison, and for good reason: the Synod itself met on Vesperad. There was no greater seat of the Chantry's holy authority, not in forty thousand worlds. I will say this for Father—whatever strings he'd pulled to land me my dark appointment, they had sung true. History will say what it will of Alistair Marlowe, but the man was a virtuoso where politics were concerned. Count Mataro continued speaking. "You turned down an appointment to Lorica College? Are you insane?"

"Not turned down," I corrected smoothly, honestly. "Ran away from." All this truth was starting to sour on my tongue, turning to the dry press of something very much akin to fear. What was to be done with me? What

were they planning to do, these lords? I half expected a liveried servant to barge in and declare that Lord Archon Marlowe was on the telegraph plate in the next room, demanding the return of his apostate son.

When nothing of the sort happened, I briefly considered falling back into the chair I'd awoken in. I refrained only for fear that in my diminished state I would fall asleep then and there in front of this great lord and his consort. "Your Excellency, I cannot go to that place." I thought of Gibson, of the blindfolded bald cathar slicing the old man's nose open. I thought of the mutilated slaves at the Colosso in Meidua, dressed to play Cielcin. I thought of Ghen and Siran and the wet-paper-tearing sound of flayed skin. That would have been my life, my legacy. It would've been me.

Luthor of the too many surnames narrowed his emerald eyes, studying my face, but he spoke to his husband. "He cannot stay here, Balian."

The count raised a hand for quiet, into which I hastily interjected, "Speed me on my way, then. I wouldn't need a good ship, lordship, or even a ship at all. Just a berth on something reliable." It was a mistake; I knew that as soon as the words passed my lips.

Balian Mataro's huge face composed itself into a frown. "I'm not in the habit of wasting valuable people, Lord Marlowe." He glanced at his husband. "What happened to the guards who brought this matter to our attention?"

"They're our guests at present," said the lord consort, picking at an invisible mar on one gray sleeve. *Guests indeed.* In a detention cell, I'd warrant.

"Have them transferred to some new posting as far from here as possible—to one of the moons, perhaps. Somewhere where their talk is just that. Camilla!" The count snapped his head in the direction of the lictor, indicating that she should join us. She crossed the floor in even, heavy-booted strides. I tensed in spite of myself, knowing full well that in my current state I could do nothing against someone armed and shielded. But it was nothing, and the count continued, "Be a dear and tell one of

your compatriots in the hall to send for Vladimir and Lady Ogir at once."

Dame Camilla—the woman was certainly a knight—looked pointedly down her genetically resculpted patrician nose at me. "But my lord . . ."

The lord count patted her arm reassuringly. "I've nothing to fear from Lord Marlowe here. Not in the thirty seconds this will take you." He pushed her gently toward the doors through which his husband had arrived. "Go on." When she'd moved away, Balian Mataro asked, "You speak how many languages, Lord Marlowe? Four? Five?"

"Nearly eight, lordship," I replied, not seeing the relevance when we'd been talking starships. "Though perhaps five fluently." A slight exaggeration—my Durantine was good enough to fool poor kitchen servants, but I was hardly prepared to have tea with one of the consuls of that far republic.

The count looked at his husband with an odd glint in his black eyes. Approval? Triumph? Whatever it was, it must have disquieted Lord Luthor, for he said, "What are you thinking, Balian?"

Smiling beneath that beard, Lord Balian pressed on. "And how old are you, Lord Marlowe?"

I hesitated on the edge of saying *twenty-two standard*. It was likely the correct figure, but I couldn't be quite sure. My own Ephebeia had passed entirely without pomp while I was living on the streets of Borosevo. I knew the local date, but the standard calendar mattered only to those who traveled beyond the circles of the world or dealt with sailors from the Dark. I'd not seen the standard date in years or had access to the nobile datasphere. "I was nineteen when I left home, lordship," I said at last, "but I don't know the current Imperial Star Date."

"Sixteen one seventy-one zero four."

Had I been drinking, I might have spat it out. Thirty-five years. It had been thirty-five standard human years since I went into fugue aboard the *Eurynasir*. Earth and Emperor, Crispin would be nearly fifty, assuming he'd never left home himself. I was not the elder brother anymore, just as I'd said in Haspida. I had expected a slip of

thirteen years between Delos and Teukros. But thirty-five? It is a fact of space travel that we get left behind. Time's arrow flies in one direction. Despite the ubiquity of this fact in palatine life, I shut my eyes and forced myself to be still.

The count put a hand on my shoulder. "Are you all right?"

In lieu of an answer, I said, "I'm twenty-three, lordship."

"I have a son, as you know."

"And a daughter, Anaïs, both a little younger than yourself," Lord Luthor interjected.

Count Mataro resumed speaking. "They have few enough companions their own ages. I have command of only four lesser houses, and two of those are offworld exsuls. I would take you as ward of the court. I would have you instruct my"—he glanced at Luthor, smiling—"*our* children in languages. They could use a little practical experience."

Luthor bristled. "I still think this is a mistake, Balian."

"This man is a palatine lord, Luthor. One of the Imperial peerage, of the constellation Victoria. Old blood." Balian Mataro raised an eyebrow to underscore those last two words, then said to me, "You wouldn't be using your true name, naturally. But as I see it, it's better to keep you safe here than to send you away."

"In case someone comes looking?" I asked. "Then I can say, 'No, Lord Inquisitor, these nice men saved me.' I can be your shield." I saw it clearly—I was to be their prisoner. Well kept, but a prisoner all the same. I felt the walls closing in around me and knew I was cornered. *Old blood*, the count had said. Whatever his noble title, Count Mataro was the ruler of a provincial backwater, a lord with little name. I was of the peerage. My family could trace its blood back to Avalon, to the first days of the Empire and to old William Windsor himself. It was surely something they couldn't have ignored.

"You object?"

"It is a cage, Your Excellency."

"Rather a nicer one than you deserve," Luthor snapped, his words directed to Lord Mataro more than myself. "Balian, I really must protest."

The doors opened again, admitting a scholiast and a woman dressed in the gray suit of an Imperial logothete. Both bowed, appearing to sense the sudden tenseness in the room. The woman—clearly the superior of the pair—said, "You summoned us, my lord?" She was older, her patrician face revealing the subtle surgical enhancements that told me she'd been born a peasant. Her graying hair was cut short above a copper face, and her eyes—also gray—seemed to look right through all they beheld. Her name, I later learned, was Liada Ogir, High Chancellor of Emesh and the power behind the Mataro throne.

The count briefly introduced me and my situation. "He'll need a set of false credentials within the day. Something that won't raise too many eyebrows. Vladimir will advise. Perhaps something patrician; that might draw less attention, don't you think?"

"Of course, Your Excellency." A column of five guards had entered as well, hoplites in gilt green with long white capes trailing on the ground behind them. They did not carry lances like the Imperial legionnaires or my father's men but instead wore ceramic long swords on their hips and phased disruptors strapped to their thighs. Better options for interior work. Judging from the scope of this one chamber, Borosevo Castle was a tighter sort of place to maneuver than Devil's Rest. "What should we call him, my lord?" asked Chancellor Ogir.

Lord Mataro looked me up and down. "They already know him as Had from the fighting pits. Hadrian is fine. Hadrian . . ."

"Gibson," I interjected, not even thinking about it. "Hadrian Gibson."

I caught Lord Luthor glaring at me and bowed my head politely. I wanted that look wiped off his too-handsome face but suffered myself to be led.

"One last question, M. Gibson," the count said, holding up a hand as the hoplites moved to escort me from the study. "You never did say: Why did you go to see the Cielcin in the first place?"

That puzzled me for a moment. I had no answer ready, so I chewed my lip, reflecting. "I wanted to know if it was

a monster, my lord." So much nuance in the change of address, mine and his. What details they implied. "I wanted to see it."

The other palatine nodded gravely. "And was it? A monster, I mean."

"I don't think so, my lord," I replied. "It was afraid."

CHAPTER 44

ANAÏS AND DORIAN

MY CHAMBERS FITTED ME like new teeth, my clothes like old snakeskin. I paced anxiously from one room to the next, stalking like a wolf in want of escape. The rooms were fine as any I had seen: I had my own bath, my own closet kitted out with formalwear machine-tailored for me, my own sitting area with leather couches, even my own small collection of passable wines. The walls were hung with oil paintings of ships, both nautical and astronomical, and the curtains were velvet dark as sin, guarding windows that overlooked the dome of the Chantry and its concrete bastille.

The four-poster bed with its smart mattress and linen sheets seemed almost to grope at me with its luxury, and I gave it up after two nights, sleeping instead in a tangle on the floor. I have long since outgrown this spartan tendency, but so shortly removed from the coliseum barracks and the streets, I found it difficult to adjust. Worse than that were the servants. It felt strange not to have to do everything for myself again. Wrong.

It was only another gilded cage, and I was far more a prisoner there than I had ever been on Emesh. I'd made a mistake. For my curiosity and mad desire to meet the Cielcin prisoner, I had traded my freedom, my dream of traveling the stars, and my friends. My friends. What must they have thought of me vanishing as I had? They'd guess—or Switch would—that I'd gone after the Cielcin in the hypogean gaol. But it would look like I'd abandoned them. If only I could've gotten word across the

plaza to the coliseum . . . but I was permitted no messages, and I shuddered to think what the count's men
would do if I tried. My every move was watched, so I did
what I'd been taught to do when observed. I behaved as
expected.

I had managed to get new drawing materials out of the
count's chamberlain, and I was just finishing a lonely supper and beginning a pencil sketch of Borosevo's skyline
from my window when a knock sounded at the door. I
ignored it, hoping that it was some nattering courtier who
would simply become bored after two knocks or three
with no response. The knock sounded again, and I was
privately glad that I had not left the holograph plate running its evening news cycle, lest the noise betray my
presence.

The locked door opened, and a pair of green-armored
peltasts in Mataro livery swept through—as if the castle's
cameras hadn't already revealed all my rooms' hidden
secrets. One took up position by the door while the other
examined my person, removing the folding knife I'd
bought with money from the Colosso and—bizarrely—my
pencil kit. He put them on the table by the door beside his
companion, then stepped into the hall. A moment later a
strikingly handsome young woman swept into the room,
leading a somewhat flustered younger man who could
only be her brother.

Before she opened her mouth I knew exactly who she
and the lordling were: Anaïs and Dorian Mataro, the
count's heirs. Both were paler than Lord Balian, the one
father's ink-black skin tempered by the other's gold complexion to something coppery as oiled wood. They had
the same almond-shaped eyes, hers green, his dark; the
same thick black hair; the same strong build and fine silk
clothing.

Already standing from my impromptu frisking, I stood
a little straighter upon seeing them, then remembered
that I ought to bow, being in that moment rather less than
palatine. When I straightened again, I said, "Lord and
lady, you honor me."

The girl offered me a hand. An ivory band with a pale

beryl shone on one slim finger. I took her hand and kissed the ring, as was only proper. As I did so, she said, "You're the one, then?" She looked me up and down, head cocked to one side. "You're shorter than I expected."

The young man behind her smoothed his oiled hair with a decidedly anxious motion. "Don't be rude, Sister!" He extended his own hand to me, clasped it warmly. "Dorian Mataro! We're to be friends, I understand." He smiled slightly in the ironic way all children have when they parrot something their parents have told them. Strange that I thought of them as children though they were not so much younger than I. So long had I been amongst the plebeians that I did not find it strange that the son of a palatine lord would deign to touch my hand.

"Hadrian," I said in answer, affecting a warm smile that slicked my face like oil. I'd forgotten how much of court life was like this. The invisible masks. At the Court of the Moons on Jadd, the courtiers at least have the decency to wear genuine masks. Remembering myself, I added, "Hadrian Gibson. A pleasure, lordship."

"Dorian, please!" His ironic smile broadened into something more open and earnest. "And—and this is my sister—"

"Anaïs!" she said, cutting him off. I swiveled to look at her, found those eyes—like star-cut emeralds—searching the lines of my face. Searching for what? I offered the girl—she couldn't have been more than nineteen—a halting smile. "Welcome to Borosevo, M. Hadrian."

Brief images flashed in the space behind my smile: Cat coughing in the storm drain, a knife buried in the shoulder of a store clerk, the cruel laughter of the other boys at night. Of the coliseum and the friends I still had there. The friends I had abandoned there. Welcome to Borosevo, indeed. *Oh, ladyship. I know Borosevo in ways you never will.* I prayed that none of what I'd thought had reached the smiling mask on my face and bowed my head. "You're too kind. I . . ." I broke off, looking to the faceless hoplite standing just inside my open door. "To what do I owe the honor of this visit?"

Lord Dorian seated himself in the chair I had so lately vacated, but it was his sister, still absorbed in the study of my face, who said, "We wanted to meet you, of course. Father says you've traveled all over, that you speak Jaddian and Lothrian and—"

"Were you really a gladiator?" Dorian asked, as his sister lowered herself onto the arm of his chair. "Truly?"

I looked down at my feet, somehow unable to look the girl in the face. I had been away from my own kind for so long that the sight of her broke something in me. Her face—all of her—was a work of art. To say this is not a compliment, not truly. She had no choice but to be perfect. I have never considered myself particularly handsome, knife-faced and severe as I am, but Valka once said I had the sort of face one saw in marble, and thinking of the statues in our necropolis, I could not say I disagreed. But I was as one of my charcoal sketches compared to the oil painting that was Anaïs Mataro.

Anaïs Mataro. Radiant as a bronze statue, dark as a summer eve. The personification of the icon of Beauty herself. And a cool, calculating opportunist. Not knowing this at the time, I smiled, wearing the face the count had asked me to wear. "I was a myrmidon, ladyship. One of the fodder fighters."

"A pit fighter?" One of her brows arched.

Her brother butted in, beaming. "You know, I remember you, sirrah! You were the one who shorted out that one fellow's shields with the sand!" Dorian swung a leg up over the arm of my chair, sitting with a casual ease that reminded me of . . . someone. I couldn't place it.

Hands clasped before me, I nodded at my boots again, genuinely abashed. I'd not grown used to my small, local celebrity. I'd spent most of my time as a myrmidon squirreled away in the coliseum, in the hypogeum, save for a few ventures out in pursuit of drink or women or starships, in descending order of success. "That was me, lordship."

"That was a damn good show, M. Hadrian," Dorian grinned. His teeth were very white.

"It's kind of you to say so," I said, so politely I felt it

might rot my teeth. Latching onto something the count had said at our meeting, I said, "I understand you've been learning Jaddian?"

"*Soli qalil,*" Dorian said, smiling round the lilting edges of the words.

"*Qalilla,*" I said, mouth crooking into that long-absent Marlowe smile. "*Qalil* is small. *Qalilla* is a little." That second L sound was a trial after so many years of disuse, made by a flapping of the tongue alien to Galstani.

Though it was risky to so correct a palatine, young Dorian—young? He was only a year or two my junior—grinned more widely. Had he made the mistake on purpose? A test? The broken smile hung on my face. "Yes, that's it. You're right." He plucked at a loose thread on the seam of my leather armchair and added, "Have you been to Jadd, sirrah?"

I blinked, mind clunking over a thousand permutations of my response. Feint and counterfeint. What was it the old philosopher had said? Just like single combat? But no. Truth was better. "No, lordship. I had the privilege of a scholiast tutor while I was with my father's company."

"And a master at arms, plainly," Anaïs said, looking me up and down in a way that . . . unsettled me. Like I was a sample on a slide. No, like I was a morsel on a dish. I shifted where I stood, for a moment understanding how Kyra must have felt. The tall girl leaned against the side of my chair. Her bright eyes tracked over the remains of my supper: the dirty plate, the half-finished glass of water with the bottle placed to the side, the serving tray hovering just off the edge of the table. Her gaze lighted on my open sketchbook, and I saw her face open. "You draw?"

Without waiting for me to grant permission, she drew up the sheaf of cheap paper the chamberlain had given me, spilling my pencils to the floor with a clatter. I clenched my teeth, biting back an importunate demand. It took a long while for Hadrian Gibson the courtier, the merchanter's son, to crush the Marlowe's offended howl. I could feel the muscles of my face knotting with mingled rage and affront while at the same time some autonomic reflex smoothed those feelings away, turning me meek as the servants who

had furnished my childhood. "Yes, ladyship. A small hobby."

I stood just behind her, looking around—but not over—her shoulder at the half-finished landscape. I'd depicted Borosevo with a heavy hand, emphasizing the shadows cast by the bleeding sun that even then squatted fatly on the horizon. The city was all low buildings but for the glass fingers of the urban farms and the odd radio tower. They sprawled darkly across the landscape, jagged and broken-looking. It was not a flattering picture.

"It's beautiful!" she said, turning to look slightly down at me.

Around a wooden smile, I said, "That's very kind of you to say, ladyship. I'm afraid it is a poor image compared to the beauty of your city."

"Nonsense! You've captured our proud city perfectly!" Proud indeed. Who was it said pride is blind? Or was that love? "Such a talent! Isn't he talented, Dorian?"

Her brother craned his neck to see. "Can you draw people, M. Hadrian?" It might astonish you to know how often this is the first question anyone with the tiniest scrap of artistic talent receives, followed shortly by, "Can you draw me? Or . . . or my sister here?" He pointed, smiling rather blandly in expectation. When I didn't answer at once, he waved a hand. "Not now, of course. I only wondered."

"I'd be delighted to, lordship." My smile was starting to feel like a wooden gash on my face, and I was certain then that I'd prefer Ghen's coarse braying to this cloying, demanding politeness any day. "Only I've had a long day, lord and ladyship. Adjusting to court life again after so long in the fighting pits . . ." I let my words trail off, counting on the others to pick up on what I wasn't saying. It is never proper to make a request of the palatine, you understand, and so much of courtly conversation is implication, two parties speaking past and around one another like perfumed nobiles in a contredanse.

They did not get the message, or else they did not care.

"I should look forward to it, then," Dorian said, smoothing down his darkly oiled hair. "Perhaps later in

the week—which reminds me why we're here." He looked up at his sister, exposing the stupidly thin line of beard he wore to accentuate the line of his jaw. Evidently the palatines did not have their beards removed on Emesh. It had the look of a pencil line along the jaw, and I had to suppress a smile. It looked ridiculous, a boy's parody of manhood. I couldn't tell if he was referring the matter of their visit to her as to a subordinate or deferring to her for quite the opposite reason. Their gene-perfect faces were so much harder to read after the cavalcade of rough plebeian faces I'd grown accustomed to since coming to Emesh, and the inner workings of their power dynamics were a mystery quite entirely beyond me.

Anaïs tossed her curling black hair. "Yes indeed!" She turned her attentions back to me, eyes bright. They held me like spotlights, pinning me as surely as the sight of a sniper's rangefinder. "We were hoping to invite you out, have you meet some of our friends, get to know the court."

"That would be nice." I bowed my head, hoping I'd hit the appropriate note of awed enthusiasm. It was a kindness, I supposed, or else a part of some convoluted scheme I could not yet see. I wasn't certain the count was keeping me around for my language acumen alone, just as I wasn't certain he'd bought my line about being able to protect him from the Chantry. I was acutely aware that I was back in a world of wheels and spirals, a place where nothing was straight. Contredanse and counterfeint. Once I had excelled in such waters. Now I was not so sure I even had gills.

"We were thinking we might borrow Fathers' box at the coliseum," Dorian offered, spreading his hands. "You could tell us your stories while we watch the fight!" He grinned again, and I realized where I had seen the way he'd thrown his leg over the arm of his chair before, that gesture of assured, dominant ownership. Crispin. The boy moved with the same careless abandon as my little brother, swaggering about because he owned the whole of his world. But I soon learned that there was one small difference between the boy and my brother: Dorian's

delight was an honest thing. He *loved* the Colosso for the sport of it, not the blood.

"As his lordship wishes," I said, bowing to hide the stiffness of my words. I tried to imagine what it would be like to sit behind the prudence field in that gilded box beneath silk awnings while the men and women I'd spent the last year with struggled and died on the brick and sand below. I felt another pang, wishing I'd stayed where I'd been with Ghen and Pallino, Siran, Elara, and the others. I hadn't made things right with Switch. None of this showed on my face, though, and when I straightened, the expression I wore was a perfect mask. "I'd be delighted."

I was among palatines again indeed.

CHAPTER 45

LOSE THE STARS

OF THE CONTESTS I watched at the Colosso that day I can recall almost nothing. Save for Anaïs and Dorian, I remember almost none of the palatine and patrician members of Emeshi high society I met, either. Each blurs into the next, perfect faces cast in shades of teak, of bronze, of ivory. They are nameless and faceless to me even as the myrmidons and slaves in the coliseum below were nameless and faceless to them. It was those fighters who drew my attention, not the giddy socialites. Alis and Light were new and more or less untested. Four others I knew only by sight—I had seen them eating in the mess not a fortnight past. And there was Erdro. Erdro had fought with me my first day in the coliseum. I liked the man well enough; Erdro was the sort of myrmidon who aspired to the position of gladiator. He made a science of his physical fitness and ate with a measuring spoon.

None of it mattered. The first arrow caromed off his breastplate, drawing a gasp from the crowd and a cheer when he kept on charging the ink-skinned gladiator captain Jaffa. But the gladiator only cocked his antique crossbow again. And Erdro died. They cheered for that too. The same sound, the same inflection. Two other myrmidons fell on Jaffa, beat him until his suit locked up and a pair of servitors had to drag the paralyzed gladiator from the field. He would have bruises. He should have been dead.

A familiar feeling came over me as I sat amid all that gold and silk and velvet: the desire to leave. Rocket

contrails streaked the southern sky over the flats of the artificial island that rose just beyond Borosevo's canal warrens. The graceful lines of the Uhran starship traced themselves against the blackness of my thoughts, and I sat stonily in a padded chair beneath the whir of air conditioning and the piping of soft music while bare-chested slaves served chilled wines from fluted cups. Below, Umandh slaves were dragging Erdro's body from the field, and—unnoticed—I set a full cup of wine on the rail for him. No one disturbed it.

But I couldn't leave. Anaïs and Dorian were near at hand, introducing me to the sons of archons and the daughters of guilder magnates. I could not leave without risking tremendous affront, which I could not afford in the present climate. Anaïs in particular was never far, and she foisted drinks on me in the hopes of wringing tales of the arena from me, and because I was young and somewhat drunk and attended by a woman of no small charm, I will confess I boasted. What's more, I lied. Where had I learned to fight? Why, from a Jaddian Maeskolos with whom I traveled for years. Why had I fought as a fodder myrmidon before finally earning my court appointment? That was complicated. I'd lost my letter of introduction, you see. It had taken some time to track down my father's ships and get a new draft delivered to Castle Borosevo, and a man had to make a living. How had I lost it? Well, Borosevo had its grimy underbelly, didn't you know?

I told a version of my mugging in Meidua without the motorbikes and transported to the canals of Belows. This titillated my audience even more than the stories of arena combat had, and since it is the peculiar quality of danger to excite those who have never experienced it, Anaïs was not alone in hanging on my arm by the end of the tale. Chained by social convention, by politeness, I knew I had lost the stars. The hangars that held the Uhran starship and the clunky Andunian were as good as empty. The count had me now. I had made my choice, traded one future for another.

Seeing Erdro die, I couldn't help but feel I'd made a mistake.

"Is it true, Dorian?" asked a heavy patrician girl with a round face, pouting ever so slightly. "Is it really?"

"You know I can't tell you, Melandra!" Dorian said, and he pulled the girl a little closer on the swallowing couch on which they reclined. "My fathers would have me in a gibbet if I talked about the triumph!"

Triumph. The Cielcin. They were talking about the Cielcin. Makisomn. Dorian glanced at his sister, then up at the canopy above us. I recognized the reflex to look for cameras, but no sooner had he done it than he looked round at us all and winked.

"You're serious?" Melandra asked, leaning closer against the young lord. Her lover? "How'd they catch one?"

Anaïs answered for her brother, as she often did. "Gilliam Vas procured it from the foederati attached to the visiting Legion!"

"Did he really?" asked the son of an industrial guild factionarius from Binah in his thick lunar accent.

Melandra made a face. "That gargoyle?" I snorted under my breath; *gargoyle* was exactly the right word for the intus. "I suppose that only makes sense. The mutant has demon blood himself." This was not the first remark I'd heard about the chanter at court. You must understand—*inti scare* the nobility. They are what we would all be but for the grace of Earth and Emperor, and a reminder that the palatines have no control over their genetic destiny, lest they risk such mutation. Gilliam Vas was a reminder that we were bound to the Emperor, and a reminder of Saltus's words to me so long ago: *We are both homunculi.* I had rejected the statement at the time, but there had been truth in the creature's words and in the chanter's mismatched eyes. And like most truths, it was not easy to learn.

Dorian swatted his paramour with a playful hand. "Watch yourself—that's a priest you're talking about!"

"He's a beast, Dorian!"

I had not known Erdro well and had seen many of my fellow myrmidons die since I'd started in the Colosso, but that didn't make his death any easier to brush aside. Feeling I had nothing positive to contribute to the discussion of the mutant priest, I drifted away from the conversation,

carrying my half-finished wine back to where I'd left the spare for Erdro's shade on the rail. One of the oiled, nearly naked servers moved to clear it away, but I dismissed her with a wave that felt too comfortable. I leaned against the rail next to it, watching a troupe of Eudoran mummers performing a scene from Bastien's *Cyrus the Fool*—part two, I think, where the prince survives atmospheric reentry by hiding beneath his mother's skirts. They played the farce in classic style amid holographs and pyrotechnics. Mother would have approved despite the players' Eudoran blood—she had no love for that itinerant people. Their masks were brightly painted, visible even from our height, and looked splendid on the massive screens for the convenience of the crowd.

"Did you know him?"

I started for the folding knife that was not there. But it was only Anaïs, who flinched, nearly dropping her wine.

"I'm sorry!" she said, clutching a hand to her breast. "I didn't mean to scare you! You didn't get any on you, did you?"

"What?" I wasn't following. She meant the wine. Some had spattered the tiles at my feet, red as the ink with which I write this account. "No, not at all, ladyship. Forgive me, I startle rather easily."

She laughed then, the hand on her chest relaxing as she withdrew it. "That makes sense. The fighting pits . . ."

I eased back, leaning against the box railing again to watch the Eudorans perform. "I . . ." I thought of my time in the streets, of the times I'd flinched away from the prefects whether I was innocent or not, of the other criminals, of broken ribs and crying in the night. "The fighting pits . . . yes."

"Did you know him?" She repeated the question, inclining her head toward the field, toward the spot where Jaffa had felled Erdro with the antique bow. One of the Umandh slaves busied itself scrubbing the blood from the brick while the troupers performed Bastien's play at the other end of the field. When I nodded numbly, Anaïs said, "What's that like? I can't imagine."

Though I was somewhat drunk by that time, I knew

enough to hold my tongue. A pained smile cut across my face, and I kept my intent focus on the Umandh slave, its trunk stooped, tentacles scrubbing at the spot on the ground where Erdro had bled from his arrow wound. Her question, the callous detachment of its premise, froze in me. I turned it over in my mind as if it were a particularly dubious gift, examined its intent beneath the crass disregard. I decided she had meant to give no insult, though I had taken it. "I didn't know him very well. You get used to it . . . down there." I swept a hand over the field, the brick studded with the concrete caps of the terrain pillars. "We weren't really friends, I suppose."

As I spoke, I thought of those myrmidons I did count as friends, and though I was not a religious man I thanked heaven it had not been Switch or Pallino fighting Jaffa that day.

"He fought bravely."

"He did," I agreed. Bravery had nothing to do with it. Erdro needed money, so he fought. I looked down over the edge, down bare meters of stone wall to the floor of the coliseum. Just past my arm's reach, a Royse field glimmered, rippling almost invisibly in the air but with enough latent force to stop a bus launched from a rail gun. And yet I felt exposed, recalling my failure to remain in my father's box at the Meidua coliseum and how visible that failure had been.

Anaïs leaned against the rail beside me, making me conscious of the smoky smell of her perfume. I could feel those green eyes on me, but I found I could not turn away from the coliseum floor. It all looked so different from the box. I replayed Erdro's demise, saw Jaffa cock his crossbow, only to become Crispin as he fired. Anaïs spoke, shaking me from my vision. "At least you don't have to risk your life anymore, right? Or do you miss it? We could get you in as a gladiator. Dorian would love that! He's always wanted to be friends with a gladiator—"

"No!" I said too loudly. Suddenly it was not Crispin with the crossbow at all but me, and it was Switch they expected me to kill. Siran. Ghen. Pallino. "Black Earth, no."

She drew a bit away from me, surprised by my vehe-

mence. I wanted to fling myself from the balustrade, to dash myself to pieces on the bricks. Why had I gone into the coliseum gaol after Makisomn? I was just as trapped as I'd ever been, a prisoner now of the count's pleasure more than I'd ever been a prisoner of poverty.

The rest of what Anaïs said to me washed by unremembered. When she went away again—called back by her brother or one of the other patrician socialites to some passing fancy or other—I stood alone again and watched *Cyrus the Fool* survive fire and death by blind luck and pure simplemindedness. Everyone laughed. I swatted Erdro's wine cup from the ledge, watched it pass slowly through the Royse field and shatter on the killing floor.

CHAPTER 46

THE DOCTOR

NEITHER ANAÏS NOR DORIAN was aware of my proper identity, or so I thought—they believed me the son of a minor merchanter engaged in trade with Jadd. Before long their scholiast tutor insisted I speak to them only in Jaddian as an exercise. I was not truly their friend, not truly anyone's friend. My possessions were recovered from the coliseum dormitories by house guards. Emperor knows what Switch and the others thought about that. I was confined to the vast palace atop its concrete and steel ziggurat, a thousand feet above the city and sea level. From my room in the outer wall, I could see all of Borosevo rolled out like a dirty carpet, a stain upon the green waters of the world.

I left an engagement with the two noble children, crossing a mosaic floor in a quadrangle decorated with tinkling fountains with green copper statues in the centers. A pair of collared Umandh stumped past, wobbling on their three legs, their scaly, coralline hides cracking in the air as they carried a massive statue of a Mataro sphinx in their strong feelers. A float palette might have been easier, but using the xenobite slaves was something of a status symbol. House Mataro kept several hundred in the palace. Mostly they performed aesthetic chores such as waving fans at important personages in the open air or carrying things about the palace as visibly as possible. Emesh may not have had much in the way of material wealth or political significance, but it had the xenobites. I watched them

retreat down a colonnade, their soft droning fading with their progress.

"M. Gibson! Hadrian!"

I turned, recognizing the voice. "Lady Anaïs." I bowed almost before I'd turned round. "Forgive me, were we not through for the day?"

The count's daughter was taller than me by a head, the perfect blend of her two fathers. She smiled down at me, hands on the soft swell of her hips. "No, we were. I was hoping I'd catch you is all."

"Catch me?" I pushed a fall of hair from my eyes, the strands already damp with sweat from the damnable press of the air.

She smiled—she smiled like an open flame—and said, "There's a boat race around the harbor at the end of the week, you know?" I hadn't, and I told her so politely as I fell into step beside her, matching her long stride as best I could. "Everyone from the city attends. It's the event of the season—not counting Dorian's Ephebeia, of course." *That* announcement had been made weeks before, along with the revelation that a Cielcin would be sacrificed in a Chantry triumph to commemorate the occasion. Perhaps that was why the lady's boat race had escaped my notice. "Lord Melluan's sons are down from Binah"—that was the green moon, a place said to be covered in woods as vast as the fabled forests of Luin—"and Archon Veisi himself is up from Springdeep. Everyone who matters in-system."

I nodded politely. "It sounds like quite the showing."

She linked her arm through mine, laughing sweetly. "It will be, M. Gibson, truly." We descended a curve of staircase, passing through the shadow of a square tower from one of the inner, higher sections of the palace toward the lower, outer wall. High above, the Spear Tower rose like a column of smoke into the firmament, tall as the ziggurat on which it sat. It looked narrow as a reed, as if the wind might bowl it over. I stopped a moment, looking down on the shaded garden where it wrapped beneath the wall of a higher terrace. Sailcloth awnings decorated with the

dyed patterns of dragons and manticores snapped above our heads.

"Is there much sailing on Emesh, then?" I stopped to let a decade of household soldiers march past, a group of peltasts with familiar energy lances. "I confess I'm not much familiar with the culture. Short of my time in the Colosso, I've not had much time to experience your fair planet." I did not mention my time in the streets. Would not.

Anaïs squeezed my arm, leaned against me a little. "Oh, you must come with me, then. Any one of the ships would be honored to have me aboard. You could be my escort, if you wanted."

"My lady, you honor me." I inclined my head in a slight bow.

"It might be fun!" she laughed, then released me. Around the corner the droning of more slave Umandh hummed softly as they were directed by a pair of servants calling instructions in raised voices. Doubtless one or the other had one of the droning communications boxes I had seen years ago with Cat in the fish warehouse.

Then a voice—*the* voice—first broke into my universe. There are moments, instants that divide. Time fractures about them so that there is a time after . . . and so that all that was before is a kind of dream. "No, no, damn it— you're doing it wrong." I did not know it then, but my life had split, was cloven evenly in two from the moment I heard those words. I peered round the sandstone pillar of a colonnade and out onto the balcony beneath a vaulted ceiling overlooking the parade ground. In a few months' time Dorian Mataro's Ephebeian triumph would begin there, processing through the streets and along the canals of Borosevo to the coliseum, where at last the Cielcin Makisomn would be sacrificed by the Chantry grand prior, Gilliam's mother.

Three Umandh were attempting to replace light fixtures in the ceiling, their cilia struggling to manipulate tools and electronics meant for the five-fingered. Even as I turned the corner, one dropped a huge fluorescent rod, shattering the bulb to dust. One of the douleters, a fat man in a house uniform of muddy green, slammed his

shock-stick into one of the creature's legs. It went to two knees, dropping tentacles to brace itself as the human screamed, "Fucking squid-tree-looking filth!" Off to one side, his companion twiddled the dials on one of the droning boxes used to communicate with the Umandh.

The man pulled his stick back for another blow, and suddenly there she was, her tattooed hand closing around the man's wrist. "Go ahead, try it." Her voice rang clear and high and polished, strangely accented. Hearing it, I recalled the tattooed doctor from the *Eurynasir* on my fateful trip away from Delos.

The fat douleter tensed as the slender woman held his arm, eyes wide. The strength went out of him, and he shook her off, casting a violent look over his round shoulder at the woman. I like to imagine now that he cast a warding sign her way, superstitiously fending off his demons. Anaïs came up just behind me. "Oh! Hello, Doctor Onderra!" she said, surprised. "Repairing the lights?"

The slender woman snatched the Umandh comms terminal from the second douleter, who was too busy bowing to Anaïs to protest, and fiddled with it for a good five seconds before responding. When she finally spoke, it was in even tones, the voice airy, musical and amused. "Lady Mataro, good afternoon!" She did not bow, curtsy, or make any gesture of deference or obeisance. She only smiled, full lips parting as she clasped her hands behind her back. "And yes, there was another brownout in this wing of the castle late yesterday. I thought I'd offer my assistance with the Umandh since *some people*"—and here she glared at the douleters—"don't understand them worth a damn."

"Brownouts?" I asked, looking to Anaïs to explain.

The palatine girl bobbed her head, wiping the newborn sweat from her hairline. "Castle generators have been a bit broken since the storm season started."

"Things break," the foreign woman said hastily, eyes sharpening on me. "Messer . . . ?"

Anaïs squeezed my arm. "This is Hadrian!"

"Hadrian . . . Gibson," I managed, offering my hand as I had learned to do in the coliseum.

She was nearly as pale as I was myself—a sailor's pallor, though so white and unblemished that I decided her skin must be proof against solar radiation, like my own. In high boots and simple trousers, she looked drab next to Lady Anaïs Mataro in her flowing kaftan, but she wore them proudly as any queen. Her arms were bare to the shoulder, the left tattooed in a dense intaglio of fine black lines, whorls, and angles spiderwebbing from deltoid down to the start of each finger. Still smiling, she moved forward, extending her right hand—which entirely lacked tattoos—and took my hand in hers. "Valka Onderra Vhad Edda, xenologist." I don't know how I responded, though I guessed I'd said the correct thing, for Valka smiled again and said, "Lovely to meet you."

I do not consider myself a great artist, though she made me wish I was. I could not have known at this first meeting how many times I would fail to capture her, in charcoal and in life. The brazen declaration of her: the pride in that upturned chin, the pointed nose, and the tidy carelessness that put her above the opinions of lesser men. There's little sign of her wit—so close to cruelty—in any of the drawings I made of her, and this poor prose cannot contain her beauty, body or soul. Even holographs fail. They are only echoes, as is this.

Any Imperial aesthete would have told you she was too much of too many things: too severe, too serious. Her skin too pale. Her eyes too wide. Those eyes. Golden eyes. I have never seen their like, before or since. They knew things, and they laughed at what they saw even as they cut it to ribbons. There exists no word for the color of her hair, such a deep red it looked black in all but the brightest light. She wore it short, and what excess there was she gathered into a bun at the top of her head, loose strands playing across her forehead and about her small ears. She smiled like a razor at a joke only she ever understood and stood like a soldier at parade rest, waiting patiently with that terminal clasped behind her.

After what I feared was an embarrassingly long moment, I managed to ask, "You work with the Umandh?" I could have melted through the floor then and there. What an

astonishingly bland question. If I had known who she was—what she would be—I would have strangled myself from the shame.

The doctor glanced back over her shoulder, frowning at the three creatures, now intent on scooping up the shattered remains of the broken bulb. "Only incidentally. My primary focus lies with the ruins on the southern continent."

"I wasn't aware Emesh *had* a southern continent." *What ruins?* I made a mental note to steer the conversation in that direction later on. I'd heard nothing about Emesh playing host to alien structures—but then I'd known nothing of the Umandh until Cat had taught me better.

"Anshar!" Anaïs offered. "It's not large. It's where Tolbaran is—the old capital from back before my great-grandfather took the planet and built Borosevo." That had been a bloody mess, I later learned. Before Emesh had become an Imperial palatinate, it was dominated by Extrasolarian interests and a Norman Freeholder group. When House Mataro descended on the planet more than a millennium ago, backed by three Imperial Legions, they'd built the oldest parts of Borosevo on an isolated atoll, leaving the old capital to molder in the hands of their servants.

Doctor Onderra smiled again. "Your companion is not from here, is he?" She said it just like that, no honorific, no *ladyship*. The doctor only clipped the Umandh comms tablet to her belt the way a chanter might his prayer book, jounced by her hip. She had not addressed me directly; she spoke to Anaïs as though she were my handler and I her servitor.

Her ladyship clutched my arm again, pulled me close in spite of my attempts to maintain distance. "No, he's from Teukros. He was a myrmidon, did you know? Fought in the Colosso for a year."

The Tavrosi academic raised her eyebrows, the sort of hollow, unimpressed expression of an adult entertaining a very small, very irritating child. "Was he indeed?" Gone was her earlier openness, her warmth, snuffed out by this new datum. Belatedly I remembered that the Tavrosi

clans took a dim view of blood sport. Among those strange men at the edge of the galaxy, violence was a thing for primitives and machines. War among the clans, such as it was, was almost exclusively economic. I could feel the doctor's temperature toward me cool. That bothered me, and it bothered me that it bothered me. I threw a glance at the palatine lady on my arm, sharply as I could. She didn't see it.

"Tell me, M. Gibson, do you enjoy killing slaves for your masters?"

It took me a moment to realize the woman was speaking to me. I had forgotten my assumed name. When her words hit me, they did so like a blow to the liver. But then, she was Tavrosi. They did not have the Colosso in that strange and distant country, nor slaves. They had sim games and mandatory public work and a peace maintained by therapy and reeducation, protest where we had order, chaos where we had peace. They discouraged families, so much so that long associations between couples were disrupted by their mongrel state, and they committed that greatest of abominations: mingling their flesh with that of machines. Deciding that she had not understood the myrmidon-gladiator distinction, I said, "I fought with the slaves, my lady. Against the gladiators."

"Against them?" Valka Onderra sneered. "Well, I suppose 'tis all right, then." She pressed a strand of that red-black hair back behind one ear. "And I'm not a lady, I'm a doctor."

She was a scholar like me, then, as she had already admitted when she'd said she was a xenologist, but that point had escaped me for the barest second, making my brain numb and the rest of me feel the fool. She broke off a moment and shouted instructions to the two douleters, gesticulating with that intricately tattooed hand. The two men responded, circling the Umandh with their sticks, and Valka tossed them the comms box from her belt clip. "Amateurs." She said the word like a curse, an effect heightened by the snapping Tavrosi accent, and tapped a finger against her temple, those golden eyes narrowing in frustrated analysis. She burbled a stream of swear words in a Tavrosi

dialect. I caught the word *okthireakh*—*Imperials*—and another that sounded awfully like *barbarians*.

Barbarians, was it? I dusted off my Tavrosi languages, cracking my metaphorical knuckles. I switched to Nordei, the most common of the Demarchy's languages. I had only the barest understanding of it, but I tried anyhow. I asked, "The device you use to communicate with them—how does it work?"

Valka Onderra's fine eyebrows rose in surprise, but the woman responded—not in Nordei, but in Travatsk, another of the Tavrosi languages. Sly. I didn't know a word of it, so I spoke instead in Panthai, the only other clan language in which I could string together a sentence, though I must have sounded like a thick child. "I didn't understand a word of what you said."

Incredibly, the Tavrosi doctor's face split into a smile. Anaïs was looking from her to me, bafflement on her perfectly gene-sculpted face. "Was that Tavrosi? Do you two know one another already?" She looked pouty beneath that sheer curtain of blue-black hair. I resisted the urge to tell her ladyship that there was no such thing as Tavrosi.

The foreigner looked at me again as if for the first time, stroking her pointed chin. "No, no, ladyship. I've never seen the man before in my life." Her attention briefly flickered from my face to Anaïs's, then returned to me. "Not many Imperials learn a Tavrosi language, much less two."

"I'm not many Imperials," I said, standing a little straighter and—I hoped—taller in the doctor's eyes.

"Plainly." She cocked an eyebrow. Then she changed tack. "The Umandh aren't like us. They don't think."

"I'm sorry?" I said. The subject change had given me whiplash.

"What does that mean?" Anaïs said at the same time.

Valka jerked her head over her shoulder to where the xenobites had returned to replacing the light fixtures under the watchful supervision of their overseers. "They aren't individuals, really. They're more like . . . well, like a neural lace." I had no idea what that was, but I kept my face impassive. In the face of ignorance I've often found that silence is the best tutor.

I wished only that someone had taught Anaïs Mataro that same lesson. "What's that?"

The Tavrosi cocked an eyebrow, "Each of the Umandh is like a cell, and they . . . The droning is not so much their communication. 'Tis not a language. They're . . . net-working."

Networking? It was a datasphere term, I knew, but I had as little understanding of the arcane workings of a plane-tary datasphere as a dog has of human mating rituals. This time my curiosity surrounding this semi-forbidden field of study overcame my trepidation. "You mean they're a combine-organism?"

The doctor brightened, glanced from Lady Anaïs to myself. Her brows knitted together, and she inclined her head in a slight affirmative. "Not entirely. They're distinct—they don't share tissue—but the droning lets them harmo-nize."

"Literally harmonize." I cracked a thin, crooked smile, which Valka returned. Somewhere in my breast, a shadow of the old Hadrian—the scholiast's pupil—stirred as if from fugue. This was what I had lived for as a boy. Had it really only been four years ago? *Four years for me,* I amended. *Nearly forty in truth.*

Clearly unhappy to be boxed out of the conversation, Anaïs leaned forward. "Are you staying in the capital long, doctor?"

"Only until the storms pass. Calagah gets a bit . . . well, 'tis underwater this time of year." The Umandh were fin-ishing their work, the pitch of their song rising, a steady beat joining the suddenly disjointed sound of their chorus. I still couldn't see how they made the sound, though I fig-ured they had to have mouths somewhere in their tops, somewhere amongst the tentacles. As one of the tripod creatures trundled past, I marked the thick white glaze it had plastered over itself, daubed in whorls down the length of its narrow trunk and radial thighs. Some sort of tribal marking? I wanted to ask about it, but I filed that away too for another time.

Instead I followed the natural flow of the conversation, resisting the temptation to pursue any number of tangents

up their blind alleys. "Calagah? Would those be the ruins you mentioned?"

To my small amazement, it was Anaïs who replied, not the doctor. "You really don't know?"

I really didn't, and I was growing a bit tired of the pattern of non-answer shaping up in this conversation. Still I kept the edge off my tongue, mindful that one of the ladies was a palatine and that I—in my current guise as M. Hadrian Gibson—was not. "No, my lady, I'm afraid not."

Valka ran a thoughtful hand up and down the tangle of lines on her arm before she turned those unlikely golden eyes upon me. "Calagah is the ruins, yes. Um . . ." She eyed Lady Anaïs, biting her lower lip. When Anaïs neither complained nor made a move to stop her, the doctor said, "'Tis very old, not human. The site predates the Norman settlement here by thousands of years."

That made me blink. "Umandh, then?" I'd never heard of the Umandh building anything so permanent. Their homes, built along the seacoast in one fenced-off ward of the city and on their island alienage—were accretive structures mounded from debris. They'd taken the wreckage of boats and starcraft, bits of crumbling buildings, and whatever else they could find and lashed them together to make lean-tos. Their village on the water—in the water—looked like nothing so much as a gyre washed up upon the shore. It would not last a decade unattended, much less centuries.

The doctor wrinkled her nose. "'Tis the obvious conclusion." Doctor Onderra eyed the palatine lady on my arm and spoke more plainly. "We are not the oldest race in the cosmos, though most seem never to leave their home worlds. Extinction catches them first."

"Like the Arch-Builders on Ozymandias?" I asked, naming the first extinct civilization that came to mind.

Valka blinked. "Quite, but the ruins at Calagah are far older. The Arch-Builders have only been extinct for—"

"For forty-three hundred years, yes," I finished, eager to prove my knowledge. Valka looked surprised, and I added, "I'm a bit of an amateur enthusiast."

The Tavrosi woman crossed her arms. "Indeed. Well,

some of us make a living at this, M. Gibson. Though I've several holographs of the Calagah site. If you're really interested, you could stop by my chambers." I smiled, sure that she was warming to me—or I was, until she came down for the sting. "That is, if you're not too busy killing people." Then she brushed past, leaving me small and sweating in her wake.

She was in the shadow of the arches back out to the colonnade, following the Umandh and the two douleters, before I found my words. "It was very nice to meet you, Doctor."

She didn't look back, but she waved. "I suppose it was."

I had no response for that, and I stood there, Anaïs forgotten on my arm. No words came to me, and for a time only the distant sounds of Borosevo came through from the balcony. The lights the Umandh had installed flicked on. The word that finally came to mind was Classical English: *dumbstruck*. Literally to be struck speechless, as by a blow. We have no word for it in Galstani, but no other word applied..

CHAPTER 47

THE CAGE

LET US LEAVE THE matter of Valka and my turbulent heart a moment. She has been brought upon the stage, but as I waited for her, so must you. I must approach her now as I did then: cautiously, curious as the azhdarch circling the matador. Besides, I did not see her again for weeks, save in the impressions she made upon my young mind. Instead I attended Anaïs's regatta, another fight at the coliseum, and two live operas put on by the same Eudoran troupe who had performed at the Colosso's halftime show. The rest of my time I spent accompanying the count's children about their business and their lessons, and I was only allowed out of the castle on such voyages.

It was like the count knew I wanted to leave. I do not think he truly did, but I felt hemmed in, locked like Daedalus in the dungeons of Knossos. And like Daedalus, I sulked in the darkness of my room, scratching new images in my journal. What had I been thinking? That the count would take an interest in my abilities and retain my services? That I charmed my way into his service by mere force of character? That indeed is the story they tell: that Marlowe the coliseum slave talked his way into the count's service and into the arms of his daughter, that he was seduced by a witch of the Demarchy and turned thence to darkness. I wish I could say it were so. I wish I could say I came to the count's service by some cleverness on my part.

Nothing could be further from the truth.

I was there because I had defeated myself. Hoisted by

my own petard, to borrow the Classical English expression. I'd had a plan to escape, to buy a starship for a song and a lie. I'd alienated my only close friend to do it, and I didn't even have a ship to show for it. I'd been so sure when I walked into that gaol that I'd be able to walk out again. I'd forgotten who I was for a moment, forgotten the secret of my blood. I'd grown too comfortable in the coliseum, sure that Had of Teukros could do as he liked.

Still, it could have been worse. I could have been in the gaol.

I wanted to contact my friends in the Colosso. Pallino, Elara, Ghen, and Siran—even Switch, if he would hear me. Palace security would have monitored any calls I made as surely as they monitored my every hour lounging alone in my room. Any talk of our plans to buy a ship might look like an attempt to flee. I'd bought my comfort and fine meals with my privacy, traded my future for that present, if unwillingly. As on Delos, I was aware that I sat in a crystal cage.

Only this time I had no one to blame but myself.

I was not leaving Emesh. My stupidity, my cupidity had seen to that. Like Doctor Faustus, I had wanted knowledge—and like Doctor Faustus, that knowledge had cost me dearly, would cost more dearly still.

CHAPTER 48

TRIUMPH

THE MUSIC OF THE parade as it marched out of the vomitorium beneath the lord's box was deafening, the martial sounds of brass and drums amplified by speaker drones arcing above the heads of the crowd. I stood in one remote corner of the box, sipping a glass of Kandarene red in the shadows of a striped awning, watching as the count and his husband waved from the fore of the box, Anaïs between them. The young lord Dorian, whose birthday it was, stood on a bier at the head of the parade in full combat armor enameled green and golden, a white cape pinned to his shoulders, a highmatter sword glowing in his hand.

I barely saw him.

I was seeing Crispin instead, seeing my brother in black and crimson paraded about the Meidua coliseum while my father and mother—had my mother even attended?—watched from the equivalent of where Lords Balian and Luthor stood. Instead of Tor Vladimir and Chancellor Ogir, I saw Sir Felix and Tor Alcuin. Instead of the wiry, hard-eyed Dame Camilla, I saw Roban, who once had saved my life. Only the presence of the Terran Chantry was unchanged: two figures in spectral black, darker than space itself, their chasubles trimmed in iridescent white. Indeed, were it not for Chanter Gilliam's disfigurement, he and his superior, the tall, hook-nosed grand prior of Emesh, might have been a match for Severn and old Eusebia.

The woman was Ligeia Vas, Gilliam's natural mother,

made unnatural by time. I tried to look past her withered visage, the long braid of silver-white hair looped about her shoulders like a scarf, the knobby hands resting on their cane. I tried to see the palatine woman who had willingly borne a child to term within herself. I couldn't see it, but then, who could see such a life in so withered a face? No young man, surely. No young man has ever seen anything in the elderly save the damage done by Time.

Fireworks crackled from the parade line, fired by hoplites in formal armor. They filled the dusk with colors: bright greens, soft golds, scarlets like falling stars. Each shock of color was accompanied by a deep concussion that shook the eardrums. The blasts were more felt than heard, the noise of them lost in the cheering of the crowd and the blaring of music. The Borosevo Sphinxes—the gladiators I'd spent two years surviving—all stood on the bier a step below Dorian, armed for the combat that was to come. Behind them on similar biers came those house sworn to Count Mataro's service: Melluan, Kvar, and Veisi, as well as a knight-tribune called Smythe and her officers, representing the Imperial Legions. The biers were followed by a platoon of hoplites in Mataro colors, and next came a full century of Imperial legionnaires in their faceless ivory armor, all of them boxed in by a double line of marching band musicians and by the firework mortars.

Draining my wine, I left the glass on a stone rail and pressed through the crowd of dignitaries flooding the box, bowing my way around Lady Veisi in search of a better vantage point. Word was that there was to be a melee followed by a staged round of duels between Dorian and the gladiators—Dorian would win, but only just and in such a way that none would question his legitimacy. But before all that the cathars would appear, dragging the Cielcin from its prison to die its sacrificial death.

I couldn't have cared less about the young nobile. He was a decent enough sort but vapid as that sister of his, though without any of her guile. My concern was the melee. Not one month ago I would have been fodder. I

could not decide if I was ready to see my one-time companions again: Pallino and Ghen, Switch and Siran and the rest. I hoped they wouldn't all be fighting that day.

"You must feel right at home."

The foreign accent gave the voice away before I saw her. "Doctor Onderra!" I spoke over the murmur in the box and over the concussive roar of crowd and triumph. "No, I don't." The truth was, I couldn't imagine there was anyone in all the Colosso that day who felt more out of place than I. I should have been arming myself, not wasting time among the nobility. *The nobility.* When had I started to think of myself as something else?

When I told her so, she frowned, "You miss it, then?"

"Not on your life, but I'd rather be down there than up here. Wine?" I seized two glasses off a passing tray and pressed one on her. She cradled the goblet in her hands, chewing the inside of one cheek. After a moment had passed, I leaned in to half shout, "I'm sorry I've not been by to see those holographs you mentioned. My lord count has had me teaching his children the finer points of Jaddian etiquette. He's expecting an emissary within the next year, I've been told." That was only part of it. Mostly I was afraid I'd make a greater fool of myself in her presence.

"Are you—" She broke off. "Were you some sort of diplomat before . . . ?" She gestured at the parade orbiting the coliseum's killing floor. A local musician danced about on one bier, clutching a microphone in her hands while she cavorted almost naked and sang into the device. At some point the martial anthem of the band had faded, blurred to join the woman's supporting artists in a raucous tune dominated by synthetic guitar.

Memory brought a pained smile to my lips, and I forced a swallow of wine to hide the expression and turned away. "I might have been." Whatever attractions the doctor held for me, I was not about to start narrating my life story to her. That particular task was a challenge for old men and not for that time or place. "Plans . . . changed." She would understand, surely, if I told her. She was of the Demarchy; she would share my feelings about the Chantry. I glanced

at Gilliam Vas's hunched form. There were places on Delos—in the vicereine-duchess's own court, for a start—where such abominations were given willingly to the fire at birth. Looking at Gilliam, I thought I understood the custom, so great was my unease. I mastered the feeling, unsure if my dislike was for his deformity or for the man himself or some alloy of the two. How easy I thought the world in those days, imagining that all enemies might be as twisted without as within.

I have since learned otherwise.

"Plans always do," the doctor supplied, taking a sip of her wine before nodding approvingly. She leaned in, more to protect herself from being overheard than out of any intimacy, and said in a stage whisper, "This all seems a bit much for a birthday party, don't you think?"

For a palatine, the potential ruler of the planet, I thought it was maybe a bit small, but then Emesh was not Delos or Ares or Renaissance or any of the old worlds. I might have disagreed but instead waved an acknowledging hand. "The palatines like their parties."

"Back home we just get terribly drunk."

"We do that here too." I stifled a short laugh and hoisted my cup of wine. "I think they do that everywhere."

Valka looked down over the triumph parade. "I've heard it said that the Eudorans don't drink."

"Remind me not to travel with the Eudorans," I deadpanned, eliciting a chuckle from the woman. I punctuated the weak bit of repartee with a swallow of wine, grinned into the brief silence.

One of the guests—a tall man, clearly palatine and wearing an earth-toned suit with white piping—pressed through the crowd, one hand raised. "Valka!" Despite his advanced age, he moved with grace and noble dignity. A collapsed highmatter sword jounced against one bony hip, marking him as a knight. He lowered his raised hand, flattening his mop of unruly white hair. The cut might have been at home on a boy of fourteen, shaggy and wild, though he might have been pushing four hundred, to judge by the deep lines on his cheeks and forehead. "Valka, my dear, it is good to see you!"

"Sir Elomas!" She smiled, allowed the older man to take her hand and kiss it, smiling all the while. "'Tis lovely to see you." I turned a politician's smile on the knight as she said, "You must meet M. Gibson. Hadrian, this is Sir Elomas Redgrave, my sponsor. Sir, this is Hadrian Gibson. He's . . ." She broke off, puzzlement stealing its way over her face. "What exactly are you?"

I bowed to the knight, careful not to spill my wine. "A tutor. I've the honor of instructing the lord's children in languages."

"Some honor—I've met the little shits." Elomas grinned, careful to keep his voice low. "I'm not familiar with House Gibson. Where are you from?"

Mindful of the false identity I wore, I raised defensive hands. "From Teukros." *If only.* "We're not palatine, sir. My father runs a shipping company. Natural fabric trade with the Principalities."

"Ah!" Sir Elomas was still smiling, all teeth. "That would explain it." As it was meant to.

Doctor Onderra leaned forward, cradling her wine cup in her hands as the heavy music blared from the parade below, almost washed out by the cheering of the crowd. "Sir Elomas is Archon Veisi's uncle."

"Uncle-in-law," the knight amended.

"He sponsors my work at the dig site."

"In Calagah?" I asked, turning my attention from Valka to Sir Elomas.

The knight brightened. "You're familiar with the site?"

"Only recently. Doctor Onderra's promised to show me some holographs on the subject." I smiled. "You're an archaeologist, then?"

The old man steadied his sword hilt against his hip, adjusted his shield-belt over his suit jacket. "Only an enthusiastic amateur."

"The best kind, surely." I glanced at Valka, then down at my own feet. I recalled that the doctor and I had had something of a debate on this very subject at our first meeting.

"Ah, Sir Knight! Welcome back." The intruding voice carried a familiar aristocratic drawl. "Glad to see you

could pull your head out of that hole in the ground long enough to come and—" Gilliam Vas was struck to silence as his mismatched eyes skated over me. "You!"

I felt Valka take a surprised step back beside me, but I turned my politest smile on the intus. "Your Reverence, it's been some time since the coliseum."

The intus wrinkled his nose as if he'd trodden on something foul. His wrist twitched—actively suppressing an urge to pull his kerchief free, I didn't doubt—and he said, "I'd heard the count had admitted a lowborn into Borosevo Castle, but I didn't expect he'd stooped so low as you." Valka and Sir Elomas both regarded me with something like curiosity. Beneath my false smile my jaw tightened, permitting the creature the time he needed to continue, "This man assaulted me in the coliseum tunnels while I was working to secure our lordship's prize."

"Prize?" Valka looked confusedly at the round-shouldered priest, her sharp brows contracting.

Gilliam puffed his pigeon's chest out. "For the triumph."

"He means the sacrifice," I said. The day's events were common knowledge. "The Cielcin."

"Do be quiet, barbarian." The ugly priest clasped his hands before him—he was not drinking wine. For an absurd moment he looked like some Eudoran parody of a priest, the slight asymmetry of his skull making his waxy face seem more mask than flesh. I squinted at him, trying to commit those features to memory; he would prove a challenge to draw. He looked, I decided, as all Chantry priests should look: as though he were the secret face of that debauched institution. "You're the one who broke into its cell, too." It wasn't a question, but I could see the wheels turning in the man's head. "I'm surprised you're still breathing. Or is the count starting a harem?"

"Jealousy looks bad on you, Gil," Sir Elomas interjected, clapping the intus on the arm in a friendly sort of way. "But I'm sure there's a whore somewhere in the city who'll *take* you." He spoke the word *take* with a vindictive alacrity that lit a fire in his mossy eyes. I had to suppress

a smile, both at the jibe and at the secret knowledge that I was what Gilliam wished he was. Had he known, he wouldn't have dared speak to me as he was, no matter his ecclesiastic post. Briefly my fingers found my house ring on its cord beneath my shirt.

Gilliam Vas turned his nose skyward. "Have a care, sir. Recall that it is my mother who sanctions your little expedition. One word from me and . . ."

Elomas appeared entirely unruffled. "Why have you come here, Your Reverence?" He had abandoned the familiarity of a moment ago. I wondered at that, filed it away for later consideration.

"I'd wished to convey my congratulations to you on the birth of your niece." Gilliam *did* draw out his kerchief now and pressed it to his nose. I caught a whiff of something like coffee and cinnamon from the fabric. He glowered past the rumpled bit of cloth. "But seeing the company you keep—barbarians and heretic whores . . ." His upper lip retreated in a curl of bespoke disdain as he glanced at Valka. "I should think the courtesy misplaced."

For a moment I forgot my imagined station, and Hadrian Marlowe spoke from my lips, not Hadrian Gibson or Had the myrmidon. "Until this moment, priest, I did not think it possible to misplace a courtesy." I felt myself scowl and smoothed it down, glad to have an answer to my earlier question: it was the man I hated. His appearance, whatever my prejudices, was incidental.

Gilliam bared his teeth as he reached for a reply. Finding one, he opened his mouth to respond, but the words vanished, boiled away by a terrific hiss that rose from the crowd like steam, drawing the unseeing forward to the edges of their seats and dragging eyes upward to the massive screens that projected views of the proceedings on the floor. How many times had my helmeted face been there amongst my fellow myrmidons? I felt almost I had never seen those screens—that coliseum—before, seeing what I saw there then: the xenobite, pale as Death. They had given it a shift, one of the white dishdasha of the sort clerics wear beneath their robes. Its horns had begun to

grow back, making a lumpy ruin of its crest, and the white hair that sprouted from the back of its head was wispy in the buffeting air. It screwed shut its massive eyes, its subterranean biology not proof against Emesh's fist-sized sun. In the angry light of day it less resembled a man. Makisomn looked like some Precambrian creature plucked from a volcanic vent. Its slitted nostrils flared, and it bared those milk-glass teeth in a snarl. The crowd screamed, hurled drinking bulbs and bits of food. The archenemy of humanity had arrived. The formal music returned, perfectly timed by some clever planner, dominated by the beating of drums large as groundcars.

The pageantry reached its climax as the two cathars emerged from the shadows of the vomitorium opposite the parade entrance. The other biers had fanned out, the legionnaires and Mataro hoplites squared off into ranked units at the long ends of the elliptical plane. Young Lord Dorian descended from his bier, accompanied by the Borosevo Sphinxes as an honor guard, lances in hand. He met the two cathars on the field, and from our box Grand Prior Ligeia raised her voice—a witch's groan—and began the invocation. "The Earth has left us, vanished into the Dark." She let these words hang in the air, waiting for the common refrain.

"She has forsaken us." The crowd grew silent in the wake of the words.

"Blessed are we, the children of the departed Earth," the grand prior declared.

"She will return."

There is something very human in quiets such as that, in the preternatural stillness of fifty thousand souls. All of them—and I myself—were cowed by the weight of that silence, animated by that spiritual communion that mankind calls God. Beside me Doctor Onderra watched impassively, a slight quirk to her lips. I tried not to stare, turned back to watch the prior from behind as she continued her ministry. In the city beyond the coliseum and in Borosevo Castle above, the great bronze bells were ringing.

"This is a joyous day," said the prior, voice amplified

and broadcast about the space, "a day of celebration. For today the son of your lord, Dorian of House Mataro, comes of age. He is a man this day!" Had it been the count administering the rite, they might have cheered, might have felt the press of celebration more than ceremony. At the grand prior's words, there was only silence and the bowing of pious heads.

Unity through justice. Justice through piety. Piety through prayer.

I never went to Vesperad, but I know their minds.

She was still speaking. "Behold this beast, this demon! Child of the Dark. Captured in battle by our brave warriors, a sacrifice now! A reminder! The Dark will not stand; its creatures will not be victorious. The stars are ours, said Mother Earth! They are for us!" Below, one of the cathars drew a massive sword from a sheath wrapped in what I knew was human skin. The blade was so long that the one cathar had to kneel for the other to draw it, and then they approached, bookending the young lord like shadows.

"Is he going to kill it himself?" Valka whispered. She'd followed me from the back of the large box. She touched my arm, suddenly very close.

My eyes would not leave the Cielcin, but I shook my head. "Not likely. He'd only make a botch of it."

"They're not . . . blind, are they?" she hissed. "Your priests?"

"No, they can see through those blindfolds. It's pure symbolism. The Chantry icon of Justice is blind." I looked away from the screen to the actual tableau unfolding on the coliseum floor. The Cielcin was forced to rise, dragged by two legionnaires from its place on the bier. From the loose way it sagged between them, the way its legs melted and tangled beneath it, I knew Makisomn had been drugged. "They sedated it." I clenched my jaw. "The cowards." But it was theater. All theater, as surely as the Eudorans' masque plays, as surely as Mother's holograph operas.

I did not hear the rest of the prior's nattering, or would not hear it. My eyes were on the White Sword, its ceramic

blade nearly five feet in length, unpointed. It was a ridiculous thing, far too unwieldy to use in combat. It shone a
snowy argent, sickly in the orange daylight beneath that
blood-cream sky. I clenched my free hand around the
railing, the veins standing out against the skin. At a word
from Ligeia Vas, the Cielcin was forced down. "They may
raid our cities, burn our worlds, but they will never break
us!" Her voice was the dry rasping of twigs on stone.
"Behold him, people! Behold the demon, our great
enemy!" I grunted at the improper pronoun, but no one
else seemed to care. "We will drive him and his kind back
behind the stars and into the final darkness from whence
there is no return."

The blow, when it came, did not fall from on high. This
cathar was too much the showman. The two legionnaires
holding the Cielcin torqued its arms back long enough for
the cathar to whirl in a horizontal arc that parted
Makisomn's head from its shoulders. Inhuman blood,
black as oil, sheeted down the front of the body, followed
by a gasp and rush of air. I knew a moment of the profound-
est anticlimax, artfully manufactured. It diminished the
dead creature.

See how easily it dies.

The cheering came moments later, falling like a storm.
Fifty thousand people cheering, their religious decorum
abandoned. I looked down and away at the floor. At my
shoes. The crowd threw synthetic silk streamers toward
the ring, white and green and golden. They drifted lazily
down over their neighbors' heads and onto the battlefield.
I looked up just in time to see them settle, a parody of
snow, radiating like the striations of a human eye from the
central figures of the young lord and his cathar companions.

The second cathar wiped the blade with a swatch of
white cloth. He pressed the cloth together, folded it neatly
in half, then opened it for everyone to see. The pressure
had made a symmetrical blot on the opposite side, a sigil
such as ancient mystics used to show men in order to peer
into their souls. That presentation ended, the torturer folded the cloth over his arm and assisted his brother

murderer in sheathing the White Sword. He then seized the alien's head, wrapping his fingers beneath the epoccipital fringe sweeping back from its horned brow. The cathar knelt and presented the head to Dorian, who nearly dropped it as he lifted it by the hair for the crowd.

Still watching my feet, I whispered a single Cielcin word: *"Udatssa."*

Farewell.

CHAPTER 49

BROTHERS IN ARMS

"WHAT'S THIS ABOUT?" I asked the guard when I arrived at the palace barbican. "Your runner said there was someone here to see me?" I had ignored all the calls to my room's holograph plate, had gone out onto the balcony until someone had sent a servant to fetch me, and so my silk tunic stuck to me, and my hair was slicked against my forehead. Still I drew myself up to my full height and tried to look presentable, trying to mask my trepidation.

The guard only looked at me, words clearly in retreat from his chapped lips.

"I'll say you do!"

Pallino emerged from the guardroom, his laugh half fading as he entered the hall, an echoing place of tiled floors and high pillars. Another pair of guards followed, chuckling at something the old myrmidon had said. He drew up short, chewing on something that didn't exist. A word, maybe. Hands on his hips, he surveyed me with his one blue eye. "Ghen was right about the 'Your Radiance' thing. You clean up, kid." Though it was a joke, there was a kind of strain in it.

"You look like shit," I shot back, eliciting the smallest of smiles from the man. I tried to smile back, but I couldn't quite bring myself to. There was something in the older man's demeanor, something frigid. How quickly his joshing manner with the guards had gone cold. A sudden dread seized me, and I asked, "Did someone . . . ?" *Die?* I couldn't get the word out. Was it Switch? Siran? It could

not be Elara—there would be no smile left in the man if that were so.

Pallino started. "What? No. We thought *you* were dead, you bastard." He gestured to my fine clothes. "It's plain you ain't a prisoner, so why was this a secret?" The old soldier looked like he wanted to spit, but he refrained, mindful of the mosaic. "You figure now you've got your fancy new friends you can just leave us high and dry, is that it? Switch was right about you."

"I . . ." I looked round at the three guards as if hoping to find some answer in their faces. Behind the myrmidon, the open gate to the castle hung open, admitting the daylight but not the liquid heat thanks to the static field that shimmered just inside the high arch. Just beyond that was the parade ground, a great plaza that stretched for nearly three miles to the low shape of the coliseum, all gray concrete and bright metal. "What?"

He wanted to do this *here*? In front of a small detachment of house peltasts? In the sight of Earth only knew how many different kinds of cameras? We were on the front steps of the castle, in Emperor's name! Behind me the incline lifts rose for dozens of stories up to the top of the ziggurat and the castle mezzanine. The place was bustling with logothetes and the civil service, both Mataro and Imperial proper. There were even brown-shirted foederati mercenaries present, a coarse company in one corner awaiting I knew not what. Pallino wanted to do this *here*?

"You up and vanished on us, boy!"

We couldn't have this conversation here. We couldn't have it anywhere near the castle. How could I answer truthfully without compromising my secret? The secret the count had all but ordered me to protect? A thought occurred to me, and I turned to the nearest of the peltasts. "Guardsman, I'd like to speak with my friend here in private. Might we take a walk around the plaza?"

The man looked to his senior, a hard-eyed woman with a lantern jaw. She shook her head. They had their orders. They knew who I was, or at least that I was not allowed outside.

"The gentleman is not to leave the castle unescorted," the peltast said in a flat voice, pointedly not looking me in the eye.

I held my wrists out to Pallino as if they were shackled. "I'm not *exactly* a prisoner, but as you see, I'm not exactly free either. I couldn't send a message." This last was not strictly true, was one of those small lies we tell to save our souls.

Pallino stood string-cut, taking in the new data. At last he managed the word, "Oh."

A snort escaped me, and I gestured the aging veteran away from the gate and the guards. There was nowhere in all the castle where we could be guaranteed privacy, and I didn't doubt that there were those in the count's service who would be very interested in my comings and goings. So I led Pallino into the shadow of a red column. Eager to restart the conversation, I asked, "How is everyone? How's Elara?" I clapped him on the shoulder, trying to take some of the tension out of the moment. Over his shoulder I could see the three peltasts watching us from the outer door.

"What's that?" The old man's eye had wandered, taking in the frescoes on the vaulted ceiling depicting the Mataro conquest, the retreating Normans unwashed beneath the ivory boots of the Legions. He had an almost wistful look on his face as he looked back round at me. Remembering some other earlier life? "Elara's fine. One of Amarei's new lads bruised her jaw in the last melee, but she's a tough old bitch." He smiled a lazy smile. "Love this mural." He reached a hand up, waving it to take in the scope of the image.

"It's a fresco," I said, unable to help myself. As I spoke the overhead lights flickered and went out for a moment. I frowned at them, but such brownouts were common in the castle. Storm damage, or so the servants said.

Pallino didn't seem to notice or care; the sunlight was ample enough. "I know it's a fucking fresco, lad. I wasn't born in no barn." The lights sparked back on.

Ducking my head, I murmured an apology, then stood square facing the older man. "I suppose we'll have to can-

cel buying that ship, eh?" There. I'd said it, and I hoped it was innocuous enough that I wouldn't be answering any pointed questions later from the count or his inquisitors.

Pallino blew out a long breath, seeming almost to deflate. "It wasn't a bad plan." Robbed of the anger of his original purpose and a chance to yell at me, the man was bereft. He didn't know where to take our conversation. That was good. That was *something*. At least he wasn't shouting anymore. At least he wasn't making a scene. "Buying the ship with some land of your dad's . . . smart."

I jerked as if stung, shocked. "Switch told you?"

"I've got to say, it don't make any sense." He hooked a finger beneath the strap of his leather eye patch, scratched his face. "Why would a rich kid like you be fighting in the pits with dogs like us? Especially when you could come on up here and get treated like some kind of royalty?"

How could I answer that? It was worse now than when Switch had asked me after our visit to the shipyard. That time I hadn't been under surveillance. What was it I'd said to Switch? *There'd be nothing but trouble until I left the Empire.* That was it. *If* I left the Empire.

"Same as you," I said pointedly. "It was my best option. That's what Switch and I were fighting about." Pallino took this better than Switch had. He only grunted, arms crossed over his barrel chest. His attentions are still on the fresco. Still he didn't answer, leaving me to question exactly how much Switch had told him. "He didn't believe me."

The myrmidon grunted again, slowly moving his eye from the image of conquest on the vault above. Beside us a door opened and a group of logothetes and guild representatives filed out of one of the conference rooms, stranding us for a moment in a sea of drab gray and violet suits. At length Pallino spoke, shaking his head. "You rich kids." That blue eye focused on me beneath furrowed brows. I was sure then that he knew, sure Switch had told, and I was grateful—so grateful—that the man had the tact to keep quiet. I had to remind myself that Pallino had been a soldier once. Discharged a First Line Centurion. He had seen active service on Imperial dreadnoughts, hadn't been one of those below the freeze line, kept in reserve for centuries

at a time. He knew what it meant to be monitored, to be under the scrutiny of other men every waking instant of his life.

"It's not like that," I said, not sure what either of us meant but knowing I was different in that way all young men do. "I *had* to leave home, Pallino." I leaned into the word *had*, pouring every ounce of determinism I could muster into it. He needed to know I meant it, but I had to let him know without saying anything to compromise the tenuous nature of the count's charity. As courtiers so often do, I was dancing barefoot on the edge of a knife. Between the truth and the necessary illusion. Between admission and security.

The man must have taken my meaning, for he backed off, changing topics instead. "They letting you out anytime soon? Be good to have you back." I gave him a look. They were never going to let me fight again. This thought penetrated, and he changed tack. "At any rate, be good to have you come round for drinks next time we win." A thought flashed behind his eye, and he added, "You heard about Erdro?"

Swallowing, I bobbed my head, and it was my turn to look up at the frescoed ceiling. "I saw." Unsure what else to say, I scrambled and added, "I thought he had Jaffa for a moment."

"It was a fool's game," Pallino replied. "Those antique weapons demos are about as stacked against our side as it gets. He should have known that, shouldn't have charged that bastard."

"He was a good man," I said simply. "A good fighter."

"He was." Pallino rubbed his sleeve above the spot where his Legion tattoos decorated the biceps. "Maybe it's good you're out. I'd have hated seeing you end like that, Had. Who knows; maybe this is a good place for you."

He was trying to be polite. It hurt. "I'd rather be off-world."

"Why?"

I had expected the question, but still it was not an easy

one. How to explain to a plebeian that wealth and power came with a cage? He would only see the silks, not what it cost to wear them. "This isn't home, Pallino." I shrugged, focused my attentions on the older man. "It's not me." I broke eye contact, unable to bear the gaze of his single eye. "We could still buy the ship."

That eye narrowed. "How, if you're stuck here?"

"I could front it with my—my dad's land. You, Elara, and Switch could work for me. You wouldn't have to risk your lives anymore. It'd be steadier work. Safer." I broke off, rubbing my jaw. "Suppose I'd have to hire a pilot, but . . ."

That snagged something in the myrmidon's mind, and again he chewed on something that wasn't there, eye flicking up to the ceiling in thought. Neither of us spoke the unspoken—that I'd implied I would still be alive to collect the owner's share of any income. If he were paying attention—and he was—he knew then that I was at least of patrician breeding. "That wouldn't be half bad, to be sure."

"You'll think about it?" I brightened. If I could not escape my circumstances, then at least I might help my friends. And although the chances were slim to none in that moment, perhaps I harbored a hope that I might find a way to escape, to get away from Emesh and onto a path chosen by myself for myself.

Pallino's mouth turned up into a tight smile. "Might do, aye." He chewed his lip, smile collapsing like a wave. "And I'll talk to Switch, see if I can't make him come round. It's not right, a man not talking to his brothers." Was that what we were? Naturally the word made me think of Crispin, the only true brother I'd ever had, though the loss of him had not stung so deeply as the loss of my myrmidon companions. Hearing that word, *brothers*, sparked a deep loneliness in the base of my soul of the sort I'd not felt since Cat died. Not because I *was* alone, but because I was not and perhaps deserved to be.

Tucking my chin, I had to shut my eyes to stop them from watering. "I'd appreciate it," I said, voice halting. "I'd go myself, but . . ." I made a noncommittal gesture in

the direction of the guard room. Seeking to lighten the mood, I asked, "What did you have the guards laughing about?"

"War stories, son," the myrmidon said, clapping me on the shoulder. "War stories."

"He say anything about me?" I turned to stand beside the shorter man, crossing my arms. We stood in silence a moment, both staring up at the image that so enamored my companion. Directly above us hung an image of an Umandh struggling against two Imperial legionnaires with glowing lances. One man had his boot on the trunk of the colonus, and I recalled the way the gladiator in Meidua had stood upon the body of his mutilated foe.

Pallino leaned away, twisting slightly to look at me. "Who, Switch? He and Ghen talk shit now and again. Reckon he misses you."

"Tell him I'm sorry," I said, clasping my hands behind my back, "and that I'd tell him myself if I could." I jerked my chin up, pulling on an ounce of aristocratic poise to choke down my emotions. "I know I owe you both an explanation for . . ."—I gestured at my fine clothes and the opulent surroundings—"but I can't discuss it right now. Can you trust me?"

The older man was smiling when I turned to look at him. "You know, in the Legion you learn to trust the men on your decade. Even the bastards. Sometimes especially the bastards. Don't matter what they're about. You're all pulling the same way, you hear me?" I said I did, and Pallino pointed a finger at my face. "You're not the worst bastard I ever met, Had. Not even close." He pointed at his own face, then at me, then himself. Pallino grinned. "We're pulling the same way."

We stood then awhile and talked of small things, of our friends and the coliseum and how stupid my fine clothes looked on me. But soon enough Pallino had to go—he had drills to conduct training the new fodder recruits. I turned to go first, to ride the incline lift to the palace proper. He seized my wrist. "This ain't goodbye, you know?"

"What?" I blinked at him, genuinely confused. "No, of course not."

The old veteran grinned like a wolf. "Good, because I'm holding you to that ship thing. Now you're in with the gentry, it shouldn't be too hard for you to manage." I wanted to correct him, but there was no time. The leathery myrmidon clapped me on the back and said, loudly and apparently in jest, "And who knows? You might need us if you ever wanted to skip town!" And with that he went out into the rippling daylight, waving casually over his shoulder.

CHAPTER 50

WITHOUT PRETENSE

SEAWATER THREATENED TO SPILL over the tops of my boots as I jumped from the deck of the flier, droplets spattering my clothes, disturbed by the repulsor jets along the underside of the silver-black craft. A decade of soldiers in Mataro livery went ahead, clearing a path along the tidal zone toward the place on the beach where the khaki-uniformed douleters waited with their Umandh slaves lined up for inspection. Remembering my courtesies, I turned and helped young Lord Dorian—a man now, by all the rights of the Imperium—down from the flier. He accepted my hand graciously, as did his sister. Doctor Onderra came last, along with an older woman in the same khaki uniform of the Fishers Guild. Valka slapped my hand away and sloshed ashore just ahead of me, carrying her Umandh comms box steadied against one round hip.

Lingering a moment by the quieting aircraft, I placed my red-glass spectacles on my nose, squinting up at the sky. Today was to be a learning exercise: a proper visit to the Umandh alienage at Ulakiel. The royal children were to learn about the native xenobites, and I—in my dubious capacity as their captive friend—had been dragged along. Given Valka's presence, I had not complained. The island, like the southern continent of Valka's stories, was one of a rare set of antique volcanic outcrops from a time before Emesh's tectonic death. Ugly black stone rose for perhaps half a hundred feet above sea level to a worn-down promontory, upon whose crown the island's human vilicus had

built his keep, overshadowing the Umandh in their grubby hovels.

"See the palisade?" Valka said, pointing out to sea where a chain-link fence rose unrusted from the green waters. "Poor bastards can't even swim away."

"Electrified?" I asked.

Valka made a face. "Heated. On contact that fence'll get hot enough to cook any organic matter it touches. The Umandh are stuck here unless they fancy burning off a few tentacles."

It was my turn to pull a face. "That's awful." I had watched the Umandh beaten in that Borosevo warehouse and had seen them brutalized at the Colosso. I had thought mine a strong stomach, but something about that heated fence tore at me.

"'Tis *your* Empire, M. Gibson." She shrugged, hurrying up the berm to rejoin our noble charges, ignoring the armed peltasts who treated her presence as slightly hostile, edging closer to their young masters. Something in the way she said the word *your* soured my stomach. I followed in her wake, shaking the salt water from my treated, still-dry clothes.

The man who greeted our party on the beach screamed offworlder almost as much as Valka and I. He lacked the rich brown skin of the majority of people on Emesh. Rather his skin was ashen, a saturated gray color, not natural at all. My first thought was that the man was a homunculus, for he reminded me of nothing so much as the little beast Demetri had kept on the *Eurynasir*, but no homunculus could have held a station in a guild on Imperial soil. Some mutation, perhaps, or a deliberate aesthetic choice purchased from some corporate bonecutter. "Lord and Lady Mataro, so good of you to pay us a visit on our humble island! I am Niles Engin, I'm the vilicus here at Ulakiel."

Dorian made a gesture to signal that the man could stop bowing. "Thank you, Vilicus."

The gray-faced chief overseer patted his curling black hair nervously. "And Earth's blessing on your Ephebeia, my lord. I watched the broadcast."

Anaïs took her brother's arm. "He was so gallant, wasn't he, sirrah?"

"He was, ladyship." His eyes lighted on Valka and myself. "And these must be M. Gibson and the Tavrosi."

Valka stiffened at being called merely *the Tavrosi*, but she offered no complaint and extended a hand. "Valka Onderra, xenologist."

"Yes, yes." Vilicus Engin clasped her by the forearm instead of the hand—a subtle thing, that—and discreetly made the sign of the sun disc with the other hand down by his hip. Subtler work still. The Demarchy's dissociation with the Chantry was well known; their autonomy maintained primarily by their isolation. "You're the xeno expert, yes? This little tour should be most educational, then. You can see how they live in their proper habitat."

Valka's lips compressed into a sharp, thin line. She glanced toward the concave bend of the shoreline, raising her slim eyebrows incredulously toward her red-black hair. I saw what she saw: the little hutment grafted to the base of the basalt rise, sprouting like fungus from the margin of the sea. Thick beards of rust hung from metal sheets; in places it had rotted through panels visible even at this welcome site. Ulakiel may have been the largest single refuge for the native intelligent species, but it was not designed to put on much of a show for guests of any distinction. The five Umandh that had come with Engin's party were curiously quiet, without even the faintest mewling or rasp. Their stony silence disquieted me, and I kept an eye on them where they loomed, tentacles seeming to taste the air, moving as blind man's hands might in the hope of finding their way in the dark.

"Tide won't be in for another few hours," one of Engin's men said, pointing at a series of stakes hammered into the beach to mark water points. Because of its two moons, Emesh's seas rose and fell wildly. On impulse I glanced up at the sky. The green moon, Binah, hung low over the horizon, dark where it occulted the edge of the giant sun.

The white moon, Armand, was nowhere to be seen, sojourning on the other side of the world. Dorian jostled me, hurrying to catch the vilicus and Anaïs.

That day—like every day on Emesh—fell hot upon us, choking, smothering as a blanket. I pushed my red glasses up my nose. The coastline stank of fish and rotting seaweed, though how any of either found its way into the alienage's limited waters was a grand mystery. I had to suppress a Gilliam-like instinct to wrinkle my nose.

"'Tis a damn waste," Valka breathed, coming off the heels of a question about population density. "A neurological wonder of the universe, and these tank-brains have them fishing." Her shoulders hunched a little as she brooded.

I could only look away and repeat, "It's awful." Not far off, an Umandh emerged from the surf, dragging a net half-filled with fishes the color of tarnished silver. It started droning, low and monophonic, rattling out from the aperture in its head whence sprouted the long tentacles. I felt Valka's eyes on me but could not turn to see the expression there, for to do so would have been to signal what an admission that had truly been. I was still seeing Makisomn's head, too-long tongue lolling as it shook in Dorian's fist. The lordling himself walked not far off with his sister and the vilicus.

I took in the shantytown the Umandh had built, watched the creatures droning along, attracted by the one's song. They moved with apparent mindlessness, directed as ants are by a communal urge to pull together. As we watched, the one newly in from the sea dispensed its catch in a flurry of tentacular motion, distributing the little fishes out one and two at a time to its brethren, who passed the morsels up over the rims at the tops of their trunks and into where I assumed their mouths must be. It was not hard to imagine their immobile ancestors rooted to the seabed, trailing tentacles through the waves to strain for prey.

"We actually just exported a thousand of the natives to Triton. A fair breeding sample, though reproduction is not a particular challenge for the beasts," the vilicus was saying. Two of his khaki-uniformed officers tapped

shock-sticks against their thighs, watching the coloni closely. Farther off, our own guardian escort stood at quiet attention, itching hands not far from their sidearms should the children prove threatened by the slave creatures.

Dorian frowned visibly, but it was Anaïs who said, "I didn't realize we were shipping the Umandh offworld."

"House Coward on Triton seems to believe the creatures can be trained to lay wiring on the seabed." Engin frowned. "Not that I've known them to do so much as screw in a light bulb." I shot a glance at Valka. Was that not what they had been doing on the day I'd first met her? Helping to repair one of the castle's frequent power difficulties? "But that's Coward's problem, and if they can find a use for the mongrels, all to the good. Even the Normans couldn't find a use for them when they ruled here."

I had the measure of the man then, could smell his place in the worlds. "You were a trader yourself?" It is said that xenobites from the other coloni races are still traded along the spaceways, coupled now with the Cielcin slave trade, my unfortunate legacy.

"Yes, indeed," said Niles Engin, puffing out his chest. "Ran a line in the Cavaraad trade from Sadal Suud to the inner systems. Helped spice up the old courts." I had never seen one of the Cavaraad, the so-called Giants with their staved-in faces, like someone had taken a clay effigy and pressed his thumb in to hollow out the face. They'd been popular in the Colosso circuit some centuries before, their massive size pitted against myrmidons such as I had been.

"Cavaraad?" Dorian repeated, confusion in his dark face. "You were a slaver?"

"Is," Valka huffed from the fringes. I watched her stalk off, shoulders hunched in that way she had as she studied the readout on her tablet. She was listening, trying to understand the Umandh's song. I left the palatine children with the vilicus and the guards and moved off to stand beside the doctor, boots giving way in the sand. She pointed, indicating a series of woven chimes hanging from the garbage houses the Umandh occupied. "See those?"

Shading my eyes with a hand, I nodded. "Are they wind chimes?" Though they looked nothing like them, they reminded me of the wooden and paper prayer cards that hung in the vestibule of Chantry temples or lay at the feet of the icona—prayers for strength, for health, for courage. Prayers for love and wealth.

"No one knows," Valka said. She moved off toward the nearest structure. "They're all over the Umandh barracks in Borosevo. Could be religious." She hissed air out between her teeth. "I hate we can't just ask them."

"Can't you use your tablet?" I waved a hand at the device that was again swinging from her hip like a legionnaire's cingulum. "Just ask them?"

She shot a glance at me with those golden eyes. "'Tis not a language, M. Gibson. The Umandh harmonize at different frequencies to accomplish tasks. One sings that 'tis hungry, say, and others harmonize with it until they are fed. They're smarter in packs, but not much smarter than chimpanzees."

"So you're saying that all the tablet does is—"

"—is spoof one of their signals. They know we're different from them when they hear our signal, but your people have taught them to obey."

I did not rise to the bait. She wasn't talking about me. "How many words—How many signals do they have?"

"Only a few dozen that we know of. Honestly, do you know how unlikely it is that the Cielcin have something we recognize as grammar? How unusual?"

"About one in twenty-five species," I said automatically.

Valka's eyes lit. "Don't be clever." But she smiled.

I crossed my arms and leaned toward Valka. "I read a theory that language like ours facilitates the growth of civilization, that it's the reason the Cielcin and we are the only spacefaring cultures in the universe."

"In the *known* universe," Valka corrected. I could sense her standing rigidly at my side, made stiff as by some hidden concern. "You're talking about Philemon of—"

"Philemon of Neruda!" I cut her off, enthusiasm overriding my native sense of propriety. *"Unnatural Grammars!"* I

twisted to regard Valka, who looked surprised to find I knew the name of the man and his treatise.

The doctor pursed her lips. Impressed? She put a hand to her face. "Tor Philemon's convincing, but our sample size . . . 'Tis too small. And the Irchtani and Cavaraad have languages but no star travel. I like his hypothesis, though 'tis only a hypothesis."

"You're saying we can't support his claim until we survey more—"

"—until we can survey other species. Very good!" She was grinning openly now. "Not bad for a *brathandom* like you." I didn't know the word, but I could tell she was mocking me. No, not mocking—teasing. She was teasing me. When had that started?

There would be time to dwell on that later, I decided, and I pushed it aside. Interesting as they were, it was hard to imagine a truly collectivist species like the Umandh developing the technical know-how to design shoes, much less starcraft. Instead I said, "So if it can't *really* translate, what does that box do?" I flapped a hand at the comms tablet on her belt.

"Have you ever tried telling a cat what to do?"

I looked up at her, shaking my head. "No." The truth was, I had never seen a cat. We did not have them on Delos, and if there were any on Emesh, they were inside where the ornithons could not get at them.

The doctor was not looking at me; she had stooped over the very tablet we were speaking of, fiddling with its dials. "'Tis not easy, Gibson." She arched one brow, hair slipping out from behind her ear to coil between us. "'Tis not like with your Cielcin. The Umandh do not think as we do. Their consciousness operates on completely different principles."

While she spoke, I studied what could be seen of the coloni hovels. Trash and bits of old buildings piled together the way a bird might build a nest. What looked like the floor of an old prefabricated house leaned against the cliff face, sagging where time and stress had bent its composites so that it clung to the fascia like limpets might. "What are those?"

I pointed to a set of metal rods the dotted the land-scape about the low structures. Hoops hung from them, their surfaces woven with bits of string and wire and some corded substance that might have been gut. Though they glittered with color, there was no apparent pattern, so the colors were meaningless and left a brown impres-sion on the mind the way paints do when mixed by a child.

Seeing them, Valka brightened and led me further along the shoreline. I followed the Tavrosi xenologist, spar-ing a glance toward the spot below the berms where Engin crouched, surrounded by what I could only guess were Umandh children. The fry were indistinguishable from the adults, save that they were shorter. Engin was passing out bits of candied fruit from a paper bag. Anaïs laughed as the creatures plucked food from her hands.

Valka had pulled one of the hoops down from its place on the pole, and only then did I see the thongs hanging from it. There must have been a dozen of them, knotted and braided with bits of shell and stone that clacked softly in the breeze and with the motion of the hoop. Noting this, I asked the obvious: "What is it for?"

She shrugged, passing the hoop to me.

Feeling as if I were being tested, I took it, turning the thing over in my hands. "These stones couldn't possibly make very much noise."

"To you or me," Valka said, clicking the tablet back into its holster at her hip. "The Umandh see with their ears." She tapped her own ear for emphasis. "'Tis louder to them." She moved a little closer, peering over my shoul-der as I examined the thing. They were the only things in that place of recycled trash that seemed crafted well and honestly. I ran my fingers over the weaving that spider-webbed the hoop, pulled gently at one of the tassels. On impulse I shut my eyes, imagining I was seeing the thing as an Umandh might.

The surface of the weaving inside that hoop stood out in ridges, some fainter and harder to feel than others. There was a pattern to it, a geometry. "It's an anaglyph," I said, opening my eyes.

Her golden eyes lit, surprised. "Have you been reading about them?"

I shook my head. "No." The truth was that I'd been too busy sulking about the loss of my freedom to do much studying.

She narrowed her eyes, chewing again on her lower lip. After a moment she said, "It took the original Norman survey teams the better part of a decade to work that out."

"Maybe I'm just lucky." I don't think Valka took me at my word, but she shrugged it off. "Is it some sort of writing system?" It made sense that a blind species like the Umandh would keep records that could be read by touch.

Valka shrugged again. "Writing, art, maps. We can't be sure." That made sense, given how difficult it was to understand the Umandh mind, and yet I sensed Valka knew something she was not letting on. "It certainly means *something,* but . . ." The way she said the word *something* had a brightness to it that defied questioning even as it invited curiosity, and yet I sensed a shadow on her words—or fancy now that I did.

Unsure, I let the silence stretch between us as I examined the tassels that hung from the bottom of the plate-sized hoop. Looking round at the others marching away down the shoreline, I asked, "Why circles?"

"What?"

"Look at the frames," I said, pausing long enough to reach up with both hands and mount the chime back on its pole. "They're perfect. Nothing here is perfect." I gestured at the hovels around us. "Why do they care about these things?" I tried to imagine all their fine tentacles twisting the bits of salvaged wire and reed into shape, teasing, smoothing them out with care of a sort I had not seen from their kind in any other task. At once I felt a sudden, crushing sense of otherness, a wall to understanding greater than any mere language barrier. I rounded a small crest in the beach and peered under the slanted bit of floor that had been turned into a kind of roof. Another question settled on me, and since Valka had turned so inexplicably taciturn, I asked it. "What are your ruins

like? I haven't been able to find any holographs on the palace's datasphere."

"Calagah?" Valka asked. "I thought you were not reading about them?" She was standing just behind me, and she followed me as I slipped down a shallow embankment and into the cool, close space beneath the old floor. It was drier than I had imagined, and the walls teemed with bits of trash tied onto strings that swayed slightly, disturbed by our passage. I wondered what they *looked* like to the Umandh, what quiet music they added to this dark and ugly place.

"No, I meant I was not reading about the anaglyphs."

"Ah," Valka said. "Why do you ask?"

"Well, if they built a civilization before the Normans landed on Emesh, I'd be interested to learn what they built it out of. There's not enough land to grow anything like wood, surely. Stone?" Somehow I could not picture the tree-like amphibians as masons. Valka was standing in the doorway, squinting back out at the shore where the others stood. I could not see what she saw, and she did not answer. "Doctor?"

She twitched, looked round at me. "What? Sorry."

"What is it?" I asked, moving toward the opening to look back at Engin and the others. The Umandh children had scattered and were spinning in the shallows, their droning high and ululating. Was it laughter? "What are you looking at?"

"See those brown stripes on that one?" She pointed. The trunk of one of the older Umandh had deep brown welts with thin lines spiraling from them in the random way an eggshell breaks. "Engin beats them."

I felt a sick knot form in the pit of my stomach and looked away. After a second I told myself I was acting the fool. I had seen men and women mutilated on the Chantry's steps. *Homo hominis lupus.* Why should this bother me more? I made myself look. "He has them whipped?"

Valka was still speaking, the luminous edge of her words cutting through the woolly cloud in my head. ". . . thought I'd gotten them to stop. *Meonvari tebon kahnchob ne kar*

akrak. He can't whip them! He has them pinned down and *chiseled*."

I felt myself flinch. "What?"

She passed a hand over her eyes and turned from the beach. "You *anaryoch* are obsessed with pain." Over her shoulder I saw Dorian Mataro lift one of the Umandh children into the air, laughing as he did so. What the creature felt I could not say.

"Chiseled?" I repeated, my earlier question utterly forgotten. Laughing, Vilicus Engin retrieved the alien child from Dorian's grasp and returned it to the water with surprising care.

Valka mimed driving a spike down with her fist and pushed past me into the hushed dimness beneath the floor-turned-roof. "It's that bloody church of yours."

"The Chantry?"

"They normalize violence. Look at you." She waved in my general direction. "The gladiator."

Myrmidon, I thought, but I did not correct her. I didn't speak at once but contemplated the braided cords hanging from the roof above. Only slowly did it dawn on me that we were standing somewhere free of cameras, of the constant, watchful eyes of court and Chantry. So I spoke not as the fictional son of a merchanter nor as the myrmidon he had been before, but as Hadrian alone, without pretense. "What they do is . . . is vile."

I felt the pressure of her strange eyes, but I would not meet them. There must have been something in my voice, a gravity. I clamped my jaw shut, suddenly afraid of saying too much, or that I'd already said too much. I wanted to say more, to tell her about my father, about my duty to the Chantry. But that was Hadrian Marlowe's duty, and I was Hadrian Gibson. For a moment we were like two puzzle pieces whose owner understood they fit together but could not see how. Had we a day or even an hour, it might have been different, and all her lingering antipathy for me might have washed away.

But it was not to be.

"I thought 'twas against your laws to say such things," she said.

"It's blasphemy," I corrected, "to be *heard* saying such things." I risked a look up. Valka stood amongst the hanging ropes the Umandh had arranged, head cocked to one side, sweating through her thin shirt, hair stuck to her pale face, an expression like unexpected moonlight. "You can say them if they don't catch you." I squared my shoulders, my old sense for the dramatic flaring up. "And if you *can* say them, you should."

Valka nodded, combing a stuck strand of hair from her face, and I understood Shakespeare's impulse to be a glove. Her hand lingered on her cheek as if in quizzical exasperation, and she shook her head. "What am I supposed to say to that?" She crossed one arm to prop up her other hand and slumped into it.

"It doesn't matter, I . . ." The impulse to look over my shoulder for listeners was too great. "I just wanted you to know we don't all think like that. It's not easy living like we do. We're not all . . ." Monsters? Barbarians? "We're not all what you think we are."

She closed the space between us and lay a hand against my triceps. Her fingers tightened even as her face formed a sad, sweet little smile. "I know that." A shout from outside shook us back to our here and now, and she said, "What were we talking about? The ruins?"

"What?" I could still feel the cool spot where she had touched me through my sleeve, knew and feared that the sensation would fade in moments. "Oh. Calagah! I asked what the Umandh built the ruins out of. You'll pardon me, but they don't seem up to building much of anything."

The woman looked at me a long while, chewing over her answer. Almost absently she stroked one of the hanging bits of Umandh art. I was aware of just how close she was standing, of the smell of her sweat and mine and the faint perfume of her hair beneath the salt and rotting fish smells of that place. She must have reached some decision, for she said, "The Umandh didn't—"

"Hadrian!" Anaïs peered under the lip of the slanted floor above us.

I sprang back from the doctor and turned the motion

into a supercilious bow, one hand pressed to my chest, making the sticky cotton cling there. "Ladyship!"

The palatine girl's jaw tightened when she saw Valka. "Oh, Doctor Onderra, I thought you were with the xenos. Don't you have shots to give them or something?"

Valka smiled like a chip of broken glass, but she bowed as well. "Not that sort of doctor, ladyship."

While she straightened, Dorian appeared over his sister's shoulder and said in a baritone on its way to his father's basso, "Oh, now this is cozy, isn't it?" He didn't sound sincere. They both looked terribly out of place in their water-treated silks with their bright colors and rich embroidery—Dorian's houppelande especially struck me as so fine as to diminish the hovel about us.

An old thought returned to me unbidden, that we palatines were not truly even human. Saltus's words cackled in my ears: *We are both children of the tanks.* I scowled. *Inhuman.* The word applied to homunculi, to the Extrasolarians, whose bodies were perverted by machines. Not to the blood palatine of the Imperium. I felt queasy all of a sudden.

"Oh, hello M. Gibson, Doctor Onderra," Dorian said. He rested a hand on his sister's shoulder, seeming to notice us for the first time. "Wondered where you'd wandered off to."

Vilicus Engin popped up an instant later. "What in Earth's name are you doing in there? Out, out! Don't just stand there!" He made a snapping gesture, then remembered who he was speaking to and temporized, "These hovels aren't stable! Come, come, my lord and lady, come!"

Anaïs was staring—no, glaring—at the doctor, as if she'd caught her stealing, her contraband midway to her purse. I wondered at that a moment, but I dismissed it when the palatine girl seized my hand. "You must come see the primitives! The vilicus is going to have them dance for us!" I shot Valka a besieged expression, but the doctor only looked glassily back at me, that hard-edged smile catching in me like fishhooks.

CHAPTER 51

FAMILIAR

"AND *IUDARITRE* IS 'to cut?'" Dorian asked, dropping out of Jaddian to clarify in Imperial Galstani.

I indulged the lordling with a pointed smile. "Quite right, lordship." Technically it was *to have cut*—the perfect infinitive—but for the purposes of our exercise it was irrelevant. I tugged at the chain about my neck, the one that held the ring I'd stolen back from the ship reclamation crews my first day on Emesh forever ago. Looking out through the shielded window, I could spy the starport at the watery edge of Borosevo, a flat, white concrete expanse dimpled with the round craters of blast pits. I returned to Jaddian quickly, recalling the mandate Lord Count Mataro had given me as the price of my secured position. "The trick with draw cuts—if you're quick enough—is to attack the arm," I said, continuing my account of a battle against the gladiatrix Amarei of Mira. She'd been a guest of the court two weeks earlier, and the lordling was still quite taken with the thought of her. "Especially if you're dealing with shorter weapons." I put down my pencil, satisfied, and turned the journal around, revealing a charcoal portrait of the young lord in gladiatorial armor of the antique style worn by the myrmidons, not the high-tech safety gear of Amarei and her ilk.

The count's son looked at it appreciatively and asked about the origin of my talent. *"Pou imparato iqad . . . rusimatre?"*

"Rusimiri," I corrected and shrugged. "I've always enjoyed drawing. Since I was little." I lifted the pencil

again, glancing sidelong to where Anaïs sat in her sim goggles, some fantasy or other piped directly onto her retinas and into her ears. Gesturing at her I said, "My father discouraged us from such things—he said they weren't holy—so I took up drawing instead. My scholiast supported it, said it was a classic hobby. A proper vocation." In Jaddian the word *muhjin*—vocation—also means talent, making it a subtle boast. The subtlety was lost on Dorian.

"You're very good! You should consider work as a royal portraitist. Anaïs, come see!" The girl did not immediately stir, so her brother scooped up a cherry from a side dish and threw it at her. Squawking, she prized the goggles from her face. "Hadrian drew me!" he announced.

The sister stood, languid as a cat, the look of petulant frustration on her pretty face morphing into one of surprised delight. "Oh, this is marvelous!" She flashed her mathematically perfect teeth, leaning over the table in such a way as to award the onlooker a view down the top of her blouse. Blushing, I averted my eyes as Anaïs settled into a chair beside her brother. "Would you draw me next?"

"We're supposed to be speaking in Jaddian, my lady," I said tartly, inserting the pencil into the cheap plastic sharpener the lordlings' guards had given me when they'd confiscated my sharpening knife.

Anaïs pouted, crossed her arms just under her chest. "Oh, all right." She rocked back onto the chair's rear legs. "I thought you were talking about the Colosso!"

"We were!" Dorian exclaimed, tapping the picture in my journal and smudging the delicate charcoal in the process. "That's why he drew me as a myrmidon." He went on to catch his sister up on my duel against Amarei of Mira, when I'd stun-locked her suit's functions with several small attacks, slowly crippling her.

When he finished, Anaïs clapped appreciatively and asked, "Will you go back?"

"*Alla* . . . Colosso?" I asked. *To the Colosso?* I didn't know the word for Colosso in Jaddian, or indeed if there was one.

"Yeah!" Anaïs brightened. "You could go back as a gladiator! You'd be perfectly safe!"

"Not this again!" I had to stop myself from standing, clamped my hands down on the arms of my chair. Valka's false charge rattled in my head. *Tell me, M. Gibson, do you enjoy killing slaves for your masters?* I looked down and away. "Many of the fodder myrmidons are my friends, ladyship."

Dorian pulled a face, but Anaïs said, "Well, that surely won't be true for very long . . ." She hadn't contemplated the full meaning of what she'd said, and when it hit her a moment later, her dark face turned faintly green. Eyes downcast, she mumbled, "Sorry."

As a palatine, as Hadrian Marlowe, I might have been able to stay offended. Hadrian Gibson did not enjoy that luxury. "Her ladyship is most kind to understand my situation." I could not even recognize, officially speaking, that she'd given me insult. Her regret seemed momentarily to have cowed her. "Forgive me, ladyship. Doctor Onderra's opinion of the games has . . . somewhat colored mine of late."

"Doctor Onderra," Anaïs repeated. "Must we talk about the Tavrosi woman? She's leaving soon."

I stiffened, turned the page in my journal to hide my reaction. Leaving soon? To Calagah, of course. Emesh's extreme tides would be changing, and when they did the halls and caverns of Valka's ruins would emerge from the depths of the sea. Valka was only here to work with the city's Umandh, to learn what she might in her off-season. Once the true focus of her life's work was available again, she'd be gone.

Dorian intruded on my thoughts. "Her opinion of the games? Do they not fight in the Demarchy?"

My mouth twitched, and I had to stifle a frown—I didn't have a concrete answer to that question. I felt sure they must've had some sort of competition, though I couldn't have guessed what form it might've taken. "I just don't think they have a proper Colosso, lordship. Perhaps this is a question better asked of the doctor."

"They're too busy worshipping their machines," Anaïs sneered, leaning over the table and resting her chin on her arms.

I sat studying her face a moment, newly sharpened pencil poised. Then I set to work. "They don't worship machines in Tavros."

"They're still heretics," the girl said, head bobbing against her arms on the table. I began tracing the contours of her face. "I don't know why Father tolerates her." My lips quirked, recalling how patently amiable she had been when she'd introduced me. I wondered at the change in naïve perplexity, little seeing my own role in it.

"Her expedition is sponsored by Sir Elomas Redgrave, Sister—you know that. The Calagah site's just some old tunnels. Why not let the offworlder dig around? What harm could it do?"

"I just don't like her is all. Gilliam says she's a witch, that she gave herself to machines." She shuddered. "He says she's not really human anymore."

The count's son raised his eyebrows, scratched at his blue-black hair. He had Lord Luthor's high cheekbones and narrow eyes, though somehow in him the effect was one of earnestness and not distrust. He looked perpetually surprised. "Gilliam's a priest. He's meant to say such things. The Demarchists are strange, I'll grant, but there's nothing inhuman about the doctor. I think she's gorgeous, truth be told. Don't you, Hadrian?"

I twitched so badly I nearly dropped my pencil. "What?" I looked him in the eye. "Oh. Yes." I did not add that I'd been spending a couple of evenings a week in her company, discussing the Umandh and the various places she had been. "She's a brilliant xenologist, you know. Did you know she's been to Judecca? To the tomb of Simeon the Red at Athten Var?"

"Really?" Dorian raised a carefully manicured eyebrow, dark eyes widening. "That's incredible!"

Anaïs sighed and seated herself, picking up her goggles. "I'm not sure what you see in her. Offworlder like that . . ."

I smiled, but a touch of frost edged my words. "I'm an offworlder too, if it please her ladyship."

The girl had the grace to look mollified, but her brother interrupted. Dorian leaned over the table, half mirroring

his sister's slumped posture. "Say, might I have that portrait you made of me?"

Against my will, my grip tightened around the charcoal pencil. The last thing I wanted was to rip a page from my fine journal. The book was perfect. And yet I could not refuse the lordling's request. "Of course, lordship." With stultifying precision I prized the thick white sheet free and slid it across the table to the young lord. Tearing it felt like breaking bone.

"Do you think Father would let me fight in the Colosso? As a gladiator?"

I glanced up at him, pencil stopping its work as I started on Anaïs's portrait. "Might do. My father let my brother fight."

Dorian heartened at once. "I feel I should after my Ephebeia. He didn't let me kill the Cielcin."

I traced a contour of Anaïs's hair with my pencil, frowning. "Beheadings aren't easy, as I understand. The White Sword isn't highmatter, you know. Your fathers only wanted to ensure the thing was done right, I'm sure."

"And it was a Chantry ceremony anyhow." Anaïs sat up again. "Old Ligeia likes to make sure everything's just right." She pushed herself away from the table, turned away, then turned back brightly, somehow catlike. "You could teach us!"

This thought didn't follow on the heels of the earlier conversation, and I sat at the table, squinting up at her in confusion. "What in Earth's holy name are you on about?" Pointedly I set the pencil down in the ruined fold of my journal.

Anaïs gestured to herself and her brother. "Sword fighting, I mean. You were a myrmidon. A good one! I looked you up on the holographs."

"Don't you have a master at arms?"

"Not a very good one—just old Sir Preston Rau. The man's hideous. You'd be so much better! Dorian, tell him he'd be better." She rounded imploringly on her brother, slapped his upper arm.

She'd surprised Dorian halfway through the process of eating another cherry from the chilled bowl on the table.

He pushed the fruit into his cheek and said, "It might be fun. Why not?"

I opened my mouth, shut it, opened it again. Anaïs beat me to responding. "You wouldn't be really fighting. Just teaching." She looked down at her hands, then up again shyly through dark curls. I groaned inwardly. I knew when I was outmaneuvered.

"But why do we have to train *outside*?" Dorian moaned when I'd disarmed him for the twelfth time. He waved off a lictor who tried to help him stand, also for the twelfth time. The swarthy man glared at me for having brutalized his young charge.

My bare feet scuffed on the fine clipped grass, and I tapped the plastic-and-foam training sword against my shoulder. We'd foregone shield training in favor of clearer channels of communication, a move that had excited my two companions almost as much as it had vexed their security. After reminding the muscle-jawed security sergeant that I was hardly likely to kill Anaïs or Dorian in front of a decade of house peltasts in broad daylight, the man had relented. I tapped the earth at my feet with the sword. "Your myrmidons train outdoors, lordship." I glanced at Anaïs, whose bodysuit clung to her like a sheen of white oil. To her credit, she'd not offered a single complaint, leaving that emasculating role to her brother. "It's good to get used to fighting in conditions like these. That way when you have climate control, you appreciate it." Sir Roban had said something very like that to me as a child when he'd first taken me running through the castle grounds in winter rather than in the castle's gymnasium.

Mopping the sweat from his face, Dorian shifted his weapon from right to left. The boy had been demonstrating a frustrating tendency toward ambidexterity, which required twice the footwork practice. Anaïs hadn't been kidding about their training. I did not wish to speak ill of this Sir Preston Rau of theirs, but the children were as

incompetent a pair of fencers as I had ever seen. Had Sir Felix been so good a teacher? Thinking of Felix put me in mind of Gibson—of what happened to Gibson—and I looked away from my two charges, fearing they might see something of my hurt in my face.

"I suppose that makes sense . . . but by Earth, it's hot."

"Would you stop whining?" Anaïs put in, taking her turn to square off against me. She slanted her training sword between us, hand forward in the traditional saber guard. "You said this would be fun."

Dorian grimaced, seated himself in the shade of an overgrown arbor against one wall of the courtyard, and propped his sword beside him. "I said might be fun. This is just . . . melting."

"Forgive me, lordship." I turned to look at him. "If you want to fight in Colosso, you had best get used to it."

"The gladiator suits are water-cooled!" Dorian objected.

It was my turn to grimace. The expression turned into a snarl as Anaïs went for a sneak attack, striking my inside hip. I parried the blow without so much as turning to look, focused in time for the riposte to take her in the shoulder. The memory fabric of her target suit bruised red where I had struck her, and she scowled. "How did you do that?"

"You favor the same cut coming off the line," I said, referring to the painted line on a proper fencer's round, were this a formal duel. I mimed the cut at half speed for her. "You take the easy shot, straight to the left hip each time. Try something—" She howled and brought her sword down like an executioner's. She wasn't strong, and so I parried the blow easily, sidestepped, and pivoted to press the edge of my blade against the flat of her stomach. Mindful of the watching guards, I did not follow through on the blow, though the pain of one might have better taught her to remember her mistake. She stepped back, pressure from the blow tracing a red line across her torso like an angry wheal. I found myself wishing we'd had the garments when I was growing up. Felix had been a traditionalist, but they would have stopped Crispin denying that I'd hit him. "You just need practice."

We continued in that vein as we had for the previous hour, with Dorian and Anaïs taking turns fighting me. Neither landed a hit, but that was only to be expected. The peltasts, armored in Mataro green and gold, shifted nervously with each blow, but they intervened less and less as it became apparent that I was not going to kill their charges with the foam training weapons.

Dorian successfully turned one of my attacks, then stumbled as he lunged for the riposte. I let him fall, muddying his knee in the grass. Dutifully I offered him my hand and helped him rise just as the familiar drawling voice of Gilliam Vas wafted into that space. "Here you are, young masters." He froze, seeing me standing above the beaten Dorian, and his uneven nostrils flared. "You again!"

"The young masters asked me to instruct them at fencing, Your Reverence." I swept my blade behind me and bowed. "I shall withdraw."

Anaïs stepped forward. "Hadrian, no!"

Gilliam Vas turned, glancing at the escort who had peeled off when he'd entered the courtyard. "Master Dorian, my lady Anaïs, your fathers sent me to collect you."

The young lordlings stepped forward as I collected their weapons and made to leave, glad to shrink into servile invisibility. Dorian asked, "What's going on, Gil?" *Gil?*

"Nothing of import. Lord Balian wishes for you to attend him." He spread his hands. "I believe a trip to orbit was mentioned." Gilliam smoothed his oiled hair back from his forehead, apparently unbothered by the heat and the thick, cloying air. As I moved past him, he caught my arm, fingers surprisingly strong. "A moment, M. Gibson."

"Of course, Your Reverence." Three swords under my arm, I stood aside, fumbling in the pockets of my trousers for my red glasses, anything to put a shield between myself and the awful priest. Gilliam showed the young lords back inside, left them in the custody of the house peltasts. I loitered in the sunny courtyard for some time, kneading my bare toes in the soft grass.

When Gilliam returned he found me standing in the

shadows of the arbor, leaning on one of the training swords. The other two lay against a pillar near at hand. Without preamble Gilliam seized me by the biceps and leaned in close. "What's your game, offworlder?"

"I beg your pardon?"

"Not too long ago you were bottom-rung in the coliseum, now you're . . . you're . . . wrestling with the young lords."

I arched my eyebrows above the oval rims of the glasses. "Wrestling? Chanter Vas, the nobile children asked me to show them a few moves from my days in the fighting pit. It would have been rude to refuse."

"Rude?" Gilliam repeated, baring artificially straightened teeth. "Rude?" He released me and took a lurching step back, as if saying the word twice had reminded him of its meaning. Standing straight as he could, the intus angled his chin upward. "Some among His Excellency's retainers feel it is improper for a man of your . . . your station to commingle so obviously with the palatine caste."

That earned Gilliam my most acerbic of grins, edged and knowing. "My *station?* The count himself requested that I attend his children."

"Lord Balian has queer notions about propriety," Gilliam said with edged glee. Was that a pun? The old prejudices were known to rear their heads from time to time, even among the palatine caste. Apparently aware of his error, Gilliam reddened. His mistake only made him angry, brows drawing down over those mismatched eyes. "Listen. You're being too *familiar* with the count's children. It isn't . . . proper. Do you understand?" And this from an intus bastard, a mutant, the fleshly avatar of impropriety. Really, it was almost too much for my cultivated sense of irony to take. I stifled a narrow smile.

"Proper?" I echoed, playing dumb. "If you think I've touched Lady Anaïs, I assure you I've no intention of doing so." What was Gilliam to them, or they to Gilliam? Was this court puritanism only that? The protection of palatine blood from the lowborn humanity Gilliam perceived me to be? He was palatine but marked by his affliction as less than a homunculus in many ways. Often I have

found that such outsiders cling hardest to those labels that are denied them. Thus weak men are the most aggressive and unskilled ones loudest to boast. Gilliam was palatine, so the fact that he thought I was not was important to him. It was petulance and little more.

"Touch Lady Ana . . ." He trailed off, voice going tight in his throat as he repeated my words. "A degenerate like you and the young lords . . ." He shuddered, his jaw working as if trying to tear boiled leather, and for a moment I thought he might hit me.

Very carefully, drawing on my guess and my politest speaking voice, I said, "Your Reverence, I assure you that my intentions toward the young lord and lady are entirely innocent. I am only at court because of the count's orders. Given a choice I would have been on the first ship out-system." I did not add, *But I'm a fugitive from my own house and trapped here to protect your lordship from the Inquisition.* I shuddered to think what a Chantry inquisitor would do to a nobile house caught harboring a fugitive like myself.

"Then explain your espionage."

"My . . . what?" I blinked at him behind my red glasses. "You mean my visit to the coliseum cells?"

Gilliam scowled. "You broke into His Excellency's gaol. You can't honestly tell me your intentions were innocent."

"They were!" I objected, perhaps too hotly. "Well, perhaps not innocent, but harmless! I wanted to meet the creature. To speak with it." Here at least was something reasonable. Even I had to admit that breaking in to see Makisomn looked far from innocent, which made the truth seem a weak excuse.

"Consortation is a grievous sin, M. Gibson. One of the Twelve," the Chanter hissed, subconsciously making the sign of the sun disc at his side. "What could you learn from such a beast?"

"I've no idea. I only wanted to see it with eyes unclouded."

"With eyes unclouded," Gilliam mocked, voice stretching to a high note, though from the way his eyebrows relaxed from their intense frown, I knew this had sur-

prised him. Not the answer he'd expected, then. Coldly he asked, "Why?"

"Innocent curiosity." I shrugged, knowing this answer— while almost true—would not satisfy the man. Perhaps I ought to have said *monomania*. "I wanted to meet a member of the only species to ever challenge mankind's primacy in the universe."

"Blasphemy!" he snarled. "No species can challenge mankind's place!" I thought he would grab me again.

Taking a step back, plastic sword twitching in my hand, I almost whispered, "Tell that to the warship recovering in orbit. Tell that to your guardsmen." Some piece clicked into place. Gilliam's dislike of me was not only due to the fact that he thought me baseborn. It was not only that he thought me a spy and a danger to his lord. He thought me a heretic. I suppose I was a heretic, given my interest in the xenobites.

The chanter's lips quirked, and I could almost see the impulse to punch me spasm across the surface of his addled brain. Instead he changed tack. "I understand you can speak their vile tongue."

"Not very well."

"Perhaps that's for the best." Gilliam half turned to go. "Call it innocent curiosity all you wish, but there will come a time when the count loses interest in you, boy. You know the punishment for consortation, surely?"

"I surely do." And despite the warmth of the day and my dislike for the malformed priest, I felt a chill, fancying that I heard the sharpening of ceramic knives and the sound of quenching iron on the wind. The cathar-torturers of the Holy Terran Chantry did not have their reputation without reason. Heretics so heinous as to consort with the inhuman were flayed, crucified, and left to die.

His threat spoken, Gilliam smiled. "Do consider what I've said, and stay away from the young lords."

He was halfway back to the doors and to his two foederati guardsmen before I said, "Your Reverence, a moment." Gilliam turned, lumbering to a halt—was one of his legs shorter than the other? He waited. So as not to make his famously twitchy guards point stunners in my direction,

I stayed under the arbor. I wanted to say something threatening, something impressive. I wanted to cow the little gargoyle of a cleric. But all that came were insults about his condition, and whatever my personal feelings about his sort, I would not stoop to such low behavior. Instead I took a step forward, removing my glasses to fix the priest with my best, most violet stare. "Don't assume you know everything."

CHAPTER 52

LITTLE TALKS

I DID NOT PAY Gilliam Vas much mind. Though he was a priest of the Holy Chantry—a chanter, no less, and no mere anagnost—my childhood on Delos had acquainted me with such high-powered antagonists. Besides, the intus's appearances were few and far between. And I had other things to distract me. My outings with Dorian and Anaïs continued as before, and their Jaddian improved, which was well. Emesh was expecting an ambassadorial visit from the Principalities, and the count and Lord Luthor wanted to impress the soon-to-be-visiting Jaddian satrap governor with their family's fluency and culture.

I had never met a Jaddian palatine, one of the vaunted *eali al'aqran*. The Jaddians had been Imperial citizens once. Drawn together by their ethnic identity—their distant ancestors had peopled the Mediterranean and were among the last to leave Old Earth—they had rebelled against Forum and the Solar Throne more than nine thousand years ago. Against all odds, those once-provincial worlds on the outer edge of the galaxy had won their independence and the right of their nobles to control the genetic destiny of their own children. Few as they were—a mere eighty-some princely families and their leal vassals—they were mighty, with armies of cloned mamluk soldiers and a strong tradition of military service that shamed even imperialist Turkey of old. Never again would those rebel princes kneel before our holy Emperor. Free of the Chantry's grasp—though many in the Principalities still worshipped Mother

Earth—those foreign nobles bred themselves beyond anything the Imperium would allow. They embraced eugenics in ways Sol never would, reassured by the supremacy of their genetics program and their way of life. They were a nation of supermen, of demigods.

I hoped to meet them. Tales of the crystal courts of the Alcaz du Badr, of the harems of Prince Aldia, and of the inhuman speed and skill of the Maeskoloi swordmasters were legend in the Imperium, exotic as the vicious Cielcin, strange as the whispers of Vorgossos and of the Extrasolarians who hid between the stars.

After that afternoon at the Ulakiel alienage, Valka and I had spent more time together. Whatever our differences, we had found common ground in our respect for the xenobites and in our contempt for the Chantry. She knew I had spoken truly that day on the beach, out from under the Imperial thumb for a moment. She had seen *me*, the boy who had fled Delos rather than be shipped away to Vesperad, and she had not despised me.

But I was still not allowed outside the palace unsupervised, and so speaking further truth to Valka was not in the cards. Doubtless there were places in Borosevo Castle where we could truly speak in private, but only the count and his senior staff would know about them, and asking them was out of the question. And so I found myself outside Valka's door, not for the first time and not for the last. She never let me inside, but we walked the palace colonnades and the vaulted halls or else descended to the terraced gardens that studded the south face of the castle ziggurat.

This time she did not open at my first knock, nor my second. I stood there in uncomfortable silence for a long while, counting the herringbone tiles—black and tawny— that covered the floor. A logothete hurried by, escorting an offworld dignitary in Durantine robes. Neither spared me more than a passing glance, and I pretended to be absorbed in the holograph display on the wall opposite the doctor's room: a swirling, impressionistic cloudscape of rose and violet mist enveloping the white geometries of a stone monastery of Mandari design. A panel in the

corner of the misty image said it was the Bashang Temple on Cai Shen.

Cai Shen was gone. Laid waste by the Cielcin. I wondered if those white stones still stood or if war had turned them black. What cruel joke of gods or Fate had tuned that holograph plate to Cai Shen? I ran a hand through the image, pressed my fingers to the metal of the wall behind. I turned away, trying not to think about how the temple and its whole world were glass now. The image fizzled, and the lights dimmed so that only the evening sunlight pierced the high windows to either side of the holograph. The brownouts had grown so common that I didn't even blink but knocked on the doctor's door again and rattled the knob. "Valka?"

It wasn't locked. Had it been left that way? Or had the power malfunction fouled the electronic lock? In any case I found myself opening the door to a room I ought not to have opened. *All right, boy. In or out?*

Despite the lack of illumination, I could see that Valka's rooms were finer than my own and larger. For all that, they were a mess. I stopped for a moment, reminded by a green undergarment left on the floor that I was intruding. The clutter humanized her, though like all young men I clung to my shattering image of Valka's perfection. Clothing littered the floor, hung from the backs of chairs, lay atop printouts and storage chits strewn on the low drinking table and the higher dining one. I forced myself to reevaluate the doctor, to remind myself that at the other end of my private affections was a person and not the dream of one. Remembering myself, I cleared my throat and said in a weak voice, "Doctor Onderra? The door was unlocked. I . . . Are we still on for this evening?" No answer. The sense that I was intruding only grew stronger—and rightly—but I felt I had pressed too far to give up yet. Unwilling to go much farther into the room, I repeated myself. "Doctor Onderra? Valka? It's Hadrian."

I spied her at last, seated with her back to me on the broad sill of one window, obscured by the hangings. Padding softly around a pair of abandoned pants, fighting the conflicting emotions accompanying the thought that Valka

might be undressed, I moved carefully into her line of sight. She *was* dressed, but her eyes were closed. Asleep? "Doctor?"

Her eyes opened, and only by degrees did she seem to become aware of where she was or who I was. "Hadrian? How did you get in here?"

Offering my deepest, most effusive bow, I said, "The door was unlocked. I wasn't sure if you'd left it that way or if the power . . ." I waved my hand around the darkened room. "They really ought to do something about it. These are the diplomatic apartments, and if doors are coming unlocked in these outages—"

Valka smirked. "'Tis fortunate for me, then, that I've a young man like you bursting into my room to defend me." Her wording confused me, and I stalled out before I remembered that Valka was much older than I was, the product of Demarchist gene editing not unlike my own.

I knew when I was being mocked and had the good grace to blush and look away. "I'm sorry."

"I'll let it go," she said, an edged smile cutting the white planes of her face. "This time."

The lights chose that moment to flicker back on, accompanied by that quiet machine whir that we do not notice until it is gone. Under the overhead lamps, Valka's clutter looked even worse. Embarrassed, I backed off, looked down at the drinking table by a couch covered in a tangled blanket. Beneath the remains of a half-eaten meal, the table was coated in papers, some fresh, some yellowed and likely older than I was. In contrast to her housekeeping, Valka's handwriting was remarkably neat. I could not read the swirling Tavrosi script, but I recognized her sketches of the Umandh anaglyphs. She had drawn several of them linked together like soap bubbles. It reminded me of . . . of . . .

"Have you ever seen Cielcin *Udaritanu*?" I patted myself down, remembered belatedly that I had neither a pen nor journal with me. There were some examples mixed in with the portraits and landscapes and illuminated quotations that were my custom.

She blinked at me. "Come again?"

"Their writing!" I smiled brightly. "Do you have a . . ."

Valka produced a pen from nowhere and lobbed it at me. I caught it without thinking and perched on the edge of the couch. Finding an unused sheet of paper in the mess, I held it up. "May I?" She signaled assent with an upraised hand, and I began scratching at the page. The ink was poor, but I set about my task. "The Pale use this nonlinear calligraphy. For artwork. Poetry, monuments, and the like." I held the sheet out to her, marked with a few quick glyphs. While she looked at it, I stood to peer past the curtains and over her shoulder where she sat on the sill. "See, they use the relative size and position of the logograms to convey grammatical structure." I pointed out a curling train of glyphs diminishing in size. "So this whole string—this clause—is subordinate to this subject." She looked up at me, one winged eyebrow raised. Suddenly sheepish, I scratched at the back of my head. "I'm sure I got one of the logograms wrong somewhere, but you see the principle."

"You think the Umandh anaglyphs are like this?"

She handed the sheet back, and I retook my seat. "I can't say—they only looked like them. Gi—My tutor used to draw blocks around the different elements in a sentence when I was learning. It looked sort of like this." I tugged her own paper free, showing her the interlocking Umandh circles. "Do the Umandh ever link their symbols up like this? Or are they just on those bone chimes you showed me at Ulakiel?" She was smiling at me. Widely. Too widely. "What?"

The lights sputtered as she reached out to snatch her notes from my hands. "I was saving paper, you idiot." She did not stop smiling, and so her words had no sting.

"Oh." I smiled too and wadded up the markings I had made.

"Don't do that!" Valka objected, rising from her place at the window. She'd dragged pillows from the other room to better make her seat by the glass. She held out a hand, waving for me to give her my drawing. "May I keep them?" I must have made a face, for she added, "For inspiration." Outside it was starting to rain again, and in the distance,

over the green waters, the umbral mass of a storm scraped its back against the roof of the world, casting heat lightning like sparks from a grindstone.

Sensing a break in the conversation, I asked, "Why were you sitting here in the dark?"

"What?" She turned toward me, plainly distracted by something I could not see. That was strange, for she wasn't staring out the window but into the corner by the kitchen, where there was nothing. "Oh, sorry. I was just thinking. You know the tides will be in retreat at Calagah before long?"

I leaned back a little against the cushions. She had the same couch in her rooms as was in mine, a plush thing upholstered in brown leather. "Will you be leaving then?"

"Only for a season," she replied, "and not for a while yet. 'Tis long, the local year. *Soon* does not mean the same thing on Emesh as it does out there." She twirled a finger at the beamed ceiling, pointing through it to the sky beyond. Valka moved to the kitchen area, and I watched her go, watched her pour a glass of water, her hair in her eyes, and slam it back in one swallow.

I'd seen the gesture before in my fellow myrmidons and in myself after a night of hard drinking following a victory in the arena. "Are you all right?"

"I get headaches," she said, putting a hand to her eyes in absent emphasis. "'Tis nothing, really."

"Can I get you anything?" I asked, unsure of what else to say.

Her smile returned. "We're in *my* apartments, M. Gibson." She poured another glass of water and returned, settling onto the edge of the sill. Framed there—curved lines against square glass, against the rain—she looked larger than she was, a statue like the bright carvings of my home. "You're staring."

"Sorry." I shook myself, looked sharply down. Unconsciously mirroring her, I said, "I was just thinking." Not strictly true, not in any concrete sense. I had been lost in some vague dreamscape of thought without lodestone or compass, caught amongst my family, the Chantry, Deme-

tri, Cat, my myrmidons, Valka and House Mataro and the Umandh. My world had grown so large, and I was so small. I couldn't tell her any of that, couldn't be myself as I had been at Ulakiel, not with the cameras watching. Instead I asked, "Do you like it here?"

"Mmm?" She spoke through her nose as she drank. "On Emesh?"

My hair, darker than hers, fell across my face as I shook my head. "In Borosevo. In the castle." I patted the arm of the couch as I spoke, emphasizing its material presence.

The woman took a long draught from her water glass, golden eyes darting to the side. "Things are very different from my home."

"Mine as well," I said, not knowing if it was completely true. "Do you want to go back?"

Valka grinned. "Gods, no. The xenobites are all out here."

"None in Tavros?" I asked.

"Only a few," Valka said, setting her glass on the sill beside her. "Some the Extrasolarians brought in before the clans drove them out, but they're . . . socialized. They're as unalien as aliens can be, and there's nothing like Calagah in the Demarchy. Nothing . . . old. 'Tis like . . . 'tis like . . ." She broke off, massaging her eyes. "You have to be there to understand. The ruins are so old, older than anything we've built. It makes you feel . . . small. It makes all of us small."

I didn't answer. Couldn't answer. It was that contextualizing, the way she placed humanity in among the creatures of the stars and not above them that called down the Chantry's ire. Valka was Tavrosi—a diplomatic nightmare, as in the Demarchy all persons of adult age controlled weighted shares in their electorate. She was both private citizen and foreign dignitary. Accusing her of heresy would be tantamount to declaring war on her nation, a war the County of Emesh did not want and could not afford. Perhaps that was why I thought of her as lonely. A person made into a state, that state embodied

in her person. She was rather like a palatine, though she would never admit it.

Contorting my answer into something for the cameras took a measure of doing, but I said, "I know what you mean. It's a big universe. Even our great accomplishments feel humble sometimes. Not so humble as the Umandh, of course, but humble all the same."

"The Umandh?" she repeated, brows knitting, then shooting up. "Oh, yes."

"Strange that they've not accomplished more in all their thousands of years," I noted, seeing a way to say the truth without saying it. "It's like Philemon of Neruda said. Language is necessary to the development of civilization. If what you say is true, the Umandh's . . . songs are little better than what the ancient dolphins had."

The Tavrosi doctor surveyed me for a long moment. I knew she would recall our earlier unrecorded conversation about Tor Philemon. A thin light shone in those gilded eyes, alight with wan sorrow. "The dolphins?" She considered this a moment, reflecting on the long extinct species. "That's a fair comparison. They're cleverer than dolphins, but perhaps only because they can use tools. Do you know . . ."

Have you ever seen someone speak of something that consumes them? That lights them up from the foundations of their soul? Valka spoke with such fervency that I forgot myself for a time. Whatever animosity she had felt toward me upon our first meeting seemed to have mostly evaporated, vanished into a hesitant respect for me and for my situation. And I? I feared her. I feared what she represented, and that I cared what she thought of me. I feared the secrets I was made to carry. My name, my blood. I feared that she would think me false, my respect for her work feigned, when it was the thing I'd shown her that was most true. Thus we are all destroyed by those things that matter to us, as she mattered to me in my loneliness.

At length I broke into her dissertation—too abruptly, I still can hear my pitchy tone—and asked, "Doctor, have you eaten?"

She brightened. "No, would you like to?"

That was the first of many meals we shared, in Borosevo and after. I could sense Valka's attitude toward me changing. I was no longer only the barbarian, the butcher of the fighting pits. I cannot say when the change began— whether it was at Ulakiel or after—but when we returned to her rooms that night, she left me with a smile and a soft word, a promise that we would speak again on the morrow.

CHAPTER 53

A GAME OF SNAKE
AND MONGOOSE

THE COUNT'S TABLE POSITIVELY dripped with food. Even in my father's house I had rarely seen such riches. Emesh boasted no royal forests in which to raise game for the high table. The meat there was vat-grown and placed as far from the palatine family as possible, to be shared amongst the artisans and lesser functionaries of the court at the low end. The natural food was of all pelagic stock, some terranic, some native-form. Platters of grilled salmon and sautéed scallops bestrode boats of white sauce and plates of roast potatoes and stuffed peppers. The main course, arranged in neat slices like geologic time, was a native congrid ten meters long, the alien eel-like creature roasted and swimming in a sauce of blue wine.

Static fields on the outer arches gave the hall the appearance of open space. Soft music played not through speakers but from an actual string quartet and harp in a far corner.

"What a lovely recipe," said one guild factionarius to her wife. "Wouldn't you agree?" The woman's companion nodded demurely, smiling all the while. The great hall was given over entirely to the one long table, as was customary on the occasion of such formal state banquets. There are such occasions at the court of every lord in the Imperium, as if it were food that truly held our society together. As the count's nominal ward, I'd earned myself a somewhat exalted position nearly a dozen places from the head of the table, the least of Lord Mataro's personal

guests, sandwiched between a perfumed merchanter from the green moon and a Legion lieutenant called Bassander Lin.

Valka was near at hand, seated beside her patron, Sir Elomas Redgrave. Further to my right and up the table, past a smattering of logothetes and scholiasts, were arranged the greats of Emesh System. Archon Perun Veisi was there with his wife, seated to the count's left at the head of the table, and Lord Luthor and the children. And there was Liada Ogir, the patrician chancellor, seated beside a hard-faced woman in Legion dress blacks with the stars and oak cluster of an Armada tribune on the collar tabs. She was the Knight-Tribune Smythe who had marched in Dorian's Ephebeia.

The Chantry contingent was present as well, just next to the Veisi couple, as close to the throne as propriety would allow. I was glad only that Gilliam and I were seated on the same side of the table, separated by several scholiasts and the leaders of the Whitehorse Mercenary Company.

"Have you been on Emesh long?" asked Bassander—Lieutenant Lin, I should say. He smiled thinly, his clean-shaven face relaxed but with an underlying dignity bordering on the formal. There was a leathered tiredness in him, as if the banquet were some trench he'd found himself dug into, and he'd spoken not at all until that moment, focusing on the fine food as though it were some chore he'd been set. He did not belong at table, despite the polish of his immaculate ebony uniform.

You have heard, no doubt, that we met as rivals and fought a duel for the command of our army. It is not so. No, I met the Phoenix at table one quiet evening in Borosevo. Bassander Lin. My last friend, my enemy. Hero of the rout at Perfugium, where Hadrian Halfmortal failed. Veteran of a hundred battles, knight, captain, traitor. He would be all of those things, but not yet. That night he was only a dinner guest, as was I.

Not knowing any of this, I set my wine down, mindful of the formal gray suit I'd been loaned for the occasion. "A few years—not too long. I'm only recently in the count's

service. I'm . . ." A prisoner? A ward? A translator? "A tutor." Pausing a moment to tear a piece from the communal loaf of white bread, I asked, "What of yourself? You've been long in the Legions?"

Lieutenant Lin pulled a face, scratched at the shaved side of his head just above his ear. "Well, that depends on how you measure. I'm nearly at eighteen years' active ship time, but . . ." He trailed off, seizing the moment to take a long draught from his water cup. He was not drinking alcohol. "But if you factor in the ice time . . . gods of my fathers, it's going on two centuries."

"Two centuries?" Across the table, Valka nearly choked on a bite of pepper and imported goat's cheese. "You can't be serious." For my part, I thought she'd focused on the wrong number—on two hundred and not eighteen. He was palatine then, or so patrician as to make no difference. Careful observation of his face revealed no signs of the scarring that marred Chancellor Ogir's, or Gilliam's, or that of the hard-eyed Dame Camilla, who sat behind the count and his lord husband. What hair he had was precisely the color of burned wood, untouched by gray, and his steely black eyes smiled far more than they cut. He might have had a hundred living years in truth, but his bones carried no more than twenty of them.

Bassander inclined his side-shaven head deferentially. "Yes, ma'am."

The guild factionarius beside Valka, a big bulldog of a woman, laid a ringed hand on the doctor's arm. "Imperial officers typically undergo long periods between thaws." She leaned forward, hand lingering on Valka's arm—a fact not unnoticed by the factionarius's pale slip of a wife—and said, "The good lieutenant should be glad he's not a conscript. Our legionnaires serve twenty-year terms, you know. And that's active duty time, not counting fugue."

Bassander Lin allowed that this was quite correct. "I knew a centurion once who enlisted during the reign of Emperor Aurelian III."

"That was twelve hundred years ago!" the factionarius said, aghast.

At the same time, Valka hissed a word through her teeth in Panthai: *"Anaryoch."* Barbarians. She did not see me, but I smiled at her in sympathy. The change to lifetime service had occurred only recently. Before that soldiers had served twenty-year terms, some as many as four. Many of the houses palatine had opposed the change. I would have, had it been my choice.

Valka came by her outrage honestly, I later learned. Her own people eschewed standing armies as a rule, preferring to rely on their technological terrors to ensure a shaky peace. The threat of planetary annihilation—of mutually assured destruction—held their clans in line. To Valka it was preferable that all men *might* die than that any man *did*. I supposed I could respect that, barbarous as it was.

The factionarius tittered, removing her hand from Valka's arm to pat the other woman on the knee. "Well, I think soldiering is more properly men's work. Wouldn't you agree, Lieutenant?"

Lieutenant Lin appeared to consider, dabbing his forehead with his napkin. "In my experience, ma'am, soldiering is soldiers' work." He took another swig of water to punctuate his statement with what struck me as the grace of long practice. He emerged from his pause with a neat turn to Valka. "If I may ask, ma'am, your accent—you are Tavrosi?"

Valka slid a fan of hair back behind one small ear. "I am."

Seizing hold of this escape from the factionarius and her awkward questions, the lieutenant said, "My whole ship was loaned to a Tavrosi company once. For the Mathuran Campaigns. I wish I could have spent my time there better." This reference to Tavrosi history went over my head, and I ducked over my plate, not seeing a way to apply myself to the conversation with grace. Bassander asked, "What brings you to Emesh, my lady?"

"Doctor," Valka corrected smoothly, wiping her mouth with her white napkin, golden eyes narrowing on the lieutenant. "The coloni, in point of fact."

The keyword commanded Sir Elomas's attention from

Valka's far side, and he broke off a conversation with a Welfare Ministry logothete. "Talking about the Umandh, are we?" He combed back his mop of white hair, set down his knife with a perfunctory clink. The old knight moved with spiderlike precision—no wasted energy, each little motion minutely calibrated. It was the hallmark carefulness of a lifelong duelist. "Have you had a chance to examine the natives, um . . ."—he squinted sea-foam eyes at Bassander's collar tabs—"Lieutenant?"

From there the conversation turned to the Umandh for the next few minutes, and I seized the moment to finish my food, signaling a server to recharge my wine cup and place another slice of the congrid on the rosy china.

This conversation topic exhausted or else played through to its natural terminus, the lieutenant—starved for conversation and apparently unwilling to engage the scholiasts on his right—turned back to me. "And what is your role here, messer? As tutor, you say?"

"Hadrian." I extended a hand as I'd learned in my coliseum days, an awkward gesture at such close range. "Hadrian Gibson."

"Bassander Lin." He shook my hand.

"The lad speaks the Cielcin tongue," said Sir Elomas with a strange glint in his eye.

"Truly?" Lieutenant Lin raised his brows, eyes nearly all whites.

I licked my lips, conscious of Grand Prior Vas and Gilliam a few places further along the table, and pitched my voice low. "Yes."

The big factionarius leaned in. "Why in Earth's holy name would you learn that?"

I felt tempted to repeat the answer I had given Gilliam in the courtyard days earlier: *To see with eyes unclouded.* But something told me my sense for the melodramatic would not be appreciated in that moment. Instead I fell on Hadrian Gibson's line. "My father—we were very fortunate for merchanters, you understand—took on a scholiast to tutor my brother and me. He was meant to be teaching us Jaddian, but I had something of a knack, if you don't mind my saying."

"For languages, you mean?" Bassander asked, signaling another of the servers for more to drink. The mousy woman brought wine. Lieutenant Lin politely declined and waited as water was brought for him instead.

I nodded. "They just sort of stick up here." I tapped the side of my head. "Even Cielcin. I'd hoped to learn to communicate with the coloni here, but Doctor Onderra tells me their language is thoroughly impossible."

"But the Cielcin," the factionarius's small wife said, looking even paler than her usual sallowness. "Such . . . horrible creatures. Demons . . ." I half expected her to make the sign of the sun disc.

Pointedly I looked at Valka; some part of me was still trying to overturn her initial impression of me. "They aren't demons, madame." She did make the sign of the sun disc then, pressing circled thumb and forefinger to her brow. "You know, when I was a child, I—"

The factionarius laughed, cutting me off. "You must forgive my wife, messer. She's very pious."

I offered the two women my most encouraging smile, feeling somehow reduced, like a biological sample on its slide. "I'm sure the Empire needs all the piety it can get, madame." Carefully I took a sip of the dry Kandarene wine. "But as to my small ability, I've always considered it an investment in the future."

"What do you mean?" Bassander Lin shifted in his seat to get a better look at me, and something in the movement communicated to me that he was far closer to the twenty years he appeared to have than he was to the hundred or so that were outwardly possible. Forty, perhaps? I could not stop thinking of him as *the junior lieutenant*.

I spread my hands. "Well, we can hardly fight forever, can we?" I asked, having said much the same to Adaeze Feng at table so long ago. "When the fighting is done, someone will have to speak to them." When the factionarius's wife was on the verge of commenting with doubtless more pieties, I raised a hand. "If only to secure their surrender."

"Surrender?" At the sound of that voice behind me, I knew the woman across from me had not been about to

argue but to warn me. Ligeia Vas stood, a witch-shadow stooped by time, resplendent in robes of Terran black, her thick white braid twice wrapped about her shoulders. In her face I saw echoes of Gilliam—those two blue eyes, frozen as distant stars, were identical to Gilliam's one. Whence his black eye came I never learned, nor did I care to. The features that were in him a twisted parody of humankind looked finely chiseled, as if from marble, in the grand prior's time-folded features. "We do not want their surrender." That said, she addressed the entire segment of the high table, speaking loudly enough to reach Lords Balian and Luthor in their matching high-backed chairs. "The Cielcin must be wiped from the face of our galaxy. Purged." She slipped then into the guise of a preacher, total and absolute. "In the Cantos it is written, 'Go out into the Dark and subdue it, and make for your dominion all that is there and will bend to you.' So too it is written, 'Thou shalt not suffer demons to live.'"

I turned my back on the priestess, brows raised. The factionarius and her wife both bowed their heads, and the smaller of the two women murmured something into her barely touched plate. Inanely I thought that anyone who would so pick at the finest food on the planet must be a madwoman or a fool. "That last was borrowed from an ancient cult's writings," I said. "The original quote refers to witches, I believe." I braced my shoulders like a man half expecting a knife to plunge between the blades. Turning my back was a dangerous play, but it was worth it for no greater reason than the brief, bright smile in Valka's eyes.

I heard the leather groan as Ligeia Vas's hands tightened on the back of my seat, and I swear even the copperskinned Bassander went white as death beside me. "You're the one my Gilliam warned me about—the demontongued boy." *Demon-tongued:* Ligeia was the first to call me such. She would not be the last. I heard the factionarius's wife murmur the words in echo of her priestess. The seed was planted to flower as it may. The priestess spoke in Classical English—the language both of the scholiasts and of high Chantry ritual—quoting directly from the

source I referenced, an ancient religious text belonging to one of the adorator cults endemic in the older parts of the Empire. "Thou shalt not suffer a witch to live." Returning to standard Galstani, she began, "It means—"

"I know what it means," I said, replying in English and drawing stares as far up the table as the high lords.

Apparently recognizing the language, Lord Mataro laughed. "What did I tell you, Ligeia? The boy's a proper talent."

The prior sniffed but did not take her hands away from the back of my chair. "This was the Colosso slave?"

"He wasn't a slave, Reverence," said young Dorian, gallantly swooping to my defense. "He was a myrmidon. Quite a good one."

I turned my attention up the table, looking past Bassander and the scholiasts, past the foederati, past Gilliam and the Veisi couple. Gilliam was smiling, a lopsided gash in his lopsided face. Recalling that old maxim about never letting the enemy see you bleed, I returned a smile just as crooked. It was all I could do not to break that smile when Ligeia Vas intoned, "Would not a man who speaks the language of demons be a witch?"

The temperature in the room—chilly for Emesh—practically froze. Gilliam, damn him, laughed. Lord Luthor's lips quirked in acknowledgment of the fact that the old woman had scored a point.

Yet there is a response to such absurd accusations—I retreated into absurdity. Speaking round the rim of my wine cup, I breathed, "I prefer the term *magus*, if it's all the same to you."

Elomas broke out laughing, a tinny, false sound that nevertheless invited his neighbors to join in. I could have kissed the man. A poor joke and an awkward one, but it had been my only recourse. "You've some stones on you, lad!" Sir Elomas barked, still grinning.

I risked a glance back over my shoulder to look at the woman. Despite the suddenly warmer climate in the dining hall, the grand prior's face was icy. "Have a care, my child."

"Always, Your Reverence." I bowed my head, turning

away from her, all too aware of her hands, like talons, grasping the brass knobs decorating the corners of my seat's backrest. "Though it is kind of you to worry about me."

That withered ice crystal of a face looked incapable of evincing such mortal emotions as worry or concern. Glancing at Gilliam's uneven face, I decided it was no small wonder the creature had turned out as unsavory as he was, victim of so unnatural a mother.

Then, like a bolt of sunlight, salvation. Valka cleared her throat. "Beg pardon, priestess, but M. Gibson was about to tell us a story when you walked up. Might he continue?" Story? What story? I scrambled, mind doing a mad dance to sort itself. Obligingly Valka said, "You said: 'They aren't demons, madame. You know, when I was a child, I—' and then our friend here interrupted you." She indicated the factionarius. Was it my imagination, or had Valka imitated the precise tone and cadence of my earlier delivery? The basic fuzz of memory jarred my sense of déjà vu. I frowned at her.

And then it came. I had been about to tell a story about Gibson sharing the holograph images of Cielcin warriors, but I thought better of it. A new thought was flowering in the shadows of my skull and growing fast. That inner part of me capered and rubbed its hands together. I went for it, saying, "When I was a boy my . . ."—*My lictor? My bodyguard?*— "my uncle Roban took me to a Free Trader fair. A troupe of Eudorans were in-system at the time, and I recall that there was one man, a trainer, who pitted animals against one another while men gambled." I broke off, permitting the mousy server to recharge my glass. "A strange fellow, as I recall. Not a homunculus, but blue-skinned. While we were watching, the man paired a mongoose against a snake, one predator against another."

One of the foederati captains cut in, "What's a mongoose?"

"A sort of terranic mammal not unlike a cat, I'm told." Taking a deep breath, I continued, turning my eyes uptable toward the lords and Archon Veisi. "I begged my uncle to let me place a bet on the contest, which I did,

backing the snake despite his insistence that I vote for the mongoose. Five kaspums—my monthly allowance. The creatures battled in a damp culvert by the roadside while we looked on. Most of them left disappointed. Can you guess who won?" I looked round the table, hands open in a gesture of invitation. "Anyone?"

Elomas—increasingly the good sport, though somewhat ignorant of terranic ecology—spoke up first. "The snake?" This elicited a chorus of nods and faint agreements from the assembled guests.

In the far corner, the string band changed its tune to something ever so slightly familiar, and I smiled before continuing. "That's what the onlookers thought. Obvious choice, really. The thing outmassed the mongoose three-to-one without question, and that's to say nothing of the venom." I took a moment to explain for the edification of the foederati captain and some others that terranic serpents carried powerful toxins in their fangs. "But no, it was the mongoose who won." I took a sip of wine, made an appreciative face, and half turned in my chair to study the still-standing prior. "The onlookers all cursed the man for a swindler, but they left when he threatened them with another of his snakes."

"Is there some point to your story, M. Gibson?" asked Ligeia Vas, arching ghost-thin brows.

"There's not. Not truly," I said, revisiting my crooked smile. "Except for an observation my uncle made at the time." The laws of proper delivery demanded my silence then for a space of some seconds, my own brows arching. "He remarked that the behavior of animals should not surprise us. They are, after all, only animals, and a tiger cannot change his stripes, if you'll pardon the cliché. Mongeese have always been great hunters of snakes, as any student of literature might tell you. This alone is not remarkable, but the Eudoran, it turned out, had altered his mongoose so that it was proof against the snake's venom." I smiled brightly at the grand prior, hoping she would see this insult for what it was. "The problem, you see, was that the Eudoran was a kind of snake himself,

rigging the fight. My uncle said that that was the trouble. You never know which men are snakes and which are mongeese. Not until you bite—or have been bitten."

Silence floated like smoke, punctuated by the soft strains of harp and viola. Somehow the music enhanced the quiet more than it broke it. After a moment I tore my gaze from the star-eyed prior and focused on my plate. Valka was smiling at me—smiling—the lone candle flame in a sea of ashen faces. By that token alone I decided the whole gambit had been worth it, whatever else happened. The band—true soldiers—had not missed a note through that awful quietude. Then the count laughed, pounding his empty tumbler against the tabletop in raucous applause. "A proper talent indeed! It would seem, Reverence Vas, that we must not make the mistake of considering the myrmidon a fool."

With kneading motions the grand prior tightened her rope of uncut white hair about her time-weighted shoulders. Her nostrils flared, but she smiled, paying me what she doubtless believed a fine compliment. "You would make a good priest."

CHAPTER 54

GASLIGHT

AFTER ANOTHER OF MY evening visits with Valka, I walked alone along a colonnade that overlooked one of the castle's inner courtyards. Below, a trio of brightly dressed courtiers sat inside an ironwork gazebo, playing at some holograph game by the soft twilight. The day had been a soaking one, not rainy but thick with steam—as was only too normal in Borosevo—and my clothes clung to me like seaweed to the body of a drowned man. A logothete stopped me, and we chatted awhile. My performance at dinner with the grand prior had garnered me some small, brief celebrity. Ligeia Vas was not well loved, it seemed, as is often the case with the Chantry's elite. But that fellow was a Colosso fan and also recalled me from my time there. When we parted ways, he left with a photograph of us both taken with his terminal, and I with a thin, amused smile.

A new place is like new shoes, I've often found, and having lived in Castle Borosevo for some months now, I felt the place breaking in around me, growing comfortable. The rounded arches of the colonnade and the pale sandstone walls beneath their red tile roofs were warm and inviting, scored in places with crawling vines and decorated with iron statues of dancing nymphs and legionnaires. Even the Umandh had become less strange, droning on their work crews as I passed them by. What is more, the servants smiled or bobbed their heads as I went by. I may have been a prisoner, but I had the run of my prison. And if my attendance on Anaïs and Dorian was

tedious, my evening studies with Valka were anything but. We had shared a bottle of Kandarene red, as was our custom, and a laugh at the prior's expense, though I was careful not to give too plain an insult to the Chantry Synod's appointed representative on Emesh.

Valka was under no such censure, and she had laughed, saying, "The look on that old ruin's face! She looked like she would have had you shot if she could've!"

"She could have," I said soberly, unable to keep down a smile of my own. Valka's laugh was a deep, musical sound that escaped her chest from somewhere near her heart. It was not the laugh of some churlish courtier, trained to demure and girlish precision. No, she laughed like a storm cloud, like the sea. And she had broken on my grim demeanor like a wave against the sea wall at Devil's Rest.

Thus I was deep in the question of her—in her foreignness and the way she made me feel half a fool—as I crossed the castle grounds on my way toward my chamber and bed. Perhaps an hour or two of drawing before sleep, I thought. Just the thing.

Valka was still a mystery. Despite her diplomatic status, she was no kind of ambassador. What I did not then recall was that since everyone in the Demarchy of Tavros holds voting power, any Tavrosi clansman might be considered a representative of that strange, distant people. It was one of the many reasons Tavrosi guests are so often frowned upon at the courts of the Imperium. They complicate matters.

My rooms lay on one of the middle levels of the Sunglass Hall, one of the newer, less opulent buildings on the palace grounds, somewhat removed from the diplomatic apartments in the north wing. There were gaslights in the yard below the edifice, and I passed a lamplighter with his wick. I had thought the lights a symbol of opulence, as servants had to be paid to man them, but I realized later that they were only a safety precaution. With the palace's power grid prone to outages, the gaslights ensured good visibility on the wall-walks and in the colonnades of the castle by night.

The man waved at me, smiled, and doffed his cap. A bird chirruped in one of the castle's ever-present bits of greenery, and not long after, an ornithon rattled in answering challenge. I stopped, standing a moment in contemplation of the unfixed stars. Pallino and I had met again a few times, on each occasion advancing our plans to buy a starship. Switch's bond with the coliseum was nearly up, but Pallino had renewed his more recently, meaning we had something like another nine local months before he was freed from his obligation. That was more than a standard year, which meant it was in Switch's best interest to renew himself, to earn another year's pay and allow the smallest overlap in their contracts. It was longer than I'd have liked.

But I let it go. For the moment I was fed, comfortable, and safe. And I harbored a flickering, private hope that when and if my plan came together and I left Emesh behind that Valka would come with me. It was not impossible. I wanted to travel the stars, meet xenobites. She was an expert in xenobitic cultures. Was there a future there? She was so much less cold toward me now than she had been at our first meeting, but though I dreamed, I did not delude myself. She had her own path to follow. But perhaps you will forgive a young man his dreams. I had suffered much; I had a right to dream.

"Boy!"

Mere steps from the door to the hall and solitude, I froze. I knew that voice, that lisping, aristocratic drawl. Before I could turn fully round, a hand seized me by the shoulder. Turning, I found myself face-to-face with Gilliam Vas. His mismatched eyes caught the gaslight, making the blue one shine. His white-blond hair hung lank across his misshapen face, and his teeth flashed between lips pulled back into a snarl as he backed me into the nearest lamppost.

"I don't know who you think you are." His breath smelled of something sweet—mint or verrox stimulant or both. I turned my head away, trying not to cough. "The count may find your baseborn antics amusing—Earth only knows why—but I will not tolerate such offenses. Not

from you, and not at the expense of my family's dignity. I pray you remember who it is we are."

Deliberately slow, I placed a hand over Gilliam's, prepared to duck at the waist and break his wrist if I had to. "If your family's dignity hangs by so thin a thread, Your Reverence, that such as I threaten it, well . . . you should rethink exactly how much it's worth." My words were a little breathy with surprise.

The priest blew air from his nose like a bull about to charge, and he rattled me against the lamppost so that I struck my head and cried out. "You dare to mock me? Me?" His uneven fingers twisted in the fabric of my tunic, as if it were a throat they held. "My family is older than you could possibly comprehend, you up-jumped little plutocrat." He was stronger than I'd imagined. "If the count didn't want you for whatever reason, and if you were not so beneath me, I would kill the man who so insulted my family."

His hand still twisted at my shoulder, I drew myself up to my full height and looked down at him. I marveled at the fact that he—who should have been acutely attuned to the blood of those around him, intus that he was—could not guess my lineage. But then, I was short for a palatine, and whatever else was unusual about my appearance could have been explained by the mere fact that I was an offworlder. No one in the palace had guessed my secret, so why should he?

"Perhaps you and yours should not act so belligerently. The prior interrupted a personal conversation with her rhetoric, and I am trying to go to bed, Reverence."

From the spasm of muscle beneath Gilliam's jaw, I knew it was the wrong thing to say. His hand shifted, and his face swung even closer to my own, though he was now looking up at me. Up close in the light of the lamp, I could make out the heavy sheet of makeup he wore to mask his pitted complexion. Well applied as it was, his sweat had caused it to bead and run a little about the hairline and shine. "I'll release you when I'm done, pissant," he said. Then, incongruously, he released me, staggering back one

uneven step. At arm's length now, he spun and back-handed me across the face with his other hand. I gasped in pain. The man had lived on Emesh all his life, and the intense gravity had put a strength behind that arm that was amplified by the thick ring he wore on his middle finger.

Not speaking, I massaged my mouth with one hand, glaring at the shorter priest. There was only a little blood when I pulled that hand away. Had I been myself—Hadrian Marlowe, the son of a landed archon—I might have challenged the man to a duel for his insult. But I was not Marlowe, not anymore, not that day. Hadrian Gibson hung his head, his lips compressed into a thin, hard line. "You were a spacer," the priest snarled, shaking out his hand as he glowered at me, "and so you're barely better than a barbarian, so I will explain it for you." The blue eye shone brightly in the firelight, but the black one drank that same radiance and seemed a socket, a hole in his waxen face. He raised that twisted hand again, as if to strike. I flinched and could have cursed myself for flinching. The chanter laughed, and it was a sound like the smashing of priceless instruments. "There it is." He pointed one finger directly at my face, the black mass of his ring gleaming wetly in the gaslight.

Gilliam put his hands behind his back and leaned forward, pointing his chin at me, offering it like a target. I think I turned to stone for a moment, paralyzed by social convention. I could not strike him and remain here as Hadrian Gibson. Gilliam's smile did not falter, and he said, "Aah, you can learn. You see, this is not the Colosso, *myrmidon*. We expect civility at court, and no matter how well trained Balian thinks you are, a half savage is a half savage. Blood tells all."

"Your Reverence is an expert on *half* savages, surely." I was careful to enunciate the half, inclining my head to reference his condition. "It is good of you to stoop to my level. And such dedication! Tell me, were you born thus, or did you pay a bonecutter to better relate to such as me?" Not for the first time, I wondered at the fire in the

man. The hatred. Was it that his deformity spurred him to act twice as viciously in his role as palatine and priest? Or was it only that he saw in me someone beneath him? Was he what all palatines looked like to the plebs?

Is this what Switch saw in me?

Gilliam hauled off and struck me again with the ringed hand. This time I did not gasp in pain, did not cry out. My hair fanned across my face, but I kept my eyes on the man. His chest was heaving, his blood up. "You're lucky the count likes the look of you. Otherwise I'd have my cathars carve that pretty nose of yours for your insolence."

"What do you want of me, priest?" I asked. "I want nothing of you."

Gilliam looked at me as if his chair had asked why he'd pulled it from the table. Instead of rebutting with the usual snide remark, he asked, "Why are you here?"

I blinked at him, confused. "Excuse me?"

"I ask again: Why are you here? What lies did you tell the count? How have you suborned him? You and that Demarchist witch?"

Though the air was hot as ever it was in Borosevo, I think my sweat changed to ice and imprisoned me; suddenly I could not move for cold. So that was it. There it was at last. An answer. Gilliam believed I was plotting some mischief with Valka, a spy and saboteur.

I scowled at the intus. "What are you talking about?"

"You consort with that Pale demon and cozy up with that backspace whore . . ." He lurched toward me, teeth bared. "You insult the Holy Terran Chantry. Blaspheme at His Excellency's table, and you think we're all too stupid to notice? I know what you are, heretic." He raised his hand again, but I was ready this time. I didn't even blink when he struck me, didn't turn my head away. His eyes bulged with fury, but there was a spark in them—a spark, I think, of fear. "Why are you smiling?"

"Do you really think the count would let me free if that were true?" I spat red on the tiles. "Be realistic, Reverence." He swung at me again, but I was more than ready now and bent away. His hand struck nothing, even on the backswing. Strong as he was, I was fast. I'd had to be, not

only as a child when Crispin was my only opponent, but again above the canals and on the rooftops of the city, and in the coliseum, too. I kept backing away, toward the stairs and my bed. Perhaps guards would come soon. They would not stop the chanter, would not lay a hand on Gilliam, but audiences changed performances, and though everything we'd said and done had been recorded for the castle's ten thousand eyes, the mere presence of other eyes might change the man's behavior. The lamplighter was watching us, face fallen, and from my vantage on the steps to the hall I saw a pair of servants in the shadow of a colonnade, but they were all remote as stars. "I'm not your enemy, priest. I didn't ask to be here at all."

Gilliam collected himself, smoothing back his flaxen hair as he stood straight as he would go. He spat, made a warding gesture. "Don't you dare insult my mother again, boy, or I'll have you thrown naked into those fighting pits of yours."

I knew better than to respond.

CHAPTER 55

THE QUIET

I STOOD WATCHING MY feet, long fingers clutching the bottle of Kandarene red Dorian had helped me smuggle from the castle cellars. Standing there I became acutely aware of the blood beating in my ears and of something small and niggling in my left boot. Uncomfortable in stillness, I fidgeted, shifting the bottle so that I clutched it behind my back. After a mere half minute, when it seemed all the stars had burned out and the universe had gone cold, the door locks cycled with a metallic whine, the latch rattled, and rose-gold light spilled into the hall, slicing a wedge across the intricately patterned wooden floor.

A naked man, handsome and gray-eyed, looked out at me, blinking, trying to conceal his genitals with a plaid blanket. I stammered an apology. "I've the wrong room, messer. Forgive me." I was sure I did not have the wrong room. Averting my eyes politely, I said, "I thought I had the Tavrosi diplomat's room. Has she been moved?"

"M. Gibson?" The voice rose from deeper in the room behind the naked man. "What is it?"

My heart—I cannot tell you what happened to it. It did not sink but rather left my body entirely and plunged toward the planet's core. I glanced briefly at the muscled young man in the doorway. Plebeian, by the slight asymmetries in his otherwise perfect face, but beyond that I could not say if he was a courtier or a servant. It mattered not. He was her lover, and she had forgotten about our meeting. She swung into view, languorous and light-

footed as a cat, those golden eyes bright in the scant light of her chamber. She had pulled a long shirt hastily over her head, and her red-black hair tumbled in wild disarray. A flush glowed on her pale cheeks, but there was no embarrassment in her. Before I could stop the silent screaming in my soul and articulate a response, she gasped, "We had a meeting!" She pressed a hand to her cheek, remembering, and pressed the other against the back of the man in the doorway.

"We did."

"What time is it?" she asked, glancing from me to her lover. I told her, and she hissed between her teeth, then said, "Out then. Out you go."

Crestfallen, I swept into a bow, doing my best to conceal the incriminating bottle of wine. "Of course, my—Doctor." I'd almost used the wrong address again, and it made me scowl. "I'm so sorry."

"No, not you!" She snapped fingers at the man. "What was your name? Mal?"

"Malo," the man said in honeyed tones, moving to wrap an arm about her slim shoulders. I wanted to scream, but Valka brushed him off. Scowling in turn, the other man slid out past me, not concerned in the least about his nakedness. One of the pleasure servants kept for the guests of the palatinate? Mother's harem sprang to mind. Surely the count kept his own such harem, if only as a symbol of his lordly authority. "Dial in if you need me again, Doctor."

Valka flashed a brittle smile and slapped the man's backside. He jumped and hurried down the hall naked—but it was not uncommon to see one of the palace bedworkers so unclothed. I winced. Her smile collapsed the minute Malo vanished. I watched him go, then bowed to Valka again, more coldly formal. "Doctor Onderra." I found my mouth suddenly dry, my words breathless. "If I should come back at another time . . ."

"No, no!" She scratched her fingers through her hair. "Not at all. Do come in." She held the door open for me. "It's my fault—the time got away from me." She bit her lip. "Would you like something to drink?"

Anxious, hesitant, I revealed the green glass bottle from behind my back. "Actually I brought something, if you'd like." There was a kitchenette in one corner with tiled counters and gas burners, every device of cold, brushed steel. I moved toward the couch—strewn with tangled blankets and the scattered remains of Valka's clothing . . . and Malo's. I do not know why the fact bothered me like it did. I might have availed myself of the palace body servants had I a mind, same as her. I never did. The two high windows dripped with dark hangings, occluding the bruised and twilit sky, admitting only scarce light. The artificial lights were similarly dimmed, glow-spheres gone faint as moonlight through cloud, hanging sensuously in the air like paper lanterns.

Valka eyed the Kandarene bottle and gestured to a cupboard near the small kitchenette in the far corner of her small quarters. "You pour. I'll find my things." She sauntered off through an arched portal to the back room while I found a corkscrew and glasses. I confess I watched her go—the sway of her—with the bemused candor of all young men who believe their attentions unnoticed.

"The capital agrees with you, I see," I called from my place by the tiled counter.

"What's that?" Valka's bright-edged voice trilled from the other room, strained a bit with the effort of searching.

"I said, the capital agrees with you!"

The doctor emerged some time later, carrying her wrist terminal and a series of data crystals. Setting the accouterments down on a low table by the settee, she said, "I wouldn't say that." She had sonicked herself clean and sorted her hair, though she still wore her loose, flowing shirt. The front and left sleeve were printed with ghostly human skulls wreathed in smoke above the logo of some Tavrosi musical group, and she'd donned trousers of some elastic weave of the sort often worn for exercise. They suited her.

In the pressuring way many young and foolish men believe passes for subtlety, I said, "I meant your companion."

"What?" She plugged one of the crystal flakes into a

read slot on the terminal, squeezed the projector. "Oh, Malo!" she snorted. "He's just . . . well, he's all right." I felt a little better as I passed her the wine, which she took with a grateful bow just as the holograph phased into laser clarity. Long legs up on the table, Valka raised her glass and said, "I didn't mean to keep you waiting." She reached out and lay a warm hand on my arm. "I'm sorry."

I bobbed my head, swallowing the little wine I'd sipped. "It's all right." I tried not to think about her gentleman companion, palace servant or no. "We all forget things."

"I don't." She spoke without boasting but said this as if it were only a fact. "I must have lost track of the time . . ." Here she glanced wryly at her lap, as if to indicate that it was a bit late for such mannered consideration. I struggled not to blush, steeled myself with thoughts of Cat that arrested my desires quite handily and replaced them with a sick, yawning guilt. "How goes it with you?" We continued in this vein for a couple of minutes, Valka gathering a blanket from the back of the settee to cover herself.

During the first lull in our conversation, I said, "There's something that's been bothering me."

One eyebrow arched teasingly. "Just the one?"

I sniffed bemusedly. "For the moment!" We exchanged private smiles, and I hid myself behind the rim of my wine cup. "You said Calagah was made of stone, but while we were at Ulakiel . . . The Umandh, well . . . they hardly seem capable of anything so complicated as masonry."

Valka sat stone-still a moment, watching me. Then, like a spider stirred to sudden movement by the vibration of a string, she stood, blanket falling to the floor. "I haven't shown you my holographs!" She hurried to her room again, then returned carrying a tablet terminal, which she deposited on the drinking table before the couch. "I've been meaning to show you . . ." She toggled through a couple of settings on the small screen, then clicked a hardware switch on the device's frame. "This is Calagah."

The image projected in a concave sweep of laser light before us showed satellite images of a complex built into

a deep cleft between cliffs of columnar basalt, vestiges of Emesh's ancient and long-since-ended volcanism. Valka described its latitude and the dimensions of the site in question, cycling through image after image with languid waves of her free hand. She recited facts and figures with a casual offhandedness that belied a level of memorization even the scholiasts would respect.

At last she cycled to ground images, revealing a geometry more precise than the natural shapes of the basalt pillars—flat faces of black stone like obsidian, pillared and arched like a mathematician's fever dream. It looked . . . how can I put this? The ruins did not seem to be a part of the surrounding rock face. Rather it was as if some immense artist had inserted them into the landscape by some malfunction of computer programming, a fault in the process of rendering that had clipped the facade through the cliff face.

"It's beautiful," I breathed at last. Surely here was one of the Ninety-Nine Wonders of the Universe, or the unlisted hundredth. "When did you say it was built?"

Valka's eyes sparked as she leaned back against the settee. "Now, that is an interesting question. 'Tis difficult to date. The material the builders used shares some similarities with obsidian, but hydration dating is out due to the site's history of flooding. But that would only date the material in any case, and there's no mortar or organic material on-site. No paints or pigments. No graves."

"But you have a guess?" I asked.

"We do. Based on the age of the surrounding strata." She smiled and encouragingly asked, "How old would you think?"

As a young boy, I had gone with my uncle Lucian to see an old stone town some of the first colonists had built on Delos in the first centuries of settlement. They had been poor, and but for a couple of prefabricated structures, they had quarried the native granite. *The stone for Devil's Rest came from the same place, you know,* he had said. *The quarry's up in the mountains.* But the stone of that town was poorly cut and worse jointed, and though it was a protected site by order of the viceroyalty, it was

showing its age. These alien ruins reminded me of that dilapidated town, thick with the caul of history and the ghosts of all that time.

"Five, six thousand years?" I said, adding in another couple of millennia for good measure.

The xenologist shook her head. She pushed her hair back before she answered, "No."

"More?" I asked. "Surely no more than ten . . . twelve thousand years?"

Her grin widened. "No."

"Twenty?"

"Hadrian." She said my name like it was a child's name—like I was a child. "These ruins are more than seven *hundred* thousand years old. Maybe so much as a million."

I gasped fishlike for a good ten seconds. "What?" I couldn't even begin to articulate all my questions. How could something possibly endure so long? What exactly was it built of? How had it survived seasonal flooding for all those uncounted eons? I spoke without thinking, so absorbed that for a moment I was heedless of my surroundings. "The Umandh couldn't have built this. That would make them . . . so much older than we are. They should have advanced *past* us." But the raw truth was staring at me out of the laser light. "They couldn't have built anything like this. They don't have the technology!"

Valka stopped my roll. "And so we come back to Philemon and *Unnatural Grammars*."

"You're not seriously proposing that the Umandh have been a static culture for the better part of a million years? We're just over a quarter of a million years old ourselves, and . . ." I held up my hands, indicating the vast expanse of human civilization, as if my spread fingers could encompass all those stars and planets and the Dark between them. Frustratingly, Valka shrugged. She looked away, playing with the hem of her shirt. Not for the first time, I felt there was something she wasn't saying. I remembered our encounter with Engin the slave trader and spoke again. "Take the Cavaraad, for example. Hemachandra's ethnography—what was it called?" I could not remember

the name of the volume and gave it up. "He describes the Cavaraad in Mattar Prefecture on Sadal Suud as approximating the late Bronze Age in their development. That's why he pushed to get the planet protectorate status when House Rodolfo sought to stake its claim."

"Claim . . ." Valka repeated, taking a sour sip of her wine.

"But as a species, the Cavaraad are only about fifty thousand years younger than we are!" I protested. "Surely you're not going to pin that delta solely on the fact that they speak."

"Sing, actually." Valka slammed back the remainder of her wine with an agility that made me wince—the vintage was worth the price of a flier. "They have no lips—they work their diaphragms like bellows. Changes the pitch." She made a gesture with her free hand, pressing on the air as if on a bladder. It made me think of bagpipes. An apt comparison, that, if you have never heard the Cavaraad sing.

"You've seen them?" I sat forward with greater interest, as she had touched upon this great obsession of my youth. "The Cavaraad?"

White teeth flashed in the dimness. "I spent a summer on Sadal Suud, actually." Valka reached out for the bottle, refilled her glass. "What is this, by the way? 'Tis quite good."

"Archduke Markarian's finest bouillir. The '969, I think?" I wrested the bottle from her, rotating the label. "Yes!"

"Markarian?" Her eyes widened. "This must be worth a fortune!"

"Lord Dorian acquired it for me from his fathers' cellars." When Valka's eyes did not contract, I dismissed the enormity signified by the vintage. I had hoped to have another conversation that night, so I said, "I told him it was for a lady." Her face darkened, and I added, "I didn't say it was for a doctor."

I looked away, covering my new embarrassment with a long drink. We fell into silence, unsettled, uneasy. The

only sound that remained was the faint, edge-of-hearing whine of the holograph projector in Valka's terminal. My nerves finally overpowered my patience. Eager to get back on track, I began, "On Sadal Suud, did you see the Marching Towers?"

In answer she bent over her terminal and keyed in a couple of commands. A moment later the image in the air dissolved, replaced by a flat image of a smiling Valka standing on a ridge line, gripping the straps of a knapsack on her shoulders. Behind her a series of black stone towers rose from the next ridge line like spines on the back of a dragon. "I hiked the old stone road with a caravan from Mattar to Port Shiell." She toggled the image, showing a series of ox-drawn wains. "I can't believe you people still make animals do things like that."

"That's why they were domesticated on Earth," I said, brushing this jibe away. "That must have been a wonderful trip. Can you go inside the towers?" I'd never seen holographs of the alien towers before, and the accounts I had read as a boy were mostly apocryphal.

"Oh no," Valka said. "They're more obelisks than towers. The Cavaraad used to drag these massive stones from the lowlands to line the ridge." I saw one of the Giants in her next holograph. It must have been thirty feet high, its gray flesh like wet clay, its face a featureless black pit. How it saw with only that gaping hole for a face, I did not know. The holograph moved, and the huge creature lumbered off into the fungal forests, dwarfing the treelike mushrooms. The holographs began to toggle then, flipping through images of Valka's trip. A close-up of one of the towers dominated the field in one. It was like a piece of night, black as the stones of my home, so dark I could not make out any features. That bothered me, but I had another thought pressing at my teeth.

Coming back round to the topic, I said, "Much as I like Tor Philemon, I'm not sure his hypothesis explains everything. If Calagah is really so old as you say, then there's something . . . something very wrong . . ." I was about to say *with the Umandh*, but I had just seen the obvious fact.

When next I spoke, it was in a voice with all the juice pressed from it: flat and lifeless, full of fear. "The Umandh didn't build Calagah, did they?"

Valka's expression was completely unreadable. I'd like to flatter myself and think that she was surprised, but the woman has always remained one part mystery to me. She seemed far away, as if focusing on a noise in a distant room. At last she stirred and shook her head, reaching for the bouillir as she did. "I don't think so."

"You don't think so?" I echoed, pressing.

"No," she said more firmly. "The Umandh are only perhaps half a million years from the evolutionary womb."

My problem with her holograph of the Marching Towers snagged suddenly like a cloak on the sharp edge of my mind, and I sat straighter. "It's all the same!"

Valka *did* look surprised then. "What?"

"The Towers, Calagah—I bet even the Temple of Athten Var on Judecca. It's supposed to be all black stone too." I stalled out, then pointed at her. "You've been to Athten Var! You don't study the Umandh or the Cavaraad. You study . . ." I trailed off, staring *through* the image of one of the Marching Towers of Sadal Suud, standing defiant against a binary sunrise. Momentarily unaware of the heresy I spoke, I breathed, "It's all one culture, isn't it? One species." I sat in a kind of fugue, in a sort of religious transport. It is said that our forebears looked up from Earth's face and into the Dark and asked if we were alone in the universe. We were not. But this. This.

We were not the first.

That basic cornerstone of the Chantry's faith was— and is—a lie. I felt myself, my world, shrink in that moment. I became smaller than an atom, crushed beneath the weight of all that space and time, and mankind shrank with me. All its proud kings and emperors; all its warriors; its great poets and artists; its farmers and sailors; its great accomplishments; its greater atrocities. All vanished into the context this conclusion provided. And it was all confirmed, rendered for me as immutable and natural law by Valka's consecrating word: "Yes."

Yes.

The Chantry knew. The Chantry had to know, or else why would they so police our words, our thoughts, in the name of our souls? This fact threatened the very foundations of their belief, of their power, and so they held on tighter, limited offworld travel, limited datasphere access. *Datasphere access.* Valka's own terminal was disconnected from the planet's network—dark, unmonitored. But that thought drained the blood from me. We were speaking heresy.

I imagined the Inquisition cutting out tongues, saw the tattooed foreheads and the branded ones. I imagined men and women sitting blind and hunched under bridges, hands out for alms, the word *HERETIC* large and dark against their skin, ragged cheeks torn in the agony of the blind and dumb. How often had I seen such people in Meidua and in Borosevo, their truth cut down by the cathars' knives, turned to rumor and folklore in the whispering of crowds? Too often. I clammed up, knowing the damage was done, knowing that Valka and I would both be questioned, that I at least would join those mutilated husks on the steps of the city temple where once I had begged with Cat. I half expected armed guards to burst through the door at any moment.

Nothing happened. And Valka, for all the worlds, seemed unconcerned. She understood what we were saying, surely! She must know what would happen. But she only smiled at me and drank her priceless wine.

It was all mad. I heard a voice—my voice—speaking anyway. "What do you call them?" I gestured weakly, nearly sloshing wine from my cup. "The builders?"

Valka glanced upward, as if checking something written under the arch of her skull. *"Ke kuchya mnousseir."*

"The . . . Grave?"

"The Quiet," she corrected. "I really shouldn't be telling you this." Her tone shifted, turning almost wooden, as if she wanted the words out of the way. "The diplomatic suites aren't officially monitored, but I don't trust a one of your bureaucrats."

Ordinarily I might have argued with that. This was the palace and seat of a palatinate. *Every* room was monitored. Every one. When the next day and the next dawned with neither of us tortured or tormented, I would decide that Valka had been right. But in that moment, my longing for knowledge—that same impulse that had driven me down into the coliseum's gaol and into the hands of Balian Mataro—pinned me to my seat like a butterfly to the mounting board.

"Why do you call them that? The Quiet?" I bit my lip, glanced nervously at the door. "It's a bit . . . dramatic, wouldn't you say?" *And I would know, eh?*

"Because at all their sites—here, on Sadal Suud, on Judecca, Rubicon, Ozymandias, Malkuth, and all the rest—there's nothing."

"Excuse me?"

"No tools, no ships, no bodies, no artifacts of any kind." The whole time she was speaking, those gold and amber eyes never left my face. At any other moment, I might have enjoyed that contact, but then it only chilled me. "Just the buildings. They're mute. Quiet."

This slammed another wave of silence down upon us, and we sat, me processing, Valka allowing me to process. Something she had said juddered into place, and I asked, "No bodies? Are you serious?" I took up my wineglass again. "How is that possible? Where did they go?"

Valka performed the least eloquent shrug I have ever seen, an achievement in itself. "No idea. It does make the Chantry's job a fair bit easier, wouldn't you say?"

"You suspect them of carrying off everything? Looting the sites?"

"What?" Valka's eyes went wide as dinner plates. "No! 'Twould be impossible." Those brilliant eyes narrowed. "Your Chantry is composed of men, M. Gibson, not gods."

I had to stop myself from grinding my teeth. "It's not my Chantry."

A small sound escaped Valka, the seed of laughter. "If you say so, *barbarian*." I looked up at her to bite off a retort, but her eyes were smiling. Only then did I note that she had said the word softly, almost teasingly.

That caught me so much by surprise that I stammered as I pressed ahead. "But surely the bodies can't be gone. They must have done something with their dead. Must have left—"

"Nothing," Valka finished and shrugged again, "Nothing, M. Gibson. Just the structures themselves."

I frowned, opened my mouth. When the words did not at once come to me, I disguised the failure with a swallow of wine. "That's not possible."

"It's true."

"Nothing at all?"

Valka waved a hand. Once, twice, several times, each gesture cycling her terminal from holograph image to holograph image. "Just the carvings I told you about, the ones the Umandh emulate with their story knots." With another gesture she conjured projections of the objects in question, though I recalled them well enough, have even drawn one in my journal. "Completely unreadable, of course."

My heart sank. "No one knows how to read them? Outside the Empire?"

"Not that I've ever heard of. Some rogue scholiasts have tried, but without any idea how the symbols relate to the spoken language, or if they do . . ." She trailed off.

"It's a Rosetta problem," I said, and when she raised curious eyebrows at me, I explained that on Old Earth there was once a people whose writing could not be read. Not until a monument was found that showed the ancient writing alongside two other known languages of the time. It was like a key that opened up all the writings of that lost empire. "And the strangest part," I added, babbling now to mask the welter of emotions churning in my stomach, "was that the hieroglyphs weren't ideograms at all, but a system of comingled logograms and alphabetic elements . . . What?"

She was smiling at me. Not with her eyes alone, but properly smiling. It lasted only a moment, then collapsed under the weight of my gaze. She shook her head. "Nothing."

"But why come here?" I gestured inchoate at the glimmering holographs, at the stone facade of Calagah, black and smooth as poured glass. "There have to be a dozen

sites outside Imperial space where the Chantry doesn't hold power."

At last she answered, "Not that aren't controlled by the Extras." She jabbed a finger at me, words slurring from Markarian's strong wine. "Only barbarians in the universe worse than your lot." She snorted, and I could not tell if it was in derision or with laughter.

"My lot?" I knew what she meant, but it helped me to distance myself. Outside the narrow windows an ornithon hissed at the setting sun.

"The Sollan Empire."

My lips pulled back from my teeth, snagging briefly on the chipped end of one incisor, relic of a bout in the Colosso. "I don't know anything about the Extrasolarians." I wasn't sure how to continue this line of conversation, so I changed tracks instead. "So these . . . the Quiet. They're the object of your study? Not the Umandh?"

Doctor Onderra took a more measured sip, conscious now of the value of the vintage. She gave an insistent nod, pushed the hair from her high forehead, fingers lingering in the red-black whorls. "As you say."

"I still can't believe this is a secret, that it's true."

Valka sniffed. "Your great houses control information. They control datasphere access and restrict offworld travel to a few and allow the Chantry to run roughshod over them at every turn. You can't have known."

"We—The great houses don't *let* the Chantry run roughshod over them. They just can. The Inquisition would sooner destroy a planet than let it go to heresy, and they have the means. Plagues, atomics, weapons the Mericanii left behind. Things that crack planets, Doctor."

"Heresy . . ." Valka snorted again, a decidedly unlady-like sound.

"Truth is treason and all that." I waved a hand, trying to recall the source of the quote. Gibson would have known, but Gibson was gone.

The woman's face composed itself into a grave mask. "Sin."

"I'm sorry?"

"You Sollans have made crime and sin the same thing.

You couldn't see the truth if it danced naked in front of you."

"I could," I snapped, defiant, a trace of my old palatine hauteur—Hadrian Marlowe's demeanor, not Hadrian Gibson's—creeping though. I gestured at the twinkling holographs, still glittering treacherously in the air above the low table.

Valka stood, leaving her emptied wine glass on the drinking table between us. "Maybe you could, at that."

My tact momentarily discarded, I asked, "Why haven't they killed you?"

She looked down at me over her shoulder. "Excuse me?"

"All this!" I waved a hand over the shimmering holographs. "You know all this. I don't believe they'd let you just . . . walk around. Breathing Imperial air."

"You think you own the air?" Her accent congealed around the question, making her seem somehow stranger and more foreign.

I waved this aside as strenuously as I could. "The Chantry can't want this spread about. If they knew you were telling me . . ." What was I saying? Of course they knew. "We'd both be dead. Worse than dead." I had to stop myself from spiraling off into a description of exactly what *worse than dead* meant.

Valka repeated her peculiar gesture of staring up at the ceiling. She scratched at the back of her neck, exhaling sharply. Presently she crossed the space between us and placed a hand on the side of my neck. I flinched but all too quickly relaxed into her grip. "They aren't going to find out, Hadrian. Peace." She smiled, but in that way that older people reserve for children who do not know any better. "I've been here for years. I told Elomas right here in this room." Her smile transmuted, turning from wood to mocking moonlight. "He's just fine, isn't he?"

CHAPTER 56

WITCHES AND DEMONS

IF IT WAS TO be believed, my little stunt with Ligeia Vas at dinner seemed to have endeared me somewhat to Lord Mataro even as it condemned me to walk on eggshells whenever I was not in the personal company of His Lordship or the royal children. Lord Mataro, I think, was one of those lords who chafed under the yoke of Chantry oversight. How many lords palatine, how many planets does that theocratic institution hold in the palm of its hand, quivering for fear of retribution, of the cathars' knives? For fear of invoking the atomic wrath of the Inquisition, the planet-burning might of weapons they would not permit even the Emperor to command? And yet, like Valka said, the Chantry is composed of men, and men can be outmaneuvered, tricked, mocked at table.

Gray-skinned vilicus Engin and the factionarius from dinner were all bows and scraping when the count, led by a trio of lictors armed and shielded, exited the conference room to rejoin those of us in his train left to wait in the hall. Doctor Onderra and I stood, ending a conversation with a junior scholiast regarding the native life forms on Emesh that everyone called bugs. "Not insects at all, really," as he put it. A quintet of logothetes in drab brown uniforms scurried toward their lord, holograph tablets projecting, preparing audio recordings and ready to make annotations with glittering light-pens.

I fell into step beside Valka, sandwiched between a double line of green-armored guards. Ahead, Ligeia and Gilliam Vas shadowed the count, the former saying some-

thing to His Excellency in a dry monotone. How many times had I followed Father thusly as a boy? How many hundreds of times? The signet ring on its new chain was clammy against my chest, hidden by the cream shirt and fashionable silver silk robe I had been given for the occasion. As the count's train resolved from chaos into a line, a logothete dodged out of my way with a muttered, "Court Translator, sir." I could not say if that was my proper title or if the man was merely confused. Self-conscious, I busied myself with fixing the wide sash that secured the light robe about my narrow waist. I wished they'd permitted me a shield-belt, some sort of weapon. But no, only the palatine were allowed to carry weapons in the presence of other palatine, and I'd my role to play. It may have won me a measure of friendship from the count, but my stunt with Ligeia Vas had put me in a precarious position. Tor Gibson did always say I was melodramatic. *One day that mouth of yours will get you killed.* Well, it had certainly gotten me exiled, and now . . .

"You know, I think I was wrong about you, Gibson," Valka said, steadying the Umandh comms box that swung heavily from her belt. We cut impressive shadows across the mosaic on the floor of the Fishers Guild's main hall, tiles patterned artfully with images of men and Umandh pulling fish from the sea to feed a hungry city. It took me a moment to recall that Gibson meant me, as if some part of me expected the old scholiast to speak up from a dingy corner, eyes bright but glassy, faded with time. He never did. By the time I realized I'd taken too long to answer, I decided to keep my mouth closed and wait the doctor out, using my silence to pull her into further speech. Presently she cleared her throat. "You aren't a barbarian."

"Not *just* a barbarian, you mean." We passed under the shadow of a holograph plate mounted on the wall, its ghostly panel displaying footage from a Colosso melee not two days old. The sound was muted, but the anchor's words were captioned along the bottom in Galstani.

Valka snorted, glanced up at the screen just at it flitted to the face of the anchor, a handsome native woman, dark complected but with waving hair so blond it was nearly

white. In Panthai, her native language, Valka said, "Everyone here is a barbarian, but you're all right." She nudged me as we stood there watching the holograph.

In a stage whisper and in Imperial, I said, "That's sweet of you to say." By my smile I made it clear I was teasing her, and she looked away, frustrated.

The doctor cocked her chin upward, mock-offended. Still in Panthai, she added, "But you're strange for an Imperial, you know."

"We're not all the same," I said, the riposte coming out before I knew what I was saying. "There's an ocean of difference between the count and myself."

"You're both palatine men."

"Is that all you see?" I asked, darting a look her way. "My class? My sex?"

"'Tis what you are."

Something twisted in me at those words. Was it not a species of the same argument used by the Chantry to dismiss the Cielcin as devils? Or by my father to dismiss his plebeians? By myself to dismiss Gilliam? These latter two were lost on me at the time, but their seeds were there, stirring that I might one day see. For the moment I saw only that Valka was blinkered herself because she did not see me.

"There's more to us than that," I objected. "More than where we're born or how. We are . . . more." I finished lamely.

That brought a frown to her strange but lovely face. "What do you mean?"

I shrugged. "You should judge people by their actions, by what they do, not who they are."

The Demarchist twitched to hear this and scratched at her tattooed arm. I didn't appreciate its full meaning at the time, but the intense fractal intaglio decorating Valka from shoulder blade and breast to the base of her graceful fingers contained in its whorls and geometric angles the coded history of her line. A cultural, visual representation of the genes native to her very bones. She wore her history and her clan's history on her sleeve, written in ideograms I could never understand. All this moved behind the lines of her fine-boned face in mute contradiction to the words

I'd uttered. "'Twould be nice if you applied that generosity to anyone who's not one of your nobiles."

"I do! I try to." She was still speaking Panthai, so I replied in kind, halting and thick-tongued though I doubtless was. "Where do you think the patricians come from? They're plebeians who have been rewarded for their actions." I had to remind myself that I was playing the role of a patrician.

"Whereas you were rewarded for being born in the right place."

I set my jaw. "Would you punish me for who my parents are? They worked for what they had, built upon what their parents gave them, the same as anyone else: palatine or plebeian. I have stolen nothing." I stopped short, afraid I was close to revealing my palatine identity.

"Enough," she said breezily, following the swish of the viridian-robed scholiasts ahead of us. "I never thought I'd see the day an Imperial prior was shamed at a lord's banquet." I took the change of subject to mean I'd scored a point, but I did not gloat.

Bogged down by my unfamiliarity with her language, I shook my head. "Is where you come from truly so different?"

"Yes." We stepped through a static field and into the cloying air. The scream of fliers greeted the new day, their noise rebounding off the low buildings of Borosevo. "The Wisp's far enough away that it can afford to be."

I looked down at my boots past the hem of the silk robes. "I would like to see it someday."

She stopped a moment, nearly colliding with the logothete behind her. She was looking at me strangely, as if I'd said I wanted to destroy her Demarchy and not visit it—or as if that were what she had expected me to say. After she stumbled her way clear of the logothete, we had to hurry to rejoin the line.

Perhaps the Chantry's icona are real. Perhaps those spirits hear our prayers. Perhaps not. I have always considered

myself agnostic, but you see, to a peasant, a serf who has never seen the Emperor—to him, our Emperor and those gods are the same. His Radiance's laws still affect the provincial, even when there is no Emperor at all. It is a mistake to believe we must know a thing to be influenced by it. It is a mistake to believe the thing must even be real. The universe is, and we are in it. And by whatever strange forces move us through time, God or otherwise, our tour of the fisheries brought us to the same warehouse where I had first seen the Umandh years and lifetimes earlier.

It hadn't changed, as if the metal walls and rickety catwalks were a museum exhibit, their artful disrepair well tended. Entering, I looked up, half expecting to see Cat crouched nervously on the walkway above. A pang spasmed through me, and I caught my hand forming the sign of the sun disc discreetly at my side—a damned stupid superstitious thing to do. *Rest easy, and find peace on Earth.* A sudden laugh threatened me, and I fought it down, imagining what Cat would say to see me dressed as I was in fine silks and high boots.

My distress must surely have colored my face, for I caught Valka watching me. Seeing her only made me feel worse. Had I truly forgotten Cat so quickly? No. No, life must move on, surely. I was no ascetic. I should not be alone.

"Are you all right, Gibson?"

Hadrian, I wanted to say, as I had said at Ulakiel alienage. *Call me Hadrian.*

"Yes, I . . ." What could I say? That I'd once robbed this place years ago? "I was just thinking, sorry."

"The workers all come in from the offshore compound, Your Excellency, as you know," said gray-faced Engin, all cordiality and polite deference. His khaki uniform was freshly pressed, pinned with medals and the collar tabs of the civil service. The uniform made him look paler, more ashen than he already was. He wrung a billed cap in his hands; the headwear might have been formal had it not been crushed in the vilicus's square-fingered hands. He glanced nervously to where a team of his people had clustered a pod of droning Umandh along one wall of the musty warehouse.

Gilliam pressed his kerchief to his face. "How many of the beasts do we still have?"

"At Ulakiel?" Engin frowned, glanced to his aide, a woman even thinner than me.

She had the look of one of Emesh's northern tribesmen, denoted by the tight braids that ran in rows to the nape of her neck. Her twanging accent confirmed my guess as she said, "Seventeen hundred and forty-three, Your Reverence."

"And globally?" The count frowned, crossing over to inspect the gathered coloni slaves. Balian Mataro was no small man—was indeed among the largest palatines I had seen—and still the aliens dwarfed him, their waving tentacles and finer cilia waving higher, swaying on their three legs.

The northwoman said, "Approximately eight million, Your Excellency." The light flashed on her collar tabs, the left with the notched wheel symbol of her rank, the right with a silvery open hand against a black enameled background, sigil of the Imperial civil service. Not an aide, then, but Imperial oversight in the Fishers Guild's offices. They may have served the count, but all their books flowed straight to the Imperial office on Forum. I ruminated on split loyalty, and on the plight of the Umandh. What was it Engin had said when Valka and I had gone out to the Umandh alienage? That they had sold a breeding population offworld? I imagined the beasts disseminated throughout the Empire, ornaments of human superiority like the homunculi wealthy men sometimes ordered as wives, the features of the women's bodies crafted to suit their desires. Hollow, childish, cruel. Prophet that I was, I imagined the Cielcin meeting the same fate. Man is a wolf to man and a dragon to the inhuman.

"That number is up since my last report on the matter. Significantly."

Ligeia Vas swept silently across the floor, staying between her son and the lord she served. "It is my understanding that you yet allow the beasts their rituals." How she wasn't sweating through her brocade chasuble I

couldn't tell you, yet she appeared completely untroubled, examining the vilicus and his assistant with those witch-bright eyes.

One of the junior ministers, a layman I did not know, exclaimed, "They ought to be brought to the light of the Chantry."

I suppressed a snort, unwilling to cite the obvious logical fallacy inherent in the man's piety. Luckily I didn't have to do so. Valka glared at the man, then spoke as if over the heads of everyone in the count's party. "Why would a xenobite ever consent to be embraced by your faith?"

The *your* was not lost on the dough-faced functionary, nor did it pass the prior and her chanter son unnoticed. Ligeia and Gilliam both held their tongues a moment as the stupid minister blundered in, "What . . . whatever do you mean, Doctor?"

Valka's nostrils flared, and she looked ready to strike the man. Gilliam visibly sneered beneath his kerchief. "You'd have better luck getting rats to worship cats."

The grand prior raised a bony hand and turned to address the vilicus and the count together. "I believe our mandate was clear when we accorded your house the terraforming technologies you required, Lord Mataro."

That had been well over a thousand years earlier, and Balian knew it. Still the weight of those years hung from him, though he had not lived them. His shoulders slumped, compressed as by a yoke. "Yes, of course."

"The native culture must be obliterated. Take the children from their parents if you must, but we need no rebellions. We can tolerate no gods but the Earth herself and her Son." She meant the Emperor.

Unseen, I glanced sidelong at Valka. The doctor stood with her hands clasped behind her back, chin angled upward as if baiting a boxer to strike. I thought of what she had shared that day at Ulakiel—what she had shown me in her holographs. That simple, secret fact, terrifying and terrible: we were not first. Did Ligeia know? Did Gilliam? Even if the Quiet were a secret known to only a few in the Chantry—those tasked with guarding their secret—surely the mother-and-bastard pair must know. After all,

they were the highest ranking members of the Chantry on Emesh. No wonder the woman was squeezing so hard. It made we wonder why they hadn't glassed the site from orbit, why none of the ancient sites had been obliterated by the Chantry over the years.

"Leave the doctor alone, Ligeia." Balian Mataro placed a hand on his prior's arm. "The girl is a foreigner and unused to our ways."

"The girl is an infidel," Gilliam put in, leering at Valka.

"And you're a self-righteous little hobgoblin," the count said, perhaps still angry and rattled by the comment about terraforming equipment.

I smiled in spite of myself, glancing down at my feet to hide my expression.

"Balian, please." The grand prior swept forward. "A measure of decorum."

"I am lord of this planet, grand prior. Have a care how you address me."

From the far wall, the Umandh's droning changed in pitch, warbling with a strange, constant rhythm. There must have been half a hundred of them, all swaying like coral polyps in a strong eddy. The noise of them was incredible, rattling the cheap glass panes in the windows. "Would someone please shut them up?" Gilliam snapped his fingers in the general direction of the coloni, then used his kerchief to dab at the beads of sweat forming on his brow.

At the chanter's command, one of the douleters clubbed the nearest creature to quiet it, doubtless counting on the message to translate to the others, linked at they were. It trumpeted in pain, splintering its portion of the great harmony it shared with its brethren. I felt a terrible pang of déjà vu, remembering the last time I'd been in this place. But instead of meekly turning to aid their fallen comrade, this time the Umandh stretched their feelers far as they would go, their droning turned to a dry rattling like air through a busted trachea.

Beside me Valka sucked in a breath, tore her tablet from her belt, and glared at it in confusion, tapping at the screen with a forefinger. The count, not recognizing that

the sound was a bit odd, turned to address Engin. "Quiet your beasts, vilicus."

Engin slashed the air, shouted an order at his dou-leters, who began fiddling with their tablets. "Get them under control and back on the ship, double-time!"

Among the adorators who dwell in the mountains above Meidua, it is said that pride is the greatest sin. I have not always agreed with that supposition, or with my friend Edouard, who first shared it with me. But it was so here. The first of the Umandh boiled from behind its invisible line, breaking from its pack like a Jaddian der-vish. It spun, twisting on its three legs in a strange, whirl-ing charge, its own drone stretching to a high shriek as it threw itself toward our party like a frenzied beast. It caught one of the count's guards, wrapping its tentacles around the man and falling atop him. They had counted on their weapons and a thousand years of oppression to cow the creatures.

Pride.

The dam broke, and the pack of Umandh threw them-selves upon us, shrieking like the tearing of metal in some deep pelagic hell. Gilliam staggered back, then turned with surprising speed to shepherd his mother away. The remainder of the guards gathered together, forming a cor-don between the suddenly animated horde and their count. I turned to look at Valka just as the other guards—the ones who had been dutifully holding positions outside—stormed in. The man the Umandh had tackled, whose green armor was slashed with white to mark him as a lictor, struggled, but the Umandh held him with countless arms, the tentacles squeezing tighter, immobi-lizing the man. I heard bones crack beneath that armor, or dreamed I did. One of the other guards fired a plasma burner at the creature, burning a smoking wedge out of its side.

The Umandh howled like a deflating elephant, but it struggled on, kept squeezing until the fifth round from the plasma burner felled it.

"Get His Excellency outside!" shouted Dame Camilla,

voice amplified by speakers embedded in her breastplate. Rounding on Valka and myself, she exclaimed, "You two, come with me!"

Valka was standing hunched, slightly aloof, fiddling with her tablet. She was not panicking, was barely sweating despite the sweltering heat in the warehouse. I nearly tripped over an upended crate of fish getting to the knot of soldiers. "Give me a weapon!" I didn't know what I was saying, but when they hesitated, I snapped, "I'm not going to kill your bloody lord, just give me something!" I snapped my fingers, held my palm out. Something huge and scaly struck me, the rough texture of it tearing my fine silk robes, scraping the flesh over my ribs. My head struck the ground and rang like a bell. I snarled, fingers trying to find purchase on flesh as hard as coral, as stone. The cloying stink of raw fish filled my nostrils, and then thin tendrils filled them, stopping my air as another appendage forced itself down my throat.

My vision blurred, and in my panic I bit down on both the tendril and my tongue. Copper blood filled my mouth, mingled with the sulfurous ichor from the Umandh's veins. I was still choking, could not remove the thing from between my teeth. I could not move.

I could not move.

The pressure was too great; my every limb felt stressed to breaking, and I imagined glass pillars splintering under weight. At once I went blind, went weak, felt the world slipping away. Would that I had died there, died and spared the universe the stink of me. Another monster strangled in its crib, snuffed out before I could be inflicted on the universe. The blood slowing in my ears carried with it the sound of tramping feet, the fall of starships, and the burning out of suns. The world faded into darkness, the true Dark of which the chanters sing. White faces bloomed like flowers in that darkness, only to be snuffed out and blown to dust. I saw my father's face and Crispin's. Cat's and Valka's and my mother's. And Gibson's, nose slit, back straight, eyes undimmed.

He shook his head. "Go back!" he said, then shrank

into shadow, leaving only green eyes that turned to glass. To starlight. To darkness and no more.

No more.

Light.

There was light. Light and the air came rushing back into me, and the glass-splintering feeling in my bones turned to raw aching. Valka had tugged the Umandh tentacle I'd bitten off free. "Are you all right?"

Why, Doctor Onderra, fancy meeting you in a place like this. My oxygen-deprived brain made me giggle at the thought. Two creases formed between her eyebrows, and she started when I sat up abruptly. "Yes." My eyes widened. "Down!" I seized her by the shoulders, nearly blacking out again as I tugged her down and rolled atop her just as another of the Umandh tumbled past, tentacles lashing. Valka lay frozen beneath me, eyes wide. I didn't want to move, but I staggered to my feet with a groan, the fat sash that held my robes in place coming undone and the garment tangling about me. With a growl I shrugged out of the garment, stripping down to my cream shirt and trousers. The shirt clung to my torn side where the blood flowed hot and sticky. I hauled Valka to her feet. "You all right?"

That I had deliberately mirrored her tone was not lost on her, and she found a small smile. I nearly missed it; she played it off as a compression of the lips, skin whitening. "Yeah."

"Come on." I seized her by the wrist, moving toward the very ladder I'd once descended to steal fish. "Up that way! Quickly!" Where was the count? I couldn't see through all the confusion, through the tangle of Umandh slaves and humans, through the haze of plasma smoke and the beginnings of fire. Valka was still lingering on the first rung of the ladder. "Go, damn you!"

Her eyes widened, and she climbed. One of the Umandh must have heard our escape, for it hurtled straight at me, nine feet of stone skin and waving tentacles. Stupidly I dove

sideways, rolling as I hit the ground on the far side of a row of open fish containers and slamming into the next. The Umandh crashed into the boxes, tumbling over them in its blindness. I scrambled to my feet, seizing a pair of frozen carp.

Numb, confused, I threw them at the staggered creature as I backed away and sought some sort of weapon. Maybe one of the douleters had left a shock-stick lying around or some injudicious dock worker had abandoned a pry bar for the refrigerated crates. *Or maybe there's an Imperial Legion waiting in ambush, buried under all the fish.*

I looked about for the soldiers, but they were too busy completing their massacre by the doors to help with my stray. There were so few of them. Most of the reinforcements who had come streaming in to supplement the men who'd been there from the start had vanished, retreating with the vanished palatines. I thought I saw Engin's gray-skinned body face down and bleeding on the concrete floor, but I didn't waste time on him.

The Umandh was on its feet, hissing past the tentacles snaking from the mouth at its crown. Translucent golden slaver flew from its mouth, and as it tipped forward I saw the little studded fangs orbiting the lining of its trunk. From that perspective I realized the tendrils weren't arms—they were tongues. I scrabbled backward and nearly tripped again over the carcass of a seven-meter-long congrid. Something metallic clattered against the row of boxes. When I saw what it was, I almost laughed aloud. The machete was one of several used to gut the massive congrid eels and the terranic sharks harvested by the Fishers Guild, no doubt left there by some careless slave or douleter, just as I'd hoped. I could have kissed whoever had left it there, and I snatched it up, rolling to face my opponent. The edge bit through two of the Umandh's tendrils, notched another, kinked a fourth. The creature bellowed and body-checked me, trying to sweep my legs with one of its own. I twisted, catching one of its tentacles in my fist. I brought the blade down, then slammed my booted foot against the inside of one of the colonus's three spindly knees.

I felt the bone break, and the Umandh's war cry warbled in pain as it fell. I placed the point of the machete against the creature's bony exoskeleton and raised my other hand to slam the pommel and pierce the tough hide. It groaned, made a sound like the crying of brass whales in the waters of my home, and lay quiescent. My hand hung there, raised like an executioner's sword, my shadow like the shadow of a cathar cast across the body of the guilty. As I hesitated, I glanced upward and saw Valka watching me from the catwalk, just where Cat had once watched me, where I had watched the douleters beat an Umandh with no name.

I pulled the machete away, raised the blade in silent salute to the doctor above me.

Then one of the count's soldiers shot the creature at my feet.

"It was the foreign witch!" Gilliam was shouting when at last I emerged into the sunlight. He was irritatingly unharmed, one arm sheltering his mother. The grand prior, looking more the part of a witch than Valka ever could, nestled against her son in spite of the heat. "She can use that terminal of hers to talk with those . . . those . . . creatures!" he sputtered. "And Mother knows what else she's capable of!"

The count wiped his sweating forehead on a patterned sleeve. "We've used those tablets since the colonization. They have nothing to do with our Tavrosi emissary."

"Then she's sullied it with some foreign perversion. Some device of Tavros!"

Dame Camilla strode forward, smoothly cutting the intus's stream of implications off at the head. She saluted and bowed to her lord, said, "All dead, Excellency."

Lord Balian Mataro sagged against a crate. "Very good. Cut them up and throw them in the sea, Camilla." He waved his dismissal, hand heavy with the weight of rings and orders.

She didn't leave, and I imagined those jewel-hard eyes

of hers locked on the count beneath her helmet. "And our own dead?"

"How many?"

"Three," the knight-lictor replied, as if it were just a number. "Engin and two of ours."

I glanced at Valka, raised my eyebrows at her as if to ask, *Did you have anything to do with this?* She shook her head, more tired than affronted, and the count addressed one of the surviving slave-handlers. "What the hell happened?"

The douleter, a woman with yellow-white hair, stood ramrod straight when speaking to the count, her eyes on some spot above his massive shoulders. "I . . . I don't know, my lord. Your Excellency. I've never seen the like. I've seen them get mad sometimes, seen them charge, aye. But this . . ."

"They were frenzied," said Ligeia Vas, shrugging free of her son's protective embrace. "Enraged." Above us the drone of Royse repulsors filled the air, and several fliers—military landers escorting one sleek, chrome blade of a skiff—circled into view, falling like samaras in springtime from the cloud-dappled sky. "They should be wiped out, the *beasts*."

"They heard you say you were the count," Valka said, thrusting her chin upward in a gesture that made her appear a cubit taller. "'Twas the moment when their droning changed. Perhaps they understand our tongue better than we thought, sir." Some of the surviving retinue winced at the overfamiliarity in her address, but she ignored them.

Gilliam stumped forward. "You will address the count correctly or not at all." He turned imploringly to the man in question. "I tell you, the witch is responsible. Who here knows the creatures better? Hmm? Who has more reason to want you dead? I've warned you from the start, Excellency! She is a foreign agent!"

I felt a muscle pulse along my jaw. "You cannot prove the doctor is responsible, Chanter," the count said wearily, going stone-faced as the first fliers settled into the sea a ways out and powered inland, sending up great clouds of mist that formed glittered rainbows in the umber

sunlight. "Do drop your accusations until we've returned to Borosevo Castle, at least." He gazed up at the castle, which rose in the middle distance like a fairy tale above the low buildings and the algae stink of his city.

"What other explanation could there be?" Gilliam limped forward, mopping his beaded brow with the kerchief from his sleeve. He pressed the kerchief to his chest. "She's a foreigner, lordship. A Demarchist witch." My mouth twitched at the word, the Chantry's label for anyone who flirted with the hated thinking machines without their divine consent. How easily it tripped from Gilliam's lips.

"It could be simple rebellion," I blurted, edging into the conversation with a perfunctory bow. "Like the doctor said, they know whose boot it is on their necks." I glanced from the count to the prior, bowed my head. "So to speak."

Gilliam's twisted jaw worked, those mismatched eyes flitting from my face to that of his lord. Whatever else he was, the man was no fool. He pointed a square finger at my chest. "See? She has the lowborn under her sway. The witch is behind this, mark my words!"

Valka's nostrils flared, and she took a step forward, her lithe body coiled as if to strike. "Say 'witch' again, priest, and I'll make you wish I were one." I swear Gilliam quailed beneath the light of those golden eyes. I like to imagine he took a step back. I fought down a smile. Unnoticed, momentarily forgotten in the wake of Valka's threat, I edged closer to the chanter. How dare he?

"She threatens me, sire!" The intus tried his best to straighten his twisted spine. He did not respond to Valka but rather spoke to his liege lord. "This foreign . . . woman." He did not say "witch." "Who else has the know-how to communicate with the Umandh? I saw her! I saw her fiddling with that device right before the attack! And now she threatens me, sire! This offworld whore with her forbidden—"

Gilliam never finished the sentence but instead went sprawling. I didn't even know I was going to hit him; the thing happened of its own accord. I stood above the priest in his tangle of black robes, shaking out my bruised fist,

alone in the eye of an abyssal silence. I didn't feel rage or contempt or even hatred. I felt . . . clean. Justified. Righteous. I rubbed my knuckles, torn side momentarily forgotten. I took in a deep breath, pushed the air out through my nose. "That's quite enough from you."

Blood dribbled from the crooked man's broken nose. Coming out of his stunned state, Gilliam pressed his kerchief to the flow as he pointed with his free hand. "Barbarian!" he squeaked, recovering his feet with surprising speed. "You hit me!"

"And would do it again!" I stepped forward, still remarkably calm. I had just struck a priest of the Terran Chantry. By rights I should have melted in fear of the cathars and their knives, but I just sucked on my teeth, staring down. "Apologize to the lady."

"M. Gibson!" Valka moved forward, but one of the surviving guards moved to hold her back, as if afraid my heretical violence was catching. "What in the hells are you doing?"

The priest bared his yellowed teeth. "You'll pay for this, peasant. Guards! Guards, you saw what this barbarian did! Seize him!" Beneath their mirror-black visors, the guards looked from one another to their lord. Balian Mataro, who had so recently survived his brush with death, just looked at me, worn out. By the gods, the man looked nearly every one of his years in that instant, his black eyes dim and distant. Gilliam was still shouting, "What are you all waiting for! Seize him! Stun him!"

Stunners came up, blue slits gleaming as two hoplites closed in to take my arms. Valka's face went white. "Wait!" I said, raising my hands. "Wait! The man gave offense, lordship. You heard it yourself." The keywords were *gave offense*, words any nobile of the Imperium would recognize. I chose them precisely, hoping to capture the sportsman I knew the count to be. I had few enough cards to play, but I'd dug my own hole. It fell to me to climb out of it. "I demand satisfaction." There was a way, slim and dangerous as a monofilament scythe, thin as a cord, a chain hanging about my neck.

"Monomachy?" The count cocked an eyebrow, but his

eyes glinted. "Surely the doctor has more right to that than you."

I watched Valka long, trying to decipher the feelings embedded in the lines of her chiseled face. Anger? Fear? She shook her head. I could practically hear her mutter the word *barbarians* again. "He said I was under her sway; he thinks me simple." A paper shield, that. And maybe I was simple, letting him goad me as I had. Now I had no recourse, no way out but forward. *Hello, Father.* Well, it was that or die. Before anyone could challenge me, I added, "And the man has assaulted me twice before, my lord." This raised a few eyebrows, but I pressed forward. People had died, inhumans had been slaughtered, and this pedant was finger-pointing. "First he ordered his foederati escort to attack me in the coliseum, and then he accosted me in your palace after your last feast."

"Excellency, this peasant has no right!" Gilliam protested.

"You don't deny it, then?" I bared my teeth.

"You've no right to a duel," said Ligeia Vas. "My son is palatine. You've no right to challenge him."

I looked Balian Mataro right in the face, expecting the man to shake his head. He knew. Knew I had no other choice and knew his delicate game was up. And mine. With unfeeling fingers, I snapped the chain from round my neck and slipped the ring onto my thumb, holding it up. "I have every right." I glowered at Gilliam. Briefly I glanced at Valka and saw surprise etched on those delicate, hard-edged features. "I told you, Your Reverence. You don't know everything."

CHAPTER 57

SECOND

"ONE HOUR, LORDSHIP," THE driver said. He was from the urban prefects' office, as were the two guards who accompanied me on my mission from the palace to ensure I did not try to flee town. We might have walked, but my minders seemed to think that would only allow me greater opportunity for mischief, and so I'd allowed myself to be shuttled across the plaza from Castle Boros-evo to the coliseum. We left the driver in the flier as the other two frog-marched me past the douleters and arena security and into the hypogeum.

The concrete vaults hung low overhead, posters and cheap prints taped to them above aluminum bedsteads strewn with the untidy possessions of the fighting poor. The bed that had been Erdro's was already filled, and my own was gone entirely—stripped, I didn't doubt, by the count's soldiers after my . . . discovery. One of my escort cleared his throat, reminding me that time was wasting. The truth was that I was dreading the next moments. I had declared war on a man, a formal challenge to monomachy. I had stirred up the count's court, revealed my nobile blood, insulted the Chantry, assaulted the Chantry, and just possibly alienated Valka in the process.

And yet . . . and yet I stood on the edge of making one thing right. That terrified me more than the rest together. As someone once said, to go to war is easy. It is peace that is hard.

Switch was sitting at one of the small tables in the sitting area at the far end of the dormitory near the old food

and hygiene dispensaries. He was alone, idly turning the pages of an illustrated novel. My guards had fallen back, so my approach was quieter than it might have been. Some of the few others in the room noticed me first, and a stillness settled over them. It was their quietude that alerted the younger man to my presence.

I am not sure if it is possible for a face to brighten and darken at the same time, but if it is, then his did. His eyes widened, but the surprise curdled instantly to suspicion, and he half stood, his mouth compressed to a thin, white line. He sat back down quickly, shutting his book with a soft thump. "What are you doing here?"

I'd rehearsed a dozen versions of this confrontation the night before. None was quite right. I believed I had been protecting my friends by hiding my right name. Fear and pride had moved me to a place I had neither meant nor wanted to go, and whatever else I might have said, one thing needed saying. "I'm sorry, Switch." I did not bow, did not kneel. I did not even hang my head.

Switch looked at me, nodding. "Pallino said you were holed up in the castle." He looked pointedly at my guards. "That they weren't letting you out?"

"Yes." I glanced back over my shoulder at the two stony prefects in their khaki uniforms. I was conscious suddenly that I'd drawn a deep breath. My secret was out, traded for the bruise I'd put on Gilliam's jaw and my desperate circumstances. There was no longer a need for the concealment I had practiced since those first days on Emesh. I would face whatever punishment my father, my house, and the Chantry chose for me, but I would face it after this duel. First I needed Switch, needed someone to stand in support of my challenge legally.

I might have asked Pallino, but if I was to die, I did not want to do so without making things right with Switch. I had so few friends in all the universe that I could hardly stand to do without a one of them. And so I told him everything. I spoke quickly, mindful of the time limit the prefects' office had imposed on this venture of mine. It was not hard. There was much I did not wish to recall or recount.

I told him about Gibson and the Chantry school on Vesperad, how I had fled, how I had beaten my brother almost to death. I told him how my mother had saved me and how it was for her sake and safety that I had not cried my blood and status to the authorities or admitted it to him. I am not ashamed to say I wept as I spoke of this, fearing for her safety anew in light of what I'd done.

Next I spoke of my time on the canals, though I did not speak of Cat, the beatings, or that moonless night in the alley. Some things should remain unremembered and unspoken. I explained how I had come to be in the fighting pits, and he understood and accepted my stupid reason for breaking into the gaol. He laughed, and when that telling was done, I said, "I need your help, Switch."

He blinked, taken aback but not offended. "With what?"

"I hit that intus priest," I said simply. "That's why none of this is a secret anymore. He would have me executed if I weren't . . ."

"A palatine?" Switch said the word like he was spitting poison from a wound.

"A palatine," I agreed, and looked away. "I know it's a lot to ask, and I've no right to ask it, but I'm to duel him in two days' time. I was hoping you'd—"

"Yes," Switch said, standing.

For a moment I must have looked a great fool. I'd frozen mid-word, my mouth open, hands spread in supplication. When I found myself again, I stammered, "You will? You'll . . . stand with me?"

"As your second?" He set his jaw, nodding. "Of course I will, Had. I wouldn't have made it this far without you." I have never forgotten that. Had, not Hadrian. The myrmidon's name and not the palatine's. "Doesn't mean I'm not still mad as hell at you."

I felt my teeth grind and just managed to conceal the gesture with a nod. "Switch, whatever . . ." I shook my head, squared my shoulders. My hair fell across my face, but I let it hang there. "Those other palatines. That wasn't me."

The younger man looked down at his graphic novel, eyes lensing shut. "I know. I know, Had. You just don't

know what it's like. You . . . You people . . ." He shook his head. "You can't see us; you never see us. We're just part of the furniture. You treat us like homunculi, and we're not. We're as human as you." Switch hadn't looked at me during any of this, only tucked his chin and raised his shoulders as if in anticipation of a blow.

"I am not those men." His argument cut both ways, but that didn't make him wrong. "I don't think there's any such thing as a kind of people," I said, "just people." He didn't respond to that, just kept looking down at the table before him, hands in his lap. Now was not the time. I let it drop. The chair legs ground against the enameled concrete as I drew it out, turned it around, and straddled it across the table from Switch. The other myrmidons had long since ceased to hover, returning to their lives. Still he did not look at me until I spoke again, saying, "Thank you, Switch."

The man nodded, still not really looking at me. At length he asked, "Why me?"

"Eh?"

"Why not Pallino? He's a better fighter."

"I don't need a fighter," I said. "I need my friend back. You're the best friend I've got."

A wicked grin broke across the myrmidon's face. "And what's that say about you, then?" I made a rude gesture with my thumb, and the grin widened.

"I wouldn't ask if I were putting you in danger. You don't have to fight. The law requires I have a second, and if it goes badly . . ."

"It won't go badly."

"*If* it goes badly," I insisted, "I didn't want this unsaid." I broke off, and it was my turn to look away. "I really am sorry, you know."

My friend dismissed the apology with a wave. "What did the priest do to piss you off so bad?"

"What?" For the briefest instant, I'd managed to forget why I was in the hypogeum in the first place.

"Why'd you punch him?"

In all the scrambling since that day in the warehouse district, since I'd punched Gilliam, Switch was the first

person not to challenge me or reprimand me for what I'd done. He was, as I have said, the very best kind of friend. It was my turn to grin. "He insulted a lady."

Switch clapped his hands together. He rubbed his palms, nodding. "Classic, classic." Still he did not criticize and acted as if I'd said the most reasonable thing in the world.

All the while I heard Gibson in my mind murmuring, *Melodramatic. Damned melodramatic.* Flushing, I smiled. Switch smiled. I pressed my forehead against the back of my chair, and before long we were laughing. For a moment Gilliam was banished like the demon he was, and Valka, and the count, and Vesperad. And my father. They would all keep for another time, be it one of the next three nights before the duel or until word was handed down by quantum telegraph from Delos or the Chantry. In that instant, all that mattered was that I had my friend back and that we had ever been friends at all.

"She wouldn't want me to kill him. I don't want to either. Not anymore." With the heat of the moment cooled into entropic collapse, I felt none of the desire for Gilliam's blood that had possessed me the day before. But I had struck the blow and sealed my fate. By Imperial law I could not withdraw my challenge, as it is only proper that such brashness be punished by the consequences of that brashness. "I'm going to need your help, Switch. It's been months since I used a sword. Reckon I'm out of practice."

"You're saying you need someone to knock you around?" A look of positive glee stole over my friend's face, and I felt a knot in the pit of my stomach even as I matched his toothy smile with my crooked one.

Where had he come from, this young myrmidon before me? It was as if someone had spirited my friend Switch away and replaced him with some fey changeling like in the stories my mother used to share with me. The indentured catamite was gone, eclipsed by the myrmidon before me. How he'd grown in those few years! Had I done this to him? But no. Those were his own legs he stood on. I had only pulled him to his feet.

"Had?" Switch was looking at me, brows knitting together. "You all right?"

I'd been staring. Not at him, but at the book on the tabletop with its darkly shadowed image of a young couple menaced by distorted caricatures of the Cielcin. Their shadows fell all around the human couple, the woman cowering, the man pale with terror. There was a single large rose in the foreground, the only spot of color against that chiaroscuro nightmare of a cover, red as arterial blood. There was a hand beside it, the fingers oddly twisted, broken, straining as if to grasp the rose. Though I have forgotten the name of the book, I have never forgotten that hand, nor that rose.

"What?" I looked Switch squarely in the eye. "Yes, I—I think so." That was not the moment to come apart, to spill all my trepidations out upon the table between us. I could feel the eyes of my escort on me, hard and unsympathetic, and the weight of all that concrete close above my head like the cathar's White Sword. "I could die on Thursday."

"You won't, though." Switch didn't sound conciliatory or even friendly. He said the words like he was stating a fact. "I've seen that priest. He's a mute, that one. All twisted up. But it's like you say: You don't want to kill him. You just cut him once well and good and have done."

First blood. I could have laughed. First blood, and I could call the duel there. No one had to die, the law would be satisfied, and I would say that I was too. Switch's manner turned suddenly cheerful. "Might turn this lady of yours onto you too, gallantry like that. I've seen it happen."

"Not this lady," I countered, resting my chin on my arms.

"Too proud?"

"Too . . ." I could not find the word. "She's Tavrosi."

Switch's eyebrows shot up. "A Demarchist? Really?"

One of the guards cleared his throat. "That's time, Lord Marlowe!"

Raising a hand in acknowledgment, I rose to my feet and said, "If you come to the palace by the main gate, I'll meet you in the public barbican. Pallino knows the way." I wanted to add that Pallino and I were talking again

about the ship, wanted to make use of this opportunity to talk without the omnipresent palace cameras, but it was not meant to be. Anyhow it would have been wrong to push the issue that had divided us so soon after our reconciliation. I rapped the tabletop with my knuckles in polite applause. "Thank you, Switch."

Not knowing what else to say, I shoved my hands into the pockets of my trousers and slouched toward the door and the palace. And the future. And the duel.

Switch called after me. "I'm just wondering—what's your name? Your real one?"

I smiled, and it was as classic a crooked smile as my knife-edged excuse for a face had ever worn. "Oh, it *is* Hadrian," I said. "Hadrian of House Marlowe. Of Delos."

Though it was significant to me to name myself for true again, Switch took this in with only a shrugging motion of his lips. "Sounds right and proper."

A hollow laugh broke from me, and I half turned back to my guards. "It is proper. You know?"

"Yeah," Switch replied. "Guess it is."

"I'll see you tomorrow, then?"

"Tomorrow." He ducked his head. "Later, Had."

CHAPTER 58

BARBARIANS

"ARE YOU INSANE?" VALKA demanded without pretext or hello, bursting through the door to the bottled garden where I was training for my duel. "This isn't the opera, Gibson—or whatever your name is. Who asked you to defend my . . . my . . ." She was flustered, words retreating from her. She swore in Panthai.

"Your honor, ma'am?" Switch suggested, finishing the sentence for her. I'd been confined to the Sunglass Hall after my visit to the coliseum to see Switch, who'd been brought to me as I'd requested. I consoled myself that Gilliam was similarly sequestered, tried not to think about the chain of dominoes I'd set in motion.

Valka's jaw worked words over soundlessly. "This isn't Old Earth, damn it! I never asked for your help!" Her nostrils flared, and she leaned on what I would one day learn was her favorite swear word: *"Imperials."* Switch pulled his lips down in a frightened grimace. I shook my head, glad to have my friend back, if only temporarily.

Burying my exasperation—*rage is blindness*—I propped my training sword against a white birch tree and turned to Valka. The truth was, I was surprised she'd not come to yell at me sooner—she'd had a night and half a day. With the air of a man resigned to wrestle a viper, I said, "I'm sorry. I know you don't approve of violence."

"Violence is not the issue!" She combed back her hair. "I'd punch the little troll in his teeth if I had my way, but I—" She broke off, made as if to bite a fingernail, then

stopped herself, closing her hand into a fist. "You're not *responsible* for me, damn it!"

I felt my eyes widen, said, "Of course I'm not." That hadn't been my intention, not precisely. I thought back to the instants before I'd struck Gilliam. He'd repeatedly called her a witch. A whore. My face went the color of Switch's hair. The myrmidon made a small throat-clearing sound, and I said, "Doctor Onderra, forgive me." I swept into a shallow bow. "This is my friend Switch."

The myrmidon bobbed his head. "Afternoon, my lady."

"She's a doctor, Switch," I murmured, curtailing the woman's classic tart response.

"She the one you punched this priest over?"

I pinched the bridge of my nose in frustration. "That's not helping." The myrmidon at least had the good grace to look cowed and spent the next few heartbeats examining his shoes.

The doctor crossed her arms, compressing her chest a little. "You Imperials . . . You backward, chauvinistic *kaunchau rhobsa mehar di* . . ." She descended into some Tavrosi argot of which I did not understand but a word in twelve.

"We're not! My mother once fought a duel over a woman," I blurted, unthinking. "Well, two women. Well, two women and a horse. This isn't helping." I knew it was the wrong thing to say the moment the words escaped my lips, thinking of the blue-skinned homunculus my mother kept in her harem.

Valka only looked at me. "Your mother—some great *lady*, was she? Lord . . . Lord . . ."

"Marlowe." I bowed again. "Hadrian Marlowe." When I straightened, I stuck out my chin a little. That this was a mistake dawned on me only a moment later—it was more of the old aristocratic hauteur than the egalitarian Valka could stomach. I felt so much the fool, the ring on my thumb more an affectation than the assumption of my true self. It felt as if it were not mine at all, as if I'd borrowed it, stolen it—and I suppose I had. Switch stayed silent and did not look at the ring on my hand. "The count

ordered me to hide my name. I'm in hiding, you see, and . . ." It was my conversation with Switch all over again. Only worse. So much worse. Because it was Valka.

"Not anymore," she said. It wasn't a rebuke, wasn't a condemnation, just a blank statement of fact. I stared at her, acutely aware of the blankness of my expression. Against all odds, Valka blushed and looked away. "I'm sorry." Strange emotions played across her face, the anger resolved and tangled with something . . . softer? I could not have named it if I'd tried.

At once I found I could not look her in the face; instead I played with a fraying bit of rubber on the edge of the practice sword's grip. "You're right. I'm the one who should apologize. Much good as punching the bastard did me, I suppose—" Here I paused, risking a look up at her. Valka was still studying the back of her tattooed hand. "I suppose it was for the wrong reasons."

Was it my imagination, or did she grow still, just for a moment? But no, the moment was gone, and Valka was all *Doctor Onderra* again. "Thank you," she said at last. Nicety stowed her outrage a moment, and turning to my myrmidon friend, she said, "Your name is Switch?"

The fighting man bobbed his head. "Aye, ma'am. Well, my name's William—after the Emperor, you see—only there are too many Williams. Switch was my working name before I bought my way out of the pleasure house. I like it fine."

"Switch it is, then. You're one of Lord Marlowe's, uh . . . friends? From the coliseum?"

For an instant, Switch's earnest nature exceeded his plebeian caution, and he said, "Had and me knocked about a bit, sure." He scratched his head. "We were both trying to buy our way offworld. Light out for wherever, you know?"

Turning back to Valka, I said, "So you're here . . . why? To tell me to drop the challenge? I can't do it."

"Why not?" Valka snapped. "I thought you palatines could do whatever you wanted."

Try as I did to resist, I actually laughed in her face. "Whatever I want? I'm sorry. Did you miss the part where

I've been living under an assumed name here?" I gestured at Switch, who was dressed in the synthetic mesh fatigues common amongst off-duty myrmidons. "Do you think I risked my life in the coliseum for love of the game? My father *sold* me, Doctor. Sold me to the Chantry. So don't stand there making assumptions."

Valka pursed her lips. "I didn't know." Her voice—her beautiful voice—lowered almost below hearing, strengthened only as she cocked her head for the rejoinder. "But what has that got to do with this Gilliam?"

"I *can't* drop the challenge. Not for you or anyone." I twisted the ring on my thumb. "Legally. You can't back out of a formal challenge. I'm committed." I looked down and away, then snapped my attention back to her as I added, "And the son of a bitch had me stunned!"

Even at five paces, I could hear Valka's teeth grinding. "That has got to be the stupidest custom I've ever heard."

"It's not!" Switch put in, taking a step forward, wiping his hands on his breeches. "If you know you have to commit to a duel, you're less likely to . . ." He glanced at me, words faltering. "Well . . . you're less likely to start something. If you're sober . . ."

I caught him looking at me. "I was sober, Switch!"

"Just checking!" Switch grinned.

A wry smile—perhaps a trifle sad—twisted Valka's lips. "You still shouldn't have done it in the first place. Even if you win you'll make an enemy of that priestess. What the hell were you thinking?"

"I didn't like him calling you a witch, all right?" I rubbed the back of my neck, turned away. "Is that what you wanted me to say?" I did not add what I was thinking: that societies without the duel replaced it with murder, and the power of Gilliam's position might have allowed him to get away with all manner of vile things. For all its apparent barbarism, our stupid custom provided a channel whereby the issue might be legitimately addressed.

She didn't answer. Switch shifted uncomfortably beside me, and I walked away, creating distance between us. Part of me wished my myrmidon friend were gone, would suddenly remember an urgent appointment elsewhere. Unjust,

that, after all we'd been through and after what I'd put the both of us through. I was being ungrateful, but I really hated to have this conversation in front of anyone. At last she said, "Yes, *my lord*."

Since I'd met the woman, she'd confounded me. Her foreign strangeness, those golden eyes, the skin like new vellum, the iron-jawed determination, the obvious intelligence. Even her subtle cruelties. Whatever it says of me to admit it, she sang to me in a chemical language beneath and beyond poetry. Perhaps it was precisely because she challenged me? There was iron in her, and more than iron. Adamant, such as starships are made of. Highmatter. *My lord.* The words rattled in my ears. In spite of myself, my shoulders slumped, and I said, "Hadrian."

"What?" She hadn't heard me.

"Call me Hadrian."

The air escaped her in a rush. *"Imperials."* She turned to Switch. "Your friend better not get himself killed." She turned smartly on her heel and left, apparently having said her piece. "If he does, I'll kill him."

Switch and I stood staring at each for a good thirty seconds, communicating wordless exhaustion. At last I said, "What the hell is that supposed to mean?"

The myrmidon arched his thick red eyebrows. "Don't die, obviously."

"Thanks, Switch."

We returned to our uneasy silence, neither of us moving. After a moment, the myrmidon jerked his chin, mouthed the words, *Go after her.*

"Wait!" I caught up to Valka in a dim colonnade, pink marble bruised by the withering sun. I felt grubby and small before the Tavrosi woman, dressed as I was in exercise clothes and my own shame. "Doctor Onderra, wait." She turned, a hand resting on one prominent hip. In contrast to myself, the doctor might have been carved from ice—but was that a small smile on those lips? Laughing at me? There was no way out of it. "I'm sorry. You're

right, I hit Gilliam because of what he said about you. I couldn't stop myself." Visions of Crispin unconscious on the floor flashed before me, and for a moment I saw him lying on the smooth marble between us. Somewhere in the trees beyond the colonnade a bird cried out, screeching at the afternoon blush. I turned away from the image of my brother, closed the fist that had struck Gilliam. In a small voice I added, "My fault."

Rage is blindness, the scholiasts say, *calmness sight*. They eschew anger as they eschew all extremes of emotion, mud in the mind's clear pool. Perhaps it is good I never made it to Teukros, to Nov Senber. Fear. Fear lay at the root of it all, a dragon in the classic sense, birthing monsters. Death to reason. Why was I afraid? What was it about Valka that took familiar feelings and turned them strange as the stars in Emesh's sky?

"You're right," she said, bright voice soft and dark as the air beneath the pillars of the vaulted colonnade. "'Tis your fault." She didn't offer anything more, but she didn't leave either. I tried to focus on that, to quiet the galloping terror in my blood. Terror of what? That she would hate me? Did hate me? Would never speak to me again? Maybe she was a witch, by Earth and Emperor, and I her thrall.

I cleared my throat. "I mentioned I was going to be a diplomat one day . . ." And how wrongly that had gone. Punching Gilliam in the face had been the least diplomatic thing imaginable. "In diplomacy you have to be willing to forgive people their . . . their differences. You have to at least try to understand them . . . for a time." I was babbling. I knew I was babbling, but I pressed on the way a drowning man might in hope of shore or of a bit of driftwood to cling to. "I'm sorry that I acted in your defense—that wasn't my place. But I can't take it back." Still she didn't say anything, only drummed her fingers against the comms tablet that swung from one hip, casual as a sidearm in its holster. "I only . . . He shouldn't have been making those accusations." A new thought occurred to me. "You're not actually under any suspicion, are you?"

Valka shook her head. "They'd have thrown me in the Chantry dungeons already, diplomatic pass or no." She

spread her arms. "I wouldn't be free if they thought me responsible for the uprising. 'Tis why you shouldn't have interfered. The Umandh acted alone, the desperate fools." She relaxed her confrontational stance, leaned against a pillar as she stooped to hitch up a boot where it had slipped down her calf. "Honestly my supposed role in this would have been forgotten already if you hadn't clocked the mutant."

"Someone had to do it."

"No!" she flared, straightening. "*Someone* didn't. I did! He was my problem." She tugged her vest down to settle it, eyes hard. "You had no right to get involved."

"I had every right! Given our history, given his insult to both you and me . . . And I didn't see you lining up to defend yourself. Did you want to?"

"No!" she snapped. "Because fighting doesn't solve anything."

"Who told you that?" I demanded, genuinely nonplussed. "If you fight to solve a problem and win, that problem's solved, Valka." I didn't know what I was saying, but if I had it might have saved me a lot of pain when the war came—or when I came to the war.

"And you've created seven new problems you have to deal with."

"Seventy-seven new problems," I agreed. "But you keep fighting, because if you can choose when to fight, you have some control. If you bury it, let it fester . . ." I shook my head. "Gilliam's done nothing but threaten me since I got here."

The doctor snorted, hardly able to contain her scorn. "And that gives you the right to try and *murder* him? That's even worse, *my lord.*"

I bit my tongue before I could say, *You wouldn't understand.* By the fire in her eyes I knew that would be a lethal mistake. Instead I paused, marshaling myself to say, "It's a formal duel, not murder."

She snorted. *"Okthireakham anaryoch kha."*

"Maybe we are barbarians. Maybe it's different where you're from—I don't know. I do know that if you let someone like Gilliam act with impunity, he will trample over

everyone in his path, a great many of whom could never hope to challenge him. I'm palatine. I can."

The doctor cut me off. "And what's that about, anyway? Who the hell are you?"

"I told you: My name is Marlowe. Hadrian Marlowe. My father is Lord Alistair Marlowe of Delos. I . . . He wanted me to serve the Chantry. I had . . . other ideas. I didn't lie to you more than I had to. Any more than the count demanded of me. All that about the Umandh, the Cielcin . . . Calagah. That is *me*." The full weight of what that meant settled on me. Old gods—the Chantry would know. Once I was released from my quasi-house arrest— if I survived—would they come for me? For my mother? I gave Valka an abridged version of the story—how I was stranded on Emesh; how I was robbed, left destitute along the canals. "I didn't have a choice about the coliseum. I had to eat."

"You could have come to this castle at any time. 'Tis not like they've punished you."

"Yet," I hissed. "The count's kept my presence a secret from my father and the Chantry. Why, I don't know."

Valka snorted. "You don't know?"

I had some theories, but none I was in the mood to share. "I am a prisoner here, Valka. Why is that so hard to explain? I can no more leave here than the Umandh. Why do you think I worked so hard to stay in the coliseum? I didn't want . . . *any* of this. I didn't ask to be here. I didn't ask for Gilliam to have it out for me. I didn't ask for you—" I broke off before I said something truly foolish and looked away. "You cloud things up." A flier arced past the castle, framed in the arches of the colonnade. Valka didn't speak, didn't move. "I sure as hell wish it were elsewise." After a moment's silence, I risked a glance.

The Tavrosi woman chewed thoughtfully on her lower lip. At last she nodded. "You know what you've done, right? Hadrian?"

"I'm sorry?" I looked up sharply from an examination of my hands. It was the first time she'd used my first name.

"You made this happen," she said, then clenched her jaw tight around the next words. "You made this about me.

Someone's going to die because you needed to prove . . .
what? That you're a man? You were a fighter, by the gods.
No one doubts that." She grew momentarily silent, her
eyes fixed like a corpse's on something beyond the mortal
world. "I don't want anyone's death on my conscience. I
don't want anyone to die because of me."

I took a step forward, reaching for her hand but afraid
to touch it, needing to and knowing I should not. "You're
right," I said. "You're right. But whatever happens, it won't
be because of you. It was my choice. I'm sorry I dragged
you into it." I pulled my hand back, feeling suddenly very
foolish. "No one has to die."

"But you said—"

"We have to fight if our seconds can't talk and resolve
our differences, which they won't, but first blood's enough.
I'll strike the first blow and have done. I swear it."

Her lip curled. "What about solving problems? What
happened to"—her tone changed, mimicking my earlier
words with frightening accuracy—"Gilliam acting with
impunity, trampling over everyone in his path?"

"That isn't fair," I said. "Do you want me to fight him
or not? You can't have it both ways."

It was her turn to look away, arms crossed. She didn't
say anything.

"I can't apologize any more than I already have," I said
truthfully. "I can't back out, and I can't run away. But I
will try to make things as right as I can." My words died
slowly, growing softer, losing force. "I hope . . . I hope you
will forgive me." More softly still I added, "I don't want
to kill anyone, Doctor Onderra."

"Valka," she said at last. "Call me Valka."

CHAPTER 59

ON THE EVE OF
EXECUTION

HAVE YOU EVER BEEN made to contemplate your death? Locked in a tower cell, perhaps, or in some bastille of the Chantry to await your end on the edge of the White Sword? Have you ever sat there through a sleepless night and counted the seconds you have left like grains of sand? I pray that you have not. It is one thing to die and quite another to have suffered the fear of death and survive. I wish neither for you, who has suffered both. You stand as does the solitary candle in chapel, flickering against the Dark. A darkness not of space but of time, of the yawning maw of some empty, echoing future forever barred to you.

It is comforting to know the sun will always rise—that is, until it does not, until it dissolves into cold ash and the universe runs down, or you do. Fire fades. And life. Or it is snuffed out. For the chapel candle, that is no tragedy—the candle knows not when it is extinguished. It is only a symbol, only the avatar of the unconquered sun lit to keep watch through the night in the Chantry temple. But the human flame *knows*, and it shivers not from the wind but from fear. From the sickness of the heart. And so I shivered in my cloying bed and on the floor beside it when I could lie amongst its folds no more. Though I was but one score and three years old—next to nothing compared to the centuries I have since counted—I felt my age and the specter of my fleeting mortality. I felt the ache in every once-broken bone, felt every scar from every wound healed on the street and in the Colosso.

I have made many mistakes and done many terrible

things on purpose. For fifteen hundred years I've haunted our galaxy and gathered regrets. Perhaps Gilliam Vas deserved to die. He was not a good man. He was wicked, petty, cruel as nature was cruel to him, as others doubtless had been cruel, too. I have stopped believing that it is up to any man to decide what other men deserve. I have met saints punished for their virtues and monsters praised for their monstrosity. I have been both sorts of creature.

Not long ago I said that I have always considered myself agnostic, but I believe that men must have souls. It was not always thus. I used to think that we were only animals, and thinking that justified the way some of us were treated as only animals. Thinking that helped me to turn a blind eye to the ugliness of the world. I know better now. Whatever Gilliam was—and there was little good in him—he was a man like any other. But I had made a choice, as we each must always do. I was young and angry, embarrassed and afraid. I did not want to die and did not want to kill, and I did not wish for Valka to hate me.

I had to choose.

Life is never about what we deserve. I do not know if there is a God, be it Mother Earth or the icona or one of the uncreated gods of old, but if there is, God alone may dispense perfect justice. It is not to be had in our fallen world. We can only strive for it. Perhaps Gilliam deserved to die. Perhaps I did. Perhaps we ought to have killed one another or made peace without the use of steel. It doesn't matter, nor is it for me to say. I had made a choice, and I have made several choices since. That is all we can ever do, then live by our choices and by their consequences. Judge me as you will. What gods there are may yet forgive me and have mercy on his soul.

CHAPTER 60

THE SWORD, OUR ORATOR

THERE WERE WORSE PLACES to die, I decided, tightening my brown dueling jerkin. The grotto overhanging the white grass field was carved with the figures of Blind Justice, Wide-Eyed Fortitude, and Death herself, sheltered from the rain by a natural facade of raw sandstone. It was the same stone from which most of Borosevo Castle was fashioned. This altar, invoking the shrines of ancient pagan deities on Earth, stood at the narrow end of an elliptical garden hedged by terranic yew, the deep green leaves black in the burnt rust of Emesh's sun. They carved a lovely contrast against the bone-grass, white as milk, that carpeted the strange place.

And then there were the flowers.

They were native, those blooms, and large as a man's head when closed. They suffused the high hedge walls, their copper-colored blossoms wet and heavy on their golden vines, filling the air with a heady perfume so lovely it made the sweaty air bearable. And they moved, opening and closing like the beating of hearts or the somnambulant blinks of so many hundred eyes. I felt transported, as if the arched gate into the grotto were a portal into faerie, as if this little garden were a slice of Cat's forests on Luin.

My wounds from the encounter with the Umandh still itched. Count Mataro had seen to it that I'd received the best of care following that afternoon in the warehouse, and truth be told I was astonished by how quickly I'd healed. The flesh had knit back together well enough, but

the new skin still prickled where the correctives had been applied. Scratching, I glanced back over my shoulder at my small crowd of supporters to offer an encouraging smile. Valka was absent, a fact of which I was equally glad and aggrieved, but Switch was there, standing in as my second—he had already negotiated this spot with Gilliam's second. Both Anaïs and Dorian had come, much to my surprise, though they stood somewhat apart among their guards. Even more surprising was the figure of Sir Elomas Redgrave. The old man was seated on a bench, sipping tea from the cap of a heating bottle as he spoke softly to Switch. I watched them both a moment, a frown creasing my face. Had Valka asked him to come? Was he her eyes?

"Scared, Marlowe?" Gilliam glowered at me from his camp across the white grass field, attended by a pair of Chantry anagnosts in black robes. The gargoyle himself wore high boots and black trousers, and even the leather of his jerkin was black. Without the heavy robes to disguise him, the myriad imperfections of his form screamed for attention: the pronounced hunch, his uneven legs, the way he carried himself as if he teetered on the edge of some abyss.

I bowed my head. "Not at all." I had been a myrmidon for years and a student of Sir Felix Martyn for more than a decade before that. I was tall, healthy, my blood untainted, my limbs straight and clean. What threat could the intus possibly pose? I watched him scuttle crab-like over the grass.

"The combatants will not speak!" piped the plebeian officiant, a square-faced man with thinning brown hair swept from a high and furrowed brow. That stopped the intus responding.

Switch hurried over, ducking round a pair of officiants in the uniforms of city prefects. "They're almost ready to start. You got this?"

The square-faced officiant drew a pair of matched backswords from a padded box. Dutifully the short plebeian checked the edges against his thumb, made a note on his wrist terminal. "I'll cut him first and have done." I

shook my head. "The doctor was right. I shouldn't have done this." Gilliam brushed his attendants off, tugging on a black fencing glove that looked tailored for his oddly shaped arm. I frowned at that. It looked well used.

"Yeah, no shit, Had," Switch said reflexively. From the corner of my eye, I saw him freeze, stiffen. "Sorry, sir, my lordship, sir."

"Stop that, would you?" I seated myself on a flat stone and unzipped my boots. "I am exactly the same person I always was."

Switch shifted uncomfortably and looked away. "It don't . . . It doesn't feel like that."

I had a real talent for alienation, it seemed. Looking up, I tugged my boots free and peeled my black socks off to bare the thick sheets of callous on my soles. Switch had seen the routine a thousand times in training, so he didn't ask. "Switch, thanks for being here. It means a lot. Truly."

He never replied, for at that moment the officiant with the thinning hair raised his clear, nasal voice. "The combatants shall approach!"

"That's my cue," I said to the myrmidon, trying to appear jovial. I wasn't sure I'd carried it off. Barefoot I crossed the bone-grass to where the civil servants stood clustered about the equipment required by law for a *duel palatine*. Camera eyes orbited the cluster of men from the prefect's office, prepared to record the duel. Even then one was recording video testimony of the legal witnesses, of whom Anaïs, Dorian, and Elomas were the principals. I had formalized my own charge days earlier, the evening of the Umandh's abortive attempt on the count's life. *For dangerous slander against a personal acquaintance and to answer past charges of assault and insult against my exalted personage.* The formal jargon chafed like a uniform collar. Maybe I had lost some of my Imperial polish.

I accepted my blade from the officiant after Gilliam took his, going briefly to one knee to receive the weapon. "You will fight until one party bleeds, at which point the unbloodied will be granted an opportunity to end the engagement, as has been the custom under the Index and

the Great Charters of the Imperium since the Assumption of Earth." The mere mention of the homeworld's name prompted discreet sun disc signs from Gilliam and his Chantry associates while I, filthy apostate that I was, stood unmoved. The intus priest noticed my lapse and sneered, but he held his silence. The little man was not done speaking. "If the opportunity to abort the engagement is not taken, the engagement will continue until one party can no longer fight. Is this clear?"

Two yeses sounded in the still air. Two men paced away from each other in the shadow of three officiant prefects. Three Chantry icona watched from the artificial wall of the grotto shrine, stone faces unseeing as funeral masks. Thin mist rose from the bone-white grass, thickening the dense Emeshi air with moisture. It was like walking through a dream, all clouded. All quiet. I did not truly hear the officiant as he recited the formal charges. Instead I watched Gilliam, his blond hair oiled back from his high and misshapen forehead, watching me with those slitted, mismatched eyes.

I pushed my sword forward, blade held at a slight angle, upthrust as I pressed my left fist to my breast. It was a knight's salute, a gesture I had little right to but one none would truly challenge. It kept the blade forward, ready.

"Have you confessed?" Gilliam asked, the ban on our silence lifted. "I'll hear your sins before you die."

I did not reply, did not move but to flex my toes in the damp grass. The day would be a hot one, the fat sun rising the color of blood. I might have been a statue, locked in that moment, every preceding second had carried to that grotto that damp and fog-bound morn. My previous decisions ensured that I could not but walk the path I was on. I had chosen.

Gilliam lunged, and I snapped the parry, retreating a step. The sound of naked steel, not the highmatter of true swords, was fine music in the stillness. My eyebrows shot up. He was fast, far faster than his uneven legs belied. And his form was good, surprisingly straight and even despite the crookedness of his frame. This would not be an easy contest, or at least not so easy as I'd believed. I allowed my

earlier arrogance to fade away. *Pride cometh before destruction.* Gibson was never far, endlessly quoting in my ear. My own pride fell with my fortunes, retreating before the advance of the priest. Teeth bared, Gilliam swept low. I turned to parry, distracting him as I lashed out with my off hand to cuff the man across the face. He staggered back, gasping, a bruise already blossoming on his cheek.

With a snarl, he pressed a new offensive, and I circled left around him, unwilling to be driven toward the wall of the grotto where our witnesses watched. I heard a woman— Anaïs?—gasp as I battered Gilliam's sword aside with a clangor. The whole situation wasn't real. It couldn't be real. Gilliam's blade made a pass for one of my kidneys, but I turned it with an elbow snap, knocking his point aside before stepping into the range of his sword and pulling my own weapon up and around my head into a rolling cut, saber-fashion, that should have connected at the joint of his neck and shoulder.

But Gilliam vanished, dropping into a roll that carried him counterclockwise by nearly ninety degrees. So stunned was I at this that I almost failed to jump aside. I felt the point of his backsword scrape the brown leather of my jerkin. Had I grown so used to fighting with the heavy myrmidon's round shield that I'd forgotten how to duel properly? I heard Switch hiss in unneeded sympathy.

Maybe Valka was right. Maybe we were barbarians. What need had I for this? If I hadn't gotten my blood up, hot off the Umandh's attack on the count, if I hadn't let my heart and my pointless feelings for Valka rule my head, none of this would have happened. But we all make mistakes and must stand by them. I cannot say if Gilliam's competence, his skill, made the whole ordeal more a farce or less of one. He beat my weapon aside, made to lunge. I outdistanced him, able to retreat on my long, straight legs more easily than he could advance on his twisted ones.

It is the mistake of poets, of librettists like my mother, to believe that fighting is ever only one thing. They believe the work of the soldier, the game of the gladiator, the art of the duelist are all the same and that those are the same as the chaos of fighting on the streets and in the country

villages of a thousand worlds. But there is fighting and there is fighting. I remembered the time I'd toppled Ghen in the training yard to get everyone behind me—to save Switch, in point of fact. Where was that Hadrian right now?

I kicked the back of Gilliam's knee, staggering him in advance of a descending overhead blow. Once. Twice. The third cut I brought in from the side, but the little goblin of a priest parried each with a strength that astonished me. He was on the retreat now, and briefly I saw the waxen expressions on the faces of the two Mataro children. What would they think if their new friend killed their priest on this sanguinary field that bleak morning? I needed first blood, needed to call off this farce I'd written for myself, needed to apologize in action as well as word. Needed to redeem myself to Valka.

Valka.

I never saw the strike that cut me, only felt the raw, rusted pain of it lance up my arm. Red blood wept into the cream of my torn sleeve, faintly brown in the fabric. How had I missed it? I hissed, staggered back, swearing under my breath in Mandar of all things, groaning as my promises ran out with my blood. Medically the wound was minor, a clean slash across the top of my forearm. In a way that transcended the facts of our dispute, the wound was mortal.

"Halt!" The officiant's nasal voice was deep now; the man was affecting a sergeant's tone of command. "First blood to the defendant!" He focused his square face on Gilliam, green eyes wide beneath furrowed brows. "Is the gentleman satisfied?" he asked in deadly earnest.

There was no blood on Gilliam's blade, none at all; he'd moved so quickly. I resisted the urge to clutch my arm and backpedaled, holding my sword at the ready in a haggard echo of my earlier salute. Only then did I realize my chest was heaving, that I was tired. Earth and Emperor, I should have kept up my regimen after coming to the palace. Ye Gods, the last few months had softened me. I set my jaw. The wound ached, but that was not the worst of it.

I had no power in that moment, waiting for Gilliam to answer. My word hung on that answer, my promise to

Valka. I had failed. I had been so sure that I would get first blood, that I could end everything at that critical juncture and bow out with some grace and dignity. I had been so sure. Now all that was taken from me and left in the hands of the asymmetrical creature holding the twin of my sword. I held my breath and felt the world suspended in that breath.

"No!" Gilliam sneered, and he lunged.

Damn my talent for making enemies!

I turned the first new attack, batting the blade down past my sinking heart. Time narrowed before me, the futures ahead of me thinning, reducing from the vague quantum smear of potential to a single pair of doors. Through one I stood above the mute's body, a bloodied sword in hand. Through the other our positions were reversed. I slammed my sword up, stepping in and to the right to block a charge and angle out of the way as Gilliam redoubled his attack.

"Surprised, boy?" he asked through gritted teeth. "Expected it would be easy? Brave of you . . ." He blocked a thrust with a neat slipping motion of his sword, stepped in with a low jab that ought to have skewered me in the thigh. I danced back, threw a retreating cut at the intus's shoulder. Strange, I reflected, that the man's mother was not here. "Brave of you to challenge a cripple."

I slashed the chanter across the front of his left thigh. The black leather sighed open, and Gilliam winced. "You should have taken the blood. I won't make the same mistake again," I said, redoubling my attack, driving the intus backward across the white grass toward the wall of pulsing flowers, steel ringing in the thick air. My left arm smarted, weeping blood as I advanced, but I ground my teeth and pressed ahead, cutting at the priest's head and shoulders. The truth of what I'd tried to tell Valka rang in my ears: I was not a killer, had never been one.

Gilliam threw himself at me, spitting. His sword lanced straight at my eyes, and I was saved from blindness or death only by a reflexive slash-block that left me open to remise, and I was lucky that the speed of my defense had startled Gilliam into stillness. We stood there a moment,

watching one another. If there were a moment to talk, to come to an understanding, it was then and there. But we never did.

The little man snarled and threw himself at me again. I parried his blade, binding it, slicing down and across to jab Gilliam in the right hip. The point of my sword hit bone, and he bit down a cry. For a moment there was a clear line of attack open to his throat. I didn't take it but backed off—as I had a thousand times with Crispin—and waited. One of the officiants murmured something to his square-faced compatriot. I couldn't make out the words, but the tone was one of anxious disapproval. I glanced at the crowd. Elomas's wizened face darkened as he watched me, sipping his tea.

"Could have ended it . . ."

I circled Gilliam, blade in a low guard, pivoting to keep my right side oriented toward him. "En garde!" I said. *Stand and fight, you bastard.* "En garde!" I cried again, and I rattled my saber, tip jouncing in anxious little circles. I wanted to goad him, to bait him into making a mistake. Crispin had gone for it nearly every time, his brain chemistry blanched in its own androgens, blinkered as surely as a horse on parade. It didn't work. The limping priest held his ground, jaw set, shoulders square as he could make them.

I could wait no longer and moved forward, sword falling in blow after blow against his guard. The priest was fighting carefully. No more of the spastic movements and quick footwork I'd come to expect. With a snap of my shoulder I brushed his blade aside and again exposed a clear line of attack, baring the man's pigeon chest.

I didn't take it. Couldn't take it. I didn't even see my opportunity, blinded as I was by sentiment. I had not killed, and so I could not. I gave ground, retreating to the safety of guard. I sensed the watchers' disquiet, though I did not then understand it, confusing it for the discomfort anyone would feel knowing they were to witness a killing. "I don't want to kill you," I said at last, crouching lower in my guard.

Gilliam circled to my right, and I followed the arc of

him, keeping my leading foot pointed in his direction. "Hadrian, you're playing with him!" The voice belonged to Anaïs, high and sick with nervous tension. There followed a moment of supreme stillness, the holo of our lives paused, suspended. Only the flowers moved; only they breathed.

Something like a shadow passed across the chanter's uneven face, worming its way through his eyes to his soul. Like gravity, it could not be seen save by its effects. The twisted lips twisted, the dark eye darkened, and the blue one froze over and cracked. Every cord in the man was taut as a bowstring, and he snarled, "I'll kill you, heretic. I'll not let you twist this place. These people. My people."

Long have I sat in my cell here at Colchis without writing a word. The vermilion ink which my hosts provided for me had dried, and the candles guttered out. I sent for a fresh bottle and new light—the night here is interminable. Perhaps there is some meaning in all this.

Gilliam's rage moved him, blinded him. It nearly blinded me, so fast did that sword move. His haste and fury made him sloppy, and thrice more could I have slain him: once with a strike to the abdomen, once with a wide slash to the throat, and again with a blow that would have staved in his ugly skull and dyed his blond hair red. Yet I couldn't do it. You must think it strange that I, who has supped on more blood than have most empires, could not kill a single man. I say again: a single death is a tragedy.

I stabbed him in the hip again instead, steel grating against bone. The point of my sword came out red, startlingly bright in the morning air. Gilliam flashed his teeth at me, and I half expected to see blood on the gums. But he spat, "Demoniac! Abomination!" What was he talking about? I staggered back, keeping my sword between us, trying not to think of the blood on its point. "Threat . . ." he was saying. "Spy . . ." He still believed me part of some conspiracy against the country, against his faith. And all because I'd been interested in his Cielcin.

Sometimes there is no climax. A thing happens, and it is over. Gilliam lunged again. I parried, extended into the riposte. In a simple motion, my blade swept across my

chest, point still aimed forward to brush the wild thrust aside. I stepped forward, tucking my right shoulder to bring the point in line with Gilliam's ribs, metal grinding on metal. On leather. On bone. And then red blossomed there, black against the black of his jerkin, and the breath went out with it in a wordless groan. *Red and black*, I thought. *My colors.*

Gilliam's forward momentum carried him straight onto my sword. He sagged there, transmuted to dead weight. He wheezed, a wet sucking sound deep in his chest. I must have punctured a lung. There was nothing for it. I shoved him back, had to plant a foot on his chest to free my sword from his ribs. He hit the grass with a moan that turned to burbling. I had to suppress an urge to throw my sword aside. I was on display, my silent audience vigilant. My knees turned to water, and I fell, propping myself on the treasonous blade in my lying hand. *Valka, forgive me.*

The intus's sword had fallen from his slackened fingers, and I had enough presence of mind to toss it aside. Tradition forbade medical intervention. We walked onto the field knowing what we were about to do. I could feel Valka's scorn already. My hands were shaking, and each beat of Gilliam's heart spat blood upon the earth. It was hot. Too hot. The chanter raised a hand, and unlike mine, it was steady. He reached out slowly, and I thought he was about to make the sign of the sun disc in final benediction. Instead he reached for the crowd, for the royal children. "My lady . . . Lord Dorian. Do not . . . trust . . ."

I looked up sharply, glaring across the swath of field with burning eyes. Anaïs and Dorian stood bracketed by Elomas and the prefect officiants. Her dark face had gone somehow white. She shook her head furiously, then darted for the arched exit. Her brother called out after her, and a pair of armored peltasts rattled in her wake. I knelt open-mouthed, watching her go.

The priest was a long time dying, chest rising and falling in smaller and smaller increments, diminishing by decay. Smaller, smaller, smaller.

Still.

I was still kneeling beside the priest's corpse when the

soldiers came for me. Their leader, a tall woman I did not know, her pauldrons marking her as a centurion in the count's personal guard, said, "Lord Marlowe, you must come with us."

I did not answer, only shut my eyes and—with a tremendous effort—stood.

CHAPTER 61

A KIND OF EXILE

"THE INTUS WAS RIGHT," said Lord Balian Mataro coldly, gathering his orange silk robes around him as he sat behind his desk. "That Tavrosi woman's got you by the balls." The small obscenity coming from the mouth of a palatine lord of the Empire cowed me more than the anger in his voice. At a sharp gesture from him, I seated myself across the desk, glancing around at the tinted glass walls of his office.

I remembered Father's office in the capitol in Meidua. The two rooms had almost nothing in common. Father's office was all dark stone and dark carpet and darkly polished wood, stuffed and cluttered in such a way that indicated a person of immense discipline, a man who dwelt in his mind more than in the wider world. This place, though, was all clean lines and modern whiteness; it might have been the combat information center on a Legion battle cruiser. I could not have said what kind of man it indicated had he not been sitting before me.

"I made a mistake, lordship, but you know the law."

"As did you when you boxed that chanter into a duel." Mataro's face darkened. "My grand prior wants your head. Strike that—she wants you alive."

Swallowing, I looked down at my hands, picked absently at the simple bandages glued to my forearm. I needed no medical correctives for this truly minor injury. "I know."

"The boy was her son."

"I know."

"Then why in Earth's holy name did you—" He broke

off, bit the inside of his cheek as he shook his head. "I need you out of my city, away from all . . . this." He waved a glittering hand. "Away from her. Until it quiets down." A servant entered then, evidently part of some routine, for the bronze-skinned young man's eyes widened in surprise to see that his master had company, and he bowed out again, carrying the tea service with its single cup out with him as discreetly as possible. "The Chantry has *me* by the balls, you know. And I can't rule my planet with the Chantry turned against me. If I don't give Ligeia what she wants, she'll stymie my trade agreements, subject my ships to search and seizure, hold my officers—anything and everything short of invoking the Inquisition. You killed her son, damn it!" He slapped his desk, emphasizing this refrain.

"Respectfully, sire," I said mildly, unable to look the man in the face, "I was angling for first blood." I watched my hands shake in my lap; I couldn't get the priest's eyes out of my head, black and blue, unchanging.

"You didn't get it." The count's knuckles whitened against the edge of his desk, then relaxed suddenly. "If I didn't need you, I'd give you over to Ligeia right now." He glanced toward the heavy metal doors, beyond which the guards who had dragged me from the sanguinary field waited. How easy it would be for them to drag me across the castle complex to the Chantry temple, to hand me over to Ligeia's cathars and have done.

I shuddered. "I could leave. You could—" Then something the count had said clicked, and I straightened. "If you didn't need me?"

The count lifted a jeweled box from one corner of his desk, disturbing a stack of leaflets and a holograph image of himself and Lord Luthor on a hunting expedition. He turned the thing in his hands, said, "Yes . . . well." He cleared his throat. "I'd meant to keep this quiet for a few years, but this little spate of idiocy has forced my hand." He swore violently, making me jump, and nearly crushed the jeweled box in one massive fist. Seeing that display, the size of him, I felt grubby and mean in my own genes. "Damn it, boy! I thought you were supposed to be clever."

"Smart," I said cleverly, "is not the same as clever. Like you said, I . . ." I had let Valka get into my head. She was still there, crouched just behind my eyes, scowling daggers. I clenched my fists in my lap to stop them shaking. I couldn't stop seeing Gilliam's face, the mismatched eyes gone hollow as glass, relaxed, fixed on some light beyond the confines of mortal sight.

With forced slowness, the count set the little jeweled box back on the polished glass surface of his desk, brows knitting as he examined me from his considerable height—by Earth, he was huge. "I was hoping to marry you to Anaïs after her Ephebeia."

I was a minute closing my jaw and another collecting the potsherds of my wits enough to stammer, "Marry? Your . . . your daughter?" For a moment the glass-eyed specter of Gilliam Vas and the crouching, furious impression of Valka both blew away like smoke, clearing the air to reveal the figure of Anaïs Mataro, slender and full-breasted. Beautiful as an ice sculpture, dull as a puddle.

"Or my son, if you preferred. I only thought—"

"No! No, lordship." I hoped my haste was not a reproach to him and softened it with a more politic, "I am honored, of course, but . . . me?" Married? To a palatine lady? I supposed it had always been among my possible fates, but it had been so many years since I'd been Hadrian Marlowe *proper* that the whole thing felt like a lying dream. A nightmare. Trapped on Emesh, on the world where my life had gone to pieces. A thousand half-formed objections blossomed like weeds, and like weeds they choked me, permitting the count to continue.

"It wouldn't have been for at least three years," he said, suddenly more awkward than angry. The change alarmed me. "Two until the Ephebeia, then another for the betrothal period, per custom. I had hoped to keep this quiet, give you time to acclimate to life here in Borosevo, to know the girl, but this lunatic behavior of yours . . ." He broke off, hissing air through his teeth.

Still drowning in the ringing noise sounding in my ears, I spluttered, "But . . . me? Sir . . ." It was not the correct address, and a flicker of contempt spasmed across

Balian Mataro's brick-chiseled face. "I have nothing to my name. I left home in some difficulty, as you know. And my father is only a petty lord, an archon. Landed, I'll grant, not posted, but all the same, I—"

"How old is your father?"

The tangential question shocked me, sent me spiraling off along a new track. "My father! Dark take me! Excellency, if he were to find out where I am—and the Chantry! They'd kill me for running!"

The count raised a hand for quiet. "How old?"

After a moment I composed myself and said, "I . . . I don't know. Just shy of three centuries, I think?"

"And his father?"

"He would've been four hundred and twenty-some? But he was assassinated by the Mandari—"

"Why?" the count asked, then waved a hand. "Doesn't matter. His mother, then?"

I squinted at the count, trying to follow this bizarre tangent to its logical denouement. "Six hundred and . . . ah . . . eighty . . . two?" I had to struggle to remember. "What is this in aid of?"

"And how old do you think I am?" Again he lifted the tiny jeweled box, made it vanish in his huge fist.

I took a shot in the dark. "Two hundred?"

"One hundred and thirty-three next fall."

"What?" I blurted, unable to contain my surprise. That was entirely too young. There was gray in the black of his hair, and the lines about his mouth seemed too firmly pressed into the skin of his face.

The day's sins temporarily forgotten, the count spread his massive hands in innocent defeat. "We are a minor world—a minor house—and our blood is not so nobile as yours. I had that lovely genome of yours scanned when we took you in. What you carry in there"—he pointed at my face—"would cost my house its title to obtain. How your family came into such patterns—how it's been able to hold onto them—is beyond me. Do as I ask, and I'll make you consort to the highest post in this system. All I ask is your genes."

"Uranium license," I said simply.

"What?"

"The wealth," I clarified, not knowing what else to say. "We have a uranium mining license." That was part of it, but I'd also inherited a great number of hyperadvanced gene complexes from my mother, daughter to a duchess and an Imperial vicereine and a distant cousin, some dozen times removed, to the Imperial house itself. Those complexes, reinforced across generations of breeding with House Kephalos and House Ormund, who had held the duchy of Delos in Lord Julian's day, made my family line as desirable as that of many lords far greater than my father. Things grew quiet between the count and me, and again I clenched my hands, this time as much to clutch my anger as to squeeze off the palsy of horror and grief attached to Gilliam's death. Something twanged within me, tinny and broken. I should have known, should have realized. Stupid. Stupid. Stupid. Then another thought, almost as dark as the first, rose from my chest and burst from me. "I'm not your damn stud!"

"Yes, you are!" The count slapped his jeweled box down on the table with such a crack that I expected to see shatter marks, but the surface was unmarred. "You are whatever I say you are. You're not in a strong bargaining position, Lord Marlowe. You've killed a member of my senior staff!" His voice grew stronger with each word, hands planted on the arms of his chair.

My fists clenched convulsively. I could still feel the sweat there, caked on from my duel. I looked into Balian's eyes, black as the one of Gilliam's. "By law that was no murder."

"By law!" the count echoed. "Do you think that will matter to my grand prior? If you think the writ of law will protect you from what you've done, you're a fool. You need my help." In tones suddenly soft and reasonable, he said, "I am not asking anything unpleasant of you. You should be glad. You know the girl, and she's fond of you, which is more than can be said of many arrangements."

Ligeia Vas's frozen gaze haunted me as I sat there, hands fidgeting in my lap. There was nothing I could do, nowhere

I could go. I could not refuse, could not run. I frowned and nodded slowly. "But what of Anaïs herself? Does she know about all this?"

The count scowled. "What do you take me for? She's known since you arrived here." At last he opened the jeweled box, peeled a sheet of candied verrox leaf from a sticky bundle. *Since I arrived.* At once her actions since we'd met came into sharper focus: the way she'd always been around me, always asking me to social events, touching me, clinging to my arm. It was all so obvious, so . . . calculated. I felt cheap, less than a person because it wasn't about me after all. "Moving forward, her children by you will inherit your gene complexes, and my grandchildren will be admitted to the peerage."

I saw a flaw in the count's plan and jabbed a mental finger at it. "But Dorian is your heir, is he not?"

"Presumptive." The count flashed a smile. "But the complexes in your blood are worth a slight change of plans. Both of the children are young; there is time yet to make a proper lord out of either of them. Wouldn't you say?" He slipped the verrox leaf into his mouth, chewed. Unbidden, his eyes drifted closed, then snapped back to alertness as he swallowed.

That dramatic expression triggered something in me, for I almost rocketed to my feet. "But sir, my father!" I'd been about to bring the question up earlier, but the tangent about age and gene complexes had driven it straight from my stress-addled brain. I needed sleep, needed focus. "He'll never approve!" I was desperate by then, grasping at straws, at whatever means of escape I could find.

Lord Balian Mataro reached into a drawer beneath his desk and drew out a sheet of crystal paper. He turned it on the glossy surface and pushed the document toward me. Ordinarily such writs were done on vellum, signed by hand. But this was a copy, clearly sent to Emesh across the vast and echoing quiet of space by quantum telegraph. I felt my blood temperature drop when I saw the seal printed beneath the holographed fractals beside the signatures: the crimson devil capering with its trident raised

above its head against a field of darkest black above the words "The Sword, Our Orator." It matched the bezel of my ring exactly, had indeed been made with an identical ring hundreds of light-years away. And the names beside it: Alistair Diomedes Friedrich Marlowe and Elmira Gwendolyn Kephalos. My father and my grandmother, the vicereine.

It was another terrible minute before I realized the nature of the thing they'd signed. So long, in fact, that the count's deep voice asked, "Do you know what this is?"

"A writ of disavowal," I said, eyes going to the graphic of the Imperial sunburst at the top of the long sheet of white crystal paper. I read: *We resolve beneath the mark of His Imperial Radiance, our Emperor, William the Twenty-Third of the House Avent, Firstborn Son of the Earth, etc., to dissolve all ties legal and familiar with the renegade Hadrian of the House Marlowe, formerly of Meidua Prefecture, Duchy of Delos, Auriga Province. In concert with the examinations of the Holy Office of the Inquisition, his conduct . . .*

". . . his conduct has been found wanting of the standards and grace expected of his station. He has betrayed his house and his lord father and brought shame upon his family name and upon the viceroyalty of Delos," the count recited—or perhaps read upside-down. "Grievous charges." I took it as a mercy that he did not keep reading.

I did not answer. There were tears in my eyes and something like tears in my throat. I could not speak. My ring was a lead weight on my thumb, dead and pointless. It was just a lump of metal. I had nothing, then. Truly nothing. Before, when I was destitute in the streets of Borosevo, I'd had the private dignity of my hidden station and what holdings were tied, however tenuously, to my name and rank. But now I was truly destitute, with nothing but the genes in my bones. Mataro was right. I *was* a stud, and in the most unflattering sense, like a famous racehorse lamed in the slip. I tried not to think about Switch, about Pallino and Elara and the ship I'd meant to buy with the ghost assets on my ring and a song.

No longer. I would almost *have* to prostitute myself to Anaïs and House Mataro to survive.

"I'm sorry to tell you this."

"No, you're not," I said in a voice like grave soil. I had just seen the date on the writ and knew what had been done to me and by whom. "You sent to him. To my father. You telegraphed him right after I arrived." The *day* I'd arrived, if I'd read the date right. He'd been planning this since we met, since I sat unconscious in his chair upstairs. That was why he'd been willing to keep me in his house, why he'd tolerated my antics in the coliseum hypogeum and at dinner with the prior. The bastard didn't even have the decency to deny it. His face did not so much as twitch. He knew he had me. "For all I know, you urged him to do this. Made some deal to keep me. What was it? Thirty pieces of silver?"

The man's face went blank. "What?" He didn't understand me. "You should be honored. You're to be my son."

"I'm to be a whore." I almost choked, took a moment to crush the sob in my throat before it could escape. *Grief is emptiness.* So chastised, I filed my grief, turned to practical matters. "What are you going to do with me, then?" There would be time to dwell on the day's horrors later— would be time to drown them, if necessary.

"You brought this on yourself, boy." The count tugged the writ back toward himself. "Now, to present matters. Once you're married, Ligeia won't be able to move against you without moving against my house, which she will not do." He stood with a swirl of orange silks and paced anxiously to the curved arc of windows—view screens, in truth, which projected an image of Borosevo in all its rusty, low glory, the canals green-choked by algae. "The problem is those three years between now and then. You've made yourself a powerful enemy, you know." He paused to peel another verrox leaf off the bale, hand vibrating visibly. "I've a mind to send you to Tivan Melluan, up on Binah, to get you out of harm's way."

I did not respond; I was staring at my hands again. They too were shaking, though not from verrox toxemia. My

long hair fell over my face, curtaining me off from the count. Tears milled across the surface of my eyes, unfallen. Too much—it was all too much.

At length I looked up from my hands, resigned, and said, "My lord, a question, if I may."

It was worth asking. It was all I could do.

CHAPTER 62

THE GILDED CAGE

THE EMPTY WINE BOTTLE bounced against the floor tiles, rolling away under the table. I let it go. I had half a mind to call Switch on my terminal. I shouldn't have been alone in that moment, and yet I knew I could not stand to be with anyone. It wasn't even dark out; that day—that interminable day—refused to end. The orange sunlight fell darkly through the narrow windows, casting my spartan apartments into relief. My wine depleted, I dragged my journal from the small table beside my short couch and keyed a control in the tabletop to polarize the light from the windows, dimming the world.

I sat sharpening my pencil, twice breaking the thing in my unsteady fingers. Gilliam's face kept asserting itself. "Don't trust," he had said, "don't trust . . ." Perhaps the Chantry gods were real, I thought. Perhaps they hated me; perhaps I was to atone. *Lord Consort of Emesh* . . . I ground my teeth. *The bird cares not that his cage is gilded.* A great honor, even if it was a kind of prison. *A kind of poison.* I would be a lord in title as well as blood, and a greater one than my father.

I scooped up the empty glass, raised it in a dramatic toast. I had to suppress an urge to dash the glass against the wall, but I settled for slamming it back onto the side table with a scowl. Slumped against the arm of the chair, I raised a hand to no one in particular—to the cameras in my suite, perhaps—and made a rude gesture. I forgot in my drunkenness that they were not the cameras of Devil's Rest.

The door cycled open. I'd locked it, wanting to be alone. Half panicking, expecting to see a cathar or Chantry assassin, I raised the scalpel I used to sharpen my pencils, pointing it like a plasma burner. In my haste my knee slammed into the arm of the couch, and I staggered and fell back into my seat, knocking my glass to the floor. "Damn it . . ." A sob shook me, blessedly quiet. Unable to look at Valka, I looked down at the shattered glass instead, at the wine puddling on the hardwood.

"If you're trying to drown yourself," she said with affected coldness, "there are larger bodies of water on Emesh."

I glared up at her from my place on the floor, then down at the scalpel in my hand. Contemptuously I threw the thing aside, watched it clatter over to the small table by the kitchenette. "Wasn't water."

"'Tis the problem, I think." She filled a glass of water from the sink and passed it to me, helped me to regain my place on the couch. "Drink." Her hand touched mine briefly, and even through my haze I felt and remember the warmth of it. There was care in the motion and a tenderness I did not deserve that day of all days.

I drank, rested my head against the back of the couch. She moved off to recover the scalpel. She turned, caught me staring, and arched one winged eyebrow. I had seen uglier statues of Venus in old archives, though surely here was Pallas. That thought forced a laugh through my nose. It collapsed into silence, and after the better part of a minute had passed—during which time the xenologist seated herself in a narrow armchair by the windows—I managed to mumble, "I'm sorry." Then again, more strongly, "I'm sorry." I pressed my eyes closed, pinched the bridge of my nose. "There's more wine . . . somewhere. Sir Elomas had a case sent up. Thank him for me?"

"I should think you've had enough." She gave me a look that diminished me, made me feel a part of the couch I half lay upon. Those golden eyes took in the bottle that had rolled onto the floor, the pencil shavings, my rumpled clothes, and the tangled blankets that lay scattered on the floor between the sofa and the open door to my bedcham-

ber. She crossed her arms. "I was going to come knock some sense into you, but I think the damage is done." She kept watching me.

"Sorry . . ." My tongue was thick and fat in my mouth, slow to follow the scant lead my brain had on it. "Valka, I was only going to wound him, but he cut me." I held up my bandaged arm for inspection. "The bastard cut me. Faster than I expected." I shuddered, shut my eyes. I couldn't look at her, not in my current state. Maybe if I closed my eyes she would go away. She shouldn't have been able to get inside in the first place. "Stupid . . . I . . ."

"You *are* an idiot," she said, but she smiled, if only barely. "But you're not a liar."

"What?" I looked blearily up from my journal. It had fallen open to an image of Devil's Rest, the castle in undetailed black as seen from the streets of Meidua— seen indeed from that very street where I had almost died a lifetime ago. Had it really only been three years? Or thirty-five?

Valka's eyes narrowed to slits, glowing in the dim umber light of afternoon, but her smile didn't waver. "You'd never killed anyone before."

"I'm not . . . I . . . No." I wanted to cry, but more than that I wanted to be all right, or at least to present as all right in front of this strange and exquisite foreigner. She was a colossus, tall and calm and remote as the stars.

After a pregnant moment, she said, "It's not easy, is it?"

She was being subtle. I was too drunk for subtlety at the moment. It was a struggle to keep my words cogent, to stop them from running like a man's makeup in the rain. "What?"

"Killing."

I cocked my head at her, numb fingers working to close my journal. "Yeah." Her voice had not been that of an academic but was drawn with painful experience. I did not press her. Valka sucked on the inside of one cheek, kept her attentions fixed on my face, lost in thought. Blearily I gathered up what wits remained me and asked, "What?"

She shook her head, pressed a fall of red-black hair

behind her ear with a determined gesture. "What will you do now?"

I shrugged, moved as if to grab a bottle from my side table, only to remember too late that it was empty and on the floor. I mumbled something about the marriage, then told her everything. About Gilliam, about Anaïs, about my father and the Chantry. "The count wants to send me up to Binah. To keep me away from Vas." I paused, cleared my throat. "But I asked him to let me go with you."

"What?" Valka's head snapped up. "Why?"

"I don't want—I don't mean to invite myself, it's just . . . I think you're right. I don't think the Empire's good for me." I stifled another sob, slammed my head back against the sofa. Once. Twice.

If ever there were a moment, a point at which Valka warmed to me, it was then. I could almost feel it the way one feels the sound of ice cracking when water is poured into a glass. Her cold and brittle smile softened. Instead of answering, she rose and tugged my empty cup from my hands, went to refill it. I was left in silence for the better part of a minute, watching the bob and dart of tiny ships against the distant celadon sea. In the evening sunlight the green waters turned the color of mud, and all the world was cheap as a bad painting. *The ugliness*, I thought. *This was what Gibson meant about the ugliness of the world.* But perhaps the world was perfect and it was myself who was hideous.

The woman returned, this time settling herself onto the low coffee table before the couch. She pressed the water on me. "Why Calagah?"

I lied, "For the aliens. The history." *For you. To escape.* "If you'll have me. I don't want to be a . . . a burden."

"The count will allow it?" Valka looked nervous. The expression did not suit her.

"I can't stay here, not after"—I waved an incoherent hand—"today." Nodding, I slumped sideways onto the arm of the couch. "I'm sorry."

"For what?"

"Came here to yell at me," I mumbled. "Right thing. Now you're being all nice."

She pursed her lips, eyes darting out the window to the painted, putrid city. "I'll yell at you later." Then, "Your father disinherited you?"

I shook my head, regretted the gesture at once as the room started to spin. So I shut my eyes. "Disowned me. My grandmother did, too." A laugh escaped me, mad and thready and broken. "I'm not really Hadrian *Marlowe* anymore. I'm Hadrian nobody." I pulled the signet ring from my thumb—the damn thing had gotten me into all this mess in the first place. With little effort I flung it across the room. Let the cleaning drones have it; let them sweep it into a bin and bear it to the incinerators. It was worthless anyhow, disinherited as I was. My holdings would have been canceled the moment it had happened. The land I held on Delos had defaulted to Meidua prefecture and to House Marlowe.

House Marlowe.

I'd believed I was House Marlowe, but I was only an extension of it. An appendage. I'd always thought my house composed of individuals, but even on that strange world I had depended on my name and on the ring that symbolized it to mean something. We think ourselves the masters of such symbols, but they are our masters. Devils. Sphinxes. Suns. I had clung to the bloody thing like a talisman, hoping it would protect me, save me. It had damned me instead, had made my idiotic behavior catastrophic. "The Sword, Our Orator!" I hissed, saying my family's words. I made of them a curse. "Would that it weren't so."

The lights dimmed in one of the castle's too-familiar power fluctuations.

Valka struck me hard across the face without preamble or warning. The sound of it startled me more than the force of it, and I pressed a hand to my cheek, stunned. "Stop it," she said, brows knitting as she leaned in. "'Tis well you're having second thoughts, but 'tis too late. You have no one to blame but yourself. You understand? This isn't happening *to* you, 'tis happening *because* of you."

The fool believes the iniquities of the world are the fault of other men. Gibson's voice, dry as old manuscript pages,

had never been more clear. *The truly wise try to change themselves, which is the more difficult and less grand task.* What need had I then for House Marlowe? For the worthless ring?

My face ached where Valka had stuck me, but the pain was far away. I didn't argue. She was right. "His eyes, Valka. His eyes. Gilliam's. I . . . I saw them . . . hollow. One minute he was there, and the next . . ." I had seen dead men before, had seen their eyes—like distant suns and with just as little heat—but never once had I seen the moment of passage. Even Cat, who had died in my arms, had crossed over with her eyes shut. "It was horrible. Horrible . . ." I fancied I saw his pale blue eye shining at me now, filmed over in death. The eye of a vulture.

The Tavrosi woman made a hushing sound, ushering in a long and agreeable silence. I teetered on the brink of sleep, that soft and temporary oblivion. Teetered but did not fall. At length I said, "Can I go with you? To Calagah? I don't want . . ." I pawed the air in the direction of my ring. "I don't want any of this."

Her lips curled, and she said, "What about Anaïs?"

I sniffed. "What about her?"

"You're betrothed." She gestured at the room around me and by extension at the castle beyond. "You have to come back here."

"I know." I drew my legs almost to my chin, blew my hair from my eyes. "But I don't have to stay here."

Valka smiled again—the warm smile she had shown me earlier, not the cold one that was her custom—and rested her tattooed hand on my cheek. She spoke words I could not hear, or perhaps she did not speak at all. The moment is a warm haze, a smear across my memory as darkness and the trials of that day washed me away.

CHAPTER 63

CALAGAH

IN BOROSEVO I'D FORGOTTEN what it was like to be anything but hot. The sprawling capital sat a mere ten degrees north of Emesh's equator, squatting across the island-shoals that dominated that vast and shallow sea, far from the planet's remote and lonely continent in the south. There the forensic remains of long-quieted volcanism showed in the time-eaten upthrust of igneous rock, black and flinty. Thence the long-conquered Norman settlers had maintained their planetary freehold, centered on the captured city of Tolbaran, now the seat of Lord Perun Veisi.

During a brief sojourn to Veisi's castle in Springdeep, I learned much of Emesh's pre-Imperial history: about the fishing culture and the network of island towns that dominated the planet from cap to shrunken polar cap; about the settlement and the first contacts with the Umandh; about the guerilla fighting and the peasant fishing junks wrecked at sea, dragged under by the coloni natives. I learned about the annexation, the decade of struggle between the free-holders and the three massed Imperial Legions under the direction of the first Count Mataro, Lord Armand, for whom the smaller moon was named.

And I learned about Calagah itself.

Valka was a good teacher, and where her information was lacking—which was rare—Sir Elomas Redgrave filled the gaps with neat concision. That I was to wed Anaïs Mataro when she came of age became something of an open secret, and indeed something of a joke to my two

close companions. They called me "my lord" to my face, echoing Ghen's mocking tendency to refer to me with the Imperial style.

Four local months to the day from my duel with Gilliam, I followed Valka and my new friends from the Springdeep research team out from under the wing of our shuttle and onto the mossy stones of the rise above the cleft at Calagah. Seaweed trailed over the white plastic-and-acrylic structures that sprouted like limpets from the black stone, lending the impression that we walked along the floor of the sea, that the gray-and-golden clouds were the dappled surface of the ocean above our heads. At this latitude the winds were fierce, scouring over the water and kicking up fine spray that rimed the world.

But at least I was cold again out under the open sky. Here Emesh felt a little more like Delos, like home. After so many years on this brave new world of mine, I had ceased to note the gravity, the heavy air like gelatin in my lungs.

"Bel, Maros, you're on kelp detail!" Sir Elomas shouted, crinkling the foil wrapper of his cheap candy bar as he waved an arm at the site. "I want it burning down on the beach within the hour." The two techs hurried about their duties without complaint while the others set to unloading the shuttle. I joined Valka and the bald scholiast, Tor Ada—one of Archon Veisi's people—at the base of a spike of columnar basalt, the hexagonal columns skewed by time so that they cast unholy shadows over the mossy crag.

The wind was rising, and here on the continent of Anshar it bit, carrying the chill of the approaching winter. I popped the collar tabs on my short jacket, leaning into the sea breeze as I trudged closer. The ocean, which at the equator was a rich, almost putrescent green, glimmered a pale aquamarine beneath gray clouds that glowed golden in the refracted sunlight. The two women and the column in whose shelter they stood overlooked the cleft itself, a deep, nearly straight gash in the world. From Valka's holographs I had deduced that we were standing *above* the Calagah site, that the black-glass facade of which I'd seen images in her chambers months and months before lay

embedded in the stone wall over whose lip we peered. My heart sank a little at that realization, for I had wanted that moment of supreme revelation, mounting the crest to see that remnant of another age lying unrolled like a map at my feet.

"It'll be another hour or so before we get the camp back in working order," said Tor Ada. She hunched her shoulders, tucking her arms into her voluminous green sleeves in an effort to shrink herself against the wind. "I should have stayed in the shuttle. The wind's fearsome."

Valka grinned. "I like it! Reminds me of home!" Home, I'd learned during our time together, was in the canyons of Edda, where the winds scoured far more fiercely than this, driving the locals to dwell in cities along the walls of chasms much like this one.

"At least it's better than the bloody heat in the capital," I put in, conscious of my dark hair snapping about my face. "Is there time to go down into the site while we wait?"

Ada shuffled her feet. "I believe so."

We descended by a rattling metal stair bolted into the face of the cleft wall. Valka's boots and mine rang loudly on the netted metal structure while Ada's slippered feet were nearly silent, drowned out by the blowing wind. As we descended the clouds broke, and ruby sunlight fell in dripping lines across the gray basalt. I felt an absurd longing for the old coat I had worn at home, for the feel of the tails snapping about my legs and the shadow it would cast against the basalt wall to our left.

And then there was the site, blacker than the stones among which it was built, a seamless part of the landscape as if melted into place. A thousand times I've tried to sketch that facade, to depict the columns and arches and angled buttresses, and a thousand times I've failed. My old journals show the scars of those torn pages, mute testaments to the inadequacy of my artistic powers.

My breath left me, leeched out with the very sunlight, for the stones of Calagah were darker than any color I had ever seen—darker than my hair, darker than the blacker-than-black uniforms of the Legion. The entrance was

perhaps three hundred feet across, dominating the western wall of the cleft where it was at its widest. The cleft itself ran down below sea level, protected by a lip of stone that held back the sea for most of the year.

What strange powers or peoples had contrived so grand a structure in so isolated a location? That vast aperture began as a tangle of angled columns, of arched supports and buttresses—some wide as a man, some thin as whispers—that processed inward by degrees, layer upon layer, all the while narrowing from three hundred feet to the width of a door. The eye rebelled at this complexity, wandered until it was lost in it as in a deep wood.

"It's . . ." There was nothing to say. Why was I even trying? "It's . . ."

Valka touched my arm. "I know."

Wrong. The word came to me as if from outside, pushed into my head from some higher space. "It's wrong," I said.

Tor Ada hurried across the sandy base of the crag, feet squishing around pools not yet dried. The world stank of dead fish, and indeed here and there were carcasses, picked clean by birds or left to rot. I pressed a hand to my face, remembering Gilliam and his damned kerchief. I hurried after the scholiast, seized by the undeniable impulse to see this strange and fabulous ruin.

"Wrong?" Valka asked, confused, moving to join me. We stopped at the foot of the stairs, Tor Ada having vanished inside. From the base of the cleft I could no longer hear the sounds of the team working to prep our campsite atop the cliff. Indeed, all the world had dropped away, the entire galaxy and universe deleted save for the contents of that ravine.

In the holographs Valka had shown me, every line and angle had seemed perfect, rectilinear, square. No longer. Every arc, every bend, every pillar in that place of darkest stone was skewed, bent as the column of basalt on the cliff by our camp. "The geometry, it . . . Nothing's parallel."

"You noticed that?" Valka's eyes widened, and she straightened her red leather coat.

I pointed with two fingers, picked out the details that had clued me in. "That spar's shorter than the ones at the

base, and they're canted upward. See? They should be parallel, but they fan up. It's subtle, but they diverge—"

"—by 0.374 degrees."

It was my turn to blink. "How did you memorize—"

She tapped her head, then paused a moment as a gust sent wet sand scouring up the ravine. "You wanted to be a scholiast, and you have to ask? I'm old enough to be your mother, remember? I've had time to practice."

"My mother is three times your age," I snapped. *A scholar and a scholiast* . . . Not that they had scholiasts in the Demarchy. That distant land had never suffered under the Mericanii, had never learned to fear them or their daimon machines, so they had no need for scholiasts. "The whole ruin is like this? All . . ." I mimed two things not being parallel.

"You'll have to tell me how you picked up on that sometime."

"No trick. I just saw it." I shrugged, but I still did not mount the first of the glassy black steps up into the ruin for the deepening chill in my blood. That place was like something out of a dream, for surely only the unconscious mind could birth so black a stone. "What's it made of?" All these months and I'd never thought to ask. Well, there was never a substitute for field experience.

A fey light lit Valka's burning eyes, and she crouched beside me on the stairs, caressing the glassy stone. The strong wind blew her hair over her face, partially concealing her smile. Not the cruel, cutting one she so often wielded, nor the warm one I had seen by chance the night of my duel, but one of genuine delight, a child's abandon glowing in that austere and hard-edged face. "I've no idea."

Crouched beside her on the sandy floor of the ravine, I said, "You're serious?"

"It doesn't scan." She traced a line over the surface, scraping caked sand from the step, leaving a deep black line. "We can't break a sample off for testing, and the field units . . . nothing. Nothing at all. 'Tis just black."

"What do you mean, 'tis just black?" She blinked, her joyous smile tamped to a subtle frown. Realizing my error, I tried again, "It's just black?"

Brief amusement flickered across her face. "We can't get a fix on its molecular structure. It doesn't seem to have one." I ran a hand over the face of one of the steps leading into the darkness beneath those canted pillars. Though the stone lay in direct sunlight, its surface was cool and smooth as wine, but it seemed no different from ordinary stone. There was nothing in the glassy texture of it that spoke of some bone-deep mystery. I pressed my palm flat to the surface as if my hand were some cunning instrument and by its ministrations I might divine the truth of that place. The stone seemed colder in places, and I frowned, moving my hand about the surface of the step, transfixed. Suddenly I gasped, yelped as if someone had staked my hand to the stair with a spike of ice. Cold. The kind of cold that crawls, shooting up my arm to my heart, circulating through every part and pore. I cried out, clutched the hand to my chest. Alarmed, Valka grabbed my wrist. "What is it?"

A gust of wind blew up, delaying my response as I clamped my mouth shut against the sand, tucked my head. Valka was still holding my wrist. Cold ached in my fingers, terrible and biting. Bitter. I laid my other hand on Valka's, gently removed it from my arm. When the wind died down I said, "It's nothing. Colder than I expected. It . . . startled me."

A frown line formed between the woman's winged eyebrows. She pressed a hand to the black glass-stone. Her frown deepened, and she withdrew her hand. "Feels warm to me." She hauled me to my feet and started up the stairs, hips swaying with each step. I confess I watched her for a good five seconds, then looked away as she turned back. "Are you coming?"

Flustered both by her and the strangeness of that alien place, I looked once more at my hand. It ached with remembered cold. I hadn't imagined it. I touched the step again and felt only the warmth of the high and distant sun radiating from the black stone. My eyes darted up to Valka, standing some ten feet above me on the dark stair. Looking up into the opening of those ruins, the black walls glittering all around, I experienced a crippling sense

of vertigo, as if the door were the mouth of an incalculable well and I were poised on its brink. I saw a figure in green standing in the archway, and for a fleeting moment I believed it was Gibson, but it was only Ada. "What's taking you all so long?"

"Our boy here was admiring the architecture," Valka said, covering my advance up the stairs.

"He can do that inside!" Ada made a snapping *come on* gesture with her right arm, pale eyes alight.

I followed Valka beneath the shadow of the pillars, past ranks of stone pilings and buttressed supports—it was like walking into a spiderweb. The walls around us grew closer as we ascended the short flight of steps. The door at the end was slightly narrower at its base than at its top, so subtle that only my artist's eye might have noticed and been driven mad. "There are other chambers all along the cleft," Valka said, "most well above ground level. They're all empty, but this is the main complex. There are other entrances farther back in the highlands. Air shafts and the like."

"But this is the only door?"

"'Tis the only door."

We were inside then, lost in the salty dark. Not a month past these darkened halls had been underwater, and the stamp of the sea still lingered. The air was cold, though not so bitterly as the stone had been. I had expected a vast hall such as we might build, high-ceilinged and pillared as outside. But the space within was low and dim, lit only by lines of phosphorescent tape plastered to the walls on either side. Valka pulled a pocket glowsphere from her jacket as we walked, heads nearly scraping the ceiling, shook it, then twisted the power circuit before she released it into the air. The thing must have been Tavrosi-made, possessed of some of their technological heresy, for it assumed a position close to Valka's shoulder and followed her as she advanced, casting red-gold highlights on the black walls.

The alien stone—was it stone?—threw the light back in rainbow coruscations; the highlights rippling across the umbral surface made the hall seem brighter than it was. "Is it all tunnels?"

Tor Ada turned in a rustle of green linens. "There are chambers, branchings, but it goes on like this for quite a ways."

"Isn't that . . . strange?" I asked, frowning. "What was it for? Not a city, surely." We'd gone perhaps a thousand feet, and the hall showed no signs of widening.

The scholiast replied, "We think it was some sort of temple, maybe. A sacred site."

"Don't archaeologists always assume something has religious significance when they have no idea what it is?"

Valka laughed. "Just so." The scholiast did not appreciate my joke, for she walked on in silence. "But Tor Ada's guess is a good one. You'll see."

We came at last to a round chamber like the hub of a wheel with several passages continuing on down, deeper into Calagah. Here we stopped, determined to go no farther in what little time we had. With a gesture, Valka ordered her glowsphere to take up a position near the domed ceiling, and there it illuminated a constellation of round glyphs. They looked exactly like the knot patterns the Umandh used in their artwork. They covered the ceiling, interlocking, superimposed over one another until the eyes grew as lost in them as in the confusion of pillars outside.

I stared up openmouthed, for the first time comprehending why no one had yet deciphered the alien symbols. The Quiet had spoken, but the words were lost to time. Nothing about the hieroglyphs—if they were hieroglyphs—was linear or logical. "It's like nothing I've ever seen." Minds had conceived them, intelligences strange and incomprehensible. "This has been here for nearly a million years?" I shook my head, choking back wonderment. "It looks new."

As the great soaring temples of the Chantry invite the eye to elevate the onlooker toward heaven, the weight of that dome, so near at hand, pressed me downward. Tor Ada was rattling off a catalog of details about the site. "The lower levels are still flooded; we'll have to get the pumps running again over the next week . . ." I barely

heard her. In that instant I was remade from hesitant skeptic to true believer.

"There's no way the Umandh could have built this," I breathed.

The pronouncement cut Tor Ada's monologue off at its roots, and Valka said, "No."

"It's unbelievable." I shook my head, tried in vain to find something to do with my hands. Starved for options, they rattled at my sides, infected with implication. "Small wonder you keep this so low-profile." There should have been cordons, security around the site. A Chantry warden force. Something, anything. Perhaps Emesh had been adjudged too small a concern since foot traffic to this remote corner of the Anshar stone lands was rare. Perhaps the Chantry underestimated the effect such ruins might have on a man's soul. Perhaps they did not *know*. I tried to imagine Grand Prior Vas standing in the mud amongst the dead fish at the base of the cleft.

I felt an echo of the feeling I'd had sitting in Valka's apartments in Borosevo. Human, Cielcin . . . Quiet. We had never been the only ascendant force in the galaxy. Small and strange as that tunnel was, it humbled me, made me recall that for all my breeding, all my family history, I was but one man. One man alone in a cosmos strange and great and terrible.

"Yes?" Valka was speaking into her wrist terminal, head ducked and turned away. I looked round at her, eyebrows raised. The scholiast did likewise. Valka pressed a finger just below her ear, listened through the bone conduction tab clipped just under her ear. "We'll be right there, sir." Ending the call, she turned back and said, "That was Elomas. The camp's cleared."

CHAPTER 64

THE LARGER WORLD

ROUGHING IT IN THE countryside means something rather different if one of your party is a knight. Sir Elomas Redgrave's quarters in our little hutment were a single-story prefabricated structure with about fifteen hundred square feet of floor space. The exterior reminded me sharply of the count's office in Borosevo, all white ceramic and black glass, scuffed and muddied by all the time it had spent lashed by summer storms. Both Binah and Armand were locked in polar orbits, and so the tides at this southerly latitude far exceeded the gentle swelling near tropical Borosevo. Weeks passed, and I followed Valka and Sir Elomas through several miles of cave tunnel, more underfoot than helpful.

Elomas had brought three servants with him when we'd departed his family's estate at Springdeep. The first was his young nephew, Karthik Veisi, a lad of perhaps fifteen who served as his squire. The second was a local woman, his maidservant, and the last an offworld cook, a chef from distant Asherah. As we entered the camp, Karthik was setting a plate of whole fishes roasted with tomatoes and herbs on the low table. Though small, the knight's home was richly appointed, with an enclosed kitchen and shower units separate from the main dining area, which doubled as a study. The floors were covered in Tavrosi carpets two inches thick, patterned with mandalas of blue and red. In his youth Sir Elomas had traveled far, ranging from Jadd and Outer Perseus to the Spur of Orion and the heart of the Empire to the Sagittarius and Centaurus colonies. He

had worked his way in a great arc across the settled quadrant of the galaxy before retiring with his niece's family on Emesh, near the galaxy's core and the edge of human space. What a life that must have been . . .

The old knight drew out a chair for Valka, moving deftly to pull out another for Tor Ada before the scholiast could grab one for herself. Only once these two were seated and I had settled into an unoccupied seat did Sir Elomas sit, saying, "Karthik, the wine, please."

"Of course, sir." The squire went away, bobbing his head to me as he passed with a muttered, "M'lord."

It had become our custom to take dinner this way—Elomas, Valka, and Ada as seniors to the excavation and myself as their honored guest. Each evening we would settle in, spending perhaps two hours in conversation before breaking for our respective domiciles.

"Food looks wonderful, sir," I said, prising a brown roll free of the bread basket. "Thank you again."

Sir Elomas poured himself a cup of tea from a red china pot before pouring for Tor Ada. "I've always believed," he began, having said something to this effect every time we sat down to have a meal together, "that food is meant to be shared. Come, come." Thence Ada launched into a description of the day's work, the bulk of which at that early stage comprised cleaning out the flooded sections.

"The truth is," I said, "I'm afraid I'm little more than a tourist, Sir Elomas. My expertise—as you well know—is limited to linguistics and getting in everyone else's way." This elicited a short laugh from the old knight and the two women.

Elomas boomed, "Nonsense, dear boy! Nonsense! Maros was telling me you were instrumental in getting the pumps running down Tunnel C! 'Couldn't have done it without Marlowe,' she said. By my word as a Redgrave!"

I smiled and worked carefully to skin the fish Karthik had placed on my plate. "That's kind of you to say, but I'm little more than a glorified day laborer." I put the knife down, hid my frustration with the task behind a drink of water. "Still, I want to say again how grateful I am to have been invited here."

The old knight set his teacup down and began sawing the head off his fish entirely without ceremony. "You've certainly livened things up. And after what you did to that bastard priest . . ." He shook his head sadly. The rancor in his tone visibly startled Tor Ada, who took a moment to reassert her customary scholiast's blankness. "I was a duelist in my day, you know? I say, there was this one time I was a guest of this Mandari minister. He was from some bioengineering firm or other—defunct now, glad to say—who specialized in one-off homunculi. Concubines, you understand, were the primary output of such an industry." He shuddered, and I was content to let him ramble. "You see, I am afraid I offended one of the man's senior staff at dinner. Just a slight joke about the man's, ah, preference for his own work, shall we say?"

"His own work, sir?" asked young Karthik, taking a seat at the far end of the small table with his own fish.

"Implying that he was cloning himself, of course!" said Sir Elomas, giving us all earnest looks. "Revolting vice, but the Mandari deal in revolting vices. As you might imagine, the fellow challenged me to a duel, and, well . . . here I am, so . . ." He at last severed the head of the fish, crunching through the spine before he set to butterflying the carcass, revealing the mixture of tomato and spinach and fine white cheese where the organs had been. "Needless to say, the minister looked askance at my having killed his underling, and when my accusations of self-buggery turned out to be true, well . . ."

"He tried to kill you?" Valka asked, having finished—more delicately—the fine work of opening her own fish. She smiled above the rim of her water glass. Like me, she abhorred tea. Just one of those biographical minutiae that made me feel, subconsciously and stupidly, that we were more similar than different.

Elomas nodded brightly. "Poison! Can you imagine? So quaint! It's good you're here, Marlowe. Safe and sound. The priests are fond of poison, and old Ligeia has a long memory."

When I had finished, Karthik rose and began to clear my plates away. Rarely had I observed so dutiful a squire.

After he took mine, I turned to Valka. "How long have you been here again?"

She finished a bite—she was eating more slowly than the rest of us—and said, "Four local years, but the flooding interrupts us."

"Since those awful storms in '68, wasn't it?" Elomas asked, pulling a face as he cut into his fish. "Nasty storms, those. The Borosevo power grid's never been the same."

Valka finished chewing before responding, "Yes. That's right."

"But this planet's been settled for nearly a millennium. Surely there's nothing left to discover here." The thought had been bothering me since we'd arrived, since I'd spent more time walking around Calagah. In the intervening weeks, I had seen almost nothing of note in the ruin save for the black halls themselves. It was a place of ghosts inhabited by no culture I could see, no people.

Tor Ada took the liberty of answering me, saying, "It's been in Imperial hands for a millennium, aye, but it belonged to the Norman United Fellowship of Emesh before that. Only Earth and Emperor know what they carried off or sold."

"No," Valka said, at last permitting the remains of her fish to be cleared away. "No, there's no record of secondary artifacts at any of the sites built by the Quiet." She cleared her throat, slipped back for a moment into her native Tavrosi.

"Purportedly built," Ada corrected with a raised finger. "We cannot confirm the Quiet hypothesis, given Chantry regulation of all data regarding extinct xenobites within their protectorate. We may never know if it's true. And everything we discover here will be sequestered too, once the Chantry gets its claws in." A slight frown creased her plain patrician face. "Calagah is a minor site, and the Chantry seems unwilling to commit a warden presence out here in the Veil. Too costly. But that means they've also deemed this place a minor risk, theologically speaking." At this she glanced sidelong at me, as if afraid I would denounce her for a heretic. I smiled encouragingly. "Their people went over Calagah in the first century of

our occupation. They tolerate us because they know our expedition is fruitless. And you won't be allowed to leave with any notes or recordings except for your memory."

She directed these last words at Valka, who only smiled in that mysterious way she had—as if the two women shared in some secret joke—and drummed her long fingers against the faux wood of the table. "Every Quiet site I've visited was empty when 'twas found. 'Twas probably nothing for the Normans to plunder in the first place save ticket sales for viewing the tunnels."

"Truly!" Elomas agreed. "The Normans certainly knew how to put a price on everything. Bloody mercenaries!" He set down his cup. "Speaking of foreigners, the Jaddians arrive soon, do they not?" He glanced to Ada, who quickly swallowed her water, coughing.

"Yes, sir. Within the fortnight, if I'm not mistaken."

"Very good! You know, I've not been to the Principalities in centuries." He rounded on me, pointing one finger around the bowl of his goblet as he brandished it at me. "Marlowe, you must visit Jadd, or at least one of the other worlds. Samara, perhaps. Remarkable people, truly."

Karthik returned from the kitchen then. He looked oddly crumpled, his square, unassuming face closed off. I failed to process this for a moment as I listened to Valka describe the problems with the Chantry's politicking. It was sobering, the stranglehold they had on knowledge in the Imperium and even in Jadd, where the icona and Mother Earth were not the only gods. What had begun as an Imperial propaganda machine and a threat wielded against the lords palatine had grown beyond the Imperium, had grown beyond all control and recognition. Even our Emperor knelt at the Chantry's altars and received his crown and staff from the Synarch himself.

"What is it, boy?" Elomas asked, noting his ashen-faced squire for the first time. Karthik hesitated, eyes flickering from his shoes to the face of his knightly master. He took a mincing step forward. "Out with it, Karthik!"

Starting, the boy stood at attention. "It's the wave, sir. Orso and Damara had it going in the kitchen. It . . ." He glanced sidelong at Valka before fixing his eyes on me.

"Come on, boy, they're just words. String them together, now!"

"There's been an attack, sir. A battle." He looked at me as he spoke, though the words were for Sir Elomas.

Whatever else he had been—a duelist, a dandy—Elomas was no soldier. He blanched. "The Cielcin?"

Karthik only nodded. Such gravity in so small a gesture. The turning of worlds.

"Where?"

Karthik swallowed. "Edge of the system."

Elomas stood, nearly knocking over his chair in his haste, its clawed feet catching in the thick, colorful carpets. "You're not serious."

"Should have the audio in here in a second."

All five of us maintained a grave silence. Years of rumors brought to Meidua by merchanters, of Chantry proclamations, of Legion reports relayed to Father's council—all of them converged in that single moment, falling like game tiles, and it all became real. I looked down at the table, wishing I could turn my water into wine like the magus of legend.

The prefab hut's speakers all clicked on, carrying the slightly tinny voice of the announcer reporting the sanitized public dispatch via planetary broadcast. A man's voice, his deep tones heightened by nerves. "—that thirty-three hours ago a joint action of the Emesh Defense Force and the 437th Centaurine Legion under Knight-Tribune Raine Smythe annihilated a Cielcin incursion force in the heliopause, marking another glorious victory . . ." I didn't hear the rest, only silence, as if I were in the eye of a hurricane. Valka's nose wrinkled, a frown line forming between those arching brows. I confess I felt a portion of that same scorn welling up within me. *Another glorious victory?* I knew the sorts of men who wrote these dispatches, the logothetes of the Ministry of Public Enlightenment. Cheap men, brassy little cynics defined by their dislike of their fellow man. The practiced ear could hear the calculation behind every word like fishhooks in the mind. We have all been those men, but most of us have the decency not to make a career of it.

I listened to the broadcast in silence, hands tightening around my glass. I envisioned the wreckage of Cielcin ships hauled back to Borosevo, alien bodies and weapons mounded at the feet of the icona in the city Chantries. There would be another triumph, this one through the city, along the streets and canals. I saw Makisomn beheaded again and again behind my eyes, heard Count Mataro's basso profundo rumbling through the speakers: "This is a glorious day for Emesh, my people! The enemy was at our gates, bent upon the destruction of our home! Let this be a warning to all those beasts dwelling in the outer Dark! We will not . . ."

Sitting in that little hut at the end of the world above the black tunnels of Calagah, it felt as if nothing at all had happened. Had Orso the cook not been listening to the planet's broadcast, if another autumn storm had wiped out our communications uplink, if he'd simply been turned to another channel, the evening would have gone on unchanged, and the world with it. A world is large, a solar system larger still. However close the war truly was, Emesh was unscarred. Strange, the way the larger world casts its shadow on our own, our moments fleeting and small when measured against the roaring thrust of time.

"That's enough!" Elomas called out, loud enough that his servants could hear him in the back room of the tiny house. The speakers clicked to silence, drowning us in quiet.

CHAPTER 65

I DARE NOT MEET
IN DREAMS

"WHY KEEP COMBING OVER the site if the whole place has been mapped and cataloged?" I asked, clambering up the black steps after Valka and Sir Elomas. We had been at Calagah for some weeks, and each day I went down into the cleft with Valka, Tor Ada, or Elomas. We walked the close, darkened halls for hours. I was only a guest, an amateur, and so I mostly shadowed Valka and the scholiast or assisted the technicians in moving equipment.

Sir Elomas stopped at the top of the stairs, shaking his tea flask to activate the heating element embedded within. "Because we're not sure if it is, boy!" He grinned, white teeth flashing as he unscrewed the cap. Above us, the angled, irregular pillars stretched and curved like thorns. The man seemed so ordinary, so common, so out of place against that alien blackness, drinking his tea. "Whoever built the damn place . . ." He shook his head. "There are entire chambers we've found with neutrino detectors sealed behind meters of solid rock. Not buried, but built that way, like someone cut in through the bedrock and slipped space inside. That's why I've got people hauling gravitometers all over."

My muscles still ached from helping to carry those gravitometers the day before. I'd known they were scanning for new chambers, but . . . "Sealed chambers?"

"Entirely separate. Built sealed," Valka put in. She popped one of her glowspheres and set it drifting, faerie-like, in her wake.

Curiosity piqued, I asked, "Was there anything in these chambers? Or were they—"

"Empty as the rest," she replied. "Emptier. The main halls had some Umandh stuff when the Normans first moved in. We've drilled down to a few along the country-side, enough to get probes in."

But for the light of Valka's glowsphere, it was totally dark in the tunnel. I fumbled in my coat for my hand lamp, following the spectral forms of my companions down and around a bend. "Why would they build separate chambers?"

"I think 'how' is the far more interesting question, do you not?" Valka asked, glancing back over her shoulder.

"I'd swear the tunnels move, Doctor," Elomas grumbled, planting his hands, tea flask and all, on his hips. "I'm already lost."

The Tavrosi glanced back over her shoulder again. "We're not even to the dome yet, sir."

Elomas laughed too loudly for the close hall. "I know, I know. But you know what I mean."

"I do," she murmured, leading us out into the domed chamber I'd seen on my first visit to the ruins. "'Tis easy to lose one's way down here." One of the gravitometers stood on its tripod in the middle of the floor, pendulum swinging steadily back and forth, indicators blinking red and green.

We went on for a little ways, following Valka's light deeper into the tunnels, past a couple of technicians applying new strips of glow tape to the walls. The air hung chill upon us, and here and there we splashed through puddles on the floor where it stepped down or lay cracked and sunken by time. Nothing seemed to move, and the only sound besides our own was the faint drip of water. Condensation fell from the ceiling to patter on the floor as the glowsphere and my hand lamp sent awkward shadows juddering over walls thick with circular anaglyphs like the ones from the dome, like the ones from the Umandh hovels at Ulakiel. I caught myself imagining the blind, tentacled creatures feeling these marks left by Valka's ancient xenobites. What had their strange communal mind thought of this place? Of the beings that had built it?

"I still can't believe this is real," I whispered. We'd stopped in another branching chamber, this one low and rectangular with a forest of pillars sprouting with no pattern from the floor. Some didn't make it fully to the ceiling, and others tapered before touching the floor, useless as broken fingers.

"You've been here for weeks," Valka breathed.

"You never really get used to it," said Elomas at the same time. He shivered. "I'm just glad the Chantry hasn't decided to frag the place from orbit. Inquisition has some nasty weapons, you know."

I ran a hand over one of the columns, feeling the faint tracery of lines there, both embedded and raised and without pattern. "If they did that they'd be saying there was something to hide. Say what you will of the priests, but they're not fools." Valka snorted, though whether with amusement or derision I knew not. I moved off toward the far end of the hall, keeping my hand lamp pointed in front of me to avoid the tangle of black pillars. "I don't think they care what those of us stuck on this miserable rock think."

"Easy now!" the affable old knight chided. "I live on this miserable rock!" He broke off a moment, and I heard the rattle of his tea flask unscrewing. "You are right, though. It's trade over the gravity well that concerns them. Let old Elomas and the foreign witch dig in the ground, so long as they keep their heads down and don't find anything." The knight's voice sounded far away, muffled. "And don't get me wrong—I'm keeping my head down. I like my blood on the inside."

A circular arch broke the wall ahead of me, opening into darkness. I turned, speaking over my shoulder. "Why do you do this, sir?"

"Sponsor the dig?" Elomas asked. I could just make out his white hair haloed in the light of Valka's sphere. "Are you seeing the same ruins I am seeing? I thought you were a scholar, Lord Marlowe. Look at this place! And besides"—he spread his arms as if he might embrace the forest of black stone all around us—"this place is a mystery. The only mystery worth solving on this world, at

least. You know, when I was your age—this was before the Cielcin invasion, mind you—I used to travel all up and down the Perseus, where I was born. Out on the frontier at the rim! I saw everything I could. Dozens of worlds. But I'm old now. I'll take a quiet adventure in my own backyard, thank you. Even if the bleeding galaxy's falling apart."

It was the sort of thing that was not easy to respond to, and I covered my quiet by wandering a ways away from the two of them. I was standing nearly in line with the round door when I said, "You don't think the war will really come here, do you?"

The silence that fell on the chamber could have choked a man. We were all thinking back to the radio report nights before. Cielcin in the heliopause. In the system. But Valka surprised me, saying, "'Tis not the first time the Pale came in-system. Your Home Defense Force caught a scout several years back, right after I arrived."

"I didn't know that!" Elomas exclaimed. "Where'd you hear that, girl?"

I could almost feel Valka's shrug in the inky air. "In the palace, a couple of high tide seasons ago. Elomas, come and look at this, would you?" Her tone was perfunctory, almost disinterested, and so I did not hurry to follow the older man but stood as a lost child in that place of alien stone. It may seem strange to say—after all, I had been in the place for weeks and had stood in that very room many times—but still I could not take it all in. I felt the unknown architects like an oppressive weight, not on my mind but on my genes. The press of my augmented mortality hung on me like a yoke when I contemplated the length of time these ruins had been here, nearly a thousand times the lifespan of human civilization. What had they been like, these ancient builders and gods? Had they been mightier than we? A great power bestriding the stars in their fiery youth? Or were they weaker? They had colonized fewer worlds than man, it seemed, and terraformed none. Perhaps they were only early and not great at all.

A breeze blew soft against the back of my neck, ruffling the wild hairs there and making me turn. The yawning doorway stood open at my back, the hall beyond lit by the greenish glow of the tape striping the walls. Frowning, I left Valka and Elomas to their examinations and passed through the arched doorway into the round hall. The floor rolled beneath me, for the hall there was a tube, and I splashed through what little seawater had not been drained away. I had not been this way before, so I moved slowly, casting the beam of my hand lamp up and around, carving deep shadows on the anaglyphs. They coated the walls here, circles of varying sizes lying tangent to one another like clumps of soap bubbles. They looped up over my head and under my feet so that I stood inside a tubular passage covered in shallow, graven circles, some recessed and others convex, stippling the surface of the stone.

Remembering the safety protocols Elomas had drilled into me during our stay at Springdeep, I shouted something back to the others about where I was and waited for a reply. Satisfied, I pressed ahead, pulling a small glowsphere from the pocket of my bridge coat. Hand lamp in my teeth, I popped the seal and shook it to activate the light source and the tiny Royse repulsor. I tossed it gently down the hall, watched it go past rank meters of tunnel until it slowed in the air and stopped. Mindful of the chill waters along the bottom of the tunnel, I followed the wall, running my fingers along the black stone, feeling the ridges and grooves the Quiet had carved there in a time beyond counting.

After a few minutes of slow walking, I came to where my glowsphere had slowed to a crawl, hovering in the air. So I snatched the orb and tossed it farther ahead, scanning for pitfalls as it went. I repeated this process for a couple of minutes, moving farther up the passage. Having done this a full six times, I elected to turn back.

And froze.

A crack yawned out of the wall I'd just passed, wide enough that a man might fit through it sideways. I stood utterly still for a long moment, sure I had not seen it when

I'd first come that way. The entire tunnel was little more than two meters wide. I could not have missed it, I swear it by all the art in me. One boot splashed into the water as I staggered toward it, having doubled back to snag my glowsphere. A light in both hands, I peered into the crack and saw that it was not a crack at all.

It was a passage. The walls were smooth and glassy, unmarred by the carved anaglyphs, and reflected the light in ripples starkly white against the inky stone. This was no stress fracture but an intentional feature of the ruins. How had I missed it? I aimed the hand lamp inside, catching sight of a chamber beyond and what looked like steps. That was strange. In all my time in Calagah, I hadn't seen any steps except the ones leading into the ruins outside. I squeezed through the crack and looked around. The meager beam of my hand lamp couldn't pick out the roof above. I knew from studying Valka's holographs that we weren't much more than a hundred feet underground at this point, but it seemed the darkness above was the naked Dark of space, forever open, starless and yawning above me. Curious and in need of better light, I threw the glowsphere upward, knowing I would not be getting it back. It sailed higher, spreading its white-gold light over the trapezoidal room I had just entered. The gleaming orb sailed up and up and up—and did not stop. Unsettled further, I stood staring at what the light had illuminated.

There *were* steps, but they were only the steps of a dais—three of them—that fronted the . . . the mural on the wall opposite. I only caught a glimpse of it by the light of the glowsphere, for a moment later the device went dark and crashed to the floor not four meters from where I stood. Dead. That could not be—these glowspheres were meant to shine for days down in that abyssal dark.

"Valka!" I called out. "Sir Elomas! Have you seen this?" I broke off, embarrassed, sure they could not hear me. "Of course they've seen it, Marlowe," I spluttered, looking back over my shoulder. "They work here." I was talking to myself—never a good sign. I would turn back in a moment. Just a moment. My hand lamp had not gone out, and I turned it on the image embossed on the far

wall. I widened the beam of my lamp as far as it would go, but even so I could not take in the totality of the single glyph carved fifty feet high.

It was a circle like the others, and yet unlike them, for within its boundaries was carved no subdivision, no geometric form or arc. The circle was plain and smooth save for where at the lowest point of its arc it was broken by a single ray that widened to a wedge as it approached the floor. I moved toward it. For a moment I thought I heard footsteps, thought Valka and Elomas had come looking for me, but when I turned I could see no one. The light reflected from my lamp seemed to shine out of the black stone as if it had come from within its depths, and I saw my thin reflection there, a ghostly shape. I mounted the three steps of the dais, reaching out a hand to caress the single ray carved into the wall. The stone within the wedge had been chipped back two inches from the smooth face of the wall, marbled and rough beneath my fingertips.

I almost felt I could see the ancient mason with his chisel, so undimmed was the carving on that wall. It struck me then that this whole chamber was dry. Not drained as the tubular hall had been, but *dry,* as if the waters of the sea had never made it to that place. I let out a breath, and it misted the air, turning white as temple smoke. How did we ever think we were alone in the universe? How did we ever think we were the princes of it? What antique arrogance had driven that superstition and cast the Chantry in its image?

As that carving dwarfed me, so its implication—the implication of all that strange stone—dwarfed us all. Again my breath frosted the air, and I felt a sudden chill steal over my bones. I decided that I had tarried long enough and was about to leave and find my companions again when I saw something move out of the corner of my eye, or thought I did. There was nothing. Only my reflection. Then the cold took me, bright and piercing as it had been that first afternoon on the steps outside, as if someone had driven a spike of clearest ice through my arm and crucified me. For a moment all thought fled me, even the instinct to pull my hand away from the wall.

My reflection *moved,* stirring in the wall. It looked right at me, and its eyes were not violet like my own but perfectly, astonishingly green. Though I did not move, it reached out its other hand for me, and I felt the cold wash over me like a wave, pouring from my extremities to my deepest core. The pain shone in me, not white-hot but blue, so agonizing that I forgot to cry out, so brief I did not have to, though I knew it must stop my heart.

Those green eyes fixed on me, and I half imagined I felt a hand take mine where it splayed against the wall. I tried to scream, but my jaw would not work. My knees buckled, but I did not fall. Those eyes. Those terrible green eyes staring at me out of my face—was it my face? I could see nothing but those eyes. They filled the universe, *became* the universe, and behind them and through them I beheld countless suns. They scattered like embers and blew out, all but one. Toward it I fell and into a city whose spires and bell towers recalled the castle of my home, but all the buildings were strange. I heard a great wailing, as from an infant, as I stood beneath the vaults of a mighty chapel. There a cradle stood amid shattered statuary, and I approached, but the cradle held nothing but air. The image crumbled, and I fell backward through thick mist. As it parted I beheld a great ship studded with statues of men and gods and devils. She stretched across the heavens and drowned the unfixed stars.

And I saw the Cielcin standing in rank and file amidst the black of space itself, marching in the night. How bright their spears! And the song of them was like the flash of cruel lightning. Where they passed, the stars fell and planets went up like smoke. And I beheld one greater than the rest. Silver was its crown, and silver the inlay of its black armor, and its eyes were terrible as the worlds burning in its wake. The great ship with her statues over-shadowed that Pale host and plunged into the nearest star like a knife descending.

Light.

I was blind, though in that brightness I sensed a presence. Shapes moving invisibly, casting no shadows. I tried

to cry out, but the words would not come, for I had forgotten them. I felt nothing, heard nothing. Knew nothing.

Save three words.

This must be.

I fell backward from the dais like a toppled tower and skidded on the smooth floor as if I'd been thrown. My body ached from remembered cold, though the sensation itself had altogether fled. Groaning, shivering like a dead leaf as the hot blood hammering in my veins, I sat up. I had thrown my hand lamp in my terror, and I crawled over the cool stone to recover it like some frightened bait beast in the arena before the azhdarch or the lion pounces.

"Valka!" I cried, forgetting Elomas in my astonishment and pain. "Valka!"

I needed to tell her, to tell her what I had seen.

She was not in the room with the forest of columns, nor was Elomas, and though I called for both, neither answered. Nor were they in the room where the gravitometer stood on its tripod under the graven dome. I ducked down several of the side passages, following glow tape and the light of floating spheres until I felt sure I should have found them, crying out all the while. I resolved instead to return to the surface and followed the slanting passage back up into the light of day. The sun blinded me after my time below ground, and I stood in the thin southern sunlight, remembering the cold.

"Where the hell have you been?" Turning, I saw Valka hurrying across the sandy base of the cleft, her red-dark hair snapping in the wind. She picked up speed as she approached me, grinding to a halt mere feet away. I tried to speak, but she punched me in the shoulder. "I thought you'd fallen down a shaft and broken your neck! Elomas went to wave Springdeep for a search party!"

I blinked at her. "What are you talking about?"

Valka didn't seem to hear me. "Do you know what the

count would have done if we'd let you die out here?" She combed her fingers through her hair in agitation.

Taking a careful step away from the doctor, I raised placating hands. "Valka, what are you talking about? I couldn't have been gone more than twenty minutes."

Her mouth hung open, and I could only stare at her as she said, "Hadrian. You've been gone for six *hours.*"

I opened my mouth, closed it. My denial died on my lips when I noticed the sky. The sun was setting, had already vanished behind the top of the cleft. A few broken words spluttered out of me, and I shook my head. "That's not . . . There was a room off the round hall. I . . ." What was I supposed to say? My reflection stirred again in my memory, moving in the blackened stone without me.

This must be.

I had never seen Valka frown more deeply. Confused, she said, "Hadrian, there isn't a room off that tunnel."

"What?"

"'Tis the way to the eastern complex. There are no branchings."

I shook my head. "No. There was one." And I described the massive glyph above the dais and the narrow door. Valka's face darkened, confirming my worst fears. I withheld the rest—the voice, my vision—for the moment. I still shook with the memory of it. A thin, hard line formed between her brows, and I broke off my narrative, saying, "You must have walked right past me."

Her nostrils flared. "Walked right . . ." Her voice trailed off, and she half turned away.

I looked down at my feet, taking a moment to reevaluate the situation. Had she been afraid for me? Worried? Had she been acting out of fear? Was she still? I did not want to lie to Valka. I knew what I had seen: the mysterious door, the too-high roof of the chamber. I had seen my reflection move, had seen its eyes, green as death and alien. Had seen . . . other things.

It could not be real. I must have dreamed it. We returned to the tunnel, water pooling about our ankles. Four times we walked the length of it, and four times we found nothing. "It doesn't make sense," I said, shaking my head. "It

was here. It was right here." I pressed my hands against
the black stone wall, fingers digging into the Quiet anaglyphs. Then, more weakly, "It was right here." Looking
round, I caught her staring at me, the light reflecting in
her golden eyes like a cat's. She had a quizzical look on
her face, as if she were trying to frown and chew the inside
of her cheek at once. "I'm not lying."

"I don't think you are, but . . ."

"There was a dais just through here." I pointed at the
wall. "A huge chamber the size of a Chantry sanctum.
Maybe . . ." I was getting desperate. "Maybe Elomas is
right. Maybe the walls move." She shook her head, half
turned to go. "I'm serious, Valka! Really! There's this . . .
mural. One of the glyphs, only it must have been fifty feet
high. I touched it and—Do you remember when we first
got here? When I touched the step and it froze my hand?"
Her face darkened, but she said nothing. "It happened
again. I touched the glyph, and . . ." I told her everything.
Earth and Emperor protect me, I told her.

She didn't speak at first. That was the worst part. She
didn't laugh or strike me. She didn't even cross her arms.
Valka stood there like one of the statues from my vision,
unmoving and unmoved. It was dreadfully quiet in that
tunnel with only the dripping of water and the faint
sounds of our breathing to break the silence. There was a
mountain of it. An ocean, concealing by its mass and
charge all that I had seen and learned.

Her nostrils flared, and she looked away, lips pressed
together. "You're unbelievable."

"I'm sorry?"

"After everything you did with Gilliam, after I let you
come down here to Calagah, you have the *audacity* to lie
to my face. If you got lost in the tunnels, just say so. You
don't have to posture for me. I'm not impressed. 'Twasn't
even a good lie!" She broke off before her voice could rise
to a shout. "Visions? Visions! Marlowe, your idiot people
might call me a witch, but that is *your* superstition. I am
a scientist; I believe in verifiable, measurable things. Not
ghosts. We are dealing with an extinct civilization here.
Not . . . whatever the fuck you're playing at."

I bit back a rebuke and implored, "Why I would I lie? Especially after Gilliam?"

"Because *you* are an ignorant savage from a backward country who still believes in fairy stories," she snapped. "Because you're bored. Is roughing it in the country with us small folk not enough for you, my lord? Do you miss your fancy wines and oiled houris?"

"That is *not* me," I almost snarled, and for all her stridency Valka stepped back a pace. I did not point out that we were hardly roughing it with Sir Elomas's servants in tow. I did not point out that it was she, not I, who made use of the palace body servants. I was crushed, but I would not be petty. "That's not me, and you know it. If you don't believe me, fine. I'm sorry I told you, but by Earth herself, I am not lying to you."

Violet eyes held golden ones, but only the gold ones blinked.

"Say what you like," she sneered, and she turned away, muttering, "Barbarian."

CHAPTER 66

THE SATRAP AND
THE SWORDMASTER

"MY DEAR SATRAP!" SAID Sir Elomas when the heralds had finished announcing our august guests, affecting his deepest, most courtly bow. "Welcome to Calagah! You honor us with this visit." He straightened, pressed his straw hat back onto his head. "Such an honor indeed that you would take time out of your sojourn to see our little hole in the ground."

The long-awaited Jaddian contingent had arrived at last.

The woman Elomas had addressed—the Lady Kalima Aliarada Udiri di Sayyiph, Satrap of Ubar and ambassador from the prince himself—stood nearly seven feet tall, her oiled copper skin and dark eyes the personification of Jaddian genetic purity. Surely she was one of the *eali al'aqran*, the pureborn of Jadd, more palatine than palatine. You could sense it in the way her slippered feet spurned the very ground on which she walked, in the subtle way she turned up her nose at Elomas as he spoke, in the tense carriage of her shoulders beneath their silk shawl. Her gown was samite, umber and gold, and gold were the chains that decorated her throat and forehead and dripped from her ears. Her sable hair fell in a thick plait, braided with golden ropes and hung with little phalerae that glittered like stars.

Behind her was a double column of Jaddian mamluks, their armor mirror-bright beneath their striped blue-and-saffron kaftans, their faces concealed by deep hoods. They moved wordlessly in perfect lockstep. I caught sight of Anaïs Mataro close behind them, flanked by lictors in

her house's green and gold. She smiled at me, and I acknowledged that smile with a nod. After the incident in the tunnel—after Valka's reaction—I did not have a smile in me.

The satrap's deference to Elomas was confined to the lifting of a single eyebrow.

"I should hope it is a good deal more than a hole, lest all this has been a waste of time." The speaker was not the satrap but the black-clad specter of a man at her side. The swordmaster's face was impassive, but his eyes were smiling, black as black. While he spoke, his gloved hand fingered the gold clasp of his belt where it held fast his ceremonial mandyas, the half robe of his order. The garment covered his left side fully, falling to his ankle, hanging loose from his left shoulder and burying his arm in folds of cloth the color of blood at night. "You are this Sir Elomas Redgrave?"

"I am, Sir . . . ?"

"Olorin," the swordsman said. "Olorin Milta."

His speaking out of turn surprised me. Swordmaster he may have been, one of the Maeskoloi, but he should not have spoken before his charge and mistress. Yet she did not rebuke him but said only, "Forgive my servant. Olorin is . . . unaccustomed to quietude." A smile flickered across the swordmaster's face, and he cocked an eyebrow as his mistress had. "We should like to see these caves. The count called them a wonder of this world." Her tone betrayed how little she thought that meant. I couldn't blame her. She'd only seen Borosevo, I guessed. Not the most inspiring first impression for one of the famed *eali* sybarites. Fetid canals and the stink of rotting fish and dying algae were nothing next to the towers and crystal terraces of Jadd, to the pleasure gardens of Prince Aldia du Otranto and the limestone bastions of the Fire School.

Elomas waved a hand. "Nonsense, nonsense. There is nothing to forgive. Come, my friends, come! You'll be wanting refreshment, of course. We've not much, but we do a little wine cultivation on my nephew's estate in the westerlands. You must have a glass! I've a bottle of gold

sweet as kissing, you'll see." He fell into easy step beside the satrap as he spoke, drawing her forward and causing the rest of us to fall into stride behind him.

"I am afraid, sir," the lady said, tossing her massive braid, golden chains rattling at her forehead and throat, "that we cannot stay. We've only three hours to spend here. Shall we go down to the ruins? I should like to be seeing this wonder Lord Balian speaks of."

From the drop in Elomas's voice, I knew his face had fallen. "Yes, well . . . Yes, of course. This way!"

Fate had brought me shoulder-to-shoulder with Anaïs, who tucked her arm through mine and said, "It's good to see you, Lord Marlowe." I returned the pleasantry, and she continued, "I understand we're to be married soon."

"I've heard the same." Ye gods, she was speaking loudly. "Though it is not for some years. You've your Ephebeia to get through." I wanted nothing more than to melt through the earth and flow to the sea. *This must be how Kyra felt*, I thought, knowing I couldn't run.

Anaïs squeezed my arm a little closer. "You *will* come back to Borosevo soon, won't you? Ligeia wouldn't dare take revenge for Gilliam. I know she wouldn't." She leaned a little closer and whispered, her breath hot against my cheek, "I'd have her killed if she did." I could feel Valka's eyes on the back of my head, but I kept walking.

Unwilling to argue or to point out all the problems with that statement, I smiled a weak smile, trapped as I was. "Soon enough, I'm sure, once your lord father says it's safe."

Ahead of us the satrap's security forces proceeded across the craggy expanse of mossy basalt, sweeping the landscape with scanners and stunners. I could just make out the energy curtain of Lady Kalima's shield as well as that of her Maeskolos bodyguard. The swordmaster's mandyas flapped in the wind, making him look like the hero in some dramatic opera. He wore the garment slip-fashion— as the traditions of his order decreed—a silken cord tied beneath the right arm to keep it from falling off. The voluminous, square sleeve hung empty, and his left arm

hung before him as if in a sling, the hem of the red silk garment nearly trailing on the stone. By contrast his right arm—and indeed the rest of him—was wrapped in black leather polished to a dark shine, so tight it fit him like a sheath does a rapier. "You like the Maeskolos?" I asked Anaïs. "You're staring."

"You're staring too," she said, dodging the question. Why had I asked that, of all the damned things? Jealousy? Gods, was it jealousy? But I didn't even care for Anaïs. Why should I feel jealousy?

"Well." I said, grasping for an appropriate response, "he's a Maeskolos, isn't he?" One of the famed swordmasters of Jadd, the greatest fighters in the human universe. Candidates for the Fire School were taken in their youth exclusively from the *eali* pureborn and subjected to nearly a standard century of training. You do not need me to regale you with tales of their prowess. Their praises are sung loudly and often anywhere human beings draw breath. It is said one of the Maeskoloi can engage a hundred legionnaires and survive and that they move so quickly they shock the very air. Much later I would see one defeat three of the Emperor's Martian Guard without drawing her blade. They had a certain allure, an attraction to them that transcended the personal.

"He is," Anaïs agreed. We were descending into the cleft along the rattling metal staircase, walking two abreast, feet ringing on the metal stairs. "I wish you'd come back with us."

"You know I can't," I said, glancing down at the landing where the Maeskolos was following Sir Elomas and the satrap in the center of a knot of Jaddian guards. It was all I could do not to grind my teeth. I did not want to go back. Though I could not see an alternative, I could not resign myself to my fate. I felt *used* by the count, little better than an animal. I shuddered. "A good thing the Jaddian fleet got here when it did. I understand the Planetary Defense Force is expecting another attack. Are they staying on Emesh long?" Anaïs did not answer at once, and I looked sidelong at her as we stepped out onto the plastic gangway we'd erected from the base of the stair to

the pillars and steps of Calagah. To my surprise, the young lady seemed sobered, folded inward, her slim figure in her silk dress bent over itself. Against my better sense I laid a hand on her shoulder. "Are you all right?"

The count's daughter—the countess, one day—brushed her face against my hand. "I thought the war would stay . . . far away, you know? It doesn't seem real."

Despite the void in my chest where feeling ought to be, I was not so cold as to pull my hand away. What could I say to the girl? I glanced away, up the basalt face of the cleft, pillars of black stone clawing blasphemously at heaven. Unbidden they reminded me of the towers of my home, and I felt a measure of the chill that Anaïs seemed to feel.

"Dolá Deu di Fotí!" The Jaddian religious imprecation snapped my attention away from Anaïs and toward the rest of our party. I caught one of the mamluks watching me from under his or her deep blue hood. Its visor was a sort of mirrored chrome fashioned in the likeness of a human face, and I saw a distorted image of myself reflected in its curves. There was something profoundly unsettling about the mamluk, and I shivered, then disguised the gesture by adjusting my short jacket. It was the Lady Kalima who had spoken. "What a sight this is!" Her bodyguard stood silently beside her, hand on one of the three—*three*—highmatter swords that swung from his belt.

Doctor Onderra began her practiced breakdown of the history of the site, carefully eliding any heretical mentions of similarities to offworld sites. I watched her as she spoke and pointed out tiny features of the alien architecture. Her eyes skated over me, caught me staring. One corner of that pointed mouth quirked, and I felt myself blush. I had to look away from her, from both her and Anaïs.

"What manner of creature built this place, I wonder?" the satrap asked, her throaty voice rebounding off the glassy pillars and spines of columnar basalt. "Your coloni?"

"The Umandh?" Tor Ada shook her head. "They—"

Elomas butted in, ascending the shallow steps at the entrance to the black labyrinth. "We're not entirely sure

of the site's provenance, ladyship. There's been much contention on that very subject. The evidence suggests that Emesh was perhaps host to an earlier species of intelligent life *before* the Umandh. But come, let us step out of the wind!" I caught the abashed scholiast's eye, smiled in sympathy.

"Is that possible?"

Tor Ada picked up on this thread with guarded reluctance. "Several worlds have extinction-level events in their histories, ladyship. It is said that even the Earth was ruled by dragons before mankind first rose up." I had never heard such a thing before, but it must have been so, for the satrap nodded, chains tinkling, and led the press inside, dismaying two of her mamluks, who hurried past her to check the forest of slanting columns for assassins. I watched them search, realizing as I did what so unsettled me about the soldiers. Their limbs were too thin, too long, reminding me more of the spindly Cielcin than of mortal men. I had heard that the Jaddians cloned their soldiers, but I had always thought them men, not homunculi.

At length we penetrated the depths of the ruins, passing the room with the branching exits, descending a gradual slope through the main tunnel and into the glow tape–lighted darkness of a room Ada and Elomas had dubbed "the sepulcher," though we'd no proof it was any such thing. Where the tunnels were narrow, low-ceilinged warrens, the sepulcher progressed airily into darkness, webbed through with graceful pillars that stretched from floor and wall to ceiling like the striated tissue in the lungs. They passed into utter darkness, into places where the light of glowspheres could not reach.

"The natives are little more than magpies, my friends," Elomas was saying. "Have you seen their hovels? Garbage tips, the lot of them."

"I am glad," the satrap said, looking round in the dark admiringly, "that we took the time to come see this." It was no mere pleasantry. Even through her thick, lilting accent, it was clear she was impressed.

Valka stepped forward into the light, her eyes characteristically—impudently—attending not upon the figure of the foreign dignitary but upon the structure at the far end of the chamber. "'Tis good to recall that we are only a small part of our universe and not its center." She smiled her bloodletting smile, waiting for someone to argue with her.

Someone in the foreign satrap's retinue—perhaps Anaïs herself—had clearly warned her about the good doctor, for Lady Kalima did not seem offended by Valka's words. Though the Chantry's power in Jadd varied from principality to principality, the doctrine of the Primacy of Man— our manifest destiny—never wavered. The Jaddians had been Sollan once and remained Sollan in their conviction that the stars were our demesne. Valka, far from embodying a proper respect for man's stewardship of the stars, often said we were no more special than the coloni, than the Cielcin. No more special even than the cattle and fishes, the birds and ornithons and congrids in Emesh's sea. One animal among animals, *animal inter animalia*. I, who once unmade a star, find no truth in that sentiment. Indeed, Valka's willingness to debase man's place in the universe so often seemed to me borne of misanthropy rather than humility. We have a place in this universe, even if it is one which we must make for ourselves.

Instead of replying and engaging with Valka's clearly heretical line of thinking, the satrap said, "It is reminding me of the insides of Cielcin vessels. Is it not, Olorin?" She turned to her companion, eyes still lost in the geometric confusion above our heads, her attention eventually shifting to the altar and the great hanging mass above it, splintered now where the pressure of geologic time had fractured the glassy material under the crushing weight of igneous rock pressing down upon the sepulcher. The room was keyhole-shaped with the structure Ada and Valka had dubbed "the altar" in its center—a stone slab, waist-high and wide enough for two men to lie upon it beneath a finger of the same dark stone that descended from the ceiling like the uvula of some sleeping giant.

This question yanked my attention from that looming mass of stone. "You've been aboard one of their ships?"

Sir Olorin—for a knight he was—looked round at me, then at Elomas. "Who is this?"

I bowed and said in Jaddian, "Maeskolos, if it honor you, my name is Hadrian."

"This is young Lord Marlowe, Swordmaster, my lady," said Elomas, brushing back his rakish white mane, his smile all teeth.

"*Ay ya!*" The swordmaster rapped his armored thigh in recognition or applause. "The duelist! I had wondered what they'd done with you." He took a step closer, as if to get a better look, then answered his lady's question. "Belike it is reminding me of the Cielcin vessels."

Valka tutted audibly, unimpressed by the foreign dignitaries, and I had to remind myself that she was such a dignitary herself. "Impossible. These ruins are nearly a million years old. The Cielcin have been a spacefaring civilization for less time than we."

Ignoring her, I frowned, casting my eyes up and away into the darkness of that crypt-like chamber, wishing they'd brought more light. "This is similar to the Cielcin vessels, you say?"

"Superficially, though perhaps it is just the cave-like nature of the place." The satrap continued turning, admiring the ruins.

The swordmaster tutted, "Not much appreciation for light, have they?"

"Perhaps the builders were blind?" Valka supposed. "The Umandh are blind."

"I thought you said the builders were not the Umandh." Sir Olorin countered, right hand checking the lay of his sword hilts against his hip. In the dimness, the light of the glowspheres rippled across the energy-curtain of his shield barrier. Strange, I thought, that he alone of the soldiers should wear a shield. I watched the mamluks in the shadowed air, their blue-and-orange robes slick and shining in the scant light. I fancied that they were not breathing and shuddered.

Valka merely said, "We have no fossil evidence whatsoever depicting what the builders were like. I only suppose they might have been *like* the Umandh. After all"—and here she paused, as if bracing herself for the lie—"they emerged from the same genetic potential here on Emesh." The doctor waved a hand, as if by doing so she might encompass the world.

"May I ask, *badonna*?" I turned to the satrap, eyes appropriately downcast. "You said this place reminded you of Cielcin ships. When did you capture one?"

"Some years back," Lady Kalima said, not looking at me, which was only to be expected of one of the Jaddian *eali* nobility, more palatine than palatine. I might have been a gnat. "We took an outrider at Obatala. It . . . They are like caves on the inside. Very dark. It is very like this."

Obatala. That had been one of the planets along Demetri's route from Delos to Teukros, had it not? This distracted me, and I nearly lost my chance to reply. I had forgotten about the disappearance of the Jaddian merchanter and his crew in the wake of everything else that had happened, buried beneath years of poverty and indenture in the fighting pits of Borosevo. If there had been Cielcin at Obatala, then perhaps there had been Cielcin in the Dark surrounding it. But I stuffed that ancient concern back where it belonged and asked, "So you're heading across the Veil for Norman space?"

Sir Olorin answered instead. "We are making for the front, beyond Marinus, at the very edge of the Veil. This was to be our last stop before the final crossing." Ubar. Obatala. Emesh. Marinus. I tried to visualize the distribution of these worlds across the blackness in that chamber as though it were the sky. The Jaddians had cut a great arc, sailing from their distant land at the galaxy's edge and spiraling inward through the old Empire to the Norman frontier near the core. Olorin kept speaking. "Your world has been most fortunate, I understand, to repel an attack recently." It had been only a couple of months since we got word of the abortive Cielcin raid on the edge of Emesh's system.

"You aren't here because of the attack, surely?" Anaïs asked. "It's much too soon, isn't it?"

"Indeed." The Maeskolos threaded his left arm up through the half robe he wore over his fighting blacks and crossed his arms, apparently finished with this line of discussion. "Forgive me, this place, it . . . We do not have such things in our corner of the galaxy. You are truly blessed, Lady Anaïs, Sir Elomas, to live on a world with such marvels." He gazed up at the massive cracked tongue of rock that hung above the plane of the altar in the room's center, shook his head.

Lady Kalima stepped forward. "Truly, though we must return to the capital. This little adventure has been . . . most gratifying. Thank you."

"Must you?" Elomas sounded distraught, but my attentions were elsewhere, fixed on the sapping darkness above and around us. "You're sure I can't interest you in that wine?"

In the darkness, no one noticed that I lingered in the sepulcher as a penitent does long after the absolution is given in temple. The Jaddians were the third group of offworld dignitaries to visit Calagah since our arrival, though they were by far the most important. Though much has been made of my interest in the xenobites, it is by no means a rare fixation. A junior director of Izumo Group had come with his family for a daylong visit before the Cielcin incursion at the edge of the system, and after him a group of Norman prospectors arrived, who on examination turned out to be little more than grave robbers. I was weary of the pleasantries, and I hoped that by sulking in the cave chamber I might be spared the farewells. Despite my brief interaction with the swordmaster, I did not expect I'd be missed. Besides, it was rare that I had time alone in the ruins. I almost fancied I felt eyes on me, staring out of the dark stone. Remembering the visions I had seen, I shivered. I should not have told Valka. She had barely spoken to me for weeks, and when she did it

was with a strained politeness and stiff formality that seemed to stem as much from embarrassment as contempt. *Because you are an ignorant savage from a backward country who still believes in fairy stories.*

"Because I'm an idiot who doesn't know when to keep his mouth shut . . ." I muttered.

I reached up, fingers stretched to grasp an arm-wide glassy spar of rock that arced from wall to ceiling, branching in two further along and joining the tangled supports like tree branches that held up the ceiling. Utterly unremarkable. No cold, only stone, as it had been since my vision.

I frowned.

"Thought you'd gotten lost."

A woman's voice intruded upon my reverie, and I smiled, turning. "No, I . . ." It wasn't Valka. "Hello!"

Anaïs Mataro stood in the doorway, slim figure dark against the dimness, her curling silken hair like a cloud about her head, falling past her shoulders. "Your friend the knight's talking the Jaddians' ears off. Figured I'd come looking for you." Her hard-soled shoes clacked loudly on the stone floor, and her skirts rustled as she closed the distance between us. "You're sure you can't come back with us today?"

"And have the Jaddians wait while I pack all my things?" A paper shield, that. "I don't want to depend on their charity, do you?"

The girl smiled, teeth milky in the insufficient light, almost blue. "No, I suppose not. Still, I'd like it if you came back."

I returned the smile more thinly and nodded. She wanted me to agree with her, to say I wished I were back in Borosevo as well, but I would not lie to her. "Truth be told, Borosevo might not be so safe right now. If the Cielcin are coming, I mean."

"You think they are?"

"Our Jaddian friends seem to think so. " I turned away, looking back at the black mass of the altar. "And after that first attack, can you honestly say you don't believe them?" Gods, it was cold in those tunnels, in that

chamber, in the darkness beneath the world, and the weight of all that rock above crushed my soul into a space many sizes too small. The Cielcin felt so close at hand, menacing as the crooked pillars of that alien warren. Shadows on the mind.

The girl came up behind me and wrapped her thin arms around me. She didn't speak but held me there. She was taller than I, and so she pressed her cheek to the back of my head. It felt good to be held—it had been so long. I didn't resist, not at once. Cat's face flickered out of the dark, brown skin paled, drawn with plague. Wincing, I prized Anaïs's arms off of me. This was the girl to whom I was to be sold.

"Let me go, Anaïs."

She started but did not draw away. The distance between us might have been measured in light-years, parsecs. "Father told me his plan . . ." I pressed my lips together, uncertain what to do. I felt sure now that this was how Kyra had felt. "How you're to be my consort."

"Your brood man, you mean."

"Is that all you see in it?" she breathed, words warm on the back of my neck. "It doesn't have to be like that, you know? We could be . . . good. This could be good for Emesh, for our children."

"Our children . . . ?" The thought would not cohere. Children. What could I say to that? They could have their genetic sample of me whether I wanted it or not. I could live out my days in a tower, in a summer palace like Mother. But I had no power, no choice in the situation. My muscles turned to marble beneath my skin, and I stood still as one of those misshapen pillars supporting the darkness above. "Anaïs, I can't talk about this now. My father cast me out. Your father poached me for . . . for my cells, like I'm some sort of racehorse."

Still she didn't answer, only clung tighter. Was she trembling? Was she afraid? Or was that only me? Wordlessly she reached up, touched my face with one hand and turned me around. Leaden, I turned to face her, to look her in the face through the gloom. I teetered on the edge of further speech, opened my mouth to find the words.

She kissed me.

I froze.

In the chill of that cavern, she was warm, willing . . . and I did not want her. "It isn't like that," she whispered.

I held her at arm's length, said, "It's exactly like that!"

"But you'll be the lord of all Emesh, at my side. Can you imagine?" I could imagine, and I told her so. But power is like magnetism—it works in two directions, repelling as surely as it attracts. My mother and my father were prisoners of their stations and their blood. They could not choose. So too was I powerless and at the mercy of Anaïs's attentions. The memory of that moonless night in Borosevo came back to me, men laughing as they dragged me from my hovel. I shut my eyes, willing the memory to go away.

I don't want that, I meant to say, but instead I heard a voice identical to mine saying, "What a day that will be." What else could I say? As the soldier before his legate, as the sailor before his captain, and as Kyra had been before me, I was powerless before this girl and the machinery she represented. I would be hers, and nothing I could do would change that. "But I don't think your court will accept me, after Gilliam . . ."

She pulled herself against me, face nuzzling the hollow of my neck. I could feel my body responding, betraying me. I was going to be sick. "I don't want to talk about Gilliam. We'll make them accept you. They are *my* court, *my* planet. My *family's* planet. We'll show them, you and I." I was petrified, and for a moment I forgot to move as her lips fixed themselves to mine. Their taste was like the taste of ashes.

"Hadrian, I—Oh!"

At the sound of the voice—*the* voice—I pushed Anaïs from me, feeling the blood that had stirred me darken my face. Anaïs caught her breath and turned round with a giggle even as my heart turned to glass as my muscles had to marble, shattered when it hit the ground.

Valka stood in the doorway of the sepulcher in silhouette as Anaïs had moments before. Even now I wonder if she scowled or if her knife-edged face smiled in bemusement. "Doctor, I . . . Anaïs came to find me."

"I can see that," Valka's bright voice said archly. "The Jaddians are waiting for the lady. Come on."

Cowed, sick at heart, I swallowed and nodded my head. "It's not what it . . . We weren't . . ."

"I don't care," Valka said. I like to think she said it too sharply, too quickly. But then she laughed. "Come on, now."

CHAPTER 67

LOST TIME

OUR EXPOSURE TO THE oceans of space has made of our vast worlds small islands. Our genetic enhancements have strained our appreciation of time. As you have read, once I dallied in the streets and canals of Borosevo without regard for the cost in years. Crowded by all that noise, that color, the verve and bustle of the city and its dying people, I thought my lost time worth nothing given the centuries my blood assured. How easy it was to believe that I could stay there, stay with Cat in our crumbling tenement until time itself pulled me down like the buildings.

The man who hopes for the future delays its arrival, and the man who dreads it summons it to his door.

Augustine once said that if there are such things as the past and the future, they do not exist as such but are only the present in their own times. The past, he says, exists only in memory and the future only in expectation. Neither is real. The past and the future—our lives and dreams—are stories. We are all stories in the end. Only stories. And it is in the nature of stories that times present and past are present in time future, and the future present in the past. Thus all time is always present in the mind, and in the story of the mind, and perhaps in those forces that shaped the mind. The poet wrote that all time is unredeemable. That what might have been is only an abstraction: worlds in quantum space, unrealized, which in turn define events by their exclusion *from* events.

What if? What might have been?

I saw myself in the dusty halls of that athenaeum on

Teukros and in the vaulted chambers of the seminary on Vesperad. Other Hadrians tramped the dust of other worlds, unmade, unreal. Footfalls echoed in memory down passages I did not take, toward doors I did not open.

They were nothing next to the thoughts of where I might be going.

The future might come only in its own time, but the scholiasts teach that there are many futures, and it is only the crashing of the waves of time and possibility against the interminable *now* that makes the world. It is not the future that is present in Ever-Fleeting Time but the *futures*. Freedom—freedom of thought and action—matters and is guaranteed because the future is not. There are no prophecies, only probabilities. No Fate, only chance. The present time is not when we are, but what we do.

Upon these and more material facts I meditated, sitting half-drunkenly upon the strand overlooking a pale turquoise sea. Night on Emesh was never truly dark, for at any given time either Binah or Armand would be visible in the sky, shining green or pink in the dimness. That night both were present: the massive, forested Binah low on the horizon and small, jewel-bright Armand set high in the firmament to outdo the very stars. Wind whistled down the cleft behind me, moaning through Calagah's fluted pillars and out into the world.

The Empire. The Chantry. Anaïs. Gilliam. Ligeia Vas . . . I fidgeted with little chips of stone, gray against black volcanic sand, making lines of them. *The Jaddians. Sir Olorin. Sir Elomas. Lords Balian and Luthor.* They were all pieces on a board. I destroyed the line of stones. *The Cielcin. The war.*

Must everything you say sound like it's straight out of a Eudoran melodrama? Gibson's words rattled out of ancient history, referred from a simpler time. I stifled a laugh, tipped the wine bottle back before screwing it into the sand. I'd walked into a melodrama, hadn't I? Or rather, I had expected one, created one for myself. I shook

the memories away and tried to finish my drawing of Lady Kalima, but I despaired of ever properly capturing the disdain in her *eali* eyes. The charcoal snapped, and I swore, dropped the journal on the beach beside me, and leaned back against the rocks.

"You all right?"

I started and cried out, nearly knocking over my wine. "You need to stop sneaking up on people!" More softly, I swore to myself and closed the journal, took up the broken pencil.

Valka stood on the rise above me, balanced with each foot on a separate spar of basalt, perched like a Mandari assassin ready for the kill. Many times we'd talked like this before the incident in the tunnels, and many nights since I'd sat alone. "You make it sound like I've made a hobby of such things." She had her hands shoved deep into the pockets of the red leather jacket she'd favored since coming south, its tails flapping about her knees in the night wind.

A sickly grimace pulled at my face as I recalled her little spate of poor timing in the tunnels a week earlier. We'd not spoken much since then; the truth was that I'd been avoiding her. "Well, don't . . . start." My grimace intensified. *Great job, Marlowe. Real coherent.* I tried to salvage my dignity. "How did you know I was here? And how long have you been *standing* there?"

"Not long. And you're out here about every other night." She leaped down from the escarpment, kicking up little puffs of sand as she landed. She peered down at me past a fringe of dark hair. In the moons' light, the subtle red there gleamed like burnished copper, glowing like the burning edges of a sheet of parchment. I think she worried for me, seeing the bottle half-emptied as it was. For when she next spoke, it was in the tone someone might employ when speaking with a plague-stricken family member. "We've . . . spoken out here before. Several times." That was true. Many times since I'd come to Calagah, Valka and I—often with Elomas or Ada or the squire, Karthik, in tow—had wandered the shoreline within a mile or so of the cleft.

"I know that." I made a face and looked down at my journal, hauling the sandy tome up into my lap. "I just . . . I was just trying to be alone is all." I tried to scuff the thing clean with a loose cuff. When she neither moved nor said anything, just kept looming at the edge of my vision, I let the journal drop into my lap and burst out, exasperated, "It's only that I—I've had a lot to think about. Would you mind?" The sea by night was the wine-dark described by old, blind Homer, highlighted a snowy white as Valka's hair was flame's honest crimson. She did not move or stir. She didn't leave. She might have been a stone, one of the basalt spires, but for the pressure of those golden eyes on me. Patience is a great teacher and silence a better one— they prize things from men's souls without the need for knives. When the lapping of somber waves had been the only sound for too long, I blurted, "About what you saw. In the cave . . . I . . ."

"We don't have to talk about it," she said. "We both said awful things."

"We both . . ." I clenched my teeth. That was a lie. This time, at least, I was innocent. But Gilliam's vulture-blue eye peered at me over her shoulder, and I stopped myself. "As you wish." Looking for a way out, I said, "And about Anaïs, I—"

"Hadrian, I don't care." She seated herself beside me, and somehow that simple gesture softened the gut-wrenching edge in her words. "I don't know what you're so ashamed of. You're supposed to marry the girl. 'Tis good that you kissed her, better than most of you palatine *inmane* can hope for."

I stiffened at the insult. *Inhuman.* It stunned me, made me feel rather how I expect a grandfather might if called an ignorant child. "Better than . . . ?" *I don't know what you're so ashamed of.* How could I explain that? I turned my face away, pawed for the bottle beside me, wishing I could vanish up inside it like some djinni and forget the entire world.

"Well, like your parents." I'd forgotten I had told her about them. She drew her knees up to her chin, heels digging furrows in the flinty sand. "Cold. You know what I

mean. This is good. Better. She's a good kid." To hear a count's daughter referred to thusly was a novelty, and I smiled. "You could do a lot worse, you know? She likes you." She punched my arm, strangely playful. "She's gorgeous, too."

An incoherent noise escaped me, and I said, "I don't want to marry her." I seized a fistful of the little stones I'd been toying with and hurled them at the sea. They thudded into the muck near the water. It felt good to say aloud. "I don't want to be stuck on this planet. I killed a man, Valka, and they will try to kill me before long. The Chantry, I mean—the grand prior. This place . . . You're the only reason I . . ." I broke off, embarrassed.

No words. I stopped and just *looked* at the sea, at the play of rosy moonlight on the black waters, the stars winking in the heavens, waves pushed by wind and pulled by Binah and Armand. The beauty of it kindled at the base of me, enough to momentarily crowd out the screaming chaos. How fragile it was, that quiet. The lapping waves, the distant scree of some night bird. Away and beyond but near at hand, the lights of orbital ships and satellites scratched a silent procession against the unfixed stars. "I wasn't supposed to be here, Valka. It wasn't supposed to be this way." I tugged the planted wine bottle free, uncorked it.

Valka snatched it from me before I could drink and took a long pull herself. "I wanted to be a pilot, you know."

"What?" I grabbed the bottle back. "You're serious?"

"Completely. I wanted to buy a ship, trade up and down the Wisp. Maybe carry passengers."

"What happened?"

"My father died," she said, her gaze fixed on some point in the sea or sky that I could not name. I bent my head, murmured an apology. "'Tis all right. You did not know." She did not sound at all rattled, though she hugged her knees more tightly to her.

"How did he die?"

Valka turned to look at me. "He was killed. Doing this." She took another swallow, then glared at the bottle with hooded eyes. "This is not so good a bottle as the last."

"Elomas hoards the good stuff for himself." As I spoke I began sharpening my broken pencil on the scalpel I carried in my leather drawing kit. Valka looked briefly alarmed, as if fearing I might cut myself, but my hands were steady. "Sorry. I wasn't expecting company." My hands stilled in my lap, still clutching their tools. "Your father was a xenologist too?"

"Why do you sharpen your pencils with a knife?"

"I'm sorry?" I looked round at her, confused. She repeated her question, waved a hand at the utensils in mine. "Oh." I held the pencil up for inspection, admiring the black point, so sharp. "It puts a better point on." Crispin had asked me the same question once.

I could feel her staring at me, not amused. "That's absurd. They make pencil sharpeners, you know." Hadn't Crispin said the same thing?

All I could do was shrug, gesturing with the scalpel. "It's not really about that. It's . . . The tools we use help adjust our thinking."

"How do you mean?"

"When I don't feel well, I draw." I opened the book, flipping through a couple of the earlier pages—pages far from the drawings I had made of Valka herself, each dark and minutely detailed, heavily shadowed. "Sometimes I'll sit and stare at a page forever, but I don't see anything. When that happens, I try to figure out what's gone wrong. Why I can't do it." I put the scalpel down on the drawing kit beside me. "I take time to sharpen the pencil again, even if it doesn't need it. It's good to practice the motions. It focuses my mind, helps it—me—work better." In all this rambling, she had not once made a sound or interrupted to mock me, so I added, "Of course, there are some times when the art comes effortlessly." I smiled up at her, keeping a hand flat on the journal for fear it would spill open, as in some torpid comedy, to reveal Valka's portrait.

She tapped her front teeth against the rim of the bottle, as she nodded. Suddenly conscious of the silliness of the gesture, she put the bottle down in the sand between us. Valka's eyes did not break contact with the wine-dark

sea. "He was. A xenologist. My father, I mean. He ran afoul of your Inquisition while on a dig at Ozymandias."

"They're not my Inquisition."

We were both quiet then for a long time, the sea and the faint calling of birds again the only sounds. The wind moaned from the cleft behind us, ragged and lonely and alone. At last I asked, "Do you hate me, Valka?"

"You do enough of that yourself." And she favored me with a small smile that bled through the pall that lay on me like ink through cloth. "You don't need my help."

A sort of madness seized me, bubbling up from somewhere lower than my throat, and I started laughing, low and quietly. A hiccup cut it off, and I had to clamp my jaws shut and hold my breath to keep the condition from worsening. "You have me there."

"You're not who I thought you were," the woman said, words bright-edged as her hair in the moons' light. I looked at her, she at me. Her smile widened.

I felt my own smile grow to match, felt the quiet laughter of a moment ago threaten to return. "Who did you think I was?" She didn't have to say it. I knew.

Valka looked at me a long time, those golden eyes bright in the gloom with a light all their own. "You can guess, I'm sure."

I could. She thought I was Crispin. Thought I was a butcher, a thug. She thought I enjoyed the violence of our world, a wolf among wolves, and though the Empire was a wilderness of wolves, I did not think that I was one of them. There must have been something of that thought on my face, for she said, "You're not, though. You wear your Imperial mantle like it chafes you."

"It does."

"Why?" she asked. "Why are you unhappy? This place . . . They want to give you everything. You have everything. You're a palatine, and they want to make you consort to a girl who rules a planet. Do you know how insane that is? Anaïs Mataro ruling a planet? Or anyone, for that matter."

We both laughed a little, her at the Imperium, me at Anaïs. When that was done I looked away, fiddling again

with the chips of stone in the sand beside me. "What makes you think that what I have here is so worthwhile?"

"Your privilege, you mean? Would you rather you were one of your peasants?"

"I was a peasant for years," I said harshly, glaring at her. "I lived in storm drains, Valka. I lost my . . . my friend to the bloody Gray Rot. I almost died in Colosso more times than I can count. I've been through things you can't imagine. Don't preach to me about privilege. I know what I am. I didn't choose it, but don't think I haven't suffered for it. And staying here would be no privilege." I couldn't keep looking at her, not just then. Not with what I was about to say. "But Gilliam . . . Gilliam was my fault. I will atone for that and beg your forgiveness. I acted wrongly. But if you think that a forced marriage to Anaïs Mataro isn't a prison for me just because she is gorgeous—your word, not mine—then you don't know what a prison is."

To my everlasting surprise, she said nothing, covered her silence with a drink of wine.

An expression so very like pain pulled on the muscles beneath her pale skin. After a moment I said lamely, "I wanted to be a pilot too. Switch and I and some of the others—the myrmidons, I mean—we were going to buy a ship, maybe start merchanting. Maybe mercenary work, traveling from Colosso to Colosso." I picked up one of the stone chips and hurled it at the sea. It didn't quite make it there. "I was going to be like Simeon the Red. Travel the stars, meet xenobites . . . rescue princesses, I don't know."

"You have a very romantic view of the universe," she said. She meant it as an insult, but I refused to take it as such.

"I would like to," I said. "I'm just sorry the universe doesn't share that aspiration."

I could feel those unnatural eyes on the side of my skull, but I didn't look her way. "Are you always this dramatic?"

"Ask anyone who knows me."

Valka snorted and passed the nearly empty wine bottle back to me. "For what it's worth, I'm sorry too."

Another problem with Augustine's common-sense vision of time: it assumes a sort of causal relationship between past and present, between present and future. True, perhaps, in the physical sense, but in the narrative? No. Stories are not subject to Time, Ever-Fleeting. They transcend time. They are eternal. In Classical English, the word "present" means both "now" and "gift." How the ancients survived such confusion I will never know, but there is beauty in such vagaries. Each moment, as it passes, is precious and so is separate from the moments that follow or precede it.

The truth? The truth is that I cannot remember if we shared that bottle on the last night at Calagah or if there was some other conversation our final night that I can no longer remember. It does not matter. In memory we rose from the shore and made the walk back to the cleft just as the sky turned to flame and thunder.

A great flash filled the heavens, red and white, channeling deep shadows across the craggy landscape. Smaller flashes followed, blue as daylight. I stood transfixed, staring up at the fading light as fire streaked the heavens. *Something* cast its flame against the clouds, turning the night to a mummer's parody of sunset, the colors all wrong even for Emesh's bloody giant sun. There was pink in that light, and blue—the colors of plasma—falling like lightning across the sky.

I had no time to remember elementary physics. Indeed I had forgotten sense in my shock and awe.

Sound followed shortly after the light, and the shock of it knocked me from my feet. It was like being one of those prophets from antique mythology, brought to my knees— to my face—by the bellowing voice of God. Like thunder, but more than thunder. Like someone had broken the sky. I clapped my hands over my ears, felt myself groan, but I did not hear it, for nothing could be heard beneath the awful crashing. The light was fading, and the sound with it, leaving a tinnitic ringing in my ears undercut by a dull,

chthonic rumble, as if another planet were grating itself against the skin of the world.

"Get up!" someone shouted. Something tugged at my arm and shoulders, helped me rise. Valka. It was Valka. Technicians came pelting from their plastic homes, some panicking, others milling, staring uncomprehending at the sky.

Near at hand, someone shouted, "A meteor?"

"Impossible!" another voice declared.

"A ship!" screamed a third. "One of ours?"

"Cielcin!" I lost track of the speakers, of the faceless members of this Attic chorus crying that the army was at the gates. "It's the Cielcin!" Fear is a strange thing, irrational, but incredible in the way it achieves truth faster than reason.

My ears still rang, and my eyes ached from the fireball. The sky above was scored with streaks of light, the stars lost in the confusion, finer points shimmering in the vaulted airs of heaven, white against the Dark. From the ground it was beautiful, well and truly beautiful, an angry red tower of flame and smoke falling as a sword upon the world. Without needing to be told, I knew our chorus was correct, knew that a ship was falling, smitten by ships more distant still. I knew those fine points of light in heaven were the drive-glows of lighter wings, tiny ships holding no more than two men each deployed to cover and blockade Emeshi airspace.

And I knew. Knew with the bitter certainty of fear.

The Cielcin had come.

The words came easily to me then. "Bel!" I shouted at the nearest technician. "Run to Elomas and tell him to wave Springdeep—we're going to need fliers. Soldiers." So small a thing, and yet when I recall that day I remember that as a proud and vital moment, the moment when I could have caved and fallen to the ground but stood fast and straight and acted.

The technician, a feminine man with high cheekbones and a pale offworld complexion, stammered and looked confused. "What?"

Beneath our feet all the world shook, punctuated by a

crash of unholy thunder loud as the dying of suns. Valka staggered against me, but I caught her, steadied us on the uneven ground. "The hell . . ." I looked west to where the column of flame had descended, a slash in the sky that now touched the horizon. Streaks of orange light yet fell from the heavens, tongues of flame tracing where the fiery remains of the ship had just fallen from the sky and crashed into the stonelands. "Bel, go! Find the old man!" I turned to Valka. "We need to round everyone up, get them onto the beach, away from here."

"Away?"

"You can spot the camp from miles off—it's a target!" The sky in the west choked on smoke, lit from beneath by still-burning flame. Remembering the crash, I was bothered by the blue bursts of light cutting through the chaos. Attitude jets? Yes, they must have been. Ye Gods, they had steered this way. Of course they had. They'd aimed for the one continent on all Emesh. They were banking on walking out of here. I tried to remember details, but the chaos had burned them all away. "It could be one of our ships. Shot down."

Valka stood off to one side. She hadn't moved for a good ten seconds. "Shot down, maybe, but 'twas not human." How she could tell through the smoke and noise I could not say. "I think you're right. We need to get everyone out of here."

CHAPTER 68

HELP

WE WERE ALL HUDDLED in a shallow spot in the seaside cliffs when the shuttles came, arcing overland and out along the coastline to come back toward Calagah from the sea. Their lights gleamed blue and white, their tread nearly silent on the air, buoyed by Royse repulsors. They came in like the longships of old, kicking up the surf with their engines, outboard attitude jets adjusting their drift. Still more shot past, drives carving blue lines in after-image across the sky, angling toward the spot in the west where the ship had crashed. They looked different in the dimness, oddly fishlike, glinting like brass as they streaked away.

The dozen that set down on the beach were squat lozenges, taller than they were wide. Their slanted front faces hinged open, turning to ramps. A moment later soldiers in rust-colored combat armor tramped out, the Veisi serpent twined across their chests and down their left arms. Their leader—a centurion, by the transverse crest on her helm—passed her lance to an adjutant and unsealed that helmet, which she tucked under her arm. She moved forward, advancing on Elomas and young Karthik where they sat on a low shelf of stone. "Sir Elomas!" She was nearly bald, copper-skinned and severe with a sheet of burn scar above one bright eye. I recalled her from Spingdeep: a good officer, resolute.

"Vriell!" Karthik rose and dashed to the woman, who stopped to embrace the shorter boy. "Are you here to take us away?"

"Aye, little lord!" She tousled the fifteen-year-old's hair, then stood and spoke to the old knight. "Sir, if you would, I've orders to return you to Springdeep directly."

Elomas had not stirred from his place on the low shelf of stone, boots dug into the beach, jacket thrown down beside him, shirt open to the breastbone as he chewed on one of his chocolate bars. He looked drawn, pressed thin as paper, and yet he smiled at the severe-looking centurion. "What's going on, Vriell?"

"I'm not at liberty to say, sir."

"Not even to me?"

"Not to anyone," she countered, standing at attention, her hand on the hilt of her ceramic short sword—mere soldiers were not permitted true highmatter swords in those days. "Not my place, sir. Orders come straight from the top."

"From Father?" Karthik asked, meaning Archon Veisi. He peered up at the centurion. "Or the count?"

"From the knight-tribune," Vriell replied, then realized she'd said too much and set her jaw. "Please, sir. Let's get everyone aboard the shuttles now." She stepped aside, gesturing with one arm to indicate that Elomas should take the lead. "This way."

The knight-tribune. I studied the centurion's face from my place against the basalt cliff, glanced at Valka and Ada where they sat huddled among the few packs the technicians had liberated from the site. *Knight-Tribune Raine Smythe?* I summoned up a memory of the woman from the banquet, from Dorian's Ephebeia and the triumph. Square-jawed and plain, face traced by patrician scars, her unremarkable brown hair cropped short. She had seized power on Emesh, citing some emergency protocol in the wake of what we all knew, officially confirmed or otherwise, was a Cielcin attack. Count Balian would have ceded authority to her as the ranking Legion officer, allowing her temporary command of his personal forces. That explained the Mataro green mixed in among the red and white of His Radiance's Legions.

Lights still flickered in the sky, bursting and sparking as lighters and other starships tracked and dragged to

high and lower orbits, bisecting the night sky with streaks of flame. Every now and again, a point silently blossomed into a rosette of pink-red flame: the death of some spacecraft. The poets romanticize space combat; holograph operas depict them as things of sound and fury. Even from within a battle it is not so, but from the outside they are only light and silence, save when the heavens come crashing down. I rose from my place, craning my neck to look back along the shoreline to where the smoke of the distant crash muddied the air, lit from beneath by plasma fires and burning metal.

"How far off are they?" I demanded. "The Cielcin?"

The centurion looked at me, recognition in her bright eyes. Her eyebrows—or rather, her eyebrow and the patch of burn scar—rose in surprise. "Lord Marlowe."

"Centurion," I said. Valka and Tor Ada moved steadily toward the fliers, pushing through the milling few dozen technicians and archaeologists. "We know it's the Pale."

The patch of burn scar above Vriell's eye whitened. "Then you understand the need for haste."

"Who's on the other fliers?" I pointed up at the sky.

"Jaddians," she answered, unsure how much my rank demanded that she share with me, "and the Legion."

I glanced at Valka, then to Elomas. "Sir, you have to let me go with them."

"What?" Elomas's eyes widened, green even in the predawn light. "Why?"

"Out of the question, lordship!" the centurion said, taking a step forward to lay a hand on my arm above the elbow. "The count would never forgive me or Lord Veisi if you were to come to harm."

I brushed her gauntleted hand off, but she reasserted her grip. What did I care if Archon Veisi lost favor in the eyes of the count at Borosevo? He was only a regional governor. A flicker of my father's aristocratic ice slipped into the edges of my voice, and I hissed, "Get your hands off me." Vriell quailed visibly, reminded for a moment that I was palatine. She released me. That I was to be the consort of her count's future heir was a secret, was irrelevant, but my own breeding was enough to engender

pause. "You're going to back them up once the dig team's secure?" She didn't respond, just set her heavy jaw, chin thrust out. I took it for affirmation and clapped my hands. "Good. I'm coming with you."

"Lordship . . . I . . ."

"I'm coming with you." I brushed past her, making for another of the drop-ships, one the dig team was *not* pouring into.

Valka's voice rose above the hum of repulsors and the lapping of waves. "Hadrian!"

I turned back, planted by chance on a slight rise in the craggy beach. My words were for the centurion, though I spoke as my father might, to the whole group. "If any of the Pale survived, I can talk to them. I can get them to surrender." Whatever Valka had been about to say, she grew quiet. "I can help! Centurion, you know I can help."

The truth was that I did not know what made me say it, what drove me. Curiosity, perhaps? Or pride? Even now, after all the centuries, all the bloodshed, after the death of a sun and the death of a species, after all the good and evil done by me and in my name and in the name of mankind, it is that instant that rings true. If you seek a moment—*the moment*—on which to hang my life, it is there. Upon that stony shore at the margin of the world, on a night when fire reigned and fell from heaven, I found a purpose. I was *Hadrian Marlowe* again. I was like a man possessed, and I stood fidgeting with the wheal of cryoburn scar on my left thumb. I had lost my ring, thrown it away in Borosevo. I'd looked for it the next morning, but it had vanished. Stolen, I had guessed, by one of the servants, or else tidied away by some unthinking cleaning machine. I had not pressed my claim at the time. It was next to worthless now that my titles and holdings had been revoked by my father, and I'd had other things to worry over.

"It's not safe." The centurion shook her head and advanced on me again. "You have to go back to Springdeep."

"Then you'll have to stun me, Centurion, and then you can explain to Anaïs Mataro why it is you stunned her fiancé." That struck true, and the color drained from the centurion's face. Seeing my opportunity, I forged ahead.

"Let me go where I can help." Vriell looked from me to Sir Elomas, but the old man only shrugged, wind pushing his mop of white hair over his face, obscuring it. "If I can talk to them, maybe I can stop further bloodshed. You don't want to lose any of your people, surely." Makisomn's head rolled behind my eyes, and I sucked in a breath, eyes screwed shut for a moment as I marshaled myself and forced words out. "Three hundred years of fighting, Centurion, and in all that time we've never, *never* seen the Cielcin surrender. We can change that."

CHAPTER 69

OF MONSTERS

EVEN AS I HURRIED down the ramp, a shield-belt heavy at my waist, I could not believe it had worked. Vriell had gone with Elomas and the others—even Valka had not objected to the retreat back to Springdeep—leaving me in the care of her adjutant and second-in-command, a coal-skinned optio whom I did not know. The man led me and the decade of troopers in our flier across the primordial countryside of wort and moss to the place where the Cielcin ship lay smoldering like a finger fallen from a burning corpse, broken at the end of a great furrow in the landscape turned up by the grinding halt of its impact. I slowed as we approached, overcome by the realization that I had never before seen so great and terrible a vessel. Unbroken, it might have been half a kilometer from end to end. Now it was a smoldering ruin of heat-blackened metal and what looked incredibly like stone. Not a castle of ice at all—what ice would survive a brush with Emesh's atmosphere?

The flames still burned. Figures stood illuminated by the few Jaddian fliers still turning in the air, black against the night. Juddering repulsors shone blue above us. A curious mix of Jaddian mamluks in blue and orange and Imperial legionnaires in ivory armor and red tabards crawled over the scene, supported by the odd Mataro staffer in green and gold. Dead ahead, a man in form-fitting leathers stood, flowing robe and empty voluminous sleeve billowing in the wind.

"Sir Olorin!" I called, passing by the optio, a hand raised in greeting.

The Maeskolos, apparently in command, turned from the helmeted legionnaire at his side to look at me. His pointed eyebrows rose, then lowered in suspicion. "Lord Marlowe, is it?"

"It is, *domi*." I bowed, hands clasped before me.

The legionnaire beside Sir Olorin slammed a fist to his breastplate in parody of a salute, his visor and the helm with its pronounced neck flange collapsed, folded away like a paper sculpture, baring his face. "What are you doing here?"

"Lieutenant Lin!" I inclined my head less severely now. "Good to see you."

Bassander Lin returned the gesture, running a hand through his ridiculous hair. The sides looked freshly shaved, but the top was a tangle the color of smoke. He tried unsuccessfully to tame it, looking a sight more harried than he had at the count's feast. "Why are you here?"

"I can help," I said, repeating the line I'd used with the centurion not ten minutes earlier. "I speak the Cielcin tongue. Not fluently, mind you, but enough. If there are survivors, I thought I could help negotiate."

"Negotiate?" Bassander repeated, face darkening. "With the xenobites? Are you mad?"

Olorin smiled warmly, looking like a caricature of some friendly devil, his features all exaggerated points. The effect might have been disconcerting on a lesser man, but on the swordmaster it conferred a certain poised charm. "We are not knowing if any of the beasts survived yet. We must prioritize containment, I am thinking." He tapped his nose.

"If we can avoid bloodshed," I put in, aware of my delicate position, "I think we've an obligation to try."

"*Ben jidaan!*" Olorin said. "You think you will be reasoning with them?"

I glanced at Bassander and swallowed. "I won't know unless I try. I know the words."

The Maeskolos crossed his arms, chin tucked like a pugilist's. "Very good, then."

"No, it isn't!" Bassander interjected, rounding on me. "Are you their commander, then? If we find a survivor, what are you going to do? Say, 'You, throw down your arms and surrender to these people?'" He snorted. "I am sorry, Lord Marlowe, but what makes you believe you can be of any assistance here? You're not a soldier."

"No, not really, but I . . ." Not sure where else to turn, I looked to Olorin for aid.

"Then you plan to, what? Talk them into submission? For your own sake, go back to your nobiles. This is soldiers' work." The lieutenant actually *smiled* as he said that, shook his head, and looked briefly skyward as one of the Jaddians' strangely organic fliers skirted overhead. He turned to the optio—now near at my heels—and to two of the chrome-masked mamluks. "Soldiers, take Lord Marlowe back to the shuttles and hold him there for his own safety. This is no place for a palatine."

"I'm not a child!" Apparently under orders to obey the Legion officer, the first mamluk placed gentle hands on my arm and shoulder, turning me. The carbon weave of the wiry, too-thin fingers was hard, but I shook free. "I can speak to them! Please." The creature closed its hands on my arm again, more forcibly this time.

"Speak to them?" Olorin repeated. "What makes you think you can get them to talk?" A deep frown creased his angular face as if the question troubled him deeply.

"I can speak to them," I repeated, tried to torque my arm free, but the mamluk held it fast. So I jerked my arm up, elbow taking the creature in the soft place just under its chin. Its head jerked back sharply, and it bent back like a child's punching toy, bent at the knees until it almost paralleled the ground. It made no noise, did not so much as grunt, then folded back upward in equal silence. I half sidestepped, half leaped away as the creature came to. "Just give me a chance."

Olorin raised a hand to call off his servant. "That is not an answer." His frown deepened, carving shadows on either side of his pointed mouth.

I looked imploringly to Bassander, who said, "We're arguing over a non-issue right now. We can't spare the

personnel to watch Lord Marlowe. We need him secured. Lock him in a shuttle if you must."

The mamluks had both frozen. The one I'd upset just stood there, fingers flexing as if in search of a throat. Its hood had fallen off in the scramble, revealing a coif of black nanocarbon that covered its scalp and neck and ears, anchoring the mask to the suit. The black lenses of its eyes watched me, dead as the eyes of a doll. I shuddered. Bassander's lips quirked in sympathy. The mamluks were cold things, unreal, as if instead of a man I might loose a colony of twitching spiders from behind the mask.

I straightened, attempted to muster what dignity I could. "We can do *better.*" I kept my eyes on the hoodless mamluk, ready for it to try . . . something. "Wars aren't won with soldiers, sir. Not unless you're willing to kill every single enemy in the galaxy. Wars are *fought* with soldiers, but they're won with words." I would rue that pronouncement—the naivety of it—and as I write it here, my heart blackens with the irony and the bitter knowledge that I was wrong. "We have to start talking to them someday."

Both Olorin and Bassander had slightly dumb looks on their tailored faces. Earth and Emperor, they were so . . . narrow. At last the Imperial lieutenant said, "That is dangerously close to heresy, lord."

"It *is* heresy," I spat. "Are you going to report me, eh?" I rounded on Olorin. "Are you?" In my moment's distraction the mamluk gained half a step on me, and I raised my hands in readiness. "Order the homunculus to stand down, damn it! Enough!"

Olorin hissed something in Jaddian, and his soldier froze. My face still screwed up in determination, I kept my eyes on the foreign swordmaster. His caricature of a devil's face glowed, touched with a wry amusement that was as unexpected as the lightning. "Better? We have to do better?"

Before I could answer, a Jaddian officer in the familiar brass armor and striped silk robes ran up. She might have been a mamluk by the styling of her uniform and the

slimness of her body. But the curves of hip and breast beneath the uniform betrayed that this was no androgyn but a human woman. In Jaddian she said, *"Dom Olorin, domi,"* then began speaking so quickly that I couldn't follow.

Olorin raised a hand and in his native tongue said, "Please take your helmet off when you are speaking to me, Jinan."

At a gesture, her chromed mask and cowl broke apart and stowed themselves, baring her head and revealing a breathless, oval-faced woman with the dark curls and olive complexion of Jadd. She glanced over at Bassander and myself, smiled uncertainly at me, then continued her Jaddian patter, her accent so thick that I had trouble keeping up. She kept looking at me and at one point clearly asked what I was doing there. Olorin dismissed her question. There was a blue silk ribbon wound through her hair, which was wrapped in a braid that circled her head like a crown. Though I knew it not then, her name was Jinan Azhar, and she was Sir Olorin's second-in-command. I waited beside Bassander, watching her speak and admiring the tallness of her.

My captain.

It is strange to think that those dear to us were at one time strangers. Another person in a sea of faces. It is stranger still to think that we would meet them again gladly, even knowing all the pain our meeting would bring.

"What is it?" Bassander asked the instant the Jaddian officer was done. "What's going on?" He hooked his hand over the hilt of the ceramic arming sword he wore on his left hip. "Is it the Cielcin? A report from your"—he looked over at the two mamluks standing nearby—"creatures?"

"Thank you, Lieutenant Azhar," Olorin said. He adjusted the drape of his crimson mandyas, reached up and drew up the folds of his winged collar to better cover his slender neck. "The mamluks do not make reports," he corrected. "Not to me. They are *haqiph*." *Vile*, I translated, not understanding. He said the word with no malice. "My cutting teams got into the ship. Apparently none

of the xenobites are aboard." He flashed me a pointed look as he said it.

"No Cielcin?" the optio asked, speaking for the first time. "On a ship that size?"

"There must be room for hundreds," Bassander breathed. "That doesn't make any sense. Why would they lob an empty ship at the planet?"

I was shaking my head. "It was shot down, wasn't it?" When no one answered, I changed tack. "Were there still Cielcin in fugue?"

"Dead," said Lieutenant Azhar. "All dead."

"They ejected on entry," I said with utter certainty. "I saw blue flashes. I thought they were course corrections, but they must have been escape pods."

"There's no such thing as an escape pod!" Bassander exclaimed, voice high with exasperation. "There's nowhere to escape to most of the time."

"Shuttles, then!" I snapped back.

Olorin shook his head. "We would have detected them, surely."

"Are you so sure? The first Cielcin incursion in-system was destroyed out in the heliopause. This second one made it all the way here, and no one noticed. Don't you have a fleet parked up there alongside the *Obdurate*?" Sir Olorin shifted his weight from foot to foot, unbalanced. I snapped my fingers, pointed at him. "It's possible, then?" I knew next to nothing of astrogation or orbital military tactics, but it was only logical.

Bassander scratched vigorously at his wild scrub of hair. "Blue flashes, you say?" I answered in the affirmative, and the lieutenant chewed the inside of his cheek. Then he swore furiously. Olorin and I exchanged glances as Bassander whirled around. It took the young lieutenant a moment to compose himself, and when he turned back his normally pleasant expression had reasserted itself, though tinged with something like pain. "Where would they go?"

I smiled, knowing I was about to have my way. "There's only one place they could go."

It took the better part of an hour to find the Cielcin shut-tle, a dark, scarab-like thing large as a city bus. It gave off no thermals, nor could it be found by radar. Some sort of cloaking field. I let Bassander's explanation roll off me. That wasn't why I was there.

The tunnel opening in the earth was one of the venti-lation shafts that pierced the stonelands, half staved in by the passing of nigh on a million years, reaching down by feet and fathoms to join the labyrinthine complex of Cal-agah below. The Quiet, apparently, had needed to breathe, or else the shafts served some other function. They were few, some deep enough that falling into them would kill a man, others safe enough to jump down. This one was of the former variety, and so we lost time belay-ing four decades of soldiers down into the tunnels. I might have argued against such a tactic, citing the close quarters and how difficult it was to move in the Quiet's narrow tunnels, but Olorin had seen the labyrinth before and would not hear a word of it.

I was among the last down, unarmed and unarmored— save my shield. With a deliberate click I activated the energy curtain of that shield, felt the static tingle as my hairs all stood on end. Briefly the light bent through the Royse field as it established, twisting the faintly trapezoi-dal hall in my vision.

"Which way, Marlowe?" asked Lieutenant Lin, omit-ting my title.

The air below the surface was still, contrasting with the surface winds. We had descended into one of the round intersection chambers and stood at the center of five diverging paths. I was not sure where we were. One tunnel looked much like another, and these interstices were but subtly different. At last I shrugged. "We're high up, well above the main chambers. I say we head down." I pointed at two of the passages, each bending visibly downward into the dark.

"Which one?" Bassander asked. In the dimness his

ivory-white armor nearly glowed, the red double stripe of his rank the color of dried blood where it ran down his arm.

"Have we got the men for both? There can't have been more than a dozen Cielcin on that shuttle."

Sir Olorin nodded. "We shall be taking the one on the right, Lieutenant."

"Very well." Bassander relayed the instructions with a series of curt overhead gestures. His soldiers immediately pulled apart from the Jaddian mamluks and their few officers, forming into a column and filing into the hall. Each man held a phase disruptor handgun, the vertical slits at one end glowing red to indicate they were set to kill. They moved off quietly as they could toward the mouth of the tunnel as Bassander said, "I'll take Marlowe."

Olorin shook his head. "No need. I shall keep watch on the *amralino*, my friend." I clamped my jaw shut, suppressing the desire to object. I'd dug myself into this mess, after all, so I allowed myself to be led off.

The mamluks moved more quietly than the legionnaires, and they did so entirely without the suit lights the Imperial soldiers used to see. Olorin himself seemed untroubled by the darkness, so I half stumbled my way into the depths, following the tunnel in an arcing spiral down and to the left. When I stumbled a third time, someone seized me by the forearm and frog-marched me deeper. At first I believed it was one of the homunculus soldiers, but the breathing sound in my ears was ever so slightly ragged. Human, then—proper human. One of the lieutenants, I decided. Perhaps the woman I had seen earlier, Lieutenant Azhar. I felt exposed in that armored company. Raw. Like a nerve. Earth and Emperor, what had I gotten myself into?

The air opened up around us. We'd entered some chamber, and the faint sounds of footfalls vanished now instead of rebounding upon us. We stopped, or at least my guide stopped. "Light," I whispered. "We need light."

A female voice sounded in my ear, muffled and close, thickly accented. "We can see."

"They can see *better*."

"If they're here," Olorin replied in a stage whisper. "Be silent."

Something heavy slammed the stone behind me, and I whirled just in time to see a flash of golden light in the darkness, reflected by my guide's shield. One of the mamluks had been flattened, and something massive squatted atop it, dark against the glittering blackness of the stone floor. That image clung to my brain, sharper than the sound of the mamluk's neck snapping.

The shouts of stunner fire illuminated the beast like lightning. Its armor repelled the stunner blasts effortlessly, and it whirled, nine feet of pale muscle in flanged polycarbon, face like the white skull of Death, eyes like rotted sockets, teeth like a bank of glass knives. Was that blood on its mouth? I stumbled back, and Lieutenant Azhar threw herself between me and the creature. Flashes came from my right, and turning I saw two more Cielcin sprinting through the darkness, growing closer with each flash. I needed a blade, a gun. Anything. *My kingdom for a horse*, I thought, and my addled brain cackled with the absurdity. *Keep it together. Keep it together.*

I scrambled back, heard Olorin cry out in Jaddian, "Stun them! Stun them!"

A stun bolt took the bloody-mouthed creature in the face, and it staggered, losing stride, but did not fall. In the phosphorescent afterglow of so many stun pulses, the Cielcin's hair shone: a thick, white braid like Ligeia Vas's. For a moment it was all I could see. A second stunner pulse took it in the face. A third. It went to one knee, groaning in pain. It tried to rise.

Someone screamed. A human voice—one of the lieutenants. He did not stop screaming. It rebounded off the walls and canted pillars in that echoing space until it filled the universe, high and shrill and ceaseless. If he was saying words, I did not know them.

"Light!" I screamed, leaning on all the force and air left in me, leaning on my passable Jaddian. "*Fos! Fos!* Light!"

Lieutenant Azhar echoed me, and white beads blazed from the breastplates and gauntlets of all the Jaddian

soldiers, mamluk and lieutenant alike. Lights blazed even on the bodies of the three dead mamluks. Four Cielcin— for four there were—all howled and staggered, struck blind. They cast hands across their faces and fell back, fingers too long and too many, hissing like an ocean going up in steam. For a moment it was all I could do not to smile. It had worked. They had stopped.

And so I had a horrible moment to contemplate the writhing form of the screaming lieutenant, his limbs flailing, scrabbling at his chest and the ground around him, fingers finding no purchase. His shrieking was amplified by speakers in his suit, and it filled the air and rattled the very pillars that held up the roof of that alien place. Blood gushed from his neck through a hole chewed in the nanocarbon weave of his underlayment, staining the orange-and-blue-striped robe he wore nearly black. Then his screaming stilled, and beneath it a wet whirring filled the air, mixed with the groaning and hissing of the Cielcin struggling in their blindness and the cough of stunner fire.

Something emerged from the hole in the lieutenant's neck, something wet and churning, an angry white snake with a drill bit where its mouth should be, still turning in the air. Someone swore in Jaddian as the thing drew itself out, rising like the smoke of sacrifice into the suit-lit gloom. It drifted into the air, long as my forearm and half as wide, and flew toward the next nearest target—and fell to the ground in two smoking pieces.

Sir Olorin held his highmatter sword casually in one gloved hand, his left arm still slung though his mandyas. The blade of faintly glowing matter rippled and shifted in the air: blue as crystal, as seawater, as moonlight. Never once fixed, the strange atoms of that blade flowed one over the other, its cutting edge fine as hydrogen.

Two of the Cielcin were down, stunned. A third crouched over the body of another mamluk, slamming its head to the ground, indifferent to the stunner bursts. The fourth threw itself at Olorin. The Maeskolos flowed like water, like the metal of his blade, stepping in a graceful arc around the alien, pivoting his wrist to slice neatly with his sword. He exerted so little effort, he might have been

sidestepping a troublesome patron in a shop. He did not even move his left arm from its casual place in his belted robe. I swear he shrugged as the creature ran across his blade. It stood frozen a moment, a shocked, almost confused look on its vaguely familiar face. Then its torso slid diagonally apart and spattered to the ground. The legs buckled a moment later.

"Don't kill them all!" I shouted, taking hesitant steps toward where four of the silent mamluks struggled to restrain the Cielcin whom stunners would not fell. "We need to talk!"

"Talk?" Olorin repeated, flicking his wrist. The bluish molecules of the rippling blade vanished, leaving a faintly bitter stink of ozone where they'd ionized the air around them.

I ignored him, walking in a wide circle round the Cielcin where it wrestled with the mamluks. I shouted, *"Iukatta!"* It was a word I was absolutely confident in, and so I spoke it with authority. *Stop!*

The shock of hearing its own language stunned the Cielcin to stillness as surely as a proper stunner would a human being. It blinked, turned its helmeted head to look my way. It cocked its head to one side, a curiously human gesture. Still in its language, I said, "Why are you here?" I repeated the question more loudly. *"Tuka'ta detu ti-saem gi ne?"*

No answer.

"Where are the others? How many are you?" I came to a stop just out of lunging distance of the helmeted xenobite, confident in the masked soldiers' ability to hold it in place, though even kneeling it was taller than they were. They held its arms pinioned, bent back in readiness to break the shoulders should it resist. When it still did not speak, I said, "My friends here will kill you, understand?" Nothing. The helmet's face plate was an arc of mirrored gray, utterly devoid of expression or detail. "Answer my questions, and I swear you'll be treated fairly."

"Fairly!" The inhuman made a high rasping sound. I knew it was looking directly at me. "Fairly?"

"Why are you here?" I repeated. "Why come here? To

this place?" I turned from side to side, taking in the cavernous space around me. *"Detu ne?"* Why?

The Cielcin snarled through its helmet and tried to lurch forward, only to groan as the mamluks twisted its narrow arms. "It is not for you!" This was so far from any response I'd expected that I stood there stunned, hands frozen in the act of forming a gesture as if I were a marionette in the hands of a forgetful puppeteer. This, by chance, was precisely the right thing to do, for the Cielcin said, "This is a holy place."

"You worship the . . . the ones who built all this?" The images I had seen in my vision marched back to me: the Cielcin standing amidst the stars, their shining host overshadowed by that massive ship and the light of that murdered sun.

"It is not for you!" the Cielcin repeated.

"What is it saying?" asked Lieutenant Azhar.

I waved her off, attentions focusing entirely on the creature pinioned before me.

"What is it saying?" Olorin asked, realizing that my earlier bluster was not bluster at all.

I stayed focused on the Cielcin. Inspired, I said, "They want to hurt you." I took a step forward, crouching beside the corpse of a mamluk long enough to prize its phase disruptor free of its skeletal fingers. I checked that the thing was set to stun, recalling Prefect-Inspector Gin threatening Rells's gang outside the corner store in Borosevo. I recalled also the shopkeeper I had stabbed, the dockworker whose arm I had broken. I saw Crispin bloodied on the floor and Gilliam dead at my feet. "I will." I wasn't sure I could. Nasty things, phased nerve disruptors. Set high, they could carbonize every nerve cell in the body. Set low, they could cause unconsciousness—or pain.

It was not hard to figure out the antique gasket that sealed the Cielcin's more primitive suit. As I removed the helmet, I reflected that the Chantry was not wrong: the Cielcin were so beneath us in so many ways. It was their tenacity, their sheer bloody-mindedness, that elevated them. The seal was like the sort I had seen in historical dramas about the beginnings of spaceflight, the helmet

bulky and made of common materials. No nanocarbons, no ceramic. The armor plating was proper metal, clumsy, weighty, and overdesigned.

"Marlowe . . ." Olorin interrupted. I could not read his tone, had no attention left to pay him.

Face-to-face, the Cielcin looked shrunken. It had no hair, and the crown of horns on its head was filed to rounded nubs. Its four slitted nostrils flared. "I do not fear you, *yukajji-do*."

I do, I wanted to say, and I clenched my fist to keep the disruptor from shaking as I pressed it to its forehead. "Where are the others?" I asked.

"No others."

I fired.

The Cielcin rocked backward, baring teeth clear and sharp as glass in black gums. Its lips peeled back in a rictus. It was not stunned, barely dazed. The all-black eyes stayed fixed on me, unblinking. Was that scorn in their depths? Defiance?

I could not read them. My hand *was* shaking now. The creature saw it—they all did. "How many of you are there?" I did not wait for an answer but squeezed the trigger again, hand jouncing at the Cielcin recoiled, arms straining painfully against the mamluks that held it fast.

"*Ubimnde!*" it wheezed, breath somewhat strained.

"Eleven?" I repeated, then said it again in Jaddian for the benefit of the humans in the room. "Where?" A part of me believed I could keep going, could press forward, but that part had not told my hand, which rattled the disruptor. I squeezed off a third shot, striking the Cielcin in the face. It slumped, groaning, and I echoed my question. "*Saem ne?*"

I'd heard stories about people dying during interrogation, about soldiers botching the job, so unskilled were they compared to the cathars. I had always thought those stories incredible, and yet there I was. I was glad Valka could not see me, though I felt the shame in her eyes, prayed she never learned of that moment. I felt her contempt for violence, for me, and lowered the gun. I tried to tell myself that what I was doing was not *really* torture. It

would recover, would not be like the cripples who lined the vomitoria of the Colosso, begging bowls in hand.

It was not like that.

The lies we tell ourselves to guard us from ourselves . . .

I lowered the weapon.

"Where are they?"

CHAPTER 70

DEMON-TONGUED

WITH THE CIELCIN BEHIND us stunned or dead and Bassander's legionnaires hurrying to our aid, we pressed forward, following the vague instructions of the Cielcin, knowing it was likely a lie or a trap. I still held my Jaddian phase disruptor, slack now in my limp fingers, the brass stock glowing in the light from our suits. I watched it as we moved deeper in until the tunnels ran straight and strips of glow tape marked passages familiar to me.

We were near the sepulcher, the keyhole-shaped chamber where Anaïs had kissed me. The legionnaires met us at a juncture, and after a brief explanation of what had occurred, Bassander sent four of his soldiers back up the tunnel to join Lieutenant Azhar and the mamluks Olorin had left behind to guard our three prisoners and the corpse of the Cielcin the Maeskolos had slain.

"You all right, lord?" Bassander asked, having heard about my ordeal in the cave above.

I couldn't say if it was concern or self-interest that motivated the question, but I nodded, murmured, "Hadrian. And yes. I'll be fine."

The Legion lieutenant nodded, face invisible behind that convex arc of jointed white ceramic. "Lead the way, then. You two!" He pointed at two legionnaires with heavy plasma rifles. "Take point—cover Marlowe and the swordmaster. They're not kitted out for this." As if to himself, he added, "Bloody stupid risk." Olorin, blessedly, did not hear him. He turned back to me. "How's the charge on your shield?"

I checked. "Eighty-one percent."

"It'll do."

The approach to the sepulcher was a single level hallway, the walls canted slightly inward, creating a trapezoidal cross section and a space wide enough that three might walk abreast.

"Scanning," one of the legionnaires said, stopping to check his suit's built-in terminal. "No life signs."

"They hid an entire shuttle," Bassander said, signaling readiness and ordering more soldiers forward with a flash of his left hand. The mamluks moved seamlessly forward, some autonomic process in their homunculus brains telling them to slip into the gaps in Bassander's formation.

Eyes still downcast, I offered, "There should only be seven. The one I spoke to said there were eleven of them."

"Unless he is meaning there are eleven ahead." Olorin looked round. "I am not liking this hall; it limits us." I glanced back over my shoulder to where five of Bassander's men—three kneeling in front, two behind—had walled off the corridor. Somewhere in the chamber ahead, water was dripping, condensation from the humid sea air on the ancient, glassy pillars about the cracked altar structure. I felt transported. Ours was not a column of soldiers but the funeral procession for my grandmother descending once more into the underworld. Strange how such memories dominate our lives, echoing back through time to places where they have no business.

Drip-drip-drip.

But for that faint noise and the sounds of quiet feet, a terrible hush lay on that darkened place. How appropriate that it should be there, of all the chambers in Calagah. The Quiet had built the tunnels with but one focus, a series of ascending and descending branches and loops and spirals that all led to this one dead end. As if all their alien musings circled back to this one thesis, this one idea. The Cielcin's words rang in my head.

It is not for you.

For us? Humanity, it clearly meant. I had the sudden impression that I stood at the heart of a vortex, in the eye of a hurricane I could not see or understand.

"Marlowe." Olorin nudged me. "Go on."

I could have been safely on a shuttle back to Spring-deep right now with Valka and Sir Elomas, could have been awaiting another fight in the coliseum or another day of thievery in the canals. I could've been hunched over an index in a scholiasts' scriptorium—as I am writing this account—or else bent over a prisoner in the bastille at Vesperad.

Drip-drip-drip.

But I was there, almost crouching in a tunnel beneath meters of basalt upon the margins of a fickle sea, hunting xenobites amid ruins more alien still. The course of my life never did run smooth, its disjointed moments collapsing inexorably toward this single one, caused by all that came before and by my single blunt declaration to the centurion upon the beach: *I can help.* My hands were still shaking. But I found my voice, my words. *"Kavaa . . ."* *Hello.* The word was small, crushed by nerves and the bile rising in me at the thought of my little episode in the cave. I got my lungs behind me and tried again. *"Kavaa, Cielcin-saba! Bayareto okarin'ta ti-kousun'ta!"* Hello, Cielcin! *You are all surrounded!* I pressed forward, moving so that only a thin cordon of soldiers stood between me and the entrance to the sepulcher.

It was not a literal translation, and I had had to make a presumption. By phrasing the statement as I had—passively—I was made to project the feminine, receptive gender on the group of Cielcin I hoped lurked in the chamber before us. Being soldiers, I knew it was customary to use the masculine, knew I was being rude. Still in Cielcin, I added, *"Nasca nietiri!"* *I want to talk.*

As a child, I'd been taught not only to speak but to orate, and as I had grown, my voice had filled out. I had been groomed to sit in that black chair in Meidua, to sit beneath the Dome of Bright Carvings and rule a continent. I had a good voice, and that night it resounded in that quiet space, rebounding off walls. When I think of myself, oft times it is thus: standing in that darkness, lit from behind by the suit lights of the legionnaires and mamluks. Yet also I feel a shadow fall across that scene, cast not by

myself and the shapes of the two soldiers beside me but by the sun of Gododdin, which I would destroy. Sometimes I feel that standing at the mouth of that hall was to stand on the bridge of the sojourner and watch that sun explode. In memory it is not the white suit lights that bathe the scene but the light of that murdered sun, cast backward across time.

Drip-drip-drip.

I repeated my declaration a couple of times, my voice rebounding off the hard walls of that airy chamber. After the third time, I tapped the disruptor against my shoulder, rested it there, and shouted in Cielcin, "Is anyone there?"

"We are here." And from the dark it came, a voice like the end of the world. "You are few." The alien voice that replied was higher than that of the one I'd questioned. "And you are small. Some of us might escape."

"Past all my soldiers?" I must have sounded like a primitive to them, a child, like Makisomn had said. "I don't like your chances."

A high, cold sound went up from the darkness ahead, like wind brushing through the crenellations at Devil's Rest in the dead of a Delian winter. Involuntarily I felt myself shiver. Then the speaker spoke again, starting with a long and sibilant hiss like gas escaping a dirigible the size of a small moon. *"Canasam ji okun ti-koarin'ta ne?" Are you threatening us?*

"Canasa ji ne?" I repeated, genuinely incredulous, unsure if the emotion would translate well. *Threatening you?* "Of course I'm threatening you!" I shot a glance over my shoulder at Bassander and Olorin. "Put down your arms. Surrender."

"Surrender?" Again, the high, cold sound. Outrage? Laughter? I couldn't say. "Why would we surrender?"

"Siajenu iagari o-peryuete, akatha." I opened my hands in a sort of shrug, letting the weapon go slack in my hand. *Because you have nowhere to go.*

"The People do not surrender to animals!" shouted another alien voice, deeper than the first.

"Be silent!" a third speaker hissed, followed by something I couldn't quite catch.

"Listen!" I cried out in Cielcin. *"Ubbaa!"* The alien voices were silent. I had an insight, a growing realization, a sense of what they might be feeling. "Whatever you've heard of my people, whatever stories . . . I will not harm you." I tried not to think of the Cielcin I'd tormented with the phase disruptor on the floors above.

"You lie!" the second speaker called down.

"If you fight now," I replied without hesitation, "you will most certainly die." I pushed past the two guards holding position at the end of the hall, took a halting step into suit-lit gloom. "You've come this far, soldiers. Don't throw it all away in some mad final push. Throw down your weapons, and I will see to it personally that each of you returns home alive."

Drip-drip-drip.

At last I saw one of them clearly as it stepped from the inner darkness, disgorged from the shadow like a child of night, all flanged black metal and rubber, face blessedly hidden behind a mask. Too tall, too thin to be real. "And who are you to promise anything?"

"I have a clear shot," one of the nearer soldiers said to Bassander Lin.

"No!" I hissed in Galstani. How did I answer the Cielcin? What could I say to it that would mean anything? I thought of stories I'd heard as a child. Stories about travelers who gave their names to the Cielcin only to be bound in servitude, tricked the way Faust was tricked by the cunning devil into signing away his soul for all time. Only the Cielcin were not devils. I was. Even so, something stopped me from giving my name out immediately. "I am someone fighting a war he did not begin. This is no more my war than it is yours, soldier. We inherited it from our parents, same as you. Surrender and we can make an end of it."

That high, cold sound filled the air between us. "Are you a soldier or a priest, creature?"

Drip-drip-drip.

"Only a man!" I replied, not stopping to think about my answer. "But I'm the only one here who can speak your words." In the Cielcin language the word for man, active-gendered, implied a doer of deeds, a creature of action, not merely a sex.

"A man?" A new voice rang out. "What is this? A joke?"

"No joke," I replied, and I threw down my disruptor toward the soldiers and the tunnel at my back. "Only the truth. Will you not treat with me?"

The muttering reigned above again. Then the fourth voice sounded. "I will treat with you. We will speak." I noted a shift in that instant, not in the alien's tone of voice but in its choice of words. Until it spoke, the conversation had been ill-matched, each side using the masculine-active gender to describe itself, describing the other with the feminine-receptive. But in that last statement, the fourth voice—the commander, I guessed—had used the feminine to describe itself and its soldiers. How telling that shift was, I realized, how truly indicative. They had lost the upper hand. Until that moment I had not realized how the shape of the language might show agreement, everyone speaking in the same mode. The would-be scholiast within me was quietly fascinated, but the part of me that thought in my father's voice silenced the fascination. There would be time for it later.

Speaking Galstani now, I turned and called past the soldiers to Bassander and Olorin. "I'm going to speak with their commander by the altar."

If they were at all surprised to hear my news, they didn't show it. After a second Bassander Lin pressed past his soldiers and said, "I'm going with you."

I nodded. "Yes, of course." I looked down at my hands. The shaking had stopped. "I think this is going to work."

Eternity is in silence. It is in the quiet of the world, in the darkness and solitude of the heart. These are the things that make forever out of instants. These are the things that

turn the time it takes to walk across forty feet of bare floor into eons. As I walked slightly ahead of Bassander Lin, it seemed as though I could feel the weight of those alien eyes on us—on me. If the Cielcin objected to the lieutenant's presence, they gave no sign. They held their silence close, watchful as the ever-present stars that lurked somewhere beyond the stone that formed the roof of our world. Bassander and I stopped, alone in that empire of silence.

Then a heavy foot fell. Another. A third.

The Cielcin captain lumbered out of the dark, leaning hard against one of the slanting pillars around the altar, one leg weak beneath it. The alien carried its helmet in the crook of its man-long arm, and it pulled its lips back from its sharp teeth as it appeared. No words of scholiast wisdom came to mind, nothing to stem the tide of rage or fear. But I didn't need them, for there was no rage. No fear. I felt clean. Unclouded. Ready. As I plunged into the dark, away from the light and order of the world in which I had toiled for so many years, the concerns of that ordered world dropped away.

"I forget"—the Cielcin sounded dry as straw, as bone, pressed of vitality—"how small your people are." This one was shorter than the one I had shot with the disruptor in the cavern above, but it still stood nearly eight feet high. The features of its strange face were more pointed than those of that other, its eyes more slanted than round, hair braided at the left shoulder.

I stopped before I spoke, noticing the hand the creature pressed to its side just below where the kidney would be if it were a human being. *"Tuka okarin ikuchem." You are injured.* I used the feminine-receptive, passive construction. The alien did not argue.

"Eka," it agreed with a clockwise roll of its head. *I am.* Then it added, "It is nothing serious. The suit took the worst of it. I can speak for my men."

"I believe you." I gestured to the lieutenant beside me. "Cielcin, this is Bassander Lin, a . . ." I cast about for a word that would encapsulate what "lieutenant" meant. "He is a small captain." When Lin noticed my use of his

name, I repeated the words in Galstani for him, then turned back to the Cielcin. "My name is Hadrian Marlowe."

"Hadrian . . ." The xenobite attempted to wrap its toothy mouth around my alien name. "Marlowe." It pulled back its lips again, and in the stark white light of Bassander's suit I saw that its gums were black. "I am Itana Uvanari Ayatomn, once *ichakta* of the ship you shot down." *Ichakta* was captain. It pointed one finger at the roof above our heads, groaned, hissed like a wounded cat, and slumped against the column.

Still in Cielcin, I replied, "Will you surrender?"

"Can you ensure the safety of my men?" It looked me up and down. I knew what it saw: a small man not dressed for war, haggard, his hair tangled across his face. The details of my dress must have collapsed into some clearer understanding, bridging the gulf between species. I was no soldier and would never be.

"I cannot, no." I knew I had said otherwise moments ago, so I curbed this revelation, saying, "But I can try. Will try." I glanced at Lieutenant Lin and relayed the Cielcin's concern.

The lieutenant shook his helmeted head. "I don't know what the knight-tribune will do with them, Marlowe."

Shifting to Galstani in order to better reply to the man, I said, "I can't tell it that." He only shrugged, face invisible through his helmet, hands ready on the stock of his plasma rifle.

"What choice does it have?" I could almost hear the eyebrows rise behind Bassander's helmet mask.

I repeated this question for the Cielcin *ichakta*, who bared its glass-splinter teeth again in a venomless snarl, rolled its head counterclockwise on its neck. "There is always a choice." It tipped its face skyward, toward the confusion of crooked pillars and black archways that supported the distant arc of the ceiling. "The People never forget how to die, *yukajji-do*." It was strange hearing the word People—*Cielcin*—pronounced in context. They said it differently than we, the consonants hard and grating. Strong.

"You want to die?" I asked.

Uvanari looked down on me from its height, lips stretched only a little, like a dog on the edge of growling. Its slitted nostrils flared, and it looked away again. *"U ti-wetidiu ba-wemuri mnu, wemeto ji."* It sounded like poetry, like scripture. I was slow to translate it: *In the time of dying, we will die.* I stifled a groan. If it wasn't poetry, it was certainly a quotation. Earth and Emperor, it was like talking to myself. I struggled to incorporate this newfound philology into my understanding of the alien captain, who seized my studied silence as an opportunity to add, "There are worse places and ways to die."

That was a mistake, giving me something easy to respond to. Aware of the other Cielcin lurking in the dark, I said, "That may be, but not today! None of you has to die *today.* Surrender!" I injected as much urgency as I could into my tone, praying to I-know-not-whom that the emotion might cross the gap between species. *Let Plato be right.* "Surrender, throw down your arms, and we will not hurt you. You can walk out of this place. None of you has to die here." I wanted to explain that I was a lord, that I could offer my protection, such as it was. But if the Cielcin had equivalent concepts in their culture, I did not know them, and so I was mute.

I heard a stirring in the shadows, a congress of whispers. Uvanari glanced back over its shoulder, shouted something coarse and inchoate to silence them. The one with the deep voice answered back, too fast to catch.

"What's going on?" Olorin called from the doorway, seizing his opportunity to mirror the actions of the Cielcin across the way.

Bassander shouted back, "I don't know."

I waved them both to silence, took a step forward. "This is not our war, Captain. We inherited it, you and I and all of us. It will go on only so long as your people and mine are willing to die for it."

"Not one of the People has surrendered to your kind, not in all our generations."

"Then it's time to start." I said the words without hesitation, without thought. With conviction. "Your sacrifice and the sacrifice of your men will change nothing." And

then I did perhaps the stupidest thing I'd done in all my life—I walked around the captain. I stood between it and its lurking people, whether six or ten I did not know. Bassander made a strangled sound, shocked, but did not move to follow me. I hoped the soldiers' plasma rifles were more effective against the Cielcin than the stunners had been in case I needed them to be. "Lay down your weapons, Captain. Please." Briefly Uvanari made that high, cold sound I had heard earlier. It winced, clutched its side.

I moved forward to catch it before it fell to its knees. Behind me the other Cielcin hissed, and one hurried forward even as Bassander shouldered his rifle and shouted, "Stay back!" The other Cielcin took his meaning, held its long, six-fingered hands up to show it was not armed.

Mirroring the lieutenant's order, Uvanari hissed, *"Lenna udeo, Tanaran-kih!"* The other Cielcin—Tanaran, I guessed—froze where it stood. It was different from the others I had seen, dressed not in an ungainly armored suit like the captain but in a form-fitting wraparound with tight sleeves that reminded me of the combat robes I had once seen on a visiting Nipponese gladiatrix in Meidua in my youth. Its white hair was wild, hacked roughly off at the shoulders, and its mouth hung open, uncertain. Something in the geometry of its face, in the tightness of the skin at the base of its epoccipital crown, perhaps, told me this was a very young Cielcin. When it did not move, Uvanari repeated its command. "Stay back!"

"Tuka udata ne?" I asked, settling the captain back against the pillar that had taken its weight.

"It's nothing, a broken rib." Black blood, still warm and cloying, clung to the layers of cloth insulation visible between the carbide armor plates. The technology on display in that suit really was ancient, centuries behind anything we had. That struck me as wrong. Surely any species so dependent upon star travel as the Cielcin would work harder at developing their suit technology? The creature might have had a broken rib, but I accounted that the least of its worries. I was no doctor, but it looked like something had punched through suit and skin and meat, pierced the torso and crushed one of the translucent bones.

I looked up at the Cielcin Tanaran. I wanted to call for a med kit, but I didn't know the word. *"Panathidu!"* I snapped, reaching up a hand to the other xenobite, who stood there confused at my inane babbling. "Medicine! Medicine!" I turned to Bassander, who was still crouched, and spoke past him to the soldiers in the mouth of the tunnel. "Bring a med kit! Their captain is wounded!"

Tanaran looked at Uvanari, massive black eyes narrowing to canted slits. It rolled its head clockwise, said, "What does it want?"

"He," Uvanari answered, using an explicitly active-gendered pronoun to refer to me, "is trying to help me." It turned its attentions back to me. "We have nothing, *yukajji-do.* Leave it." It grunted, forced itself to sit up a little straighter. "Perhaps I will die here, peace or no peace." The alien face composed itself into an expression of nearly human solemnity. "And we were so close . . ."

"Close?" I asked. "Close to what?"

Uvanari screwed its eyes shut before answering, and its words grew thin as ghosts and whispers. "They are not here . . . not here." It rested its head against the pillar, prompting the other Cielcin, Tanaran, to hurry to its side. "You can have your peace, little human."

Tanaran sucked air past its teeth. *"Veih,* no. Captain, you can't."

"Eka de," Uvanari said. *I can.* It opened its ink-spot eyes. *"Uje ekau." And I will.* It crossed its closed fists over its chest. A salute? A surrender? A gesture of fealty? I couldn't say. "We surrender, human."

CHAPTER 71

INQUISITION

AND WE WERE SO *close.* The words rattled in my head, turning over as they had half a million times since I had first heard the Cielcin captain speak them. *Uje ekurimi su keta.* So close to what? *They are not here . . .* I could have broken my hands on the tabletop in frustration, would have given my left arm for a chance to speak with Uvanari again, to wring an answer from it if I could. No, not *wring.* I had wrung enough. I glanced across the petrified wood of the council table to where Sir Olorin Milta sat beside his satrap, not looking my way. He had not spoken of my interrogation of the Cielcin in the tunnels of Calagah, and I was not about to mention it.

They are not here.

They.

Did Uvanari mean the Quiet? Was that even possible?

". . . should be ready in a week or so," Knight-Tribune Smythe was saying, her blunt-featured face turned down in intense concentration. The subject had just turned from the frequent brownouts in castle power and surveillance to the Cielcin. To my surprise, Centurion Vriell's pronouncement that the hard-edged Legion officer was running things in Borosevo seemed to be true, though I could not have said whether that was by some Imperial fiat or simply because the count had stepped aside. Balian Mataro sat in the high seat on a dais above the council table, chin propped on one fist like an image of bored Zeus done in black marble. "The creature's wounds are healing nicely, my medics tell me."

"And the others?" asked High Chancellor Ogir, steepling her hands before her. "Have we started on them?"

The subtext beneath those words dragged my eyes to the one personage at the table whom I'd most struggled to avoid. Ligeia Vas wore her customary black robes. Her face was powdered, drawing further attention to her off-world pallor, and her white hair was in its customary double coil about her thin shoulders. Worst of all, her icy eyes found mine, sharp as knife-missiles—she had been staring at me. They did not stray from my face as she answered, "We have not, per the request of our Jaddian emissary." At last she turned, glancing briefly at Lady Kalima di Sayyiph. "They requested we suspend operations pending this meeting, a suspension we granted out of respect for our visitors and for their assistance in apprehending the xenobites." From the way she said the word *respect*, I gathered that respect only stretched so far.

I studied the almost celestial Jaddian satrap from my lonely place at the end of the table, a lonely spot of color in a cloud of gray-suited logothetes. Rubies glinted at her throat and from her ears, and so much gold jewelry hung about her neck and from her hair that I was astonished she did not bend from the weight of it. Sir Olorin Milta stood just behind her, hand toying with the three high-matter sword hilts strapped to his thigh, eyes fixed somewhere far away, on a point out to sea through the broad arc of alumglass that made up the opposite wall of the council chamber. I had the sudden sense that the Jaddians really were on my side, willing to try and speak with the captives. To make peace.

"In any event," the knight-tribune said, drumming her square knuckles on the tabletop, rippling the water in the glass at her elbow, "thanks to Lieutenant Lin, we find ourselves in possession of ten Cielcin prisoners."

"Captives." I couldn't help myself. "They surrendered to us. If the *ichakta* were human, we'd be trying to ransom it back to its liege."

The grand prior slapped a hand on the table, demanding attention. "The beast is *not* human, heretic."

"That beast is an enemy officer," I said, addressing

myself to Raine Smythe. The knight-tribune pressed her lips together, but she seemed willing for the moment to hear me out. "There's no procedure in place for dealing with inhuman officers, is there? Should we not treat it honorably?" I did not add my private suspicion, that Tanaran might be something other than an officer. Whatever it was, the younger Cielcin was no soldier. It was certainly not dressed as one. Nor, for that matter, did I share Uvanari's implied connection between its people and the Quiet. I would save that little bit of information for Valka when she returned to Borosevo within the week, all activity at the dig site having been suspended in the wake of the attack as the recovery teams worked hard to salvage the wreck of Uvanari's ship.

The chancellor looked like she'd been fed a tablespoon of lemon extract. She licked her teeth, ashen face darkening and pinching as she spat, "*Inmane!* I remind you, Lord Marlowe, that you are here on sufferance."

"He is here, Chancellor, because he alone has spoken to the prisoners and can offer insight," Sir Olorin interjected. I looked to him, bowed my head in thanks. He returned my nod, dislodging a tangle of dark hair.

The surgical scars that marked Chancellor Ogir as patrician whitened as her lips compressed. "When I want your input, lictor, I will invite it."

"Enough, Liada," Lord Balian said. "That's quite enough. The Jaddians are our guests." Somewhat mollified, the reedy little chancellor backed down, seeming to find something entirely fascinating about the pattern of angry veins on the back of her leathery hands. It surprised me then that the satrap did not leap to her servant's defense herself. It surprises me more now.

Olorin's interjection served a secondary function, as was revealed in the next moment when Raine Smythe said, "Lord Marlowe's done the Empire a service; that cannot be denied. And his consideration is a goodly one. If we seek to negotiate using the captured Pale as hostages, we must consider their treatment." Feeling I had scored a point, I smiled at the grand prior, but the witch-priestess did not deign to look my way. The knight-tribune drummed

her knuckles on the tabletop again. "But we have an opportunity here to extract real tactical information. Why did the Cielcin come here to Emesh? Why now?"

There followed a moment of pregnant silence punctuated by the drumming of those knuckles and of the nervous sounds of the logothetes at each extreme of the arc of the speckled rose-green table. All of us knew what we were really discussing. Perhaps that was why the count was silent, preferring to let the military and the clergy take the reins. I peered down at my lap, at the hands folded tightly there, recalling the way they'd shaken in the tunnels, recalling the fear that had edged up into panic.

"The prisoners must be questioned," said Ligeia Vas into that pregnant silence, lacing her hands on the tabletop, her stillness counterpoint to the knight-tribune's nervous movement.

"The prisoners—the captives—must be made to give us something, aye." Raine Smythe bent her ear to listen to a whispered word from Sir William Crossflane, the white-haired first officer at her side, then shut her eyes a moment.

"The location of their fleet?" suggested the Jaddian satrap, eyes still locked on the city far below.

Undaunted by this benign interruption, Raine Smythe continued in her rough contralto, "Perforce what remains is to decide what manner of information we believe we can extract."

"Without jeopardizing the creatures' value as hostages," said one of the count's ministers, earning a glare from the chancellor.

"And so," said the scholiast Tor Vladimir, speaking up from his place near the count at the center of the semicircular table, "we must weigh the value of our prisoners as diplomatic assets against their strategic value." The man's soft words, utterly without inflection, filled the room like a kind of sleeping gas.

I still couldn't believe we were even having this conversation, and I blurted, "You're talking about torturing them."

"They would do no differently in our place, son," the elderly first officer beside the knight-tribune said. "This

is war. We—" Dame Raine put a hand on his arm, quieting him. He blustered a moment, lips working between massive, bushy sideburns like those of a gasping fish. "They launched two attacks against us in the past few months. Who's to say they won't launch a third?"

Ever the antagonist, Sir Olorin said, "I was under the impression that the first attackers were only . . . what is the word? Outriders? Scouts for the second attack. That it was all one battle fleet."

"Was it?" the grand prior demanded, twisting in her high-backed chair to face the Jaddian swordmaster. "For a human, Maeskolos, you seem to be intimately familiar with the plans and intentions of our enemy. Perhaps Lord Marlowe's heresy is catching."

"Lord Marlowe's dedication to the faith is not the issue up for discussion at the moment, Your Reverence," the knight-tribune interjected, gazing sidelong at Ligeia Vas but not turning her head. "Please, if we could stow the piety long enough to come to some decision?" She hid her face in her hands, massaged her eyes with short, hard fingers. Everything about the woman was blunt: her features, her manner, her movements. But she was one used to power—not the comparatively small power of a landed nobile, but the fist of the Imperial Legions. Her authority was the authority of the Imperium, of the Presence and the Solar Throne itself, and it did not tiptoe around the priors of provincial chantries. She took a deep breath, expelled it. "While I see the case for preserving the captives for ransom, I believe that they—particularly their captain—are of far greater interest to the Imperium for the information they hold regarding Cielcin fleet movements."

The gross incandescence of Ligeia's smile curdled every fluid in me, and I clenched my teeth so hard that I fancied they cracked. *No. No, no.* Still I had to respect the play for what it was. Raine Smythe had played the grand prior right into her hand in a matter of moments by first chastising her, then giving her what she wanted to silence her, ensuring that the last word on the subject subordinated the priestess to the tribune's will. The politician I

might have been applauded within me even as my spirit choked on the sound of screaming.

Whatever happened, there would be blood. I saw that then. Always blood. Blood is not the foundation of civilization—ours or any other's—but it suffuses its mortar at every level, drips from its walls. Despite the glass and airy light of that room, I felt hemmed in, as though I cowered in some catacomb of the mind, dank and musty and lost. When we think of War and her atrocities, we imagine that the unforgivable is prosecuted on the battlefield, in the heat and fire. It is not. Atrocity is writ by quiet men in council chambers over crystal glasses of cool water. Strange little men with ashes in their hearts. Sans passion, sans hope . . . sans everything. Everything but fear. For themselves, for their own lives, for some imagined future. And in the name of safety, security, piety, they labor to found future heaven on present horror. But their kingdom of heaven is in the mind, in the future that will never be, and their present horrors are real.

"You cannot be serious, knight-tribune," said Lady Kalima. Her attention flickered to the tribune's face. "Surely the prisoners are of more use to us, ah . . . unmolested."

Raine Smythe glanced briefly at the count in his high seat before leaning in to address the Jaddian noblewoman. "If you've an alternate suggestion, satrap, I would love to hear it. But this planet is under threat. I know it's not one of *your* planets, but it is in the Imperial interest that Emesh remain, ah . . . unmolested." She mimicked the satrap's cadence, if not her accent, on the final word. Olorin's hand tightened briefly about the wine-red grip of one of his three swords, prepared to unclip it from his belt. For a moment I thought we were about to have another duel in Borosevo, but the tall swordmaster released his weapon without comment, face composed as that of a scholiast by the next moment.

"They weren't an invading force." All eyes turned to look my way, even the satrap's. I could not figure out why for a good moment, and then it clicked. I'd opened my fool mouth again. Forced now to explain, I said, "They were looking for something. Sir Olorin, sir, you were

there. You're the soldier, Knight-Tribune—you have the reports. Is the design of the ship shot down over Anshar consistent at all with the design of a military vessel?" When no one answered I looked round, spread my hands. "No, really. Is it? I'm no expert in ship design. Anyone?"

One of the minor logothetes, a thickset plebeian man with graying hair and a drooping face, cleared his throat and tapped his stylus on the petrified wood surface of the table. "There were no ship-to-ship armaments found on the wreckage of the xenobite craft. It would appear that—"

I raised my eyebrows. "No ship-to-ship armaments, eh?" I imitated the knight-tribune's knuckle-rapping gesture and surveyed the lords of two nations, the Chantry prior who wanted me dead, the high officers of the Imperial Legion, and the crowd of logothetes before continuing, "Perhaps there is no third wave. Perhaps our Cielcin friends knew there was no hope of rescue. Perhaps their retreat into Calagah represented a last desperate stand? The *ichakta*—their captain—only surrendered when I promised medical aid." That was not strictly true, as you have seen, but the only persons capable of corroborating that story besides Uvanari and myself were Bassander Lin and the Cielcin Tanaran, neither of whom were present or spoke the other's language.

"Get to the point, please," said Chancellor Liada Ogir.

"Our Cielcin *friends*?" the grand prior repeated, blood darkening her whitened cheeks.

"A figure of speech," murmured Tor Vladimir, his sleepy voice coming to my aid.

I let the prior's tangent die down, again affecting the knight-tribune's knuckle-rapping gesture. "Look. I'd wager that the ships you destroyed in orbit were an escort sent to cover the crashed vessel's approach. They weren't kitted for an invasion."

"Then what were they after?" First Officer Crossflane croaked from beside Raine Smythe, a frown tugging on his chops. "Are they spies?"

Mouth open, I stared at the man. I had a suspicion, of course. The *ichakta*'s words still echoed in my skull: *They are not here.* I needed Valka, needed to talk to Valka. She

would understand, could help me make sense of things. She would *know*. That the grand prior was sitting right *there,* a vulture in black robes, malice wafting from her like perfume, did nothing to help my burgeoning courage. Balian Mataro sat watching me, head no longer propped on his fist. His black eyes glittered like beetles, like the black stone of Calagah, and his lips were pressed shut. My patron. My sponsor. My jailer. A mad smile threatened to steal its way onto my face, and I drowned it. *Joy is a wind.* With every word I dug myself into more danger with the Chantry, but it wasn't the Chantry I was playing for. Thinking of Anaïs, of the marriage pact that hung informal between us, I thought, *Let's see you keep your claws in me, you bastard.*

"Spies?" I said. "I'm not sure how that would be possible, sir." From the quartered shield plaque on the breast of his black uniform, I knew the man was a knight, though his name was a mystery to me. I leaned forward, addressing myself wholly to Knight-Tribune Smythe. "But if you were to allow me time with the captives—with their captain especially—I'm sure I could get something more out of them." There was more I could have added. I could have mentioned the Cielcin's association with the Quiet, only that it would have meant something only to Ligeia Vas, who for all I knew might torture *me* for my trouble.

"Something *more*?" The first officer sneered, turning with incredulous rage to his younger superior. "Raine, this boy can't be serious."

"Let me try! Hold local space for . . . a week. Blockade the planet if it helps you relax. Give me a chance. Their captain will speak to me, I'm sure of it. I'm sure I can—"

"Enough, Marlowe." The count did not shout. He did not even raise his voice. He was just like Father. Exactly like Father. He just . . . said it. Shook his head. In his high-backed seat raised above the level of his guests and councilors, Balian Mataro shifted, squaring his bull shoulders. "I concur with the knight-tribune and Grand Prior Vas. The enemy shall be questioned. I'll hear no more about this."

Exactly like Father. I opened my mouth to respond,

eyes fixed on the tribune and officer, both in uniforms black as funeral shrouds. I had to convince them, to prove I could be of use. If I could persuade them to take me, they could recruit me right out from under Balian Mataro's nose. I glowered at the man. "Your Excellency . . ." I stood, bowing low over the dappled jade pink of the table surface. "Forgive me. I have pressed overmuch. I apologize." The tip of my long nose scraped the surface of the table, and I jerked my chin up and looked at the dais. Briefly I considered making a farce of the whole thing: throwing myself on the floor, beating my breast, and begging forgiveness. It wouldn't have helped, but the mockery would have made me feel better.

Must everything you say sound like it's straight out of a Eudoran melodrama?

Yes, Gibson, I thought. *It does.*

"Take your seat, Lord Marlowe. We are not done with you yet."

I retook my seat, eyes downcast. Something in the way the count spoke those words twisted knives in my belly, but in my distraction I did not reflect on their meaning overlong. I was hearing Gibson's old lessons again. *Obedience out of loyalty to the office of the hierarch.* True enough—my obedience certainly wasn't out of love for his person. Not that I hated the count, for he was at his foundations a decent man. Rather I resented what I was to him. I felt as I imagined a particularly adroit princess might have felt in one of Mother's fantasies of Old Earth: not only lowered to the level of a breeding animal but dismissed as a person, as an intellect.

Knight-Tribune Smythe resumed control of the conversation as if there had been no interruption. "I propose this: the bulk of the prisoners will be kept in the bastille and treated gently. Meanwhile we will isolate the captain and give him to the Chantry for interrogation. Agreed?" A murmur went around the table, and she continued, "We are agreed, then. The"—she looked at me—"*ichakta* will be given over to the Chantry for interrogation. The Jaddians will sit in, as they are party to this affair already and all intelligence is to be shared between our parties."

With the sweep of a hand she took in Lord Balian, Lady Kalima, and herself.

Behind my eyes every degradation of the body and spirit practiced by the cathars of the Chantry ran like video reels played at a hundred times natural speed. The cutting and burning, broken bones and peeled skin, foreheads branded, noses slit, the disembowelments, decapitations, and rapes. The screams I imagined echoing out of Vesperad, out of steel-walled prison cells, blossomed and withered and blossomed again like flowers season after season. And these men and women sat in sunlight and in warmth, not smiling but still contented as Ligeia outlined the next phase in the operation.

And I was made a liar. I had promised the Cielcin they would not be harmed, had given my word as palatine. By the Great Charter, my word was a kind of law, and they were asking me to break it. More than that, it was a personal blow, an affront to my sense of self, to who I was on this new world of mine: Marlowe again, but not of Meidua.

". . . must be present, of course. We'll need a translator."

Translator. The word—its special associations, its affinity with myself—stuck out of the morass of failure that remained of that meeting. Translator. And then it hit me, sunk in like an arrow shaft, like a blade. "No!" I almost stood again. "No, I won't!"

Ligeia Vas was smiling. It was a moral victory for her, if not one ending in my death. "You have no choice. As you say, it seems there is none better suited to the task."

"No!" I did stand then, startling the two logothetes I sat between. I turned wild eyes on Raine. "You mean to tell me you don't have a translator on that ship of yours?" The *Obdurate*, up in orbit, was a supercarrier containing dozens of smaller frigates, thousands of crew. "Not one?"

"Not many scholiasts aboard Legion vessels, lad," Sir William Crossflane replied.

Desperate, I turned to Lord Balian. "Your Excellency, please. You must forbid this."

"You wanted to talk to the demons, boy," the prior said, answering for the lord she nominally served. Her

white face glowed the same hue as my family's funeral masks, and those blue eyes might have been violet but for a trick of the light. They glittered, and then they were only the blue of Gilliam's eye, sightless, staring, fixed beyond sight. "Talk to them."

CHAPTER 72

PALE BLOOD

THE PLACE GLEAMED LIKE a surgical theater, which I supposed it was. The interview chambers beneath the Terran Chantry's bastille—a surprisingly unassuming brutalist structure at the base of the ziggurat atop which Castle Borosevo perched—were all built to the same model, like stainless steel balloons inflated inside cubes. The walls and floor and ceiling of the room we occupied all blurred, melting into one another, and glow panels were fixed to the ceiling, colder than space. There were no shadows in that awful place.

Uvanari's back was toward me as I entered, led by a white-robed Inquisitor and two black-robed cathars, bald and blindfolded. It recalled for me an icon of the pagan god Andreas, its legs and arms spread in an X. Though it was turned away from me, I saw the white blur of its reflection in the brushed metal wall of the cell, so I knew that it was naked. Per the inquisitor's instructions, I stayed out of sight, waiting in a corner beside a rolling cart laden with surgical implements and glistening pale tubing. My breath frosted the air, and frost crunched beneath my feet. I felt the weight of eyes: the human watchers, the same ashen-hearted little men who had ordered this inquest. Ligeia would be there, and Ogir. And Smythe.

Smythe. I had thought better of the one-time plebeian officer.

The cathars busied themselves attaching sensor tape to the xenobite's body in different places, and then one came for the cart beside me, wheeled it around the cross

Uvanari clung to so the creature could see it. A thin, high wail escaped the Cielcin, bringing a smile to the inquisitor's flat, native face. She thought them signs of pain and fear, those expressions which colored my own face.

Uvanari was laughing. *"Qisaba!"* it swore, stopping the piercing sound, the words of its language a guttural contrast to the grating height of that inhuman laughter. "Why did you bother healing me?" It grew quiet, tried to crane its neck to look round, but it couldn't see me. But it must have known someone was there from the blur of color reflected on the metal wall, if nothing else. What it said next cut through me: *"Raka Marlowe saem ne?"* Where is Marlowe? "I was promised sanctuary."

The inquisitor looked at me to translate. She had not picked my name out of the string of alien words. I realized I was holding my breath, "It asked why you healed it just to hurt it again." I did not bother with the part about sanctuary. What was the point?

"Marlowe!" Uvanari turned its head, trying to see me. *"Bakkute!* You said! You promised!" Its earlier amusement with the situation was gone. It had an enemy: me.

To the inquisitor I said, "It asks for me." Then in Cielcin I added, *"Asvatatayu koarin o-variidu, Uvanari-se."* I wasn't given a choice.

"You will not speak to the prisoner unless translating!" the inquisitor snapped, stepping backward off the grating in the floor that waited, hungry, beneath the cross. She slipped a recording nodule from her wrist terminal and held it to thick lips. "Sixteen one seventy-two zero two thirteen. Inquisitor K. F. Agari presiding. Subject is the Cielcin xenobite named Uvanari in the Calagah report. Brothers Rhom and Udan assisting with lay translator." Her black eyes narrowed, face turning down as she made a note on a holograph image that sprouted from her wrist. "You are the captain of the ship shot down on this world?"

The interview began in this vein: cool, detached, clinical almost as the room itself. I was only an interface, a substitute for the translator devices it is said the Tavrosi, the Normans, and the Extras take for granted. Indeed I tried to be less than myself, to put myself away from that

terrible place. *Just go away inside*, I told myself. Not a
scholiast's aphorism, only the scrambling thought of a
young man in too deep and far from home.

"I am Itana Uvanari Ayatomn, Ichakta of the ship *Yad
Ga Higatte*." From the flat tone of the creature's voice, I
knew this was the Cielcin equivalent of confining itself to
name, rank, and serial number. My heart grew leaden in
expectation of the blood that was to come.

Inquisitor Agari accepted this translation with a nod.
"Why have you come to Emesh?"

I translated this, swapping *Emesh* for *this world*, know-
ing the proper place name was meaningless to the Cielcin.
To my horror, Uvanari only repeated, "I am Itana Uvanari
Ayatomn, Ichakta of the ship *Yad Ga Higatte*."

Whatever the inquisitor might have been, she was not
so stupid that she failed to recognize the repetition. At a
gesture, one of the two cathars approached, circled round
behind the Cielcin, and worked a mechanism on the back
of the cross that swiveled one arm down within easier
reach of the humans. The arm still restrained, the cathar—
without speaking, entirely without hesitation—removed
one glassy claw from the end of Uvanari's first finger. It
made a dry cracking sound as it snapped, thicker than
human nails. And yet the principle was the same, and the
xenobite bit back a cry as blood welled up, blacker than
the cathars' robes, and dripped onto the grate below the
cross.

"Tell him he has eleven more."

Instead I said, "I'm so sorry. I tried to stop this, but . . ."
What more could I say? I stopped, tried to find somewhere else to look, found only our dull reflections in the
brushed metal walls. I imagined doing this over and over,
with each of our prisoners, until each creature collapsed
into fury, then madness, then death, bled and cut away
until nothing remained. The ancients used to believe
there was no science in torture, nothing to be gained. I
will not say they were wrong, and yet the Chantry's power
in torture was never that it found the truth, even when it
did. Rather it was that it taught the great to fear, even the
Emperor. It was teaching the Cielcin then.

Just go away inside. I prayed to no one and to nothing. But then I froze, stalled a moment, realizing I had not translated Agari's last statement. I had not threatened Uvanari but apologized, and no one had noticed. *No one had noticed.* I could say whatever I wanted, could take my own path—such as it was—to answers. I only had to be careful.

"Why have you come to Emesh?"

"I am Itana Uvanari Ayatomn, Ichakta of the ship *Yad Ga Higatte.*"

"Why have you come to Emesh?"

"I am Itana Uvanari Ayatomn, Ichakta . . ."

"Why have you come to Emesh?"

"Why have you come . . . ?"

"Why have you come . . . ?"

They took seven of Uvanari's claws from its hands before it answered, before it gave a single word. *"Balatiri! Civaqatto balatiri!" We came to pray.*

I swore, eliciting raised eyebrows from Inquisitor Agari, and said, "It said they came to pray." The torn-off talons sat in a steel bucket on the cart. Beneath the frosty chill of the room I could smell the fetid metallic stink of blood.

Her follow-up question drowned under more words from the *ichakta.* Uvanari's deep voice cracked with pain, but it was lucid. "Your people were not supposed to be on this world. We jumped in blind. We did not know."

"Did not *know*?" the inquisitor repeated when I finished translating, and at a gesture from her, one of the cathars prodded Uvanari with a shock-stick. The current ran through the creature, and its flesh strained against the leather restraints as it bucked. "How could you not know?" She made a slashing gesture when I automatically began to repeat her. I fell silent, watched the inquisitor as she brooded on this, tapping her way through prompts on her wrist terminal. A flow chart. She had her questions on an Earth-blasting *flow chart.* The awful mundanity of that fact took me like a physical blow. This wasn't even religion. This was business.

The inquisitor took a moment, then asked me in Galstani, "The Cielcin have religion?"

"I don't know much about it," I said, wishing there were a god and that he might crush this little bubble of a room with me still inside it. "Their word for 'god' means . . . watcher? Teacher? That's all I know. I'm sorry."

She waved me into silence. I could see the connections forming in her hunter's mind. The Cielcin. The ruins. The Quiet—did she know about the Quiet hypothesis? She saw xenobites coming to a world with other xenobites. Coloni. She would make the connection, rightly or not. The Umandh would burn for this, doubtless seen by Chantry zeal and human supremacists as somehow complicit in the Cielcin war against mankind. Another pogrom, another march of the faithful.

"Are there more of you coming?"

Blood dripped from seven of twelve fingers, black as oil. Uvanari rolled its head counterclockwise. "No."

Unable to speak, I shook my head, and the inquisitor raised a hand. Instead of peeling the eighth claw from its fingertip, the cathars removed one mutilated fingertip, severed it at the joint. The second cathar placed the amputated little stump in the steel bucket on a bench against the back wall of the room alongside a deep-bellied washbasin. They did it without malice, without pomp or melodrama, just broke the fingertip off with a push knife and a light tap. I almost expected the glassy bones in the hand to crunch, for Uvanari to shatter like a sculpture. It only screamed. "What did you do that for?" I shrieked, "It answered you!"

"Too easily," the inquisitor replied. She looked up at one of the cameras as if she were a prophet and it her god, as if answers would come pouring from it. In that pose she waited out Uvanari's screams.

When Uvanari's wailing had quietened, I said to it, "I'm sorry. I didn't know."

It glared at me, glassy teeth biting down on one lip, cheeks heaving, four nostrils flared. But it did not speak, would not.

"No speaking to the prisoner, translator!" the inquisitor snapped. I glared her down; in my present state, I was too far past caring to concern myself with the fact that

this was a Chantry inquisitor, that even though I was palatine I ought to fear her. The facts of the moment had
crushed all caring out of me. But for a quirk of fate, but
for my mother, it might be me in inquisitorial white, head
shaven, asking these questions. I confess it was this
thought and not compassion for the bleeding xenobite
that consumed me. I experienced a moment of curious
double vision, seeing myself in the inquisitor and again in
the tunnel at Calagah, a stunner pressed to the head of
that other Cielcin.

Inquisitor Agari rephrased her question. "When does
the next invasion fleet arrive?"

I translated it as fast as I could and added, "I believe
you, but you have to give them something." One day the
recording of this exchange would be reviewed by Legion
military analysts, perhaps, or by anagnosts of the Chantry, or by the logothetes of the Emperor's own court. A
translation would be made, and my addition would be
discovered. But for the moment I could get away with it.

Uvanari was still breathing hard, and it leaned forward,
sagging against its restraints, its ruined arms akimbo.
"Asvatoyu de ti-okarin, hih siajeu leiude."

"It says it can't tell us what it doesn't know," I translated, then half turned away. Away from the inquisitor,
away from Uvanari and the cross, away from all of it. The
woman twitched in the corner of my eye, but I stepped
toward her. "A moment, please! Give it a moment! Let me
try." I waited, and when the inquisitor nodded her consent I turned to Uvanari and spoke in hoarse tones. "You
weren't an invasion fleet, then. You said you came here to
pray? What do you mean, here to pray? In the ruins?" I
could feel the inquisitor's eyes boring into the back of my
head and waited for her to change her mind, to object, but
this time she held her peace.

At last Uvanari managed to say, "You have seen the
ruins." Its chest rose and fell, sweat beading on its forehead beneath the bony fringe, runneling down the fine,
scale-like lumps of skin where horn transitioned to white
smoothness. I nodded, then realized my mistake and

instead rolled my head in imitation of the creature's own affirmative gesture. Seeing this, the creature bared its glass-scalpel teeth in the snarl I was starting to realize was a smile.

"You worship the . . . the ones who made that place?" I didn't know the word for "builders" and so had to improvise. Funny how that of all things should stick in my memory, that little failing. When the inquisitor made a noise, I turned to her and in Galstani said, "Inquisitor, please." Uvanari tipped its head to the right, a curt Cielcin affirmative. It winced, then sagged back against its restraints. There was no headrest, so its crown sagged between the spars that held its arms akimbo. "Ichakta, please," I said. "There's nothing they've done so far that cannot be reversed. Tell me, is this planet threatened?"

"*Veih!*" the captain spat. "No, it is not! We were here because *they* were here, not you. The gods. They built those caves, same as the ones they built on Se Vattayu." *On the Earth.*

It took me a second to work that little bit out—the word *vattayu* meant earth, ground, dirt. For a moment I imagined our Earth—the Homeworld-goddess of the Chantry—and had to shake off the idea.

"On your homeworld?" *Se Vattayu.* That was new information, at least to me. They called their homeworld the Earth too. I hadn't known that. The implications clicked into place a moment later. "You had such ruins on your homeworld?" Scholastic consensus was that the Cielcin were a subterranean people, a theory reinforced by the cavernous, unlit nature of their ships and by the trick I'd pulled with the suit lights in the tunnels of Calagah.

"What is he saying?" the inquisitor pressed.

I didn't want to tell her, for I felt certain that to do so was to threaten Elomas, to threaten all who worked on the Calagah dig site. To threaten Valka. I imagined those unlighted tunnels melted to slag, atomic charges transforming the delicate arches and non-Euclidean parallels to cinders. "There won't be another attack, Inquisitor."

"That's it?"

"That's it," I lied.

"You can't be serious," she sneered, broad nose wrinkling. She stepped forward, seized the shock-stick from one of the silent cathars, and jammed it into Uvanari's ribs. She held it there, an animal glee in her eyes that sickened me. What had they done to her on Komadd, or wherever she'd been indoctrinated? How had they made such a woman? Or had she always been broken? "What are you planning, *inmane*? Another invasion?" She pulled back, then slapped the heavy stick across Uvanari's face. It grunted but held itself still. "Is it the people you want?" One of the cathars hurried forward, gloved hands on the creature's face, checking for unplanned injuries. This intervention of her subordinates got through to Agari, and she staggered back. I hadn't translated anything, and she hadn't noticed.

I glanced up at the ceiling, wishing that some voice—Olorin's or the chancellor's, maybe—would sound from the speakers and call an end to the horrible experience. Yet the horizons of reality were bounded by the steel bubble of that cell, and it was hard to imagine that anyone was out there to interfere.

The cathar checked for concussion, for broken bones in the face, for shattered teeth. Then he screamed and fell backward into the arms of his brother, cradling one of his hands. For a moment I did not see the blood against the darker-than-black of their robes, but the wet glint was unmistakable, and the red that dribbled down Uvanari's chin was not the black of Pale blood. For a horrible instant I saw the stubs of two human fingers poking out from between the captain's lips. Then they vanished, crunched between Uvanari's teeth, and were gone. *Oh,* Crispin's voice sounded in my memory, *so they aren't all cannibals?* Suddenly the technical distinction between what was and was not cannibalism did not matter. I staggered back, unable to master the thrashing horror in my gut.

The second cathar stopped the inquisitor from exacting retribution with an upraised hand—they were forbidden to speak during the rite of inquest by ancient custom. Horrified as I was, I could not help but admire the

Cielcin's spirit, its refusal to be cowed. I liked to imagine that I might show such spirit, were our positions reversed. I would have spit out the fingers, but I wasn't Cielcin.

While the inquisitor busied herself helping the wounded cathar, I said, *"Biqathebe ti-okarin qu ti-oyumm." They will hurt you for that.*

"Let them." Uvanari could not wipe the blood from its chin, and it dripped carmine onto its chest. Its blue-black tongue slithered out, smeared the blood on its lips. "You humans are all the same, always the same."

At the time it did not strike me how curious a pronouncement this was, and I said, "I'm sorry." I could not look Uvanari in the eye. The muscles beneath the waxen flesh pulled it into shapes and feelings strange to me. In a way they were stranger than the Umandh, though they walked and talked like men; the minds behind those eyes were the minds of persons incomprehensible. What I interpreted as bravery or stubbornness may have been no such thing. Seeing that—seeing them—I reasoned that perhaps the Chantry was onto something.

Perhaps all we shared was pain.

The creature spat at my feet. There was no malice in the gesture, as if it were no particular insult amongst the Cielcin. There was blood, though, blue-black in the sputum. I stepped back, rattled into the cart, and froze.

"What are you doing?" the inquisitor demanded, rounding back on me as the steel door sealed with a pneumatic whir. "What did it say?"

"Brave talk," I said, cocking my head to one side. "I told it that it shouldn't have done that."

The inquisitor straightened, dots and streaks of red marring her otherwise immaculate robes. "He shouldn't have."

"I think it's telling the truth, though," I said, taking a fractional step to place myself between the cross and the inquisitor, hoping that might quiet her rage. "I don't think there's another fleet coming. Question the others." The gravity of what I was saying hit me, and I backpedaled. "*Just* question them. They're not . . . They'll tell you. Isolate them. Get them to talk. Either they tell you different things and they're lying, or they all say the same and you

know we have the truth. That's standard procedure, is it not?"

The inquisitor took the shock-stick from the cart, hefted it, ready to resume her work, and echoed the horrible words Ligeia Vas had once said to me. "You would make a good priest." The blood in me thickened to poison at the words, and I turned away, hiding my eyes. Uvanari howled as the current ran through its body. The sound collapsed into a high-pitched, nasal whine as it forced air through the slits that passed for a nose. She hadn't even asked a question. She did it again, and only after she had made the creature scream a fourth time did she say, "Ask it who it serves. Ask it where its people are right now."

CHAPTER 73

TEN THOUSAND EYES

IN THE ENSUING WEEKS I was witness to dozens of separate interrogations. To my relief, all of them were simply that: interrogations. Uvanari was kept in a private cell, isolated as Makisomn had been in a place just above sea level at the base of the Chantry bastille. The others were similarly isolated, kept from one another to grow truth from lies in separate gardens. Those whose stories diverged from that of the majority were noted, watched, compared against the others and against the tortured Uvanari. I was present for each session. Lord Mataro would not see me, nor Lady Kalima, nor Knight-Tribune Smythe.

From all this, we concluded surprisingly little. Tanaran, who it seemed was some sort of clerk or minor logothete equivalent, spoke the determined truth the entire time, and from it and those that corroborated its narrative we discovered that I had been correct to trust Uvanari's word. The Cielcin were not attacking Emesh, or else had not attacked it. The orbital forensics groups under the joint direction of House Mataro and the 437th Legion corroborated this revelation, to even zealous Agari's satisfaction. Theirs was not an invading force. It barely counted as military.

However I suffered for all this, no one seemed to care.

I sat alone in the suite appointed me, the same one I had occupied before my flight to Calagah. The count had appointed a pair of hoplites to stand watch in the hall. I suspected they were there as much to police me as protect me, but I offered no complaint, nor did I try to leave my

chambers except when the Chantry sent for me. Anaïs visited and left messages on the room's comm console. Sometimes she brought her brother along, hoping to persuade me into some game or idle distraction. I did all I could to keep my distance, and to my surprise the girl seemed to get the message. More than that, she seemed to understand. Perhaps I was too cruel. They meant well, she and Dorian.

And so I was not surprised when a knock sounded on my door on the fifteenth day of interrogations. Whoever it was had been cleared by the guards, and so I opened it without hesitation. "What is it? What do you—" I shut up.

Valka Onderra stood in the doorway. She had cut her hair, removed the topknot she'd favored and cropped the sides and back short, leaving stray threads of black hanging about and across her face, obscuring one eye. The red in it glowed as she stood there, one hand drumming on the Umandh comms pad clipped to one broad hip. Conscious suddenly of the darkness of my chamber, I waved a hand over the sensor pad, keying up the room's illumination and casting the dark accents and darker oil paintings of space into relief.

"Valka!" I said, trying to sound bright. "I didn't know you were back."

She smiled, a sad little thing—she must have heard what was happening—but she didn't seem angry. "Just this afternoon." I half expected her to hit me. She did not hit me. "Home Defense Force closed Calagah for the season, wouldn't let us out of Springdeep until yesterday."

"And Elomas?"

"Trying to negotiate with the HDF to let him return to clean out the campsite. I think he left his wine."

"Not the wine!" I did my best to affect an imitation of horror, but my heart wasn't in it. Stepping aside, I waved a hand. "Would you . . . Would you like to come in?"

The Tavrosi doctor stood in the doorway surveying me, one hand still feeling the comms tablet. I was glad to see that she was allowed to continue carrying one in Borosevo even after the events that day in the fishery packing house. A part of me—a small and stupid part—needed to claim

some of the credit for that tiny victory, and I brightened to see it there. I know now that it had nothing at all to do with me. I only wished to believe that I had helped in light of everything else.

At last she spoke. "You look awful."

I was sure I did. I had seen my face in the looking glass in the bathroom not ten minutes earlier. My face, always severe and angled, had acquired a waxen, sunken quality. My violet eyes were hooded and bruised; my ink-dark hair, once neatly combed, fell in a curling tangle past the point of my chin. I probably smelled bad. The time I'd spent homeless in the canals below the castle ziggurat had broken my autonomic need to shower, and after what I had seen . . . well, I'd been forgetting to eat, much less do anything else.

But Valka came inside without further comment, permitting me to shut the door. Aware of the cameras, I slumped into an armchair near the holograph plate and the low coffee table. The doctor surveyed the room, taking in the casual disarray of it, the drawing supplies scattered on the low table, the rumpled jacket flung over a chair, the empty wine glasses and half-filled water cups on shelves and counters and tables. She crossed to the window and pulled the paisley blinds, admitting the burgundy sunlight with a snap. "You should clean up." She stood framed by the window, darkly feminine against the glass and the city below. I sighed.

"Servants will do it," I said, but I began plucking the pencils from the table and from the broad open face of my journal, the exposed page depicting the image of an alien hand: six fingered, clawed, each finger with an extra joint, each joint too long to be human. Only three of the six fingers had claws, and one had been shortened to the knuckle. The skin at the wrist was flayed in a band two inches wide, the muscle exposed. At a glance it looked like a work out of some antique but fanciful anatomy text. It might have passed for just that were it not for the pain. Pain was always easy to portray, easier to feel.

"When was the last time you went outside?" Valka asked, then repeated, "You look awful."

"There hasn't been time!" The words came out harder than I'd intended, brittle and glassy. "I've been . . . I don't want to talk about where I've been."

Valka seated herself on the arm of the sofa opposite me, side-lit by the window. Her lovely face shone in sharp relief, both golden eyes shining, though one was in darkness. The music in her voice broke. "I . . . I've heard. Anaïs told me."

"You've seen her?" I cradled my head in my hands, looked down at the thick carpet, a mandala-patterned thing in black and white done in imitation of the Tavrosi fashion popular in the Veil and the colony worlds. I tried not to think about Anaïs, about what she was.

"She's worried about you. Says the Chantry has been forcing you to translate while they *question* the Cielcin." I bobbed my head, looked around for an abandoned glass that might still hold some wine. None was visible. "But she also says you're the reason they were all brought in alive. She said you're a hero."

The wry amusement Valka forced into her words was more than my exhausted, scream-addled mind could handle. "She doesn't know what she's talking about. She thinks it's all some grand adventure, Valka. It isn't." My voice rose with each staccato pronouncement, and my fingers curled into claws. I was nearly shouting by the end, eyes blazing.

The woman swore in her native language, then hissed, "Imperials." Her favorite curse. Somehow her scorn was comforting; the knowledge that someone else in the universe shared my present fury helped, like light reaching for light across the dark material of civilization. "Can't they use an autotrans like the rest of the civilized universe?" She shoved her hair back past her ears. I'd wanted to do that.

"A what? Oh." A machine intelligence, one of the slave devices the Tavrosi saw as commonplace and the Chantry saw as sinful. "You know they can't."

Her strange eyes blazed. After a moment of companionable silence, she asked, "What are they like?"

"The Cielcin?" I looked away, out the window and

over the red roofs and the metal ones to the vast swath of the landing field, trying again to find the place in the labyrinth where another, younger Hadrian had been dumped naked to die. I had never gone back, never repaid the debt I owed the old crone in the hospital flophouse, never revenged myself on the dock workers who had robbed me. I'd never figured out what happened to Demetri and his crew, either. How had it all turned out this way? Earth and God and Emperor, I should have been on Teukros, at Nov Senber. I should have been Tor Hadrian by then—should be Tor Hadrian now, dressed all in green. But there are other powers that move our world, powers greater than man. Powers that, like time and tide, wait for none. Even Emperors, like starlight, bend to the blackest forces of natural law. I waited for the space of several breaths before saying, "They're . . . They're like us, but not so much as I first believed."

I told her everything then: about the descent into the tunnels, about the standoff at the Quiet's sepulcher, about Uvanari and Tanaran. I omitted my own messy role in the interrogation of the Cielcin in the tunnels. It is easy to say only that I did not want Valka's recovering opinion of me overturned, but the truth was that I didn't think I could share that particular episode then and there. The thought made me sick.

"We're safe, though." I rubbed my eyes with my knuckles, pressed myself back into the cushions of my armchair. "At least I think we are. It doesn't seem as if the Cielcin were an invasion force. Even the Chantry has started to believe that." I smiled my weakest smile.

Valka leaned in a little, eyes intent. "And they haven't tried to . . ." She made a slashing gesture across her own throat.

"Kill me? No, no. They need me right now." I stood up, gathered a few of the stray glasses from counters between my chair and the little kitchen area in one corner. I filled one with water from the filter unit, drained it, filled it again. "Do you want some? I may be out of wine." Valka declined with a raised hand, and I leaned heavily against the granite counter. "I'm trying to convince the knight-tribune to use

the captives as leverage, to open peace talks with the Cielcin, but no one will listen. The count won't even attend council meetings. I think he just wants it all to be over."

And I think the Cielcin worship the Quiet, I wanted to blurt out, but leaden exhaustion and the sick, scalp-prickling sensation of being watched that had vanished while I stayed at Calagah crawled over my skin. I eyed the most obvious camera in the room, a tiny black lens embedded in the room's lighting and climate control panel. One of ten thousand eyes, I did not doubt, networked and feeding information into house security's monitoring station that was cataloged, if not actively reviewed by voyeuristic police.

"Can you blame him?" Valka asked, ringed fingers tracing the black lines on the back of her exposed left forearm.

"Gods, no!" I spun the cup like a humming top, the weighty glass rattling. I closed my hand around it to stop it spinning out of control. "But we need to be better, not *anaryoch*."

She sniffed, but there was laughter in the sharp lines of her face. "Your pronunciation . . . 'Tis terrible, you know."

"I'm sure it is." I spun the glass again. What I was saying was probably safe enough, but the vast number of things I wanted to say and couldn't was making me nervous. "I wish I could tell you more, Valka. I really do." One never knew who was listening. Officially the recordings were exclusively for castle security, but he was a fool who thought the Chantry couldn't gain access through one channel or another.

Valka hung her head, a little too crestfallen. "I understand. Imperial business." To anyone who knew her, this sudden hangdog surrender was like a slap. I nearly let my cup fall again, but I caught it at the last second, still surprised. Briefly her jaw stiffened, muscles in her temples flexed, and her eyes drifted closed. And then the lights flickered and faded, leaving us in darkness. Another of the castle's frequent brownouts. I despaired, fearing the climate control would break down and leave us sweating in the dark.

She looked up, eyebrow arched, all Valka again. "I forget those stupid things are there."

"What?"

"The cameras. 'Twill be a few minutes before they get them back online."

The cameras. "Ah." It took a moment for what she'd said to fully process. Then I realized, remembered, and my eyes went wide. Ten thousand eyes had closed; we were alone. "How did you . . . ?" My eyes flicked to the room's control panel. The tiny red light beside the camera was gone. "Are you sure?"

"Completely." She tapped her temple. "What shall we talk about? Murder? Treason?" I felt the blood drain out of my face, lurched to my feet. Valka laughed, actually laughed, pointing at me. "Oh, your face!" She wiped her eye with a finger, tapped her temple again. "I'm saving that one, Marlowe."

I wasn't laughing. My words escaped through my teeth. "Are you insane?"

"You're the one acting crazy." She smiled her most cutting smile. "No one heard me."

I was slow to sit back down, certain that at any moment the guards outside would blast the wooden doors inward with a riot cannon, guns blazing. When nothing happened, I said, "But how?" I looked at the dead lights on my room's environmental control panel. "The brownouts? It's you?"

For the third time she tapped her temple. "Neural lace." She'd used the phrase before in our first meeting.

"I don't know what that means."

She hissed something incomprehensible in her native tongue, then said, "I keep forgetting. Here." Valka turned away, long fingers feeling the back of her scalp, parting the red-black hair. "Feel just here."

"What? I—"

"Just do it." I did, pressing my fingers against the base of her skull. There was something there, a lump no wider than a pea. Through the strands of hair, I could just make out the gleam of something white as porcelain against her pale skin. I wasn't sure what it was, wasn't sure what to say, so I stood in confused silence, my hand still in her hair. "In Tavros," she said, "we all get these as children,

if our parent has the social credit. You can take your hand out of my hair now."

I withdrew my hand as if shocked. "Yes. Sorry," I stammered, turning away. "But what . . . is it?" Even as I asked, fragments of my cultural heritage whispered in my ear. *Demoniac. Witch. Sorceress.* It was a machine, of that I'd no doubt. The perversion of the body with machines. She had committed one of the Twelve Abominations, one of the arch-sins for which the Chantry would execute anyone, *anyone*, without trial or second thought. I recoiled inwardly, feeling a compulsive religious need to cleanse myself. But I knew one thing—Valka was not kidding about the cameras being dead. How she had done it I could not say, but she would not have revealed such a thing without the utmost certainty that she was safe. *I'm afraid*, I told myself. *Afraid of Valka.*

But fear was a poison, and whatever I was, I was better than that. "You can just"—I waved a hand—"do it?"

Her laughing demeanor collapsed like a wave. "There's no *just* about it." She pulled a face. "'Tis expensive." She crossed her legs, the fading ripples of her smile ebbing from the cream of her face. "It has its advantages, however."

With the same fascination the sheltered student shows for the macabre, I leaned forward. "Like what?"

Those golden eyes blazed. "Not now. You were saying?"

"Hmm?" I was a shadow of my best self, pressed flat and spread at distorted angles across the universe of truer things, distorted by the relativistic gravity of events. "Oh! The Quiet." What I had discovered had been more or less entirely stamped from my mind, washed out by the woman's diabolic display of power. I told her everything then. I repeated Uvanari's confession that the Cielcin expedition had come to Emesh not for war but to pray in the chambers at Calagah. That was why they had steered their damaged ship for the ruins, of all the places on the vast globe—so that they might die in the halls of their dead gods.

"Why didn't they turn around when their scout ship was attacked?" Valka asked, straightening her earthen vest.

"I think they were looking for something," I said. *"They*

are not here." Valka's brows rose, and I repeated the
ichakta's words in its native tongue. "'*Rakasuryu ti-saem gi.*'
That's what it said. They could be looking for anything. The
Cielcin have a culture based on plunder. That's why they're
fighting us: for resources. Before we came along they had to
parasitize their own fleets. It makes sense that they'd carry
off any Quiet technology they could find."

She shook her head. "What Quiet technology? You've
seen Calagah, Hadrian. 'Tis just stone."

"Maybe on Emesh! But that can't be true of all the
ruins in this part of the galaxy." I did not bring up my
vision. I would not talk about it. Not again.

"I've been to Sadal Suud, to Rubicon. There's nothing.
We don't even know how developed they were. They've
left nothing."

Mania wrestled with the flattened shadow of depres-
sion, and I sat up straighter, pushed my long hair from my
face. "Nothing we understand, but the Cielcin . . . Valka,
the Cielcin evolved surrounded by all this. They must
know something we don't."

She was quiet a long moment, beautiful face downturned. At last she nodded. "All right, what do you—" A
knock sounded at the door. I froze. Valka froze, and then
her eyes slowly widened. "Are you expecting anyone?"

All I could do was shake my head. I had to swallow
once, twice before I could find my words again. "Are you
sure you stopped the cameras with your . . . whatever it
is?" She looked hurt, but I didn't waste time on egos.
"You'd best . . ." I tapped the back of my head to indicate
the demon machine crouched at the base of her skull.
"We'll talk later."

"We'd better."

As with Valka, I knew whoever it was at the door must
have been vetted by the two Mataro hoplites standing like
display armor in the hall, and so I opened the door without fear. "Sir Olorin!" I had trouble banishing the surprise from my voice. "To what do I owe the honor?"

"No honor!" the man said with a jovial wave, shaking
a dark bottle at me. "Pleasure! I was told I might find you

here, that I had only to be looking for the guards." He smiled an absurdly toothy smile at the two masked and helmeted hoplites at attention on either side of my door, pointed cruciforms painted over the convex planes of their faces, doubtless hiding a profusion of sensor equipment. The Maeskolos still wore his customary blacks, but they were silk and not leather. He had discarded the flowing crimson mandyas as well, and the shirt he wore hung open to the breastbone, displaying a plane of bronze chest and a square-cut gold medallion that reminded me of the one Demetri had worn, this one stamped with a single unbroken circle. I wondered at that a moment, doubtless appearing either tired or a fool. Or a tired fool.

At last the other man said, "May I come in?"

I blinked. "I . . ." I stepped aside, one slippered foot nearly tripping over the other. "Yes, yes, of course. Please." He passed over the threshold, and I latched the door after shooting an unreturned smile at my guards. Mindful of the swordmaster's declaration, I tried again. "To what do I owe the . . . pleasure, then?"

Sir Olorin Milta pivoted smartly on his heel, knee-high boots squeaking on the hardwood, three sword hilts swinging freely, knocking into one another like wind chimes. "I've come to be understanding that the last few weeks have been . . . somewhat . . . trying. I thought you could use a drink."

My politician's reflexes, native-born in me and sharpened somewhat since my time in Borosevo began, activated my fight-or-flight response, and the question began ringing like a klaxon in my ears: *What does he want? What does he want? What does he want?* But I smiled. "Even if the times weren't trying, I could hardly refuse. But may I introduce my . . ." My what? My friend? My colleague? My muse? Valka had not stirred from the couch, unaware of or unmoved by the swordmaster's lofty station. That surprised me—I may have been a stuffy Imperial palatine, but the Maeskoloi were the stuff of legend, even in Valka's distant, ensorcelled home. "My . . . This is Valka Onderra, *Doctor* Valka Onderra, of Clan Onderra Vhad Edda."

"Xenologist," Valka added, her accent suddenly thickening as she rose and offered her hand to the effete Jaddian swordsman. There was a look in her eyes not unlike that of a gourmand faced with a particularly grand cut of meat. She offered a hand to shake, which the Jaddian took and—to my private relief—did not kiss.

Olorin smiled, all teeth again, so white I thought them synthetic. "Sir Olorin Milta. Lovely to be meeting you. I . . ." He looked round at me. "Is this a bad time, Marlowe?"

"Ah . . ." I hesitated on the verge of saying, *Yes, I'm afraid so.*

My eyes went to Valka, who was still examining the swordmaster, and she beat me to the punch. "Not at all. I should be going."

"Must you?" Olorin's eyes darted, weirdly, to me. He seemed to be mulling over some private thought, then refocused his attentions on the Tavrosi woman with deliberateness. "Please. My call is a social one. I've brought zvanya." He proffered the bottle of pale orange brandy for the lady's inspection. "Any friend of our friend the translator is a friend of mine."

Friend? I eyed the swordmaster warily, glad his attentions were elsewhere. *When did that happen?* To be sure, he hadn't argued against capturing the Cielcin as strongly as Lieutenant Lin had, but I wouldn't have named him as a friend.

"What is it?" Valka asked, stooping over the peeled foil label.

"Zvanya!" the swordmaster repeated, rubbing his thin lips and the fine stubble growing over the hard planes of his face—evidently the Jaddians did not lase their pores in puberty. "You have not had it?" Valka said she had not, prompting the man to uncork the liqueur on the spot. "*Tavmasie!* Then you must stay, please! Please!" At his request I found a trio of clean tumblers and waited while Olorin poured three drams of the rose-clear liquid.

I sniffed speculatively at my glass. "Gods, that's strong."

"It is strong as it needs be! *Buon atanta!*" Olorin said with gravity, then slammed the entire glass back.

One after the other, Valka and I imitated him. The

taste of raw cinnamon overpowered me, undercut with the flavors of strong wine and the barest trace of orange. All those notes were drowned, however, in a medicinal alcohol bite clean and bright as fire. My eyes watered. Valka coughed. Olorin laughed. *"Ehpa!"*

"Cheers," I said back. "But forgive me, Maeskolos—I don't mean to seem ungrateful, but . . . well, I'm rather surprised to see you here." Valka had hurried over to the small kitchen area, where she was filling her tumbler with water. The Jaddian liqueur had not agreed with her, it seemed.

Catlike, the swordmaster settled into the armchair I had occupied moments earlier, his large, dark eyes scanning over my open journal with an air of detached interest. "I'd been wanting a word. Since Calagah."

Valka cleared her throat. "You're sure you don't want me to go?" To my surprise she made a questioning gesture at the bottle of zvanya, prompting a polite wave from the swordmaster. "If you boys want to talk, I'd be happy to go elsewhere. I don't want to intrude."

"No!" I said too quickly, eliciting a sly smile from the Jaddian. "It's not an intrusion. I wasn't doing anything anyway." *And we aren't finished talking, Valka, remember?*

"Did you draw this, Lord Marlowe?" the swordmaster asked, changing the subject abruptly as he lifted my journal from the table.

I turned on the spot, looking over the swordmaster's shoulder at the image of the Cielcin's flayed wrist and broken fingers. Olorin lingered on the image a moment, his own fingers barely touching the charcoal-blackened claws. "I did. Am." I shook my head, trying to clear it. "It isn't finished."

He flipped back a page, revealing a concept sketch of a Jaddian mamluk leaning on a ceremonial glaive. I am no longer sure where I saw one with such a weapon, but the overlong bladed plasma spear made the spindle-legged homunculus appear even more like a marionette, knock-kneed and all elbows. He flipped back through the book quickly, passing a cloud of portraits—himself, Lady Kalima, Sir Elomas, Balian Mataro, Switch and Pallino. My mother. "These are remarkable. Quite . . ."

"Thank you," I said, moving forward, teetering between politeness and a desire to demand the book's return. I hovered just out of reach of the chair, as if my closeness could prompt the swordmaster to stop flipping. Somewhere in the journal, nearer to the middle, was a drawing of Valka, one I did not want shared. Nothing tasteless, you understand, but neither was it meant for anyone but me.

Olorin closed the journal with a resonant bang and set the volume back on the table. "Another drink?" Valka, who had vanished a second shot in the interim, brought the bottle round and passed it to the swordsman, who filled his glass and mine before passing it back to her. When this second round had vanished, he said, "I wanted to be the one to tell you; I did not want the Chantry to be surprising you." His voice fell to a whisper, and he closed long fingers around his newly emptied tumbler. "I've just come from a meeting. My lady and the count and your knight-tribune. They feel we've not made much headway in the past few days, and they want to try . . . something else."

"Something else? Have they not tried enough?" Then another question hit me, and I glanced briefly at Valka, who stood impassive by the high counter that separated the kitchen from my sitting room. "Just the nobiles and Tribune Smythe? Not Grand Prior Vas?"

"The Chantry *bruhir* was not present, no." Olorin slung one long leg over the arm of his chair and cracked his knuckles one at a time with a practiced calm. No, it wasn't that—it calmed him, each popped joint bleeding tension away as surely as a scholiast's aphorism. The man was marshaling himself, preparing to say the thing he'd obviously come down to my humble quarters to say. "They want you to speak to the captain. Alone."

"What?" I nearly dropped my glass, had to crouch in order to catch it. When I straightened, I asked, "Are you serious?" That was what I'd wanted from the start. Ye gods, the damned bureaucrats had gone and done everything backward.

The Maeskolos inclined his head, tangled black hair falling over his eyes. "I wanted to be the one to tell you."

A faint smile appeared on his olive face, flashed like lightning, and was gone. "As a friend. You'll get the call tomorrow." I signaled my understanding, still standing there gormlessly with the empty zvanya glass in my hand. All at once I found myself unequal to the task of speech. "They'll be monitoring your conversation, of course, but the creature won't be harmed."

Valka's eyes hung on me like chains, and I resisted the urge to turn to her. I wanted to scream, to sag onto the hardwood floor and beat my hands against it until the flesh peeled from the bones and I smashed those too to flinders. It wasn't over. I had not expected it to be over, but the desire was there, hot and remote in me. What I needed was to be home again, to be safe in my own bed beneath painted constellations in a tower by the sea, to walk with Gibson on the high wall in peace and quiet.

I had no words for Olorin, who said, "What you did in those tunnels. You did . . . *better*. You made us do better." It was my word, thrown back at me out of yesterdays. My word and my curse: *Better*. "You were right. I've never heard of the Cielcin surrendering before. You did that." He cast his gaze round at the disarray and clutter in my room, perhaps sensing the apathy and dysthymia it implied. There was no judgment in his face, no pity, as there was in Valka's. There was nothing, nothing at all. That should not have been a comfort, and yet it was. "You can refuse, of course."

The first words that came to mind had to be stamped down, ground out. Instead I snarled, "This isn't . . . I'm not playing good prefect, bad prefect!"

"What?" The Maeskolos looked confused. Valka had to stifle a grin. "I know how hard all of this must be for you. That's why I wanted to tell you myself."

"No! Damn it!" I almost shouted, surprising even myself. "You don't understand. How could you? It's not you in there every day. You don't have to hear it scream; you don't have to stand there and repeat everything it says and everything she says. You. Don't. Have. To. Be. There." I could feel the ten thousand eyes of castle surveillance upon me. "I do."

"There's a saying," Valka said, bright voice shining through the cloud I'd gathered around myself. "Back home. That the galaxy is curved—that if you go far enough and fast enough, you wind up right back where you started."

Something about the way she said it—or perhaps only the fact that it was Valka who said it—took the wind from me. My shoulders slumped, then squared. "Fine," I said in a voice like wind-etched stone. "I'll do it."

CHAPTER 74

THE LABYRINTH

THE DOOR'S PNEUMATICS HISSED behind me, leaving me embalmed in darkness. The weeks had taken their toll, and as the prisoner had suffered, so too had its cell. The place stank of rotting meat. If you have passed by a peasant's shack in the country and smelled the carcass of a poached deer skinned and left waiting too long for the stew pot, you can imagine the stench. Red lights shone low on the walls, their dimness a perverse courtesy to the night creature that was the cell's sole occupant. Part of me envied poor dead Gilliam. The stench of rotting flesh and blood and raw, inhuman sewage filled the air, and I longed to press a perfumed kerchief to my face to mask the odor as the priest might have done.

In the dim I beheld Uvanari. The *ichakta* was again strapped to its cross. It had been there for two days, the whole ensemble canted backward to keep the patient conscious, moved at intervals by automated controls to reduce the incidence of pressure sores.

Its crowned head looked up at the sound of the door, black eyes narrowing to slits as it saw me. "You," it hissed, and then it saw the object I held. "What is that? Have you come to kill me?"

"*Veih,*" I said in answer. *No.* I held the hypodermic up for its examination. "For the pain. Our doctors examined your blood chemistry; they think this will work. Please." I held the thing up again, offering. Uvanari turned its head, weak but . . . defiant? Resigned? It was the turning away of a broken predator who knows the hunter has

come to fell it, exposing its neck. I jabbed the needle into its arm instead, then stepped back to let it take effect. While we waited in silence, I reflected on all the ancient legends that spoke of truth serums, of magic drugs that made a man reveal his innermost secrets. All false. No such medicament exists. Scopolamine. Thiopental. Amytal. All alter the mind, open doors, but truth—*truth* is something else entirely. Something separate from knowledge. Besides, whatever effect such poisons have on the human spirit, Uvanari was not human. It was a miracle we could do anything for its pain, much less make it talk. Still, I dared to dream.

After a minute had elapsed, the Cielcin began to relax visibly. Its appearance had degraded badly in the time since its imprisonment. The right arm was flayed, skin stripped bloodlessly from wrist to elbow, the bluish tissue salved with something wet and glutinous that kept it from rotting. I had been present when the skin was peeled off like a woman's stocking. I can still hear the screaming, as I heard it then in the silence of that cell. *Good prefect, bad prefect,* I told myself, and I said, "I am sorry, Ichakta. I didn't know they would do this." But I had known, hadn't I? I had seen what the Chantry had done to our own people. The butchered criminals and branded heretics that littered Meidua and Borosevo and doubtless every city on every planet in between. Ignoring a thing is not ignorance, and he who holds his silence is an accomplice every time.

"Okun detu ne?"

The question surprised me so much that I echoed it. "Why me? What do you mean?"

"All this time, you. You stand there with those . . . *creatures.* The others. You speak for them. Why? Who are you?"

Time fell past while I struggled to answer this. I set the anesthetic down on the cart with the torture equipment, one piece of mercy amongst all that pain and suffering. "I told you, I'm just a man. I'm not anybody. Just . . . I just know the words. That was why I was in the cave, and it's why I'm still here."

"I thought you would say that." While it spoke, I moved behind it, changed the angle of the adjustable bit of scaffolding that held its arm in place, angled it down so that blood and feeling might return to the injured limb. The cathars had bandaged the declawed and shortened fingertips, and the dried blood shone black against the white gauze. Uvanari moaned softly as its flayed arm moved against the padded backing of the rig. I winced in sympathy, but the creature said, "You are a slave, then?"

I shook my head, then realized that it could not see me. "No."

I had spoken in Galstani reflexively, but the Cielcin seemed to understand. "You are not *diyugatsayu*."

"Free?" I repeated. "I am free."

"He who works for others is not *diyugatsayu*," Uvanari said. "You are a slave." I walked around again to face the creature. Was it really nine feet tall? Its suffering had shrunken it like a silhouette crushed by intense light. "That is well—we are all slaves, Hadrian." My name pronounced by its inhuman tongue was a kind of accusation, and I flinched away. I felt eyes watching me: the two inhuman ones, and the countless artificial ones in the walls and ceilings through which humanity present and future looked in on me. I knew I should not flinch. I had no right to. I was not myself in that moment but humanity's avatar, speaking for us all to Uvanari, who spoke for its kind. Humanity must not flinch, whatever Hadrian felt.

Much as I wanted to explore philosophy with this mind so unlike the minds of men, I had a script, a mission to obey. As Uvanari said, I was a kind of slave. The good prefect. I cleared my throat. "They want you to give them *something*. If you do, they will stop all this. Heal you. They can graft your arm." The word for graft was a mystery to me, and I spent the better part of ten seconds stumbling around a way to say it. I settled on using the word *caenuri*, to heal, again. "Please. Who is your leader? Your *aeta*?" The word was typically translated as *prince*, but it shared etymological connections to words like *maker*, *owner*, and *master*.

"I am done speaking with you, Hadrian." The alien looked away, shut its eyes.

Though its arms had been stretched wide when I entered, the cathars had folded their victim into a sitting position on the adjustable cross and cast a blanket over the *ichakta*'s grubby nakedness. It just sat there, arms half-open, face turned away. Not speaking. As a child I had learned of the blessed victims of ancient religions, men and women slain for their unwavering conviction to their now-forgotten gods. The Chantry had adopted such images and used them in the worship of the Heroes, those men and women who had devoted their lives to the realm or given their lives for it. Images of men tied or chained to trees or crosses, their faces turned to the heavens, composed not in rictuses of pain but in quiet piety. With so demonic an alien visage crowned with horns of white bone, the parody was almost obscene. Almost a sacrilege, even to one like myself who could not pray.

"You need to give us something."

"All I have left to do is die," Uvanari said, and I could almost hear Gibson decrying the creature for its melodrama just as he had me for mine. "It was a mistake to surrender. I knew it would come to this."

I took in the burns, the dried blood on its fingertips, the flayed band of flesh. "Then why did you do it?"

"For the same reason you gave." Then the creature did something I have never forgotten, something that remains etched in my memory as if in laser light. It shook its head. Not the neck-stretching gestures by which it typically signaled yes or no. It did the human gesture, having learned it in speaking with me. "This is not my war, as it is not yours. We inherited it, same as you. When you said that, I dared to hope."

"We have a saying." I straightened my back, thrust out my chin. "My teacher always said that hope is a cloud."

Whether it was introspection or pain that slowed the alien's response, I couldn't say. "It sounds very wise."

"He." The Cielcin blew air from its angled nose slits. I continued, "I want to return you to your people, Itana

Uvanari. To your *aeta*." *Your master? Your owner? Your maker?*

Was that light in the ink spots of Uvanari's eyes? Hope?

Hope is a cloud, Gibson's voice said in my ear. A part of me.

Uvanari turned those eyes to the ceiling, spoke as if to the congress of invisible watchers: the inquisitors and logothetes, or perhaps the more invisible and unhearing gods. "To my people? After all your people have done? You think my master will thank you for this?" It tried to move its flayed arm against the electromagnetic restraints.

"I thought you said you were a slave. What are your lives worth to your master?" I twisted my questions as though they were a knife. "How much more will those lives be worth in trade with us?"

"We are *kasamnte*," it whispered. "*Nothing*. Do you understand? Not even Tanaran matters to *him*."

I stopped my slow circling of the Cielcin on its opposable cross, hands frozen at my sides. For a moment there was only the frost of our breath misting the air, going up in steam. There was so much to unpack in that sentence; had it been a lesson with Gibson, I might have asked him to repeat himself. *Tanaran?* I tabled the bit about Tanaran a moment, focusing on the pronoun: *him*. Uvanari had definitely used the active-gendered pronoun, *o-kousun*. But it was the object of the sentence, following the neuter-neuter structure one expected around a linking verb. It felt wrong, like a broken tooth.

"Him?" I asked. Uvanari didn't answer; it wouldn't even look at me. This was the part where Inquisitor Agari would strike it, or tear the blanket from its nakedness, or order another tooth or claw removed with pliers. I was not Inquisitor Agari. "What do you mean, him? Your master? Your *aeta*?"

"My . . ." Uvanari clamped its jaw shut, head lolling in the counterclockwise negative gesture. *No.*

I changed tack. "What do you mean about Tanaran? 'Not even Tanaran matters to him,' you said. *Hejato Tanaran higatseyu ti-kousun.* What is Tanaran in this?" I reflected on the younger Cielcin as I stood facing

Uvanari, worrying at a thumbnail. Tanaran had not been dressed in the combat armor Uvanari and the other soldiers wore; it had worn only light fabrics in green and black. "Is Tanaran *aeta*?"

"Tanaran?" The Cielcin almost laughed, hazy now with the painkiller I'd administered. "Tanaran is *baetan*."

I blinked, tore a sliver of the thumbnail off with my teeth. "A root?"

"Will you kill me, Hadrian?" The words came as if from nowhere, a non sequitur, but their presence had hung over all that preceded, over every word we'd exchanged that day. It had all been tipping forward to this . . . this . . .

I looked sharply up at the creature through my lank hair. Uvanari was looking at me, its inhuman face drawn and paler than milk. One of the horns in its crown had been snapped off, I saw, and none too cleanly—what remained of it was a jagged nub. I had missed that somehow in all my observations, all my sessions of standing like a ghost in the corner of this room. Not a ghost—a daimon, same as the machines Valka's people used to translate.

"Biqa o-okarin ne?" I asked. *Kill you?* "I can't kill you. And what did you mean about Tanaran?"

"It will . . . could be *aeta* one day," Uvanari said, then changed tracks. "You have to kill me. It is the way. If you are truly sorry, it is the way."

A cold stone sat in my throat, a cold, hard, dead lump of coal without the fires of redemption in ancient fables. I could not speak past it, not to Uvanari. The words that found me were in Galstani. "I wanted to help. I wanted to . . . to make things *better.*" The floor gleamed the color of knives, scuffed and scratched, brushed clean. How many people had ended their lives in this room, their stories snuffed out, pasts and futures erased? "It's my fault." This was what Gibson meant: *the ugliness of the world.* I switched back to the Cielcin language, said, "I can't do that."

"You *must.* It is *ndaktu.*"

Mercy. No—*a sort of formal mercy.* I tried to remember the precise definition of the word, the almost legal implications of it. I tried again. "Where is your fleet, Uvanari? Your people?"

It rocked its head in the counterclockwise negative, seeming almost to have some sort of fit. "No. No."

"I want to contact them. There must be a way. A way that doesn't put them at risk. I want to see you and Tanaran and the others returned. Really." I was not a liar, but I was made one by the machinery of context. I knew that whatever I did, whatever I learned would be twisted. I recalled the last words of an ancient general, their meaning lost or never understood: *How will I ever get out of this labyrinth?* But I had to keep walking as Theseus had: always forward, always down, never left or right. I was complicit in these horrors only as a fox is complicit in the hunt or the rabbit in a dog race. I sought escape. I knew everything I did and said would serve their cause. And yet how could I do anything else?

The *ichakta* spat onto the grate at the base of the cross. "I will not betray my people. Not to you *yukajjimn*."

"Do we have to say 'vermin'?" I muttered in Galstani. I hung my head, rubbing at my eyes in frustrated defeat. We were not on a first-name basis any longer. But I had learned one thing—that I should speak with Tanaran, not Uvanari—and so I turned to go.

"Wait," the xenobite said. I stopped, already halfway to the door. "His name is Aranata."

"Whose?" I asked, though I knew what Uvanari meant the moment I'd finished the word.

"My master's," the captain said. It had used the masculine pronoun again—who else could it have meant? "Aranata Otiolo. You will not find him. But . . . you will stop now?"

Turning fully around to face the prisoner, I asked, "Are you going to cooperate, then? Are you going to tell us where your people are?"

There was silence for a moment, terrible as the death of stars. Then, "No. I cannot. I do not know. We move."

"You must have some way to find home again," I said, unbelieving.

Its head lolled in the negative direction. "No. *Veih*. No."

"Then I can't make them stop." I couldn't make them

stop anyway, no matter what Uvanari told us. I could never make them stop.

Another pause, shorter this time. "If I tell them what they want to know, will they kill me?" When I didn't answer, the Cielcin spoke again, its voice little more than the dry whisper of leaves on broken glass. *"Biqaun ne?"*

Will you?

CHAPTER 75

MERCY IS

NIGHT HAD FALLEN ON the castle, and lights settled on the canals of Borosevo like the shimmering of swamp gas. Corpse fires burned, too, in plazas and on street corners, reminders of the plague, so long fallen away from my everyday experience, that wracked the unhealthy commons in the world below. This high up, one could not smell the smoke, much less the stink of sickness and of rotten fish and algae that was the perfume of the city.

A pair of watchmen passed me on the stairs up to the corner tower and terraced gardens that clung to the southern face of the ziggurat atop which the castle stood. In a strange way, the path recalled the winding stair down from Devil's Rest to the abandoned wharf I haunted in childhood. I no longer noted the heavy, cloying dampness on the air or the dull weight of Emesh's stronger gravity. The sea breeze cut wild and clean across me, gathering my hair in its fingers. High above I made out the blue-white spot of the *Obdurate*, locked in stationary orbit above the city and playing host to a constellation of glittering repair crafts dimmer than the stars. Debris from the engagement with the Cielcin still fell at times, carmine scars on night's blue curtain. I watched just such a piece fall across the heavens, turned to ash by the heat of entry.

A wind tousled the terranic palms planted like sentinels in the earth, and somewhere an ornithon hissed. That garden high above the sea was a beautiful place, as the wharf had been, and Calagah, and the seawall at Devil's Rest. I think I might have been a sailor in another

life—or perhaps we all were—for always in such pelagic climes I have found a fleeting but instantaneous peace. Ignoring the printed warnings, I clambered up onto the parapet and turned my face windward, loose shirt billowing.

And I was alone.

There were always the cameras, but there at least I was free of the servants and courtiers and their incessant whispering. Unsteady, I seated myself on the stone rail, feet dangling above the next terrace fifty feet below. Part of me felt like a child, and I must have looked like one compared to that mighty edifice of stone. The castle lurked behind and above me, hanging like the Sword of Damocles above my head. A thousand feet below, the bastille crouched, an ugly concrete structure beside the Chantry's copper dome and slim towers.

I did not weep, though I had cause for weeping.

The only sound was the rustle of wind in the cedars, broken here and there by the quark of a night bird or the hiss of ornithons. Somewhere a frog croaked, and more distantly a man's voice carried on the wind.

I heard none of this, could hear only the screams and animal snuffling of Uvanari in pain. Whatever differences there were between our species, pain was not among them. I clenched my jaw until it ached, hearing in my head its desperate plea: *Will you kill me, Hadrian?* I wasn't sure I could.

The Cielcin fought for themselves, for their right to exist. We were no different. So long as their existence threatened our colonies, so long as our soldiers destroyed their worldship fleets, there would be no peace. So long as atrocity was met with atrocity, murder with murder, fire with fire, it mattered not at all whose sword was bloodier. The Chantry would torment Uvanari unto death. Then they would start on Tanaran or one of the others and achieve . . . nothing. All the torment in the universe could not give the priests coordinates the xenobites did not know, and nothing would change.

Where had I gone wrong? My good intentions had all boiled away, leaving only this labyrinth. Every choice I had

bred suffering. Kill Uvanari—if I could—and Tanaran would be next upon the cross. Or I would. Do nothing, and the captain suffered, and I suffered with it, if only in my soul. We were at war, I told myself, and hard times called for hard choices. Images out of spiritus mundi crowded my mind, recalled from that horrible nightmare I had seen in Calagah. The Cielcin marching across the stars. A great host, beautiful and terrible, its white hair streaming in the sun. I saw them burned away by that dying star and heard screams louder still. My hands shook, and again the screams became the wailing of the infant I had not seen. Then there were only the three words spoken to me by that Quiet voice:

This must be.

Despite the heat of the garden, I shivered. And after what seemed half of eternity, I called up a holograph on my wrist terminal and keyed a message.

I waited.

"You know, I think Gilliam was right," I said, hearing the approach of feet. "You really are a witch, sneaking up on a man like that."

The footsteps stopped, and Valka's bright voice rang out in the gloom, flattened somewhat by the wind. "How did you know it was me?"

"I didn't," I said soberly. "Glad it was, though. I'd have looked ridiculous if it had been anyone else." I looked back over my shoulder, patted the rail beside me. Whether more afraid of heights than I or less foolish, she declined. "I was hoping we could talk. You know, quietly."

She looked round the garden terrace, smoothed her shortened hair as she took in the palm trees and the bright flowers tamped to vague colors in the scant lighting set into the stone wall behind us. Behind her the safety lamps that lit the wall-walk dimmed, fuzzing silently out, then back on again. One continued to blink softly as if palsied. "All right, I'm running a loop on the three cameras out here, but we shouldn't talk long."

I chewed on the remains of my thumbnail. "That's actually what I wanted to talk to you about: this thing you can do."

"What of it?"

"I need your help. Uvanari, the Cielcin captain . . ." I shook my head. There was no good way to say it. There was no way not to say it. "It asked me to kill it, and I think I have to." I was not looking at her but down at the hulking bastille far below. She didn't speak, and I might have thought her gone but for the glaring sense that I was being watched. "They're torturing it, Valka, despite all their promises and all the promises I made. I have a responsibility. I can't save the captain, and it's my fault it's in there in the first place, so . . ." I told her my plan, all of it, withholding not even the smallest detail. I spoke quickly, mindful of what little time we had. "I might be able to get something out of it, something that will keep the Chantry from harming the others. I want to return them to their people, to use them to open a dialogue with their leaders. To stop the fighting." I swallowed. "To end the war."

Only then did I turn. Only then could I bear to see the judgment in those golden eyes.

There was none.

"You said once that what happened with Gilliam was my fault. You were right. But if I do nothing this time, then that's my fault, too. And I can't do it alone."

The way her lips pressed together, the way her eyebrows drew down . . . I could not read it. She chewed her lip. "Very well, I'll do it," she said. And then she added two words I have never forgotten or deserved: "For you."

The other Cielcin shared a single cell in the bastille. Unlike the steel bubble of the interrogation room, the holding cell was sectioned concrete, walls and floor and ceiling. What lighting there was hung from pendant cables, the yellow bulbs dialed low. I was not allowed inside, but the Chantry's own melodramatic tendencies had conspired to wall the front of the communal lockup with actual metal bars, the white paint on them chipped and flaking. One of the Cielcin saw me—the one I'd shot with the stunner in Calagah, perhaps—and nudged its

companion. Like a set of sails filling with the wind, the ten Cielcin rose and turned to face me. Were they human, I might have said they waited in quiet curiosity, or else that hatred burned cold in their corpse-like faces, but they were not human, and what they felt I could not say.

They had all been stripped of their armor, and but for Tanaran, they had only skintight unitards glistening with the coiled patterns of moisture-recycling and temperature-regulation tubing. Their clawed feet were bare and looked more like hands than seemed right. One hissed, baring its teeth, *not* in the gesture its kind took for smiling. "You!"

Weeks had passed since last I had spoken with any of the xenobites save Uvanari, and never before had I addressed them as a group. Conscious of Inquisitor Agari standing at the end of the hall and of the cameras like spiders in the corners, I said, "I am sorry you are being kept this way. I had assurances it would be otherwise." *Always speak to one in a crowd,* my father often said. *A crowd can ignore you, but a man cannot.* Tanaran was no man, not in any sense of the word, but I spoke to it all the same. "Tanaran, I know what you are."

The Cielcin noble narrowed its eyes. "You do not."

A weak smile stole over my face. "The *ichakta* told me you are a root. *Baetan.* I do not know what that means, but it means you are important." I darted a glance at Inquisitor Agari, then turned to speak to the other Cielcin, singling Tanaran out of the crowd.

But Tanaran spoke first, standing straight as the too-low ceiling would allow, its need to stand at attention defeating its good sense. "How is Uvanari?"

I thank the Chantry's imagined gods that the creature could not interpret my facial expressions, for I opened my mouth, distressed. Again I looked to Agari. "They ask after their captain," I said to her in Galstani.

"Tell them he's being well treated but that the wound he took before his capture is not yet healed."

Swallowing the lump of shame in my throat, I rounded on the Cielcin. I might have vomited had the past few weeks not put me off food. How was I to say that? But say it I did. It seemed to comfort Tanaran, who looked down

at its bare, clawed feet, teeth glinting as it smiled. Unable to help myself, I added, "This wasn't what I wanted. If I had to choose, you would all be on your way"—I paused for a moment to draw them in and to ruminate on my next words—". . . on your way back to Aeta Aranata."

The sound that greeted this was like nothing human, a ululating wail of equal parts grief and fury. I had to stifle an urge to cover my ears. Tanaran padded closer to the bars, prompting the two legionnaires near me to stiffen reflexively. It had to stoop a little in the cramped cell, so tall was it. *How can such a creature bear the Emeshi gravity?* I wondered, remembering how I had suffered in my first months on this outsized world. And these creatures dwelt in space, on ships with a fraction of the gravity of Delos, much less Emesh. They must have laminated their bones, reinforced their muscles. Changed themselves, adapted in order to survive.

Tanaran wrapped its too-long fingers around the bars, pressed its flat face between them. "The *ichakta* would never betray *him* like that. What have you done to it?"

"To Uvanari? Nothing." I blinked, taking a step back in response to a nervous twitch from one of my bone-colored guards. *Nothing*—how hard that word had been to say, *Nothing*. And how easy. Almost I can still taste it on my tongue. "I spoke to it just last night." I glanced up at the pendant lights, frowning. Valka had said there would be a signal, said she would cut the lights in the bastille with her Tavrosi magic so I would know the audio pickups were severed. What was keeping her?

"What else do you know?" The young Cielcin let out a quieter, mewling version of the wail the collective had emitted mere moments before and shut the liquid shadows of its eyes. "You know where our *scianda* is? Our fleet? You will destroy it."

"*Veih!*" I stepped forward again, coming to a halt at the painted red line on the floor that marked the minimum safe distance. "No. The *ichakta* would not give us that. It said it couldn't." I looked at Agari again. I had to wait. Had to wait for Valka.

"That is what you would say!" shouted another of the

Cielcin, this one more square-jawed and strongly built than the skinny Tanaran. Without warning it lunged at the bars, thin arms stretching between the peeling steel beams. They seized my shirtfront, and I realized too late that the line had been painted to account for the length of human arms, far shorter than Cielcin ones. I moved without thinking, assuming the creature's skeletal structure was similar enough to my own to make the break feasible. I shoved both arms up between the xenobite's closed fists and slammed my elbows down on its wrists even as I went face-first into the bars. I staggered free, fell square on my backside.

Agari shouted an order, and the two legionnaires advanced, tugging stunners from thigh holsters.

"Stand down!" I shouted, finding my feet again. My hair had fallen in my face. I blew at it, almost petulant. One of the legionnaires helped me to my feet. I thanked her and glowered through the bars at the other Cielcin, teeth clenched. *"Rakur oyumn heiyui."*

"It was stupid," Tanaran agreed more vehemently, glaring at its companion.

"This *yukajji* is the reason we are prisoners—"

Tanaran cut the larger creature off. "I know, Svatarom. *Svvv.*" It made a buzzing, hissing sound that I took for hushing. Tanaran pawed at its roughly cut hair as if lost in thought. Presently its eyes narrowed. "You say our people are safe?"

"Uvanari has not betrayed you, no." I stayed carefully back from the red line now, estimating the full reach of Svatarom's arms. Glancing up the dingy hall, I caught Inquisitor Agari watching me, offered what I hoped was a reassuring smile. "Besides the name of your *aeta*, we know nothing. Only that yours was not an invading force."

A third Cielcin spoke up in a voice higher and more feminine than the others, though such a gradation had no meaning amongst the xenobites. "Are we the only survivors? The other ships . . . Did anyone . . ."

Again I glanced at Agari. She would not want anything revealed to these creatures, no betrayals of fact or data. She'd tell me to give them nothing. I shook my head.

"Veih." This was so vague an answer that I had to start over. "The other ships broke in orbit." *Broke.* What a telling euphemism. The creature hung its head, air whistling from its nostrils as through broken teeth. Two other Cielcin hurried to catch the creature as it sagged to its knees. Was it sobbing?

Tanaran's own face hardened, and it shut its eyes. "I see."

The lights dimmed, replaced by red emergency lights low on the floor.

Agari said, "What's going on?" She repeated the question into her wrist terminal. "Another outage? I thought support had this sorted!"

Valka had done it—or at least I hoped that she had. There wasn't much time; whatever she'd done with the neural lace implanted in her head, she had said it would not hold for long. Tanaran looked around, confused.

"Look," I said, words soft beneath Agari's confusion and shouted orders. "Look. Listen. I have a friend who's grayed out the surveillance here, and none of the others speaks a word of this language. We can talk a moment. You and me."

"Iugam!" Svatarom slammed its hands against the bars. "It is a trick!"

"I don't lie!" I said, though I had lied for too long. "What's wrong with the lights?" I asked Agari, feigning ignorance, pretending I knew nothing about the Tavrosi witch camped on the castle walls, her mind interfacing with the datasphere and the bastille security systems. She was, I reflected, precisely the reason the Chantry kept so close a watch on technology within the realms and polities it policed. The inquisitor shot back the answer I expected, and I rounded on Svatarom and the others. "This has not gone like I hoped, and we're wasting time. Uvanari asked me for mercy."

"Ndaktu?" Tanaran echoed, its voice etched with a grief any species could recognize. "Why?"

I chewed my lip, then hissed under Agari's shouting from the end of the hall, "Because they're torturing it, the *ichakta.*"

My words seemed not to penetrate for the better part of a minute, and we stood in half darkness, staring at one another. At last, Tanaran spoke. "They're . . . hurting Uvanari?" I nodded, then realized the futility of the gesture and made the wordless grunt that was Cielcin for *yes*. For a second I thought the xenobite might break into tears, saw a muscle in its jaw tense. "Your people do not want us to know." It was not a question.

"Veih." I shook my head, forgetting to make the alien gesture instead.

Tanaran cast its eyes down at the barren concrete floor, long scarred from countless eons of metal doors dragged across its surface. "Then we thank you."

Svatarom's jaw hardened, glass teeth flashing. "The *yukajji* must make it right. It is responsible." The Cielcin whom Uvanari called a *root* was silent for a long while. Too long. "Tanaran."

The robed xenobite stretched its lower lip down past its teeth. The expression meant nothing to me, but it said, "Svatarom is right. You are responsible."

"What does that mean?" I asked. "It asked me to kill it."

"Yes." In Cielcin, the word was barely even a syllable, an unvoiced breath of air. "Among the People, it is not right that one such as the captain should suffer."

It was what I had feared it would say, what I had feared was true and why I had come here in the first place. It was why Valka had grayed out the cameras. *Not long now. Not long.* "So I have to kill the *ichakta*?"

"The one who causes dishonor must do everything—*everything*—to end that dishonor. You say this is your fault. You are right. You say you wish you could send us home. But it is too late . . ." Its voice broke. ". . . too late for the *ichakta*. To return home as it is . . ." It could not finish its sentence.

"Would be disgrace," Svatarom spat, then actually spat. "You did this. You promised we would not be harmed. You gave your word."

The safety lights flickered, causing me to glance at Agari as I said, "I know! Why do you think I'm here? I

understand what I have to do, but I need your help to do it." I had told Valka much the same thing the night before, whispered beneath the wind on the garden terrace beneath the terranic palms. *I need to get them to leave me alone with Uvanari. That's when you short the cameras, and I . . . I . . .* My voice had broken then, choked off into something very, very small.

Valka had lain a hand on my arm, had murmured that she understood. *But you don't have to do it.*

I can't do this anymore, I can't. I tried to explain what I thought the Cielcin had been trying to tell me: that it wanted—needed—to die.

"What are you going to do?" Tanaran asked.

"What are you saying to it?" Agari demanded.

I waved her into silence. The cool air in the cell stank of rot, as if something damp had died and taken up residence in the concrete. But I breathed deeply, eyes never leaving Tanaran. The lights flickered again, and I heard the faint whine of distant generators coming online. No time. No time. "I am going to kill Uvanari. *Ndaktu*. Mercy." I tried to find refuge in a scholiastic aphorism, something to reassure me that I was on the right course. *Mercy is . . . Mercy is . . .* There was nothing, or none that I had ever learned. "I need you to do something next time these lights go out."

And I told them.

The lights came on again within a minute of the end of my little speech, and the cameras with them. "Another thing, Tanaran," I asked, stopping as I pretended to turn away. "Uvanari called you *baetan*. What does that mean?"

The young Cielcin's chalky skin flushed a dark gray, black blood flooding capillaries in its cheeks. The other xenobites nearest Tanaran hissed, startling the guards nearest me. I held up a calming hand, repeated my question.

"It means I belong to him. To the *aeta*."

"I thought all Cielcin belong to their *aeta*, to his dominion." I caught Agari watching me, nodded as reassuringly as I knew how, though I am sure now the expression was strained. "Are you not all his slaves?"

That outrush of breath, the slitted nostrils flaring *yes*.

Tanaran took a mincing step back toward the bars. "I am his."

A concubine? A wife? I squinted through the bars. I had begun to think of Tanaran as male—had begun to think thus of all the Cielcin, truth be told. I reassessed, reminding myself that neither was this a woman before me but something more, something less ... something else entirely. I was beyond humanity here, beyond the grasp of translation. The Cielcin's sexual modes did not even map onto ours, not biologically, not sociologically. It was only our desire to humanize them that did. "What does that mean?"

"I am his. He is carried by me." It pressed a hand to its stomach in some gesture I did not understand.

"Carried?" I repeated. "Does this have something to do with children?" It occurred to me that I had no notion of how the xenobites reproduced.

And I still have none, for Tanaran stepped back, startled. "What? No!" It rolled its head in a furious negative. "I carry a piece of him. His authority."

Images of the Imperial auctors flashed before me. Those elite were gifted with all the Emperor's authority, the ability to act in his stead, in his absence, so titled that they were equal with the Emperor in authority, though they had none without him. They shared in the Imperial Presence, spoke with its voice. Was this like that? Or something else? Perhaps it was like that, and so Tanaran was the leader of this ... expedition? Pilgrimage? I did not inquire further, pressed as I was for time.

"One other thing," I said hurriedly, conscious that I was once more under the ten thousands eyes of the state. "Uvanari said you came here to pray. To the others? To the ... first ones?" I wanted to say "the Quiet" but knew the label would mean nothing.

"The gods," Tanaran agreed. "The Watchers." It seized the bars. "They made us, *yukajji*. Us." It bared its fangs, somehow fierce all in an instant.

Sensing the change in Tanaran's attitude, the inquisitor approached. "That's long enough, Marlowe." Agari

grabbed me by the elbow. "What did it say?" She jerked her shaved head in the direction of the cell.

"Nothing—they told me to go to hell," I said, shaking my head. "I thought I was getting through to them, but . . . they blame me for it all. I can put together a transcript. Did you get a recording?"

"Partial," the inquisitor said in answer. "Another one of those brownouts. They'd been localized up in the castle, but . . . It shouldn't be possible."

I tugged my arm free, bowed my way into the lift carriage that would take me back to the bastille's processing level and the exit. "I'll get the transcript written as fast as I can. It isn't much, but I've confirmed one thing." There was nothing for it; I had to give Agari something. Something to distract her and her superiors from what the Cielcin wanted of me.

"What's that?"

I opened my mouth. Anything, to mask the true purpose of my visit. I only hoped that I was not dooming the young xenobite to hang on a cross of its own. Perhaps its *baetan* status would protect it. I hoped so as I said, "The one without the armor? The little one?"

"Yes?"

"It's nobile, or whatever passes for nobile among the Pale."

CHAPTER 76

DEATHBED CONVERSIONS

ALWAYS FORWARD, ALWAYS DOWN, and never left or right. I needed a way to deliver Uvanari from the torment I had brought it. I needed to appease the other Cielcin by following a cultural script I barely grasped. I needed to protect myself from my own people when my translations were inevitably compared against the recordings. I needed to protect Valka, my accomplice now, a machine witch guilty of one of the Chantry's Twelve Abominations. Most of all I needed to get myself away from Emesh, from the count and the grand prior and all the people who insisted I was a fly in their web.

I think Gibson was right about me—melodramatic to the end. Besides the Cielcin, I told no one of my plan. No one but Valka.

I walked into that interrogation cell for the last time with acid where my blood had been. Nerves fired in every fiber and tissue I possessed. I had to be careful, so careful. We were flying blind. If Valka failed to hack into the bastille's network a second time, if Tanaran and the others moved before Valka had worked her technologic wizardry, if Uvanari was too injured to play its part . . . well, there's a minotaur in every labyrinth, sometimes more than one.

"We are aware," the inquisitor began, "that the one called Tanaran is the leader of your expedition."

When I translated this, Uvanari bared its teeth, strained a little against the electromagnetic clamps that held it wrists and ankles. It looked at me. "You told them?"

"Ekaan," I said, adding the breathy sound that meant

yes in their language as best I could. I continued, "I had no other choice. Is Tanaran related to Aeta Aranata, your master? His . . . *child*?" While I spoke, I studied the bandages wound about the flayed arm and the patch that leaked anesthetic through the back of the ruined hand and into the bloodstream. My hand closed about the knife I wore, a main gauche like the ones I'd worn at home, purchased during one of my infrequent trips to the city.

"Why would Tanaran be *his* child?"

I repeated the question to Agari, adding, "However they manage succession, it isn't hereditary. If that's what this is." While interesting, the information was academic, and the inquisitor was no scholiast.

The inquisitor sniffed, and instead of allowing me to answer its question, she asked a new one. "Would your master negotiate for Tanaran?"

"Reverence," I said, brows rising and pulling together, "are you serious? I had not been told we were considering—"

Agari's nostrils flared. She glanced briefly to Cathar Rhom before answering. "Just ask the question." My heart weighed a little lighter then, and I turned to do just that.

Uvanari clicked its jaw a couple of times, jerking its chin upward. "It is possible. But the *aeta* has other heirs." It used the same word it had earlier: *baetayan*, roots. But here the context was clearer, and I saw the word for how we might use it. *"Masvii iagami caicane wo ne?"*

"It asks if you will let the others go free," I said, wanting to hear the answer for myself.

Agari's flinty eyes narrowed to slits, the wheels in the mind behind them turning in ways I preferred not to understand. The muscles in her jaw worked as if trying to chew through gristle, teeth grinding. It was as if her brain were powered by the friction of them. "Tell the *inmane* we're considering all our possible options."

This I did, omitting the Imperial slur. Uvanari's inhuman face split into the snarl that passed for smiling. "I see you have politicians amongst your kind too."

I grinned, realized what I was doing, and instead bared my teeth in as close to the Cielcin smile as I could manage. Uvanari seemed to get the point, for it returned the

gesture as I said, "Yes." When Agari asked for clarification, I said, "It said it knows that line is nonsense."

The inquisitor sniffed in understanding, then toggled the holograph panels, advancing her questions another step. While she read over the change of direction, I took a long, calming breath, listened as the inquisitor took notes into her terminal. ". . . way to salvage the prisoners. The one cataloged as prisoner A009 is to be detained privately pending further deliberation. Recommendation: Agari, KF . . ." She rattled off the date. For a moment I suspected the horror was over. I glanced at the holograph panels on the wall, each depicting an identical live feed of the other Cielcin in a holding pen. I felt an absurd desire to wave, though they could not see us. Maybe all my planning was for naught.

"Captain," Agari said, voice suddenly so cold that I felt my spinal fluid crystallize as I straightened, "if we are to attempt such a negotiation for your people, we will need their location."

A lump formed in my throat. Of all the lines of inquiry, I knew this one would bear no fruit, no matter the near politeness the inquisitor had just demonstrated. Every detail of the room snapped back into focus then: the cross with its adjustable beams, its magnetic clamps; the grating on the floor; the sterile walls; the array of tools on the cart, instruments of both medicine and torture. And then there were the cathars themselves, identical in their baldness, their black robes and aprons more clinical than liturgical, darker than any fabric had a right to be. This was not a place for jest, even in defiance. I closed my hand around the hilt of my knife until the bones ached, waiting for Uvanari's response.

The Cielcin refused. "I cannot tell you this."

At a sign from the inquisitor, the cathar lifted a device from the rear of the cart, long as my forearm and with a knob at one end so that it resembled a mace. Wordlessly it held the thing out for the *ichakta*'s examination, then triggered some mechanism in the haft. The composite material at the head of the item heated rapidly until it glowed

like a coal fresh from the fire. Fear lighted in Uvanari's eyes, and it tried to shy back, spluttering curses.

The second cathar stooped, tugged the cloth that covered the xenobite's genitals away. Then it worked on the leather straps that secured the Cielcin, leaving only the electromagnetic clamps in place. In a Eudoran masque, the character of the Torturer always speaks in mustache-twirling detail about the excruciations he intends to perform on his victim, usually the Heroine. He winks at the audience and rubs his hands together, cackling all the while. The cathars did not speak, did not offer explanations. They only acted.

"What are they doing?" Uvanari asked, deep voice at once much higher. "Hadrian, what are they doing?" When the last of the flammable belts were removed, the second cathar stepped back from its victim, its charge, and stood with hands folded.

I did not have time to answer. The first cathar swung its mace, showering the Cielcin with cherry-red droplets fine as tears. Uvanari screamed, and the cold air of the cell filled with the smoky metallic stink of burning flesh. Its thin chest heaved, sucking in air to fuel more screaming, the sound collapsed and sunken through pain into the vestibule of madness. Angry welts began to rise on the creature's white skin, gray and black and jaundiced a sick yellow at the edges. Blood like ink leaked from the wounds, and something else, something silver.

Lead.

The bastards had used *lead*.

"Inquisitor!" I couldn't stop myself. "No!"

Uvanari gasped something as thin tongues of smoke coiled upward toward a sucking vent in the ceiling. Agari ignored me, the whites of her eyes too visible in the stark cell. I expected her to rebuke me, to scream at me, to ask how I dared say a word against her. Instead she only asked, "What did it say?"

I listened again, shook my head. "I can't make it out, you maniac. You've gone too far." Only a tremendous effort kept me from drawing my long knife then and there.

The inquisitor actually shrugged, then repeated her question, her order. "Tell us the location of your fleet."

"Air rot you!" Uvanari managed. Some sort of curse? There was no way to be sure. "Would you betray your own?"

The inquisitor waved a hand, and the cathar struck the Cielcin with his mace, leaving a medallion of burned flesh larger than my fist. "Tell us the location of your fleet!" the inquisitor repeated, and I echoed her in my smallest voice, eyes on the cathar and not the prisoner bracketed to its cross. I only hoped Valka would not be much longer.

My eyes met Uvanari's. Glass teeth shone in black gums, thin lips pulled back. To the untrained, the panting wheeze of its breathing might have been the Cielcin word, "Yes. Yes. Yes." I took a breath of my own, knowing that it was not that. Any time now, any time, Valka would knock the power out in the lower levels, and Tanaran and the others would turn on one another.

"Tell us the location of your fleet."

Screaming.

"Tell us the location of your fleet!"

Smoke.

"Tell us the—"

Screaming.

Uvanari hung limp on the cross, face sunk to its chest so that only the horns of its epoccipital crest presented itself. Without the leather restraints, tied at only the wrists and waist and ankles, it looked barely attached to the cross at all. As we watched, all silent as the cathars, Uvanari vomited, blue fluid spattering the grate. It vomited again, spat to clean its mouth. "You humans. Are all . . . all the same."

I frowned, caught on the verge of delivering this statement to the inquisitor. "You said that before!" I said in Cielcin, cutting the inquisitor out of the loop. "You said that before! At the very beginning." I had missed it. How had I missed it?

"What is it saying?" Agari demanded, raising a hand to forestall her cathars. "Marlowe?"

"Shh." I did not turn to look at her, so distracted was I

by the implications. I forgot the Chantry, forgot *ndaktu*, forgot the plan. "You've spoken with humans before?" It wasn't a figure of speech, surely? "Where?" I brushed past the cathar, repeating the question, the word. "*Saem ne*? Where? *Saem ne? Saem ne?*"

Agari was not so thick as to miss that. She grabbed me just above the elbow and hissed, "What the hell is going on?"

I told her what it had said, added, "If they've met other humans before, then maybe those people know how to find their fleet. We don't need to do this."

At a gesture from Agari, the cathar with the sprinkler mace slammed the head into Uvanari's stomach, just about where a navel should be on a human. The wheal it left grayed the white skin to bubbled slickness, and Uvanari clamped down on its teeth, hissing, "Tell him to stop."

It meant Agari. I shook my head. "She won't."

"She?" It bled from half a hundred tiny wounds, and looking on I was as numb as Uvanari was in agony. Valka was taking too long. Had she changed her mind? Had she abandoned me and the whole plan? She wouldn't, surely. Surely not. With a tremendous effort, as if it were lifting a portcullis and not a head, Uvanari looked squarely up at me, eyes narrowing. "Your kind . . . monsters, taking what you want."

"We are not monsters. We don't eat your kind," I shot back, and all the stories I'd heard in childhood came back to me, all the tales of men spitted and roasted over plasma fires, of the Pale eating brains and children in the night. Chantry propaganda, or so I then believed.

"We do," Uvanari hissed, "if we have to."

"This is useless," Agari said, closing out of her terminal's holograph prompts with a wipe of the hand. "Useless!" She turned to the cathars, hesitating on the cusp of some unvoiced decision, unsure how to proceed. She was in the labyrinth too, just as lost as I was.

Vwaa! Vwaa!

Warning lights pulsed scarlet from the corners of the cells, klaxons blatting their wordless alarm. Uvanari's eyes—two wells of deepest dark—swiveled to look me in

the face. Agari froze, glaring at the ceiling. I had expected the interruption, and even I jumped. I was careful to speak first. "What's this?"

The inquisitor checked her terminal, cursing under her breath. "Another brownout. I don't care how much damage the generators took in the plague riots—I'd swear this is deliberate." I struggled to keep my face intent, thinking of Valka and her heretical Tavrosi implants. Diplomatic status or no, I'd asked her to cross a line.

Vwaa! Vwaa!

Agari's terminal started blaring an alarm too, and she slapped a button on it, held it to her lips. "What?" I couldn't hear the response—it was relayed to the inquisitor through the conduction patch obscured behind one ear—but the color drained from her dusky face, and she said, "Well, stop them! No! No, damn it! Use the stunners. *The stunners*." Her eyes darted between the two cathars and myself. "No! I'm on my way!"

Vwaa! Vwaa!

Though I suspected I knew the answer, I hurried forward and asked, "What is it? What's happened?"

"They lost power in the west wing. Cameras are down."

I loved Valka in that moment.

"Another outage?" Then, "Wait, the west wing? That's where the others—" I broke off, eyes snapping to where Uvanari hung on its cross. Whether it was listening or not was hard to say, for its head sagged again, breathing now more ragged.

The inquisitor scowled—was that accusation in her black eyes?—and swept toward the door, which hissed open on its hydraulics. "Come, Marlowe." I didn't move, glanced back over my shoulder at Uvanari. "Come on. You're needed. The other Cielcin—"

"Let me stay."

"No."

"Let me talk to it." I glanced at the cathars. "Alone."

"They're *attacking* each other. You are coming with me, now."

I ground my teeth as loudly as I knew how and jabbed one finger at the floor beneath me. "The last time you left

me alone with this one, I made more progress than you did in two weeks of cutting and burning. Give me five minutes. Ten." The alarms still blatted their screeching cry, lights red and white spiraling on the metal walls and ceiling. As an afterthought, I added, "Just until you've secured the others."

Vwaa! Vwaa!

The woman might have been a century responding. She was not the sort of person used to the pressures of time; she was used to being in utter control, to being in command of every line and detail of a situation, to power. The chaos was chafing at her, breaking whatever discipline she had. Fear was a poison, was poisoning her. I bit my cheek to stifle the crooked Marlowe smile that threatened to steal over my face and steal my plan from me. The word that left her was all air, flat of sound and shapeless as the Cielcin *yes*.

She pointed. "Rhom, stay with him. You, with me." She departed in a whirl of black robes and a hissing of door hydraulics, taking the other cathar and all my hopes with her.

The cathars. I had forgotten about the thrice-damned cathars. They never spoke, and so they had slipped beneath the level of my notice entirely. Stupid, stupid thing to do. Cathar Rhom stood in the corner, not speaking. I dared not argue. When this was over, when I had done as I had promised myself I would do, there would be blame enough directed at me without the cathar's testimony that I had demanded he be sent away. Yet with him present, I was done for.

I moved close to Uvanari, hoping my whisper would carry under the *vwaa-vwaa* of the alarms. *"Eka yitaya,"* I apologized, hand clenched around my sheathed dagger. "I cannot do as you asked."

The xenobite's face lifted, and even clamped to the torture rig it looked down on me, glassy teeth the color of human blood in the red light of the alarms. Though it was hard to say for certain, I thought the black eyes tracked over the figure of the cathar in his corner. Its eyes shifted to the ceiling, to the pulsing of the alarm lights high on the metal walls. "You did this?"

Hoping that whoever came after me would miss the subtlety of the gesture, I bared my teeth. I wanted to tell the creature what was coming—needed, in fact, to step back—but I also had my part to play, Eudoran melodrama or no. I asked, "You have met humans before, then?"

Uvanari made that awful keening whistle that passed among its kind for laughter, though the sound was smaller than I had ever heard it before. It thrust out its chin, one of those gestures we coincidentally shared with its kind, and said, "You are asking the questions now?"

"Please?" I looked nervously over my shoulder at the cathar. He was still there, unmoved, a terrible specter of failure, all too visible. I took a step back.

The Cielcin blew air past its nose-slits. "Yes."

"Saem ne?" I asked. *Where?* It didn't answer but retreated into sullenness and the certain knowledge that its torments were not over. This was only a moment of calm, or would have been were it not for the sirens.

And then it was.

The sirens died, all lights snuffed out but for the still-glowing service lights on the cathars' surgical cart, tiny indicators like stars that cast almost no radiance in that dark place. The power was gone. The cameras. Everything. But for the cathar, we would have been alone long enough for me to fulfill the Cielcin's wish and my unvoiced promise to deliver it from this place.

Something thudded to the floor in front of me, heavy and hard as bone.

I stumbled back, one hand still on my knife. Something moved ahead of me, blacker than the darkness. The reality clicked into place a couple of moments later.

The clamps.

The electromagnetic clamps.

By the Earth, the cathars had removed the analog straps to keep them from catching fire during the Cielcin's lead torture and had not restored them, leaving Uvanari free when Valka cut the power. I expected it to lie in a puddle at the base of the cross, to hold itself, to cry. It's what I would have done, what any human would have done having suffered what Uvanari had suffered.

The Cielcin was not human.

It stood, snarling through the slits in its flat face.

Brother Rhom realized this all far too late. With a speed I could not have imagined, the Cielcin barreled past me, ruined hands outstretched, pale gray in the dimness. A hollow crack filled the cell, rebounding in the quiet: Rhom's head smashed against the wall. Uvanari groaned, its flayed and bandaged arm thrown across the cathar's throat, the other hand closed over the human's too-small head. I should have stopped it, should have stabbed it in the back. It would have been perfect, would have been justified. I see that now. I did not then. I stood frozen, transfixed, jaw slack as Uvanari twisted the cathar's neck, displacing the blindfold. Briefly I saw the cathar's eyes—white and pure, without iris or pupil, glowing in the black—before the Cielcin sank what pointed teeth remained to it into the meat of the cathar's throat. Those eyes went out like sparks, and Uvanari tore.

The darkness spared me the color of the blood. Only the shape of it, dim as thunder, impressed itself upon my petrified mind. Uvanari hunched over Rhom's new-made corpse, and I swear it drank of his blood. After a moment, still shocked, I drew my knife. The Cielcin hear more sharply than we. How this is possible when their ears are but sunken holes, as lizards' are, I cannot say. The quiet rasp of ceramic on leather seized the Pale captain's attention, and it turned. Red blood coated the creature's face, dribbled down its chin and fell upon its pointed chest. "You mean to do it, then?" Its bluish tongue, black in the darkness, snaked down, visible by its glistening. It tasted the air.

"That's what you wanted. Why I'm here." I hoisted the main gauche. Its dull white blade shone blue-gray in the gloom, almost the color of the Maeskolos's highmatter sword. Fervently I wished it were that weapon I held and not this piece of common zircon.

The Cielcin stood, obscene, Satanic in its nakedness. I heard its nostrils flare. "Yes. I'm not sure how you did it. But here we are."

"Ndaktu!" I said, keeping up my guard. "You said it

was my fault. You wanted me here!" I knew I was trying to reason with Death, that one never reasoned with Death. I had worked so hard—*so hard*—to achieve this moment, to undo what I had done, to spare a creature its obvious suffering.

"And if you die here," Uvanari said simply, "who will question my people? They need you to speak with them!"

"They'll find another translator!" The desperation cracked its way into my voice. "Your people are dead without me."

"They're dead anyway," Uvanari returned, "but I will not see them suffer."

It lunged again, gait jagged and uneven, thrown off by pain and by so long on the cross. I threw myself sideways, getting the cross rig between myself and the Cielcin, forcing it to slow. Even on a good day, one-to-one, armed as I was and unarmored, the xenobite would have shredded me. It was larger, taller, had the better reach, had claws and horns and fangs all sharp enough to kill, had muscle reinforced by alien praxis to resist the degradations of space. Against that, how could I hope to stand with only my grubby knife? Uvanari slashed at me with its left hand—the one that still had four claws—and I raised my knife so that the forearm cut itself on the edge of my blade even as I looped sideways, ducking one arm of the cross to keep it between myself and my attacker.

"I mean it!" I said through gritted teeth. "I want to save them! To speak—" I seized the arm of the cross and torqued it upward, using it to strike the creature in the face before dancing back. "I want to contact your *aeta*. Everything I said was true."

"*Paiweyu.*" *I don't care.*

Gilliam. I clearly remember thinking this. I saw the crook-backed intus clear as day, facing me across that cell. *It's Gilliam again.* My stupidity, my arrogance had pushed me forward into a place and time I did not wish to be in and robbed me of any freedom to choose. I was now a victim, not of fate but of a kind of logical proof.

Hissing like a nest of snakes, Uvanari boiled at me from under the arm of the cross, flayed and bandaged arm

tucked against its chest, the other reaching out to seize me.
I slashed at it, but the creature drew its arm back, and my
knife whistled through air. It clanged against the metal
backside of the cross, ringing up my arm. The xenobite
stumped past me, fingers clattering across the top of the
instrument cart. It came away with the mace, the lead
sprinkler, still vaguely orange from its cooling tray. Swearing, I ducked a savage blow, unwilling to risk a parry.

The wild sweep cleared a space between us for a
moment, and we stood an arm's length apart, my knife
raised in a low guard while the creature fiddled with the
mace, shifting its grip. "You need to stop this. The power!"
I lunged, but Uvanari swatted my arm aside with its own
longer one. "It won't stay out for long. They'll come *back*!"
My opponent slammed its mace downward, nearly taking
me in the side of the head. It smashed into one of the
cross's arms, bending the metal rig backward with a
crunch. It didn't answer me; at last it had unraveled the
mystery of the little bronze ring on the handle of the torture device that activated the heating element in the head
of the weapon.

An orange glow like the death of a fire blossomed in
the dark, carving red highlights into the naked inhuman's
twisted face. Only the eyes were dark, pits so deep they
reached up through the floors of the bastille and the air
to channel the fathomless night of space. It smiled, crystal
teeth glinting like obsidian in the hell-light from the torture mace. It jerked its arm back, brought the weapon
down.

In sword fighting, one parries the blade, fighting sword-
to-sword as often as not. The knife fighter attacks the arm.
I advanced inside the blow, snagging the Cielcin's wrist
with my open hand, torqueing down even as I stroked my
knife along the inside of the creature's arm, shaving it as
a carpenter does hardwood. By rights, blood ought to have
streaked blackly from the wound. It only dripped.

But Uvanari cursed all the same, withdrawing back
toward the corner and the cart with the surgical implements. I pressed my advantage but hesitated a moment on
the verge of another lunge. The Cielcin swung the mace

again, and my hesitation saved my life. The lead fell like burning rain against my shoulder and my left side, where I'd thrown my arm up just in time to catch and stop the blow. Heat blossomed on my side and back, pain sprouting like the new grass from my flesh. I heard myself scream, somehow remote, as if the sound were echoing up a deep well. Something hit me in the back, but the pain of it shrank beneath the fire. I felt myself hurled into the corner, crashing into the cart. The surgical instruments and torture devices tumbled off, clattering to the floor as I tried to rise. The air stank of smoke and burning meat, and I fancied the fabric of my shirt still smoldered. Brother Rhom's torn corpse lay not far off, the meaty gash torn from his neck sickly wet and all too visible. His killer stood naked over me, its shadow flickering on the steel walls from the light of the glowing mace. I laughed, shaking my head as I scrabbled around on hands and knees, free hand searching in the dark for something, anything that could protect me.

"Dein?" Uvanari paused, prone to the same error of curiosity that was my great sin. "What are you doing?" It had never heard a human being laugh before and did not know what to make of the sound. Nor did I. I thought I was sobbing.

I made no sudden moves but said, "I saw one of your kind executed once. I just realized this is the same." My voice broke, torn by the heat still ebbing into my flesh, the lead cooling, hardening against my skin like wax. The Gibson part of my mind whispered, tried to tell me that fear was a poison again and again, but I didn't need it. The fear was gone, burned away. My back and side ached, throbbing where the molten metal ran and cooled on my flesh. The pain had taken it all away, left me clear and unable to think of anything else. I risked a glance back over my shoulder and saw the Cielcin raise his weapon, ruined forefinger hooked through the loop that opened the slotted head to the lead filings bubbling inside. My hand seized at last on something heavy, and I felt my knuckles creak.

Uvanari grunted, smashing the mace downward, slots

open to pour forth their horrors. I twisted, taking up what I had grabbed. Twisting, I slammed the heavy tray the tools had rested on into the descending mace, batting it aside. Specks of lead hissed against the steel floor like fallen suns. The tray rang bell-like in my hand, and time stretched as I cast it down, rising to my feet and stepping inside the Cielcin's reach. I closed my left hand over its right wrist and brought my knife's point up into its abdomen, striking once, twice, three times. Uvanari barely made a sound each time, each more gasp than word. With the third stab I twisted the knife. The Cielcin swore, dropped the heated mace with a clang. It bumped against my leg. I stepped forward, the knife still in Uvanari's gut, and slammed the Cielcin into the wall. The air went out of the xenobite, and it slid down the wall, lubricated by the black slickness of its own blood.

"Stay down," I hissed through clenched teeth, through pain. I had said much the same to Crispin once, long ago. "Stay down, or I'll—"

"Or you'll what?" I could feel Uvanari's breath on my face, and only the steady twisting of the knife kept it from lashing out with those horrid fangs. "You'll kill me?"

I barked, "No! I'll let you live. It won't be long before the power's back on—before they're back in here—and then what do you think they'll do with you after what you did to Brother Rhom here, eh?"

"You wouldn't!" Uvanari's round eyes went wider, still naught but shining pits in its skull of a face. "You wouldn't!"

"I would!" I nearly shouted the words. "I'll ensure you live. I swear by Earth!" Now I wonder if that last bit meant anything in the xenobite's tongue. *Eyudo Se ti-Vattaya gin:* I swear by Earth. I wonder if it had some comparable significance to the old captain as it does to us humans. "I'll do everything I can to keep you alive, Ichakta. But give me something . . ." The word hung between us, ripe with implication. I felt the lines of my face harden into stone, heard my voice go cold until it was Lord Alistair speaking and not Hadrian at all. "Where did you meet humans? Where have you met humans before? Tell me that!" I

reversed my grip on the knife, held it firm against the creature's ribs. *"Marerra ti-koarin!"*

"Fusumnu!" Uvanari said between quickening breaths. *A world?* No. World was *fusu'un*. I felt my brow furrow.

"A dark world?" I asked, pressing the knife a shade deeper.

The xenobite grunted, air rushing out in juddering steps. "Y-yes! Between!" The word *vohosum, between,* literally meant *between the stars.* I drew back a fraction, grip slackening as understanding filled me.

In Galstani I said, "The Extrasolarians." Barely human shapes twitched in my mind like spiders, men who had given themselves wholly to daimon machines. My grip tightened again, and I used the knife to slam Uvanari against the wall again. "Where?" When it didn't answer, I said, "Tell me, or I'll have them start on Tanaran!" I didn't mean it, couldn't mean it, and I was ashamed, glad the creature could make little sense of my facial expressions. Uvanari didn't answer but tried to free itself, clawing at my eyes. I torqued the knife up, angling the blade deep within its body, grinding it along the curve of a rib. Its grip slackened from the pain, talons scraping my face. I slammed its right hand down against the floor, felt bones snap. The Cielcin screamed, and I screamed back at it, "Where?" I slammed the wall beside its head with my open hand. "Coordinates, damn you!"

"I don't know! I was not *ichakta* then! I was a child!" Someone was pounding on the door, words muffled and strange. How long had they been there? What did they want?

"A name, then! What was the planet called?" The Cielcin shook its head, shaking it in the counterclockwise negative that had become so familiar to me. "What was it called? Uvanari?"

Perhaps it was the sound of its name that shook the answer free. Something in the creature broke, pulled the wind out of it, and shrank it until it was a husk that sprawled beneath me. It rolled its head again spasmodically. I could not say if it was a yes or a no or the inchoate gesture of a dying thing. The pounding on the door intensified, the

press of the immediate future and necessity against the interminable now. "Tell the others my wound took me," Uvanari said. "Tell them anything, but do not tell them it was like this." I could hear the defeat in its tone, the surrender. I nearly choked on it, having already betrayed the truth to Tanaran and the others. I offered a stiff nod, a gesture wholly meaningless to the creature. At last it spoke again. "The world? Vorgossos."

I froze, and the sensation of shapes crawling spiderlike in my mind intensified. *Vorgossos* . . . "Vorgossos is a myth!" But a myth the Cielcin had heard of? Surely such a myth set its roots in truth, in the world of atoms and darkness? The *ichakta* was dying, threat or no; that last twist of the knife had severed some vital artery or nicked some precious organ. The blood fell hot past my hand in galloping spurts, darker than ink.

And then the lights returned, returned as Uvanari, weak now, murmured, "Vorgossos."

"It's not real," I said, unable to say anything else. "There's no such thing as Vorgossos."

The door hissed behind me, and I panicked, drawing the knife up sharply and deeply notching a rib as more blood spilled like the dark between stars onto white flesh. As legionnaires poured in, I staggered backward, slumping to the floor at the foot of the torturer's cross.

My knife had done its work. Uvanari was dead before even the first of the soldiers could reach it.

CHAPTER 77

A RARE THING

"WE MUST BEGIN AT once on a second prisoner!" Inquisitor Agari said from one knee before her betters. "The one Marlowe identified, their political leader."

Two chairs sat at the base of the count's dais, each straight-backed and fashioned entirely of gilt wood, each attended by a lictor. Lady Kalima sat on the left, attended by Sir Olorin, and Knight-Tribune Smythe was on the right, flanked by her aged first officer, Sir William Crossflane. Smythe leaned forward. "Were we to do that, Inquisitor, we would compromise the remaining Cielcin. We were lucky not to lose any when they rioted. We can play off their leader's death as an unfortunate accident, but they'll start to notice if we pick them off one by one." She looked at me as she said it. I wondered if she knew I'd already compromised that part of the script in an attempt to ingratiate myself with the enemy.

From his place upon the high seat—a hulking confection of native corals grown in a radiating, treelike pattern of greens and gold—the count waved a ringed hand. "Besides, you cannot honestly tell me, Inquisitor, that you believe this *Vorgossos* nonsense." When Agari opened her mouth, Lord Balian continued, "If it ever existed, Vorgossos is long dead. Just a thing in old stories."

"So is the Earth," Lady Kalima interjected, mouth carefully prim and eyes studious in their avoidance of Ligeia Vas, who hovered wraithlike in the shadow of the Mataro throne. "Yet it is out there somewhere."

To my utter astonishment, Vas did not rise to this bait.

Instead the Knight-Tribune surprised me with a measured, "Perhaps it's less than charitable to compare the Homeworld to a fairy tale pirate planet." The statement struck me as rather placatory from the typically strident officer, and I shifted uncomfortably behind the kneeling inquisitor, hands clasped. My left side and arm ached, warm where the corrective patches worked to mend my lead burns. I fidgeted with one just below my elbow through my sleeve. The throne room, with its high windows and the slivers of glass paneling set into the dome, was hot enough already without the warmth seeping into me from under my clothes. At least I'd not broken anything. The thought of the corrective brace I'd worn after my mugging a thousand years ago made me shudder, and I gripped my arm as tightly as I could, counting on the pain to distract me.

Agari still knelt, head downcast. "With respect, Your Excellency, Your Reverence, ladies, I cannot see how the dead xenobite could have known of Vorgossos unless it is real."

"He had it off some prisoner, girl," said Ligeia Vas, though her frigid eyes addressed the words directly to Lord Mataro. "Must have done." The count nodded his agreement and fussed with the drape of his green-and-yellow silks but said nothing. Had he always been so spineless? Or was it only the matter of the Cielcin that had taken the iron from him? Lord Luthor sat beside his husband on a smaller seat not unlike those the Jaddian lady and the Legion officer sat in, narrow eyes narrowed further in his contemplation of the inquisitor and me. At least the children were absent. I could not have faced Dorian and especially Anaïs, not with everything else.

"A prisoner that spoke the Pale's tongue?" The count sounded unconvinced.

"Your Reverence, Excellency," I said, stepping forward, keeping my burned arm crooked up and tucked across my chest, holding my opposite shoulder. "It said this *as it was dying*. As it was trying to save its crew. It wouldn't pin what hope it had on some obscure human fable it had heard somewhere. It wasn't stupid."

Lord Luthor cleared his throat. "But we have only your word on that, Lord Marlowe. The room's surveillance was down for most of the conversation."

Agari finally stood, keeping her shaved head bowed. "And how did that happen, anyhow? Are we any closer to finding a solution to the problem?"

"The house service staff insists there was more damage from the storms than originally thought," Lord Luthor said, glancing at his husband and indicating by his tone that he did not believe a word of this. My jaw tightened, and I glanced back to the ranks of logothetes and minor ministers seated on the tiered pews to either side of the hall, half expecting to see Valka seated among them. But she was not there. I bit my lip, prayed that the truth behind the issue stayed hidden.

"Can we return to the matter at hand?" the knight-tribune asked, drumming her fingers against the arms of her chair. When silence greeted this question, Raine Smythe composed herself, planting her square jaw on one fist. "I'm not convinced that starting this Eudoran farce of a procedure over from the top is our best course of action."

That set the grand prior on the offensive. The old harridan took three clattering steps down the dais, looped braid swaying against her black-and-argent robes, one finger raised as if in accusation or incantation. "And what is, soldier? Would you treat with these devils?"

Raine did not stand. Instead she shut her eyes, voice hardening to glass as she replied, "Yes."

The grand prior shouted over whatever words might follow. "You dare blaspheme in the presence of His Excellency?" She swept an arm at the count, added, "In my own presence?" Rounding on the count, her lord and—I thought—her thrall, she said, "Sire, this has gone on long enough. The prisoners have confessed that Emesh is not under threat. They should be killed and given to the people, that all may know the Blood of Earth is strong."

"No one doubts that!" said Sir William Crossflane, rounding on the priestess.

"I would rather talk with men," Raine Smythe said,

"than kill them." The line carried the weight of much use, as if she were in the habit of deploying it during staff meetings.

Ligeia seized on a technicality with all the ferocity of the zealot she was. "These are not men, Tribune! You have seen them! They are beasts, demons of the Dark shaped in a mockery of human form! They must be purged from our skies!"

"Speaking as someone doing the purging, Grand Prior," Raine Smythe said, voice surprisingly delicate from so indelicate a woman, "you can rest assured that I am aware of my duties."

"If I may." The voice that interrupted was surprisingly small, made thinner by its breathy, lilting accent. Sir Olorin pivoted on a heel behind his lady's seat. "What have the Chantry's methods gained us but the loss of a prisoner and a couple of names?"

To my astonishment, the grand prior actually quailed, retreating a step up the dais toward the lords Mataro and the coral throne. I took a sympathetic step forward, past Agari, marveling at the way Olorin had cowed the Chantry priestess with so slight a question. Ligeia glanced a moment at Lord Balian, who only shook his head. Her voice now carrying a fraction of its earlier forcefulness, she said, "What, then? Conciliation? Surrender?"

"No one is saying anything about surrender, ma'am," said old Sir William Crossflane from his place beside the tribune.

Lady Kalima stood, pivoting in a mirror of Olorin's gesture as she said, "We should be considering the original proposal: using the Cielcin captives to negotiate peace with their leader."

"One little clan? Out of how many?" interjected Chancellor Ogir from a pew along the wall, drawing the eye of all those about the throne. "We don't even know where they are."

"Vorgossos!" I said brightly, clutching my arm as I turned to the chancellor. "You all heard the name, but before the power cut on, the *ichakta* indicated a relationship between the Cielcin and the Extrasolarians."

Ligeia found her voice, perhaps emboldened by her hatred of me. "Demoniacs! Allied with the Pale? Traitors and apostates!"

"But men," I said. I turned my attention to Knight-Tribune Smythe. "What if it's not a myth? What if there's some Extra trading post out there?" We all knew the stories, had seen the holograph operas. "What if they know a way to contact the Cielcin? We could take the prisoners, find this place—"

"The Extras would never consort with us. If I went looking for this place, the Extras would turn tail and run, or worse. Have you seen an Exalted Sojourner, boy? Biggest ships you've ever seen. Nasty pieces of work. Still . . ." Raine leaned her chin heavily on her hand, muscles of her neck and jaw working, as if her teeth were trying to cut leather.

I took advantage of the momentary silence. "What if it weren't you? What if it weren't the Legion?"

Crossflane spoke before his superior could find the words. "The hell do you mean?"

I glanced around the room, looking for but not finding the brown-and-white uniforms I sought. Commandant Alexei must have left Emesh with his fleet. Disappointed, I turned back and said, "Foederati! We could hire foederati mercenaries."

Luthor Shin-Mataro sat forward in his small throne. "You're not serious. Who would lead these romantic soldiers of yours? You?"

Could it really be so easy? I could see the mute anger in Lord Balian's face as his planned marriage unraveled. I shrugged. "Why not?"

"You have *no* experience," Lord Luthor sneered. "Your carelessness lost us the prisoner in the first place."

"I had to defend myself!" I snapped, prepared for just that accusation. "You saw what Uvanari did to the cathar left with me. What it did to my arm!" I shoved my sleeve back, baring the black tape of the medical correctives warm against my flesh. "You cannot honestly hold me accountable for defending myself." I shook my head. "My lords, ladies. How long until the other Cielcin and this

aeta come looking for Cielcin here? Is it not better to head them off, to take the fight or the olive branch or whatever as far away from here as possible? Lord Mataro, I do not want to see your world attacked by the Pale—you know that. Let me go. I've some small rapport with the leader of the surviving Cielcin. It will work with me, I swear it."

Raine Smythe looked away from me to glance at the Jaddians, a frown creasing her plain, plebeian face. Pensive, she turned back to me, resumed drumming her fingers on the arm of her chair. "There's a big gap between letting you go and putting you in command of an army of foederati, Marlowe."

Olorin turned to whisper something to Lady Kalima, who nodded, patting her guardian and advisor on the arm. Seeing this, I cleared my throat. "Not an army, ma'am. A ship. One ship. The *Obdurate* is a carrier, is it not? You must have captured a pirate ship in your time?"

"A pirate ship?" Ogir sneered from the pews. "How old are you, boy?"

A moment passed while I composed myself, unwilling to rise to the chancellor's bait. "I've fought the Cielcin, Chancellor. Spoken with them, which is more than you have done." I turned my laser focus from the gray-haired chancellor to address the high lords of the Empire and Jadd. "Not foederati, then, but . . . but the appearance of foederati! Again, you must have a derelict in your holds. What do you have to lose?" I directed this last bit directly at the count, who of course had *me* to lose. I had banked on precisely this moment, prayed that the Chantry would be compromised by their failure with Uvanari. The way out—the way away from Mataro's marriage plot—lay just on the other side of this confrontation.

"The *appearance* of foederati?" Raine repeated, lacing her fingers together and leaning forward in her seat. "A covert mission?"

"The Emperor's own mercenaries." I nodded. "There's precedent! Kasia Soulier."

"Kasia Soulier?" Ogir snorted. "Are you a walking literary cliché?"

"Yes!" I snapped. "Ask anyone who knows me." That

Kasia Soulier was real—a privateer admiral in the Foundation War and a childhood hero of mine—did not seem to matter to the chancellor or indeed the crowd, for they laughed and tittered like birds. I cast my eye up and down the hall, looking for an ally in the pews and seeing none. Had I ingratiated myself with so few people at court?

Smiling, Sir Olorin said, "Is Lord Marlowe's plan so without merit? I am recalling a time when attempting contact with the Pale was a consideration shared by all of us." By the angle of his head, he took in the throne and all those seated or standing upon the dais. The Maeskolos had a way about him that was indefinable. Something in the lilt of his voice, perhaps, or in the casual way he stood, or in some unknown fact of his history that commanded attention as easily as a shout. He was like my father in that regard, as though there were some nobility in his blood that even my attenuated genes recognized as superior, a quality of person that ran down to the nucleotides. When Olorin spoke, men listened.

"The boy is needed here!" Balian Mataro shouted, breaking down some internal wall of control or disquiet. He leaned forward on his coral throne, a god in all but blood. "He is to marry my daughter!" He pawed blindly toward Luthor with one hand, who seized it in mute support. I could see the white in his furious eyes.

But Raine was nodding, fingers beating out their tattoo against her chair. "Is that finalized? The marriage contract?" She glanced back over her shoulder, eyebrows rising. Earth's bones—I had her.

"Well, I . . ." Balian stammered.

"No," Lord Luthor said, squeezing his husband's hand. "The girl has not had her Ephebeia yet."

The knight-tribune stood, tugged the bottom of her uniform jacket into place, jackboots clacking on the marble floor as she approached me where I stood in the center of the hall beside Agari. She stopped a mere two paces from me. For the first time it dawned on me how small she was, not quite reaching my shoulders. She peered up at me, faint white scars glinting against the dun of her face, brown eyes hard and knowing. "You know, I think you're

right, boy." No "my lord," no "lordship," no deference in her tone. "The other Cielcin are unaware of what happened to their leader?"

I nodded. "Yes, ma'am. I was specifically told not to tell them."

She pursed her lips, massaged her jaw. "Good. Keep it that way. Tell them . . ."

"It was wounded when it arrived," I interrupted, clearly perturbing the woman. "I shall say we could not save it." I felt my own hands closing at my sides, closing as if about the knife that slew Uvanari.

The tribune studied me another moment, somehow managing to look down her nose even as she looked up at me. "See they learn nothing." She turned back to the dais. "I agree with our Jaddian emissary. I believe there is little to be gained by questioning the remaining captives. I propose that we revisit the motion to send a party after this Cielcin prince—what did you call him?"

"Aranata," I said.

"This Aranata," Smythe finished, somewhat lamely.

Chancellor Ogir stood from her place at the end of the bench. "Knight-Tribune, this is most irregular. You pushed for the inquisition in the first place."

"I did!" Raine Smythe agreed, planting her fists on her hips as if challenging anyone to disagree with her. "But I have since had time to reconsider my position, Chancellor. Do you know what *reconsider* means? It means I changed my mind." That cowed Ogir a moment, and she looked to the dais for support. Even from Ligeia Vas, none was forthcoming. "The Chantry's investigation has produced some useful intelligence, in no small part thanks to Lord Marlowe's interference in their standard operating procedures. I did not become Tribune of the 437th by squandering strategic and diplomatic advantages, and I am not about to start doing so today." She looked back at me a moment. "Under Article 119 of the Great Charters and by virtue of my office, I hereby conscript Lord Hadrian Marlowe into my service, as well as any experts he may recommend. A full list should be provided to you by the end of the week." The look of pain on Balian Mataro's face was

the only reaction in the hall. But Raine was not finished. "I also request delivery of the Cielcin captives to the *ISV Obdurate* in the name of His Imperial Radiance, Emperor William the Twenty-Third of House Avent."

That drew gasps from the logothetes dutifully taking notes and listening from the pews, and it stirred Ligeia to action. The old sorceress tottered down the steps of the dais, a shadow in flowing black, one finger upraised. "The Synod will never allow it!"

"Your Synod is not here!" Raine Smythe said firmly. "The Imperial Legion is. I am making this request in the name of our Emperor and in the light of the Faith. Truly, Your Reverence, a handful of prisoners is worth more to the war effort than to propaganda." Hands still on her hips, she looked down at her boots a moment, nearly rocked back on her heels. A curious gesture, but it kept everyone hanging on her words, sure that she was about to continue. I made note to use it. By Earth, the woman commanded a presence. "If we're hunting an Extrasolarian world in order to make contact, this business of foederati makes sense. But I agree with the chancellor and—I believe—with our Jaddian friends when I say it would be a mistake to leave this in the hands of Lord Marlowe, who, it has been noted, has no experience with such matters. I'd like to put one of my officers in charge."

"Who?" I asked, unable to help myself.

"Bassander Lin," Raine replied, and she launched into an outline of her plan. I glowered at my feet, thinking of the tall, rather severe officer who had not wanted me at Calagah. Perhaps I was not about to come out of this as on top as I'd imagined.

When it was over, Raine Smythe stopped me in the hall in the shadow of a stained glass mural of a battle between House Mataro and the Norman settlers of long ago. Jewel-bright shadows tessellated their way across the herringbone tile and enameled pillars that rose to the vaulted ceilings. "I'm not sure how you did it," she said, fingers

tight around my biceps, "but I know you had the power cut." I didn't answer, gave the hard, scarred woman a startled look. "You can cut the charade, Marlowe. They can't touch you now—you're mine."

Old habit compelled me to look up, to try and pick out the cameras among the Rococo scrollwork and baroque embellishments of the high palatine architecture. I could not find them, and I was also aware that this was not the gesture or habit of an innocent man. I only smiled and by way of an answer said, "I don't approve of torture."

"Nor do I," the knight-tribune said, eliciting a nod from her lictor, the aged Sir William Crossflane. "But war begs hard answers of us, eh? And I don't approve of soldiers who play games like yours. I'm taking you, but I'm not taking you because you wanted it. I'm taking you because I think I need you and because Lieutenant Lin can keep a firm hold on you." I opened my mouth to reply, to say I knew not what, but the tribune was not finished. "For what it's worth, I think you're right. You did a rare thing. A stupid thing, but a rare one. You may not have seen much of it safe on this rock, but the war's gone on for far too long . . ." She broke off, shaking her head, disturbed, I thought, by visions. "Do you have anyone you want to bring with you? Anyone I can conscript?"

I paused a moment, hesitating because the obvious choice was someone who lay outside the tribune's admittedly long reach. "I'd like to talk to the Tavrosi xenologist, Onderra."

"She's a foreign national," Smythe said. "We can't recruit her."

"I can," I said, though I was not sure how I knew it was possible. "If we're to look like foederati, we shouldn't all stink of the Legions, should we?"

That brought a faint smile to the tribune's lips, and she nodded. "Anyone else?"

In spite of everything, I smiled. "Oh, yes."

CHAPTER 78

QUALITY

SLAVE UMANDH LOADED THE shuttles as I stepped from the groundcar onto the private airfield beyond the edge of Borosevo. The red sun watched from the morning horizon, presiding over a day already hot, as my last day on Emesh must be. Setting my case at my side a moment, I pulled my dark red glasses from a pocket of the charcoal greatcoat the castle staff had found for me. My ridiculous coats, Gibson had named them. Well, he wasn't wrong. I should have waited to put it on, for I could feel myself starting to sweat. The effect was made so much worse by the lingering medical correctives taped to my side and arm.

The driver hurried from his door and dragged the rest of my meager luggage from the back of his car, then fell into step behind me as I took up my case and hurried along the tarmac to where a few figures waited—some to join me, others to see me off. Valka hurried forward, and I quickly urged the driver to leave the luggage with the Umandh and their douleters. I eyed the creatures nervously as Valka approached, recalling the lumbering, spinning way they'd attacked us that afternoon in the warehouse. I had not been so close to them since, and my spine stiffened.

"You sure 'tis a good idea, this?" Valka asked, voice low so as not to carry across the open field. Above us a flock of ornithons tumbled through the air, white wings beating the sky.

"No," I said, unable to keep the humor and the relief

from my voice. "But I'm glad you're coming, Doctor." Instinct cried out in me to take her hand, but my mistake with Kyra tasted of iron on my tongue, and I recalled Anaïs's kiss, and so limited myself to a smile.

Valka stepped closer, forcing that instinct into screaming panic, but I held my ground and my breath, too. She smiled, whispered so only I could hear, "Well, it isn't like I had a choice after helping you." She drew back, her smile unmoved, unrepentant. "Though it may be I'll learn more with you than I would here."

"The Cielcin will have answers," I said, confident I was right. "That's what you want, isn't it? And a peaceful galaxy to find them in?"

She smiled, stepping back. "I hope you're right." Valka glanced over her shoulder to where the others were clambering up the ramp onto the shuttle bound for the *Obdurate* and whatever wreck of a ship Raine Smythe had selected for our use. "That swordmaster's here. Your friend."

"Olorin?" I craned my neck, looking past her. "Why?"

"Said he wanted to say goodbye."

I nodded stiffly. "All right, then. Guess I should speak to him."

"I'll be on the shuttle."

Olorin Milta stood to the side of the black beetle shape of the shuttle, wreathed in the clouds of chilly vapor from the fuel lines. At my approach he strode forward, one arm slung through his ceremonial half robe, the heavy silk snapping out behind him as he raised a hand. "Lord Marlowe!"

"Sir Olorin!" I bowed. "What an unexpected honor."

To my astonishment, the swordmaster *returned* my bow, extending his right arm in imitation of the highest Imperial courtly style. "I wanted to see you before you went. I have something for you." And to my greater astonishment, he unclipped one of the three sword hilts he wore on his right hip and handed it to me, pommel first.

My numb fingers reached out to receive it without thought. Words fled me.

It was a sword such as Emperors might wield without shame. All the art and craftsmanship of the swordsmiths of Jadd was in her, and as it is the purpose of such crafts

to render beautiful that which would be otherwise without them, no craft could elevate her. So fine a work I have not seen in more than fifteen hundred years. Not even the great mosaics and frescoes of the palaces of the Imperial Presence can compare, for they are gaudy and elaborate things. Her craft was honest and clean: the hilt wrapped in leather so red it was almost black, her pommel and fittings of plated silver, with a single finger loop in her rain guard near the mouth whence the blade would spring.

"I can't accept this—it's worth more than I am."

Olorin's smile collapsed into grave seriousness. "You undervalue yourself. And you must take it. You are the commander of this strange expedition, are you not?"

I shook my head. "Only in name. Bassander Lin has the command. I . . ." I was being ungrateful. "Thank you, *domi*."

He made a noncommittal gesture with his left hand that hung in the sling of his mandyas. "Try the balance. Please, please!"

At his word I squeezed the twin buttons, and the blade hummed, flowing upward like water into the red dawn. It was not the one Olorin had wielded in the dark of Calagah, but it shone the same way, its blade a spike of crystal like moonlight.

The weight of it was a kind of poetry. Its shining blade shimmered in the light of the sun, sending silver highlights flashing. Extended, the balance was so exquisite that it felt more than a part of me and less than weightless. And it sang, humming as the exotic nuclei of its atoms shifted, moving so that its cutting edge always matched the direction of its motion. It flickered, vibrating as I brought it up between myself and the swordmaster, the surface rippling like the sea.

"*Innana umorphi,*" I said, the word *umorphi* implying not only that it was beautiful in appearance but also in function and ability. That it performed beauty like a painter or a poet. A dancer.

"It is!" Olorin agreed. "I am glad you like it!"

I squeezed the triggers again, and the blade melted like smoke into the crimson sunlight. "I still can't accept it."

"When I return to my country and am kneeling before my prince, do you know what it is I will say?" The question seemed not to follow from anything that had come before, so I stood confused, still holding the sword hilt in my hands. I could see the heat shimmers where the ramp's static field trapped the cold air within and longed to be on the other side of it. Valka waited in the shuttle along with the others I'd asked Raine to conscript. Olorin took a step back before answering. "I will tell him I met a man, a lord of the strange Empire. I will tell him of your quality." His smile capered on his face. "And your quality will be known in Jadd and on the battlefields of our war before ever you find yourself there. You will have friends."

"My . . . quality?" I repeated, words unsteady. Uncomfortable with this praise, I asked, "You helped me—in the council meeting, I mean. You made sure this would happen." I gestured at the ship. "I don't think Smythe would have listened to me if you hadn't pointed out how useless the Chantry's been."

The Maeskolos took a half step away, slippered feet scuffing the fused ceramic of the tarmac. "In Jadd we say a man must be either a swordsman or a poet. This is not true, of course—we are having all sorts of men. And women. But these people . . ." He made a vague gesture toward the city and the castle looming like a weathered finger above it. "They are swordsmen, though they call themselves priests and politicians. The war has had enough of such men, I am thinking." He leaned forward and clapped me on the arm. "So we are sending them you! Make peace, my friend. *Iffero fosim!*" Bring light. He retreated then, step by careful step, bowing slightly as the wind over the tarmac gathered the sleeve and flowing hem of his robe and spread them like the pinion of a one-winged angel. Mamluks I had not seen before emerged from the shadows of other beetle-shaped shuttles, the fabric of their uniforms flowing from matte black to striped blue and orange. And for a moment the morning light cast their shadows back across the landing field, silhouettes blotting out the sun—none greater than his—and Olorin Milta stood tall and straight as a king.

When at last he'd left by the tatty gate in the wired chain fence of the airfield, I slipped the sword hilt into the inside pocket of my heavy coat and, sweating, turned and climbed the ramp into the shuttle, breathing a sigh of relief as I passed through the static field. A cry went up from the shuttle's occupants, raucous, joyous, and clean. I found myself grinning, surrounded—undeservedly—by friends. Valka smiled languidly in a corner seat, the one beside her empty, reserved for me. Behind her sat a mix of Imperial and Jaddian officers, all strangers to me but for Jinan Azhar, the Jaddian lieutenant who had accompanied Olorin into Calagah. She alone smiled at me, black eyes bright in her olive face. I smiled back, and then my eyes went to the others, to the motley crew I'd requested be added to our gang of pretend mercenaries.

I had promised them a ship, after all.

Ghen was first on his feet, pounding me on the back, bellowing something about "Your Radiance!" and grinning like a bull shark. Siran followed, then old Pallino, who said something about being a soldier to the end. A few other of the myrmidons came forward to shake my hand and pound me on the back in turn, each glad to be there and free of their fatal contracts or their prison sentences. Switch was the last to approach with a small, sheepish grin.

I embraced the fellow, saying, "I'm glad you're here, Will."

He pushed me back, punched my arm. "Just call me Switch, lordship—or whatever."

"Only if you call me Had!" I said, and I looked around at the friends who had known me as such. "With you all, I'll always be just . . . Had." I turned, still grinning, then felt the smile harden on my face and sag. Bassander Lin stood in the narrow arch of the pilot's cabin, his wood smoke hair neatly combed, the sides of his head freshly shaven. He alone wore the blacker-than-blacks of his Legion uniform, collar tabs depicting the triple sunbursts and silver diamonds that marked his new rank of captain. I took my arm from Switch's shoulder and saluted. "Are

the Cielcin ready for transport, Captain?" I asked, fist still pressed to my chest.

Bassander inclined his head, polite but stiffly formal. "Very nearly, but we're ready here." The ramp had retracted while I spoke to the others, the hatch sealed. "You all'd best strap in. Dust-off's in five if we're to rendezvous with the *Obdurate*." He turned smartly and returned to his pilot officer in the cockpit, door hissing coldly behind him.

The Legion officer was a problem for another time, I decided, settling into my seat beside Valka. I wanted to laugh, to cry, to do *something*. "Are you all right?" she asked.

I looked round. Valka was staring at me, eyes filled with something rare and precious: concern. Swallowing, I nodded, not trusting myself to speak. Her hand was on my knee, fingers warm. I smiled at her, then out the window to the landing field as we began to move. "I am now."

So much had happened, so much had changed, all of it lasting, all of it . . . over. I had departed Meidua in a storm, but here we rose through clear sunlight and heat, passing through cloud and air to the silence beyond night.

There are endings, Reader, and this is one. Some part of me will forever lie on Emesh, in the canals and the coliseum, in the castle and the bastille of Borosevo. It lies with Cat at the bottom of a waterway and on the killing floor of the Colosso. It lies with Gilliam and Uvanari, dead at my hands; and with Anaïs, whom I never saw again. If what I have done disturbs you, Reader, I do not blame you. If you would read no further, I understand. You have the luxury of foresight. You know where this ends.

I shall go on alone.

HOUSE MARLOWE OF DELOS

The Sword, Our Orator!

FIRST ELEVATED FROM PATRICIAN standing in the mid-eighth millennium by Duke Tiberius Ormund, House Marlowe has ruled Meidua Prefecture on Delos for thirty-one generations. Prior to that the Marlowes were military patricians, officers in the Orionid Legions with blood harking back to Avalon and the Kingdom of Windsor-in-Exile. Julian Marlowe was strategos of the 117th Legion of Orion and proved instrumental in the defense of Duke Tiberius's claim to the throne of Delos in the Second Aurigan War. For his service, he was elevated to the palatine caste and accorded the demesne of Meidua, then a fishing village of no consequence on a scrap of rocky upland. It was only later that the region's uranium deposits were discovered. While under the reign of Lord Hadrian's great-great-grandmother, the Archon Lady Sabine, House Marlowe's wealth grew until its coffers outstripped those of House Kephalos. The Marlowes are distant members of the Imperial peerage both through their marriage into House Kephalos and more distantly through their ancient Avalonian connections. They can be identified by their alabaster complexions, black hair, and violet eyes. Their sigil is a crimson devil rampant on a black field.

Lord Hadrian's grandfather, the Archon Lord Timon, was assassinated in ISD 15861 by a homunculus concubine gifted him by Yuen Starcrafts, a starship manufacturer aligned with Delos's exsul houses. They were outraged that Lord Timon had used his powers as the vicereine's

executor to secure a writ of monopoly for House Marlowe over all uranium mining in Delos System, destroying their profits. With the vicereine away at Forum, young Alistair was thrust into the role of system executor and into war with the exsul houses when they declared poine against the Houses Marlowe and Kephalos. The other houses had underestimated Lord Alistair, however, and were crushed at the Battle of Linon in ISD 15863. House Orin, the leader of the rebellion, was utterly destroyed, and system authority was more tightly concentrated in the planetary houses. For this and for defending her title, Vicereine Kephalos married Alistair to her youngest daughter, Liliana. Lord Alistair's reign was hard but prosperous, characterized by the rule of law.

Here follows a list of those members and retainers of House Marlowe mentioned in Lord Hadrian's account:

LORD ALISTAIR DIOMEDES FRIEDRICH MARLOWE, Archon of Meidua Prefecture and Lord of Devil's Rest, former Lord Executor of Delos System, the Butcher of Linon.

—His wife, **LADY LILIANA KEPHALOS-MARLOWE**, a celebrated librettist and filmmaker and notorious womanizer, youngest daughter of the vicereine-duchess. Frequently away from Devil's Rest, preferring her own family's summer palace at Haspida.

—Her mother, Her Grace **ELMIRA GWENDOLYN KEPHALOS**, Vicereine of Auriga Province, Duchess of Delos, Archon of Artemia Prefecture.

—Her sisters: **AMALIA**, **CIARAN**, **RHEA**, **ALIENOR**, **ELENA**, and **TALIA**.

—Her servant, **MIKAL**, a plebeian man from the Haspida house staff.

—Their children:

—**HADRIAN ANAXANDER MARLOWE**, The Halfmortal, The Sun-Eater, Starbreaker, Palekiller, Deathless. Responsible for the death of the entire Cielcin species.

—**CRISPIN MARLOWE**, presumptive heir of Devil's Rest, a violent and callow youth.

—His parents, {**LORD TIMON MARLOWE**} and {**LADY FUCHSIA BELLGROVE-MARLOWE**}, both dead.

—His brother, {**LUCIAN MARLOWE**}, killed in a shuttle crash.

—His ancestor {**LORD JULIAN MARLOWE**}, awarded the demesne of Meidua Prefecture for services rendered to the now-defunct House Ormund. Began the construction of Devil's Rest.

—His household:

—**SIR FELIX MARTYN**, Castellan and commander of the house guard. Also tasked with the martial instruction of the Marlowe heirs.

—His knights:

—**SIR ROBAN MILOSH**, lictor tasked with the personal protection of the Marlowe family.

—**DAME UMA SYLVIA**, lictor tasked with the personal protection of the Marlowe family.

—**SIR ARDIAN TULLO**, captain of the Marlowe pilots' corp.

—**KYRA**, a shuttle pilot.

—**TOR ALCUIN**, chief scholiast advisor to the archon.

—**TOR GIBSON**, tutor to the Marlowe children and a minor functionary on the archon's advisory council. A graduate of Nov Acor on Syracuse.

—**TOR ALMA**, personal physician to House Marlowe. Authorized to do work with High College birthing vats in the delivery of palatine children.

—**EUSEBIA**, prior of the Holy Chantry in Meidua Prefecture and a chief advisor to the archon.

—Her acolytes:

  —**SEVERN**, a young chanter who serves as secretary to the prior.

  —**ABIATHA**, an old chanter who runs the Chantry services at Devil's Rest on most occasions.

—**HELENE**, chamberlain of Devil's Rest and chief of the domestic and social servants, including the wait staff, cooks, maids, and grooms.

ON THE PLANET DELOS

Delos is one of the older examples of successful terraforming in Imperial history. Formally settled in the fourth millennium ISD, the project took several centuries to complete. It originally had no biosphere, oxygen cycle, or oceans, but the gravity and magnetospheres were just right. Comets were brought in to introduce water, and many of the animals introduced were of terranic stock, leading to a world as much like Old Earth as could be

readily produced. Due to its clement environment and strategic placement on the Imperial trade routes with the Sagittarine provinces, the world has always been prosperous. It flourished first under House Ormund, then again under House Kephalos when the Ormund Dukes fell into disfavor during the Chablon Rebellion in the thirteenth millennium and were removed from power. This prosperity was compounded by the discovery of the system's amazing uranium deposits, which have long been the subject of internecine struggles between the palatine houses of the system.

A cultural and commercial hub, Delos has attracted interstellar trade among Nipponese and Mandari corporations as well as the Eudorans, Durantines, and Free Traders.

Here follows a list of those persons appearing in the Delos episode of Lord Marlowe's account:

ADAEZE FENG, Director of the Wong-Hopper Consortium for the Auriga Province.

—Her retainers:

    —**XUN GONG SUN**, a junior minister dealing with the trade of raw materials.

    —**TOR TERENCE**, a scholiast advisor to the director's personal office.

LENA BALEM, factionarius of the Delian Miners Guild, Meidua chapter; tasked with the oversight of all uranium mining in-system.

JEM and **ZEB**, two criminals.

DEMETRI ARELLO, a Jaddian Free Trader, captain of the starship *Eurynasir*.

—His wife, **JUNO ARELLO**, co-owner of the ship.

—Their crew:

—**BASSEM**, a fellow Jaddian and the ship's helmsman.

—**SARRIC JUGO**, a Tavrosi expatriate and the ship's physician.

—**SALTUS**, a homunculus of inappropriate humor.

—**EMAR** and **IMANI**, twins.

HOUSE MATARO OF EMESH

Borne by Conquest

A comparatively young house, the Mataros of Emesh are one of several nouveau riche families that rose to prominence during the years of Imperial conquest in Norma and in the Veil of Marinus in particular. Only plutocrats some few generations ago, the Mataros made their money buying and selling slaves, particularly bulk-order homunculi for agricultural and industrial labor in new colonies. Exceedingly wealthy, Armand Mataro— only a patrician—outfitted three private legions and used them to conquer Emesh without Imperial mandate. Such private wars typified the Norman conquests, and those who were successful were granted palatine status. The Mataros are not yet aligned with any of the great ancient constellations of the houses palatine, being of relatively low blood and low status.

Emesh is an unimportant demesne on the very edge of human-civilized space, constantly under the shadow of the Cielcin threat. Relatively poor, the residents have been trying to capitalize on the planet's Umandh coloni,

though the natives are so biologically alien that their usefulness as slaves is questionable at best. Still, the planet gets by on the export of seafood and petroleum extracted from the seabed. House Mataro's sigil is a golden sphinx dormant on a green field, sometimes trimmed in white.

Here follows a list of those members and retainers of House Mataro mentioned in Lord Hadrian's account:

LORD BALIAN MATARO, third Count of Emesh, Archon of Borosevo Prefecture, and Lord of Castle Borosevo.

—His husband, **LORD LUTHOR ASTIN-SHIN-MATARO**, a Mandari man, Minister of Finance for the county and formerly of the Marinus office of the Wong-Hopper Consortium.

—Their children:

   —**DORIAN MATARO**, presumptive heir to the County of Emesh, a young man in the year of his Ephebeia.

      —His friend, **MELANDRA**, a patrician from a loyal family in Borosevo.

   —**ANAÏS MATARO**, a young and canny socialite.

—His ancestor {**LORD ARMAND MATARO**}, first Count of Emesh, conqueror of the Norman United Fellowship. Oversaw the construction of the military base in Borosevo and the beginnings of the city itself.

—His household:

—**LIADA OGIR**, High Chancellor and chief of the palace logothetes, head of the civil service.

—**LIGEIA VAS**, Grand Prior of the Holy Chantry on Emesh.

—Her acolyte, **GILLIAM VAS**, a chanter and the grand prior's bastard son, a genetically mutated intus.

—**K. F. AGARI**, chief inquisitor of the Holy Chantry in Borosevo.

　—Brothers **RHOM** and **UDAN**, cathars of the Chantry Inquisition.

—**SIR PRESTON RAU**, the elderly fencing instructor tasked with teaching the count's children.

—**DAME CAMILLA**, a lictor tasked with the protection of the count and his family.

—**TOR VLADIMIR**, chief scholiast advisor to the count.

—**MALO**, a palace concubine in the count's service.

—His vassals:

—**LORD PERUN VEISI**, Archon of Tolbaran Prefecture and Lord of Springdeep Castle.

　—His wife, **LADY LYDIA REDGRAVE-VEISI**, an offworld palatine.

　　—Her uncle, **SIR ELOMAS REDGRAVE**, a famous traveler, adventurer, and duelist. Retired to a life in the country as an amateur xenologist.

　　　—His associate, **TOR ADA**, a scholiast, director of the archaeological dig at Calagah.

　　　　—Her assistants, **MAROS** and **BEL**, lay archaeologists from the University of Tolbaran.

　　　—His servants, **ORSO** and **DAMARA**, brought with him from his travels.

—Their children:

  —**ALEXANDER VEISI**, presumptive heir to the prefecture.

  —**KARTHIK VEISI**, a young man, squire to his greatuncle Elomas.

—His mother, **LADY KAMALA VEISI**.

—**ETAN VRIELL**, a centurion in his service.

—**LORD TIVAN MELLUAN**, Archon and Exsul of Binah Prefecture.

—**LORD IVANIS KVAR**, Archon and Exsul of Armand Prefecture.

ON THE PLANET EMESH

Emesh was colonized by the Norman United Fellowship, a small-state direct democracy, in the early sixteenth millennium. The planet is mostly oceanic with a diverse native aquaculture, and as such many of Emesh's settlements were built on atolls or islands that are all that remain of the planet's long-dead volcanic past. It has only one continent, Anshar, a small, volcanic outcrop a mere fifteen hundred miles across. There the NUF built its capital, Tolbaran. When House Mataro invaded, they built an advanced military base on Borosevo atoll, which in the centuries since has grown into a sprawling labyrinth of canals and platforms. Tolbaran has now been relegated to a secondary role in civic life. Much of Anshar's land in given over to agriculture, as the volcanic soil has proved amenable to agriculture and viticulture.

The planet has two moons, Armand and Binah. Binah, the larger moon, has recently been opened for terraform-

ing, and algae cultures have taken hold extremely aggressively. Armand is too small to hold an atmosphere but plays host to vigorous mining operations, especially of heavy metals.

Here follows a list of those persons appearing in the Emesh episode of Lord Marlowe's account:

VALKA ONDERRA VHAD EDDA, a xenologist and de facto dignitary visiting from Edda in the Demarchy of Tavros. A researcher of the Umandh and of the ruins on the southern continent. Attached to Sir Elomas Redgrave's amateur expedition.

CAT, a poor girl eking out a living in the streets.

SEPHA, an old woman who runs a clinic for the city's poor and homeless, often for free.

—Her assistant, **MARIS**, a young woman.

GILA, head of a reclamation dock for abandoned lighter ships.

—Her employees, **SKAG** and **BOR**, starship mechanics.

RELLS, the head of a street gang that menaces the city and terrorizes the other homeless and disaffected people.

—His underlings, **JOI**, **KALLER**, and **TUR**, common criminals.

GIN, prefect-inspector of the Criminal Response Division, chief enemy of the street gangs.

—**KO**, **REN**, and **YOH**, all urban prefects.

NILES ENGIN, vilicus of the Umandh alienage at Ulakiel, high-ranking member of the Fishers Guild.

—**QUINTUS**, a douleter in the employ of the Ulakiel sanctuary and the Fishers Guild.

CROW, a traveler from an antique land.

—In the colosso:

—**WILLIAM OF DANU**, called **SWITCH**, an inexperienced fighter. Formerly a chartered catamite and cabin boy aboard a Mandari starship.

>—His former master, **SET**, a ship owner, pederast, and merchanter.

—**PALLINO**, a one-eyed, forty-year active-service veteran of the Imperial Legions. One of the de facto captains of the myrmidon team.

>—His lover, **ELARA**, a local woman with a taste for the sarcastic.

—**GHEN** and **SIRAN**, prisoners forced to fight.

—**BANKS**, a grizzled veteran. One of the de facto captains of the myrmidon team.

—**KIRI**, a middle-aged woman fighting voluntarily, hoping to earn enough to send her son to school.

>—Her son, **DAR**, a young man on the cusp of being old enough to take the civil service exams.

—Among the others, **KEDDWEN**, **ERDRO**, **ALIS**, and **LIGHT**.

—**KOGAN**, a former Whitehorse Company mercenary, veteran of the Battle of Wodan. Recently joined the myrmidons at the Colosso.

—**JAFFA** and **AMAREI**, professional gladiators.

—**CHAND**, a slave and physician to the myrmidons. A Lothrian ex-patriot and former Imperial auxiliary.

—**STROMOS**, chef in the coliseum's hypogean gaol. Considers himself too great an artist for his post.

—**SLOW** and **SLOWER**, prison guards tasked by the count with guarding special prisoners.

—Their charge, **MAKISOMN**, a Cielcin gifted to the count by the Whitehorse Company, meant for public execution.

THE WIDER WORLD

Here follows a list of those persons tied neither to Delos nor Emesh in Lord Marlowe's account:

His Imperial Radiance, **EMPEROR WILLIAM THE TWENTY-THIRD OF THE HOUSE AVENT;** Firstborn Son of the Earth; Guardian of the Solar System; King of Avalon; Lord Sovereign of the Kingdom of Windsor-in-Exile; Prince Imperator of the Arms of Orion, of Sagittarius, of Perseus, and of Centaurus; Primarch of Orion; Conqueror of Norma; Grand Strategos of the Legions of the Sun; Supreme Lord of the Cities of Forum; North Star of the Constellations of the Blood Palatine; Defender of the Children of Men; and Servant of the Servants of Earth.

—His Strategos, **SIR TITUS HAUPTMANN**, Duke of Andernach and First Strategos of the Legions of Centaurus.

—His tribune, **DAME RAINE SMYTHE**, a Tribune of the 437th Legion of Centaurus, captain of the *ISV Obdurate*.

—Her first officer, **SIR WILLIAM CROSSFLANE**, Commander, First Grade. An elderly palatine.

—Her lieutenant, **BASSANDER LIN**, a promising young senior security officer aboard the *Obdurate*. Frequently serves as a lictor to the tribune on political affairs.

—**SIR ALEXEI KARELIN**, Lord Chairman and Captain of the Whitehorse Company, a group of foederati composed primarily of Imperial ex-legionnaires. Attached to the 437th Legion.

—**VARRIC COUSLAND**, Lord Chairman, founder, and Captain of the Cousland Drakes, a foederati company operating out of the Norman Freehold of Monmara. Attached to the 437th Legion.

—**EDOUARD ALBE**, a Legion intelligence operative.

His Royal Highness **ALDIA AHMAD RODRIGO-PHILLIPE DI OTRANTO**, High Prince of Jadd; Prince of Laran; First-Among-Equals of the Princes of the Principalities of the Jaddian Peoples; Lord of the Encircling Moons; Keeper of the Planet of Fire; Chief of the *Dham-Eali*.

—**LADY KALIMA ALIARADA UDIRI DI SAYYIPH**, Satrap of Ubar, loyal to the Prince of Thessaloniki. A formal envoy to the war front on behalf of the High Prince.

—Her lictor, **SIR OLORIN MILTA**, a Maeskolos swordmaster of the Fire School.

—His lieutenant, **JINAN AZHAR**, a promising young officer.

UTSEBIMN ARANATA OTIOLO, *Aeta* Prince-Chieftain and Captain of Its Scianda; Master-Keeper of its People; Servant to Its Slaves.

—Its property:

    —**CASANTORA TANARAN IAKATO**, *baetan* priest-historian of the *scianda*.

    —**ITANA UVANARI AYATOMN**, *ichakta* captain of the starship *Yad Ga Higatte* and a proud military officer.

      —Its property and slave-soldier, **SVATAROM**.

INDEX OF WORLDS

A Note on Astrography

IT IS CLEAR FROM reading Lord Marlowe's account that the man was acutely familiar with the astropolitical landscape of the seventeenth millennium. He references several dozen settled worlds, whereas most among the peasantry of the time would not have known more than a handful of names. This is no surprise, given his training in interstellar diplomacy.

As of today, human colonial efforts have seeded more than a half-billion habitable worlds distributed across five of our galaxy's arms. Nearly half of these worlds owe their allegiance to the Sollan Empire, with the remainder distributed amongst smaller polities such as the Lothrian Commonwealth, the Principalities of Jadd, the Durantine Republic, the Demarchy of Tavros, and in microstates such as the freeholds common in both the Norman Veil of Marinus and the Outer Perseus. Since the Exodus and the first peregrinations from Old Earth system before the fall of the Mericanii, human colonial efforts have trended in two general directions. The first is toward the galaxy's core, through the Sagittarius and Centaurus Arms and across the Sullen Gulf to Norma. The other is toward the galaxy's edge from the Spur of Orion into the Perseus Arm, where rapid expansion led to the breakaway of the Jaddian states.

Broadly, the Sollan Empire is divided into four primarchates: one in Orion; one in Perseus; one in Sagittarius; and most recently, one in Centaurus. Efforts to establish a fifth primarchate in Norma were stymied by the Cielcin invasion, and following the Battle of Gododdin and the death of Emperor William XXIII Avent, the

Norman colonies remained unincorporated and under the oversight of the Centaurine primarch at Nessus. The primarchs are appointed by the Emperor, who is himself the Primarch of Orion. Each of the Imperial primarchates is subdivided into several provinces, each governed by an Imperial viceroy appointed by the primarch. Nominally, the title of viceroy is an appointed one, but in practice the viceroyalties of many provinces pass from parent to child, as do the palatine titles of archduke, grand duke, duke, marquis, count, viscount, and baron. Each of these lords rules a palatinate comprising their planetary demesnes and the attendant solar systems. The difference between a baron and a duke, for example, is determined by the relative import of the palatinate in question. Archons serve these palatine lords in administering districts of said demesnes. They may pass their holdings on to their children, though many archons are appointed and are little more than governors. An appointed archon, as in the case of a colonial consul, is said to rule a fief, not a demesne, as his claim to said territory expires in the event of his death and does not pass to his children.

For the convenience of the reader, I have also appended this index of the planets mentioned by the magus in his account, offering a brief description of each, enough to understand the significance of the references made by Lord Marlowe.

—Tor Paulos of Nov Belgaer

Andun   An Imperial planet in the Sagittarius Arm known for its starship manufacturing facilities.

Ares   One of the oldest Imperial worlds in the Spur of Orion. Site of the Ares Command School, where the best Legion officers are trained.

Armand   One of the two moons of Emesh; small and white. It has a few underground settlements and is ruled by House Kvar. Named for Lord Armand Mataro, who took Emesh from the Normans.

Ascia   A planet in the Lothriad.

Asherah   Arid, tectonically active world known for its mountains and for a species of massive reptilian creatures.

Avalon   One of the original human colonies and site of heavy European colonization by generation ark. Birthplace of the Sollan Empire.

Bellos   Imperial colony in the Norman Expanse; site of the Battle of Bellos.

Binah   One of the two moons of Emesh, ruled by House Melluan. A successful case for early terraforming—its surface is green from massive tree-growth.

Cai Shen   An ethnically Mandari world in the Imperium famed for its Bashang Temple. It was ruled by House Min Chen until ISD 16130, when it was destroyed by the Cielcin.

Colchis   The first Imperial colony in the Centaurus Arm. A moon of the gas giant Atlas. Never an important colony, it is nevertheless known for the massive scholiast athenaeum at Nov Belgaer.

Cressgard   A lost Imperial colony in the Veil of Marinus. Site of the first contact with the Cielcin in the Battle of Cressgard in ISD 15792.

Delos   Birthplace of Hadrian Marlowe and seat of the duchy of House Kephalos in the Spur of Orion. A temperate world with wan sunlight, famed for its uranium deposits, which made it extremely wealthy.

Durannos   The capital of the Serene Republic of the Durannos. Tectonically dead and marshy, much of its surface is covered in a massive city.

Edda   An arid, windy world in the Demarchy known for its canyons, sinkholes, and subterranean oceans. Its people are primarily Nordei and Travatskr.

Emesh   A watery world in the Veil of Marinus; seat of House Mataro. Home of the coloni Umandh and the subterranean ruins at Calagah. Originally a Norman colony.

Forum   The capital of the Sollan Empire. A gas giant with a breathable atmosphere in whose cloud belt are several flying palace cities that serve as the administrative hubs of the Imperium.

Gododdin   A system between the Centaurus and Sagittarius Arms of the galaxy, famously destroyed by Hadrian Marlowe during the final battle in the Crusade.

Helvetios   The ancient name for the star 51 Pegasi, whose principal planet is Bellerophon.

Ilium   A Norman Freehold famous for manufacturing starships. Considered one of the best starship manufacturers operating at present.

Jadd   The planet of fire and the sacred capital of the Jaddian Principalities, on whose soil none may tread without the express permission of the high prince.

Judecca   A frigid, mountainous world in the Sagittarius Arm. Famously the site of the Temple of Athten Var and birthplace of the Irchtani species. Site of Simeon the Red's famous struggle against the mutineers.

Kandar   An extremely wealthy agricultural world in the inner Empire, frequently considered the definitive source for luxury products, especially wine and genuine livestock. Seat of House Markarian.

Komadd   An Imperial colony in the Veil of Marinus and site of a Chantry seminary.

Linon   Moon of a gas giant in Delos system. Formerly the demesne of the exsul House Orin and site of the Battle of Linon in ISD 15863, in which Alistair Marlowe killed the entire house.

Luin   A planet famous for its xenobitic forests; considered something of a fantasy land. Known for the phasma vigrandi, a species of floating organisms that glow like faerie lights.

Malkuth   An Imperial planet bearing the signs of an extinct xenobite civilization.

Marinus   The first Norman Freehold seized by the Imperium and among its first colonies in the Expanse.

Mars   One of Old Earth's sister planets and the site of the first major offworld colonial efforts during the Exodus but before the Peregrinations.

Mira   A planet orbiting a star of the same name in the Spur of Orion. Naturally airless, its cities are all either domed or hermetically sealed. The surface contains enormous quantities of methane ice, which is quarried.

Monmara   A water world and a Norman Freehold known for the cheap mass production of starships.

Neruda   An old Imperial world in the Sagittarius Arm. Known for its fungus-like flora, it is home to a prominent scholiasts' athenaeum.

Nessus   Seat of the Centaurine Primarchate.

Nichibotsu   Most important of the Nipponese worlds and home to the archduke of House Yamato.

Obatala   An Imperial colony in the Sagittarius Arm that
                  lies along the trade route from Delos to Teukros.

Old Earth   Birthplace of the human species. A nuclear ruin
                  and victim of environmental collapse, she is
                  protected by the Chantry wardens, and none may
                  walk there.

Ozymandias   Old Imperial colony in the Sagittarius Arm; arid.
                  Known for being home to the extinct Arch-
                  Builders and for the massive stone arches they
                  purportedly left behind.

Perfugium   An Imperial world in the Centaurus Arm used as
                  a military base and refugee camp during the later
                  parts of the Crusade.

Renaissance   One of the most populous worlds in the Empire
                  and located in the Spur of Orion. A cultural
                  center almost entirely covered by urban
                  development.

Rubicon   An Imperial planet bearing the signs of an extinct
                  xenobite civilization.

Sadal Suud   A wild world in the Spur of Orion that is mostly
                  untrammeled. Home to the Cavaraad Giants, a
                  huge species of xenobite, as well as the Marching
                  Towers, one of the Ninety-Nine Wonders of the
                  Universe. Ruled by House Rodolfo.

Se Vattayu   The mythical homeworld of the Cielcin. Its
                  surface is apparently honeycombed with
                  labyrinthine tunnels like those the Quiet dug at
                  Calagah on Emesh.

Siena   An Imperial colony in the Sagittarius Arm that
                  lies along the trade route from Delos to Teukros.

Sulis   A Norman Freehold that is effectively a client
                  state of the Sollan Empire. Site of a repelled
                  Cielcin invasion.

Syracuse A temperate world in the Imperium, notably the site of the scholiasts' athenaeum at Nov Acor.

Teukros A desert world in the Imperium, notably the site of the scholiasts' athenaeum at Nov Senber.

Thessaloniki Seat of one of the Eighty Principalities of Jadd.

Triton A water world in the Imperium; seat of House Coward.

Ubar An arid Jaddian satrapy loyal to House di Otranto, who have been the high princes of Jadd for generations. Loyal to the Prince of Thessaloniki.

Uhra A Norman Freehold that recently transitioned from a kingdom to a republic. Renowned for its starship manufacture.

Vesperad A moon orbiting the gas giant Ius. The oldest Chantry-controlled planet, boasting its largest seminary complex.

Vorgossos A mythical Extrasolarian world said to be the domain of demons and of pirates.

Wodan An Imperial colony in the Veil of Marinus seized from the Normans. Site of the Battle of Wodan in ISD 16129.

LEXICON

THERE WAS SOME DIFFICULTY rendering this text into Classical English from the Anglo-Hindi of Galactic Standard, as there exist many words in Galstani whose coinages postdate the death of English as a living language. Several of these, such as *sakradaas* (anagnost) and *hauviros* (centurion), I have elected to render in words borrowed from ancient Greek and Latin. To the English-speaking ear, these are steeped in a tradition comparable to that which these terms—themselves steeped in seventeen thousand years of Imperial tradition—enjoy for those reading Lord Marlowe's alleged autobiography in its original form. In other cases, such as with *groundcar* and *cryoburn,* I have cobbled together portmanteaus in Classical English which I feel approximate the looser feel of these more contemporary, plebeian terms. The names of certain living creatures—many of which were undiscovered or unmade during the Classical English period—I have substituted for mythic coinages or for names derived from scientific nomenclature (e.g. *azhdarch* and *congrid* respectively).

Proper names, such as the names of persons or planets, I have maintained exactly as Lord Marlowe recorded them, including those of the Cielcin xenobites. However, I should note that these names were transliterated using Marlowe's own system and not the systems codified by the Petersonian Order or the Legion Intelligence Office. As such, these spellings may differ from official spellings found both in scholiastic and official records.

References made to ancient, classical, and contemporary literature are precisely as written in the original and

have not been modified to better communicate symbolic connections for a modern audience. Lord Marlowe has an especial fondness for the Late Golden Age writings of the second and third millennium, old calendar, for which we must credit our brother Tor Gibson of Nov Acor, a classicist by all accounts.

Please find appended a list of the special terms relevant to this first volume of Lord Marlowe's account. I am deeply grateful to those of my brothers and sisters who have aided in my exploration of this text and pray that in time we may be sure of its authenticity.

—Tor Paulos of Nov Belgaer

adamant Any of the various long-chain carbon materials used for starship hulls and body armor.

adorator A member of any antique religious cult maintained by the Empire and tolerated by the Chantry.

aeta A Cielcin prince-chieftain with ownership rights over its subjects and their property.

alchemist A heavily regulated device used to transmute chemical elements using nuclear processes. Alternatively, a technician trained to use such a device.

alienage In the Sollan Empire, a ghetto or reservation intended for the isolation of a xenobite population.

alumglass A transparent ceramic form of aluminum, stronger than glass, commonly used in windows, particularly in starships.

anagnost An initiate in the Chantry clergy.

androgyn A homunculus exhibiting no sex characteristics or those of both males and females.

apatheia The emotionless state pursued by the scholiasts to facilitate their computational function. Has roots in classical stoicism.

Arch-Builders Extinct species of xenobite native to the planet Ozymandias. So called for the massive structures they built above the plains of their home.

archduke/ archduchess Highest rank of the palatine nobility. Rules over a planetary demesne. Title may be inherited.

archon Lowest rank of the Imperial noble hierarchy, ruling over a planetary prefecture. Either a posted or inherited position.

Arma   A constellation visible in the night sky on Delos, shaped like a medieval shield.

Assumption of Earth In the Chantry religion, the departure of Mother Earth following her destruction. It is said she will return when men are worthy.

Astranavis   A constellation visible in the night sky on Delos, shaped like a starship.

athenaeum   A research compound/monastery of the scholiastic orders.

atomics   Atomic weapons. Legal for nobile houses to own under the Great Charters but illegal to use.

auctor   Appointed by the Emperor to serve as his proxy when he cannot be present.

Autotrans   A machine that automatically translates between languages in real time. Illegal in the Imperium.

azhdarch   A xenobite predator common in the Colosso. Similar to a lizard with a long neck open from top to bottom in a fanged mouth.

backspace   Territory within Imperial space not formally colonized by the Empire. Often a refuge for the Extrasolarians.

badonna   A Jaddian honorific applied to *eali* women.

baetan   In Cielcin culture, a sort of priest-historian of the *scianda*.

baron/baroness   Lowest rank of the Imperial palatine nobility that may rule an entire planet, above archon but below viscount. Rules a planetary demesne. Title may be passed on through inheritance.

bastille   Chantry judicial and penal center, usually attached to a temple sanctum.

Battle of Cressgard First battle against the Cielcin. Fought in ISD 15792.

Battle of Linon Battle fought in ISD 15863 between House Marlowe and the rebellious Exsuls of the Delos system.

Battle of Wodan Battle with the Cielcin fought in ISD 16129 above the planet Wodan.

bit Steel coin used among the Imperial peasant classes. One hundred and forty-four bits equals one kapsum. Different printed denominations exist.

Boedromion The eighth month of the Delian local calendar, which marks the beginning of autumn in the northern hemisphere.

bonecutter A black-market genetics surgeon not sanctioned by the High College.

Book of the Mind An anthology of several texts compiled or composed by the scholiast Imore. Forms the basis of their philosophy.

bouillir A class of spicy red wines made on several worlds, most famously by House Markarian's vintners on Kandar.

brass whale A large, air-breathing sea creature brought to the oceans of Delos from offworld.

Cantos The Chantry holy book, a collection of songs, laws, and parables.

captain Naval officer rank in the Imperial Legion, above commander but below tribune. May command a starship.

castellan The chief military officer on a nobile estate, tasked with the defense of the castle and holdings. Usually a knight.

cathar A surgeon-torturer of the Holy Terran Chantry.

Cavaraad   Species of giant xenobite native to Sadal Suud. Humanoid, averaging twenty to thirty feet tall. Approximately Paleolithic level of development.

Centaurus Arm   One of the five arms of the galaxy settled by humankind. Lies between Sagittarius and Norma, comprising mostly Imperial colonies.

centurion   A rank in the Imperial Legions; commands a century.

century   In the Imperial Legions, a unit comprising ten decades under the command of a centurion and optio.

chanter   The average priest or priestess of the Chantry religion.

Chantry   See Holy Terran Chantry.

chimera   Any genetically altered or artificially created animal, usually achieved by blending the genetic codes of two or more animals.

Cielcin   Spacefaring alien species. Humanoid and carnivorous. The principal enemy of humankind during the Crusade.

cingulum   A belt worn by legionnaires and other soldiers in the Sollan Empire.

clan   In Tavrosi culture, all members of a kin group drawing their genes from the same gene bank. Analogous to an Imperial constellation.

Classical English   The ancient language of both the Mericanii and the early Imperial settlers on Avalon, still used by the scholiasts.

cloister   A scholiast's living quarters, kept clean of all technological devices.

coloni   Intelligent, preindustrial races of xenobites on human-occupied worlds, particularly in the Sollan Empire.

Colosso A series of sporting events held in a coliseum involving professional gladiators, slave myrmidons, animals, races, and more.

commander Naval officer rank in the Legion, beneath captain but above lieutenant. Assists in the command and management of a starship.

congrid An eel-like creature native to Emesh, considered a delicacy.

constellation Among the palatine, a supergroup of interrelated families, usually possessed of certain signifying features and traits.

corrective Medical device used to treat physical trauma from accidents or combat.

count/countess A title in the Imperial palatine nobility. Rules a planetary demesne. Title may be inherited.

crèche A cryonic storage pod for transporting people on long interstellar journeys.

Criminal Response Division The subdivision of law enforcement in each local prefecture tasked with responding to and investigating crimes.

Crusade The Imperial war against the Cielcin.

cryoburn A burn incurred from improper cryonic freezing.

Cult of Earth See Holy Terran Chantry.

daimon An artificial intelligence. Sometimes erroneously applied to non-intelligent computer systems.

Dark/Outer Dark Space. In the Chantry religion, a place of desolation and torment.

datasphere Any planetary data network. In the Empire, access is strictly restricted to the patrician and palatine castes.

decade   In the Imperial Legions, a unit of ten soldiers comprising three groups of three and their decurion.

decurion   A rank in the Imperial Legions. Commands a decade.

Demarchy of Tavros   A small interstellar polity found in the Wisp. Radically open to technology. The people vote on all measures using neural lace implants.

demesne   An Imperial territory held by a palatine. May be passed on at the ruler's discretion.

demoniac   A person who has incorporated machines into his or her body, particularly with the intent of altering cognitive processes.

diyugatsayu   In Cielcin culture, the concept of freedom, of not being owned by another Cielcin. Heavily stigmatized.

dom/domi   A Jaddian honorific usually applied to *eali* men.

douleter   A slave overseer or trader.

drone   Any subintelligent machine operated by simple programming or human control.

duke/duchess   A title in the Imperial palatine nobility. Rules a planetary demesne. Title may be inherited.

Durantine Republic   An interstellar republic of some three thousand worlds. Pays tribute to the Empire.

eali   The Jaddian ruling caste, product of intense eugenic development. Practically superhuman.

Elegy for Earth   The Chantry call to prayer performed at sundown each day. A funeral hymn for Mother Earth.

Emperor   The supreme ruler of the Sollan Empire, considered a god and the reincarnation of his/her predecessor. Holds absolute power.

energy lance   A bladed spear with a high-energy laser built into the shaft. Used as formal weapons by guards, especially in the Imperium.

entoptics   Augmented reality device that projects images directly onto the retina.

eolderman   The elected head of a plebeian community. Typically seen in more rural regions on Imperial planets.

ephebe   A young man or woman between the ages of eleven and twenty-one standard years.

Ephebeia   A celebration held on a boy's or girl's twenty-first birthday to celebrate his or her ascension to adulthood.

Eudoran   Any of the spacefaring bands claiming descent from the failed colony on Europa in Old Earth's system. An ethnic group known for their interstellar wanderings.

Exalted   A faction among the Extrasolarians noted for their extreme cybernetic augmentations.

executor   An official appointed by a palatine lord tasked with the management of that lord's estate and holdings in his absence.

Exodus   The expansionist period following the environmental collapse of Earth. The peregrinations from Old Earth System before the Foundation War.

Expeditionary Corps   Branch of the Imperial Legions tasked with exploring the galaxy and laying the groundwork for colonization.

exsul   Any palatine lord not based on a habitable world. Can also refer to his/her entire household.

Extrasolarian   Any barbarian living outside Imperial control, often possessing illegal praxis.

factionarius   The chief officer of a trade guild.

fief   An Imperial territory granted a palatine or
                      patrician by appointment. May not be passed
                      on through inheritance.

Fire School   Famous monastery and academy on Jadd
                      where the Maeskoloi are trained.

flier   A flying vehicle about the size of a groundcar,
                      used for in-atmosphere flight and rapid travel.

foederatus   A mercenary.

**Foundation   The war between the early Empire and the
War**   Mericanii, in which the Mericanii were
                      destroyed and the Sollan Empire was
                      founded.

Four Cardinals   In the Chantry religion, the four most
                      important icona: Justice, Fortitude, Prudence,
                      and Temperance.

**Free Traders   A coalition of smaller trading companies and
Union**   independent merchanter vessels that lobbies
                      for shipping privileges and dock space on
                      planets.

Freeholders   A citizen of any of the Norman Freeholds or
                      of any planetary or multiplanetary
                      government not associated with one of the
                      great interstellar powers.

fugue   The state of cryonic suspension induced to
                      ensure that humans and other living creatures
                      survive long journeys between suns.

**Galactic   The common language of the Sollan Empire,
Standard**   descended from Classical English with heavy
                      Hindi and Franco-Germanic influences.

Galstani   See Galactic Standard.

genestock   In terraforming, the genetic base material,
                      both terranic and otherwise, used to establish
                      civilized ecologies.

Giants			See Cavaraad.

gladiator			Professional fighting athletes in the Colosso.

glowsphere			A bright spherical light source floating on Royse repulsors. Powered chemically or with batteries.

gods			See icona.

Golden Age of Earth			The mythic epoch leading up to the Exodus, culminating in the Assumption of Earth and the colonization of the solar system.

gravitometer			A device for measuring the density and structure of matter by examining the distortions of gravity.

Gray Rot			An offworld plague brought to Emesh in the seventeenth millennium ISD. Wiped out eighteen percent of the population.

Great Charters			Ancient collection of legal codes imposed on the Empire by a coalition of the houses palatine. Maintains the balance between the houses and the Emperor.

groundcar			An automobile, usually powered by solar energy or internal combustion.

guild			Any professional organization with legal approval to perform its trade. A trade union beholden to a planet's lord.

guilder			Any member of a guild.

haqiph			A Jaddian caste term meaning "untouchable" or "base." Refers to homunculi and others considered subhuman.

high chancellor			The chief appointed official in a palatine lord's civil service. A prime minister.

High College   Imperial political office tasked with reviewing palatine requests for children and overseeing those pregnancies. Prevents mutations.

High Litany   In the Chantry religion, a weekly ritual held to commemorate the destruction of Earth and to pray for a better future for humankind.

highmatter   A form of exotic matter produced by alchemists. Used to make the swords of Imperial knights, which can cut almost anything.

holograph   Any three-dimensional light image projected by scanning lasers. Used for entertainment, advertisement, communication, etc.

Holy Terran Chantry   State religion of the Empire. Functions as the judicial arm of the state, especially where the use of forbidden technology is involved.

homunculus   Any artificial human or near-human, grown for a task or for aesthetic purposes.

hoplite   A shielded foot soldier. Heavy infantry.

hoplon   An antique-style round shield used in the Colosso.

hudr   A Jaddian word for scholiast, literally "green."

hurasam   Gilded coin used among the Imperial peasant classes, worth their mark-weight in gold. Print notes for various denominations exist.

hypogeum   The underground maintenance complex beneath a coliseum. More generally, any underground complex.

ichakta   A Cielcin title referring to the captain of a ship.

icona   In the Chantry religion, a spirit or god embodying an ideal, virtue, or natural law such as Fortitude, Evolution, or Time.

Imperial mark — Digital currency of the Sollan Empire and Mandari corporations. Highly competitive, unlike the hurasam and other hard coinage.

Imperial Office — The Emperor's administration—those ministries and civil services, including the palace staff, that comprise the Imperial central government.

Imperial Presence — The formal personage of the Sollan Emperor and the area about his person.

Imperial Star Date — The standard calendar. Months and weeks correspond to Old Earth's Gregorian calendar. The year is reckoned from the coronation of the first Emperor.

Imperium — See Sollan Empire.

Index — The catalog of punishments—monetary, corporal, and capital—maintained by the Chantry and enforced by the Inquisition.

inmane — An offensive slur meaning someone less than human. Literally "impure."

Inquisition — The judicial branch of the Imperial Chantry, primarily concerned with the use of illegal technologies.

inquisitor — A Chantry official tasked with conducting judicial investigations and overseeing the torture of criminals.

intus — A palatine born outside the oversight of the High College, usually possessing several physical or psychological defects. A bastard.

Irchtani — Species of xenobite native to the planet Judecca. Birdlike with massive wings. Considered an exemplar of coloni assimilation.

Izumo Group — A Nipponese interstellar corporation specializing in the heavy metal trade.

Jaddian   The official language of the Principalities of
                     Jadd, a patois of ancient Romance and Semitic
                     languages with some Greek influences.

jubala   A powerful and popular offworld narcotic.
                     Can be inhaled or ingested in a kind of tea.

kaspum   Silver-plated coin used among the Imperial
                     peasant classes. Twelve kaspums make one
                     gold hurasam. Print notes for various
                     denominations exist.

knife-missile   A kind of drone, little more than a remote-
                     controlled flying knife. A favorite of assassins.

knight   Sollan military honor conferred by the
                     nobility for services rendered. Usually
                     includes a small fief. May carry highmatter
                     weapons.

lance   See energy-lance.

Law of the   A philosophical precept that the world is a
Fishes   wilderness and that survival is the highest
                     virtue. The law of the jungle. Survival of the
                     fittest.

Legion   The Empire's military intelligence, espionage,
Intelligence   and foreign intervention agency.
Office

legionnaire   Any soldier in the Imperial Legions,
                     especially a common foot soldier.

Legions   The military branch of the Sollan Empire,
                     loyal to the Emperor and Imperial house.
                     Comprises naval and ground forces.

lictor   A bodyguard for a nobile or other dignitary.
                     Usually a knight.

lieutenant   Junior naval officer in the Legions, beneath
                     commander but above the crewmen.

lighter   Any starship small enough to make landfall
                     on a planet.

logothete   A minister in any of the governmental agencies of a palatine house. Used colloquially for any civil servant.

logothete pluripotentis   A logothete whose office oversees the transfer of land and other titled holdings between palatines and patricians.

Lothriad   See Lothrian Commonwealth.

Lothrian   The spoken language of the Lothriad.

Lothrian Commonwealth   The second-largest human polity in the galaxy, a totalitarian collectivist state. Longtime antagonist of the Empire.

Lowtown   The poor seaside district of the city of Meidua on Delos.

Maeskolos   A legendary swordmaster of Jadd drawn exclusively from the *eali* caste. Credited with superhuman speed and skill.

magister   A lay judge who tries plebeian cases.

magus   An intellectual, especially a scientist or natural philosopher.

mamluk   Any homunculus slave-soldier of the Jaddian Principalities.

Mandar   The language of the Mandari trade corporations.

Mandari   An ethnic group semidetached from Imperial society, most commonly found staffing the massive interstellar trading corporations.

mandyas   Traditional garment of the Maeskoloi. Half robe cinched at the waist with one flowing sleeve worn over the left shoulder.

Mathuran Campaigns   A series of battles between the Tavrosi clans with Imperial aid. Reached an armistice shortly after the appearance of the Cielcin.

medica   A hospital, typically aboard a starship.

Meidua   A port city on Delos, seat of the Meidua
                      prefecture and ancestral demesne of House
                      Marlowe.

merchanter   A salesperson or businessman, usually
                      plebeian.

meretrix   The madame of a brothel or, more often, a
                      palatine lord's harem.

Mericanii   The first of the ancient interstellar colonists.
                      A hyperadvanced technologic civilization run
                      by artificial intelligences. Destroyed by the
                      Empire.

messer/   Polite address in the Empire, used for anyone
** madame**   without a formal title.

Mother Earth   The deified homeworld of humanity and
                      principal god of the Chantry religion.

mute   Slang. Short for "mutant." Refers to a
                      homunculus or to an intus.

myrmidon   In the Colosso, any contract or slave fighter
                      who is not a professionally trained gladiator.

nanocarbon   A fabric made of carbon nanotubes. Related
                      to adamant.

ndaktu   In Cielcin philosophy, the weight of moral
                      responsibility placed upon an individual
                      whose actions directly or inadvertently led
                      another to suffer.

neg   A worthless person. Emeshi slang.

neural lace   A semiorganic computer implanted in a host's
                      brain. Illegal in the Empire.

Ninety-Nine   Ninety-nine of the greatest structures, both
** Wonders of**   human and alien, in the known universe.
** the Universe**

Nipponese   The descendants of the Japanese colonists who fled Old Earth system in the Third Peregrination.

nobile   Blanket term referring to any member of the palatine or patrician caste in the Sollan Empire.

Nordei   The principal language of the Demarchy. A patois of Nordic and Thai with some Slavic influences.

Norman United Fellowship   The former Norman democratic government on the planet Emesh prior to Imperial annexation.

opera   Any scripted narrative entertainment, whether musical, dramatic, or serial, interactive or otherwise.

optio   The second-in-command to a centurion in the Imperial Legions.

Orbital Defense Force   The fleet maintained by any palatine lord for the defense of his or her planet or system.

Orion Arm   One of the five arms of the galaxy settled by humankind. See Spur of Orion.

ornithon   A flying feathered snake native to Emesh. Nonvenomous, eats primarily sea life.

Outer Perseus   The expansion region along the end of the Perseus Arm. A colonial frontier.

palatinate   Any demesne or fief comprising an entire planet.

palatine   The Imperial aristocracy, descended from those free humans who opposed the Mericanii. Genetically enhanced, they may live for several centuries.

Pale   The Cielcin. Slang, considered offensive by xenophiles.

panegyrist A Chantry priest tasked with performing the call to prayer at sundown.

Panthai A Tavrosi language developed by the Thai-, Lao-, and Khmer-speaking peoples who settled the Wisp alongside the Nordei.

patrician Any plebeian or plutocrat awarded genetic augmentations at the behest of the palatine caste as a reward for services rendered.

peerage Palatine constellation comprising the Imperial family and its relatives. Members are all in line for the throne.

peltast An unshielded foot soldier. Light infantry.

Peregrination Any of the historical evacuations from Earth's system for the extrasolar colonies.

Perseus Arm One of the five arms of the galaxy settled by humankind. Lies beyond Orion at the outer rim. Contains the Principalities, Durantine Republic, and Imperial colonies.

phase disruptor A sort of firearm that attacks the nervous system. Can stun on lower settings.

phasma vigrandi Luminescent, floating creatures native to the forests of Luin, sometimes called fairies.

phylactery An ampule in which genetic samples are kept, especially for use in reproduction.

planetbound In Imperial law, any plebeian not permitted to travel offworld. A serf.

planeted lord Any nobile who has acquired or may pass down his or her planetary demesne within the family. A landed nobleman.

plasma burner A firearm that uses a strong loop of magnetic force to project an arc of superheated plasma across short-to-moderate distances.

plebeian The Imperial peasantry, descended from unaltered human stock seeded on the oldest colony ships. Forbidden to use high technology.

plutocrat Any plebeian who has earned enough money to buy expensive genetic augmentations. Effectively patrician.

poine A structured, small-scale war between imperial palatine houses. Subject to the scrutiny of the Inquisition.

Praetorian Any member of the Sollan Emperor's Praetorian Guard, drawn from the best of the Imperial Legion.

praxis High technology, usually of the sort forbidden by Chantry law.

prefect A law enforcement officer.

prefecture In the Empire, any administrative district ruled by an archon.

primarch The chief Imperial viceroy in each arm of the galaxy: Orion, Sagittarius, Perseus, and Centaurus. Essentially co-Emperors.

primarchate Region of the Empire ruled by a primarch, comprising several provinces.

primate The highest administrative office of a scholiasts' athenaeum, akin to a university chancellor.

Principalities of Jadd Nation of eighty former Imperial provinces in Perseus that revolted over palatine reproductive rights. Heavily militaristic and caste-driven.

prior In the Chantry clergy, the chief cleric in a prefecture.

prudence shield   A form of Royse field used for security, especially in coliseums and starship hangars. Traps air and fast-moving objects.

QET/quantum telegraph   A device that uses entangled quantum particles to communicate instantly over vast distances.

Quiet   The hypothetical first civilization in the galaxy, allegedly responsible for several ancient sites including those on Emesh, Judecca, Sadal Suud, and Ozymandias.

repulsor   A device that makes use of the Royse Effect to allow objects to float without disturbing the air or environment.

Rothsbank   An ancient, privately owned banking house tracing its roots back to the Golden Age of Earth.

Royse Effect   A method discovered by Caelan Royse for manipulating the electroweak force. Allows for the existence of force fields and repulsors.

Royse field   Any force field making use of the Royse Effect to stop high-velocity objects from penetrating an energy curtain.

rus   A young man. Emeshi slang.

Sagittarius Arm   One of the five arms of the galaxy settled by humankind. Lies between Orion and Centaurus, comprises the bulk of Imperial colonies as well as the Lothriad.

satrap   A planetary governor in the Principalities of Jadd, subordinate to one of the regional princes.

scholiast   Any member of the monastic order of researchers, academics, and theoreticians tracing their origins to the Mericanii scientists captured at the end of the Foundation War.

scianda	The Cielcin term for one of their migratory starship clusters. A fleet.
seed stock	See genestock.
serf	Any Imperial plebeian forbidden by birth to travel away from the planet of his or her birth except in the case of Legion military service.
servitor	A menial laborer.
shield-belt	A self-defense device worn about the waist. Uses a Royse field to stop bullets, plasma, and other high-energy weapons.
shock-stick	A nonlethal weapon primarily employed in crowd suppression. Little more than an electrified stave.
sign of the sun disc	A gesture of benediction made by circling thumb and forefinger and touching forehead and lips before holding the hand up to the sky.
signet ring	A device worn on a palatine's finger containing his or her genetic information, financial accounts, and land holdings.
sire	An honorific used to refer to one's social superiors, usually males and usually patricians or palatines.
sirrah	An honorific used to refer to one's social inferiors, usually males.
Solar Throne	The Imperial throne. Carved from a single piece of citrine quartz. Sometimes used as a synonym for the Imperial Presence or Office.
Sollan Empire	The largest and oldest single polity in human-controlled space, comprising some half-billion habitable planets.
spinship	Any starship that uses centripetal force to generate the illusion of gravity.

Spur of Orion   The oldest of the Empire's four primarchates, comprising the oldest parts of the Empire and Old Earth System.

Standard Registry   An index kept by the Imperial High College of all the houses palatine along with blood samples of all their constituents.

static field   A highly permeable variant of the Royse field used to keep conditioned air inside buildings.

strategos   An admiral in the Imperial Legions, responsible for the command of an entire fleet, comprising several legions.

stunner   A low-power phase disruptor used to cause temporary paralysis or loss of consciousness. Weapon favored by law enforcement personnel.

Sullen Gulf   The huge gap of empty space between the Norma and Centaurus Arms of the galaxy.

Summerfair   A midsummer holiday celebrated throughout the Imperium. Its date varies from world to world, depending on local calendars.

swordmaster   See Maeskolos.

Synarch   The highest ecclesiastic office of the Imperial Chantry. Their most important function is the coronation of new Emperors.

Synod   The ruling body of the Holy Terran Chantry; a college of archpriors presided over by the Synarch.

Tavrosi   Any of the languages from the Demarchy of Tavros. Most often refers to Nordei.

terminal   A telecommunications device that accesses a planet's datasphere, usually worn on the wrist.

terranic   In terraforming and ecology, refers to any organism of Old Earth extraction. Not extraterrestrial.

Travatsk A Tavrosi language named for the Travatskr ethnic group, recognizable by its lack of vowel reduction.

tribune A Legion officer in command of a cohort, four of which make up a legion. Commands both ground forces and naval officers.

triumph A parade held to celebrate victory in war. Usually the vanquished is marched out in chains for execution.

troglodyte A human being without higher brain functions either voluntarily for personal or religious reasons, or as the result of an accident.

Twelve Abominations The twelve most grievous sins according to the Chantry's Index. Legal privileges do not apply in such cases.

udaritanu A complex, nonlinear writing system used by the Cielcin.

Umandh A coloni species native to the planet Emesh. Amphibious and tripedal, they have an intelligence comparable to that of dolphins.

vate Any preacher or holy man who is not formally a part of the Chantry clergy.

Veil of Marinus Territory contested between the Empire and Norman Freeholds. Comprises most of the front in the Crusade against the Cielcin.

verrox A powerful pseudoamphetamine derived from the leaves of the verroca plant. It is taken by ingesting the leaves, which are usually candied.

verrox toxemia A chronic medical condition brought on by verrox abuse. Includes muscle tremors and eventual atrophy.

viceroy/ vicereine The ruler of an Imperial province appointed by the Emperor. The title is typically heritable but is not always so.

vilicus   The head of a team of douleters; chief overseer.

warden   Any member of the Chantry's private armies used to defend holy sites from unwanted incursions and pillaging.

wave   To contact someone by radio or telegraph. Alternately the communications device itself. Slang.

White Sword   A ceramic greatsword used by Chantry cathars for formal executions, especially of the nobility.

The Wisp   The thin string of stars housing the Demarchy of Tavros located above the galactic ecliptic, far from the Imperium.

Wong-Hopper Consortium   The largest of the Mandari trading corporations, holding several government contracts, especially in the terraforming industry.

worldship   Any of the massive Cielcin vessels—some as large as moons—that make up the cores of their fleets.

Writ   The Chantry's legal and moral code, enforced by the Inquisition and the Index.

writ of disavowal   In Imperial jurisprudence, a formal document wherein a nobile lord disowns one or more members of his or her family.

xenobite   Any life form not originating from terranic or human stock, especially those which are considered intelligent. An alien.

Yamato Interstellar   An interstellar manufacturing company owned by House Yamato and based out of Nichibotsu.

Your Excellency   Form of polite address used for ruling nobiles above the rank of archon.

Your Grace   Form of polite address used for viceroys, vicereines, and primarchs of the Sollan Empire.

Your Radiance   Form of polite address reserved exclusively for the Emperor.

Your Reverence   Form of polite address for members of the Chantry clergy, particularly priors.

yukajjimn   The Cielcin word for humanity. Shares etymological connections to their word for *vermin*.

zvanya   A cinnamon-flavored distilled alcohol popular in Jadd.

The saga continues in

HOWLING DARK

Hadrian Marlowe is lost.

For half a century, he has searched the farther suns for the lost planet of Vorgossos, hoping to find a way to contact the elusive alien Cielcin. He has not succeeded, and for years has wandered among the barbarian Normans as captain of a band of mercenaries.

Determined to make peace and bring an end to nearly four hundred years of war, Hadrian must venture beyond the security of the Sollan Empire and among the Extrasolarians who dwell between the stars. There, he will face not only the aliens he has come to offer peace, but contend with creatures that once were human, with traitors in his midst, and with a meeting that will bring him face to face with no less than the oldest enemy of mankind.

If he succeeds, he will usher in a peace unlike any in recorded history. If he fails…the galaxy will burn.

The Sun-Eater: Book Two

978-0-7564-1303-3

DAW 218

CJ Cherryh
The Foreigner Novels

"Serious space opera at its very best by one of the leading SF writers in the field today." —*Publishers Weekly*

FOREIGNER	*978-0-88677-637-6*
INVADER	*978-0-88677-687-2*
INHERITOR	*978-0-88677-728-3*
PRECURSOR	*978-0-88677-910-3*
DEFENDER	*978-0-7564-0020-1*
EXPLORER	*978-0-7564-0165-8*
DESTROYER	*978-0-7564-0333-2*
PRETENDER	*978-0-7564-0408-6*
DELIVERER	*978-0-7564-0414-7*
CONSPIRATOR	*978-0-7564-0570-0*
DECEIVER	*978-0-7564-0664-6*
BETRAYER	*978-0-7564-0714-8*
INTRUDER	*978-0-7564-0793-3*
PROTECTOR	*978-0-7564-0853-4*
PEACEMAKER	*978-0-7564-0965-4*
TRACKER	*978-0-7564-1075-9*
VISITOR	*978-0-7564-1208-1*
CONVERGENCE	*978-0-7564-1241-8*
EMERGENCE	*978-0-7564-1414-6*

"Her world building, aliens, and suspense rank among the strongest in the whole SF field." —*Booklist*

To Order Call: 1-800-788-6262
www.dawbooks.com

Tanya Huff
The *Confederation* Novels

"As a heroine, Kerr shines. She is cut from the same mold as Ellen Ripley of the Aliens films. Like her heroine, Huff delivers the goods." —*SF Weekly*

A CONFEDERATION OF VALOR
Omnibus Edition
(*Valor's Choice, The Better Part of Valor*)
978-0-7564-1041-4

THE HEART OF VALOR
978-0-7564-0481-9

VALOR'S TRIAL
978-0-7564-0557-1

THE TRUTH OF VALOR
978-0-7564-0684-4

To Order Call: 1-800-788-6262
www.dawbooks.com

DAW 73

Suzanne Palmer
Finder

"A breakneck-paced and action-packed science-fiction adventure featuring an endearing con artist whose current mission to retrieve a stolen spaceship ignites a war.... A nonstop SF thrill ride until the very last page." —*Kirkus*

"Fergus Ferguson makes an excellent lead in this fast-paced hard-sf repo adventure set in space opera's sweeping scale and balanced on the heart of one very finely wrought character. Suzanne Palmer's writing is delightful."

—Fran Wilde, author of the Bone Universe trilogy

"Palmer makes short-distance space travel feel as comfortable as riding a bicycle, and concludes this entertaining caper with a clever resolution and a hint of intrigue. Fans of space adventure will find this a fine example of the form."

—*Publishers Weekly*

"Wicked, fast-paced, and fun. This is a total romp, and I loved it." —Elizabeth Bear, author of *Ancestral Night*

ISBN: 978-0-7564-1635-5

To Order Call: 1-800-788-6262
www.dawbooks.com

DAW 219

Patrick Rothfuss

THE NAME OF THE WIND
The Kingkiller Chronicle: Day One

"It is a rare and great pleasure to come on somebody writing not only with the kind of accuracy of language that seems to me absolutely essential to fantasy-making, but with real music in the words as well.... Oh, joy!"
—Ursula K. Le Guin

"Patrick Rothfuss has real talent, and his tale of Kvothe is deep and intricate and wondrous." —Terry Brooks

"[Rothfuss is] the great new fantasy writer we've been waiting for, and this is an astonishing book."
—Orson Scott Card

Hardcover (978-0-7564-0407-9)
Trade Paperback (978-0-7564-0589-2)
Mass Market Papeback (978-0-7564-0474-1)

10th Anniversary Special Edition Hardcover
978-0-7564-0474-1

To Order Call: 1-800-788-6262
www.dawbooks.com

**DAW Books proudly presents
the novels of Christopher Ruocchio:**

The Sun Eater
EMPIRE OF SILENCE
HOWLING DARK